Joel Manners

The
Martyr's
Tears

Book Two of
THE CHRONICLES OF THE MARTYR

The Martyr's Tears

By Joel Manners

This is a work of fiction. Names, characters, places, and incidents either are the product of the author's imagination or are used fictitiously. Any resemblance to actual persons, living or dead, events, or locales is entirely coincidental.

Copyright © 2018 Joel Manners

All rights reserved. This book or any portion thereof may not be reproduced or used in any manner whatsoever without the express written permission of the author, except for the use of brief quotations in a book review or scholarly journal.

This book is available in print and electronic format at most online retailers.

Cover art by Bayard Wu

Map by Joel Manners

ISBN 978-0-9972594-1-4

Colquhoun Books
2407 Pruett St.
Austin, TX. 78703

www.JoelManners.com

For
Gabriel and Sean
whose ability to devour books
at a fantastic rate
has inspired me to make certain
their imaginations never go hungry.

Table of Contents

PART ONE

Chapter 1. Bandirma _____ 1

Chapter 2. Karsha Hali _____ 6

Chapter 3. Wyn _____ 18

Chapter 4. Killock _____ 34

Chapter 5. Rowenna _____ 51

Chapter 6. Eilidh _____ 67

Chapter 7. Killock _____ 95

Chapter 8. Maeglin _____ 110

Chapter 9. Rowenna _____ 129

Chapter 10. Karsha Hali _____ 144

Chapter 11. Danielle _____ 156

Chapter 12. Whitebrooke _____ 179

Chapter 13. Karsha Hali _____ 200

Chapter 14. Wyn _____ 218

Chapter 15. Karsha Hali _____ 239

Chapter 16. Killock _____ 247

Chapter 17. Gwydion _____ 253

Chapter 18. Wyn _____ 271

PART TWO

Chapter 19. Cormac _____ 287

Chapter 20. Killock _____ 314

Chapter 21. Maeglin _____ 323

Chapter 22. Danielle _____ 336

Chapter 23. Gwydion _____ 368

Chapter 24. Maeglin _____ 393

Chapter 25. Cormac _____ 407

Chapter 26. Maeglin _____ 435
Chapter 27. Rowenna _____ 451
Chapter 28. Wyn _____ 465
Chapter 29. Gabrielle _____ 494
Chapter 30. Maeglin _____ 510
Chapter 31. Gabrielle _____ 526
Chapter 32. Whitebrooke _____ 541
Chapter 33. Ranald _____ 568
Chapter 34. Danielle _____ 577
Chapter 35. Mairi _____ 597
Chapter 36. Epilogue _____ 606

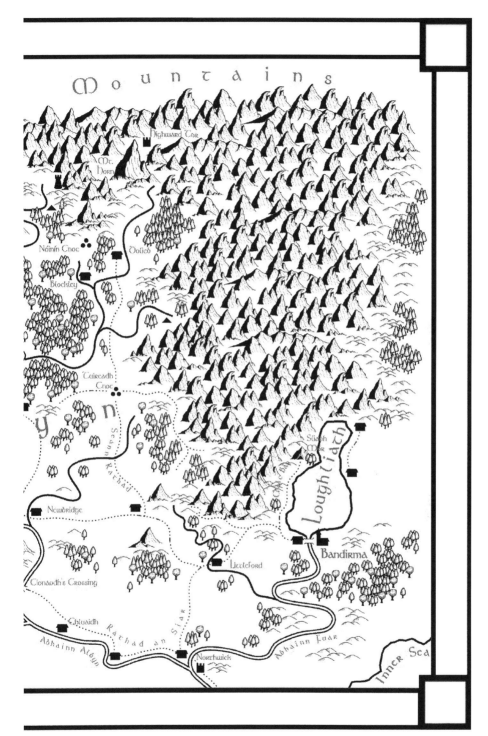

Part One

Bandirma

Two figures crept through the shadows that lurked between the weathered buildings surrounding the docks.

One of the figures clung desperately to the other. Her boots dragged with every step and her blonde hair swung about her face in long, tangled strands.

Her arm draped around the shoulders of the second figure, although there was no strength in her embrace. But the young woman who bore her weight held her close with fierce determination, and half-carried, half-dragged her across the quay.

They staggered across a stretch of open wharf, boots splashing in the puddles that filled the dips and divots of the paving stones, toward a damp pile of netting, and collapsed against it, breathing hard. The blonde woman moaned softly and fought with feeble hands to roll onto her back, and her companion helped her settle before crouching to peer cautiously over the nets.

No lanterns or torches pierced the gloom that smothered the deserted wharf. She watched silently for a moment, her raven-black hair a shifting splash of thicker darkness amongst the shadows, then knelt next to the figure sprawled on the nets.

"I must go for a moment, just a moment, I promise," she whispered. "Stay right here."

"… not going anywhere…"

The dark-haired woman paused to brush strands of hair from her injured companion's face with gentle fingers, then rose and hurried toward the edge of the quay.

The sound of her light footsteps was quickly swallowed by the ever-present roar of the nearby river in its stone channel. The blonde woman struggled to sit up, groaned in pain, and fell back onto the pile of nets. Her chest rose and fell in short gasps, and sweat beaded on the pale skin of her brow despite the chill air.

A new sound intruded upon her isolation. Footsteps, heavy and slow, grating with the sound of metal on stone. A yellow glow accompanied the footsteps, infusing the murk. It flickered faintly at first, but it grew stronger with each step.

Soon a lantern appeared, held aloft by a stocky, hooded figure. The mist that enveloped the docks swirled around the lantern like shimmering gauze and the figure's cloak gleamed with a thousand sparks reflecting from the water beaded on its thick weave.

For a moment, the figure seemed intent to pass the mound of netting without pause. His hood was drawn low against the mist, and the sound of the river rumbled in the stones, masking the strained sound of labored breathing. Then his step faltered, and he swung the lantern in a wide arc, as if unsure of what he had heard, but certain he had heard it.

The watchman pushed back his hood, revealing a bearded face with deep lines etched into its craggy cheeks. He stepped toward the nets, paused, and stepped closer again, his head cocked to the side and a frown deepening on his brow. The gasping breath of the young woman behind the nets drew him closer, until the light from his lantern had driven the concealing shadow of the netting almost to the tip of her boot.

"Who's there?" he called out, his voice a low growl. He slipped his axe from its loop, and tested the weight of its hooked steel blade. "I said, who's there?"

A flash of movement swirled behind the watchman's head and there was a sharp impact like a mallet striking a dowel. The lantern shattered on the stone as he crumpled to his knees and pitched forward onto his face.

The dark-haired woman stepped over the sprawled body. She held a heavy shaft of wood in her hands, and she raised it to strike again as she glared at the supine form between her feet. But the watchman did not move, and she lowered her weapon.

Blood plastered her hair to the side of her head and grime streaked her cheeks in long lines that spread from the corners of her eyes, but neither the filth nor the distress in her eyes could obscure the elegant beauty of her high cheekbones and graceful neck.

She swiftly knelt next to the young woman struggling to breathe and touched her gently on her arm.

"I found a boat," she whispered. "It is not far, and then you may rest."

The blonde woman suddenly opened her eyes, her gaze desperate with pain and confusion. "I can't breathe…" she gasped. "Oh, Martyr, it hurts."

"I know," the dark-haired woman consoled her injured companion. She wiped fresh tracks through the dirt on her cheeks with her long fingers, and took a deep, juddering breath. "I will help you."

The blonde woman groaned and slowly rolled onto her elbows and knees, her hands held protectively away from the ground. The skin on her hands was streaked with livid tracks of red interrupted by patches of raw flesh and long slashes that dripped blood onto the paving stones. Her fingers were curled into rigid claws by the pain, and she struggled to kneel upright while protecting them.

"I'm all right… I'm ready…"

THE MARTYR'S TEARS

She draped the blonde woman's arm across her shoulder and raised her unsteadily to her feet, but as careful as she was, her companion gasped with pain and sagged against her.

They staggered together toward the river. Her long legs quivered with fatigue, and the blonde woman's breath hissed through clenched teeth, but they forced themselves forward.

"It is a small boat," the dark-haired woman panted between ragged breaths. "I can sail it on my own… while you rest…"

"…easy as wishing…"

"That is right… as easy as a wish."

The edge of the docks materialized from the murk ahead of them, a harsh line of stones with black water lying motionless beyond.

A lean shape was moored along the quay. A sharp bow arced from a narrow deck, and a single mast rose from the roof of a low cabin.

The dark-haired woman carefully lowered her companion into the boat's cockpit and scrambled in after her. The hatch to the cabin swung into impenetrable darkness, and the three small steps leading down proved an almost insurmountable obstacle.

She laid the injured girl in a narrow bunk and pillowed her head on her cloak before hurrying back onto the deck. Her fingers raced along the bundled sail, desperately searching for the ties that held it in place, tearing at the knots in her haste. She cursed as the sail snagged on one missed tie, and groaned in despair as it caught again on another.

The boat slipped across the still water toward the heavy thunder of the river. Water slapped against the boat's prow as it met the first small ripples that crept around the breakwater. The young woman wrapped the tiller in both arms and clutched the smooth wood to her chest. The bow dipped suddenly and twisted to the side, and the boat rushed forward as the current caught it.

The high stone wall of the channel suddenly loomed at the boat's rail, and the woman wrenched the tiller to the side. The boat reared and slid forward smoothly as the sail trembled and the polished wood under her arm thrummed with the surge of the water around the rudder. Her dark hair streamed in the wind of their passage like a pennant as the boat flew from the town.

By the time pale light crept into the sky, the boat was far to the south of Bandirma. The river widened as it meandered between low hills, and the boat's brown sail caught every scrap of wind possible as the current slowed. Water frothed and curled in long waves that arced away from the boat's sharp prow. A raven swooped low and challenged their speed with furious beating of his wings before soaring northward with harsh cries, but the woman kept the boat knifing southward, away from the grey hill that lurked behind them.

Karsha Hali

Ragged, uneven snores emerged from the tangled nest of blankets that filled the single habitable chair in the room, interrupted frequently by horrible snorts and even more frightening silences. The chair was ancient and deep, covered in soft leather that was so mottled and cracked that its original color was no longer discernible, and it slumped so close to the stone fireplace that sparks had scarred its surface with dozens of burns.

A feeble glow from embers in the fireplace lit the small, cluttered room. Unsteady piles of leather-bound books cast black shadows that obscured the dim recesses. Stacks of ancient scrolls smothered a desk and laid siege to the few remaining sections of bare floor. The remains of a tray of food teetered on the edge of an end table. Tall bookshelves surrounded the room and reached to the heavy beams of the ceiling, filled with more haphazard stacks of books and a multitude of chests and locked containers.

A hesitant knock sounded from an adjacent room, but produced no more than a series of deep grunts from the tangled blankets, as if a family of boars had taken up residence in the chair.

The knock sounded again, more insistent this time. The noises from the chair stopped and were replaced by the silence of hiding and waiting.

But the knocking did not relent, and, finally, the bundle of blankets rose from the chair and shuffled on small, bare feet across the cluttered scriptorium and down the narrow, winding stairs to the lowest level of the turret, where the offending door rattled on its iron latch.

The door creaked as Karsha Hali swung it open. He peered from deep within his wrapped blankets at the young soldier who stood quivering before him.

"M'lord, you are summoned," the soldier blurted out.

Karsha considered the news for a moment in silence and allowed his baleful stare to shrivel the messenger further.

"Well done," Karsha croaked, then kept the messenger waiting with a series of deep, satisfying coughs and accompanying clearing of his throat. "Most who carry messages simply tell all, leaving no mystery. You are a bard at heart."

"Yes, m'lord, I mean no, m'lord, I'm not a bard, m'lord."

"No?" Karsha said sympathetically. "How sad. Will you come and sit while we wait for the rest of your message to arrive?"

"No, m'lord, I mean yes, m'lord, if you please, except I have the rest of the message, m'lord."

"Wonderful news," Karsha yawned. "Shall we hear it? Or shall we wait?"

"Yes, m'lord. Hear it, m'lord," the messenger stammered. "The Queen requests you attend her, m'lord. In the private audience chamber, m'lord."

"You are right." Karsha regarded the messenger sadly. "Not a bard."

Karsha ambled behind the messenger as they made their way through the echoing halls of the Silver Keep, deserted save for a few silent sentries. They passed through tall, pointed arches and across wide rooms with polished floors that appeared as dark mirrors in the dim light. Elegant pillars lined the open spaces, thin and delicate as they soared to the balconies and the inlaid ceilings above.

THE MARTYR'S TEARS

They passed through the Queen's reception chamber, its wide windows shuttered and curtained against the night. At the far end, a curved staircase spiraled around a ring of pillars, and Karsha followed the messenger up, his bare feet slapping the cold stone as he climbed after the long, hurried strides of his companion, forcing the messenger to wait anxiously on each landing. The stairs ascended through the ceiling and past several landings before finally reaching the series of rooms that were the royal apartments, the crown of the Silver Keep.

Soldiers stood guard in the hallway outside the apartment's entrance, with Sir Ceridwen dominating the door itself, but Karsha was vexed to see two soldiers who did not wear the Queen's arms. Instead, they bore badges of two swords, crossed in a semblance of the Queen's arms, with a crown perched above them, black on a white field.

Sir Ceridwen nodded a greeting to Karsha as he approached, and Karsha gave the knight a lopsided grin in return. He liked Sir Ceridwen, for the knight was fond of sharing stories over a mug of ale, and appeared to have an endless supply of both.

Karsha opened the door and shambled into the room beyond, his feet padding soundlessly on the thick carpets that covered the floor.

The Queen's private audience chamber was coldly formal, as unsuitable for the Queen as it was an impeccable reflection of her father-in-law, King Conall, and Karsha wondered if the Queen would ever order the furnishings altered. *King Arian never dared to change his father's house, either,* Karsha reminded himself sadly. The walls bore massive paintings that reached to the ceiling, portraits of great kings and depictions of great battles. Wide windows draped in thick, red curtains covered one wall that curved to match the gradual arc of the tower. Comfortable chairs and settees in matching red were perfectly arranged around the outskirts of the room. Flawless sculptures and other works of art stood along the walls.

Plaster flowers and swirling leaves crowned the tall ceiling around a chandelier that boasted two hundred candles, but none were lit this far into the night. Instead, the room was illuminated by the glow of a snapping fire and a candelabra placed on a small table by the settees.

Three people waited in the room. Sir Liam stood watch in the shadows by the door, as unobtrusive as a man in heavy steel armor could be, but it was the other two who waited in front of the fire for Karsha.

Duke Campbell stood tall and proper in a long coat of heavy, black cloth bearing traces of gold embroidery, and a tunic of a warm red with a high collar. The duke had a craggy face with a strong chin and a long, aquiline nose, and he boasted a thick beard streaked with grey along his jaw.

He turned slightly to regard Karsha as the southerner entered the room. Campbell's deep-set eyes wore their customary expression of slightly disapproving appraisal, although Karsha did not take it personally. The duke disapproved of everyone, as far as Karsha could tell.

Queen Gabrielle rested on a settee. She had been recently asleep, for she still wore her nightdress under a long, richly-patterned housecoat so hurriedly donned that the sash was not tied, her feet were bare, and her hair was bound in a loose knot. She sat attentively, her back straight and her hands folded neatly in her lap, but Karsha knew her well enough to see that the young Queen was already impatient with her stern cousin.

"Karsha, thank you for coming so quickly," the Queen greeted the wizard, her rich accent tripping over the words in her weary disregard for the common tongue.

"Your Majesty." Karsha stood by the duke and settled his robes more firmly, as they tended to wander from his boney shoulders while he walked. "Your timing was excellent. I was under the spell of a treatise on the nature of stones. It had driven me into a deep slumber, but I suspect its real intent was to drain all life from me."

Karsha turned to the duke as the Queen graced his humor with a slight smile. "My lord," Karsha nodded to the duke and received a frown in return. "I did not expect you in Kuray until tomorrow."

"You were mistaken." The duke's voice carried effortlessly through the room, each word rich and resonant. "I came as soon as I received Her Majesty's message and did not pause for rest." The duke lingered on the last word.

"It is good to be mistaken in such things," Karsha mumbled through a gaping yawn.

"Indeed." The duke hesitated, unsure whether he was being mocked.

"Indeed," Karsha agreed solemnly.

"Cousin," the Queen interrupted with a quick frown at Karsha, "you have our thanks for your swift arrival. The matter we must address is most urgent."

"Indeed," the duke said again, and he scowled with displeasure. Karsha knew the duke fancied himself a great orator and rarely was at a loss for words. Karsha busied himself with an itch on his nose as the duke gathered himself and started anew. "Yes, Your Majesty, so your message stated."

The Queen glanced to Karsha for an instant, and Karsha nodded to the Queen from behind the duke's elbow.

"My lord," the Queen said graciously, "my husband often spoke of your family's endless courage and devotion to the Crown, and of your strength and guidance, in particular."

"Thank you, Your Majesty. The Campbells have had the honor to defend the Silver Keep for generations. In past days, before the creation of the Royal Army, the Marshal of the Tower commanded all the forces guarding Kuray. Of course, that title is little thought of now, but it is not forgotten."

"It is not, your Grace," the Queen replied without hesitation. "I recently instructed Karsha on that very thing."

Karsha bobbed his head in agreement when Duke Campbell glanced at him, which seemed to satisfy the Queen's cousin.

"And in what urgent matter may I serve you, today?" the duke asked.

The Queen stood, stepped to the fire, and gazed at the flames, to all appearances lost in thought. Karsha coughed and rummaged in his robes until he found the message container he wanted. He absent-mindedly tapped his finger on the small, silver tube and watched the duke's eyes narrow as Campbell's gaze was drawn to Karsha's hand. Karsha fiddled with the container until the Queen's seal on its latch caught the candlelight.

"Your Grace," Karsha said gravely. "I must tell you of treason and murder."

"Treason? A serious charge. I assume it is not made without consideration."

"There is no doubt of the accused's guilt," Karsha said sadly.

The duke's mouth set in a hard line. "An unfortunate situation. Who stands accused?"

"A Temple priest. A man named Whitebrooke."

"A priest? What did he do?"

"He led an attack on the Queen and her guard while they were guests in Bandirma."

"What?" Campbell asked sharply, his brows furrowed as he studied Karsha. "Are you certain?"

"Certain?" The Queen rounded on her cousin. "Sir Ceredor and Sir Osythe were slain defending me. A score of our soldiers were also killed or taken captive. If not for Karsha, I would have been under their blades, as well. Yes, I am certain."

"Your Majesty, I am sorry, I had no idea you had endured such a…" Duke Campbell gathered himself. "This priest, Whitebrooke, was the man responsible for the attack?"

"Oh, yes," Karsha nodded eagerly, and produced a slip of parchment from another pocket in his robes. "Here are his lies."

The duke unrolled the parchment and read it carefully, a black scowl settling on his face as he did. "This is a Temple message? You are certain?"

"Undoubtedly so," Karsha cackled. "Their pigeon was waylaid by one of my friends. Not a good way of sending messages. I told their Bird Master. But it made a tasty pie." Karsha smacked his lips at the memory.

"You see, your Grace?" The Queen's voice was warm and consoling now. "Whitebrooke accuses my sister of murdering Bishop Benno, of murdering a dozen other priests and priestesses, and of being a Crunorix, of all things. He ordered her arrest, and when they came to do it, they attacked my guard."

"I'm sorry, Your Majesty, but this message accuses Karsha of those acts." Campbell held up the parchment between his fingers. "Lady Danielle is only accused of aiding him."

"Yes, very true!" Karsha agreed vigorously. "And for me, perhaps not a story at all, not one worthy to be told to lords of great families at the top of silver towers, all would agree. Even for the sister of a queen, maybe just a small story, full of sorrow, but what can be done? But they drew swords on the Queen, they cut down her guards, all because of Whitebrooke's lies."

"Yes," the duke said uneasily, and he tapped his finger on his lip as he considered the Temple message again. "This could be problematic. There is a law, signed centuries ago, that gives the Temple the right—"

"Fionn's Law, yes, I know it," the Queen said impatiently.

"Then Your Majesty will know that Fionn's Law exempts the Temple from Royal decree. You cannot command the Temple to do... anything."

"Reverend Whitebrooke has committed treason," the Queen said defiantly. "He has attacked me and my family."

"Yes, Your Majesty, and we must demand Reverend Whitebrooke be given to us," the duke replied. "I would be honored to serve as your embassy in this matter. But beyond that, there may not be much we can do."

"We have thought of something to do," Karsha said, and he raised the silver message container with the Queen's seal on it.

Karsha handed the tube to the duke and busied himself with untangling the long chains he wore around his neck, setting the myriad charms that bedecked the chains chiming and tinkling softly. Campbell smoothed the small pieces of parchment that had been curled inside the container and read them, his expression darkening as he did.

"Is this truly your decree?" the duke asked, disbelief and disgust warring on his face.

"Yes," the Queen replied. "What disturbs you, cousin? It seems clear to me."

"But this violates Fionn's Law," the duke snapped. "It violates the oath you swore when you assumed King Arian's throne. Have you considered the ramifications?"

"Almost all of them," Karsha intervened, for the Queen's golden eyes had narrowed dangerously.

" '…lords are commanded to seize the temples within their lands and all attending properties… restitution for the Temple's crimes against the Queen…'," the duke read from the Queen's message. "Which temples?"

"Almost all of them," Karsha replied.

"All of the temples, in all of Albyn?" Campbell's voice trailed to a whisper.

"Almost all," Karsha reminded him.

"Your Majesty, this is madness!" Campbell found his voice again, and his words echoed from the marble walls.

"Have you not attended Karsha's story, your Grace?" the Queen asked coldly.

"Yes, Your Majesty," Campbell's voice soothed. "Nevertheless—"

"Good," the Queen continued. "Whitebrooke's actions must be answered. Perhaps he is the one who should have considered the ramifications."

"Of a certainty, and yet…" Campbell glanced shrewdly at Karsha. "This was General Boone's counsel, was it not? Boone believes steel is the answer to every problem."

"It is not just one priest," the Queen reminded her cousin, exasperated. "He has somehow tricked the Temple into attacking me, and then blaming my sister for his deeds, and Karsha as well. The Temple must be convinced to listen to us, and those in the Temple who believe us must be supported. That is General Boone's plan."

"Boone can be convincing," Duke Campbell agreed, "and in matters of war, his counsel is unmatched. But he does not speak for the lords and ladies of Albyn. Your Majesty cannot be expected to understand the intricacies, nor control Boone. Your father-in-law was a master of both, but, of course, he had many years of learning how to rule, and came from family rich in the traditions of Albyn."

The Queen's face grew pale despite her dark skin, but Karsha spoke before she could gather her ire.

"A family like yours?" he asked the duke.

"My family is the king's family."

"The queen's, you mean."

"Of course," the duke stated. "Hopefully, my counsel can help curb any more of Boone's enthusiasms."

"Joyous news." Karsha bobbed his head vigorously, sending his charms ringing, again. "You have named the duty that is to be yours. Take the Queen's command to the noble families of Albyn. They are to take arms and seize the temples within their lands and you are to lead them in this."

"You wish me to take this order to them?" Campbell indicated the parchment held in his hand. "My counsel is to throw it on the fire. My lady, you must reconsider. It will not be popular."

"Not popular?" The Queen's eyebrows arched menacingly. "He tried to kill me. When the truth of that is revealed, the people will cheer our soldiers and cry for Whitebrooke's head."

"Ah, yes, of course the people will want action taken."

"His Grace meant that it will not be popular with his nobles," Karsha chuckled.

"Yes, of course," the duke agreed brusquely. "It will be they who bear the brunt of your command.

"Yes," Karsha continued. "Which is why you must lead them, to rally them while Boone is away."

"Where is General Boone? Why does he not execute his own counsel?" Campbell's eyes narrowed to slits as he stared at Karsha, and the wizard stifled a grunt of displeasure. *I should not have let that slip. I am playing carelessly. The duke is a snake, never forget. He may blow like a summer storm, but he is fast, deadly, and ever watchful.*

The Queen remained silent, staring at the fire, so Karsha continued.

"He has gone to be convincing." Karsha burrowed further into his robes. "Some say that he is good at that."

"Yes, he is," Campbell said slowly. His gaze never left Karsha's, and the wizard pondered how the story might end if the Queen was not in the room. "He has taken the Royal Army with him, has he not? That is how Boone likes to persuade. That is why you need the nobles to deal with the Temple." At last the duke turned from Karsha and addressed the Queen. "Your Majesty, this is dangerous, it is reckless, it is futile, and the lords will not support it. Perhaps I can—"

"Thank you, your Grace," the Queen interrupted, and she gave Duke Campbell a flashing smile. "I am afraid I am so exhausted right now that I cannot put two thoughts together. Perhaps we will speak more on this tomorrow?"

The duke gathered himself instantly. "Of course, Your Majesty. Such discussions are best with clear minds."

"And when we are finished with our discussion, you will leave immediately to convey my commands to the lords and ladies of Albyn," the Queen continued. "Whitebrooke must be brought to justice, your Grace, and if the Temple will not cooperate, they must be given incentive. That is my decision. Do you understand?"

The duke clearly wished to say more, but he mastered his displeasure, bowed, and strode to the door.

The Queen silently watched her cousin depart. When the door had closed on his back the smile left her face and Gabrielle took a deep breath, her eyes closed, and released some of her anger.

"Damn that man." She took another breath and opened her eyes, still furious. "He travels through the night, just so that he can wake me up to tell me how unfit I am to rule, with his 'cannots' and 'you musts'."

"And an offer to provide you counsel," Karsha reminded Gabrielle helpfully.

"That as well." She turned her glare on Karsha. "What were you thinking, telling him that Boone had gone? Birds will be flying to all of Campbell's lordlings in the morning, and you may count on that being in every one of their messages."

THE MARTYR'S TEARS

Karsha bowed as low as his back would allow. "My apologies, a clumsy mistake, very poor."

Gabrielle nodded slightly, mollified. " 'Have you considered the ramifications?', he says. Does he think I am a girl awaiting his lecture with raised quill? Imbecile." She risked a glance at Karsha. "Can I throw him in the dungeon?"

"We would find out how many supporters he actually has," Karsha said thoughtfully. "But we need him to gather the good will of the nobles. General Boone is correct. Without the duke's voice, there would be more complaining than action, and the Temple must be persuaded to give us Whitebrooke. Fionn's ancient law is not as important, nor is the pride of the Queen's cousin."

"The duke clearly does not agree."

"He hears our story and thinks of intrigue or simple murder, and he tells us we are using a hammer to mend a locket. 'Boone is a warmonger', he says, forgetting the general dreams only of destroying the enemies of the realm. 'Karsha Hali is a crazy fool who deals with spirits', he says, and he is right, but he forgets I have pledged my life to your family."

"And if he decides that Albyn would be better off without a warmonger and a crazy fool, or the queen who listens to them?"

Karsha shrugged. "It is always best to beware the sting of a viper. Especially those you invite into your home."

"Would he be a viper if he knew the truth? That fouler crimes than murder and treason have been committed? That the Crunorix have returned?"

"If he believed us, the duke would hesitate at nothing to defend Albyn, this I am certain of," Karsha admitted. "But Duke Campbell will not believe, because Duke Campbell does not believe in myths. But how can we blame him for this? Even I did not believe the Crunorix could be amongst us, not for many months, and I do believe in myths. No, we need Campbell's aid. Not his doubt, not his resistance."

Gabrielle nodded to herself. "And what does the duke say about his queen?"

" 'The Queen is young and lets her passions rule her, as do all who come from the hot climates'," Karsha told her. "He forgets that the kingdom is the Queen's family now, and that her fire does not melt the ice of her home, but protects it."

Gabrielle laughed softly. "Does it? I hope that is true." She sighed wearily and her smile fled. "I am worried, Karsha." Gabrielle wrapped her robes more tightly around herself. "Look at the two of us, after all. Campbell is not wrong. We could hardly be more out of place here in the Silver Keep."

"I think we understand Albainn nobles very well," Karsha mused. "We knew exactly what Duke Campbell would say, in any case."

Wyn

Voices drifted in the darkness that surrounded Wyn, indistinct and unintelligible. One of the voices was low and rumbling, the other beautiful. But the beautiful voice was distraught, and it frightened Wyn.

Wyn tried to move, but she could not. Someone was sitting on her chest, a crushing weight that drove shards of pain through her sternum and shoulders and made breathing arduous. Cold stones pressed against her back, and she squirmed to escape from the weight, but she could not get free. Her left arm was numb, save for agonizing pins and needles that throbbed deep within her shoulder.

Get off, she tried to say. She struck feebly at whoever was sitting on her. *You're hurting me.*

Pain twisted in her chest and nausea flooded through her. She tried to gasp, but the weight on her chest was too much, and she could not catch her breath. *Oh, Martyr, please get off.*

The pressure was relentless, and Wyn felt herself ground between the stone beneath her and the impossible weight on top of her. Her gasps became shorter and shorter.

Her head was gently lifted and then placed onto something soft and warm. Tender fingers traced across her forehead.

Please help me, she begged, but the weight would not move, and the pain would not relent, and they flooded over her until she drowned in their endless depths.

***

Wyn stood in front of her mother's small house. Weeds completely choked the tiny garden, the shutters were warped, and the roof was in dire need of fresh thatch. Wyn had forgotten how awful the leaks had been in the main room when it rained.

Wyn could have easily weeded the garden herself and learned what to plant. She could even have figured out how to patch the roof, Wyn realized now. But her mother had always said that she would do it. Once she was better.

And that had suited Wyn fine. She was rarely in the house anyway, sometimes staying away until long after the evening bells, confident that her mother would have succumbed to an exhausted sleep before then.

Wyn walked to the faded yellow door and stopped with her hand on the old latch. There was something that she desperately wanted to tell her mother, but she could not remember what it was, and the uncertainty made her hesitate.

Bother, what was it? Wyn glanced up and down the darkening street. *Where's Dani? She will know what it was.*

The street was deserted.

Never mind, Dani must be inside already. Oh! That's it! I need to tell Mum about Dani. Tell her that I'm in love with a princess, and she's in love with me. Let her know that I'm happy.

Wyn lifted and pushed on the thumb latch at the same time in a practiced motion to free the bar from its twisted hook.

She was surprised to see that the main room was filled with people. A towering man wearing the ornate robes of a high priest eyed her suspiciously, and Wyn shrank from his gaze, terrified of him, although she was not sure who he was. Two acolytes farther into the room stopped in mid-conversation and stared at her.

"Where have you been?" the tall priest demanded, his thick beard bristling, the three long scars on the back of his hand shining white as they stretched over sinew and bone.

"I don't know." Wyn stared at the priest's clenched fists, too fearful to raise her eyes to his face. "Is Danielle here? Please, I'm trying to find her."

"It's too late," the priest answered. "She's in the bedroom."

Wyn fled from the main room. She grabbed at the bedroom door and stumbled through, slamming the door behind her.

The bedroom was dark, with only small candles on the old dresser to light it. Her mother lay on the bed, dark hair spread across the pillow, the thick quilt pulled up to cover her face. Wyn crept across the floor, not wanting to disturb her, but as she approached the bed she realized that her mother was not moving. The blankets did not rise and fall, and there was no sound of the labored breathing that had afflicted her mother for so long.

"Mum?" Wyn's voice was that of a child, small and scared. She reached a hand for the blanket and her fingers remembered the touch of the old, patched quilt. "Mum? It's me."

She slowly pulled the blanket toward her. It slid from her mother's face, revealing elegant, high cheekbones and full lips under raven hair.

Wyn screamed. Danielle lay beneath the quilt, not her mother, and her skin was grey and cold.

Wyn screamed again and staggered back, knocking into a small table and upsetting its contents. A wooden box crashed to the floor with the tinkle of breaking glass and its lid twisted open. Wyn saw that it contained a small, silver mirror, now shattered from the fall. She crouched on the floor, trying to gather all the pieces, but her sobs shook her so badly that the shards laced her hands with long lines of red blood.

Then Danielle turned in the bed and stared at Wyn. Danielle's skin withered and blackened as if it were parchment in the heart of a fire, freezing shadow whispered between her lips, and Wyn screamed until she tore herself from the horrifying gaze and fled from the room.

The hallway outside stretched endlessly in both directions. Wyn sobbed as she stumbled down its length, beating desperately on locked doors with her fists as she passed. The hallway grew dark and cold, and the walls became rough-hewn stone that tore her fingertips when she brushed against them.

Wyn stopped in front of a door. It had a cracked brick over its top hinge, the same one that she remembered from when she had found it, years ago. She pushed through the door and fled across damp earth toward the shapes of trees that loomed like ghosts in the thick mist that surrounded her.

Wyn ran between trunks the color of ash, and twisted branches clawed at her hands, tearing her skin. She pushed further, but the branches grew thicker with every step, until she found herself climbing from branch to branch as the earth disappeared in the mist below.

She continued to climb until she reached the top of the tree. The branches flexed and swayed gently under her weight, a serene rhythm that never ceased, up and down, side to side, over and over again, and she surrendered to the exhaustion that weighed on her eyelids. There was no wind, and Wyn felt comfortably warm, so she was not sure where the tree might be. Somewhere far from ice and snow.

A stream burbled underneath her, soft and playful. Wyn tried to find it, but when she opened her eyes she could not see. The world was an unbroken, thick, velvety blackness that covered everything.

Wyn grabbed the branch firmly with both hands, but it swayed far to the side, and she could not hold on. She strained to keep her balance but the branch leaned further and further until Wyn was teetering on the edge. She twisted desperately and screamed as she slid helplessly off—

Her eyes snapped open and the world buried her dream. It was a confusing world, and she lay still as she tried to make sense of it. A low, wooden ceiling sloped an arm's-length above her face, and Wyn realized that she was under a thick pile of warm blankets on a narrow bed.

But the rest of the room made less sense. It was narrow and dim, with strangely curved walls and only a small window high on the wall to let in light, and it moved in a way that a room should not. The wood creaked and groaned as it shifted back and forth, and Wyn realized that the far wall was below her, as if the room had been tipped at an angle.

The sound of the stream from her dream filled the room, water burbling past somewhere nearby. A tall tree drifted across the tiny window and Wyn suddenly understood that she was in a boat. She smiled to herself, and as her confusion vanished, her eyes closed and she sank into a dreamless sleep.

***

Wyn awoke when the motion of the boat ceased. Small thumps sounded through the wooden walls of the cabin and the boat rocked once and then settled. Wyn heard the rush of a line across the deck above her head, and then a low creaking as first one end of the boat and then the other touched lightly against something firm. Trees filled the small window, tall pines that thrust their tips against a leaden sky.

Wyn thought briefly about crawling from her blankets, but she was far too warm and far too weary. Footsteps pattered lightly across the ceiling, then a small door at the end of the cabin opened, freezing air swirled into the room, and the feeble light of a winter dusk stabbed Wyn's eyes cruelly.

Danielle stepped through the hatch and closed it behind her. She blew furiously on hands clenched against the cold as she moved to a small, iron stove at the center of the cabin and busied herself with the softly glowing embers inside.

Wyn watched Danielle for a moment as profound relief flowed through her. Danielle appeared exhausted, her face drawn and her black hair in tangles from the wind and wet. Her cloak was soaked and she shivered as she waited for the stove to warm.

"Hi, Beautiful," said Wyn softly.

Danielle whirled and a smile of joy transformed her, fatigue washed away in an instant. A single step took her from the stove to Wyn's side, and she brought her lips to Wyn's in a kiss filled with the tender urgency of long loneliness, fear, and the rush of relief.

Wyn squirmed to release her arms from her blankets and held Danielle tight. Deep, comfortable moments quietly passed, their gentle breathing the only sound as they lay in each other's arms.

Then Danielle sat upright as far as the low ceiling would allow and gently stroked Wyn's hair from her face. Danielle's gaze roamed across Wyn's features, meticulously taking in every detail.

"How do you feel?" Danielle asked.

Wyn ooched into a sitting position and rested her back against the bulkhead. She was not yet certain how to answer Danielle's question. She felt warm and tired, but as she moved she could feel that there were unfathomable aches of wrongness. Her chest throbbed painfully and her hands felt thick and awkward and were wrapped tightly in bandages. Worst of all, there was a strange cloud of confusion in her mind, as if her thoughts were smothered, although it receded into the background as she took in a breath of the chill air.

"Terrible," she admitted. "How long have I been asleep?"

"Two days," answered Danielle. "Can you tell me what feels wrong?"

"My hands sort of hurt and are numb at the same time, and I feel weak as a kitten, like the time I had the fever when I was little. And it hurts right here." Wyn frowned as she placed her fingertips against her sternum. "Was I sick?"

"No, not sick," answered Danielle, and Wyn saw concern flash across her eyes. "Do you not remember?"

We were in a mountain, Wyn thought. The obscuring clouds thickened as she tried to recall. *We were in a mountain talking with God! How did I forget that?* She gently probed the pain in her chest as she tried to think, but the ache extended further than her fingers could reach.

"We were in the Mountain, right?" Wyn asked. "I met God." *And a chamber lit by lanterns… where was that? Markings on the floor… the dungeons beneath Bandirma? Or was that a dream?*

Danielle gently stopped Wyn's fingers. "Yes, we were in the Mountain, but after that, you do not remember?"

Markings on the floor, and fire… but the clouds were too thick. "No, nothing else… it's all hazy." Wyn searched Danielle's face anxiously. "Dani, tell me what happened."

"We were captured as we left the Mountain. I am not sure what happened during the fight, but when I awoke we were prisoners somewhere beneath Bandirma." Danielle paused for a moment, as if unwilling to give new life to her memories, and when she continued her voice was strained, and each word heavy with sadness and anger. "Reverend Whitebrooke freed us from the dungeons, but it was a trap. He had stolen the Martyr's Blade from my room, but it was useless to him without its Word. He tricked me into using the Word when we were attacked."

"Whitebrooke?" Wyn felt a memory seethe in her mind. *A man standing over us… then the flash of fire and pain.*

"Yes, he is the Crunorix priest," Danielle's face hardened, and Wyn quailed at the pain in Danielle's voice.

"Did he hurt you?" Wyn asked quietly.

"Not my body." Danielle glanced away.

"Martyr, what… what did he do?" Wyn asked desperately.

"Whitebrooke boasted that he had found a way to use fuil crunor to bring back his wife from beyond the shroud. But he needed the Blade for some reason, and I said the Word where he could hear it." Danielle's hand sought the ring that no longer hung around her neck, then dropped, as if strengthless, into her lap. "I told him…"

Wyn tried to think of some words of comfort, but she felt only relief, and she simply rested her bandaged hand carefully on Danielle's thigh, wishing she was not as useless as she felt.

Danielle stroked Wyn's hand gently. "You were so brave, Wyn. When he revealed what he had done, you leapt after him so quickly, I did not even know you had moved. But he was protected by a Wardpact, one designed to kill anyone who tried to harm him."

"That was it for me then, was it?"

Danielle turned to Wyn. She nodded, and her sad smile crumbled into bottomless pain. "You were barely breathing, and I could not feel your heart, it was so faint. I thought I was going to lose you."

"It's 'get stabbed in the face' for him then," said Wyn, and she tried to force lightheartedness into her voice. "What about these?" She held up her wrapped hands. They throbbed and burned under the bandages, although the pain was strangely numb and distant. She flexed her hands tentatively. Pain flared anew as the fingers of her right hand curled as far as the bandages would allow, but far worse was the panic that churned through her stomach as the fingertips of her left hand barely moved, no matter how hard she tried.

"Let them rest," Danielle said hurriedly. "They are burned, and I put a salve on them to dull the pain. There was only a little and that is used up now, so be gentle and let them heal."

"But it doesn't work!" Wyn tried to gulp back the shrillness that had crept into her voice. She twisted her left hand back and forth, straining to make her fingers respond further than a small twitch. Her arm trembled as well, and Wyn realized that she could barely hold it aloft. "And my arm, what's wrong with it? What happened?" she blurted out.

"It was Whitebrooke's ward," Danielle tried to soothe her, but Wyn could see the strain on her face. "When you attacked him, there was fire, and your knives shattered. That is how you were hurt."

Wyn laughed hopelessly. "A one-handed thief with no knives, that's wonderful."

"They will heal, I promise." Danielle held her gaze, and Wyn felt some of the pressure recede from her throat. "Wyn, I promise you, and I will take care of you until they do."

"You're sure?" Wyn wanted to believe.

"Yes, I am certain," Danielle said encouragingly. "They will hurt quite a bit, I am afraid, once the salve wears off, but I did not see anything that would not heal, given rest." Danielle tenderly stroked Wyn's hair. "You must promise me you will rest. It will help your hands, but it is even more critical that you rest your heart. I fear that Whitebrooke's ward damaged it when it injured your hands, and I can do little to help with that."

"Damaged my heart? Is that why my whole body hurts and I'm so weak?" Wyn sank against the bulkhead. "This is, so far, not my favorite day."

"I know it must be awful, but you are past the worst of it," Danielle assured her. "I have heard some say that it feels as if a horse is standing on your chest, and you cannot breathe."

"I remember that, but I thought it was a dream." Wyn brushed at a hair tickling her cheek, winced as her fingers sent new shards of pain lancing across her hands, and then groaned in exasperation. "Martyr's tears! You say this will get worse? Fine, all right, I'll be good. Rest. Lesson learned."

"Just for a little while, until the skin has healed and your heart feels strong," agreed Danielle. "I can manage the boat easily enough and take care of you."

"How did we get here? You haven't said. Did Shitebrooke let us go?"

"No, it was you." Danielle managed a smile. "They threw us into the dungeons again. I tried to help you, but all I could do was call your name. Then you opened your eyes and you asked, 'Did I kill him?' You were so exhausted and in so much pain I thought you were going to faint at any moment, but you did not. You freed us from our cell and led us through some passageways that must have been hidden for centuries, they were so coated with dust and dirt."

"I don't faint. And the boat?"

"The passage led to the river docks. It must go all the way under the river. I picked the smallest boat with a cabin and helped you on board, and we were gone before anyone came searching. No one could have caught us, not with how fast the river runs there."

Danielle made it sound easy, but Wyn could well imagine what it must have been like. Fingers that fumbled in their haste to untie ropes, a half-dead girl to drag across the open dock, all the while on edge for the shout or cry that meant you had not moved fast enough.

"What's the plan for killing that shit-stain?"

"There is no plan," Danielle laughed desperately. "I have been running so fast I have not thought of anything else. Wyn, we have only the clothes on our backs and I have no idea where to go that we might be safe. We cannot know what Whitebrooke has told the rest of the Council, or how long he can conceal his treachery, but we dare not risk revealing ourselves."

"Yeah, that makes sense, especially seeing as I couldn't fight off a sheep right now. Do you think anyone would notice if we just kept sailing until we reach your home?" asked Wyn. "We could spend the winter swimming in the ocean."

Danielle laughed and a real smile returned to her lips, and Wyn felt her heart lift in return.

"Swimming sounds wonderful. I dreamed of us together in the ocean, did I tell you? It was the night we spent in the Mountain. We had spoken of traveling home and I suppose it was on my mind." Danielle swept her hair from her face as she attempted to detangle some of the strands with her fingers. She sighed contentedly. "It was a good dream."

Danielle closed the stove and hung her cloak from a peg on the wall near the stove's heat. Wyn watched her as she made them some food, hard bread and salted meat pillaged from the boat's stores. Danielle still appeared tired, of course, but less weary than when Wyn had first glimpsed her entering the cramped cabin. Sleep weighed heavily on Wyn's eyelids as she chewed on her food, and she realized that she was a long way from recovering from Whitebrooke's attack.

That's fine, she told herself, *as long as I'm ready when it's time to kill him.*

After dinner, Danielle doused the lantern, kicked off her boots, and crawled into the narrow bunk, her body warm where she pressed against Wyn. Wyn snuggled into Danielle's arms and drifted into a blissful slumber filled with dreams of smooth, gleaming bodies in deep, blue water.

***

Danielle made them a thin soup by boiling the dried meat with some onions and a fistful of crumbled biscuits, and then they argued over how best for Wyn to eat it, with Danielle insisting that she did not mind feeding her patient, and Wyn stubbornly insisting that she was not a baby, too self-conscious to accept Danielle's aid.

They compromised in allowing Wyn to cradle the bowl in her mittened hands and slurp the broth, although Danielle raised an eyebrow at some of the noises that ensued and Wyn's hands ached with fresh pain from the bowl's weight.

Neither woman spoke as they ate, but Wyn found the silence restful and she soon relaxed and took the opportunity to watch Danielle again. The subtle twist of her wrist as she scooped the broth, the delicate grip of her fingers on the old, bent spoon, the purse of her lips as she blew to cool it.

"You know, a girl could get used to this," Wyn said happily.

"It is my pleasure," Danielle told her softly. "I am sorry the fare was so meager."

Wyn leaned against the bulkhead, exhausted by the effort of feeding herself. Her hands did seem to feel a little better, but she did not want to risk flexing her fingers again to find out how much. She had learned her lesson.

"You said we escaped with just the clothes on our backs?" Wyn asked. "So, where did I get this from?" Wyn spread her arms and let her nightshirt hang from her like a tent, the sleeves drooping from her fingertips.

"It was here, on the boat," Danielle replied. "I suppose it belongs to the owner, whoever he is. He left us a bit of food and a small box of medicines and bandages, but little else."

"Does that mean I have clothes somewhere?"

"Of course," said Danielle, and she opened the small locker under the bunk and placed a neatly folded pile on top of the blankets.

"Oh!" Wyn exclaimed. "Look, it's my dress! It's all clean and mended."

"It is still not a dress," Danielle laughed. "Not even a skirt, not by a hand's-breadth."

"I wear pants with it," Wyn admonished her. "So just you keep your naughty ideas to yourself. Actually, don't keep them to yourself. Share."

Danielle blushed. "How do you always know when I am thinking of such things? You can read my mind, I believe."

"Dani, you can look at me anytime you want to." Wyn smiled. "It's sweet that you're shy about it, but we are together, right? Maker knows I stare at you all the time, so if you want to watch my bum, knock yourself out."

"I…" Danielle's flush rose from her throat to cover her cheeks.

"That was an easy guess," Wyn giggled. "My bum's my best feature."

Wyn climbed from the bunk, slowly and cautiously. Danielle quickly moved to support her but Wyn waved away her hands. "I better be able to dress myself, or else we're in real trouble."

In the end, Wyn managed to struggle out of her nightshirt and into her leggings and tunic, but had to ask Danielle for help with her boots. Her heart beat so frantically that she grew breathless and faint when she tried to pull the boots onto her feet, and her bandaged fingers had no strength and shook uncontrollably as she tried to tie the laces. Danielle kept her face lowered as she fastened them but Wyn saw the concern on her face before she glanced away.

Wyn leaned against the bunk to steady herself and gasped, "He really did a number on me, huh?"

"Bodies heal given time," Danielle consoled. "Especially if the spirit is strong."

"You mean, if I stop moping." Wyn took a resolute breath. "Fine, I've more than enough mad at Reverend Shitebrooke to get me motivated."

"We survived him, that is what is important," said Danielle fiercely. "You will get your strength back, never fear, and we will make sure Whitebrooke pays for what he did to us."

"Oooo, I like that sound of that. Gave me a nice shiver, that did," Wyn said.

"Yes, it sounds extremely dramatic, does it not?" Danielle frowned. "But I have no idea what it might entail."

"Well, last night you said we needed to stay safe, and that still makes sense." Wyn took an uncertain step and grasped the small railing by the door, then snatched her hand back as pain flared from the contact. *Stupid girl, stop bloody touching things.* Wyn gathered herself and took another wobbly step. "So we go and hide, nice and quiet, until they've forgotten all about us. Then we kill that murdering son of a bitch. Oh, and get your Blade back, just like God told us to."

"Where are you going?" Danielle hovered anxiously behind Wyn, her hands raised to catch Wyn as she teetered on the steps that led through the hatch.

"Out." Wyn tried to push open the hatch with her elbow, then let out a stream of curses as she staggered and whacked her hand on the wall.

Wyn sat on the step and seethed as the pain slowly dissipated, one throb at a time. Danielle silently opened the hatch, letting cold, damp air into the cabin, and then sat on the top step, her hands folded in her lap to avoid the chill.

"Is there anyone about up there?" Wyn eventually asked.

"No, there is no one." Danielle twisted and glanced around. "We are in the middle of nowhere."

"Oh, good," Wyn replied, and vented her rage and frustration and pain in a scream that tore her throat and doubled her over as it ripped from her. The sound was thin and weak and left her panting with the effort, but it took with it some of the throbbing dread that coiled beneath her bandages, and she felt it whirl into the grey mist with satisfaction.

Wyn leaned against the wall and drew in a deep breath as the scream finally passed.

"Lovely," she said, and met Danielle's gaze. "Sorry about that."

Danielle nodded, and hurried to help Wyn up the steps and into the small cockpit of the boat. Danielle's hands were strong and warm where they held her, and Wyn sagged against her with relief until Danielle maneuvered her gently onto the small, wooden bench.

Wyn saw that they were moored in a small inlet, the water flat and grey, a blurred mirror of the low clouds scudding overhead, and a steady mist coated their cloaks with beads of water. Trees crowded the banks, the bare branches of the oaks and elms scratching together while the pines rustled in the gusts of wind from the north.

"Much better," Wyn said half-heartedly.

"I am sorry your reward is so poor." Danielle poked a gloved hand free of her cloak long enough to indicate the muddy embankment. "But at least you are outside. The cabin is so terribly mean."

"Oh, it's not so bad." Wyn tried to sound convincing. The wind blew strands of her hair into golden streamers that waved around her face, but she did not make a move to corral them, and instead peered disinterestedly about the cockpit and across the water.

"Perhaps at the next town we might buy some real food," Danielle suggested. "I believe I should bleed crumbs if I were to eat one more biscuit."

Wyn smiled and nodded. "Some tasty tuck sounds good to me."

"Perhaps we could find a tavern with a fire," Danielle continued. "One with some music? I still owe you a dance, I…" She trailed off, suddenly realizing her misstep. "I am sorry, Wyn, that was thoughtless of me."

"That's all right," Wyn shrugged. "I forget sometimes, too."

Wyn stared fixedly forward, furious, although she could not tell who she was furious at. There were too many choices. Whitebrooke, for the pain he had caused them both. Her body, for the weakness that made her feel so helpless and vulnerable. And, most of all, herself. Wyn felt the silence strain for the first time between her and Danielle, and she cursed herself for her stupidity.

"Well, some warm food, in any case," Danielle ventured lamely.

"Sounds lovely," Wyn sighed sadly.

The quiet stretched as Danielle began to ready the boat to sail. Wyn watched the sails billow and fill as they swung from side to side, and Danielle balanced the boat against the wind as she piloted it out of the inlet and onto the main river.

"Where shall we go?" Danielle asked.

"You're asking me?"

"We need to escape and hide," Danielle pointed out. "You are the master of stealth and concealment, not I."

"I suppose. All right, well, we don't go near anywhere they might think to look. That means not Glen Walden, not Kuray."

"Not Kuray?" Danielle asked, frowning. "I would have thought Kuray was the safest place for us to be."

"I'm sure those who are looking for us will think that, too. They will be watching for us to go there, I promise, and we'll never make it. They'll know I lived there most of my life, and of course that your sister lives there."

"My sister," Danielle said wearily. "Wyn, I am worried about Gabrielle. After the attack on her in Bandirma, I was confident that she would be safe, that whatever was happening, Karsha Hali would protect her until the Crunorix could be defeated. But with Whitebrooke guiding the Temple from within, the situation is much worse than I feared."

"I'm sure she got away," Wyn objected. "Karsha was ready to shove her out of the room, I'd say, and he seemed the sort to have a trick or two up his sleeve."

"True, they might have escaped, and may well be fugitives, just as we are," Danielle agreed, "but we do not know, and that is what scares me." She took a deep, steadying breath. "Very well, not Kuray. Then where? Irongate? I am sure Bradon's cousins would help us."

"Um. Could be," Wyn said doubtfully. "Seems a bit obvious, as well, honestly. I'd say the first thing to do is find out as much about what they're up to as we can, then we'll know where's best to hide."

"How do we do that?"

"We go to a town and ask around, easy as wishing."

"We go into a town?"

"Yeah," Wyn replied. "Littleford, I think."

"Littleford!" Danielle was aghast. "But it is so close to Bandirma."

"That just means its rumors will be fresh, is all," Wyn laughed. "It's on a river, so we can sail up nice and close and get away fast once we're done."

"It will certainly be swarming with people searching for us."

"Yeah, for us," Wyn agreed. "Really for you. Not a poor crippled girl traveling by herself."

"No!" Danielle's eyes widened with fear. "Oh, Wyn, no."

"Dani, I've done this hundreds of times." Wyn put as much confidence into her voice as she could, although her stomach was squirming with terror. *You can't even walk, you stupid girl. And look at what you are doing to Dani.* But her anger was even stronger, hatred for the weakness that caused her to hesitate and fear. Wyn swallowed to try to clear the constriction that suddenly encircled her throat, and hoped that Danielle could not hear the quiver in her voice. "I promise I'll be fine, and then we'll know and we can figure out what to do."

Danielle nodded her head miserably. "I shall be cross if I have to carry you out of another dungeon," she tried, but she could not hide the desperation in her voice, and it stabbed Wyn's heart so cruelly that she felt tears sting her eyes.

Wyn blinked furiously and did not trust her voice to make a reply.

THE MARTYR'S TEARS

Killock

Killock opened his eyes and lay still as his heartbeat gradually slowed, and he listened to the soft sounds of water trickling amongst the leaves and roots of the forest around him. Fat drops plopped as they hit the puddles amongst the roots, pattered as they fell on the leaves and branches above, and vanished with dull, flat splats when they hit the thick moss that covered the rocks.

He saw a faint, grey light through the branches, signaling the far-distant approach of dawn, but the forest was still thick with darkness beneath the trees, and the knight could not see farther than the dim shapes of the trunks that reared from the mossy floor in a circle around the camp.

"Your dreams have disturbed your sleep," a familiar, sonorous rumble murmured from the black shadows on the far side of the camp. Killock followed the voice to a heavy shape sitting with its back against a tree. Killock could not make out Lord Faron's wide shoulders or thick cloak, but the knight knew that Faron's dark eyes would be gazing, unblinking, across the camp at him.

Killock sat up and arranged his cloak around his shoulders, then laid his sword across his lap. The worn pommel felt dry and smooth under his fingers, and he let them rest gently on the grip for a moment before slowly drawing a hand's-breadth of steel free from the sheath. His fingers slid down to the blade, cautiously tracing the elaborate shapes that were now engraved onto the steel, a pattern still utterly unfamiliar to his touch. Then, reassured the sword still bore its fresh runes, Killock slid the blade home again with a quiet snap.

"It was not a dream," he told Faron.

***

The thin, grey rain that had drenched the low hills all day trickled to a stop as dusk leached the pale winter light from the world.

A wide road wound through the forest, reduced by the rain to a maze of standing water and deceptive, soft islands, ready to envelop wagon wheels and engulf boots. As the road climbed it swept past massive trunks of trees until it finally crested the last of the rumpled hills and saw the lights of Bandirma glowing in the valley below. Three riders stood on the ridge and their horses stamped impatiently as their masters silently watched the city from beneath dripping hoods.

Golden streams marked the meandering paths of lantern-lit streets, and the buildings were studded with warm glows from windows and doors. The wide surface of Loughliath etched a line of black against the lights, a stroke that traced the city's northern edge in sharp contrast as it curved beneath the hill upon which the riders stood.

Beyond the city loomed the great, black bulk of the hill into which the Temple of Bandirma had been carved. Even on a night thick with clouds, the hill was clear. Its shadow mocked the lesser shade that cloaked the valley around it. Constellations of light scattered across the face of the hill, windows and terraces beyond count, a twinkling field to replace the hidden night sky.

The riders urged their mounts toward the city and the horses' hooves clattered on worn cobbles as they raced across the final distance. But the riders were soon forced to rein in their headlong rush, as, despite the late hour, the streets of the city were alive with activity. Mounted soldiers passed hurriedly toward the dark forest roads on urgent patrols, while the townspeople paused to stare and point and wonder at the interruption in their normal routines. A line of wagons waited on the side of the road, their drivers seated in circles playing dice, smoking pipes, and complaining about missing a day on the road, while a squad of soldiers slowly made their way down the line, scrutinizing the loads that filled the wagons.

Similar consternation enveloped the lake dock, where empty boats awaited cargoes that should have been loaded long before, and armies of tired, bored stevedores watched more soldiers crawl over stacks of crates and barrels on the quay.

At last, the riders reached the entrance to the temple, the massive bulk of the Tùr Abhainn. The sheer face of the River Wall blazed with torchlight as it loomed over the Abhainn Fuar and the wide stone bridge that spanned it. Grim-faced knights stood at the end of the bridge and motioned for the riders to halt before they could pass through the long tunnel and into the temple.

"State your names, friends," a knight instructed, staring into the shadows under the riders' hoods.

"You know me, Sir Hollis." One of the riders swept back his hood, revealing cropped hair so fair that it blazed white in the light from the lanterns, and fierce eyes the color of ice gleamed above a mouth set in thin-lipped disapproval.

The knight's eyes widened with shock, and he quickly nodded his head in deference. "Sir Roland, I apologize, I was not expecting you."

The other two riders pulled back their hoods as well, and Sir Hollis quickly included them in his greeting. "Lord Faron, Sir Killock, welcome home."

Killock ran gloved fingers through his shaggy hair and scratched away the rough wool of his hood as he returned Sir Hollis' nod.

"Gate duty, Sir Hollis?" Roland asked the knight, and Killock saw Sir Hollis glance to the stone surface of the bridge for an instant before returning the Templar's gaze defiantly.

"Just while I recover from a wound, Sir Roland."

"Is the Temple closed, that travelers must be stopped and questioned at the gates?" Roland's eyes followed a squad of scouts as they thundered across the bridge and into the city.

"Yes, Sir Roland, I'm afraid so. Until we catch the fugitives who murdered Bishop Benno."

"Still no word of success?"

"No, sir, not yet."

"Perhaps you fear that my saddle bags conceal another assassin?"

"No, Sir Roland, of course not. You may pass."

Roland tapped his horse on its flanks and the black stallion snorted and strode into the tunnel, stepping high as its hooves rang from the stone. Killock nodded silently to Sir Hollis and followed Sir Roland, but the third rider paused beside the knight on the bridge.

"You seek redemption, a chance to atone." Lord Faron's voice was a quiet rumble, resonant and clear despite the roar of the river through the stone channels beneath their feet. Sir Killock turned in his saddle to watch. The rider dwarfed the knight on the bridge, but it was Lord Faron's gaze that made Sir Hollis take a step back. Lord Faron remained silent for a moment more, watching the knight, before shaking his head in sympathy. "You will not find it here, a dog watching a door closed far too late."

Only then did Lord Faron ride into the tunnel, and Killock fell in beside him.

"They have not found her," Faron observed as they dismounted at the far end of the tunnel and walked their horses across the wide bailey to the stables. He studied the courtyard, his dark eyes serene as they took in the sentries who lined the walls. "You must be pleased."

Killock followed the lord's gaze. "I had hoped they would have discovered reason by now." Killock's horse nudged his shoulder, a gentle reminder that the knight had stopped walking and that rest and food waited within sight. Killock patted the chestnut stallion on its neck and resumed his walk, feeling the ache of days in the saddle in every step.

Lord Faron did not seem to share anything as mundane as weariness. He was unhurried as he walked beside Killock, but his gait held a slowness of dignity and noble grace unaffected by the toil of the road. Long, dark hair draped across the shoulders of his fur-lined cloak, and he appeared unaware of the thick steel armor that he wore over his heavy frame. Even Faron's horse followed him without any apparent effort on the lord's part, and the reins hung loose and forgotten in his gauntleted hand.

"They have heard one tale." Faron's voice was a smooth rumble, and a soft smile spread across his heavy lips. "Perhaps you will tell them another."

Killock held Faron's gaze for a moment. "A tale?"

"It cannot be otherwise. Words are a story, nothing else. You know this."

"I know that there are lies," Killock drew in his breath and let it run out in a long, calming sigh, "and there is truth. If you seek it long enough, you can find the proof to reveal one from the other."

Faron granted the tall knight a slight nod of his head. "That will give strength to the telling."

They joined Roland and gave their horses to the care of the stables, and the three Templars walked side-by-side across the bailey to the tall doors of the temple. A crowd began to form around them as word of their arrival at the gates summoned every acolyte and priest with a chance to slip away from duty, and by the time the three Templars reached the wide steps before the doors the space between the tall pillars was packed with figures in robes of brown and white, their faces filled with awe.

Two figures waited for the Templars in a small gap at the top of the stairs, silhouetted against the brilliant light that shone through the open doors.

Reverend Nesta greeted the Templars with her hands held out to welcome them. The high priestess was dressed in simple, white robes and her ash-grey hair was tied in a severe bun. Beside Nesta stood Sir Maeglin, tall and stern in his steel armor, his eyes hooded as they flickered over the new arrivals.

"Sir Killock." Reverend Nesta grasped his hands, holding them firmly as she met his gaze. Her round face was etched with lines of concern, and she gave the knight a small, sympathetic smile. She squeezed his hands again and then greeted Roland and Faron in turn, exchanging quiet words with each.

"I've asked the others to join us in the Council chamber," Nesta informed them as she led the way through the Atrium, guarded by its stone saints, and the Sanctuary, presided over by the benevolent gaze of mighty Taliesin himself. "It is a marvelous surprise to find you on our steps this evening."

"Especially you, Sir Killock." Maeglin's voice was a dry rasp against the stone walls of the passageway. "Sir Lochlan sent a bird saying that you were on your way here. We expected you long before now."

"I was delayed," Killock replied, matching the Knight Commander's gaze for a moment.

"By duties more urgent than defending your home? You should have returned here at once."

"I should have. Then, perhaps I could have prevented the insanity that has affected you all. Accusing Danielle of being a Crunorix? Imprisoning her? It is absurd."

"Is it?" Maeglin replied coldly. "Evidence was presented, Killock. Lady Danielle could have contested the charges. Instead, she chose to flee."

"Did she? Or is that another lie?"

Sir Maeglin's face paled with anger, but Nesta spoke first.

"What do you mean?" Nesta asked. "Speak clearly, Sir Killock, I don't wish you to be misunderstood. Are you accusing Sir Maeglin, or myself, of secretly imprisoning Lady Danielle without trial? Do you really think we are capable of such a terrible thing?"

"I would not have thought either of you capable of believing Danielle was a Crunorix priest," Killock replied. "But I will render no judgments without proof. There has been enough of that.

Whether Danielle escaped, or she was taken captive by the real Crunorix, or she is still imprisoned here, I will find out the truth, I promise you that."

"That is all we want, as well, I assure you," Nesta said.

"Good. Where is Wyn? I want to see her, immediately. I want to hear this story from her lips."

"Bronwyn? Lady Danielle's friend?" Nesta asked, puzzled.

"She escaped with Danielle," Maeglin interjected. "She also faces charges."

"What charges? Do you think she is a Crunorix as well?"

"She resisted the soldiers sent to arrest Lady Danielle, and she aided Lady Danielle in her escape."

"I am sure she did," Killock said. His jaw clenched as worry and pride twisted through him. *Of course, she would have fought. Against armored soldiers...* Killock's heart quailed away from the cruel images that pushed into his mind. *I must find her.*

"Do you wish to interview the soldiers she injured?" Maeglin scowled. "Do you accuse us of conspiracy in this, as well?"

"Enough, for goodness sake. We have been attacked, and terribly hurt, and we haven't managed to do a bloody thing except make it worse," Nesta said with finality. "Don't look so dour, Maeglin, you know we haven't. Karsha Hali escaped, and Lady Danielle slipped through our fingers before we could help her, or ask her a single question. We could hardly have done worse, and standing here bickering about it does not do us any good."

"No, it does not," Roland said with steel in his voice. "Our enemy gathers his strength while we whine and lick our wounds. Killock has seen it."

"What have you seen?" Maeglin asked.

"The rituals in the hinterlands opened a passage and summoned a magus through. This, I am sure Danielle told you. But beyond the passage lies far worse than one magus, for it leads to the Black Grave itself."

"The Black Grave?" Nesta stopped in the center of the hallway and faced Killock, her brow knotted with concern. "Are you certain, Sir Killock? The Black Grave?"

"I am certain."

"It does not seem credible, does it?"

"As fanciful as tales of magi, fuil crunor rituals, and the return of the Crunorix." *Or of Danielle a willing Crunorix.*

"I wanted nothing to do with believing those, either, so it shows you how marvelous my judgment is," Nesta admitted.

"Benno believed them enough to fear that they might be true," Killock reminded her, "as did He."

"Yes." Nesta glanced away but Killock caught the flash of pain that darted through the high priestess's eyes and the sudden stillness that surrounded the Knight Commander beside her.

"Tell us of the Black Grave, then," Nesta brushed away whatever had troubled her with a sigh. "I know little, outside of the legends, and I am afraid by 'legends' I mean exclusively the tale of Sir Corvicus and Lady Elizabeth, which I read repeatedly as a girl. One assumes it is very grim?"

"It is unimaginable," Killock answered softly, "foul in every stone, and even in their sleep, the presence of the magi is everywhere, a presence that presses against your thoughts and your breath."

"Was there not a seal on the Grave? To trap the magi after the Nameless King was defeated?"

"Yes, and the Seal yet stands. The Gravewardens have guarded it for a millennium, and not even the Cataclysm interrupted their vigil. But these recent fuil crunor rituals, in the hinterlands of Albyn and here in Bandirma, have opened a new portal, one not guarded by the Seal."

"It is that easy to circumvent the Seal? A single priest, a few rituals?"

"Unfortunately, it appears so. The Gravewardens were bewildered by this news, as well. They thought the Seal to be inviolate. Perhaps the Conclave held after the defeat of the Nameless King felt that destroying all traces of the Crunorix would prevent anyone from learning the rituals required? It worked for a thousand years."

"Hmmm. Or perhaps the Conclave were fools. Now we must deal with the mess they left us. This new portal beneath the

Fellgate that Lady Danielle described… the Crunorix can use it as well?"

"There is nothing to stop the magi from coming forth," Killock concurred, "and they are stirring within the Black Grave. We have little time."

"Sir Lochlan has moved his army to guard against that," Reverend Nesta pointed out.

"True," Killock agreed. "But he will need our help. Swords alone will not stop the Crunorix if they are freed."

"Do we even know… if we stop Karsha Hali, if we stop his rituals, will the portal close? Will the magi be trapped once more?" Nesta asked.

"No one knows. The Gravewardens fear that it has created a tear that will stay open until mended, but they are guessing as much as we are."

"I remember the Gravewardens were extremely proud and mysterious in my reads." Nesta smiled. "However, I seem to have stopped us in the middle of the hallway, so despite wanting very much to relive my childhood right this moment, shall we find the rest of the Council, and allow you to tell your story just once?"

They passed in silence through the bustling passages of the outer Temple, a grim troop in the midst of hurrying acolytes, dignified priests, imperturbable soldiers, and the hubbub of hundreds of voices, earnest and lighthearted in seemingly equal measures.

Killock passed an acolyte with a sheepish expression and bowed head being scolded by a stern priest, then a cluster of young clerics arguing dogma and dinner with equal passion as they swarmed toward the dining hall. Two soldiers stood easy, laughing as they were teased by a chambermaid with a basket on her hip, as if they stood in the marketplace of any village in Albyn. The soldiers straightened and nodded respectfully as Sir Maeglin walked by, but the smiles never left their faces, and they soon returned happily to being mocked by the young woman.

I had forgotten the noise, the life which infests Bandirma. It is sometimes too easy to think of it as merely a place, or a symbol, when you are far away on the edges of the world. It is good to remember that it is much more.

They eventually departed the outer rooms and entered the precincts of the inner Temple, as solemn and imposing in its dignified work as the outer hallways had been lively. Hardly a murmur of voices reached the wide hallways, and Killock could clearly hear the scratching of quills on parchment as they passed the open doors of the scriptoriums.

At last, they reached the Council Chamber, its curved benches empty, its balconies silent. In the center stood the raised dais with its circle of chairs where the Council held court as they met with the stewards, knights, and priests who needed their guidance and judgment. But the Council had eschewed their customary roost, and instead clustered together in the space before the chairs, as if unwilling to be too far apart.

Reverend Liadán smiled sadly as she greeted Killock, but Reverend Ail could hardly meet his eye and offered only a quick greeting before turning awkwardly away.

"Sir Killock," Reverend Haley welcomed him warmly, but there was a trace of sadness in her voice as well that could not be fully concealed. "Welcome home."

"Your Reverence."

"We won't wait for Reverend Dougal," Reverend Nesta decided. "There is no telling when he might finally arrive, and Reverend Whitebrooke is not able to join us."

"That would be best," Faron agreed, "for there is dark news that looms over you all."

"I am afraid that is true." Nesta paused to take a deep breath, and Killock saw that her green eyes were lined with red. *It cannot be about Wyn or Danielle...* his mind refused to complete the thought.

"You know already that Bishop Benno was murdered by a Crunorix priest, but what we have hidden from everyone is that Reverend Benno was not the only victim of that evil. The Crunorix somehow managed to force their way into the Mountain, and there was a terrible battle."

"Rúreth?" Roland asked.

"I'm sorry," Nesta said sadly. "She fell, guarding the entrance. There is, however, even worse news to tell. God… He is gone."

Killock's mind groped for words, but none came. A numbness surrounded him as if he were enveloped in soft webs that somehow stopped sense from forming thoughts. Killock watched Roland shout and rage in fury, his pale eyes fierce, his skin ashen. He watched Nesta helplessly nod, misery etched in the kindly lines of her face. Faron's voice flowed past Killock, but for once it held no power, and the words slipped away without penetrating the cocoon.

"Rowenna and Gwydion…" Killock heard himself say. "They journey to the Mountain."

"When?" asked Nesta quickly.

"We parted ways on the Rathad an Sliabh."

"We will send a bird to the guards on the road," the high priestess said, "and hope that it arrives in time to stop them."

"Are they in danger?" Roland demanded.

"Of course they are," Reverend Haley said sharply. "No one we've sent to the Mountain has come out, not since Reverend Whitebrooke returned."

"Whitebrooke? The Archivist?" Roland was baffled.

"Yes. He was there. He's the one that told us what happened."

"Then I have many questions for him," Faron said.

"You will require patience, my lord," Nesta told him. "Reverend Whitebrooke lapsed into coma after his ordeal in the Mountain and has only recently awoken. I fear the strain that more questioning may inflict on him."

Killock heard little of what was said after that. His mind retreated again, chased by pain and shadow. The red eyes of the magus watched from the center of the pursuers, and Killock once again felt the bitter cold of the Black Grave and smelled the corrupted stench of Nóinín Cnoc. He tried to imagine those eyes in the sanctuary deep within the Mountain, but he could not. The two images refused to exist together, nor could he picture the black shadow of fuil crunor staining the stone, nor could he understand how the great Voice might not sound through those halls again.

Is that why He called us home? A cry for help that we were too late to answer? I would have been here, with Danielle and Wyn, if I had not returned to Twin Pines. I could have stood next to Rúreth, with Danielle at our side, if only—

But Killock was pulled from recrimination by the hollow boom of the chamber doors opening to admit a tall figure dressed in the robes of a high priest, his powerful frame filling the doorway, and Killock recognized the thick beard and craggy visage of the Archivist.

"Reverend Whitebrooke." Nesta regarded the priest with surprise. "I am pleased to see you arisen, thank the Maker. But should you not be in bed?"

The Archivist strode across the room and stood behind one of the chairs that faced the dais, and Killock saw the priest's knuckles turn white as he clutched the high-back chair tightly in his massive hand. *He does not appear well.* Whitebrooke's usually ruddy face was waxen, and his eyes were sunken and lined with red. Beads of sweat glistened from his high forehead and matted his thick hair, which was wild and unkempt.

"There is no need, Reverend Nesta." Whitebrooke dismissed the idea with a wave of his hand. "My idiot steward told me that the Templars had arrived, and I should be here."

"You are unwell." Heartfelt concern throbbed in Faron's voice. "The wounds from your struggle have left their mark."

"The battle took its toll," Whitebrooke spurned the Templar's concern. "I will recover."

"Yes, the battle in the Mountain. We are told that you are the only person who has survived entering the Mountain." Faron stepped to meet the priest face-to-face, a sad smile of such compassion and sympathy on his face that Killock felt his own heart labor for the release of the pain caught within it.

"That is correct," Whitebrooke answered shortly, disconcerted as he glanced around the circle of waiting faces. "What of it?"

"Tell us everything of what you saw, and how you came to survive. Leave nothing untold," Faron urged, and for a moment Killock saw Whitebrooke open his lips as if to reply immediately. But then the Archivist swallowed heavily and shook his shaggy head as he collected his thoughts.

"There is little new to tell. I was summoned to the Mountain, as I safeguard the Bishop's ring until the Convocation. But I arrived too late. The Crunorix had already penetrated the Mountain and Rúreth had fallen. By the time I reached the sanctuary the sounds of struggle were fading, and I was set upon by white-skinned creatures and a dark shade whose power I could not match."

"How did you survive?"

"I wielded the Martyr's Blade," Whitebrooke glared at the Templar, his dark eyes flashing. "I drove off the Crunorix, albeit only temporarily."

"You did?" Killock managed to keep his voice flat and emotionless, although surprise threatened to leave his mouth gaping for words. "How? Danielle is the only one who knows its Word, and she was driven from Bandirma. How did you end up with her Blade, or its Word?"

"We secured the Blade after Bishop Benno's murder," Whitebrooke ignored the Templar's concerns with a shrug, "and after she was captured on the Rathad an Sliabh I was able to persuade her to give me the Word. I had hoped that was a sign that she was beginning to break free of Karsha Hali's control, but that proved not to be the case."

Killock clamped his jaw shut as anger and disbelief threatened to burst through his control. He was not sure whether they would emerge as a laugh or a curse, but either would reveal too much as his thoughts collided with each other in an avalanche of confusion. *Danielle gave him the Word? Gave him the Blade? That is… beyond belief. And what does Whitebrooke mean, he 'persuaded' her?*

Killock found himself watching Whitebrooke as if from a distant hide, remote and yet also as intimate as the feathery touch of a flight against the cheek as the bow is drawn back within the shadows. The Archivist glared defiantly as Faron asked him questions, his bushy eyebrows furrowed, his beard jutting, a sneer flickering at the edge of his lips. *Has his anger always been there, hidden away where it could not be guessed at? Or has something changed since last I saw him?*

Whitebrooke said Danielle's name again, and Killock realized he had little idea what the priest had been saying.

"There was another ritual?" Killock slid his question into a gap in Whitebrooke's booming rush. "In Danielle's apartments?"

"Yes," Whitebrooke snorted, "as I have been explaining."

"I hadn't realized there was more than one," Killock said quietly, and Whitebrooke hesitated for an instant before replying.

"There were five, at least," Whitebrooke said, "and I witnessed several with my own eyes."

"But the first one, the one that killed Bishop Benno, you did not see? Was that one enough for you to determine the guilt of both Karsha Hali and Danielle? You knew before you saw the other rituals?"

"They are arduous to decipher," Whitebrooke waved away the question, exasperated. "As well as dangerous. I have had to be cautious."

"But you have persevered," Faron reminded the priest.

"Of course," Whitebrooke agreed.

"And you were able to uncover the people who created the ritual?" Faron prompted.

"Yes, that's correct. There is a mark, or perhaps better to call it a stain, left behind, that can be read if you have the skill."

'Like a stain or an old scar', Wyn's voice echoed in Killock's thoughts, and he felt the frozen breath of Nóinín Cnoc slide across his cheek, and saw the grey light of a winter day catch a wisp of golden hair as Wyn stared across a frozen valley. Killock watched Whitebrooke turn to answer other questions, the Archivist's gaze hesitating for a heartbeat before sliding away from Killock's. *I remember. A trail that Danielle followed to the magus which fed on the ritual's power. But it never revealed to her who had created the ritual. Those signs came from boot prints in the mud, nothing more mystical than that. There is much here that I do not understand. Much that does not make sense. But none of it helps me find Wyn.*

THE MARTYR'S TEARS

Killock strode to the door but was stopped with his hand on the latch by the rasp of Maeglin's voice.

"Are we boring you, Sir Killock?"

The Knight Commander stood next to the door, apart from the rest of the group, watching in silence. Killock met his gaze and wondered at the challenge in his pale eyes.

"I have heard enough. It's time to see for myself."

Maeglin nodded, a movement so slight that only the shifting of shadows across the steel cords of muscle along his neck revealed it. "Good luck."

"You cannot go to the archives," Whitebrooke announced, and Killock saw Maeglin's gaze shift slightly as the Knight Commander turned his attention to the priest. "It is still far too perilous."

Killock pulled the door open and strode through without a response, but Faron's words followed him into the hallway.

"He has seen far worse, and survived it."

Killock left the inner Temple and entered the deep quiet of the residential district, where wide passageways contained heavy doors of polished wood, far enough apart that rarely could one door see more than one or two neighbors, leading to the apartments of the highest echelons of the Temple.

He turned one last corner and entered a short hallway which contained only one door. Killock rested gloved fingers against the polished wood, lost for a moment in gentle memories of friendship and laughter and long evenings beside a fire with a glass of wine in his hand, enjoying the happiness of simply being with those he loved.

The door opened as he thumbed the latch, revealing a cold, dark space. He stepped inside, and his boots echoed on bare stone where thick rugs had once welcomed their tread. A hearth gaped empty in the far wall next to deep, comfortable chairs. Silver and crystal on the mantle gleamed sharp and cold in the light from the hall, an empty mockery of the brilliant sparkle that usually adorned them.

A dozen steps took Killock to the bedroom door. Inside, the bedroom was illuminated by a ghostly shaft of moonlight through the windows, enough that Killock could see that the once-magnificent room was in shambles. He stepped inside, and his boots crunched shards of glass against the stone floor. The light from the window was enough to reveal the elegant canopy of the bed hanging ripped and torn, chairs tipped over and shattered, clothes bought especially for the cold winters of a new home strewn haphazardly across the floor, and the debris of small mementos of far-away sun and waves, now smashed and splintered beyond recognition.

Gleaming scars crossed the walls, the stone slick and raw as if it had been blistered, then frozen into solidity. The scars crossed the room in wide sweeps, then traced a path across the ceiling.

In the center of the floor was a black stain. Killock could see that the discoloration had seeped into the stone itself, and had resisted what must have been vigorous attempts to dislodge it, judging by the stink of soap and lye that hovered in the room.

Killock squatted warily near the mark on the floor, vigilant to avoid its fluid shape and the out-flung tendrils that lay like the shadow of spilled oil sprayed across the floor. There were no signs of a fuil crunor ritual. No black runes, no shapes of withered bodies outlined in blood. Only the scars of battle etched on the walls, and the abhorrent stain of something unknown to the knight spread on the floor before him.

It doesn't matter what it was, Killock realized. *It came into Danielle's home, into her bedroom, that much is certain. It attacked her, and she destroyed it.*

Killock circled the stain, hunting for more knowledge, but whatever had been destroyed here was long gone, and its traces told him no more than the fact of its existence.

As he moved deeper into the room he stopped suddenly, then smiled as if the bare walls and blank stone had brought glad news unlooked for. *They found each other.* Their scent was twined together, bright laughter curled around a hot summer sun. *I feared Danielle might never speak her heart. I am glad she did.*

Killock's heart ached with the need to find them, but the black stain mocked his tardiness. *They survived you,* he cursed the stain, *but after that, what? Escaped, as Maeglin claims? I must find the*

THE MARTYR'S TEARS

truth, and quickly. No matter the path, Wyn needs me, Danielle needs me. I cannot fail them.

Rowenna

Wind chased across the wide surface of Loughliath, spreading dappled patterns in strange whorls that merged and spread and faded away. A wan winter sun tried to gleam from the small wind-stirred waves, but the lake refused to give up its leaden grey, and the wind conspired to wipe away the few glimmers with roaming gusts.

As the wind reached the western shore it swirled up the steep, forested hillsides. The tall fir trees sighed as the wind curled through them, and their swaying limbs caused the moss-covered statues lurking on the forest floor to play peek-a-boo in the small shafts of sun that darted through the trees.

Still the wind climbed as it pushed westward and the hills became mountains. Grey clouds slid past jagged peaks of white ice and black rock, revealing one knife-edged ridge after another as the mountains climbed to the west and north. Here, at last, the wind curled back upon itself, heavy with the cold smell of ice. It sank into the folds of the valleys where it chilled the shadows and lurked in patches of rotten snow.

Two riders followed the winding road through the forest. Thick moss and pine needles coated the road and muffled the hoofbeats of the horses. Both riders were garbed in layers of rich fabric, lined and embroidered, with warm cloaks and gloves and boots. Despite the chill air that brought red to their cheeks, they rode with their hoods on their shoulders and the breeze in their hair, enjoying the weak sun as only those from the icy north could.

Lady Rowenna breathed in the cool air and enjoyed the scent of the forest, pine mixed with a heavy wetness that was earthy and lush. The smell reminded her of the winter festival, when boughs were hung throughout the home and scented candles were lit, and her family would take long rides through the woods after the noon meal.

The trees shifted in the breeze and a face of stone peeked from the shadows under a tall fir. Untold years had smoothed its features into vague lumps and hollows, but the moss had given it a beard and a crown to compensate.

"King Conall," Rowenna said happily, pleased with herself. "Nine."

"Bother," Lord Gwydion replied, although his frustration was clearly rote. He gave her a smile that had only the smallest of wry twists to the corners. "Do I have six, or seven?"

"Five," Rowenna corrected him, deducting one simply because Gwydion should have kept better track himself. Gwydion frowned and kept Rowenna's glance for a heartbeat, suspicious, but let it pass. He rode through a small patch of sun at that moment, and the light made his dark hair gleam and brought out the feathering of dignified grey along his temples. Rowenna smiled as she saw their father for a moment.

"I won't be able to catch nine," Gwydion said regretfully.

"You are hardly trying," Rowenna laughed. She pulled her cloak over her shoulders and settled it comfortably. The soft fur lining brushed gently against her neck and instantly warmed her shoulders. She had chosen a long, dark red dress, elegantly embroidered with gold thread, that draped exquisitely from her slender frame. It meant that she was forced to ride side-saddle, but Rowenna did not mind, for the dress accentuated her long arms and thin waist, and swirled majestically around her legs when she strolled. But it was not warm enough without her cloak.

"I am certainly trying," Gwydion objected. "They are simply hiding from me, I swear it."

"I'm not surprised. You were horrible to them the last time we were here. You called them fat and ugly."

"I feel certain that I was speaking of my horse. Oh! Six, I believe. Um… Reverend Gurley, there, behind that clump of snowflower."

Rowenna laughed again, a vibrant, joyful sound. "He does look like Reverend Gurley. He even has a pot belly to rest his hands on while he naps."

"Excellent," Gwydion congratulated himself. "I believe I have a chance after all."

***

The score was fifteen to eight when they spotted the encampment next to the road. A dozen small tents had been rigged amongst the trees, and a tidy horse-line stretched behind them. A squad of soldiers stood attentively as the riders approached. They wore heavy armor of grey scales under their cloaks and carried spears and shields in addition to the swords sheathed at their sides. Their leader was a tall knight with a handsome, open face, who stood in the center of the road with his hand raised.

"No one is allowed on the road." The knight was apologetic but firm. "Sir Maeglin's orders."

"Interesting," nodded Gwydion. "Why would you think that I cared in the slightest what Sir Maeglin ordered?"

The knight's face hardened. "Because until Sir Maeglin says that you can go, you're not going anywhere."

"How very droll," Gwydion was unimpressed. "And I was being so incredibly charming, too. Why is our noble Knight Commander so keen to keep people from the Mountain?"

"There was a battle." The knight crossed his arms. "A magus attacked the Mountain."

"There *was* a battle," Gwydion raised an eyebrow, "but there isn't one now."

"No." The knight looked wary.

"Gwydion," Rowenna interrupted. "Just tell him who we are instead of torturing him."

"Was I torturing again?" Gwydion sounded surprised. "I suppose I was." He returned his attention to the knight. "My sister has a kind heart, you see. I am Lord Gwydion, and my sister there is Lady Rowenna, and we are Templars." Gwydion smiled brilliantly as an expression of comprehension cascaded across the knight's face. "But I see you recognize us now, don't you?"

"Yes, my lord." The knight looked abashed. "I'm very sorry, my lord."

"Good, so we'll just pop along to the Mountain, and if we see any magi we'll let them know that they aren't allowed on the road."

"Yes, my lord."

Rowenna urged her horse up the road before the knight could change his mind, and she did not glance back until a switchback had taken them from his sight. There she reined in and waited for her brother. Gwydion arrived a moment later, his face grim and his brow furrowed.

"An attack on the Mountain?" Rowenna said anxiously. "By a magus?"

"Yes, although I am not sure our friend Sir Barricade there would know a magus if it introduced itself to him."

"Of course not, but someone told him, and he said 'a battle', Gwydion. I'm sure he would recognize one of those, with or without an introduction," Rowenna snapped.

"I know," Gwydion agreed with a sigh, "and after what Sir Killock told us, of what he and Lord Bradon found under the High Fells, I am inclined to believe the possibility."

"Did it seem strange to you that the knights were guarding the road instead of the Mountain itself?" Rowenna asked, suddenly fearful. "If there were a battle, wouldn't the soldiers be up there, making sure that the Mountain is safe? Not down here telling people to turn around?"

"Don't armies usually have scouts and people standing guard all around them?" Gwydion replied, then shrugged. "I know very little about it. We could go back and ask, but I fear that suddenly revealing that we don't have an inkling as to what is going on might somewhat diminish his awe of us. And I'm not very good at humble, I admit."

"No, I cannot stand not knowing for myself." Battles meant casualties, and if one had taken place within the Mountain, the wounded would be people she cared about. *Rúreth would have been in the heart of it, of course she would. Did anyone stand beside her, or was she alone? Surely, she had aid. With Benno murdered, the Council must have sent guards.* Rowenna felt a cold hand clutch at her heart. *Benno murdered, Lord Bradon slain, and if The Bear could fall, what chance do the rest of us have? Rúreth…*

The horses pounded up the twisting road, their hooves striking sparks from the cobbled surface in the sharp bends, and soon they entered the narrow cut that presaged the end of their journey.

And still we have seen no other soldiers. Why are they not guarding the Mountain? Are they all inside?

The tall, grey doors stood closed, the great urns cold and unlit. Rowenna dismounted and led her horse to the gates and rested her fingers on the stone. They opened at her Word and the ground trembled as they slowly swung outward. No light spilled forth and the room beyond was dim and cold.

She stepped over the threshold and entered the Mountain. Her horse's hooves echoed loudly on the stone floor as they crossed the wide entrance hall. Rowenna stopped at the end of the grey shaft of light that fell through the open doors and she strained to distinguish the dim shapes beyond.

"Rúreth?" Her voice sounded thin and worried as it echoed off the bare stone walls. Rowenna cleared her throat. "My Lord?"

The echoes died in the tunnels, and then silence.

Gwydion moved to stand beside her. He caught her eye and gave a slight shake of his head. *He's worried too. I've never seen the Mountain so… empty.* Rowenna shivered as a chill passed through her, and she pulled her cloak tightly around her shoulders. It was far colder inside the Mountain than it had been outside.

Gwydion rummaged in his saddlebag for a moment and pulled out a small chunk of quartz set in an elegant silver pendant.

Its simple Word pulsed faintly as Gwydion hung it from his belt and the Diviner filled with a soft golden light that bathed the room.

"There we are." Gwydion glanced around the hall. "Now at least we will be able to see whatever awful thing is about to eat us."

Rowenna nodded her head. She felt it too, a dread that seeped in with the chill. The halls of the Mountain had always been safe, welcoming, and sturdy in a way that made their silence all the more frightening and wrong. *There can't be something awful here.*

"Lead on, Ro," Gwydion said gallantly. "I will be right behind you."

"Me?" Rowenna protested. "A fine Templar you are."

"You have the stabby thing," Gwydion pointed out reasonably.

They left their horses at the door and crossed the room, walking side by side. Rowenna's dress whispered as it brushed the floor and her boots knocked echoes from the stone. Gwydion strode beside her, tall and confident, his elegant green robe catching the light in its intricate weave.

The sanctuary loomed dark and abandoned at the end of the hallway. Its great hearth was cold, the furniture shattered and torn. The shadows lingered even as Gwydion's light shone on them, as if reluctant to let go. Rowenna saw frost glimmer on the bare stone of the room, and her breath formed white clouds that hung in the chill air.

"Well, this is cozy, isn't it?" Gwydion's smile was as cold as the stone around them.

Rowenna laid her fingers on his shoulder. "Gwydion, look." Her voice was low and strained as she pointed to a huddled shape on the floor, barely beyond the light's reach.

Rowenna felt herself quail at the realization of what the shape must be. She had dreaded finding Him from the moment they had entered the Mountain, but she had denied the thought and pushed it down deep. *It can't be.*

Gwydion moved two steps closer to the shape and stopped as the light made it clear.

The massive body lay pale and still on the floor. A wound gaped in the center of the chest, a cavernous hole with its bottom lost in shadow, surrounded by ragged fissures in the alabaster skin.

"Is it Him?" Rowenna asked quietly.

"I don't know," Gwydion replied tersely. "How could I? How could anyone?"

"I thought…" Rowenna said helplessly. *How would we know Him, if His voice is silenced? Is this body all that remains? How can He be gone?* The cavernous rumble of God's voice filled her thoughts, but it echoed falsely, as if it already contained the knowledge of its absence. Her memories felt as cold and ominous as the shadows that lurked all around her, in this room that had once been as warm and comforting as God's voice. "I hoped there would be some sense, some feeling…"

Her brother shook his head. "No, nothing at all. But it must be Him. His voice is gone… He's gone. And this…" Gwydion pointed hopelessly at the huge body.

The body's face appeared calm, almost beatific. A smile of contentment was sculpted on the wide mouth, and its eyes were open and relaxed. But there was no fire in them.

Rowenna knelt by the head and brushed her fingers across His brow, then snatched her hand away in shock. The great body was ashen stone, granite smoothed and shaped into a form.

"It must be, yet it seems to be no more than a statue. I don't understand." She sought out Gwydion's gaze in the dim light but found only a mirror to her baffled pain.

Her fingers trembled, and she felt a deeper ache begin to grow in her chest and the back of her throat. She pushed it down and locked it away for later.

She stood and faced her brother. Gwydion's mouth was set in a cold line, and his eyes were slits. She could see muscles jump in his jaw and cheek as he stared fiercely at the body behind her.

A long, rasping sigh slid from the dark hallways.

"Ro, do you think it might be time for your sword?" Gwydion kept his eyes locked on the distant end of the chamber where his light could not reach.

Rowenna nodded slowly in reply. She pulled aside her coat and drew the thin Weapon from its sheath. The sword sat comfortably in her long fingers, its nimble weight a comfort to her. The hilt bore a guard shaped like a bird's wing, the feathers spread in a long arc that swept across her fingers and along her wrist, with a simple cross guard at the base of the blade. The grip itself was soft leather wrapped in threads of steel, perfectly shaped to fit her hand. The blade rose in a long curve, never more than the width of two fingers, to a needle-thin point. Runes and intricate shapes etched the back of the blade in minute patterns, but the cutting edge was unadorned, a single pure length of metal.

The chamber throbbed with her Word. Rowenna's blade wavered and swam as if quicksilver ran across its surface, and she felt the hilt pulse through her fingers into her arm and shoulder.

She was ready.

Something dragged across stone from the dark recesses of the passageway, the scrape of movement chased echoes around the chamber, and shapes began to emerge from the dim shadows beyond the light's reach. Withered forms, their bloodless flesh scarred with corrupting marks, clutching the weapons and shields they had once proudly born in life to guard the Temple. They loped toward the Templars with a strange, halting gait, their desiccated faces gaping blankly at their foes.

"What do you say, Ro?" Gwydion's voice was strained. "Shall we kill every one of these fucking things?"

Rowenna nodded and felt anger fill the emptiness that had been left behind when she pushed down her sorrow. "Yes, Gwydion. Every last one of them."

Rowenna moved to meet them. The steady pulse of her sword beat through her body and she kept her Word attuned to its rhythm. The first husk loomed before her, and its sword jerked through the dim air as a jagged blur. Quick as thought she altered the intricate pattern of her Word and her sword obeyed instantly.

Quicksilver steel flashed, the husk's blade was swept aside and yawning gashes appeared across its trunk and neck.

The husk fell and more lurched forward. Rowenna's will poured into the blade and it blurred around her. The husks fell upon her implacably but no attack could penetrate the silver blaze, and they were thrown back and cut to pieces.

A tall shape loomed from the swarm, and the remains of silver armor flashed in the light. It clutched the broken tip of its once-great Weapon in its hands as it strode forward, and it moved with a quickness and strength that were not matched by any other in the horde. The corpse's silver armor was unmistakable, but the rest was no longer even vaguely human. Its skin had been blackened as if from a great fire, and its flesh was withered as if consumed by years of desiccation.

"Rúreth, oh…" Rowenna felt a sob of grief and anger tear from her throat as she guided her blade onto the husk. Quicksilver flared and the husk was rent and thrown aside.

Her Weapon throbbed steadily in her hand as it waited for another foe, but there were no more targets for Rowenna's blade. No husk moved, but there was a shift in the shadows, a thicker patch that slid from darkness to darkness as she watched, as if the shadow were cast from some unseen lantern that affected no other object in the chamber. Rowenna followed its path warily, her sword ready. The shadow crept from pillar to pillar and across the vault of the darkened ceiling as it slipped in and out of sight.

"Gwydion, do you see?" Rowenna whispered.

"I do," Gwydion replied. "Although *what* I see I couldn't say."

The shadow faded into the deep black space behind the pillars, and for a moment Rowenna could not find it. But her sword could. The Weapon drew a silver line through the shadow as it suddenly coalesced above her. The sword sliced neatly through the half-glimpsed shape, but the shadow did not pause. A blade as insubstantial as smoke lashed out across Rowenna's arm, shards of burning cold lanced through her, and she cried out. Her sword carved through the shadowy shape as if it were mist, and each time the shadow rejoined, countered, and drove the Templar back.

Golden light flared as the thunder of Gwydion's Word echoed from the stone walls. The light flooded the chamber, so bright that Rowenna had to shield her eyes. In the blaze, she saw the shadow clearly, the dark shape of a man, translucent, as if crafted from smoke. At the light's touch, the shadow flashed and burned. A thin wail scratched down Rowenna's spine, and the shadow was gone, leaving behind only a half-seen blur of movement as it roiled into the dark passageways beyond the gaze of Gwydion's light.

Gwydion let the light fade away until only the gentle glow from the Diviner on his belt illuminated the room.

"I'm afraid it isn't dead," Gwydion stepped close to Rowenna and bent to examine her arm, "and I'm very sorry to tell you it has put quite the gash in your coat. Spiteful creature."

"You don't think perhaps the wound on my arm might be more consequential?" Rowenna grimaced. "It does actually hurt."

"If only I could stitch as well as you, I could do something helpful. Ah, the irony." Gwydion peered more closely at Rowenna's arm. "It looks only mostly mortal, and it hasn't made you any more hideous."

"It feels terribly strange. It's numb, but it burns too." Rowenna sucked air between her teeth as a cold ache thrust long fingers of pain into her shoulder. "I'll be all right."

"Brave girl." Gwydion shook his head sadly. "Can you imagine the fuss I would be making if it were me, instead?"

Rowenna tried to give him a smile of appreciation, but she knew it must have appeared as weak as it felt, and Gwydion's self-mocking grin fell and was replaced by a concern he could not quite hide.

"Come on, Ro, let's get you out of here." Gwydion held out his hand to her. "We can deal with that bloody shadow thing later."

"We might as well finish while we are here," Rowenna shook her head. "Besides, what help could we find? Those soldiers won't have anything that could treat a wound like this."

THE MARTYR'S TEARS

Gwydion hesitated a moment longer, then accepted with a bow. "You are right, as always. Then shall we see what is behind the Deepest Door? I have always wondered. My money is on a privy."

"Yes, but watch for the shadow… whatever it was," Rowenna said.

"It will be my pleasure," Gwydion assured her.

They crossed the chamber and approached the massive stone doors in the far wall. They gaped open, an unheard-of sight, and through them, the Templars saw a dark passageway descending into the mountain.

Rowenna followed her brother with measured steps. The numbness spread to her fingers and into her chest, and extended frozen roots that throbbed and ached fiercely into the flesh and bones around it. Rowenna kept her breathing steady and let the pain flow through without controlling her. But she knew she could not withstand it for long. Not if it kept growing.

The passage curved in a gentle arc, and no longer showed signs of having been carved by any man-made tools. Rowenna guessed that they followed an ancient water channel, so smooth were the walls.

She ran fingers along the stone. It was polished and shone as if wet, but was dry to the touch. Gentle whorls and lumps flowed under her fingers, but soon she found herself leaning heavily on the wall just to remain upright, uncaring of the origins of the tunnel. Gwydion said nothing, a sure sign of his concern, and took her weight on his shoulder. She could feel the numbing cold encircling her heart now, causing it to labor.

Ahead of the Templars, the passage twisted and descended again. A final turn and they entered a natural cavern, carved eons ago from the granite heart of the mountain by the long-vanished stream that had fashioned the tunnel.

In the center of the cavern, a gnarled tree grew from a crack in the floor, and a small spring bubbled from the crack and splashed onto the smooth stone.

The siblings approached wearily. Rowenna was hardly aware of her surroundings as her will faded before the endless cold that filled her. The bright burble of the spring water was the only thing that broke through the numbing ice, and it captivated her as she staggered toward it with Gwydion's help. The freezing water splashed over her cupped hand but she felt nothing, as if someone else's palm were collecting it. The water cast a faint light, a luminescence only visible against her skin as she held it, and she watched it flicker with the gentle movement of her hand.

She was suddenly taken by a great thirst and she brought her hand to her lips and drank gratefully. The water left a slight tingle on her lips and tongue, a glow spread from the tingle into her chest, and the numbness retreated.

Rowenna quickly cupped her hands in the pool and drank again, and the sensation spread farther until at last there was only the ache of the wound in her arm, the throbbing heat a welcome relief from the searing cold.

She sat with a sigh and met Gwydion's concerned gaze.

"I am all right, now," she told him weakly.

"You look mostly dead." Relief filled Gwydion's words. "Which, I'm ecstatic to tell you, is a vast improvement over a moment ago."

"Perhaps next time you should kill the shadow creature before it can hurt your sister." Rowenna closed her eyes and rested her head on the trunk of the tree.

"Well, I will think about it." Gwydion stood and glanced around the cavern. "What do you suppose this is all about, then? It's not what I imagined."

Rowenna craned her head to consider the tree above her. She was not sure if it was alive. Its bark and leaves were a uniform color and texture that appeared golden in the light of the Diviner. Thousands of leaves clung to the tree's limbs, and they rustled slightly as the air in the cavern shifted. The limbs themselves were as convoluted as any tree's, with hundreds of branches and knots and twists. She touched a tentative fingertip to the bark of the trunk. It was cold and felt metallic.

"Apparently, all He did down here was sit and watch His puddle," Gwydion mused. "I had hoped this was where He kept His hundreds of angelic servant girls, all desperate for a new master. Don't glare at me like that, Ro. Death and destruction make one think of life and sex. Live for today, and all that."

"Who told you that?" Rowenna clambered to her feet, still weak from the recent numbing cold. She motioned for Gwydion to bring the light closer.

"You know, I don't remember her name," Gwydion confessed. "It seems irrelevant now, in any case."

"How very gallant. What do you suppose this is?" Rowenna pointed to a long shape amongst the tree's roots. Held in the lap of the tree, carved deeply into a massive root, was a long indentation in the shape of a broad-bladed sword. Hundreds of smaller roots clustered around the shape as if they stretched to drink from some now-absent source of water within it. The surface of the indentation was covered in runes etched directly into the root. It appeared as if a sword had sunk into the tree, and had then been removed, leaving behind its shape.

"Now, that *is* interesting." Gwydion tapped his lip, immersed in thought. "A mold, do you think? And a pool to quench in? It must have been a very special blade, to have been forged here."

"I think so," Rowenna agreed. She knelt and ran her fingers across the runes that covered the inner surface of the mold, then glanced at the tree overhead. "It is no mere statue. I think it is a Device of some kind."

"A Device that created the Martyr's Blade, think of it." Gwydion smiled to himself. "Who made it? And why here?"

"*Perhaps* the Martyr's Blade," Rowenna corrected her brother, but he waved away the doubt.

"Of course it was the Blade." Gwydion surveyed the room again. "Do you suppose He did it? Is that why the tree was created here?"

"I'm not sure." Rowenna stroked hair from her face and peered at the ground at her feet. "Have you noticed this?"

Gwydion held the light higher and joined his sister. The floor of the chamber was covered in wide ridges as if waves had been captured in stone at the time of the cavern's creation. They rippled in concentric circles from the center of the room where the golden tree stood. As the light shifted, Rowenna found it hard to believe the stone was solid.

"It looks like a pond, just after a stone has fallen into the center," Rowenna smiled. "You can practically see the startled ducks."

"Yes, but it's not a pond, is it?" Gwydion tapped his boot on the floor. "It's solid stone, Ro. Although this is interesting." He stood next to the crack in the floor and peered at the ground. "I wonder what this means?"

Rowenna examined the ground in front of his boots and saw that the stone was scarred by a shallow indentation that formed a single great rune. The crack ran through the rune, marring it, but enough was left to show Rowenna that she had never seen a symbol like it. It was elegant and complex, made of shapes far different from the runes the Guild Artificers crafted to create the great Devices. A quick glance around the cavern confirmed that the rune was the epicenter of the frozen waves of stone, as if marking the location of whatever impact had caused them.

"I think it means that something amazing happened here." Rowenna crouched and traced the side of the rune's shape with a gentle finger. It felt completely smooth, like polished glass.

"I wonder if He left a note," Gwydion sighed. "What do you suppose are the chances the Archives hold some ancient explanation? I never came across anything like this while I was at school, Priest's or Knight's. I must say Bandirma has a shockingly awful selection when it comes to the more interesting works of the Artificers. Perhaps we should ask the Guild? Or connive our way into their library? You could bat your eyes at the Grandmaster, give him a little smile and a wink. He would probably give you anything you wanted after that."

Rowenna straightened and smoothed her dress into place. "Yes, an excellent plan. Hopefully, he doesn't have a heart attack. I believe he's quite ancient."

"As long as he waits to shove off until after he lets us in, I think that might actually be for the best," Gwydion shrugged. "Unless you fancy cuddling up with a dry old stick. Although, now that I think of it, that is a fairly good description of… what was his name? Count Carollan's son? You remember him, Ro… the tall one with the cough? You sighed deeply at him all summer. Did you ever get him to glance up from his books?"

"I did not sigh at him all summer," Rowenna's eyes flashed dangerously. "I was just being nice to him because you were so horrible."

"Gérard!" Gwydion crowed. "I knew I would remember. Ridiculous name for a Carollan. I wasn't horrible to him. Well, yes, I was, but he was just so awful, I couldn't stand to see you mooning over him. It was for your own good, don't you see?"

"I wasn't mooning over him!" Rowenna snapped, but then she laughed, unable to help herself. "Gérard really was a horrible little reed, wasn't he? It was very hard not to laugh when you demolished his ideas on the Third Council."

"Well, they were so very rote, weren't they? Just mouthing Cian over and over."

"Yes," Rowenna sighed. The laughter lifted her heart, but she knew it would only last a short while before they would need to return to the cares of the present. Still, it felt good to remember a long-ago summer, before she had followed her brother to the Temple school to begin her training. That year felt like another lifetime.

Rowenna cleared her throat. "I do regret letting him kiss me in the boathouse."

"You let him do what?" Gwydion spluttered in shock.

Rowenna nodded contritely, but then could not mask a sly smile that grew uncontrollably as Gwydion groped for words with mouth agape. He laughed when he saw she teased him.

"Very good, Ro," Gwydion bowed to her. "I believe you have fully recovered from your hurt."

"I don't know what you are talking about. My dress is ruined. I'll have to ask Cillian to mend it, and you know what she charges." Rowenna laid a hand on the golden tree for a moment, then turned to the passageway. "Come on then, we need to go and find Roland and the others and let them know what we have found. Perhaps we will be in time to help them catch the Crunorix priest."

"I do hope so," Gwydion snarled. "I would hate to miss out on all the fun. I was promised I could be a tool for justice."

"Some sort of tool, in any case," Rowenna said thoughtfully.

THE MARTYR'S TEARS

Eilidh

The tavern quickly filled with people from the Littleford market seeking their midday meal. Farmers satisfied with their morning business and the heavy clinking of newly acquired silver pennies in their purses. Townsfolk happy with the noise and bustle of the market. Travelers content for a break before using the river crossing that gave the town its name.

Sir Eilidh's armor and her Temple badge of rank kept the seats next to her empty for longer than most, but in the end, they, too, were claimed. Her first neighbor was a pretty, quiet girl not much younger than Eilidh, with blonde hair and sad eyes, who had to be helped to her seat by a doting farmer with a grey beard that reached to his belt. They were joined on the other side by a formidable woman with red cheeks and redder knuckles and a basket filled with winter vegetables.

"We'll only be a moment," the greybeard told the blonde girl as he helped her onto the bench. "You rest here and we'll take care of everything, don't you worry."

The young woman whispered her thanks, her voice too quiet to be heard above the roar of the tavern, but her eyes brimmed with such gratitude that it did not need to be. The farmer patted her arm gently, arranged for the tavern-keeper to bring her food and drink, and departed.

But when the food came the young woman could hardly manage to eat it. Eilidh saw that both her hands were heavily bandaged, and she fumbled quietly with her spoon before giving up and sitting silently, staring at the steaming surface of her stew.

She caught Eilidh's gaze upon her and quickly lowered her head in embarrassment.

"Do you need some help?" Eilidh asked kindly.

"Oh, no, m'lady, please don't bother yourself, I'll manage."

"No trouble," Eilidh assured her. "I have five sisters, all younger, so I'm well-used to helping. And never mind 'm'lady', I'm just a knight, so there's no need for that."

"Yes, sir, I'm ever so grateful, sir," the girl replied with a smile that flashed for the briefest of moments.

Eilidh cut up the chunks of carrots and potatoes that floated in the stew until they would easily fit in a mouthful, then helped place the spoon more securely in the young woman's wrapped fingers. Eilidh could not help but notice the flinch of pain as she tried to grip the wooden handle.

"Whatever happened to your poor hands?" Eilidh asked.

"Nothing, sir," the girl answered quickly. "I mean, they're burnt, but it were just an accident, no one's to blame."

Eilidh felt her jaw clench as she saw the flash of fear in the girl's green eyes, and she realized what type of 'accident' had most likely left the girl with two badly burned hands.

"The greybeard farmer who brought you here, is he your…"

"No, sir, I just met him this morning, and he's been helping me travel. He's very kind, he is."

"Good," Eilidh replied, unsure what else to say. *At least she has escaped whoever did this to her and has found someone with a kind heart to help her on her way.*

"If you don't mind, sir, are the roads safe to travel right now? Only we saw so many soldiers on our way."

"You are in no danger," Eilidh assured the young woman, although she was not sure she truly knew the answer. "They are hunting for a man responsible for murdering a priest in Bandirma."

"Why would someone murder a priest?" the girl asked, her eyes wide with astonishment.

"They say he is a wizard, from the south. Who knows what such a man might do," Eilidh answered. The reports from Bandirma revealed little more, only that the murdered priest was the Bishop himself, and that the Queen's sister, the Lady Danielle, had also gone missing, and may have aided the wizard in his crimes. Eilidh had never met Bishop Benno, and had only ever seen him at a distance, but he had seemed kind from what she had heard, and always reminded her of her grandfather. But there was no reason to burden the young woman with those details.

"How could he have gotten into Bandirma?"

"He was posing as one of the Queen's counselors, I believe, and traveled with her when she visited Bandirma."

"The Queen?" the young woman asked in a tiny voice. "Is she all right? He didn't hurt her, did he?"

"Oh no, never fear," Eilidh comforted the girl, for she appeared to be on the verge of tears. "We would have heard if that had happened."

They spent the rest of their lunch chatting about the road to Bandirma and the great Temple itself, which the girl eventually revealed was her destination. Eilidh dared to think that the young woman shed some of her sad trepidation as they talked, and even gave Eilidh another small smile when the greybeard farmer returned to collect her. Eilidh was surprised to see that the tavern was mostly empty, the midday crowds having satisfied their hunger and departed while she lost herself in her conversation.

"Perhaps I will see you when next I am in Bandirma," Eilidh told the young woman as the farmer helped her from the bench. "What is your name, so that I may ask after you?"

"Mairi," the girl gave her another small smile. "Thank you for your time, sir."

Mairi and the farmer departed, the girl leaning heavily on his arm. Eilidh finished her drink in contented silence. Mairi had not noticed the small handful of pennies that Eilidh had slipped into her purse when she was not attending, but Eilidh hoped that they would help her on her travels.

***

The temple in Littleford stood on a small rise overlooking the town. A cluster of sturdy stone buildings surrounded a wide courtyard that opened onto the road as it wound its way from the river. The sanctuary was the largest of the buildings and could seat dozens comfortably during worship. There was also a scriptorium with wide windows that overlooked the temple's farms, and a low dormitory that housed Reverend Finnobharr, the two priests, and the dozen acolytes who lived in the temple. Behind the sanctuary stood the barracks and training field for Sir Eilidh and her ten soldiers.

In the hour before dawn, the temple began to stir. Light leaked through the shutters on the kitchen window as the acolytes who had drawn kitchen duty began to prepare breakfast, and the tenant families who worked the temple's farms tended to the small herd of cows in the chill morning air.

A lantern glowed dimly at the back of the stables as Eilidh crossed the courtyard. She hurried across the last few steps, paused in the doorway, and leaned against the frame.

Inside the stable, an acolyte blinked sleepily as he held the light but otherwise offered no assistance to the soldier who was readying his horse. The soldier did not seem to mind. He worked silently save for a few whispered words offered to his dappled grey mare as he fed her a small, yellow apple, and she munched contentedly as he sorted her saddle.

Eilidh gave brief thanks that she had caught the messenger before he left, although to call him a messenger still felt wrong to her. He was obviously so much more than that. *Ridiculous to waste a veteran with his skills on carrying a message, no matter how vital. Give the message to a pigeon and let the warriors train the new soldiers.*

The messenger had come to Littleford the day before, and Eilidh had spotted him watching her soldiers training in the yard, the whack and bang of their wooden swords and shields a ragged chorus accompanying her shouted commands. Eilidh had been curious about him from the first glance, for he bore a tattoo that spiraled around his left eye, a pattern she had seen once or twice before, always on veteran soldiers who had served on the western frontier. And at his side hung a long sword with an elegant silver pommel in the likeness of the Queen's arms, a valuable weapon she would expect to be in the hands of a great knight.

The messenger had not said much when she approached him, but the few words he offered quickly revealed that he knew far more about soldiering than all but the most experienced of her instructors from the School of Knights.

"Off so early, Cormac?" Eilidh asked.

Cormac did not seem surprised to see Eilidh standing in the stables, and a small smile flickered at the corner of his lips as he greeted the knight.

"Yes, sir," Cormac nodded. "Still a long way to go, so there's not a moment to lose."

"I'm sorry to see you go," Sir Eilidh frowned. The hour she had spent in the training yard picking his brain for ideas on how to best improve her soldiers' skills had convinced her that she needed the veteran soldier to stay. Indeed, she had lain awake for most of the night envisioning what it would be like to have him by her side in the training yard, and she liked what she saw. *Only two months into my first command, yet I could create a squad of soldiers that train like five-year veterans.*

"Yes, ma'am," Cormac nodded as he adjusted the saddle and girth.

"Still, not as sorry as you are, I'll wager," Eilidh tried to make her voice sound merely light-hearted. "I hear Irongate is under enough snow to bury a man."

"Aye, but I'm used to it." Cormac smiled in return as he double-checked the contents of his saddlebag. A pack filled one side completely, its water-stained leather a strange contrast to its elegant Venaissine stitching and sturdy construction.

Eilidh stood mute as Cormac gave the cinch one last tug. She could not think of what she might say to convince him to stay at the last moment, and was desperately concerned not to make a fool of herself under his easy gaze and slight smile.

So Eilidh stood in awkward silence as Cormac opened the stall and led his horse from the stables. Sir Eilidh accompanied him across the cobbled courtyard, the clop of the horse's hooves loud in the hushed morning.

"Godspeed on your journey," Eilidh said.

"Thank you, ma'am," answered Cormac as he turned to the knight. Eilidh saw his gaze suddenly snap to stare over her shoulder, and his eyes narrowed.

Eilidh whirled to follow his gaze. Movement caught her eye from across the courtyard. The scriptorium was a black mass against the faint grey of the dawn light on the fields beyond. Dark figures scurried through the gap between the scriptorium and the dormitory and disappeared into the shadows beneath the buildings. She heard horses approaching along the road, a vague rumble that swelled rapidly in the still air.

The shining sword came into Cormac's hand with a hiss.

"We are attacked!" he cried. "To arms!"

Sir Eilidh drew steel and took up the call, and she saw the two soldiers who guarded the gate come to alert and raise their lanterns, but she knew it was far too late to rouse the soldiers who still slumbered in their barracks. Cormac swung into the saddle and turned his horse in a tight circle as he searched for the foe.

Figures with dark cloaks and blackened weapons emerged from the shadows. Several rushed the guards at the gate and Eilidh heard shouts and the ring of steel on steel. More figures charged across the courtyard toward Cormac and Sir Eilidh.

Cormac spurred toward them. The courtyard was not large enough for a proper charge, but the mare leapt forward gamely and speared between two of the figures. Eilidh saw Cormac lash out and then his horse carried him past.

Light spilled into the courtyard as the door to the barracks flew open. Half-dressed Temple soldiers poured out, weapons raised, but more enemies emerged from the shadow of the scriptorium and charged into the fray. In the center of the courtyard, Sir Eilidh yelled defiance as she rained blows on a swarm of dark figures that surrounded her. She glimpsed steel helms and heavy armor, and a bearded face behind a raised sword. Her long sword sent one foe sprawling with a vicious cut to the side of his helm, then sliced through the wrist of another with a splintering of bone. But Eilidh knew that most of her strikes were turned aside by her opponents' thick armor, and they slowly drove her toward the sanctuary.

Cormac fought his way back to her, striking heavily on both sides. Bright blood sprayed across the cobblestones in front of the barracks as a Temple soldier fell beneath a heavy war axe. The attackers pinned another soldier against the barracks wall with long spears.

Three knights thundered into the courtyard astride warhorses in full barding. The horses' hooves struck sparks from the cobblestones as they wheeled. Then two of the knights spurred forward, one toward Cormac, the other at Eilidh. The third knight raised a steel-headed mace and roared, "For the Queen!"

Cormac gripped his horse with his knees and urged her toward the charging knight. At the last moment, Cormac veered aside, and Eilidh took grim satisfaction as the knight's heavily armored warhorse slipped and crashed to the cobblestones as the knight tried to turn too quickly to follow.

But Eilidh had only a moment to revel in the knight's fall. Already the second knight descended on her. The great warhorse reared and Eilidh dove away from the iron-shod hooves as they crashed down a hand's-breadth behind her. The knight pursued her, his great cavalry sword raised high as Eilidh scrambled desperately away.

Then Cormac was there. The enemy knight turned in surprise as Cormac struck. He thrust upward and his point took the knight in the soft padding under his raised arm and slid home. Cormac wrenched the blade free and blood poured across the knight's steel breastplate.

Cormac did not wait to see the knight slowly topple from his saddle. He extended a hand to Eilidh but she refused it.

"Get to Bandirma!" Eilidh yelled. "Warn the temples!"

Then she returned to the fight. She caught a raised axe on her blade, then whipped her sword to the opposite side and knocked down an enemy with a heavy blow to the crown of his helm as she carved a path to join her soldiers. She caught a last glimpse of Cormac as he raced through the narrow path between the scriptorium and the sanctuary. His horse cleared the garden gate at full gallop and then they were gone into the fields beyond.

More enemies rushed toward her, and her time ran out. Pain ripped through her shoulder as an axe sliced through her light practice armor. She staggered and thrust desperately toward that side, then jagged light exploded from the back of her head and blasted the world into darkness.

***

There was little light in the cellar, even by day. Only a few sickly shafts of grey slipped through the wooden door that led into the temple courtyard, but enough that Eilidh could see the heavy, low beams of the ceiling, the stacks of barrels along the far wall, and the shelves that groaned under the weight of the food stores for the temple kitchens.

It was also light enough to see that the dirt-encrusted bandages wrapped around her left shoulder had turned black with the blood that continued to seep into them.

But at night the cellar faded into a darkness so thick that Eilidh could not see the brick pillar to which she was chained. If she moved just right she could see a thin line of the dimmest light between two planks of the cellar door. She passed her hand in front of the crack, a movement of shadow in the dark the only proof that she had not left the world behind and somehow descended into an abyss.

Eilidh lay back and slowly eased her head to rest on the stone floor. The throbbing burn of her wounded shoulder was nothing compared to the deep roots of pain that threaded through her skull, and any quick movement or careless bump was practically unendurable. But lying down was better than sitting up.

Her iron manacles clinked as she cautiously probed the bandages that swathed her head. They were damp over her temple, where the pain was worst, and were crudely wound so that they twisted and tugged despite her best efforts to keep them in place. She was uncertain why she bothered, for if they were as foul as the bandages around her shoulder then they likely were doing her little good.

At some point in the endless night, the cat came to visit her. Eilidh was not sure how it found a way into the cellar, but it had come each night since she had been imprisoned there. She was not even certain what the cat looked like. She knew it was amiable, had short fur, and many scratches and scabs. But whether it was orange or white or black she had no clue.

The cat padded softly across the floor to her, then jumped to its preferred place on her chest and settled down. Eilidh scratched its ears and it purred in response, and she felt the tiny pinpricks of its claws kneading her through her coarse, woolen tunic. Eilidh did everything she could to make the cat welcome each night. It was warm, and it kept away the rats. But most of all it was another creature that shared the long darkness with her.

***

The harsh scraping of iron brought Eilidh suddenly awake. Cold light filled the cellar as the courtyard doors were opened, and heavy boots clattered down the wooden steps. Two soldiers unlocked her manacles and drew the chain from the pillar while a third glowered fiercely at her. *Are they still so worried about me? I could not harm a mouse.*

The soldiers re-fastened her manacles and pulled her roughly to her feet. Eilidh stood uncertainly, the room and her stomach swaying to the same rhythm as the pulses of pain that throbbed through her skull.

The soldiers worked quickly. Only a few words were exchanged between them as they maneuvered her up the stairs and into the courtyard, and none of them spoke to her.

Eilidh was grateful for their silence. When she had first awakened as a prisoner three days ago she had feared far worse. Eilidh had heard tales of the repercussions that usually followed such an intense battle as the surviving victors took their revenge for fallen comrades on the unfortunate prisoners.

She and two other wounded Temple soldiers had been placed in one of the stalls in the stables at first, and left to endure their wounds in agony while Brother Ewan, one of the young acolytes from the temple, tended to Sir Cathan's wounded men. Of course, she had not known they were Sir Cathan's men at the time. It was only when the knight came to inspect his wounded and his prisoners that she learned who was responsible for the attack.

The knight was not a large man, although with wide shoulders and thick arms that carried his steel armor and heavy mace easily. Wiry grey hair clung to his skull above a high forehead, and he had narrow, red-rimmed eyes above a fleshy mouth. He was clean-shaven, and his cheeks shone bright pink in the frigid air of the morning.

"These are the survivors?" he had asked the soldier who accompanied him. His voice was surprisingly soft.

"Yes, m'lord, these three and the priests we captured in the sanctuary."

Cathan had stepped into the stall and peered at Eilidh with his fists on his hips. Eilidh had wanted to curse him and spit on his face, but she had not even been able to raise her head.

"This was their leader?" Cathan murmured.

"Yes, m'lord. Sir Eilidh, they said her name is."

"*Sir* Eilidh?" Cathan shook his head slightly. "This is no knight. She is just a Temple dog. Chain her in the temple until I am ready to deal with her."

"Yes, m'lord," answered the soldier. "And her wounds?"

Anger had flashed across Cathan's face for just an instant. "She can pray for healing."

But Eilidh had not prayed for healing. She had prayed for vengeance.

Eilidh had expected Cathan to visit her right away, but no one had come save for the soldier who brought her water and a thin mush that tasted faintly of turnips. Her shoulder hurt worse, but her head began to clear and the vomiting had stopped. The pain was no less, but at least she could think.

Eilidh shivered as she stepped into the courtyard. A fine mist wafted across the stones and chilled her skin. Rotten snow lay in the shadows of the buildings, hiding from the feeble winter sun. In the center of the courtyard a wagon was waiting, a battered and crude conveyance that appeared more suited for hauling farm goods to market than prisoners to their fate. But Eilidh saw that was indeed its purpose, for Reverend Finnobharr sat huddled and alone in its bed. He was dressed in the simple brown robes of an acolyte, rough and torn, and his magnificent white beard was matted with dirt and blood and soaked by the mist. One ear had been smashed and blood caked the side of his head and neck, and his eyes were dazed and unfocused as he stared around the courtyard.

The soldiers pushed Eilidh into the bed of the wagon with the priest and chained her to an iron bracket in the floor. Two of the soldiers climbed into the back with her and Finnobharr while the third sat on the bench next to the driver.

The wagon creaked as it moved through the temple gates. Eilidh was surprised when it turned toward the town center.

"Reverend? Reverend Finnobharr?" Eilidh ventured. The soldiers did not seem to mind her talking, but the priest was confused.

"Fiona, is that you?" The priest's voice trembled, a faint echo of the refined and soothing sound that Eilidh was accustomed to hearing.

"No, Reverend, I'm sorry, I don't know where your wife is." Eilidh hoped the priestess had survived the attack. "It's Eilidh."

"Eilidh? Where is Fiona?" Finnobharr peered at her with perplexed eyes. "It's cold in here. We need a fire I think, except, are we going on a journey?"

"No, we're just going to the town." Eilidh tried to sound reassuring, and the priest accepted her words as he sank into a befuddled silence.

The wagon splashed across the low-water crossing and creaked up the road to the town square.

In the center of the open space stood a low stone dais used by the village crier and by bards and performers when they passed through town. Eilidh could see that it was now occupied by a pair of stocks, newly cut from heavy planks of wood. Behind the stocks stood a simple gallows, also freshly built, a high pole with a thick rope strung through a pulley on its cross beam.

Lord, give me the strength to bear whatever happens next with honor, she prayed, but fear churned in her stomach.

A crowd gathered around the dais. Farmers and townsfolk, old and young. Eilidh recognized a few faces from the town that she had learned in the brief time she had been stationed in the Littleford temple, but far more were strangers to her. A squad of ten soldiers wearing Sir Cathan's livery kept them from approaching the stocks.

The crowd watched in silence as the wagon slowly pulled up beside the dais and Eilidh was led to stand in front of the stocks. Then the soldiers escorted Finnobharr from his seat. The priest staggered and fell to his knees, and cried out in pain. An ugly murmur swept through the crowd at the sight, and Eilidh saw the soldiers pass wary glances between themselves. Reverend Finnobharr was well loved in Littleford, and its inhabitants muttered and shook their heads at the sight of the priest battered and bloody on his knees in the mud.

The soldiers quickly pulled Finnobharr to his feet, pushed him onto the dais and left him to stand shivering next to Eilidh.

Hoofbeats echoed against the stone walls of the buildings and five horsemen entered the square. Sir Cathan and another knight rode at their head, and the crowd was pressed into the walls of the buildings as they passed. The two knights dismounted and removed their helms as they strode to the dais.

Eilidh saw that the second knight was Cathan's son. He had the same wiry hair, although still a dull brown instead of his father's grey, and the same full mouth and narrow eyes. But he was much taller than Sir Cathan, and powerfully built, with a barrel chest and thick, muscular neck.

Cathan paced in front of his two prisoners as he examined them, and a furious scowl twisted his face. Eilidh met his gaze defiantly.

"This won't end well for you, Cathan," Eilidh's voice carried clear and strong. "I'll make sure of that."

Cathan's lips twitched slightly, and he turned his back on her and addressed the crowd.

"By the power granted me by Her Majesty, Queen Gabrielle, I find these prisoners guilty of treason and murder," Cathan's quiet voice carried effortlessly across the square.

"Treachery? What treachery?" Eilidh shouted the knight down. "We have committed no treachery. And the only murder here is at your hand, you bastard."

Cathan deigned to face her as he pulled a parchment from his cloak. He took his time unrolling it, his eyes never leaving hers, then held it aloft to the crowd as he announced its contents.

"Her Majesty, attacked by Temple cowards while a guest, barely escaping with her life. Treason."

Dark, furious faces in the crowd now turned on Eilidh as she searched for words, too stunned to respond immediately. *The Queen attacked? When, and by who?* None of the news from Bandirma had hinted at such an act.

"That cannot be true," she finally stammered.

"You doubt the Queen's word?" Cathan asked archly, a cold sneer twisting his face. He brought the parchment down and read from it to the crowd. "By command of Her Majesty, Queen Gabrielle. All lords shall immediately take possession of any temple within their lands and arrest all within as restitution against the Temple for their unprovoked attack upon Her Majesty and her loyal soldiers."

Cathan turned the parchment so that its words faced the crowd. "Signed by Duke Campbell, himself."

"But we didn't attack the Queen!" Eilidh felt she must be dreaming.

"Treason," Cathan ignored her as he rolled up the parchment and slipped it into his cloak. "And the murder of my youngest son, foully struck down while he carried out the Queen's orders."

"His blood is on your hands, Cathan," Eilidh snapped. "It was your unprovoked attack—"

Anger twisted Cathan's face again, and he stepped to Eilidh and struck her open-handed across the mouth. His armored gauntlet tore her lip and sent fire through her aching skull, and she staggered and dropped to a knee. But she forced herself not to fall, and slowly pushed herself to her feet. She met his gaze steadily, then deliberately spat blood across his polished boots.

Furious pink spots blazed on Cathan's cheeks and his hands clenched into fists, but he did not strike again. Instead, he kept her gaze with slitted eyes as he pronounced her sentence.

"They shall endure three days in the stocks, then be hanged at dawn on the fourth day."

Soldiers grabbed Eilidh and Finnobharr and drove them to their knees in front of the stocks. Hands pushed her neck against the rough, unfinished wood and she was held as the locks were fastened.

Cathan's son delivered the first blow, a brutal punch that struck Eilidh on her brow and drove her head into the wood with such force that the wooden plank splintered. Eilidh clung to consciousness as she sagged against her restraints, her body too stunned to hold her up.

But as he approached Reverend Finnobharr a surge of cries from the crowd made him hesitate. Townsfolk pressed forward and shouted their disapproval until Sir Cathan gave a furious shake of his head and his son stepped back.

The knight and his son departed then, but left the soldiers to stand guard. The crowd slowly dispersed, and none approached the stocks, and none threw mud or stones at the two imprisoned in them.

By nightfall, Eilidh's legs had gone numb and her back spasmed in agony from her enforced position. Reverend Finnobharr was far worse. For hours he mumbled in confusion, until the muttering gave way to cries for water, desperate pleas all the more heart-breaking as the old man could not understand why no one answered them.

Eilidh begged the guards to show some mercy, but they listened stone-faced. The townsfolk were not so cruel. Soon they arrived, one or two at a time, and brought water to drink and blankets to wrap over the old priest's shoulders. The guards watched but made no move to interfere.

A small figure approached Eilidh carrying a flask of water. Eilidh recognized her grey hair and red knuckles, a washerwoman who served as a steward at the temple. She had a scolding tongue and a sour expression, the last person Eilidh would ever expect to show compassion for her. But the woman held the flask gently to her lips and helped her drink, and cleaned the blood from her mouth with a handkerchief before she left.

Eilidh thought sleep would be impossible, so great was her discomfort, but exhaustion eventually overwhelmed her for brief moments, stretching the night hours into an endless series of confusing vignettes.

She had no idea what hour it was when the heavy tread of boots brought her awake to find the dais lit by torches, and long shadows of people moving on the stones in front of her.

Horsemen filled the square before the dais, a strong squad in heavy armor, tall spears held aloft, and long swords and steel shields strapped to their saddles. Two of the horsemen had dismounted and stood in conversation with one of the guards. The guard nodded and bowed and said, "Yes, sir!" repeatedly, so fast that his words tumbled over each other in his haste.

The man to whom he spoke certainly appeared intimidating. He stood tall in full metal armor, painted black and adorned with a sigil of two swords crossed beneath a crown. His hair was cropped and his beard streaked with grey, and ice-blue eyes appraised her without emotion from a lean face with a patrician nose.

"Go," he ordered the guard, who scurried off the dais without hesitation. "Unlock them." His voice was calm and quiet, and the other guard hurried to obey without question, dropping his keys in his haste as he did so.

Eilidh felt the weight of the bar come off her neck and she slumped to the ground in relief. Finnobharr thanked God and the guard and blessed him.

Eilidh crawled to Finnobharr and offered him what comfort she could as she watched the quiet square and waited to see what the tall lord would do next. The silence was broken by the small sounds of the troop of horsemen— the jingle of a harness, the creak of a saddle, the stamp of a hoof. The lord talked in a low murmur to one of the horsemen, and absently stroked the horse's nose as they spoke, but Eilidh was far too distant to discern their words.

Then she heard hoofbeats from the north, riding fast and fording the river. Sir Cathan clattered into the square a moment later, his horse lathered and pulling at the bit as he reined it in with a clash of iron-shod hooves on the cobblestones.

Cathan swung from the saddle and crossed the square, sparing only a quick glance at the open stocks and the two prisoners huddled free next to them. The knight approached the lord and bowed low.

"Duke Campbell, I did not expect you," Cathan said warily.

"No?" The duke patted the horse's neck once more and turned to face the knight. "I am surprised. When I heard of what had occurred here I made all haste to see for myself. I did not wish to pass judgment in absentia."

Eilidh saw Cathan blanch at the word 'judgment'.

"I carried out the Queen's orders, that is what happened here," Cathan blustered. "Seize the temple, arrest the traitors. Why wouldn't the Queen be pleased?"

"Pleased?" Campbell's voice was harsh. "You think the Queen will be pleased to hear of a knight who slaughtered priests and acolytes without mercy? Who attacked without warning, without giving terms? Who used her name to commit a massacre?"

"My lord!" Cathan drew himself up haughtily. "You commanded the temples be taken in the Queen's name. I only did my duty."

"And what is your intent with these prisoners here?" Duke Campbell glanced at Eilidh and Finnobharr.

"Hanging, of course," Cathan replied. "They are traitors."

"Aye, traitors are hanged," Campbell agreed thoughtfully, "but these two are not traitors."

"My lord, they bore arms against the Queen's soldiers! The Temple tried to take Her Majesty captive!"

"I think it safe to say that these two did not have a hand in that," Campbell disagreed curtly.

"They killed Her Majesty's soldiers. They killed my son," Cathan spat in disgust.

"Yes, and I think it is clear where the fault for that shameful loss of life truly lies."

"My lord knows I am your loyal knight!" Cathan spluttered.

"No, I do not." Campbell's voice was steel. "I relieve you of your title and your lands. I only wish we didn't need you, or I would hang you from your gibbet right now."

"You can't do that!" Cathan's face turned the color of ash.

"Of course I can," Campbell frowned. "Your son may keep your house, but the lands and title belong to the realm, now. If you wish to disobey my command, then draw your blade and defend yourself."

"But, my lord…" Cathan glanced quickly around the square. There were no friendly eyes, and his soldiers would not meet his gaze. "But surely there is a chance for penance. You said you needed me… perhaps there is some leniency for that service?"

"You misunderstand." Campbell motioned to his soldiers, and two dismounted and approached the knight. "I need to turn you over to the Temple to stand for war crimes against them."

Cathan's mouth gaped open like a fish, then he made a grab for the hilt of his sword. The soldiers were on him before his blade could clear the sheath.

"Far too late for that, Cathan." The duke shook his head. The soldiers dragged Cathan, screaming and cursing, from the square.

Campbell watched them go, then glanced at Eilidh and Finnobharr. "Give them aid, and food, then bring the priest to my camp," he commanded.

"And the knight, m'lord?"

Campbell mounted his horse and rode close to the dais. Eilidh forced herself to return his gaze without blinking, trying to match his calm intensity, but it took all the rage that churned within her just to keep her head raised.

"Will you give your parole?" the duke asked, still holding her gaze.

Eilidh knew she should say yes. *One word and I will be free. Free to return to Bandirma, free to tell others what has happened here, free to warn the Temple. But no longer free to fight.* And she desperately wanted to fight. Campbell may have put chains on Cathan, but Cathan's soldiers still stood unpunished for their crimes, as did Cathan's son, warm in the rambling manor that he was being allowed to keep. Even the duke, despite his fair words and condemnation of Cathan. *He is not a friend. These men acted on his orders.*

"No." Eilidh tried to keep her voice flat and emotionless, but her rage made the word growl from her throat.

Campbell nodded, unsurprised. "I thought not. After her needs are attended to, place her in quarters suitable for a prisoner of war." He turned away and rode from the square.

She was taken to an inn in Littleford commandeered by the duke's soldiers, where a gruff soldier with the arms of a blacksmith cleaned and stitched her shoulder and head with a skill that rivaled any healer. She bathed away the filth of her captivity and dressed in warm clothes that were left for her. She wished they were her own, but they fit reasonably and at least bore no insignia of the Queen.

Then she was returned to the temple and given a small cell that had belonged to a young acolyte named Afallon, who had cared for the horses in the temple stable. A quick search revealed that the small chest in the room still contained Afallon's simple woolen clothes, and on the shelf of a small nook, Eilidh found the collection of rough wooden horses that Afallon was so proud to have carved.

Eilidh sat on the small cot and examined one of the simple statues. Anger seethed within her, hatred for Cathan's soldiers, who still guarded the temple, standing at ease in the very rooms and hallways where they had slaughtered innocents. But the rage twisted within her and burned her eyes so that the wooden horse blurred, and Eilidh held it tight within her fist as the anger became pain that tore from her in sobs that shook her uncontrollably.

***

A thin silver light outlined the shutters of the cell's small window when Eilidh awoke. She had been ripped from her exhausted slumber, but there was no sign of what had occurred. The temple was silent, and only the distant whisper of the river rushing across the shallow ford came through the window.

But Eilidh was certain that the silence covered something, an echo of a sound that had been there moments before. She scrambled from the cot and crept to the door, listening with her ear pressed against the keyhole in the iron lock. She held her breath and cursed the heavy beat of her heart as she waited for the sound to repeat.

Her vigilance was rewarded by a faint rasp of metal on stone, and the creak of a leather strap. Then the soft clink of metal on metal, instantly silenced, just outside the door. Eilidh pulled back as a key was quietly inserted into the lock and turned cautiously, with only the smallest of scrapes.

Eilidh quickly glanced around the small cell, hunting for any type of weapon, but the room was as bare as it had been the first time she had searched. She could think of one reason a prisoner would be visited in the middle of the night, and she readied herself to fight against that fate.

When the door whispered open there was no light from the hallway, only a black hole in the shadowy wall. Eilidh crouched against the wall of the cell, praying that the room was equally as dark to those surely peering in through the open door.

"Sir Eilidh?" The whisper was a breath that barely stirred the silence.

Eilidh bit back her response. *It cannot be one of the guards, surely.* But she knew not to trust hope, and remained still.

"Sir Eilidh, it's Cormac," the whisper came again. "It's time to go."

Thank the Maker. "Cormac?" Eilidh's reply was no louder than a sigh. "How…?" Eilidh bit off her questions. There would be time in plenty later for a chat, but for now, she allowed herself to simply accept the soldier's miraculous arrival. The veteran warrior had not appeared in any of her dreams of escape, but she could not think of a better ally to be her rescuer.

Cormac entered the cell with a soft brush of cloth on stone, and a long steel blade caught the dim light as he offered it to her. The worn grip settled comfortably in her hand.

Cormac motioned for her to follow and slipped into the hallway. Eilidh crept silently in his wake past the small doors of the other acolyte cells, and past the coal bins and the kitchen garden in the deep shadows behind the temple. The sky was filled with the soft light of the pre-dawn hour, but the ground remained in black shadow, all the deeper for the dim light in the sky.

They reached the gate that led to the temple fields before Eilidh halted Cormac with a grasp of his arm.

"Where are we going?" she whispered.

"I have horses waiting in the trees, just beyond the fields," Cormac indicated the black mass that covered the hills on the far side of the valley.

"What of the others?" Eilidh demanded. "The other prisoners?"

Cormac regarded her silently for a moment, his face hidden in the shadow under his hood.

"They have three of your soldiers," Cormac finally answered. "Two are badly wounded, and cannot walk. They also have five or six of the acolytes, I am not sure who."

"Do you mean to leave them here?" Eilidh hissed in disbelief.

"Yes, sir," Cormac replied bluntly. "None can help us, and all are safer here than trying to escape, on foot, with no weapons and no supplies." He paused to let his words sink in. "If you want to escape and fight, then come with me. If you want to try to save everyone, no matter the chances and the cost, then stay. Sir."

"I suppose I am lucky that I can walk, then," Eilidh hissed her reply, anger and disappointment swirling bitterly within her stomach. But she knew that the soldier was right. *What could I do with a bunch of acolytes and two soldiers who cannot be moved? Barricade the doors and hope to be left in peace?* But it was hard to think of abandoning her men, and her hand twisted the pommel of her sword until the hilt groaned.

"Very well," she muttered, the words ash in her mouth.

Cormac nodded and led the way across the fields to where he had left the horses. *Just two,* Eilidh noted sadly.

They led the horses through the dark forest as the gaps in the canopy slowly brightened and the trees shifted and stirred in the cold breeze.

By the time they reached the Rathad an Thuaidh, Eilidh knew she could not go much farther. Nauseating pulses of pain lurked deep within her skull, ready to cascade from its depths at every slight turn of her head or sway of her body. Her shoulder ached and screamed for her to lie down, and sharp stabs of fire across her skull greeted her every step. She gratefully clambered onto her horse and clung to the reins.

"What now?" she asked, too weary to think further than the next breath.

"Now?" Cormac swung into his saddle and moved his horse next to Eilidh's. "Now I must continue on my mission. I hope you will join me."

"Your mission?" Eilidh struggled to remember what Cormac had told her, a few days and a lifetime ago. "What message could be more important than what is happening here? Duke Campbell was here. They were talking about traitors, Cormac, and a plot to kill the Queen."

"I know, I heard him." Cormac adjusted his cloak in silence for a moment before continuing. "I am not carrying a message. I am searching for some people."

"Who?" Eilidh could not keep her confusion from her voice.

"Some people." Cormac shrugged in apology. "It is crucial that I find them."

"More important than what is happening here?"

"Much more, to me, and to the Temple." Cormac held her gaze.

"And I should join you, just on that? You are asking me to take a lot on faith," Eilidh replied. "How can finding a person possibly be more urgent than defending the Temple?"

"Bandirma lies in that direction. If you ride fast you can get there before Duke Campbell, and I am sure Sir Maeglin would welcome one more sword." Cormac spread his hands helplessly. "I need to find these people. I swore I would protect them, so I have no decision to make, but you should know that their safety means much more to the Temple than any one sword in Bandirma."

"Their safety?" Eilidh pondered Cormac's choice of words. "I had thought perhaps you sought vengeance or some other threat. And you will not tell me any more?"

"It's safer if I don't," Cormac said without apology.

"At least tell me where you are traveling. It isn't Irongate, is it?"

"No, not Irongate." Cormac frowned in thought for a moment before continuing. "I am traveling north. To Kuray."

"Kuray?" Eilidh was astonished. "That's… absurd!"

Cormac laughed. "Now you see why I want your help. It's a long ride, and likely a dangerous one. We will need to conceal our Temple allegiance, to start."

"Yes, to start." Eilidh shook her head, and immediately regretted the movement as fresh pain throbbed with each twitch.

Cormac stayed quiet and let her ponder his words, his face impassive save for a slight smile at the corner of his mouth, as if he knew her decision already and was merely waiting for her to confirm it.

"You find this amusing?" she accosted him in her best knightly voice.

"Not at all." Cormac's smile grew into a proper grin. "I was just thinking of what I would say, in your place."

THE MARTYR'S TEARS

"What would you say?"

"I think I would likely say, 'good luck'." Cormac leaned forward to pat his horse's neck. "But I would be wrong."

"I could order you to come with me to Bandirma." She tried to make her voice sound casual, as if this were one possible option that she was mulling, but she was fearful it merely sounded ridiculous, and it certainly did nothing to wipe the smile from Cormac's lips.

"Of course you could, sir," he replied, and his smile grew broader.

Eilidh sighed and searched the empty road for an answer, but it only mocked her with its clear path. *It comes down to trust. If I believe him, I should go with him. If I don't, I should return to Bandirma. It is that simple.* Eilidh wanted to trust Cormac. His easy confidence and veteran authority were comforting, and she wanted desperately to prove herself his equal as a soldier. But her heart screamed for her to race to Bandirma and help defend it as her training and oath demanded.

I believe him, and he is correct that one more sword in Bandirma will make little difference.

"All right, I will come with you," she told Cormac. "At the least, I owe you for your rescue. But do not make a fool of me for this decision."

Cormac nodded silently and began to turn his horse to the north, but Eilidh halted him with a raised finger.

"There is something I must do before we leave, and I need your help to do it."

***

The manor stood at the end of a short track in an open meadow not far from the Rathad an Thuaidh. The ruins of an orchard spread on one side of the track, the fruit trees overwhelmed by the incursion of the nearby forest. The house itself was similarly dilapidated. One wing lurked shuttered and dark, with gaps in the roof, and the rubble of cracked stone littered the ground around it. The other wing showed that it was still occupied. Smoke rose from several chimneys along its slate roof, and Eilidh saw that a mason had started to repair the facing of one of the walls, although his work had been abandoned and covered until warmer weather would allow the mortar to set.

Her horse's hooves squelched in the thick mud of the lane as they approached the house, and dogs in the low kennel behind the manor barked at the noise, but the house showed no sign that anyone was aware of their approach.

"This is a mistake," Cormac told her for the umpteenth time. The warrior rode at her side, his small shield already strapped to his arm.

"Good luck on your mission, then," Eilidh replied curtly.

"I said I would help you, and I will," Cormac said reasonably. "But that doesn't make this any more sensible. What does it matter what happens to Cathan's son? Vengeance is not worth this risk."

"Have you never craved justice for someone?" Eilidh asked through clenched teeth.

"I have," Cormac replied shortly.

"And?"

"Justice was served."

"By you?"

"By a friend."

"And that was the right thing to do?" Eilidh waited for Cormac to answer, but the soldier remained silent. Eilidh risked a glance to her side and saw that Cormac's face was set in a grim mask, far from his usual demeanor. He caught her gaze upon him, and held her eyes for a moment before relenting with a nod.

They rode in silence through the avenue of bare-limbed trees that lined the end of the track and reined to a stop before the heavy door of the manor. Cormac swung easily from his saddle, but Eilidh dismounted far more gently, anxious to avoid another bout of nausea and pain.

Cormac led the way to the door, his long, silver blade shining in the winter light. Eilidh drew her own sword and followed. It was a simple blade, too heavy in the tip, and with a stained hilt that was starting to fray. But the blade was keen and rang true when tested.

Cormac did not pause at the door. A quick twist on the iron ring and the door swung inward without complaint. They found themselves in a dimly lit room, dark with heavy wood and a staircase that was far too wide for the hall's cramped size. Their boots thumped loudly on the wood floor, but there was no challenge from within the house.

"No soldiers?" Eilidh was surprised.

"With any luck, they are all still guarding the temple, or seeking you in the forest," Cormac said softly. "They would not think to find you here."

"Then let us hope Cathan's son has stayed warm at home while his men do his bidding."

They pushed farther into the manor, down a long hallway hung with dark paintings of ugly men with wiry hair and thick lips. Then, at last, they found signs of habitation, the flicker of orange fire against a doorframe, and the grumble of a guttural voice.

Cormac cautiously led the way down the hall. Although they stepped lightly, the ancient wood of the floor creaked and groaned with every step. Yet no questioning call nor shout of alarm disturbed the dusty quiet.

As they reached the open doorway, light footsteps hurried toward them from within the room, and in the next instant a young servant bustled into the hallway. Eilidh caught a glimpse of eyes wide with shock under a tumble of brown curls as the young woman suddenly came face-to-face with the two Temple warriors. Eilidh quickly held a finger to her lips, but the servant could not help a shrill cry of fright, and the small tray she carried crashed to the floor as she covered her mouth in shock.

"Damn your eyes, Neave," a voice bellowed from within the room. "If that's another bottle broken I'll whip it out of you."

"Go," urged Eilidh, and Neave fled down the hall. Eilidh paused to gain a firmer grip on her sword and stepped through the doorway.

The room was lit by the ruddy glow of a fireplace and the few shafts of grey light that managed to slip between the heavy drapes.

Three men occupied the ancient furniture that cluttered the room. Two were clearly favored soldiers, sharing a drink with their master in the manor house as their comrades stood guard in the temple or rode the winter roads. Both were young, near the same age as Cathan's son, and their faces shared an identical sneer of contempt and glee as they peered toward the door, expecting to see a girl in fear for her life.

The third man was Cathan's remaining son. He lounged in a deep chair with his boots at rest on the brick hearth, his powerful frame blocking the heat from the fire. He slowly turned to confront his servant, then leapt to his feet as Eilidh stepped into the light.

"You fucking bitch," he snarled. "You've got balls to come here." His laugh turned into a sneer of contempt as Cormac followed Eilidh into the light. "And I see you brought one of your dogs with you."

The two soldiers also climbed to their feet, and Eilidh saw that all three bore long swords at their sides and knives at their waists, although none wore armor.

"Make your peace, you arrogant ass." Eilidh was surprised by the coldness in her voice. The rage that screamed in her veins was so fiery and insistent she felt that it would explode from her mouth. "And pray the Maker can forgive you for what you have done."

"What I've done?" he screamed in fury. "You killed my brother, and my father has been dragged to your fucking temple!" He drew his blade with a savage motion and whipped it through the air, his powerful arm wielding the long sword as if it were weightless.

His companions drew their blades as well and moved into the room to flank Eilidh, but Cormac slid toward them to block their path.

Eilidh focused on Cathan's son. He bellowed in rage and charged her, his sword held high. He was fast and strong, and well-used to his sword, and the long blade flashed in a silver arc as it descended upon her.

Eilidh did not wait for the blow. She extended in a long, perfect thrust, just as she had practiced for endless hours, month after month in the School of Knights. The tip of her sword took him in the center of his chest and plunged into his body with barely a tremor. She twisted the sword free and ducked to the side as he fell upon her, his sword clattering to the floor from suddenly strengthless fingers, his legs buckling as blood burst from the wound.

Eilidh staggered as the room spun around her, and fresh shards of glass stabbed her skull, but she caught herself on the mantle before she could collapse.

She was dimly aware of Cormac fighting the two soldiers, but it was all she could do to remain upright as she leaned heavily on the mantle. Cormac did not need her help. The first of the soldiers lunged at him, and Cormac took the sword on his shield and blocked it to the side as he stepped the other way, placing his opponent between him and the soldier's friend. Cormac jabbed with the iron-bound shield, smashing its rim into his opponent's face. The soldier recoiled from the blow, one hand desperately seeking to stem the rush of blood and shattered teeth. Cormac followed him and slid the long, shining blade of his sword precisely between his opponent's ribs.

The last of the soldiers screamed for mercy, but Cormac put an end to his noise with a wide sweep of his sword, its tip leaving a bloody spray across the wall as it tore through his throat.

Eilidh let herself sink to the floor, her eyes now seeking out the man she had felled. His body lay motionless, and Eilidh knew her thrust had been true and had split his heart, killing him instantly. Pride leaked through the pounding pain and nausea, but she pushed it down. *There is no glory here. I doubt he had ever faced someone without his armor on.*

Cormac checked the bodies and finished one of the soldiers with his knife before coming to offer Eilidh his hand. She took it gratefully and pulled herself to her feet, then clung to Cormac as the room once again spiraled dizzyingly around her.

"I've got you," Cormac said quietly, and he held her firmly, his shoulder pressed under her arm, his arm around her waist, and she stumbled with him from the house.

Eilidh managed to clamber into her saddle with his help, then watched Cormac swing into his own.

"He didn't deserve mercy," she told him. "You were right to kill him."

Cormac shook his head, a sad smile twisting the corner of his mouth. "Perhaps, perhaps not, the Maker will decide. But whether it was justice or murder, it doesn't matter. In a battle, you kill your enemy, or else he will kill you, quick as you turn your back on him. In any case, we don't need witnesses to tell who we were, or which way we departed."

"What of the girl, then?"

"What of her?" Cormac snapped, anger twisting his face for the first time that she had seen.

"Nothing," Eilidh shook her head carefully. "I just needed to know what type of man I traveled with."

Cormac regarded her silently for a heartbeat, then nodded his head. "And I now know the type of woman I travel with."

They shared another moment of silence, then returned to the Rathad an Thuaidh. Sir Eilidh turned northward on the road and put her heels to her horse, and they raced from the small valley through a fine mist as grey evening crept across the sky.

Killock

Killock hurried up the long passageway that led to the gardens as the evening bells rang faintly within the hill. The last streaks of sunlight gave the thin clouds dramatic bands of pink against darker shadows of indigo, but the garden trees were already no more than black silhouettes against the sky.

Lanterns dotted the garden paths, creating small patches of warm yellow amongst the meandering trails, but Killock soon left the gardens behind him and crossed fallow fields of winter grass that whispered against his cloak as he passed. The night air grew rapidly chill as the last, feeble colors in the sky leached away completely to the west, and Killock's breath steamed into the air.

He doubted that he would meet anyone. The farmers knew better than to waste their time wandering their fields in the dark, and the priests and acolytes of the Temple were unlikely to stray from the garden at any time without cause, let alone during a freezing night. So Killock ignored the concealment of the trees and shrubs along the fence line and simply walked straight to the northern cliff.

Once he reached the edge, he began to search, peering along the lip and moving east and west to find familiar landmarks. The moon had not yet risen and the stars offered no light through the haze of now-black clouds, but there was enough light to see the motion of Loughliath far below, and to make out the darker black of the cliff rock beneath him. Far more useful to Killock were the hundreds of warm embers that were the windows of Bandirma. The wide balcony and enormous windows of the archive reading rooms were especially evident, directly below Killock, and from that landmark, he could trace patterns of smaller balconies and windows across the cliff until he was certain of his location.

Once he was sure, he dropped the heavy coil of rope he had brought with him to the ground and fastened one end to a gnarled tree that had weathered decades of the ferocious winds that howled across Loughliath. *If its roots can withstand those gales, they can easily hold my weight.*

Killock swung the coiled end of the rope over the edge and watched it fall into the night. Then he removed his cloak and diligently wadded it under a bush for safekeeping.

The Templar wound the rope around himself and took firm hold of it as he backed toward the edge. He leaned into the rope and allowed it to feed through his fingers and across his back as he dropped slowly down the cliff, scrambling with his boots from perch to perch as he descended.

He soon warmed from his exertions, until the frozen trickle of sweat across his back was a welcome relief. Lower he dropped, until the knot he had measured in the rope slid through his fingers, and he knew that he was close. The uneven stone of the cliff face was bare, and Killock could clearly see a small balcony below him and a stone's-throw to his left. He lowered himself until he was at the same level as the balcony, then walked across the sheer rock wall toward it. It was farther than he had hoped and he pulled himself across the last distance and grasped the stone balcony with relief.

Killock squirmed over the railing and dropped to the balcony floor, breathing deeply and silently, his senses chasing every small whisper of the wind, every waft of scent, every glimmer of light behind the curtained windows. No alarm was raised by his presence, so he tied the rope to the balcony and crept to the heavy, iron-framed door. A further silent check gave Killock the confidence to quietly push the door open and slip through the narrow crack into the Archivist's apartment.

The room beyond was illuminated by a single lantern hung from a sconce on the wall, turned low to conserve oil. The light revealed mountains of leather-bound books on every surface and more books packed into shelves along the walls. The musty scent of leather and parchment filled the air, and the only sound was the faint rustle of papers in the breeze from the open balcony door.

Killock closed the door behind him with a gentle click of the latch. Still he waited, learning the room as it returned to its natural stillness. Only then did he move slowly amongst the books. He ran a finger over the ancient leather cover of a book, then sorted through a sheaf of parchments covered in elegant, flowing writing in a language Killock could not identify, let alone read. Fresh ink crawled across the pages of a book whose vellum sheets still smelled faintly of lime. The handwriting was powerful and had been written quickly, with broad loops and flowing shapes. It was obviously a transcription of part of the book that lay open on the desk, along with passages from other works, but the language continued to elude Killock, and he put the book down, disappointed.

He paced slowly through the rest of the apartment, taking care to disturb nothing. The small drawing room looked as if it were a reflection of the bedroom in a mirror, and could be distinguished only by virtue of it being slightly larger, and having a cluster of comfortable chairs in lieu of a bed. A silver tray was placed on the table next to the chairs, its covered platters giving off the sharp smell of mint and the dull aroma of cold, congealed fat.

But as he entered the study, Killock felt a familiar tug on his senses, and with three quick steps, he crossed the room to a small, wooden box on the desk, secured with a steel lock that opened readily to the key that had been left carelessly on the blotter next to it.

The box was lined with a soft, brown fabric that cradled two objects, and Killock felt his jaw clench as he gently retrieved them.

Danielle's lance appeared tiny in his gloved hand, the sculpted hilt far too small for his grip, the long blade no more than a sliver of light. Her Diviner rested easily in his other hand, a silvery egg of metal whose rings of elaborate runes appeared as only vague patterns in the shadows. He tucked both Devices securely inside his tunic.

Killock closed the box's lid firmly and re-locked it, then pocketed the key with a smile.

He returned to the drawing room and drew a soft leather wallet from his pack. Killock carefully unrolled it on the table. Nestled in the wallet's folds were a dozen metal hoops of assorted sizes, crafted of delicate strands of metal. The knight drew the hoops from the wallet and fitted them together, carefully aligning them so that they overlapped, then secured them with a twist of the small inscribed studs that lined their frames.

The Templar stilled his thoughts. He put aside the smell of vellum and ink, of cold ashes, abandoned meals, and glass and stone. In their place a Word formed, as intricate as a snowflake. Killock shaped the Word carefully, focusing it precisely, and when it was uttered it was no more than a whisper that could only have been heard by the most skilled of listeners.

The Word flowed into the Device's hoops and its bindings released in a cascading wave, like a gentle breeze stirring the heavy leaves of a summer forest. The empty space within the hoops stirred as if heat passed through the air.

Killock raised the Diviner and peered through it. Gone was the simple shroud of darkness, and the apartment stood revealed in stark detail. Every whorl of wood, every crease of leather was plain to see, and more. A touch of ice colder than the stone walls, a shadow of emptiness that slid away from the Diviner's gaze, and he knew he had found his prey.

Killock returned to the bedroom and examined it through the hoops. He paused as his gaze crossed the cover of an ancient, leather-bound tome which bore a gilded title. There was no stain, and yet the leather was marked with cold shadow, a gossamer touch of mist that dragged for a heartbeat across his mind and was gone. Killock knew that touch. He had felt it before, in a baleful gaze that watched him from a dark tower, and he knew the shadow that had come into this room and had touched this book. It coiled against his senses like vertigo and the world twisted unnaturally.

Killock approached the book and considered it as he carefully repacked his Diviner in its wallet. No sign of the dark stain he had seen through the Device was visible, and Killock closed his eyes and rested his fingertips on the book's dry leather. The faintest touch of shadow brushed against him like the first whiff of spoiled meat. Killock raised his hand from the book and examined his fingers, slowly passing his thumb over them as if the touch of shadow were dirt that could be rubbed free from the skin. Then he quickly passed once more through the apartment, ensuring that nothing was out of place, firmly shut the balcony door behind him, and began the long climb to the cliff top.

***

The middle of the night had lingered and fled by the time Killock reached the furthest depths of the dungeons. At the end of a narrow stairwell that twisted like a corkscrew into the stone, beneath the cells for common criminals and miscreants, dwelled the dark recesses of the Pit, unused save for the foulest of prisoners.

The passageway at the bottom of the stairs was low and made of rough-hewn stones, placed for strength rather than beauty. Killock had to bend under the frequent arches that supported the ceiling, and even in the spaces between the arches, he could not raise his lantern above his head.

Small iron doors lined both sides of the passageway, spaced a dozen paces apart and never facing one another. Small windows in the doors were sealed by a sliding iron plate over thick iron bars, and massive latches were sunk into the stone frame and locked in place.

Killock moved quickly, the soft echoes of his boots swallowed by the heavy stone walls. Shadows danced behind each arch as he passed, and filled the passageway behind him with swaying curtains of black.

The knight halted abruptly in front of one door that appeared much the same as all the rest. He approached it hesitantly, warily, as if it might sense him and lash out. He reached with one hand and gently touched the latch on the window, then with a quick movement he released it and slid the iron panel back. It squealed in protest as it scraped along its rusted track.

The cell beyond was too dark to see any details, even with the lantern held to the bars. Killock saw only a rough floor made of pale stone, a few links of a black iron chain, and scattered straw. The air was musty, but there was a damp echo that tasted like copper as it crept through the narrow window.

Killock's face set into stone. He turned the latch on the door and rammed the bolt free with a clash that echoed down the passageway. The door swung open on groaning hinges, and Killock let it shudder to a halt against its frame, sending more reverberations cascading into the darkness.

The cell revealed little more to his lantern with the door open, for there was little more to be revealed. The straw came from a small palette in the corner, sour and rotten with damp, and the chain linked two empty manacles to a heavy ring in the far wall. There was dried blood near the ring, a long scrape and spatter marks on the stone beneath, and flecks that adorned the manacles.

Killock squatted in the doorframe and placed the lantern on the floor. He bowed his head, not in weariness, but in misery and despair.

The signs were clear to him. She had been hurled against the back wall with such force that her blood had stained the stone, and had lain on the filthy floor, stunned, as the blood spread under her and they fastened the manacles to her wrists. She had eventually dragged herself upright, pulling on the chain so that it had twisted and rubbed her skin raw.

And she had been alone.

A growl of pain leaked from his throat before a sharp breath stifled it. Killock stood abruptly and strode farther down the passage until he came to another anonymous door, which he threw open violently, sending more crashes tolling through the dungeon.

The cell beyond was identical save for irrelevant details. Here too the signs were easy to read. A body had lain crumpled on the floor. She had been dragged into the cell and fastened in the manacles. Blood had gathered underneath her head as she lay there, until at last heavy boots had entered the cell and helped her struggle through the door.

Killock followed the small dragged boot prints as they led to the first cell. Again, he crouched in the door and stared into the small room, his eyes lost as he raised a hand to cover his mouth, his fingers mindlessly stroking his stubbled cheek.

"The guards said you had come down here." The voice was cold and harsh.

Killock straightened and faced the sound. The newcomer had brought a lantern with him, and its light revealed the dull gleam of thick, scaled armor and a hard face with a strong jaw and a heavy brow.

"You put them *here*, Maeglin?" Killock strained to keep the rage from his voice. "They risked their lives for the Temple, time and again, and yet you hunted them down and disposed of them in the deepest, darkest cells. They were injured too, was that your doing?" Killock's grey eyes stared unrelentingly at the Knight Commander. "Her blood is on your hands, isn't it?"

Maeglin glanced unwillingly at his mailed gauntlets before clenching them into fists, and he returned the Templar's gaze in fury. "Damn you, Killock," Maeglin spat. "She ran. I did no more than necessary to apprehend her." The straps of the Knight Commander's armor creaked as he shifted his weight firmly onto both feet. "Benno was murdered."

"They are *our* people," Killock snarled. "Ours! How dare you treat them like this."

"How should murder and fuil crunor be treated?" Sir Maeglin walked slowly forward until he stood close enough to Killock that he could have placed his hand on the Templar's shoulder. His gaze never left Killock's.

Killock felt his fingers curl around the hilt of his sword on their own volition. "Show me, Commander, show me the evidence you had to convict them of either of those charges." Killock saw Maeglin's lip curl and his head twist slightly, and he knew he had scored. Killock's voice sank into cold contempt. "You know Wyn and Danielle had nothing to do with any of that, and yet you did this!"

Maeglin's face went blank. "I don't *know* they had nothing to do with it any more than you do, Killock. There are as many stories being told as there are mouths doing the talking, but there are only a few things that I know. I know the Bishop was murdered. I know our Lord was murdered. And I know nothing is going to stop me from finding the ones responsible." Maeglin paused and let his gaze burn into Killock's before he continued. "Nothing, and no one."

Killock turned from the Knight Commander and glanced around the tiny cell once more.

"You should be ashamed," Killock told him.

The Templar refused to glance at Maeglin, but his ears told him everything he needed to know. Breath hissed through narrowed nostrils, rapid and strong. Leather creaked as a gauntleted hand twisted the haft of a sword. Boots scraped against stone as he tensed to move. Then the Knight Commander turned suddenly and strode into the darkened hallway without another word.

Killock breathed in deeply and let the breath run out through open lips. Then another breath, sharp and purposeful, and he settled his shoulders. One last glance around the cell and Killock left, striding in the opposite direction from Maeglin's departure. He was not sure that he would pass another conversation with the Knight Commander without steel being drawn.

He had nearly reached the end of the corridor when he was brought up short next to another cell door, his senses suddenly alert. Killock tilted his head, then crouched and brought the lantern close to the floor. At first, he saw nothing, but as the dim light played across the grey stone he found it, a speckling of small, brown dots that ended in a blurred smear. Killock gently scraped at the edge of one of the dots with his finger and held the flecks that had adhered to the leather close to his face, first examining them under the lantern's light, then sniffing them, then finally touching the tip of his tongue to them.

He nodded to himself and stood again. He brought the lantern to the cell door and ran the light over the rough stones that framed it. Killock raised his hand and let his fingers brush over the long crack that ran through the brick over the door's top hinge. A smile played at the corner of his mouth, and he quickly unlatched the door and stepped into the cell.

***

Killock watched dawn ooze across the river docks in a fine, grey mist that left beads of water on the shoulders of his cloak and dripped from the eaves of the silent buildings that faced the river. A wide barge bumped against the quay a stone's-throw from Killock's perch, and stevedores hurried to and fro between patches of glowing lantern light to fill the barge for its voyage downriver. But the bustle did not touch Killock, sheltered as he was under a broad tarpaulin stretched between a shuttered tavern and a neighboring storehouse. Crude trestle tables had been crammed into the narrow alley, served by an ancient bargeman-turned-cook who spent every morning frying bread for the sailors and dock workers.

Killock had claimed a rickety bench near the edge of the alley and had dragged it alongside a stack of barrels to rest his back against as he stretched his legs and enjoyed his hot breakfast. Slowly the mist brightened, but there was no other sign that it was day. The diaphanous curtains thickened and became more rain than mist, and the drips from the eaves became a steady patter onto the cobblestones.

Killock pulled a chunk of steaming bread free and popped it in his mouth. He chewed thoughtfully as he watched the rain form puddles that reached for each other through the narrow cracks between the cobbles. A short distance from his seat, along the wall of the storehouse, the puddles gathered around a heavy iron drain. To a casual glance, the drain appeared like any other serving the docks, but this drain had a solid cover with no latch or handle to open it, and the water gathering around it drained only sluggishly.

The bread cook stepped in the puddle that had formed over the drain and cursed as the water sloshed into his boot. Killock smiled slightly as he pictured what the cook might have said if he had arrived a few hours early, in time to see the drain open and Killock clamber out.

Once Killock had discovered that Wyn and Danielle had used the cisterns to escape it had been easy to follow their trail under the river. And once he had tracked them to the quay and realized that they had, in fact, made it safely onto a boat, Killock finally drew a breath of relief. True, their trail was littered with the fact that they had been grievously hurt. *But they made it. They escaped, and are not captive in some hidden Crunorix catacomb, or behind a sealed door in the archives. On a boat, and gone.*

Killock popped the last of the bread into his mouth and sucked the chill air to cool his tongue, then sadly brushed crumbs from his tunic and donned his gloves. With his hood pulled low against the rain, the Templar walked slowly along the dock, speaking casually with the dockworkers and sailors, hunting now for knowledge. And he soon found his prey. Many of the dockworkers recalled the fast boat that had been stolen in the night, and the calls for the guard the next morning that had provided such theater. For the boat was a Temple messenger sloop, primed and ready to take urgent messages downriver the very morning it had gone missing, and the soldier that had been charged with patrolling the docks that night had been found snoring amongst piles of netting, with a bruised head and bruised pride, and a tale of being assaulted by a horde of heavily-armed assailants.

Satisfied, Killock returned to the still-empty stretch of the dock where the boat had been moored. He had investigated it the night before as he followed the women's trail, but now he focused instead on the traces the boat might have left behind. He had a vague description from the dockworkers, but he needed more if he was going to be able to find one small boat on the vastness of the Abhainn Fuar.

But his efforts did not repay him. Wood and canvas and tar, varnish and hemp—nothing that a thousand other boats did not also have.

Killock squinted into the rain and decided that he would need to come back later and try one last time while no one was near, but he had little hope that he would find anything helpful.

I would go after them, but how to anticipate their path? Would they flee for the distant safety of Danielle's home? The promise of shelter with her sister in Kuray? Or would they hide, unable to flee because of their wounds?

Killock began to walk toward the center of town, where he watched soldiers huddle miserably under their steel helms and waterlogged cloaks, and a young child dressed in a bright blue cloak diligently stomp in every puddle as he followed his impatient nanny across the square.

There is no way to know for certain, only to guess, and hope. It does not matter. It could take weeks, months even, to search the length of every river between here and the Inner Sea, and a lifetime if they chose any of a hundred other destinations, but I will do it. How could I not?

The puddle stomper finally splashed from view, and Killock began to retrace his steps to the bridge when he was stopped by the sight of two riders entering the town square. Both wore exquisite cloaks that appeared immune to the thickening showers, his of deep grey, hers black with a rich red that shone from the edges. Killock waited in their path, a wry grin twisting against his lips.

"... my point was that the owl is the sigil for Eloriel. Not a falcon. So, naming a falcon 'Eloriel' is ridiculous. He should have actually opened a book about Elvhen mythology before he opened his mouth," Gwydion was saying reasonably.

"Yes, and making sure we all knew that while the poor man was standing there with the bird on his wrist was certainly the kindest way of telling him." Rowenna rolled her eyes.

"Kindest to me," Gwydion assured her. "His stupidity was giving me a headache. Oh, hello, Killock. I mistook you for a rather damp Korrigan. Have you come to welcome us?"

"Of course."

The siblings dismounted, Killock embraced them warmly and they led the horses toward the bridge.

"I am relieved to see you both."

"It was touch and go for a bit. I was not at all certain that we would survive." Gwydion shook his head in disgust. "It's a bloody long way, and we nearly had to camp one night," Gwydion snorted. "Camp, Killock. Can you imagine?"

"No."

"Exactly."

"Were you able to reach the Mountain?"

"We did travel to the Mountain, and the news is as terrible as it could be," Rowenna replied sadly.

"Is He truly dead?" Killock asked. "And Rúreth?"

"Yes." Gwydion considered the knight keenly. "You knew?"

"We were told, but I had hope the bearer of the news was mistaken."

"I'm sorry," Rowenna said softly. "It is true. We found both of them."

"The Crunorix had been there," Gwydion scowled at the memory. "There were husks of the dead soldiers who had been sent into the Mountain, and a shadow that nearly killed Rowenna. It was fuil crunor, beyond any doubt, but I'm afraid whoever did it, whether it was Karsha Hali or not, did not sign his name to it. However, we did find something that I would wager you were not told about."

"Yes?" Killock prompted.

"The door in the sanctuary was open, you see, so we decided to have a bit of a snoop around."

Killock waited silently, and Gwydion continued after only a heartbeat, unable to contain his tale.

"I was certain it would be a privy, but as it turns out, well, do you recall the window behind the high altar in the Cathedral? I have always wondered about that image because I've never heard of any kind of tree in any of the stories about Taliesin, ever, nor about the Maker, and I was convinced it was apocryphal—"

"Maker's breath, Gwydion," Rowenna interrupted. "We don't need to hear about Taliesin right now."

"Of course, my dear, I merely sought to enlighten," Gwydion said testily. "I shall simply reveal the end of the story, shall I?"

"Only if you wish to avoid being hit. Really hard," Rowenna replied pleasantly.

"I yield, as ever, to the threat of violence. Behind the door was a chamber that contained a Device, a tree made of metal, absolutely stunning, and a pool of water, which appeared to be a curative for the effects of fuil crunor. It fed the tree, although why a Device needs water… and there was a strange glyph, one I have never seen before, fused into the floor of the cavern." Gwydion paused dramatically, unable to help risking Rowenna's wrath. "And in the roots of the tree was a mold of a sword."

"A sword?" Killock frowned. "You think this cave was where the Martyr's Blade was forged?"

"Yes!" Gwydion crowed. "You see, Ro, everyone thinks so. Yes, a Device to make the Blade, fed by a pool of water that we know is anathema to fuil crunor."

"It cured one little wound, Gwydion," Rowenna reminded him gently.

"Exactly. Anathema by any definition. Well, perhaps not, but so much grander than saying 'a pool of water that is a bit helpful in dealing with tiny fuil crunor wounds'."

"And you are certain that none of the Crunorix had entered the chamber?" Killock asked.

"They were all around the sanctuary, but none beyond the door," Rowenna assured him. "And Gwydion is correct, underneath all of his hyperbole. The pool did wash away the effects of fuil crunor."

"That's… astonishing."

"I *am* sometimes correct, thank you," Gwydion objected. "Oh, you mean the pool."

"Yes," Killock replied quietly as his thoughts churned. *The forge of the Blade. But what does that mean? That Bronwyn the Martyr was no mere warrior who rushed to Ruric's side. She bore a Weapon crafted specifically to fight the Crunorix. Crafted in the heart of the Temple's most holy place. Who was she? And why was the forge kept concealed, guarded by God Himself? Did they simply fear the Crunorix learning of its existence?* Killock thrust the unanswerables away and cleared his mind. "How can we use this knowledge against the Crunorix?"

"Oh, I am sure there's something squirreled away in the archives that I can dig up, now that we know what we are searching for."

"We hope there may be," Rowenna corrected.

"Which brings us full circle to the astonishing fact that I was *almost* willing to camp, so great was our haste. We would have been here ages ago if not for all the time we wasted explaining to the dim-witted that I am not an old man."

"We saw several patrols along the road, all very keen to question us," Rowenna explained. "They said they were searching for a noblewoman and an old man from the Summer Coast. I take it you have not yet convinced the Council of Lady Danielle's innocence."

"No. The further I have looked, the more questions I have found," Killock laughed bitterly. "No answers, however."

"Well, that's… terribly mysterious." Gwydion exchanged raised eyebrows with his sister.

"There seems to be no proof of Karsha Hali's guilt, nor Danielle's, of course, save for one man's accusations," Killock explained. "Yet Maeglin will not listen to any other conjecture."

"Bother Maeglin, I am happy to listen to conjecture," Gwydion smiled brilliantly. "Prefer it, in fact. Who is the accuser?"

"You know the Archivist, Reverend Whitebrooke?"

"Loud man, very hairy?" Gwydion asked.

"Yes," Killock agreed. "All the proof pointing to Danielle and Karsha Hali are stories told by Whitebrooke."

"And you cannot find fault in his accusations?"

"There are many suspicions, details that do not make sense, but he explains them away by claiming knowledge that no one can challenge."

"Well, he is the Archivist," Gwydion pointed out. "That is rather part of his job."

"Yes," Killock admitted, "although I am convinced there is some way of proving his claims against Danielle are false. We just need to find it…" Killock hesitated, testing his earlier resolve one last time. "*You* need to find it," he concluded.

"You are leaving?" Rowenna asked.

"Yes. Last night I found Wyn and Danielle's trail. Now that I know they truly escaped, I must help them."

"Good luck to you," Rowenna said softly. "I am certain you will find them quickly."

The three Templars reached the bridge over the Abhainn Fuar, but Killock paused on the edge of the stone channel, unwilling to enter the halls of Bandirma. Instead, he watched the ceaseless roar of the river through the bridge's stone arches, unconcerned by the icy rain that dripped from his nose.

"I don't think they are down there," Gwydion said thoughtfully. "But, then again, I am not a ranger."

A small smile twitched the edge of Killock's mouth. "Faron and Roland will want to hear your tale right away. Please tell them that I am sorry, but I have to go. I fear if I enter the temple, I shall never leave."

"Don't worry," Gwydion assured him. "We will have it all worked out by the time you return with Lady Danielle, never fear. Just don't take too long, or you will miss all the heroic stuff."

Killock nodded his thanks and left the siblings on the bridge. He strode along the river road and quickly disappeared into the swarm of the bustling docks.

Maeglin

Maeglin watched with disgust as fog seeped through the forest around him. The tall trees disappeared into the ghostly blanket less than a stone's-throw from the Knight Commander, and only a vague, watery light showed him where the trees gave way to the valley at his feet. Drops of water beaded on the grey steel of his breastplate and cascaded across the wide plates in rivulets whenever he moved, and his cloak hung wet and heavy from his shoulders.

A road lay somewhere in the valley before him, little more than a dirt track that led from farm to farm along the valley, but Maeglin could see no trace of it from where he stood amongst the trees. A distant rooster's crow echoed forlornly, lost in the endless clouds.

A soft jingle of metal and a muffled thump sounded from the trees behind him, a sure sign that the horses of the patrol were becoming as frustrated with waiting in the mist as he was.

The rooster called again and was answered by a chorus of crows. *Long enough,* Maeglin decided. He scowled and faced the dark shapes of the riders waiting in the trees.

"They are not coming," he announced to the soldiers, and strode to his horse, a massive shadow waiting stoically for him under the dripping branches of a tall pine. Maeglin paused to smooth away clinging droplets from the stallion's neck, then swung easily into his saddle. The stallion shifted once under Maeglin's armored weight, then stood easily.

"The fog will have delayed them, sir," one of the mounted soldiers ventured, a young knight with a black cloak across his wide shoulders and the first shadow of a beard tracing the outline of his jaw.

"*We* were not delayed, Sir Breandán," Maeglin reminded the knight.

"As you say, sir," Sir Breandán agreed. "Shall we shelter in one of the farms for the night while we wait, sir?"

"We are not waiting." Maeglin turned to the rider next to the knight. "How far to Littleford?"

"Two days," the rider answered without hesitation. He was a tall man with a thick beard that crawled across his cheeks and down the neck of his woolen tunic, interrupted only by a long, ragged scar that ran bare and pink along his jaw.

"You are certain?"

"Yes, sir."

Maeglin motioned the bearded rider forward, and the two led the other five riders of the patrol into the valley. Maeglin let his horse find its way through the fog, and long fronds of dripping grass brushed against his boots as they passed. The bearded rider would be hard to distinguish from a simple trapper if he were seated in a tavern, but Maeglin knew the man was one of the most skilled of the Temple rangers, a veteran by the name of Logan. He had guided Maeglin's patrol from Bandirma with unerring accuracy, leading them without hesitation through the rain and mist that had coated the countryside to their rendezvous in the valley.

Dozens of similar patrols had left Bandirma, each led by a ranger like their own guide. Hundreds of scouts and soldiers spread across the forested hills like winter's first snow. Pigeons had been dispatched to every temple within a week's ride of

Bandirma, carrying orders to patrol every road and search every farm. All fruitlessly seeking two women, an elderly wizard, and a Queen.

And not a sign of them, the Knight Commander scowled. *Not a single trace. And now this.*

Maeglin had expected to meet a patrol from Littleford in the valley, finally closing the gap between the inner and outer nets of searchers, but the valley remained silent, save for the steady drip of water and the lonely crow of the rooster.

A small stack of white stones loomed from the mist, and beyond it, the dark rut of the mud-choked trail. Maeglin turned his horse to the west and urged it into an easy canter that sent the mail of the soldiers following into a steady jingle and clash. A simple fence made from crossed wooden planks appeared alongside the road, and eventually a small gate upon which stood the valley's rooster, tall and black and magnificent as he watched in shock as the horses thundered past.

Two days. The thought tasted foul to the Knight Commander. *Two days wasted, just to find out what they are playing at in Littleford. At least I will be able to send messages from there, and perhaps there will be word from the farther temples. If the damn birds can find their way through this fog.*

***

Maeglin watched Littleford from a fringe of trees that tumbled into the valley along one of the many streams that fed the river.

Fields curled over gentle rolls of hills as they descended to the dull sprawl of Littleford along the lazy curve of the river. Bands of mist still clung to the folds of the valley, while low, somber clouds covered the crests with thin veils of rain.

Smoke rose from the town, a charcoal smudge drifting through the rain from hundreds of chimneys to form a darker blanket that hovered over it.

THE MARTYR'S TEARS

He squinted against a swirl of wind that blew freezing rain into his eyes, refusing to glance away. Across the river, dark shapes perched on the slope of the valley above the town. An orderly row of tents huddled close together, and a small pavilion crouched above them. A banner hung from the peak of the pavilion, but its sodden weight barely stirred as the air brushed against it, and Maeglin could not make out its sigil.

"Fifty," Logan announced, and he spat into the mud at his feet. "All mounted."

"At least," Maeglin agreed. "And the train?"

"I don't see a train," the ranger said thoughtfully. He scratched deep in his beard under his chin, then shrugged. "No wagons anyway, and the horse line is tended by men in armor. Might be squires, I suppose."

"What do you see above the temple?"

Logan squinted through the rain for a moment, then spat again. "There's a banner stuck on a pole on the bell tower. Can't make it out."

"That is what I saw, too."

"Why would the temple fly someone's banner?" Sir Breandán asked.

"No choice. Not if those fifty soldiers had anything to do with it," Logan replied.

"You think they were forced to?" A heavy scowl settled on Sir Breandán's face, and his mouth set in a thin line. "Who would dare?"

"Sir Cathan's the local nob," the ranger volunteered. "He's an arrogant prick, that's for certain, but he's never had fifty mounted soldiers, not by a long shot."

Maeglin returned to his horse and took the reins from the soldier who had tended it. *The town seems untouched, and the soldiers are just camping in the field. Not what you would expect from bandits or raiders. In any case, this is Littleford, not some outpost in the Ironbacks. But it feels wrong, nonetheless. Fifty mounted soldiers is a formidable force, which means a rich master. Rich masters don't travel without wagons and tents and cooks, not unless they can help it. And I mistrust that banner hung over the temple. By itself, it is troubling, but combined with that army and the missing patrols…*

Sir Maeglin swung into the saddle and turned to the ranger.

"Wait here. If we have not returned by sundown, make for Bandirma and report."

Logan nodded silently and slipped into the shadows under the trees as the patrol followed Maeglin down the slope toward the town. Maeglin urged the stallion into a gallop, and they flew across cropped pasture, scattering sheep in terror as the horses thundered past. A tidy wall of stacked stones marked a narrow track that wound between fallow fields, and the stallion leapt the wall without slowing, lowered its head, and pounded down the path, spraying mud and water to either side.

Soon the track joined another path, then another, passing farmhouses and barns as the riders approached the town proper. Maeglin avoided the main road and instead cut through the fields until they reached the riverbank and could hear the rush of the shallow river crossing. Maeglin slowed the stallion, who snorted and stamped in protest, and the patrol forded the river at a trot, sloshing their way across in a wave of white foam and a cascade of droplets. They passed a heavily-laden wagon coming the other way, a load of cabbages bound for the market. The farmer gaped at the riders, his round face a study in astonishment as his unguided mule slowly wandered to a stop mid-stream.

Maeglin crossed the ford and headed straight for the temple gates. Soldiers on the guard platforms shouted warnings as the patrol neared the gates, and Maeglin grimly urged the stallion to greater speed, now certain the temple was held by interlopers. The patrol was through the gates long before they could be closed and entered the courtyard. Surprised soldiers tumbled from the low barracks, still buckling on armor and weapons. With the four on the guard platforms, Maeglin counted only a dozen, all young with hardly a beard amongst them, but they were well-equipped, with steel breastplates and helms, and wooden shields with steel bosses.

Several of the soldiers drew their blades, but Maeglin saw that they were uncertain, shying away from the powerful horses and grim steel of the riders, and the tips of their swords drooped toward the courtyard's cobbles.

"How dare you?" Maeglin felt his voice scrape through his clenched teeth, and the soldiers flinched.

One of the soldiers stepped forward at last, his mouth a thin line and his eyes wide with fear. "By order of the Queen—"

Maeglin silenced the soldier with his boot, driving the steel-plated heel into the soldier's face. Bone splintered and the soldier reeled backward, clutching his hands to his nose.

"You're no Queen's man. Who is your lord?" The soldiers shrank farther away, their faces bloodless. Maeglin spotted a sigil of a blue chevron across a green field sewn onto the tunics of several of the soldiers. "Are you Cathan's men?"

"Yes, m'lord, but the Queen—" one of the soldiers attempted, but Maeglin needed only a glare to silence him.

"Next one of you who mentions the Queen gets gutted," Maeglin scowled. "Where are my people?"

The soldiers exchanged nervous glances. "They're in the cells, m'lord," one finally ventured.

Maeglin's eyes narrowed. "All of them? Bring them to the main temple, you two." He dispatched two of Cathan's soldiers who had yet to draw their swords, and they hurried to obey. "The rest of you, drop your blades or prepare to use them."

All fight had left the soldiers, and their swords clattered to the cobblestones at their feet. Maeglin's patrol herded the soldiers to the corner of the courtyard and collected their weapons while Maeglin and Sir Breandán entered the main temple. Their boots echoed hollowly from the high beams of the arched ceiling as they approached the altar. No candles or lanterns were lit, and the tall, peaked windows let in little light on such a gloomy afternoon.

Soon a shuffle of feet approached from the back of the room, and a small procession of acolytes entered, led by the two guards Maeglin had sent to release them. The acolytes stared about the room anxiously with wide eyes. Maeglin could see that most of them wore robes that were torn and ragged, and several bore bandages, or moved with difficulty, supported by those on either side.

"Where are the rest?" Maeglin said quietly, for only five figures stood before him. "And where are my soldiers?"

"There are some in the town stockade…" one of the captured guards ventured timidly.

"Dead," one of the acolytes answered, his voice choked and raw. He swallowed heavily and tried again. "Killed by these murderous bastards."

"We were ordered—!" the other guard stammered. Maeglin crossed the floor to him in one long stride, and the soldier grabbed desperately at the hilt of his sword as he stumbled away from the Knight Commander. Maeglin's armored fist caught the soldier on his cheekbone and rocked his head back, his helmet tumbling across the floor with a clatter of buckles and steel. The soldier staggered, his hands held uselessly above his head, and Maeglin's lip curled in rage as his next strike unleashed his fury into the soldier's face. The blow lifted the soldier from his feet and sent him sliding across the floor, but Maeglin was on him again in two quick steps. The soldier managed to raise his head from the floor, blood pouring from his torn lips, before Maeglin grabbed his shoulder and spun the soldier onto his back. Maeglin gripped the collar of the soldier's breastplate and rained blows on his head until at last the soldier hung as dead weight.

Maeglin released him and stood over the body, the staccato spatter of blood dripping from his gauntlet the only sound in the room. He faced Sir Breandán, who stood with sword drawn and disbelief written across his slack jaw and staring eyes.

"Put him with the others," Maeglin commanded, pointing at the remaining guard, and Breandán hurried to obey. Only then did Maeglin face the acolytes. "Now, tell me everything."

***

Maeglin stood on the guard platform and watched the column of riders approach the gate of the temple. Twenty of them, in heavy armor and armed with spears and swords, winding their way toward the temple from the camp on the hill.

The rain had finally ceased, but in its stead the wind began to gust, cold and spiteful as it swirled around the watching soldiers and slid through the cracks in Maeglin's armor. Two of the approaching riders had pennants fastened to the tips of their spears, and the wind caused them to snap and flutter, revealing a sigil of three black dogs on a field of white, and in the corner the stag and cross of the Queen's arms.

"Baron Arledge," Sir Breandán said softly, and pointed toward the riders.

"Who is Baron Arledge when he's at home?" Maeglin muttered.

"The Queen's cousin. I think he's Duke Campbell's uncle?"

"I suppose I can't gut him for claiming to be the Queen's man, then."

Breandán glanced at Maeglin in horror before quickly returning his gaze to the approaching riders. The column had reached the road already and was soon drawing up outside the closed gates of the temple. Maeglin watched them, curious to see their disposition. *If they are here to fight, they will flank us. The buildings are open to the fields, and impossible to defend against horsemen. Leave a few men here in front, to ensure we don't slip out the gates, and the rest dance their way in through the back. We'll be dead before sundown.*

But the approaching horsemen did not veer into the temple fields. They crossed the gates and turned to face the temple, their spears raised high in a thin wall. In the center of the line, the two riders carrying the pennants walked their horses forward and were joined by a third rider astride a tall chestnut horse. The rider wore a cloak lined with thick fur and a heavy coat embroidered with a leaping dog. Long, grey hair swept from his high forehead in dignified waves, and dark, bristling brows shadowed eyes set deep on either side of a long, aquiline nose.

"Lord Arledge," Maeglin called down, and the grey-haired rider held up a gloved hand in greeting.

"Whom do I have the pleasure of addressing?" Baron Arledge's eloquent voice carried smoothly up to Maeglin.

"Sir Maeglin, Knight Commander of the Temple."

"Sir Maeglin, excellent." Arledge graced Maeglin with a courtly bow, somehow unaffected by the fact that he was mounted on a horse. "May we converse?"

"We are doing that already."

"As you say. Then, perhaps I may have your safe passage to approach, so that we need not hurl our words at each other as if we were selling fresh fish in the marketplace."

"Very well," Maeglin nodded curtly, and the lord walked his horse forward until he sat directly below the Knight Commander.

"Why are you here, Lord Arledge?" Maeglin slid his words past clenched teeth. "Are you responsible for what happened in this temple?"

"No, my lord Commander, that tragedy falls on the shoulders of that man, there." Arledge raised a hand and pointed a precise finger toward the line of horsemen. As if waiting for the signal, three riders walked their horses forward to join the two bannermen. The rider in the center wore an embroidered tunic and a fine cloak, but he was bareheaded and his hands were bound behind his back. The rider glared at Arledge, then at Maeglin, and his face was mottled with rage. "Sir Cathan," Arledge introduced the bound rider, "the lord who presided over the massacre that took place here."

"By the Queen's orders!" Cathan bellowed. Arledge made a gesture of dismissal, and the soldiers guided Cathan's horse back to the line. He continued to yell, his words carrying clearly to Maeglin. "The Queen! You'll hang for this, Arledge, I swear you'll hang!"

"The soldiers here sang a similar song," Maeglin observed coldly. "They tell me they were ordered by the Queen to attack the temple."

"I have the order in question here," Arledge answered, and he removed a small roll of parchment from his cloak. "When you have read it, you will see that Cathan's brutality was his own. Yet before I give it to you, may I explain it? As you will see, there is far more for us to discuss than simply bringing a murderer to justice."

"Let me see the order," Maeglin scowled, "and I will tell you if I want your explanation."

"As you wish," Arledge accepted gracefully. He stood in his stirrups and held the parchment aloft, but his reach fell far short of the top of the palisade. "It is a touch… awkward, my lord Commander. Perhaps if I may be permitted to read it…"

Maeglin nodded, impatient, and Arledge quickly unrolled the small scroll and announced, "By command of Her Majesty, Gabrielle, Grand Duchess of Kuray, Knight of the Most Noble Order of the Sword, Keeper of the North, Marquessa d'Lavandou, and Queen of Albyn. All lords and ladies of Albyn are hereby instructed to seize the temples and all attending properties within their lands and arrest all within as restitution for the Temple's crimes against the Queen and her loyal soldiers." Arledge meticulously rolled the parchment and tucked it back in his cloak. "Signed by Duke Campbell."

"All—" Maeglin snapped his jaw closed and breathed heavily against the rage that threatened to burst from him. *All lords… every temple… my God, this cannot be true.* "How dare you!" he spat at Arledge. "How dare you attack the temples, how dare you murder my people!"

"Duke Campbell wishes me to convey his heartfelt sorrow at the actions of Sir Cathan and his men. His orders were to arrest, as you heard. Not to butcher, not to murder. Which is why I am ordered to turn Sir Cathan over to the Temple, to execute justice upon him as you see fit."

"What of the other temples?"

"Fortunately, there has been little resistance to the Queen's order so far, and no other deaths," Arledge replied, and Maeglin's eyes narrowed as he caught the faintest trace of mockery in the lord's voice. *Little resistance? How could the Temple garrisons be overwhelmed so easily?* But Maeglin feared that it might be true. *Knights and soldiers, armed with orders from the Queen, arriving in force… how many Temple soldiers would draw their blades against a Queen's knight, acting in her name?*

"The Queen was not attacked," Maeglin stated flatly. "Bishop Benno was murdered by one who sheltered in the Queen's company. In the confusion, her guard attacked the men sent to apprehend him."

"The Queen believes you are mistaken—"

"I was there," Maeglin snarled. "It is no lie."

"No, my lord Commander, you misunderstand. You are mistaken about who murdered Bishop Benno. The true villain is within your house, not the Queen's. Until you turn him over to the Queen, we will keep the Temple lands as bond."

"Prove it or be damned."

"I am not privy to such matters, only that Duke Campbell believes—"

"Damn his 'believes'. He is the one deceived, tell him that, he and Her Majesty, both. They should clean their own house before coming to mine. And you can tell Campbell that we will see how long a few country squires and their thugs can hold the temples when I come to take them back, just like this one."

"I am sorry you feel that way. Make no mistake, sir, my soldiers will carry out the Queen's orders as soon as you have departed. I urge you not to leave behind any token force, as they will certainly be quickly overwhelmed."

"I'll kill the first of your soldiers to enter the temple myself."

"My dear sir, if you wish to imprison yourself inside this temple, please do so. My soldiers will not inconvenience you, nor the five soldiers you brought with you. But we will carry out the Queen's order as soon as you are gone. Please consider that while you decide on a course of action. Surely you can serve your Temple in some better way."

"We will see."

"Regardless, think over what I have told you, and again, please know that you have Duke Campbell's most heartfelt condolences for the crimes of Sir Cathan, and he hopes you will exercise your rightful justice on him in short order." Baron Arledge bowed again, as serene in his elegance as if they had merely had a disagreement over the quality of wine, and walked his horse to the line of his soldiers. Two of the riders immediately returned to the gate, leading Sir Cathan's horse. The bound

THE MARTYR'S TEARS

knight sneered at the Temple soldiers standing on the platform above him, but he quickly turned from Maeglin's gaze.

"Sir?" Breandán asked.

"Open the gates and collect that refuse. Then send two riders into town to buy two wagons and teams to pull them. Tell them to check the stockade while they are there, on the chance that Cathan's man wasn't lying about some of our people being imprisoned there."

"Yes, sir." The knight hesitated, then continued in a murmur. "We're not leaving, are we, sir? Just let these bastards walk in and take the temple?"

"We are leaving," Maeglin said flatly. "We are fucked, and Lord Arledge knows it. He'll sit up there on his hill and watch us rot here, useless, while we should be riding for Bandirma as fast as we can. Get the acolytes and whatever food you can find into the wagons, and find some chains for the prisoners. They're coming to Bandirma with us."

***

Maeglin dismounted the stallion before it came to a halt, handed the reins to one of his soldiers, and strode across the empty courtyard toward the dark mass of the hill into which the Temple of Bandirma was carved. Maeglin removed his gauntlets and helm as he passed through the wide doors, and his boots rang from the polished floor and echoed from the high arches and shrines that lined the Atrium. A few candles flickered around the feet of the stone saints, casting an orange glow along the ridges of their sculpted forms, but their faces were lost above the reach of the light, and Maeglin paid them no heed as he passed, his thoughts far away behind the deep frown that hooded his gaze.

Pale light was beginning to seep into the Sanctuary as he entered, tracing cold fingers across the feet of the tall statue of Taliesin who welcomed all to the Temple. Stewards were cleaning the entry, the soft slap of their mops undisturbed by the march of Maeglin's boots on the stone floor.

The thick smell of simmering oats and sugar drifted into the passage as Maeglin passed the kitchens. The doors opened and a steward hurried through them with a silver tray crowded with polished covers, and Maeglin caught the scent of sizzling bacon as he passed. Maeglin continued, ignoring the pang that twisted his stomach, for his duty drove him harder than any hunger.

Beyond the cathedral lay the Council Chamber, the auditorium in which the Council held court. A single lantern hung on the far wall of the chamber, next to a small, wooden door. Maeglin stepped onto the dais that dominated the floor of the room and stood for a moment, facing the arc of high-backed chairs in which the Council sat when in session, the dark wood lonely in the quiet room. The center chair was shrouded in black cloth, to some a reminder of sadness and grief, to Maeglin a reminder of failure.

Maeglin nodded his head to the cloaked chair, then crossed the dais and opened the small door. Beyond lay a short passage and a series of small rooms, the domain of the Council. A scriptorium for their clerks stood, dark and quiet, to one side of the passage, a small dining room on the other. At the far end of the passage, a single lantern shone on two junior priests who scrambled to their feet as Maeglin approached, stifling yawns and smoothing rumpled robes into place.

"Knight Commander—" one of the priests managed.

"Is she in?"

"Yes, sir. Shall I announce you?"

Maeglin ignored the priest and let himself through the door. It opened into a long, thin room, dimly lit by a cluster of candles set on the desk at the far end. The room was strangely shaped, with a vaulted ceiling that was much higher on one side than the other. Pillars along the walls made deep alcoves between them, filled with shelves that groaned under the weight of books and scrolls. Maeglin had been told that, at one time, the room had been a chapel for the Council to use to seek guidance, but those days were faded ink on cracked parchment. In recent centuries, it had served as the study of the Bishop of Bandirma. *And now Reverend Nesta makes it hers.*

The High Priestess sat behind the desk, peering at a long scroll of parchment, a quill in her hand scratching tidy lines of ink on a sheet of fresh vellum laid precisely on the desk in front of her. Small, silver spectacles balanced on the tip of her nose, with a silver chain dangling from their frame that danced as she peered back and forth between the scroll and her writing. She was dressed in the simple robes of a junior priestess and wore no badges or symbols of her station, save for a single, silver bracelet around her right wrist, from which hung a small charm.

Maeglin trod the length of the room, his boots muffled by the thick pile of the rug spread across the stone floor. Nesta glanced at him as he approached, set the quill precisely in its rest, and laid the scroll on the desk.

"Sir Maeglin," she greeted him with a small frown of displeasure. "You are dripping on the carpet. Have you been standing in the river?"

Sir Maeglin glanced at his mud-spattered boots and heavy, sodden cloak that was indeed dripping steadily onto the exotic patterns of the carpet.

"My apologies, Reverend Nesta. I have just returned, and the rain has not ceased in days."

"Never mind, then. It is good to have you home." Nesta sat back in her chair and folded her hands in her lap. The candles cast a warm glow across the High Priestess' grey hair, worn as always in a tight bun, and held in place by a silver pin. Her green eyes sparkled as she smiled her welcome to the Knight Commander. "I did not expect you back for some time. Is there news?"

"Yes, your Reverence, but not of the fugitives. The Queen has ordered all of our temples seized."

Nesta's round face grew pale. "The Queen is alive?" she asked.

"Yes, and apparently extremely angry."

"That is hardly surprising, given the way we bungled things," Nesta said sternly, her mouth set in a thin line. "What will happen when they try to take the temples? What should we do?"

"It may be too late to do anything. The order has already been given, and temples have already been taken. How many, I do not know, but we haven't had a bird from any temple between here and Greymouth in a week. And there was violence. In Littleford. Many of our people were killed."

"Maker, no," Nesta gasped. "I cannot believe it."

"I have brought back the survivors and the man responsible, a knight named Cathan."

Nesta sat silently for a moment and watched the candle flames dance on the ends of their wicks. "What is your counsel?" she murmured, her gaze still far away.

"We re-took the Littleford temple without difficulty, and we could send out forces to do the same for the other temples. But I think we may have a worse problem. Sir Cathan and I had a talk on our way here. He had some interesting things to say, between his threats and his groveling. Most interesting was that it was Duke Campbell himself who arrested him."

Reverend Nesta turned her gaze to meet Maeglin's, one eyebrow raised. "Why is that interesting? Good for the duke, I would have thought."

"If Cathan is to be believed, Campbell arrived within days of the massacre, and with a strong force of knights. That means he was nearby. And Baron Arledge is in Littleford with another powerful force. That is a lot of soldiers to just happen to be nearby."

"Baron Arledge is in Littleford? What on earth is he doing so far from Glen Walden?"

"He appeared to be waiting. What for, I am uncertain, but he took the opportunity to deliver Sir Cathan to me when I arrived. Sir Cathan, and the Queen's demands."

"Queen Gabrielle takes our temples, then issues demands?" Nesta's eyes narrowed. "I see. What does Her Majesty desire? Reparations for what occurred to her here, I presume?"

"No. Lord Arledge accused us of harboring the Crunorix who murdered Benno. They want us to deal with it, or else."

"Us?" Nesta blinked in surprise.

"Yes."

"Does she believe we hold her sister? Or her counselor? Is this a demand to return them to her?"

"Arledge mentioned neither Lady Danielle nor Karsha Hali."

"There is too much uncertainty," Nesta sighed. "Does she know Karsha Hali is alive, or not? Is she under his power, or not? Does she know we arrested her sister, or that Lady Danielle has escaped? We cannot respond without knowing more."

"Does it matter?" Maeglin shook his head, a scowl twisting his mouth. "There is no trace of Lady Danielle. If she had anything to do with the Crunorix, it doesn't matter. We don't have her to turn over, even if we wanted to."

"And Karsha Hali?"

"No trace of him, either. Nothing at all, not since the battle in the Queen's apartments. At least Lady Danielle left tracks the first time she escaped."

"You mean, no trace of Karsha Hali since his attack on the Mountain, do you not?"

"Do I?" Maeglin glanced sharply at the High Priestess. "Do we now know he was there?"

"Interesting that you should ask." Nesta sat up straight in her chair. "I have sent word that I would like to speak with Reverend Whitebrooke as soon as he is feeling up to having a chat. I thought it past time I asked him a few more questions."

"That will be interesting."

"In the meantime, what do you advise we do to deal with the Queen's demands?"

"We need to call all of the search parties home and send scouts beyond Littleford. I want to know what Campbell has out there—" Maeglin was interrupted as the door to the study opened suddenly, banging off the stone wall behind it with a crash.

"Reverend Whitebrooke," Nesta greeted the Archivist as he crossed the length of her study, his robes fluttering about his legs with the length of his stride. "Have a thought for the door, please."

"I do not care to be summoned like a steward, Reverend Nesta," Whitebrooke rumbled. "You have interrupted my research."

"I am sure it doesn't mind. Sir Maeglin and I wondered if you might have a moment to tell us more about what occurred in the Mountain?"

"I have told you before. I barely survived. Thank the Maker I had the Blade."

"Yes, thank the Maker," Maeglin said quietly.

"Maeglin, I don't think you understand," Whitebrooke said gruffly. "God is dead, that is what is important. We are on our own. Reverend Nesta, as the leaders of the Temple, we must now find our own way. A new path—"

"I'm not sure that's necessary, is it, dear?"

"Of course it is," Whitebrooke snapped. "With God gone—"

"We are perfectly capable of remembering what he taught us, and of telling others about it, thank you. We will not honor His memory by forgetting all that He has taught us as our first act. No, that is enough." Nesta placed her hands deliberately on the desk in front of her, her gaze sharp and unwavering.

Maeglin studied the Archivist carefully. Whitebrooke's powerful hands clenched around the arms of his chair as if he would twist the wood free from its joins, and his face shone like wax behind his bristling beard, his eyes slits under a dark scowl. Maeglin shifted slightly, and the buckles of his heavy breastplate creaked as he settled his weight more firmly on the balls of his feet. The sound caught Whitebrooke's attention, and his eyes glanced toward the Knight Commander and then quickly away, and the Archivist settled into his chair, dismissing the High Priestess with a wave of his hand.

"I know that it is time for us to lead in His place. When next the Council meets, we will discuss that, and we will see if they share your blindness."

"You may certainly do so."

Whitebrooke stood abruptly and drew himself up to his full height, towering over the desk and the priestess. "If that is all?"

"All?" Maeglin snorted in amusement. "By no means. I want to know exactly what you found in the Mountain. You said it was a magus? And you defeated it?"

"I do not know what it was," Whitebrooke snapped. "But yes, I drove it away with the Blade."

"Yet, when we sent soldiers into the Mountain to investigate, they never returned, and when Lord Gwydion and Lady Rowenna entered the Mountain, they found it infested with husks," Maeglin said pointedly. "It does not sound as if you drove away anything."

"Karsha Hali could have returned after I departed. Or Lady Danielle," Whitebrooke sneered, "as she was able to escape so easily from your Pit."

"We are lucky you caught her in the tunnels the first time," Maeglin said coldly.

"The fuil crunor betrayed her. It was her ritual that led me to send a warning to the Mountain, and in turn was the reason I was summoned there."

"A warning? Why did you think to warn the Mountain?"

"Something she said when I captured her," Whitebrooke replied.

"But you didn't think to warn anyone else? Then, or when you detected a fuil crunor ritual occurring in the temple? Nor did you think to take more than a handful of knights with you?" Maeglin asked.

"I have told you already." Whitebrooke faced Maeglin. "What is your point, Maeglin? Or do you simply wish to cast aspersions all day?"

"No. I think your failures are clear enough to speak for themselves."

"Failures? I drove the magus from the Mountain, damn you! I defeated Karsha Hali!"

Maeglin felt his lip curl into a sneer. "You failed to capture Karsha Hali, and because of that dozens have died and our temples have been taken from us. You failed to protect the Mountain until it was far too late."

"I rode at once," Whitebrooke replied haughtily, "only I could wield the Blade—"

"You told no one!" Maeglin thundered. He wrapped his hand around the hilt of his sword to stop it from striking the priest and swallowed his fury so that his next words leaked through his teeth as a cold snarl. "No one. You went alone, where I would have sent hundreds. Your damn ego has cost us dearly, and continues to, every day."

"There was nothing your hundreds of soldiers could have done but die, you fool."

"We will never know, will we? And you certainly did not know that when you left for the Mountain. Even now, you have no idea what you faced there."

"I know that I defeated it with the Blade," Whitebrooke sneered. "A Weapon only I can wield. You should remember that fact while you are ranting. Where is the Blade?"

"Safe," Nesta replied quietly. She had watched the two men rage without a change of expression, her eyes keen with disappointment. "Reverend Ail and Reverend Hayley have veiled and warded it."

"It should be at my side," Whitebrooke boomed. "Who knows when our enemies might strike at us again. You will regret it not being in my hand when they do." The Archivist stalked from the room, his fists clenched as they swung at his sides, and the door crashed home behind him.

"That poor door," Nesta sighed.

THE MARTYR'S TEARS

Rowenna

Rowenna shifted the heavy book to her hip and strolled across the floor of the archives, her boots muffled on the thick runners that lined the walkways between the long tables. The whisper of scratching quills, the brush of leather on wood, and the dry rustle of parchment filled the expanse of the vaulted ceiling as dozens of priests and acolytes explored the vast collection of knowledge contained within the archives.

"Is this all?" a voice rumbled through the chamber, a deep roll of thunder that seemed more suited for a battlefield than its studious environs.

Reverend Whitebrooke dominated the center of the reading room, his thick mane of hair and shaggy beard towering over the heads of a cluster of robed attendants who surrounded the Archivist.

"No, this is not satisfactory. Not at all," Whitebrooke admonished the circle. "I ask for fact, and you bring me supposition. I could find the same in the marketplace."

Whitebrooke bent low to listen to the quiet mutter of one of the priests standing near him, then threw back his head and laughed, the sound of his booming voice reverberating against the stone pillars of the room. "What nonsense," he growled in response to whatever the priest had ventured. "Perhaps you are unaware that we fought a war against the Crunorix a thousand years ago. Don't tell me that nothing is known about them. Find it." Whitebrooke glowered at the ring of bowed heads. "Now!"

The group fled, all except one priestess who dared to stand and hold out a bulging leather folio that she had been clutching to her chest. Whitebrooke took it with more care than Rowenna had expected, and unfastened the leather ties.

The priestess who had given the folio to Whitebrooke was much younger than Rowenna had guessed from a distance, and had short, brown hair and a round face.

Rowenna watched as Whitebrooke examined the parchments contained in the folio, each sheet covered in tidy script and meticulous diagrams.

"I do not see it, Meara," Whitebrooke rumbled. "These patterns you claim to have found are merely arbitrary. You are wasting your time. Please complete the recording of the ritual before digressing."

"Yes, your Reverence," the young woman replied, but her twisted mouth and frown of puzzlement clearly showed she disagreed with his command.

Whitebrooke did not seem to notice the priestess's reluctance and he turned from her to find Lady Rowenna in his path.

"Lady Rowenna," the archivist greeted her brusquely. His gaze lingered for a moment on the book in her arms before returning to her face.

"Beledain's *History of the Temple*... ponderous reading, my lady."

"It is not my favorite of his works," Rowenna admitted, "although that may have more to do with how often Reverend Ezekiel assigned pages from it in first year."

"Ezekiel loved Beledain," Whitebrooke agreed, his voice strangely subdued, and Rowenna glanced at the towering priest to find that his gaze had turned to the tall windows and the dazzling vista of distant mountains and sparkling, white-capped waves they contained. " 'Our greatest scholar', Ezekiel always told me. He would hear of no other challenger."

"I am sorry, your Reverence. I did not mean to remind you of his passing."

"He should never have left Bandirma," Whitebrooke shrugged. "A mind like his, wasted on planting crops and officiating at farmers' weddings. Perhaps if he had chosen more wisely…"

"I am certain he did not regret his choice," Rowenna said softly. "We should not regret it in his place."

"Perhaps you are capable of such a feat, but I am not," Whitebrooke shook his head. "But you did not seek me out to reminisce about Ezekiel, I take it. Why do you return to Beledain?"

"I had hoped to find some reference to the construction of the Cathedral."

"Ah… you pursue your golden tree."

"Yes, your Reverence, but I have found only the briefest of mentions. It seems that Reverend Ambroise ordered the window in the Cathedral built with a golden tree depicted on it, but no explanation of why he chose that design."

"Ambroise? Yes, that would make sense. The Cathedral was finished while he was bishop."

"I know very little about Ambroise. Did he leave any writings that might reveal the source of his inspiration for the window?"

"Really, my lady, this does not seem the ideal time to revisit your schooling. We have many more pressing needs, do we not?"

"More pressing than the Crunorix?" Rowenna asked, an eyebrow arched elegantly.

"More pressing than ancient architecture," Whitebrooke replied brusquely. "We will not challenge the Crunorix by examining painted glass, we will challenge them by unravelling their rituals and understanding their power."

"I take it you mean your own research? Have you found success?"

"The rituals are revealing their secrets to me. It is slow work, of course, but I have already learned more than any scholar I have read. Of course, it would be faster if my archivists could complete their work without chasing ill-considered theories for days at a time."

"Was that what you were discussing with the priestess when I arrived?"

"Yes, unfortunately. Meara is one of my most gifted archivists, but she insists on pursuing theories that I have already considered and discounted."

"She is very young."

"She is. Does that concern you?"

"No, of course not. Do you not recall the excitement of youth? The urgency… no, that is not correct… the *certainty* that there are undiscovered treasures, if only one searches off the prescribed path? It still teases me every day. I hope none of us ever truly lose it."

"As you say, my lady."

"I am sorry, I did not mean to lecture."

"There is no need for an apology. You have spoken to a cause that is dear to my heart, as well. Every day, it seems, I see resistance to discovery and inspiration build walls around the weak-minded, shielding them from their fear of all that is unknown. I have fought against it all my life. It grieves me to have my own words cast in that same light. I assure you, if events were not so pressing, if the risks were not so great, if I was not certain that her effort was wasted, I would gladly have allowed Meara to explore as was her whim. She has an astounding mind."

"I spoke out of turn."

"Not at all. I am always happy to encounter a comrade in spirit. You seem surprised to hear me say it."

"I suppose I am."

"You were taught by Ezekiel. For all his brilliance, he was convinced an archivist should be satisfied to be merely the custodian of knowledge, bringing it forth when needed as if it was a precious gem to be admired, but never to be altered, save, perhaps, for the polish and filigree a jeweler would attempt. We are fortunate that many of those claimed by the ritual in the archives were amongst the hidebound who agreed with him."

"Fortunate, your Reverence? How can their deaths be fortunate?"

"Fortunate, because we need to look to our best and brightest minds to face the challenge of crafting a new Temple in the wake of God's death. To face the threat of the Crunorix, with new ideas, new ways of understanding that which has remained unquestioned. Of course, the deaths are distressing, but I must grieve for them later. I am not heartless, Lady Rowenna. I have endured more sorrow than you can imagine, but it has taught me to use that passion to inspire my greatest work, not to lose my way in endless mourning."

"I am not certain I could do the same."

"I hope you shall never need to. But I am convinced you would find strength, not despair. We have suffered greatly, these past months, yet your instinct is to fight and to find new hope."

"Have you found hope for us, in your research?"

"Yes, I believe so. Fuil crunor is slowly revealing its secrets to me. It is not so dissimilar to our own teachings."

"In what possible way is that true?"

"I am surprised you do not see it. The first lesson that Taliesin brought back from the Mountain told us of the gifts that the Maker had given to each of us, and how to use them properly, given the proper training."

"Yes, I do recall, your Reverence."

"As a Templar, you should. Your gift is very strong, your mastery of it as complete as can be taught. And yet, what if the lessons that God taught Taliesin were not the only way to use our gifts? What if they were not even the best way?"

"Are you suggesting that fuil crunor allows the Crunorix to control the Maker's gift?"

"I am certain of it. The rituals allow the Crunorix to manipulate the gifts in ways Taliesin never imagined."

"Fuil crunor destroys the victims of the rituals. It corrupts them and transforms them into husks, or worse."

THE MARTYR'S TEARS

"Yes," Whitebrooke agreed gruffly. "It is my considered belief that the rituals are designed to consume the gift utterly and grant that power to the Crunorix. But that does not mean it is the only outcome that is possible. There may be many ways to manipulate the gifts without depleting them."

"Do you suggest that we pursue fuil crunor?"

"Not as such, no. I merely point out that it is not as unthinkable as some would have us believe. In the end, what difference is there between training oneself to exploit our gift, and using a ritual to control it?"

"Perhaps all the difference in the world."

"You are not thinking clearly," Whitebrooke grunted. "You fear them, and you are letting that fear blind you. Remember your own caution not to dismiss the rewards of searching beyond the familiar. Regardless, some investigation is prudent, if only to help us defend against the attacks of the Crunorix."

"We have Weapons that can destroy them, Wards that can protect us."

"Not everyone is blessed with the gift to use Devices, nor is every Device effective in combating fuil crunor. Learning their rituals will allow any one of us so trained to directly counter their power. It is the best way."

"Not if there are consequences to its use."

"Of course there are consequences. Do you imagine those consequences are uniformly deplorable?" Whitebrooke paused and stared at Rowenna from beneath bristling brows. "Do you care for your brother?"

"Of course I do. He can be annoying, but—"

"But you would grieve to see him hurt, yes?"

"Of course."

"Will you be saddened to see him age? To grow infirm? To wither in mind and body?"

"I will."

"Will you mourn him when he is gone?"

"I am sure I will. Is there a point?"

"There is power within the fuil crunor rituals to control all of that. What is sickness, except for a weakness of your body. What is age, save for a withering of life? And death... Why should we suffer any of these things?"

"I don't understand... you said the rituals fed off the Maker's gifts. What has that to do with sickness and age?"

"Perhaps everything. If you could save your brother from death, would you not?"

"I would fight against any threat to his life, but that is not what you mean, is it? You speak of using fuil crunor to challenge death itself. Is that not what the Crunorix boasted, that their rituals gave the magi eternal life?"

"I see you remember that part of Beledain, at least. Of course, there is no reason to think that Beledain had any special insight into the truth behind the Crunorix. But even if he did, why are we to assume that fuil crunor is a tool that can only be used for Crunorix purposes? I am not speaking of using fuil crunor as the Crunorix do. No more death, Lady Rowenna, no more sickness. Never suffering terrible loss because of unforgiving misfortune. This could be our legacy, the Temple's legacy, if only we have the courage to embrace it."

"You still mourn your wife's passing, of course—"

"Aislin is already beyond the shroud. I would save others from that grief."

"We are not the Maker... of all the Maker's gifts, we were not granted the power over life and death."

"Perhaps the Maker did give us that gift," Whitebrooke rumbled, "and it has been kept hidden from us. Perhaps it is time to reveal it."

"Is that what you are researching?"

"Of course not. I seek only to understand how to defend ourselves against the Crunorix. All else is mere speculation, but one day we will need to answer the question of how the Temple will guide humanity. Into a new age, or clinging to the decreed canon? Those of us who understand that the greatest rewards have yet to be discovered must be prepared to lead the others from behind their walls of fear. But, for today, we have more pressing issues. I will ask one of the archivists to try and find Bishop Ambroise's papers for you."

"Thank you, Reverend."

Whitebrooke departed with a nod, mounted the steps to the upper level of the chamber and swept through the main doors with barely a glance aside, and Rowenna watched his exit with a small frown betraying her thoughts.

Then, with a shake of her head, she returned to the rows of shelves that surrounded the reading desks, eventually finding her way back to the sheltered alcove where she and Gwydion had been searching amidst faded and cracked histories of the Temple's construction.

As she approached she heard voices, her brother's refined tone followed by soft laughter.

"… I informed him that he was no gentleman, and that, if he persisted, I would be obliged to prove it with my blade."

"What did he do, my lord?"

"He wilted. For all his bluster, he proved to be a coward, as is so often the case."

"Were you not afraid he would set his men on you?"

"I was, my dear, I am not ashamed to admit it. But I could not bear to see a lady suffer in such a manner. I never considered the threat further than to prepare myself to fight, if that was required."

Rowenna stepped quietly around the end of a shelf and was greeted by the sight of her brother surrounded by four figures in priestly robes, their faces glowing with enraptured delight as Gwydion smiled dazzlingly at each in turn.

"You were terribly brave, my lord," said one of the young women, an acolyte with wide, doe-brown eyes.

"Not at all! I am certain you would have done the same, given the chance."

"What happened after? Did he leave the ball?"

"He fled, but he could not outpace the scorn that hung from his name. And as for the lady, she graced me with the honor of a dance, a reward far beyond any I could have hoped for."

The end of Gwydion's story was met with deep sighs from the attendant crowd. Rowenna rolled her eyes in exasperation and stepped out to join them.

"Hello, Ro," Gwydion greeted her with a smile. "Do you know Reverend Anariel?" Gwydion introduced a willowy blonde priestess, who curtsied and smiled. "And her acolytes, Rileigh, Meadow, and the astoundingly fortunate Dayfdd, who has the incomparable privilege of escorting these ladies every day."

"Anariel?" Rowenna asked the priestess. "What a lovely name."

"Thank you, my lady. My mother was quite obsessed with the Song of Joy."

"Discussing Reverend Anariel's namesake made me think of Lady Anariel. Do you remember, Ro? The Summer Ball?"

"Is that what that story was? I hadn't recognized it."

"Never mind. Now then, ladies, would you spare me? I must speak with my sister, for a moment."

The acolytes nodded and turned away with reluctance, but before the priestess could do the same Gwydion took her hand and brushed his lips against it.

"Until tonight, your Reverence."

"Yes, my lord… I look forward to it," she replied, and she departed with a leisurely step that emphasized the long sway of her hips.

"Research going well?" Rowenna asked.

"Mmmm, quite well," Gwydion nodded as he watched the departing archivists disappear into the maze of shelves. "Did you know," he continued, "that lovely woman is an absolute fountain of knowledge about Bishop Ambroise? Astounding. About anything to do with the construction of Bandirma, really."

"Is she?"

"Yes. Remarkable. Young Rileigh found me drowning in Beledain and took pity on me."

"Did she? This Beledain, right here, that I have been lugging around with me all afternoon?"

"Is that where it got to? Well, perhaps not Beledain, but something very similar, I am certain. In any event, Rileigh introduced me to Reverend Anariel, and she very kindly agreed to join me for supper, tonight, to help me delve into the mysteries of the construction of the Cathedral, and, of course, the image of the tree."

"While you were arranging for your dinner, I had an interesting talk with Reverend Whitebrooke."

"Did you, indeed? And what did our Archivist have to say?"

"I am not sure. In fact, it was rather odd."

"I am awash with curiosity."

"Well, he spoke at length about how we needed to fully master our gifts by using fuil crunor."

"What?"

"Yes, I rather felt the same way. I think I kept my mouth closed, though."

"He actually said we should use fuil crunor? To your face?"

"No, he was quite adroit in his reasoning. He spoke in terms of understanding fuil crunor better to defend against it better, but I certainly got the impression that he felt it should become something much more. The 'Temple's legacy', he called it."

"How amazingly pompous of him. I suppose he could be right, at least, the part about needing to understand it to fight back."

"It seems rather insidious, to me. The Conclave chose to destroy all records of fuil crunor, instead of using it, for a reason. They knew much more about it than we do, surely. And before you get too comfortable playing the apologist, he also spent quite some time asking me how I would feel if you suddenly grew sick and died."

"He… what? I find that leaves me deeply disturbed. And you know how much I enjoy being talked about, usually. Whatever did you say?"

"Oh, that I wouldn't mind, really."

"I love you, too. Well, all that enthusiasm for fuil crunor makes me want to have a bit of a peek at Reverend Whitebrooke's research. See if it might be a bit more practical, and a bit less theoretical, than he would have us believe. Do you suppose he might acquiesce?"

"It seems unlikely, as he has said 'No' to everyone else."

"True, but in this instance, it would be me asking."

"Yes, and he did just spend a considerable time talking to me about your death, so I imagine that will turn out to be a marvelous plan."

"Hmmm, on second thought, perhaps your plan is better. What is your plan, by the way?"

"I don't think we need to ask Reverend Whitebrooke about his research. We need to speak with Reverend Meara."

***

A gentle tap sounded on the door to Reverend Nesta's drawing room, and the door was opened by a steward to admit the young priestess that Rowenna had seen speaking with Reverend Whitebrooke in the archives, earlier that day. Reverend Meara stopped in the doorway, staring in surprise at the group awaiting her.

Rowenna reclined in one of the deep, comfortable chairs that faced the fireplace in an arc, while Gwydion leaned against the mantelpiece near her, a glass of sweet, golden wine in his hand. Reverend Nesta was nestled in a chair next to a small table that held a pair of silver-framed spectacles and a small silver box, and Lord Faron filled the chair beside hers, his somber robes and tunic immune to the cheerful light of the fire.

"Come in, dear, don't lurk in doorways," Reverend Nesta welcomed her with a kind smile. "Sit if you wish."

"Yes, ma'am," Meara replied uncertainly, but the young archivist ignored the empty seat next to Lord Faron and chose instead to stand awkwardly in the middle of the arc of chairs, her gaze firmly on the thick carpet under her feet.

Nesta introduced Meara to the Templars, and Meara risked a glance to meet the gaze of each in turn. Rowenna smiled to set her at ease, and received a quick nod in return, and Gwydion greeted Meara with a dazzling grin, but it was Lord Faron's soft, unchanging gaze that finally caught her attention, and Rowenna saw Meara's shoulders relax, and brows that arched high in anxiety returned to a more natural line, then creased slightly in an interested frown.

"I believe that you have been examining the Crunorix ritual in the archives?" Nesta asked.

"Yes, your Reverence, m'lords," Meara nodded her head solemnly. "I have, since Bishop Benno's death. Nothing else."

"And what have you found?" Faron said kindly, his gaze never leaving her eyes.

Meara hesitated for a moment, lost in his gaze, before answering in a rush.

"It is similar to the fuil crunor rituals that were found in Nóinín Cnoc by Lady Danielle. The ritual that was performed here is, I mean. In the archives." Meara blinked and collected herself. "I have correlated all the fuil crunor markings that were found at both sites and recorded their placement and their combinations with other markings. Lady Danielle wrote that the ritual in Nóinín Cnoc opened some sort of portal, and sent the essence of those sacrificed through it to a place she called the Abyss. Knowing that, and referencing the placement of the markings in that ritual, I have made some deductions as to their effect in the ritual that was used here. But they are only guesses. If we could observe what the fuil crunor in the archives accomplished, then we could start to decipher the rituals."

"Can you not observe the ritual as Danielle did?" Lord Gwydion asked.

"I don't have Lady Danielle's skill with a Diviner, so I doubt I could repeat her success."

"Never mind," Nesta consoled her. "There are few that could."

"No, your Reverence," Meara agreed, "but without help, I'm afraid I cannot determine much more. Could we not ask Lady Danielle? Her notes have been extremely helpful, but having her aid would let me solve it, I know it would."

"Ask Lady Danielle?" Nesta glanced at Rowenna for an instant before quickly returning her attention to the young priestess. "Reverend Meara, do you not know…"

"No, she does not." Faron tilted his head back slightly and regarded Meara silently for a moment. "Her attention has not wandered from her work."

"I haven't, I mean, it hasn't," Meara agreed as she glanced between the others. "What has happened?"

"Lady Danielle was accused of aiding the Crunorix," Nesta explained.

"Oh," Meara frowned. "That will make the research much harder. Do you think I could at least speak with her?"

"I'm afraid she has left Bandirma," Rowenna replied.

Meara considered that news for a moment as she worked through various possibilities. "If the ritual that killed Bishop Benno is similar to the one in Nóinín Cnoc, he may have been attacked by some power that came through from the Abyss. But I don't know how to determine whether that is what happened."

"You said that you had found some similarities… some patterns?" Rowenna prompted her gently.

"Yes, m'lady," the young priestess replied eagerly, but then she frowned. "At least, I believe I have. Reverend Whitebrooke disagrees. He considers it to be chance repetition."

"Reverend Whitebrooke has deciphered a significant portion of the ritual, has he not?" Gwydion asked, waving his hand in a casual arc to encompass the sum of the Archivist's knowledge.

"I believe so," Meara replied.

"Oh, I am certain of it. He has told me so, himself," Gwydion continued. "He knows who created each ritual, and much more. How they work, how to defend against them, and so on. Even how to use them. Isn't that right, Ro?"

"It is," Rowenna agreed. "He described to me how fuil crunor uses the gifts. I admit I do not fully understand, but perhaps you can explain it for us."

"Gifts?" Meara replied, puzzled. "I'm sorry, m'lady, I don't know about that. I don't know how Reverend Whitebrooke determines any of the things he knows."

"He has not explained his discoveries to you?" Nesta asked.

"No… I wish he would. It would be extremely helpful for my research. Do you think you might speak with him, your Reverence? I have asked, but he says it is too dangerous."

"I am sure it is, my dear."

"Then I am not sure what to do, your Reverence. The few patterns I have found seem to be worth investigating, but Reverend Whitebrooke says to abandon my research into the patterns, and I don't know how else to discover more. Not without repeating the ritual."

"Repeating it?" Nesta arched an eyebrow. "My dear girl, I don't think that would be a very clever idea, do you?"

"No, Reverend, I mean, not the same ritual, just a small one." Meara shook her head. "With just the patterns of markings I have managed to isolate between the two rituals. And just with my own blood."

"No, I don't think so, dear. Not even a little one," Nesta pursed her lips sympathetically.

"But, your Reverence, since Reverend Whitebrooke won't share his research with me, and I don't know what Lady Danielle did to examine the ritual in Nóinín Cnoc, the only avenue left is to experiment." Meara spread her hands in exasperation.

"Continue with your research," Reverend Nesta told her kindly. "I am sure you will do everything that can be done. But no experiments."

"Yes, your Reverence," Meara replied, her lips compressed into a thin line of frustration.

"Perhaps you could show us your research, when you have the time," Rowenna suggested. "I would be very interested in seeing the patterns that you have found."

"Yes, m'lady." Meara brightened immediately, and produced her leather folio, fat with parchments, that she began to quickly untie. "Some of the patterns show promise."

"I meant, taking a look at the ritual, itself." Rowenna felt a twist of guilt as the young priestess blinked in surprise and disappointment.

"Oh," Meara said. "Yes, of course. I would be happy to, Lady Rowenna, but you will have to ask Reverend Whitebrooke.

The ritual is in a sealed chamber, and Reverend Whitebrooke is the only one with the key."

"Is that right?" asked Lord Gwydion. "The only one."

"Yes, m'lord."

"Thank you, dear," Reverend Nesta told Meara.

Meara nodded and hesitated for a moment, then abruptly hurried from the room.

"She's a bit of an odd one, isn't she?" Gwydion mused as the door closed behind Meara. "And when you said 'young' I didn't realize you meant she was still a child. Is she really a priestess?"

"Not odd," Faron corrected solemnly. "Her mind is astounding. It drives her beyond the normal concerns of you or I."

"She is quite the prodigy," Nesta agreed. "Gwydion, be a dear and pour me a glass. Thank you. A touch more. There, I knew I could count on you not to skimp. She earned her entrance to the School of Priests when she was barely thirteen, I believe. Terrified her instructors for four years before she was anointed, and Whitebrooke snapped her up for the archives immediately. A perfect fit for her, of course."

"Four years?" Gwydion asked, incredulous.

"Yes, dear, faster than you," Nesta consoled him.

"Is it strange that Whitebrooke has not shared how he is gathering so much knowledge about the fuil crunor rituals with Meara?" Rowenna wondered. "Someone of her intellect… why would he exclude her? Or ignore her theories? She seems to have discovered something, despite the fact that she has been completely isolated."

"You should ask Reverend Whitebrooke," Nesta advised.

Karsha Hali

The great raven launched into the air with a thunder of wings that sent dozens of lesser ravens cawing and scrambling in fear and shock. The raven croaked in amusement as his smaller cousins fluttered in circles and cried out in indignation, but he quickly lost interest as he spread his wings to catch the wind that twisted and shrieked around the spires of stone that the silver people had raised into the sky.

The raven flashed across the face of the slender tower that had served as his most recent perch, then dove beneath one of the many bridges that arced between the outer towers and the citadel that soared behind them. Silver people who hurried across the spans cursed and clutched at their cloaks and hats, and the raven would sometimes watch them, his head tilted to one side and his wicked beak open as he bobbed his head in amusement. But better than that was catching the wind in his out-flung wings and streaking between the curved supports of the bridge, the stone walls a white blur, his scream of delight echoing in the vast open space.

Far below the raven, the thin tower rose from a massive edifice of stone, tiers of ramparts stacked one upon another as they circled its foot until they merged with the sheer walls and stacked keeps that surrounded the gates of the castle. The raven swooped over the wide, paved square that faced the gates and came to rest amongst the carvings that surrounded them. Hundreds of stone people stood above and to the sides, forming a wide circle across the front of the castle with the gates at its center. There were stone people with swords, stone people riding horses, stone people fighting, stone people bowing, stone people building, stone people kneeling, and stone people dying.

The raven perched in a crown atop the head of one of the tallest stone people. The crown had seven long spikes surrounding it, and the raven liked to wrap his talons around the spikes and feel them scrape against the rough stone.

From his perch, the courtyard extended like the prow of a ship, jutting over the deep valley and the endless grey roofs of the city that filled it. The valley was covered with the haze of the city, hundreds of chimneys sending soft streams of smoke into the air between the snow-covered hills on either side. Tall towers grew from the undulating sea of tiled roofs, but none reached as high as the courtyard that fronted the castle.

The raven carefully shit on the face of the stone person who wore the crown, then swooped across the courtyard and over the city itself. The chill air was suddenly full of enticing smells, and his eyes caught countless interesting glimpses in the twisting streets between the rooftops. The raven cawed to the city in delight as he passed over it, then he dipped suddenly, twisted and dropped onto the sharp ridge of a steeply-pitched roof. He scurried to the end of the roof, his talons slipping and scraping on the stone tiles, and peered into the bustling street beneath, his head bobbing from side to side in excitement.

A person in a brown cloak was giving fat loaves of bread to other people who swarmed around the open window of her house, and the smell of the fresh bread made the raven caw happily. He dropped from his perch onto the wooden table that held the bread, causing the bread person to shriek and wave her arms, but the raven had his prize and was gone long before anyone could catch him. He circled into the air, laughed raucously at the still-screaming bread person, and returned to his perch on the steep roof, where he quickly tore the hard bread into chunks with his curved beak and ate it, all the while watching the bread person to see if another loaf would be left unguarded.

But his feast was complete before there was another chance of pillage, and so the raven continued his flight over the city, eventually reaching the building that was his destination. It sat in the lowest depths of the valley, where the dark shadows of the tall hills never quite receded, and where the chill damp accumulated. The circular building swelled out of the peaked roofs of its smaller neighbors like an angry blister, and the thick, greasy smoke that trailed from its many chimneys smelled of melted fat and burned meat.

The raven swooped through one of the numerous gaps between the heavy, stone roof and the ancient, blackened beams that held it aloft, and settled in the rafters. The room below was filled with people and their noise and heat, and the raven hopped to and fro along the rafter in excitement.

In the center of the room was a raised platform, and on it, a person was doing something extremely interesting. She was clothed only in swirling red, gold, and orange paint, shining in the light of the burning brand she held. As the raven watched, the person held the brand to her lips and blew out a gout of flame that roiled in the air over the heads of the people clustered around the platform, causing them to shriek and cheer. Then she raised the torch above her head and plunged it into her mouth, extinguishing it, and the room exploded with more people noise. The raven cawed raucously at the dragon person, but after eating the fire from the torch she had no more fire to breathe, and, disappointed, the raven scurried along the beam and dropped to the small table where his Whisper huddled in the shadows, clutching a mug of rich, foamy liquid that smelled of dark earth and honey.

"Hello, Bran," his Whisper chuckled, and he rummaged in the pockets of his robe and produced a handful of corn which the raven eagerly gobbled, clutching the Whisper's hand in his talons to hold it still. "Did you like the fire eater? I had hoped she was a true fire spirit, but alas. The tales were… fanciful."

The raven croaked his agreement and regarded his Whisper with a sharp glance, for he knew he had not been called to this people place just to see a fire spirit, or even a pretend dragon person, no matter how brightly she was painted.

"What stories did the mountains tell you?" his Whisper asked. Bran settled his wings into place and began his tale, of his journey to the home of the king of the eagles, and the feather Bran had stolen while the king slept; of the war Bran had waged with the north wind; of the great cry of the spirit of a mountain that had sheared a wall of stone free from its millennia-old home, sending it crashing into the forest below; of the steel people spreading across the knees of the great mountains, always watching, always searching; of the shining stone Bran had found in a deep pool under ice so thick his beak could not break it, guarded by a lord of fishes, lurking amongst the mud and weeds, jealously watching over his treasure.

When Bran had finished, his Whisper sat back and sighed in satisfaction.

"Excellent," his Whisper congratulated him. "I am sorry I have only people stories to tell you."

Bran cawed and shook out his feathers in derision.

"I agree," his Whisper said morosely. He ran a wrinkled hand over his smooth scalp, and Bran watched his fingers pass across the black lines that swirled over his dark skin, stretching and pushing them into glorious new shapes. His Whisper sank into his robes, his thoughts far away, and Bran took the opportunity to taste the dark liquid in his Whisper's mug.

"South, I think," his Whisper muttered. Bran waited, his dark gaze locked on his Whisper's face. "Yes, we need your eyes. South."

Bran croaked and drank deeply from the mug again before the Whisper could notice.

"You are correct, I am uncertain," his Whisper smiled apologetically and retrieved his drink, cradling the mug in both hands. "I mistrust the absence of our foe in the north, but events approach their crux in Bandirma."

THE MARTYR'S TEARS

Bran bobbed his head. The flight south would be a long one, but Bran did not mind. He spread his wings and cawed fiercely, startling the people at the nearby tables, and launched himself into the air. He soared through the gap in the roof and circled the city until he had climbed above even the snow-capped hills, and only the white castle and the mountains behind it rose higher. Then Bran caught the north wind beneath his wings and let out a cry of triumph as his recent foe now flung him southward, toward the dark forests of the lowlands.

***

Karsha took a gulp from his ale and returned the heavy mug to the table. Bran's departure had drawn many eyes to him, but Karsha was accustomed to inquisitive stares and had spent countless years of his life in the theaters, taverns, and inns of the Old City. The gaze of his neighbors did not trouble him.

But he left soon after, his robes pulled tightly around his shoulders, his jaw clenched to keep the swell of disappointment from leaking through his teeth. The chill air slid across his scalp and made the brass rings in his ears ache, but it kept the frozen slush that covered the ancient, pot-holed streets from becoming a river of mud, and for that Karsha gave thanks. He weaved back and forth as he made his way, his small, brown feet seeking the shallowest deposits, unaware of the chaos his meandering path caused to the traffic around him.

Where are they? Waiting in their Black Grave? Or have they found a way that is concealed from Bran's gaze, hidden from Sir Lochlan's scouts? Karsha stopped in the middle of a narrow alleyway and half-turned to gaze behind him. *And I have forgotten to ask the fire-eater where she learned to paint the Symbol of Flame. A great pity that she only used it for decoration, but I should like to know where she found it.*

Karsha gradually became aware of the baleful stare of the heavily-burdened porter waiting for him to move in the narrow passageway, and the little wizard scurried out of the way with an apologetic smile. Pressed against the weathered stone of the alley's wall by the wide canvas sack the porter was carrying, Karsha felt part of his anxiety loosen. *I should instead be happy the Crunorix delay. It gives Boone time to prepare, and for Duke Campbell to finish dealing with the Temple.*

The thought of possible news from the duke made Karsha hurry down the alley until he could find a twist that offered a glimpse of the soaring towers of the Silver Keep, its white walls catching the low sun and shining as if covered in precious metal. Thus guided, Karsha made good time through the labyrinth of the Old City. The streets and alleys wound between the walls of buildings that had stood since before the Cataclysm. Some had even watched the sack of Kuray and had somehow survived the devastation that the Nameless King's army had visited on the city. Each bore the signs of centuries of repair and disrepair, and each was stained by the hundreds of hard winters that had been endured.

Karsha found the grand market almost where he had expected to and hurried beneath its wide arches. Inside was another city. Long streets lined with open shops wound their way under the high, vaulted ceiling, packed with people searching for everything from exotic spices and tapestries, to bags of wool and iron nails. In the center was the stock exchange, a circular room lined with bleachers where the merchants of the city traded their goods to each other.

Karsha eventually reached the northern entrance and entered the New City, built a millennium ago by King Ruric's engineers to replace the districts that had been razed to the ground during the Nameless King's attack. Calling the lower districts 'Old' and the upper ones 'New' had always amused Karsha, since there had never been any real difference in their age, and what there had been was now long obscured by the centuries of building and repair that had taken place since.

But he knew better than to show anything but appreciation for the difference in front of the citizens of the city. The Old City was the original, damaged in the war, but rebuilt as it had been. The New City had replaced that which had been destroyed, the work of the same engineers who had constructed the Silver Keep on top of the ruins of old Kuray Castle. *And who continued on to build Fellgate Castle, if every tavern keeper in Kuray is to be believed.*

But Karsha had to admit that there was no mistaking which part of Kuray was which. The streets of the New City were sweeping avenues, wide enough for several carriages to pass side by side, with small parks nestled amongst the rows of houses, and the open space let in the weak winter sun, making the New City seem brighter and warmer. The streets gradually rose with the valley floor as it approached the steep, rocky hill on which the Silver Keep was built, and the height allowed the New City to look down upon the Old, whose roofs spread in an endless wave of confused peaks and troughs.

Karsha finally reached the Bath House, the massive series of imposing buildings that housed the hot springs. Karsha desperately wished to detour through the tall doors and into the steamy, hot saunas, but he steeled himself and pressed on, for he was nearly returned to the Silver Keep. The great cliff of sheer stone that supported the entrance of the castle and its wide courtyard loomed above the Bath House, so high that the Bath House towers reached less than half-way to the top. The road curled back and forth across the cliff a dozen times before it gained the top, yet a traveler, congratulating himself after his climb, would have only just reached the gates.

The castle itself climbed another four times as high, a series of ever-smaller towers thrusting into the sky, surrounded by the thin spikes of attendant towers with their peaked roofs appearing at seemingly random intervals, attached to the main tower by soaring bridges. By the time the main castle reached its peak, the multi-pronged summit of the Royal Tower, it appeared to be taller than the grey and white mass of the mountains behind it, and thinner than the tip of a sword.

A small turret jutted from the side of the Royal Tower like a crooked thumb, almost unnoticeable amidst the columns and rooftops of its mighty peers. This was Karsha's destination, and he hurried through the stairs and passageways of the Keep until he reached it, despite his weary legs.

Once safely ensconced in his rooms, Karsha poked despondently at the cold ashes of his fire and retrieved a battered volume bound in cracked leather from the bottom of a chest packed with books. Karsha retired to his chair clutching the book and reverently turned the brittle pages as he examined the carefully drawn symbols within.

He had not found the illustration he was searching for when a harsh knock sounded on the door to his tower, dispelling his contented smile in an instant.

Karsha levered himself out of his chair, muttering in disgust, and hobbled on aching legs to the door. It opened to reveal a tall soldier, apparently immune to the piercing stare Karsha tried to humble him with.

"M'lord, a bird has arrived," the soldier informed him.

"How nice," Karsha prompted. "A prodigy, this pigeon, to find its way to us. Thank you for bringing me this story."

"Yes, m'lord, except Sir Avery said to fetch you right away."

"Is it not more customary to bring the message to the recipient?" Karsha stifled a yawn.

"Sir Avery said—" the messenger tried again.

"Right away, yes, so that I may see this marvelous bird that brought a message. Very well."

A dusting of snow glistened on the roofs of the towers and crunched between Karsha's gnarled toes as he followed the soldier to the aerie. Karsha shivered and clutched his robes closer around his shoulders as chill air swirled up his legs and sent him scurrying across the battlements and into the thick tower that housed the Queen's messengers.

Sir Avery was easy to spot amongst the stacks of cages that filled the interior of the tower. The Queen's Bird Master had the arms of a blacksmith and a chest as wide as a barrel, with a fiery-red beard that reached to his belt in a cascade of tangles that appeared as if it might provide a home for a dozen of his charges.

"Karsha, good." Avery motioned for the wizard to follow him to the back of the room, where tall cages draped in blankets sheltered a small desk covered in bits of parchment. The knight offered Karsha the wooden stool behind the desk, then chewed on what he wanted to say for a moment before speaking. "We've had a bird from Duke Campbell, addressed to the Queen," he began. "In cipher, so I wrote it fair for Her Majesty."

"Commendable," Karsha congratulated the Bird Master.

"I think you should take it to the Queen."

Karsha thanked Sir Avery and pocketed the sealed message tube. But as soon as he was through the doors he had the container open and was pouring over the tiny pieces of parchment within, checking and double-checking Sir Avery's deciphering. At last Karsha let the parchments roll back on themselves and he carefully replaced them in their tube.

Karsha chewed thoughtfully on his cheek with a few of his remaining teeth as he pondered the message, then hurried to the Queen's apartments.

Sir Ceridwen escorted him to the Queen's private study, where he found Gabrielle seated regally on a settee near a crackling fire, a small, elegantly bound book resting conspicuously on the cushioned seat beside her. But Karsha could see that the Queen's desk was covered with a half-dozen letters filled with General Boone's rigid handwriting, alongside maps and an unsteady pile of musty books, including a ponderous tome that Karsha recognized as containing the laws of Albyn. *Little wonder that Gabrielle looks weary.*

In truth, the Queen appeared exhausted. Her eyes were glossy and there were faint wrinkles above her sweeping brows as she struggled against the weight of her eyelids. Her lustrous hair cascaded around her shoulders without a single braid or pin, and she wore a simple dress and coat, far from the elegant gowns and dresses her handmaidens typically insisted on clothing her in.

"Karsha," the Queen greeted him, her accent warm and melodic.

Karsha bowed low.

"A bird has arrived from Duke Campbell with a terrible story. I am very sorry, but I must tell it to you right away."

"Yes, of course," the Queen replied, but Karsha saw that her face had paled.

"There was fighting, in Littleford, when the temple there was seized."

"Was anyone hurt?" Gabrielle asked quietly.

"Yes," Karsha replied. He hesitated, wishing there was some way that he would not have to lay the grim news on Gabrielle's shoulders. "Campbell tells us that the knight sent to take control of the temple has killed most of the priests and soldiers who lived there. He attacked them before dawn, without warning."

"No…" Gabrielle gasped, and her fingers covered her mouth, her eyes wide with shock.

Karsha nodded sadly. "It was a massacre."

Gabrielle closed her eyes and drew in a deep, shuddering breath. "No," she whispered. A tear gleamed on her cheek. Then she opened her eyes and shook her head slowly, her lips clenched into a thin line. "Damn him, no." Her golden eyes shone, but her voice was defiant. "What has happened to the knight who is responsible for this?"

"He will find justice at the hands of the Temple. Duke Campbell stripped him of his title, and gave him into the unforgiving hands of Sir Maeglin, the Knight Commander of the Temple."

"At least the duke has accomplished that much. Maker's breath, Karsha, we sent Campbell to control the nobles, yet we have already received the worst news."

"Steel will draw blood, no matter how gently it is wielded."

"A world of difference exists between an unfortunate death and a massacre, planned and executed in my name," Gabrielle snapped.

"It is assuredly so," Karsha said quietly.

"Littleford… how could such a thing happen in Littleford?" Gabrielle's voice ached with pain. "It does not seem possible."

"Even the gods cannot know their fate."

"That is little comfort," Gabrielle's laugh became a sob. "In my name, Karsha… those poor people. What can we do?"

"Do? You may order Duke Campbell to send his nobles home. Release the temples, before there are any more deaths.

THE MARTYR'S TEARS

Show the kingdom that your heart is a compassionate one, and that no cause is greater than the love you bear for your people.

"You may order Duke Campbell to complete the seizure of the temples. Hold fast and show the kingdom that your heart is a fierce one, and that you will not abandon the safety of the kingdom for fear of a difficult path.

"You must choose, but remember, there is a Crunorix priest hidden within the Temple. The realm is at risk. Not a faraway risk. Not a whisper, or rumor of a risk. No, he is a poison already swallowed, a tumor already burrowed into flesh. The Temple must cut him free, or we must do it for them, or else many more people will suffer than just the poor spirits of Littleford."

Karsha stepped to Gabrielle and took her delicate fingers between his boney, twisted ones. Fresh tears traced shimmering paths down her perfect cheeks, but her hands did not tremble.

"How could the gods be so cruel," Karsha muttered, "to have forced this burden on you."

"They were not cruel," Gabrielle inhaled deeply and wiped her cheeks with Karsha's sleeve. "They were wise." Gabrielle abruptly turned from Karsha and approached the fire. She poked the blaze a few times with an iron, then faced Karsha with determination furrowing her brow.

"We can do more than just pray that fate is kind to us," she declared. "We can ensure that it is."

"We can?"

"Yes. You must go to Bandirma. Do what you see fit with Duke Campbell, although he has had his chance and failed, in my mind. But, do what you must to expose the Crunorix priest for what he is, and bring an end to his control over the Temple."

"I preen like a rooster under your praise, but it is undeserved. The great families of Albyn will listen to me crow and will serve me with stuffing. And the Temple thinks I am a Crunorix priest."

"Karsha, you are the wisest, kindest, most cunning, most relentless man I have ever known. Arian said the same, as did King Conall. You will find a way to make right what happened in Littleford, as well as persuade the Temple that Whitebrooke is a traitor."

Karsha swallowed heavily as his throat tightened. "Your Majesty, you remember that this journey is extremely… hard."

"I do remember, and I am sorry." Gabrielle met his gaze for a moment and smiled sadly at her wizard. "But it must be done."

"This is not wise," Karsha shook his head and set his long strands of charms tinkling and chiming against one another. "You will be alone here. I will be in Bandirma, and Boone is already approaching Dolieb."

"It is," Gabrielle objected. "It is a marvelous plan."

"I will be trapped between a viper and a scorpion."

"Which one is the viper?" Gabrielle wondered.

"I think Whitebrooke and the Temple. Perhaps Duke Campbell and the nobles," Karsha pondered the question. "Yes, Campbell. Probably."

"I doubt the duke even knows what a scorpion is, and, anyway, you just squish them with your boot," the Queen declared with nonchalant bravado, "and a viper you hold by the tail and do not let go. You see, I know how to deal with both."

"I am astonished," Karsha admitted. "You have crushed many scorpions, and wrestled with many vipers?"

"No, but that is what they did in the stories Danielle would read to me."

"Very well, I will go, but I fear the end of this story."

"Thank you, Karsha," Gabrielle said. "You are our best hope." She paused for a moment, and a small line appeared between her brows. "And find the Martyr's Blade. We cannot risk the Temple controlling the Blade, once all of this is done."

"I will hurry, then," Karsha declared. "And if the gods are kind and I find the Blade and bring it to you, it will be a glorious story with no ending. Who, then, will wield it?"

"We will find Danielle by then. I am certain of it."

Danielle

A single-masted boat with a flat deck and a long, narrow hull slipped upriver. Its brown sail was drawn tight against the wind, and its sharp bow knifed through the muddy water and left a narrow wake, making good progress despite the current that clung to it.

Danielle huddled deeper in her cloak in the cockpit of the small boat, watched the banks slip by, and listened to the dappled burble of the water along the hull.

The Abhainn Albyn eddied ponderously as it swept around its great bends, dragging its silty water past dark banks thick with reeds that choked the shallows, and willow trees that trailed long fronds in the current. The river flowed slowly, as if it had congealed in the frigid air, and a slush of ice crept along the embankments and in the backwaters.

The river was far too wide for a bridge to span. The townships and villages that clustered on the banks of the river clung to the northern shore for the most part, where the long Rathad an Siar crawled toward Irongate.

Despite the freezing air and the low, grey clouds, boats plied the river. Heavily-laden barges cruised easily downstream, conveying goods from the north and west. They returned up-river empty, their crews rowing endlessly to beat the current. Around the villages, fleets of small fishing boats bobbed in the water as the villagers spread their nets. Occasionally a galley would churn through the water, long and lean and fast, with the Queen's colors snapping from its mast, or a big-bellied merchant with wide sails would plough a great furrow as it fought its way upriver to Kuray.

The clouds promised rain, and likely sleet and snow after dark, but that meant little to the rivermen. A steady wind blew from the north, and that was all that mattered. They could sail with it, or anchor against it, but there was no worry of squalls that could split sails or overturn loaded barges, nor of thick fog that could hide mudflats or drive ships upon one another. Just a bit of wet and cold, which was the same as any day on the river.

Danielle swung the boat's prow through the wind and settled her on a fresh tack toward the far embankment, grateful to be busy with lines and sails and finding the perfect balance against the wind for a few moments. Then she wrapped her cloak around herself once again and nestled against the tiller. And worried.

Days have passed now, and I know she is still in pain, although she says nothing. And every night the terrors.

Danielle did not know what to do, so she worried, and pretended not to notice when Wyn stumbled, for it was too embarrassing for Wyn to bear, and she grew frustrated and angry when helped.

But Danielle could not look away when Wyn cried out in her sleep, or when she sobbed silently in the darkness, although what good it did to comfort and soothe and hold, she was not sure. Danielle hid her own tears. That little she could do to lighten whatever troubles weighed on Wyn.

The small hatch to the cabin slid open and Wyn slowly clambered into the cockpit, reached tentatively for the rail, and sank onto the bench. Danielle smiled a greeting.

"Well, I made it without breaking my neck, so that's something," Wyn scowled.

"Nonsense," Danielle frowned at Wyn. "You are clearly stronger every day."

"I suppose," Wyn replied through a yawn. "How long have you been up here? Why didn't you wake me up?"

"You need rest," Danielle reminded her.

"Well, I'll not say no to a bit more kip, although I feel about as guilty as a cat in a milk pail."

"I am happy to give you a bit longer to sleep," Danielle waved away Wyn's concern. "Would you like to try piloting?"

"No, maybe later. It's just…" Wyn waved one bandaged hand half-heartedly at Danielle. "Where are we, anyway? Do you think we'll reach Greymouth today?"

"I am not certain," Danielle replied. "But we must be extremely close."

"Maker, I hope so. I'd do just about anything to get off this boat for a bit."

"I agree." Danielle shifted on the wooden bench. "I believe I know every knot and splinter on this board."

"It'll be worth the trip." A ghost of a smile curled the corners of Wyn's lips, but vanished before it could touch her eyes. "There's no way they will be hunting for us in Greymouth, and there's never been a better place for hiding and hearing stuff. We'll be well-vanished, and we'll hear all the latest while we hide, so we'll know if we need to escape a bit more, or if we're safe. And wherever your sis has gotten to, they'll know about it in Greymouth."

"I hope you are right." Danielle felt her stomach twist, as it always did when she allowed herself to think of her sister. "I still cannot help but fear that she and Karsha are held prisoner in Bandirma."

"That knight I pegged in Littleford was pretty intent on finding Karsha, and she certainly didn't know anything about something happening to the Queen. Unless she was a better liar than me, they escaped."

Danielle allowed herself to be consoled once again, but she knew the dread of hearing that her sister was at the mercy of Whitebrooke would never truly leave her. *Not until we find where she has gone.*

They sailed for a time in silence, each lost in their own thoughts as the boat slipped through the water upstream, until the wind became fitful and threatened to fail entirely, and the promise of rain was fulfilled with a steady, chilling drizzle that seemed intent to linger.

Danielle moored the ship against the south bank and secured the sail, shivering as the rain found every gap in her cloak and jacket.

It has been a long trip, and truth be told I am exhausted. There were aches in muscles across her back and shoulders that she had never known existed, and her thick, soft traveling gloves had ripped along the seam from hauling on the wet lines. *But I am grateful Wyn has had the chance to regain some of her strength, even if she still struggles at times.*

Danielle found Wyn curled up on the small bench behind the cabin table, still wearing her sodden cloak. Wyn glared sullenly at her bandaged hands as Danielle replaced the cloak with a blanket wrapped around her shoulders, and lit the stove.

"Time to change your bandages," Danielle said, cringing at the forced levity that rang hollowly in her voice.

"Is it going to hurt?" Wyn screwed up her face. "Because it doesn't really feel good already, so I'm not sure 'worse' sounds too wonderful."

"It may hurt a little as I am removing the bandages," Danielle smiled sympathetically. "But we can bathe your hands in cool water before we put the new ones on, and that will soothe them."

"Are you sure we have to change the bandages?" Wyn asked again, her words tumbling out with a tinge of panic. "We can't hurt them more, or what will I do? Maybe if they just healed a bit more first, then it wouldn't be so bad?"

"I am sorry, Wyn, but they must be changed." Danielle filled a bowl from their drinking water. "The skin is blistered, and it is broken in several places. It must be cleaned."

"Shit," Wyn muttered as she extended her hands toward Danielle. But she could not help but turn her head and bite her lip as Danielle reached for them.

Danielle slowly unwrapped the bandages, taking care that the cloth did not pull on the raw skin underneath, but still Wyn gasped at each small tug. At last the bandages were gone, and Wyn gratefully lowered her hands into the bowl of cool water.

"Maker, that burns." Wyn dared to peek at her hands in the bowl, but she did not risk inspecting them too closely. "But the coldness feels lovely." Danielle let Wyn leave her hands in the water until it no longer felt cool, then gently patted them dry.

Danielle lifted first one hand, then the next, to examine them. "They are healing very well. Would you like to see?"

"Martyr, no!" Wyn said hastily. "Just wrap them up again before I catch a glimpse."

"We may leave you some fingers free this time, if you would like," Danielle decided.

"That would be nice." Wyn met Danielle's gaze for a moment and then looked away. "Dani, are you sure they're going to get better?"

"Yes, I am certain."

Wyn nodded, clearly unconvinced. "It's just, it still hurts so much. Deep inside, sometimes, and then sometimes it burns like it's still on fire."

"Where?" Danielle gazed at Wyn's hands again, concerned.

"It's this one," Wyn said, raising her left hand. "The other just hurts normally."

Danielle could see little difference between Wyn's hands, and certainly nothing that would explain such fresh pain. *If only I had my circlet. I am certain some great healer will have encountered something similar and would have the answer for me.*

"I do not see any signs of festering," Danielle told Wyn as she began to wrap fresh bandages loosely around Wyn's hands, "and only a few of the blisters have ruptured."

"Ewww," Wyn grimaced and stuck out her tongue.

"No, that is good," Danielle reassured her. Danielle looped the last of the bandage around Wyn's wrist and tied it securely. "If the blisters break, they may become raw, and could fester."

"If you say so," Wyn shook her head, bewildered. "Whenever I get a blister I just squeeze it until it bursts."

"Now who is disgusting?" Danielle wrinkled her nose.

"Ha, you don't know disgusting." A grin began to twist Wyn's lips, and Danielle watched it anxiously, as if it might flee like a startled bird at any moment. "Mellon had this horrible pimple one time, right on his—"

"No, no, please no." Danielle held up her hands as if warding against a blow. "I am happy to not know disgusting."

"Probably wise," Wyn considered thoughtfully. "Because it was really nasty."

***

The town of Greymouth clung to the banks of the Abhainn Albyn where it was joined by the Greywater River. The two rivers combined into a wide curve of turbulent water as eddies swirled and collided in the current. The Greywater brought the smell of stone and ice from its source high in the Ironback Mountains beyond Irongate, and was unwilling to merge peacefully with the slow waters of the Abhainn Albyn.

Greymouth had always provided a wide harbor and safe haven for travel between the far-flung reaches of Albyn, and the town had prospered from gorging on the trade that flowed across its docks and through its gates. Long storehouses lined the waterfront, and the tall homes of the merchants proudly overlooked the rivers. Taverns and inns crowded between shipwrights and smithies, and a wide marketplace dominated the center of town.

Danielle stole a glance across the narrow cockpit at Wyn. She was curled up in the back corner, her legs and arms tucked into her cloak as she stared morosely upriver at the approaching town. The breeze had blown her hood off and her blonde hair waved in long strands like pennants around her face.

"Can't believe I'm back here," Wyn shook her head. "Haven't been back since I left for Kuray. Seems a long time ago, now."

"We stopped here every year on our way to Irongate," Danielle said. "But we always stayed in the castle. I do not think I ever entered the city." Danielle could see the rambling mass of Lord Owain's castle sprawled across the top of the low ridge above the harbor. Its heavy walls and massive keep seemed impossibly far away.

"You're in for a treat, then," Wyn assured her. "The town is always full of travelers so no one ever looks twice at a stranger, and you can always find a hidey-hole."

"As long as you are sure," Danielle said doubtfully.

"Yeah, we'll be all right. I know just the tavern to start at. It's right by the market, so it's always full of travelers and news, and folks looking to, uh, relieve the travelers of their money."

"It sounds marvelous."

"It's not so bad," Wyn shrugged. "The food was always tasty, and there wasn't any real crime, just folks helping themselves, as it were. If you watch your purse you won't come to any harm."

Danielle docked the boat in a berth at the far end of the quay, as distant from the chaos of the barges and ships loading and unloading as possible. Then she linked arms with Wyn and helped her through the twisting streets toward the marketplace.

Wyn walked gingerly beside her, with none of her usual happy movements, but also with none of the shaking or stumbling that had plagued her since her injuries, and as they passed between the stalls that filled the marketplace, Wyn walked with Danielle's arm linked through hers mostly for comfort, not for support.

Wyn transformed the few remaining pieces of Danielle's jewelry into a small purse of silver coins at a silversmith's shop, and left the smith scratching his head in bafflement as he tried to determine exactly how much he had just spent, and for what.

Wyn disappeared briefly and returned with a bag of hot chestnuts that they nibbled as they strolled through the market.

"Do I dare ask if we should be listening for the cries of a furious chestnut... person?" Danielle blew steam off another chestnut and popped it into her mouth.

"Not at all," Wyn grinned mischievously. "I beat him three rolls out of five, fair and square. Well, three rolls out of five anyway."

"You know how to cheat at dice?" Danielle lowered her voice. "Is it terribly hard? What happens if they catch you?"

"Oh, you don't want to get caught, or you had better have a place to run," answered Wyn. "But it's easy. I'll show you if you want."

"Yes, please," Danielle grinned joyfully. "I have always wished to know, it sounds so wonderfully thrilling."

"It can be," mused Wyn.

"And your hand? Was it…"

"You only need one hand for dice, and Righty is a bit fumbly, but she'll do for that. Wouldn't want to try anything with Lefty, though."

They finished their chestnuts while watching a wagon filled with stuffed bags of wool get auctioned to a crowd of weavers and dyers.

"Do you know how to do… other things like that?" Danielle asked in a conspiratorial whisper as they watched.

" 'Other things', she says." Wyn chuckled. "I do know a few things. You need a skill or two so that the big bosses want you around."

"Skills such as?" Danielle glanced around and leaned close. "Oh, please tell me, Wyn, it is like a story! I have never met anyone who could actually do such things."

"Well, when I was just a wee one I was a dipper for a spell, and then later I was a cracksman, that was the best I'd say. High demand for that, so the bosses have to ask nicely," said Wyn thoughtfully. "Especially if you can get into fancy houses and crack the kinds of locks they put on vaults and such. You just need to be careful you're not nicking something that the boss doesn't want anyone to know he has."

"A cracksman," Danielle sighed in wonder. "Creeping across rooftops and along dark passageways, slipping through the shadows."

"Oh my goodness, what *have* you been reading?" Wyn laughed gleefully.

"You may scoff, but there is nothing wrong with tales of adventure," Danielle scolded Wyn.

"They're just so ridiculous, with their knights always laying down their life to defend… whatever it is they're defending. Some forbidden love with heaving ditties, usually."

"Adventure reads are not ridiculous. Well, they are, but they are so romantic," Danielle sighed wistfully. "And you are hardly in a position to scoff, are you? 'Bronwyn's Adventures Under the Fellgate', we should call your story. Or perhaps 'The Secret of the Red Panties'. A charming rogue from the streets, and the mysterious, foreign noblewoman who loves her."

"I might read that one," laughed Wyn.

"Of course you would," Danielle said with certainty. "But what is a dipper?"

"It's this." Wyn winked as she handed Danielle her purse.

Danielle cradled it in both hands as if she were holding a precious egg. "A cutpurse," she whispered reverently.

"I suppose so, but we were always called 'dippers' when we were little." Wyn grimaced. "It was mostly horrible because the boss would take most of the coin, and if you were caught you always took a beating. Still, I was never a troll, I can say that. Those that murdered, or set fires, or snatched people. It was best to steer clear of that lot. Most ended up murdered themselves."

"Oh, I think I shall swoon," Danielle sighed deeply, then burst into laughter. "I am quite hopeless, I know, but I cannot help myself. Gabrielle and I would read adventures to each other late at night by the light of a candle. I paid the scullery girl a silver penny to bring them from the town."

"A silver penny?" Wyn was aghast. "For a read? Your scullery girl was a bigger thief than I ever was."

"Was she? I did not know." Danielle shook her head. "But it was worth it to me."

They strolled their way down a wide street that led from the market, avoiding groaning wagons stacked with goods that crept through the town toward the north gates and the Rathad an Siar. They reached their destination, a cheery tavern with the promise of hot food and a drink, and made their way through its crowded benches and settled between an apprentice silversmith with a long nose and a threadbare coat, and a jolly drover with his two sons and their ginger beards.

The tavern keeper had roasted a boar, and Danielle insisted on a cut from the loin for each of them. It arrived covered in drippings on a thick trencher of black bread. Danielle pretended not to notice as Wyn struggled to cut her meat, her left hand still refusing to grip with any strength from within its bundle of bandages. But her right wielded her knife with little hesitation, her fingers deft and sure now that they were free of their bandaged prison. *She took my purse without me feeling the slightest touch, whereas a week ago she could not bend her fingers without pain.* Danielle exhaled as she felt the knot of worry that lurked in her throat loosen. *And she laughed!*

It was far too much food, of course, and Wyn took pity on the silversmith's forlorn glances and donated her excess to replace the grey slab of boiled mutton he had acquired.

Danielle relaxed against the wall behind her and let the thick heat of the tavern lie heavily on her eyelids while Wyn busied herself with a long and agreeable discussion with the silversmith regarding the intricacies of his master's business. Danielle ignored them and listened instead to the cheerful sounds of the room. They felt a world distant from the horrors of the bleak High Fells, or the turmoil that they had left in Bandirma.

But Danielle gradually became aware that the endless stream of anecdotes regarding cows from the drovers at the table had ceased, and had been replaced by low, strained voices. She sipped her wine and listened vigilantly.

"He's sitting right there," one of the drover's sons was whispering. "Da, you know it's him."

"Might be, might be," the drover answered evasively. "Just looks like him, I reckon."

"Da, it's him, you know it," the son insisted. "And he's sitting next to that acolyte… Craig?"

"Crevan," the other son whispered. "It's them, Da."

"What would Reverend Kerry be doing here?" The drover tried to end the conversation with a deep gulp from his cup.

"You know why, Da," the first son answered. "Dressed in normal clothes and a long way from Overcombe... he's hiding, Da, run from the Queen's soldiers."

"What if he were?" The drover refused to leave his beer alone. "No business of ours, is it? Reverend Kerry never did any treason, and who can blame him for running after what happened in Littleford? Just leave him be."

The drover's sons gave up, clearly unconvinced, and Danielle surreptitiously followed their glances to try and find the supposed fugitives. It took only a moment, for the boys were not subtle in their stares. Their attention was focused on a group pushed as far into the corner of the room as possible. A half-dozen figures with their hoods drawn low and their eyes fastened to their food and drinks, obviously, and unsuccessfully, attempting to avoid attention.

Danielle sipped her wine, her heart suddenly beating loudly in her ears.

"Wyn," Danielle said softly as she leaned close and smiled toward the kitchen. "I think those people in the corner are from the Temple."

"I was wondering that myself. They looked a bit priesty."

"The drovers recognized two of the men over there as priests from some village. They said something about treason, and the priests hiding from the Queen, and that something occurred in Littleford. I wonder what has happened?"

"Patches here says that the Queen's soldiers arrested everyone in the Greymouth temple, but that 'at least it wasn't as bad as Littleford'." Wyn indicated the silversmith's apprentice sitting on the other side of her. "Says there's a sign on the door to the temple that says it was seized for treason against the Queen."

"It sounds as if that happened to the temple in this village the drovers were talking about as well," Danielle mused.

"Well, there's a nice piece of parchment that explains it all, just waiting for us at the temple."

"Do you think it is safe for us to go to the temple?" Danielle asked.

"Well, they are all arrested and such," Wyn shrugged, "and I doubt they're searching for us here, anyway."

They pushed through the bustling room as quickly as they could, but it was agonizingly slow, and Danielle resisted the urge to glance toward the temple priests as they eased through the door into the chill, evening air.

The Greymouth temple was an imposing structure near the north gates, with tall stone walls and wide steps leading to its heavy wooden doors. Torches burned on either side of the doors, but otherwise, the temple was dark, and the doors were closed.

A piece of parchment in a wooden frame was nailed to one of the doors, and two soldiers wearing the badge of the city watch stood guard nearby.

"It says the temple has been seized," Danielle read with growing astonishment. "Because of a Temple attack on the Queen. Oh, Wyn, they did attack her."

"Does it say if she's all right?" Wyn leaned close and peered at the parchment as well. "Look, Dani, it says she escaped."

Danielle nodded, not trusting her voice. She blinked to clear her eyes of the burning tears that had suddenly overwhelmed them, and tried to clear her throat of the terrible pressure that had accompanied them.

"Phew... treason this, and treason that," Wyn continued to read as Danielle stood silently beside her. "Murder's mentioned quite a few times, too. Who's Duke Campbell?"

Danielle swallowed past the pressure in her throat, but her voice still came out as no more than a faint whisper. "He is King Arian's cousin."

Wyn turned in surprise at Danielle's voice, and her eyes widened in sympathy. "Oh, Dani, she's all right, it says so right here."

Danielle nodded miserably.

Wyn put her arms around Danielle, awkwardly at first, not knowing what to do. But as Danielle gratefully pressed against her and took shuddering breaths, Wyn gathered her in close and Danielle sank into her embrace.

When Danielle's breath became easier, she wiped the tears from her cheeks and gave Wyn a smile of thanks.

"I am sorry," Danielle told her.

"That's all right." A small smile flickered at the corners of Wyn's lips. "Tears don't scare me."

Danielle nodded her gratitude as she tried once more to clear her eyes. "Tell me what else it says," she asked Wyn.

"There's not much more, actually." Wyn poured over the parchment again. "Seize all the temples. Treason. Murder. Love, the Duke."

"All of the temples?" Unease began to grow through the terror that had seized her at the mention of the attack on her sister.

"That's what it says."

"What can Campbell think he is doing?" Danielle shook her head, horrified. "He will start a war when we should be allied against the Crunorix."

"Actually, it says 'by order of the Queen'. It says they tried to kill her, and they killed her soldiers," Wyn objected. "Seems like that might make her a bit angry, and your sis didn't seem like the type to get angry without doing something about it."

"They could not have, could they? Even if they were after Karsha they would never attack Gabrielle. It would be madness. It must all come back to Whitebrooke, although I cannot see how." Danielle sighed in frustration.

"All right, then." Wyn glanced toward the two nearby guards. "Hold on two shakes."

Wyn approached the soldiers and flashed a timid smile and wide, hopeful eyes.

"Please, was the Queen really here?" she asked in an awed whisper.

"No, lass," one of the soldiers answered with a kind smile. "She's not been to Greymouth for ages."

"But, the parchment there was signed by her." Wyn let disappointment echo forlornly in her voice.

"That's not the Queen's name, that's Duke Campbell's." The second soldier was much younger, and his smile was amiable. Wyn somehow managed to blush as she dropped her gaze.

"Oh, I feel so foolish," Wyn sighed.

"Never mind," the younger soldier smiled again.

"Is it true what the parchment says? Was the Queen attacked? Is she safe?" Wyn's eyes grew even wider, and she clutched her hands to her chest as if she might swoon at the thought.

"Aye, it is true, but the Queen's safe," the younger soldier assured her. "Safe in the Silver Keep, no fear."

"Will there be… fighting?" Wyn's voice dropped to a whisper that Danielle could barely hear from where she stood. Wyn's lip began to tremble, and Danielle fought the urge to reach out to comfort her.

"There already has been," the older soldier said grimly. "Place called Littleford. But I hear Duke Campbell's already sorted that."

"Thank the Maker," Wyn sighed, and she rested one hand gently on the young soldier's arm, and pressed the fingers of her other against her chest in relief, before thanking the soldiers and walking away with a light step.

Danielle joined her as they made their way from the temple.

"That poor boy never stood a chance," Danielle said in astonishment. "You have made me quite jealous."

Wyn beamed with pleasure. "Well, now we know your sis is in Kuray. Plus, now I have a knife!" Wyn opened her cloak slightly to reveal a long dirk with a polished blade.

"Is that the soldier's?" Danielle asked. "I did not see a thing! Were you not worried he would catch you?"

"That one?" Wyn scoffed. "He wasn't ogling my hands, that's for sure. His friend might have noticed, but I got in close so he couldn't see, easy!"

"For you, perhaps. For me, it seems magical."

"Now, that sounds a bit strange, coming from you," Wyn laughed.

"Perhaps," Danielle admitted, "but I cannot imagine being able to take a soldier's weapon without him noticing."

"That's because you haven't had any practice with taking a man's weapon," Wyn said innocently. "You have to hold it just right, and, of course, it helps if the sheath is well-oiled and slippery. Then taking it is no problem."

"No, thank you," Danielle frowned. "I have no desire to hold any man's weapon, in any way."

"You'd be wasted on dipping, anyway," Wyn continued airily. "You'd be a natural for finding out secrets. Persuading folks and such."

"I would have no idea what to say," Danielle insisted.

"That's no problem," Wyn said mischievously. She admired the front of Danielle's tunic and smiled. "Open up a few buttons and let the girls do the talking."

"I am certain it is not so easy as simply baring my breasts at someone," Danielle objected, trying to conceal the delight she felt under Wyn's gaze.

" 'Course not. You have to touch their arm and say 'oh my' or some such rubbish."

"I feel sure I would blush and be useless," Danielle laughed.

"That would do the trick," Wyn assured her.

They returned to the market with a light step, and for a time Danielle thought of little else besides green eyes and joyful laughter. But the sight of two city guards, so alike to the pair standing watch at the temple doors that Danielle looked twice before deciding they were not the same men, brought her mind quickly back to the concerns that had clung to her for so many days.

Her smile faded and the sound of the market grew distant as Danielle tried to work through what they had learned. *So much has occurred, and all I have done is run and hide and worry. I have placed my family before everything else.*

But as Danielle watched Wyn walk beside her, she realized that she would make the same choice again, without hesitation. *I have lost so much, so quickly. Did the terror of nearly losing Wyn, as well, reveal who I have always been, deep inside? Or did relinquishing my title, my responsibilities, for love, truly change me?*

Danielle frowned as the thoughts circled without resolution. *All that is certain is that events have proceeded without us, and we must hurry to catch up. If fighting were to begin again, or worse, all because we hid away and had not told of Whitebrooke's treachery, I should never forgive myself.*

"Wyn," Danielle said, and pulled the blonde girl to a stop with a gentle tug on her arm. "I know that we are here to conceal ourselves from Whitebrooke's hunters, but the news of the conflict between the Crown and the Temple concerns me. What if it grows worse? We could stop that, if only we could tell Gabrielle who was really responsible."

"I'm all for stopping war and murder," Wyn declared. "But how do we tell your sis? That guard said the Queen was in Kuray."

"We could go to the castle and tell them who we are, and I am certain they would allow us to use a bird to send her a message."

"If we did that, we might as well ring a bell in the marketplace to let Whitebrooke know where we are," Wyn objected.

"We would be safe in Lord Owain's castle."

"I don't think I'd trust some lordling to know how to protect us from what's hunting us. Those walls and guards would mean bugger-all if Shitebrooke sends a shadow demon after us. We came to Greymouth for a reason. Keep on hiding's my thought."

Danielle considered carefully. It was not surprising that Wyn would counsel stealth and concealment, but Danielle conceded that it was equally as predictable that she would crave a castle and an escort. *But she is right. The little lords would be small help. Would I trust Lord Lucious to protect me? To protect her?*

"You are right, Wyn." Danielle smiled at her and was rewarded with a flashing grin. "But there must be ways to send a message while remaining hidden, if only we could think of them. I cannot bear to think of a war beginning while we had the means to stop it."

"I know, me neither," Wyn agreed, and tucked her hair behind her ear with a quick stroke of her fingers. "We could maybe send a message with a merchant. Or find ourselves a smuggler to take it. They're better at staying out of sight, though it would cost us. Either way, they would know where we are, which could be a problem…" Wyn's voice trailed away as she pondered.

As Wyn considered their options, Danielle's attention wandered to the busy street, and she realized with a shock that she was being watched. A figure stood behind a group of merchants, deep in the shadows of a wagon, and locked eyes with her between two of the gesticulating merchants. Danielle glimpsed a craggy visage, then glanced quickly away.

Was he watching the merchants, or was he watching me? I dare not look again.

"Oh! What if…" Wyn's smile faded as she saw Danielle's worried expression. "What is it?"

"There is someone watching us," Danielle leaned close and spoke quietly. "A man in a hood, on the far side of those merchants."

Wyn glanced over her shoulder as she adjusted her hood, then turned to Danielle with a shake of her head. "There's no one there. He was watching us, not those silly merchants?"

"I do not know." Danielle could not help but peek for herself, but Wyn was correct. The spot next to the stall was now empty. "I think he was watching us. Yes, he was, I am certain of it."

"A man staring at you isn't that strange, is it?" Wyn asked.

"Wyn, I think he was in the tavern where we stopped to eat." Danielle was not sure why she suddenly knew that was true. She could not actually recall seeing the man in the tavern, but she knew that she was correct.

"Followed us from the tavern, huh?" A small frown gathered between Wyn's brows, and she glanced around again. But nothing disturbed the normal hustle and bustle of the street, and Wyn eventually shook her head in disgust. "That's it, then. Fuck."

"What is it?" Danielle asked, her stomach suddenly twisting with dread at the grim anger that clouded Wyn's face.

"They've found us, Dani. We have to go, the sooner the better."

"Could we not hide here, as you planned? It is a big town."

"No." Wyn shook her head firmly. "Now they know we are here, I'd not like to risk it. We will find another place to hide, just as good, not to worry."

But Danielle could tell that Wyn was not convinced of that herself, and her reassuring smile did nothing to assuage Danielle's concerns either. *What is done is done, no matter how I wish it otherwise, and Wyn is right that all we can do now is leave as soon as possible, and hope she is correct.*

They headed toward the docks as quickly as they could without drawing further attention to themselves. Danielle watched Wyn, concerned that the strain might take its toll on her. They turned from the main street and left the crowds behind. Wyn changed her path at every intersection, and let the twisting streets become a maze between them and any pursuer. Wyn's steps never faltered, but as they descended farther into the alleyways sweat appeared on her brow despite the cold. They reached the great storehouses that lined the docks, and there at last Wyn halted to catch her breath.

"Not bad, right?" Wyn panted in disgust. "At least I didn't fall on my face."

"Do you think he will follow us?" Danielle peered behind them.

"Probably." Wyn straightened and tucked her hair behind her ear. "Maybe. Don't know. But if he does there's not much we could do to stop him. If only we hadn't eaten all those chestnuts, we could throw them at him."

"Perhaps we should go, then?"

"Perhaps we should," Wyn agreed. They linked arms again and started along the quay, passing bustling taverns and quiet storehouses, and boats silent save for the bored crewmen standing watch at the ends of their gangplanks. Wyn was now clinging to Danielle's arm for support, her steps dragging and her breath short, but she pressed on without complaint.

They boarded their boat after a final, tense journey across the seemingly endless stretch of dark storehouses that made up the end of the quay. Danielle quickly untied her and set the sails, catching the brisk northerly breeze.

The lights of Greymouth shimmered on the dark water of the harbor as they sailed from the docks. Danielle glanced behind them across the widening stretch of water and saw a hooded figure standing on the quay, watching them depart. From a distance, she could not tell if it was the man from the market, but Danielle was certain.

She swung the tiller and pointed the prow of the boat northward. They sailed up the Abhainn Albyn until it grew so dark that they could no longer tell water from land, trusting that no other craft would be desperate enough to sail without lanterns, then crept to the eastern embankment and searched until they found a small inlet surrounded by a thick screen of trees where they anchored for the night.

Danielle hurriedly started a fire in the stove and sighed in contentment as warmth began to creep into the cabin. But as she turned away from the stove her smile faltered.

Wyn had retreated to the corner of the bench, her cloak pulled tight around her shoulders, scowling in fury at her hands.

"I'm sorry," Wyn said, so softly that Danielle held her breath to hear. "It's all my stupid fault."

"What is?" Danielle asked, taken aback.

"That I pretty much killed myself, and ruined everything."

"Wyn, that is ridiculous." Danielle groped for words. "It was Whitebrooke's fault, not yours."

"Well, I do know that," Wyn gave a ghost of a giggle. "I've not lost any more of my marbles. But I was definitely the one who nearly got herself killed right when you needed me, there's no way around that. You even told me all about Wards and such, way back in Nóinín Cnoc, and I knew he had one, I *knew* it. But I thought, I thought I'd just get him, fast, and maybe it would work, you know?" Wyn shook her head angrily. "Stupid, that's what it was."

"It was brave," Danielle pleaded with Wyn.

"It's nice of you to say, but it wasn't, and don't go shaking your head at me neither." Wyn huddled lower in her cloak. "It was the kind of thing I did when I couldn't give a shit, and no one gave a piss about me. But now all I can think about is how close I was to losing everything, and hurting you, and it makes me angry. I can see it in your eyes, Dani. I know I hurt you badly, and it was all my own stupid fault."

Danielle was quiet for a moment, a frown creasing her brow as she worked through her thoughts. When at last she spoke, her voice was quiet and uncertain. "Wyn, you are right. I have never felt such fear, and the pain continues every day as I am forced to watch you suffer. But you are wrong in every other way, and in the most crucial way."

Danielle stood and stared unseeingly at the bright flames dancing in the belly of the stove.

"I was thinking of Nóinín Cnoc," Danielle said thoughtfully. "When the wight attacked us, do you remember?"

"I'll not likely forget that," Wyn scoffed.

"Bradon fought the wight, but nothing he did appeared to hurt it." Danielle frowned at the memory. "And then Bradon was injured."

"I thought it might turn very tragic, then," Wyn wrinkled her nose in disgust. "A bit nerve-wracking, wasn't it?"

"Do you know, I did not have the sense to be worried," Danielle admitted. "I knew I was going to save Bradon, you see. I had the Shape of Fire, and I thought, 'I will take care of this'. But it did not work. The fire did not kill the wight, it just earned its attention. I still remember its eyes as it stared at me, and how quickly it ran toward me."

Wyn quietly nodded her head.

"I could not think of what to do," Danielle continued. "I could not think of what to do except to try the Shape again, but there was no time for that. So, I stood there, and the wight was going to kill me. I was certain of it, as certain as anything I have ever known. But then something amazing happened. A young woman who I barely knew saved me. She jumped in front of me and attacked this monster, and she did not hesitate, that is how brave she was."

Danielle allowed silence to hang for a moment as she watched Wyn. Wyn frowned and studied her boots as she considered Danielle's words.

Danielle continued softly. "You saved my life, Wyn. And when I thought of it later, the thing that astounded me the most was that you did not think it was brave or heroic. In fact, I know that you are about to tell me that very thing right now. No, you did it because you fight to protect those who need protecting. Even if you have just met them. And you do it fiercely, without reservation. I told you that you caught my eye when you defied Lord Lucious, and that is true, but it was when you saved me in Nóinín Cnoc that I realized how special you were."

"Special? Touched in the head is more like it," Wyn tried to dismiss the idea, but a proper smile crept across her face, and she squirmed under Danielle's attention.

"No, Wyn, special. It is why I love you. If you did not do such things you would not be you." Danielle knelt in front of Wyn, extended a hand and rested it on Wyn's knee. "It does hurt to care, and to worry, and to hope, but changing who you are… losing the *you* I am in love with, would hurt far worse."

"I see what you're saying, Dani, and I hadn't thought of it like that." Wyn shook her head. "But that doesn't mean be stupid and reckless all the time either, does it?"

"No, of course not, but what happened in Bandirma was not reckless, what happened in Nóinín Cnoc was not reckless." Danielle squeezed Wyn's leg reassuringly. "Reckless is seeking out danger, not fighting against it when it seeks you out."

Wyn nodded thoughtfully. "But I don't understand one thing still."

"What is that?" asked Danielle.

"Well, I saved your life at Nóinín Cnoc, which I don't mind saying was very brave of me, and obviously extremely heroic, but then you waited until we were half-way home before you told me you fancied me?"

"I have mentioned before my great difficulty in asking for what I want," Danielle laughed.

The small stove was now steaming with heat, and Danielle slowly rotated in front of the stove until warmth seeped into her fingers and toes. She held her fingers to her cheeks and enjoyed their touch.

THE MARTYR'S TEARS

"That feels so good," Danielle sighed contentedly.

"What?" Wyn asked.

"Hmmm?" Danielle realized that she had drifted into Venaissine in her weariness. "Oh, I only said that it feels good to be warm," Danielle smiled apologetically.

"Was that how you speak in the south?"

"Yes. It is a very easy language, not at all like the old languages of the north."

"Do you think maybe I could, I don't know, learn some, or something?" Wyn mumbled. "That's probably stupid, isn't it?"

"Not at all," Danielle replied. "I would love to teach you. I so rarely have a chance to speak Venaissine with anyone, and we do have many hours as we travel to practice."

"If you think we could." Wyn glanced up but quickly looked away again. "Then maybe, when we visit your home, maybe I can talk to people and not be so embarrassing."

"Wyn, I would never be ashamed of you, never, and if someone were to make a scene I would challenge them to a duel and teach them manners with a blade." Danielle patted the bunk next to her, and Wyn came and sat. "But no one will dare because I will tell everyone that you are the Queen of Thieves, and they will all be far too frightened and excited to know what to say."

Wyn finally relented and laughed at that, and scooted all the way onto the bunk with Danielle.

"All right then, but I'm going to learn Venaissine anyway. What do we do?"

"When I was learning the Common tongue, my tutor always said that listening to others speak was the best way to learn," Danielle said. "Shall I do that?"

"What, you just say stuff, and I have no idea what you're on about?"

"I would explain, of course."

"I don't know, Dani," Wyn shook her head, and a small crease appeared between her faint brows. "It sounds silly."

Danielle's gaze drifted slowly across Wyn's face, lingering on every beloved detail. The stove's warmth had restored color to Wyn's smooth cheeks, and the lantern's warm light revealed the faint constellation of freckles across her high cheekbones and the bridge of her nose. Shadow fell along her slender neck and created a sharp ridge as it traced long muscles into the deep triangle where throat met collarbone and shoulder. Danielle could see the soft pulse of Wyn's heart under her jaw, and the slight twitch in her full lower lip that meant she was about to smile. Wyn's hair had escaped her braid, again, and hung in a golden arc across one side of her face to her chin, but Danielle left it there for once, unwilling to disturb its perfect fall.

"I promise your Venaissine will be as good as my Common by the time we are finished."

"I think we should try a bit harder than that," Wyn teased. "All right, I'll give it a go. A Queen of Thieves should know a bit of Fancy, I'd say, to be a proper queen."

"I absolutely agree," Danielle said with a smile. "Now, what would Your Majesty like me to talk about first?"

"Knickers," Wyn decided.

"Knickers?" Danielle repeated, incredulous.

Wyn burst into laughter. "Oh, Dani, please say knickers again, please please please, oh it sounds absolutely *filthy* when you say it."

"Knickers," Danielle obliged. "It is a ridiculous word when you could say panties or undergarments. Knickers… knickers… it is absurd."

"Oh, my God, stop, I'll pee myself," Wyn begged.

"You will wet your knickers?"

"I would if I were wearing any!" Wyn burst into fresh laughter until tears rolled down her cheeks and she clutched at her sides.

"No, you have asked about the knickers, and I will tell you," Danielle said as she fought against barely restrained giggles. "Why do you want to know about knickers?"

"Well," Wyn gasped as she tried to catch her breath. "I've never had a conversation with a queen without it coming up, so it seemed like the place to start…"

Wyn burst into giggles again, and Danielle joined her, and bright laughter filled the small cabin and banished the cold darkness that surrounded them.

Whitebrooke

Whitebrooke wrenched himself from his dream. He slowly pushed himself up and sat on the edge of his bed, his shaggy head lowered into his massive hands. The dream was gone, but the pain remained, a brand that burned endlessly between his eyes.

His bedchamber was cold, and the darkened world revealed a time far too early for the stewards to come and kindle the morning fire. Whitebrooke welcomed the chill air. It washed the clinging memories of his dream from him like spume in a mountain stream.

He forced himself to his feet and swayed a moment, the pain from his head causing the tall Archivist to lurch and clutch at the bed post. He twisted the polished wood savagely, and tried to drive the pain away with anger. The bed groaned as if it suffered along with the priest, but his pain lingered and throbbed sullenly beyond the reach of his hands. Whitebrooke released the bed post with a snarl of disgust and felt his way between the dimly seen stacks of books that cluttered the room.

Thick curtains across the far wall cloaked tall windows and the door that opened onto a small balcony. Whitebrooke yanked the curtains aside and pulled the door wide, letting the wind tug on his nightgown and blow papers from the stacks littered across his desk. The balcony perched high on the northern cliff of the massive hill of Bandirma, and the endless grey surface of Loughliath spread before it. Deep blackness roiled beyond the balcony rail, and for an instant Whitebrooke recoiled as an image from his dream, of thick, oily smoke rising from his blackened skin, loomed in his mind.

Whitebrooke stepped to the railing, his bare feet splashing in shallow puddles that seeped across the ancient stone.

Slowly his mind cleared, the clinging fingers of his dream drawing away in the cold, wet air, until all that remained was the bitter pain that lodged deep between his eyes.

Only then did he return to the room and fasten the door behind him. A moment's search across the familiar shapes of the desk revealed a lantern, and a quick twist of its lighter filled its glass with warm flame. He sat at his desk, and his fingers rested on the lid of a small box that nestled amongst the stacks of books. The image of golden eyes that blazed with fire filled his thoughts.

Who is she? he pondered.

Pale light began to reveal the shapes of the windows and drew thin lines along the edges of the room's contents. A wide table took up most of the available space, its entire surface dedicated to tall stacks of books arranged in careful towers and unrolled scrolls weighted with ink stands and a magnifying glass. Shelves of more books hid the walls of the chamber, and the small study adjacent to the bedroom was no different, its space sacrificed for the same cause.

"I am not for you, priest," her voice hissed from his dream. Wisps of fire curled between her lips on each word, and licked across her cheeks and into her hair.

Whitebrooke used the muted light to examine the back of his hand. Dark hair covered his skin save where three long scars traced parallel tracks. His knuckles also shone with scars, the results of countless encounters in the training ring, but the three across the back of his hand held his gaze. He ran his fingertips along them and gently traced the slick skin from his wrist to the small valleys between his knuckles.

Whitebrooke's reverie was disturbed by the sharp sound of the door latch being thrown. A tall, thin man stepped through the doorway carrying a basket of wood for the fire. He recoiled in shock as he saw Whitebrooke's imposing form waiting for him. The Archivist crossed his thick arms over his chest and he glared at the unwelcome disruption.

"Your Reverence, I'm sorry," the steward stammered. "I didn't realize you were awake."

"Light the fire, and get out," Whitebrooke said sharply, and he frowned at the man until the steward scurried from the room, leaving behind a snapping blaze.

He retreated to his bed chamber and quickly donned his robes. The beautiful fabric with its intricate embroidery draped elegantly from his wide shoulders. Its comforting weight and grandeur lent Whitebrooke new strength. He ran thick fingers through the tangle of his hair, then pushed his hands away, frustrated with the subconscious gesture.

The vision of a ruby, gleaming as it tumbled from a tangle of chestnut curls, permeated his mind. The gem chimed sweetly as it pinged off stone, as bright and sharp a sound in his thoughts as if it were real, and not an echo from his dream.

Whitebrooke grunted and pressed his hand over his mouth, seeking to stifle the groan of pain that swelled in his throat. He swallowed heavily, but he could not calm the labored beating of his heart. *She is not Aislin, she is not!* He tried to force his thoughts away from the fresh visions of his dream, but his gaze sought out the three scars on the back of his hand without volition, as if eager to probe for misery like a tongue pushing into a rotten tooth.

"*Oh,*" Aislin whispered faintly from his dream, and his thoughts filled with the image of her eyes wide with surprise. She pressed her fingers against the side of her head as more rubies trickled across the back of her hand and fell to the ground like rain. Whitebrooke quickly covered Aislin's hand with his own, but still the rubies fell, faster and faster, pouring from a glimmering wound beneath her chestnut hair. The gems filled the folds of her dress and formed a pool of glistening red around her. She clutched at his hand, in agony, and tore long strips of skin from the back of his hand.

Whitebrooke smashed his fist onto his desk, knocking pen holders and candelabra over with a clatter. *She is not Aislin!* he insisted furiously. *Why does she torment me with Aislin's form?*

Stewards from the kitchen arrived with his breakfast and he ate hurriedly and without pleasure, barely tasting the food. He washed down the few impatient mouthfuls he could stomach with a deep draught of scalding tea and strode from his rooms and through the quiet halls to the archives, his glare keeping the few early risers from meeting his eye.

The wide reading rooms of the archive were as solemnly silent as the halls. Stewards opened the heavy curtains and lit the candelabras as he passed, bathing the gloomy vaults in soft light, but Whitebrooke's step did not pause until he had passed from the reading rooms into the warren of chambers that were the domain of the archivists. A narrow hallway lined with dark wood and an ancient, threadbare carpet led to a small, high window and a heavy door, its wood dark with centuries of polish and care from generations of stewards.

Beyond the door was the archivists' scriptorium. Elegant pillars supported soaring vaults, each one carved into beautiful representations of fantastic tales and mythical creatures.

Tall, narrow windows brought the thin morning light into the room, illuminating rows of writing desks angled to catch the natural light. Deep shelves lined the walls and groaned under the weight of countless books, small chests and artifacts, while the center of the room was dedicated to a wide table.

Whitebrooke had the room to himself, but there was ample evidence of recent use. Stubs of candles trailed long curtains of wax from candelabras scattered around the room, thick tomes lay open on the tables, and empty ink jars clustered on the writing desks.

No, she is not Aislin, though she takes Aislin's form for a time, in my dream.

He retrieved a box from the shelves and approached the end of the room. At the foot of one of the windows was his own desk, a broad piece of polished mahogany angled just so, surrounded by enough silver stands to hold an array of books and scrolls for his attention. Whitebrooke sat in the heavy, high-backed chair and rested his hands for a moment on its arms, feeling the smooth carvings fit as comfortably into his grip as a sword hilt.

The box contained a stack of small pieces of parchment. Each was covered in elegant, precise handwriting, messages that had been carried the length of Albyn.

Whitebrooke began to read, setting each piece carefully aside when he had finished with it, preserving the sequence. Despite their number, he finished with the stack quickly, and set the last message in its place with a grunt of displeasure.

Lady Danielle's letters recounted enough details of Crunorix rituals, the catacombs beneath Sliabh Mór, and the battle with the magus that had lurked there, to satisfy even the most meticulous of researchers, but Whitebrooke's hope that they would aid him in understanding his dream was fading. *No mention of the Blade burning Danielle, although it bathed her in fire,* he pondered. *I thought I recalled… but clearly not.*

Whitebrooke placed the letters back into their box, closed the lid and his eyes, but he could not rid himself of the images from his dream. Her hair shone golden like the sun, and her eyes blazed like coals. Fire clothed her in a vortex that licked greedily over Whitebrooke. His hair turned to ash and his robes became an inferno of roaring flames. *Who is she?*

He rose abruptly and replaced the box on its shelf. *There is no guidance here, and I do not need it. I know what must be done, and there is little time for useless meditation if I am to be ready when next I hear the King's voice.*

He locked the door to the scriptorium behind him and retraced his steps across the wide space of the reading room, but his long strides were interrupted by a small figure standing in his path.

"Good morning, your Reverence," Reverend Meara greeted him. She clutched a leather folio filled with parchment and stared determinedly at him with unblinking, brown eyes.

"Meara," Whitebrooke replied.

"I have finished documenting the fuil crunor ritual, your Reverence, as you requested." Meara shifted the folio in her arms but did not offer it to him. "May I show you what I have found?"

"More patterns?" Whitebrooke asked, holding out a hand for the folio.

Meara hesitated. "Yes, your Reverence, but I have documented another series of fuil crunor markings that fits, and I am sure that you will agree that it is very compelling." The young priestess unbuckled the folio and withdrew a sheaf of parchment tied between leather covers. "I have also written a precis that explains my findings, you will find that on the first sheet, and I have diagrammed—"

"Let your work speak for itself, Meara," Whitebrooke interrupted. He took the parchments and opened the bound stack.

The diagrams were beautifully precise, every detail of both the runes and the bodies that bore them captured in black ink. Whitebrooke noticed with a shock that Meara had correctly identified several of the most critical elements of the ritual, and her deductions as to their nature were growing eerily accurate. *Astounding. I would never have thought it possible, not without the Sanguinarium as a guide.*

A thin acolyte approached them and stood awkwardly close as Whitebrooke read, as if unaware that they conversed. Meara frowned and glanced quickly at the acolyte, but he only smiled in return.

"What?" Whitebrooke demanded, and the boy flinched.

"Begging your pardon, your Reverence, but Reverend Dougal has sent me to ask for Cian's letters to Lord Fergus."

"Again?" Whitebrooke fixed an irritated glare on the acolyte. "Does he not have them memorized?"

"No, your Reverence, it's just that he is certain he remembers a reference to—"

"I am sure he does." Whitebrooke pondered the request for a moment. "Tell him that I will bring them immediately."

"Thank you, your Reverence."

Whitebrooke watched the acolyte hurry away, then faced Meara again. "Do you know of the letters Dougal wants?"

"Yes," Meara replied.

"Go and fetch them. Bring the whole box."

Meara frowned, puzzled, then left for the stacks, returning a brief time later with a small, wooden box. "Why does Reverend Dougal want to see these useless letters?" she asked as she passed the box to him.

"Cian is Dougal's life's work," Whitebrooke replied. "It does little harm to humor him, Meara."

"I see," the young priestess replied, unconvinced. "May I return to my research?"

"Come with me." Whitebrooke tucked the box under his arm and strode from the archives, Meara trotting in his wake to keep pace. A quick walk brought him to the cluster of apartments reserved for the Council, their doors opening into a circular chamber dominated by a statue of Saint Taliesin in priestly garb. The same gangly acolyte opened the door in answer to Whitebrooke's heavy knock, and escorted the Archivist to Reverend Dougal's cluttered scriptorium.

"Here, Dougal," Whitebrooke rumbled. He set the box on Dougal's desk and turned it so the latch faced the aged priest.

"Ahhh, thank you Whitebrooke, thank you!" Dougal chuckled like a child given a sweet, and he began to paw through the ancient parchments nestled inside the box. "I was suddenly struck by a memory... perhaps in his letter regarding the Northwick temple..."

"If you would leave the letters in the archives for a few weeks, we could make you a copy."

"Of course, of course," Dougal muttered. He glanced sharply at the priest looming over his desk. "What? No, that won't do, Whitebrooke. A few weeks? My work cannot wait."

"Cian has been dead for hundreds of years," Whitebrooke pointed out. "A few weeks will make no difference, and might spare the letters for another generation, Dougal."

"Yes, of course you are right," Dougal sighed unhappily. "I imagine there is much demand for his wisdom."

"You would be surprised," Whitebrooke allowed. "The scribes tell me that you have asked them to start on a new draft of your work. Will this be the complete opus?"

"Tolerably complete, tolerably complete," Dougal replied evasively. "I am sure you will agree that an historian of Cian's stature can never be fully encompassed." Reverend Dougal paused in his shuffle and peered at the towering priest. "I trust your own research proceeds well?"

"It does, Dougal," Whitebrooke replied, his voice booming in the hushed room. "Our progress is steady, but it is slow."

"Shame," Dougal tutted. "Still no sign of this book that Reverend Turlough misplaced?"

"He did not misplace it," Meara corrected the High Priest. "Someone took it from its vault."

"Who is this?" Dougal squinted at Meara, his nose wrinkled as if he detected a foul stench.

"Reverend Meara," Whitebrooke informed him. "She is one of my archivists."

"Is that so?" Dougal sniffed and turned away from Meara to face Whitebrooke again. "In my day it was expected that junior priestesses were taught to address their superiors with more respect."

"Apologize to Reverend Dougal," Whitebrooke commanded. "You know better."

Meara's ears turned red with embarrassment. "I am very sorry, your Reverence," Meara said to Dougal.

"Hmmm," Dougal grunted, unwilling to be satisfied. "I should hope so. Do not let it happen again."

"No, your Reverence."

"What was I saying?" Dougal wondered. "Ah, yes, well, I am happy to hear you have had some success, even if it is not as much as we were hoping."

"We have learned enough to send Karsha Hali running," Whitebrooke reminded Dougal. "Enough to control the power that he released with his rituals."

"Control?" Dougal asked. "Destroy sounds more like what we need."

"Perhaps," Whitebrooke shrugged. "But perhaps there is more we can learn, more we can use, ourselves."

"Set fire to it all," Dougal sniffed. "Should have done it right away, then we wouldn't need to worry about it now."

"It may come to that," Whitebrooke granted, "and we are ignoring the best Weapon we have for that task. We should be examining the Martyr's Blade to determine how it can so easily destroy the Crunorix. Then we will know how to properly wield it, how to create more Weapons like it."

"I told Nesta that very thing, but she insisted on hiding the Blade away. She and Hayley." Dougal frowned thunderously at the remembered slight.

"Foolishness," Whitebrooke intoned gravely. "The Blade belongs in my hand. How else will we discover its secrets?"

"Reverend Whitebrooke," Meara ventured cautiously. Dougal squinted at her but did not instantly reprimand her for speaking, and Meara pressed on. "Is it true that the Blade is a Device? Not a mystical weapon as is told in the *Necronix*?"

"That is correct," Whitebrooke replied. "A Weapon of unrivaled intricacy, but it is a Device. Beledain was far too willing to believe the myths that surround the duel between the Martyr and the Nameless King."

"Yes, your Reverence," Meara continued hurriedly, "but if that is the case, it must have been crafted by the Guild. Can we not ask them? Perhaps they could make similar Devices."

"What a delightfully simple mind you have," Dougal laughed mockingly.

"Why is that so foolish an idea?" Meara asked, puzzled. "Your Reverence," she added, a heartbeat too late.

"On its surface, it is not." Whitebrooke's voice rolled over whatever Dougal had been about to say. "However, the Guild is notorious for keeping its secrets to itself, and, even if it were not, creating a Device is not as simple as forging a sword. There is no mold that could stamp out copies. Each is a work of art, a sculpture, wholly a product of the master's skill. Unless that master is alive, his work can only be imitated, never duplicated."

"I see," Meara replied vaguely, already lost in thought.

"We don't need the Guild," Dougal declared. "Arrogant, tight-lipped bastards, the lot of them. We have the Weapon we need, already."

"Do we?" Whitebrooke asked. "Not while it is hidden away. It is instructive that some of us would choose to hide, instead of defying our enemies. They have even abandoned our temples to the Queen without a whimper."

"I agree that something must be done," Dougal grumbled. "We cannot continue with such… impetuous… yes, impetuous, decisions ruling us. Not with the Convocation delayed indefinitely. We need proper leadership! Thank the Maker for Sir Maeglin. If not for him, they would have cowered before the Queen like a cur."

"Perhaps we should speak with Sir Maeglin about this, just you and I," Whitebrooke pondered. "Although our Knight Commander can be very obstinate. He fails to see his proper place. Still, a useful ally."

"He's not afraid to defend his Temple," Dougal said with relish.

"No, he is not," Whitebrooke agreed. "Perhaps the three of us can convince the others that hiding the Blade away is a mistake."

"I hope so, I hope so," Dougal sniffed. "But until we do, the Blade must remain hidden away, I'm afraid."

"And, is it hidden?" Whitebrooke had not moved, but he suddenly appeared taller, more massive, and far more threatening. "You are certain it is hidden properly?"

"Yes, of course," Dougal replied quickly, stumbling over his words. "I insisted on the place… very hidden… no one else knew of it, ha, ha! You would approve Whitebrooke, you would approve."

"Would I?" Whitebrooke challenged.

THE MARTYR'S TEARS

"Of course!" Dougal chuckled gleefully. "Of course, oh, and the irony... if only... well, you will appreciate it when I tell you that I must thank you for the histories you located for my research. The ones regarding the founding of Bandirma? So many interesting stories, all *hidden* away, if you see, in those books. Astounding."

"I am happy they were helpful," Whitebrooke replied. "I knew you would appreciate them."

"Absolutely, absolutely," Dougal assured him. "Well, as I said, it is a shame that Nesta and Hayley and the others are not more attentive to our concerns, but perhaps we can change that, hey?"

"I hope that we shall," Whitebrooke agreed.

Dougal grinned and returned to praising Cian, but Whitebrooke paid scant attention, and soon excused himself.

"Should we tell someone?" Meara asked as soon as the door had closed behind them, her voice indignant.

"Tell them what?" Whitebrooke asked brusquely.

"Reverend Dougal shouldn't be... he shouldn't be talking like that, should he?" Meara frowned. "Telling people."

"Telling people what?"

"Where the Blade is hidden," Meara continued doggedly.

"Is that what he was talking about?" Whitebrooke laughed. "You forget how dim-witted most of our colleagues are. Let Dougal ramble. No one will know what he is muttering about. I am more concerned with the protections that Reverend Ail has supposedly placed around the Blade. I would not trust him to ward a privy."

"But, if—"

"That is enough for now," Whitebrooke declared, suddenly irritated by the incessant questions. He stared at the young woman as he pondered the insights into fuil crunor she had already achieved. *She is on the trail, and commanding her to ignore it will not deter her, obviously. Perhaps... perhaps she should be encouraged. She would never accept proselytizing, but if she uncovers the truth of what we can accomplish for herself? Meara has always been dedicated to finding the truth, and not being swayed by rumor and fearmongering. It would take a little*

THE MARTYR'S TEARS

guidance, to make sure she understands the work correctly, but surely worth it. It is either that, or ensure her research is stopped, and it would be a shame to lose her. With the right instruction, Meara would make a fine priestess for my Temple.

Meara had stood silently while he mused, shifting uncomfortably under his gaze but refusing to look aside. "Continue your research," Whitebrooke instructed. "It shows great promise."

"Thank you, your Reverence," Meara nodded eagerly. "May I return to the ritual chamber? I could—"

"No, Meara," Whitebrooke cut her off. "You may not. It is far too dangerous. I fear the ritual is nearing some new stage." He nodded grimly to himself. "I am certain of it."

***

The stone chamber lay deep under Bandirma, far from the grand rooms of the main temple, beneath the labyrinth of tunnels and hidden rooms that made up the stacks of the Temple archive. A single staircase burrowed from the archives toward the chamber through endless rock. Each landing it passed as it descended had only one door, each door heavy with Veils to keep whatever lay beyond hidden from all knowledge. These chambers contained secrets that could never be known to exist, let alone that the Temple possessed them, and only the most trusted of the archivists knew the complex Words that would release the doors.

Two doors needed to be opened to enter the stone chamber, one after the other, with an empty antechamber between them. The doors were crafted of the same pale rock as the walls and floor, and they bore only the smallest of marks to distinguish them from the walls, a small circular hole in the center, no wider than the tine of a fork.

Whitebrooke turned the stone key in its lock and twisted his Word, and the final stone door was sealed behind him. He raised his lantern high and stood for a moment, relishing the absolute silence of the chamber.

Beyond the cold sphere of the lantern light, the stone chamber extended into dim shadows on all sides. The domed ceiling was high enough that only vague details were visible, and the curved walls passed from the color of ash to the somber hues of a winter cloud, heavy with snow.

There were nine bodies arranged in the center of the room, although there had been a tenth at one time. There was little remaining of this last corpse save for a wide splash of blood, long since dried to a crusty, brown stain, and a scattering of flesh that could no longer be identified as any particular body part.

The other nine were still intact, but no less corrupted. They were placed in a circle, their heads surrounding the remains of the tenth in the center, as if their bodies were the spokes of a giant wagon wheel. All were withered to dried husks, their skin pulled tight across rigid skeletons, their faces unrecognizable behind lipless mouths and gaping holes where once had been gleaming eyes or a pointed nose.

Each of the bodies was covered in the jagged markings of fuil crunor. The patterns were cut deep into the flesh, and more markings had been painted on the floor around the husks with the blood from those wounds so that it was difficult to tell where the desiccated skin stopped and the stone began. There were hundreds of the markings, spiraling inward in wide sweeps toward the center.

Whitebrooke breathed in the frigid air that filled the chamber and felt the sharp pain behind his eyes recede. He walked around the circle of bodies, ensuring that none had been disturbed, that the markings were still complete. It took some time for him to complete his circumnavigation, but he found it soothing to retrace the intricate ritual, and by the time he had finished he found that his thoughts were sharp and focused.

Whitebrooke released the Veil that concealed the far end of the chamber. As it withdrew the stone wall shimmered like heat over a forge, and through the wavering curtain a shape emerged. A tall pedestal made of black wood, its surface stained and warped as if it were an ancient ruin far older than its true age. On this surface a massive book crouched, bound in black iron and tarnished silver. The shadows of the darkened chamber seemed to cling to the book, as if drawn toward its surface.

Whitebrooke approached the pedestal slowly, absorbed in the touch of the chill shadows that curled around him, and the dull ache of the book's presence deep within his chest.

He whispered a twisted word as he passed his hand over the book's bindings and the great iron clasps which secured it released with a snap. The book's spine creaked as he opened it. Page after page slipped past his fingers as he reverently turned them, each one heavy with elegant script in black ink, drawn in harsh characters that twisted and squirmed on the thick vellum.

He soon found the page he sought, and he gently smoothed it as he silently absorbed the symbols one more time.

Then Whitebrooke spoke, his voice harsh as his throat filled with the sharp sounds of fuil crunor. The ritual on the floor of the chamber stirred. It had lain dormant, awaiting his command. Now his words drew thin shadows from the corpses. The frozen air of the chamber ripped open, and the fetid cold of the abyss filled the room.

With the cold came a presence, a hunger that consumed the shadows and then receded. The twisted gap in the air dissipated as if it were a ripple on the surface of still water, a betrayal of some lurking presence that disappears even as it is noticed.

But as it faded, Whitebrooke became aware of another presence in the chamber. Black eyes watched him from the shadows, and pale skin drifted at the edge of the lantern's light. The figure stirred, and Whitebrooke heard the scrape of claws against stone.

The priest closed the book, locking its bindings with an abrupt wave of his hand. He retrieved the lantern from the floor and approached the figure. The light touched white skin stretched over muscles as hard as steel, black talons as long as needles, and white fangs that filled a lipless mouth as black as coal. The figure rose from a crouch, stretching to its full height, higher even than the massive priest who stood before it. Skin as dry as parchment rasped as it stood, and a sigh of breath slid between the long fangs.

Whitebrooke nodded his head in approval. *It is magnificent.*

"Feed," he commanded, and the wight raised its head and opened its mouth wide. A shriek tore through its fangs and filled the chamber, growing louder with each echo, until it coursed through Whitebrooke's chest like the endless rending of metal.

As its cry faded, the bodies on the ground began to stir.

Whitebrooke unlocked the chamber's door and strode across the antechamber to the outer door leading to the stairwell. He threw the door open and passed through, calling out to the knight who led the small squad of soldiers guarding the entrance, "Young man, a moment."

The knight hurried to join Whitebrooke, a frown betraying his concern. "Yes, your Reverence?"

"I am disturbed by what I have found in the ritual chamber, today," Whitebrooke told the knight. "I believe it would be prudent to increase the size of the force guarding the entrance, and perhaps to alert the Knight Commander."

"Yes, your Reverence," the knight replied, "right away."

"Good," he said. "Now, tell me—"

Whitebrooke saw the young soldier's eyes widen with shock and fear as he stared past the priest's shoulder. The knight shoved Whitebrooke violently aside as he cried a warning, and Whitebrooke followed the knight's gaze to the open doorway.

The wight stood in the opening, a blade the color of ash now gripped in its hand. It paused at the edge of the yellow light from the stairwell and drew in a long, hissing breath, its black eyes gleaming as the wight's gaze swept the room. Figures moved behind it, twisted and grotesque, as the husks pressed close to the doorway.

The knight cursed as he tore his blade from its sheath with a ringing note of defiance. The sound broke the stunned paralysis of the other soldiers, and there was a rush of steel as weapons were drawn and shields raised.

The wight leapt at the knight, crossing the distance between them in an instant. The knight thrust desperately, his sword flashing outward to meet the pale figure. The wight's blade swept the knight's aside with such force that the steel shattered, flinging

THE MARTYR'S TEARS

splinters against Whitebrooke's hastily raised arms. The knight staggered back, raising his shield high, and the wight's second blow tore the shield apart. The knight fell to his knees, clutching at his shattered arm.

The wight did not hesitate. A third strike of its blade caught the knight across his breastplate. The shining steel was torn as if it were merely cloth, and the wight's blade bit deep into the knight's flesh, ripping through skin, muscle, and bone. The force of the blow lifted the knight into the air, limbs splayed uselessly like a rag doll, and hurled him against the wall of the chamber, leaving an arc of bright blood that rained onto the floor.

The wight stepped toward the shattered body, its fangs gaping open eagerly. The ferocious thrust of a soldier's spear drove the wight off its feet and into the wall. The spear's shaft bent with the force of the blow, but the steel tip of the spear left only the shallowest of wounds in its bloodless skin. The wight twisted away in an instant, splintering the wooden shaft with its fist. The soldier staggered forward, and the wight struck her between neck and shoulder with a blow from its sword that cleaved through her armor and lodged deep in her torso, splitting her heart.

The wight wrenched its sword free and lowered its fangs to the gaping wound, tearing into the ruined flesh.

Her comrades rushed toward the wight, but even as they did the husks poured into the room, leaping forward with a strange, lurching gait. The soldiers lashed out with sword and axe, and their steel blades ripped through withered flesh and rotted bone. But skeletal hands clutched at the soldiers as the husks fell, and more husks leapt onto the soldiers as they staggered back, wrenching desperately to free their weapons.

Screams of agony and terror filled the stairwell as the husks brought down the soldiers under the weight of the horde.

Whitebrooke watched the soldiers fall with interest. As fear overwhelmed their training and they turned to flee they were dragged down all the faster, until only three were left standing, maintaining the discipline of the shield line.

THE MARTYR'S TEARS

They backed toward the stairs, and Whitebrooke felt they were certain to escape. Then the wight was amongst them, so suddenly that Whitebrooke did not see its approach, did not know it had moved from its feast against the wall. The soldiers' blades rang against its skin without effect as it plunged into them, bearing the soldier in the center of their small line to the stones with its weight. The wight's blade sliced through another, and the last turned to flee.

The wight caught him in two strides, pinning him to the floor at the base of the stairs. Its black talons tore open his armor, and it buried its terrible fangs into the soldier's unprotected back. His screams cut off abruptly as the wight fed, and it raised its bloodstained maw to the ceiling and shrieked in triumph.

The husks surged toward the stairs, but Whitebrooke was not ready to let them loose in the Temple.

"Stop!" he commanded, and their rush was halted instantly. Without another word from the priest, the husks began to lope back to the ritual chamber, wordlessly obeying his will.

The wight approached Whitebrooke, blood staining its pale skin in a glistening sheen. The priest silently rehearsed his ritual, ensuring its convoluted phrases were certain in his mind. Then he spoke, the sound of the words harsh, tearing at his throat as he uttered them.

The wight stiffened, then staggered, as if it had been struck a blow. It fell to its knees and its mouth gaped wide, straining. Whitebrooke's chant grew stronger, and the wight convulsed. Shadows as thick as ink poured from its mouth. They slid across the stones toward Whitebrooke, spreading and becoming thinner until they drifted into the air, surrounding him.

Whitebrooke breathed in the shadow. Its frozen touch filled his lungs with fire, but more intense by far was the strength that suddenly rushed into him, quelling an empty hunger that he had not realized lurked within him until that moment. His chant trembled as the sensation swept over him, but he forced the words out, and the room echoed to his voice as he absorbed the lives the wight had consumed.

At last, no more shadow leaked from between the wight's fangs. Only then did Whitebrooke end his chant. "Return to the chamber," he croaked, his throat raw.

The wight rose obediently and Whitebrooke followed it through the antechamber to the inner chamber. "Guard this room," he told it. "Defend the *Sanguinarium*."

The wight hissed its understanding, and Whitebrooke closed the door on it. He gathered his Word with difficulty, fighting against the ache in his skull and the surge of shadow that he had taken in. He could hear the echo of approaching footsteps on the stairs, urging him on. The Word slipped between his lips and the Wards rippled through the stone. A twist of the stone key and the door was sealed.

Whitebrooke pocketed the key and hurried back to the stairwell. He had only a moment to look around the area, searching for any sign that would contradict the story he needed to tell, but found none. There was barely time to kneel on the floor, as if only now recovering from a great struggle, to face the squad of soldiers clattering down the stairs.

There were only four of them, those assigned to guard the top of the stairs, drawn by the sounds of battle from below. They halted at the bottom of the stairs, overwhelmed by the carnage confronting them.

Whitebrooke rose to his feet and the soldiers shrank from him as if he were a specter.

"Thank God." Whitebrooke strode to meet them.

"Your Reverence," one of the soldiers choked out.

"Hurry, bring help," Whitebrooke commanded. The soldier took one, last, stunned look at the scene and fled up the stairs.

"Your Reverence," another soldier called out to him urgently. "Sir Dylan... he's alive!"

Whitebrooke crossed to the knight's twisted body and joined the soldier in kneeling at his side. The great wound across the knight's torso glistened with torn flesh, and bright blood spewed around the shapes of ripped muscles and bone. But Whitebrooke could see the soldier was correct. The knight's chest still moved, although each breath was shallow and produced a thick, gurgling sound.

"There's another, over here! He's alive!"

Whitebrooke hurried to where a soldier lay against a pillar, a gaping wound laying open his leg.

"You two, do what you can for Sir Dylan," Whitebrooke commanded the soldiers. "You, try to stop this bleeding. I will examine the others."

Whitebrooke made a show of kneeling next to each of the remaining bodies, but, to his satisfaction, the wight had done its work well, and there was no sign of life in the mutilated flesh. *Still, I am fortunate I took the precaution of staging my role in this assault.* Whitebrooke returned to the bottom of the stairs, and watched as the soldier's wounded leg was wrapped in strips of cloth torn from his tunic. Blood soaked the fabric immediately. *If either of them survive, is there anything they could say that would reveal me? I doubt it. In fact, perhaps I can turn this further to my advantage. Perhaps it is an opportunity to show what the future should look like.*

Boots clattered on the stairs, announcing the hurried approach of another squad of soldiers. They filled the room at the bottom of the stairs with bright steel, but their steps faltered as they stared, aghast, at the slaughter.

Their leader was a powerful man with rugged cheekbones that appeared to be carved from stone, but even his face turned pale as he looked about the room helplessly.

"What has happened?" the soldier asked.

"The Crunorix," Whitebrooke snarled. "The ritual beyond the stone door summoned terrible creatures of shadow. A wight attacked Sir Dylan and his men before anything could be done."

"A wight?" the soldier repeated, stunned. He stared at the open door to the antechamber, his sword ready, as if to strike an unseen foe.

"I was able to drive the wight back to the inner chamber, and seal the door before it could recover," Whitebrooke assured the soldier. "The Wards will hold it prisoner, for now, but we need more guards against the chance the Crunorix summon something worse than a wight into that chamber."

THE MARTYR'S TEARS

The soldier eyed the stone door with trepidation, then nodded. "I will send for Sir Hollis, your Reverence, right away."

"Good," Whitebrooke nodded sternly.

More footsteps sounded on the stairs, and figures in brown or white robes appeared. At their head was Reverend Cliodhna, a healer renowned throughout the Temple for her skills as a surgeon. Whitebrooke nodded in satisfaction as he recognized her tall silhouette. *Cliodhna is perfect for this. Very well, I will take the risk.*

Cliodhna took in the scene in an instant, and hurried to the two soldiers desperately trying to staunch Sir Dylan's bleeding. She pointed to the soldier with the wounded leg as she crossed the room, issuing commands to her healers. "Beatha, examine his leg, I want to know if it can be saved."

She knelt at the side of the stricken knight and peeled back the sodden cloaks the soldiers had wadded against his wounds.

More blood poured onto the floor, shockingly red, but its flow was much weaker than before. Reverend Cliodhna probed the wound, exploring with her fingers amongst the ripped flesh.

"Pressure here," she instructed her healer, "and here… Martyr's tears, more light."

Whitebrooke watched her work, her long fingers unhesitating as they moved amongst the unrecognizable shapes.

"Thread, hurry," Cliodhna demanded.

"Your Reverence, there is blood in his breath," her healer announced, and Cliodhna nodded grimly without pausing her work.

"What does that mean?" Whitebrooke asked.

"His lungs have been torn, and so much blood fills his bowels there must be more severed vessels that I have not yet found." The healer pushed deeper into the wound, trying to follow the ebbing flow of blood, but when she met Whitebrooke's gaze, she shook her head. "I'm sorry, your Reverence. It is too much."

"You have done what you could," Whitebrooke said gravely. "Now, stand away from him." The healer gazed uncomprehendingly at him, but she did what he commanded.

THE MARTYR'S TEARS

Whitebrooke gathered himself. He began his chant, his voice a low rumble, softening the harsh sounds of fuil crunor as much as was possible as the healers and soldiers looked on. Shadow drifted into the air around him, drawn from the lives that still throbbed inside of him. The onlookers shivered and gasped as they drew back.

Whitebrooke changed his chant, and the shadow swirled around the body of Sir Dylan. Where it touched, flesh knitted, bone fused, until the lives of the other soldiers had all been consumed and the knight was whole. Dark scars ran jaggedly across his abdomen, and his skin was sallow, but his chest rose and fell with deep inhalations.

"Maker's breath," Reverend Cliodhna gasped. "How have you…?"

"Our enemy has brought death and pain to us," Whitebrooke spoke gruffly. "But they have revealed much more to me. Secrets that they would grieve to hear us speak of. Secrets of healing… and of life, itself." He paused for a moment, as if overwhelmed by the weight of his own words.

"I have exhausted my strength, for now, but perhaps, when I have recovered…" Whitebrooke met the healer's gaze. "Perhaps I could show you. This knowledge should be used where it is most needed." He turned and gestured to the corpses that littered the floor. "We have paid dearly for it."

"Yes," Reverend Cliodhna agreed. "Please do, your Reverence."

Whitebrooke nodded gravely, then strode up the stairs, his expression stern, assured that he left behind hope for a better future.

THE MARTYR'S TEARS

Karsha Hali

Wind swept across the steep hillside with an endless sigh of thrashing pine needles and scraping wood. Bran clutched the thin branch he had chosen as his perch and rode the swaying wave, his beak open to taste the fresh smells the south wind brought with it, rich earth stirred from its long sleep, and a hint of salt. The swirling air ruffled Bran's feathers, and he shook himself after every gust.

The tree bent before a fresh blast, sending Bran's perch bowing and lurching in unpredictable circles, but Bran welcomed it. The wind was interesting, and Bran was bored.

A sea of people stretched across the valley below Bran's hill, packing their tents and wagons and assembling on a snaking road, just as they had done every morning since Bran's arrival, and Bran knew what would happen next. The steel people would march steadily eastwards along the road for the remainder of the day, then rebuild their tent city in a slightly different valley. Even the plodding oxen dragging heavy wagons in the steel people's wake had no trouble keeping pace. Bran's Whisper was extremely interested in exactly where the steel lord's people were each day, but the long, snapping pennants and bright, sparkling steel had soon grown repetitive, and Bran quickly lost interest.

Bran spread his wings and swooped from his tree, cawing angrily at the steel people as he streaked over their heads. He turned east with powerful thrusts of his wings, slipping between the gusts of wind with practiced ease, until Bran could see in the misty distance the dark mass of a stone hill standing beside wide, grey water, surrounded by thin towers rising above the sea of roofs that clustered against them.

Bran's Whisper wanted to know where the stone hill's people were, wanted to know where the raven woman was, wanted to know where the shadow priest was, and most of all, wanted to know where the great blade was, so each day Bran searched.

The stone hill's people were easy to find. They huddled inside their tunnels and peered anxiously at the distant trees, or scurried through the forests until they could catch a peek of the steel people, then ran home.

The shadow priest had been harder to find, so Bran returned each morning to the stone hill to search for him. He soared over the walls and landed amidst the rocky crags of the hill itself, where he found a perch that gave him a clear view of the wide courtyard in front of the hill's massive doors.

Bran preened his feathers into place and settled in to watch the life of the stone hill's people. The kennels filled with a chorus of joy as the pack spotted a brown-robed person approaching with their morning food. Proud horses snorted and stamped as their people adorned them with their polished leather and steel. Red-faced people shouted at each other as they unloaded their wagons into stone buildings. The stories were the same every morning, and Bran enjoyed watching them, but there had been no sign of the shadow priest.

Today was different. The dogs were still barking with excitement when he spotted the shadow priest striding across the bailey to the tallest, thinnest tower. Bran swooped from his perch and circled the top of the tower, searching for a way in. The highest windows were all shuttered that morning, but Bran soon found a gap in the weathered stone roof of the tower where an ancient wooden beam poked through, and the raven landed and followed the beam inside. The gap had been filled with a wad of cloth, but Bran tore it free with his sharp beak in an instant and soon found himself perched in the shadows above a cramped room.

The chamber was filled with the senseless mutterings of the pigeons that perched on the rafters, shelves, desks, and chairs of the room. Dozens of bright eyes blinked at Bran as the raven settled on his beam to watch. There were two people in the room, as well, a bird priest with wrinkled skin and white hair, and a young priest carefully balancing a tray of cups and a steaming pot in her hands.

The door to the room suddenly burst open as the shadow priest entered, causing the young priest to drop her tray with a clatter. The room filled with the awkward flutter of wings as a score of pigeons suddenly took flight and desperately sought safety in the rafters with Bran.

"Reverend Whitebrooke," the bird priest peered at the shadow priest with a sour look on his face. "You must be more careful, you will terrify the birds."

The shadow priest glared at the bird priest. "Perhaps you should find yourself an acolyte who can carry a teapot. Regardless, why are the birds loose in here, shitting on everything, instead of in their cages?"

"They enjoy it," the bird priest said archly. "We did not expect so much commotion. Dear, will you clean up and see if there is any more tea?"

The young priest nodded quickly and busied herself with the puddle on the floor, never raising her eyes.

"Just get out," the shadow priest said impatiently, and the young priest fled. "I have messages that must be sent immediately."

"Well, I shall do my best," the bird priest waved a hand vaguely across his desk, which was covered in small slips of parchment and their waiting containers. "I have so many important messages, each to be sent 'immediately'. More notes regarding the Convocation and the funeral, and who knows when the clergy will be allowed to travel again. And of course, there is all the normal Temple business. That cannot wait, oh no."

"Stop playing with your birds and you might find the time to send your messages." The shadow priest stepped to the desk and placed his secrets on top of the bird priest's work. "Immediately."

The secrets were small pieces of parchment, covered in cramped scratchings of black ink, and Bran cocked his head to the side so that he could see them more clearly.

The bird priest leaned back in his chair and met the shadow priest's gaze for a moment. Then he carefully gathered up the shadow priest's secrets and examined them, his boney fingers delicate as they sorted the pages.

"A request for a check on the supply of coal in Newbridge," the bird priest read, "and a query on the price of coal in Greymouth. And so on…" The bird priest continued reading in silence, sorting each parchment with a precise, dry flip of his fingers. When he reached the end, he shuffled the secrets into a tidy stack and placed them on the center of his desk.

"Yes," the bird priest pondered, tapping his lip. "I can see now why there is such a rush."

"Immediately," the shadow priest repeated. "All the rest can wait if needs be."

"Hmmm, very well," the bird priest tutted.

The shadow priest turned to leave, but the bird priest's croak called him back as his hand grabbed the door latch.

"I had heard you were ill." The bird priest rose from his desk and pottered to the mantle, now covered with cooing pigeons. "There is no need for you to deliver your messages in person, not in your condition. Send an acolyte, for your own sake."

"I am fine," the shadow priest replied sharply. "My wounds were not serious."

"Ahhh, wounded, of course. That is what I heard." The bird priest selected one of the birds, carefully scooped it up, and carried it to his desk. The pigeon blinked happily at the bird priest as he set it down and rolled the top secret in the stack into a small, wooden container. "Leave the fighting to the Templars next time, that's my advice."

"There were no Templars here, Sebastian," the shadow priest growled. "Which is why I was called."

"Of course." The bird priest tied the leather straps of the container securely around the pigeon's leg and carried the bird to the window. The bird priest opened the shutter and the bird instantly flew off in a frantic beating of wings. Bran watched it go with open beak, his wings aching to give chase. He slowly sidled along his beam until he reached the gap and crouched there, his gaze fixed on the next secret in the pile on the bird priest's desk.

"Spit it out, Sebastian," the shadow priest growled. "Whatever it is you want to tell me. I have work to do."

The bird priest returned to his desk and busied himself reading the next of the secrets, then hobbled to the mantle again to peer at the birds.

"I thought you would be relieved."

"How so?" the shadow priest ground the words between clenched teeth.

"No one from Newbridge here, that's a pity," the bird priest muttered to himself, and he shuffled to the door that led higher into the tower. "Back to your books, back to your research. No more interruptions."

"Maker's breath, Sebastian, what of it?"

The bird priest opened the door a crack and peered into the chamber beyond. "Newbridge, dear, as quick as you can. Leave the tea, I shall survive." The bird priest closed the door firmly and faced the shadow priest again. "It seems to me that you have had great difficulty making progress. The interruptions, I am sure, and your wounds, of course."

"My research is proceeding very well," the shadow priest insisted. "There is much more to fuil crunor than we have been told. With God no longer here to guide us, there may be ways to learn from fuil crunor, to—"

"I am sure it is fascinating," the bird priest interrupted with a dry cough. Bran watched the shadow priest's face darken, but before the priest could move, the door opened and the young priest entered with a pigeon cradled in her hands, and the shadow priest stormed from the room without another word.

THE MARTYR'S TEARS

Bran watched the bird priest attach a secret to the pigeon and carry it to the window. The raven scurried through the gap and followed the eager pigeon when the bird fluttered from the tower. Bran took the secret from the pigeon as soon as the stone hill was out of sight, and hid it in his treasure place before launching into the freshening breeze.

Bran turned into the wind with a cry of defiance and fought his way south over gentle, rolling hills, always keeping the stone hill in sight, until he reached a frothing river, and he followed its twisting path.

A wagon was stuck in the churned mud of a small road that followed the river bank. Two mules had already given up on hauling the wagon and its teetering mountain of hay out of the deep rut its wheels had sunk into, but the people driving the wagon had not. They yelled and cursed and plunged into the mud to shove on the wagon's wheels, and Bran cackled in delight at their struggles, but the raven had seen mules trick people into doing their work for them many times, and he did not linger. A herd of sheep was trapped on the road behind the wagon, and their nervous bleats filled the air as Bran flew over their wooly heads.

The raven passed another wagon on the road, and another, and then a herd of cows, all heading slowly northward, blissfully unaware of the obstacle they would soon face. None were interesting.

At last, the pastures and fields gave way to more forest, dancing in the swirling wind. Bran swept over the thick trees, his eyes darting into every shadow, every twitch of movement. Rabbits and squirrels fled from his dark shadow, and a family of boars raised their bristling snouts to snuff at him. But pigs were only interesting when they were seeking treasure in the mud, and so Bran pressed on.

As the day passed and the shadows shortened, a gleam of metal catching the sun's light flashed from the top of a steep ridge overlooking the river. Bran circled eagerly, peering through the thick tree canopy as it blurred beneath him.

Four riders stood on the edge of the ridge at the end of an overgrown track. One of the riders held on to their horses while the other three approached the lip of a long plunge down a rocky escarpment, and Bran swooped low and perched on the gnarled limb of a twisted oak to watch.

All four riders belonged to the steel lord, which was a little bit interesting, as Bran had never seen steel people as far south as these four were. The leader of the riders began to point into the river valley and at the gentle curve of the far shore, but Bran paid him little attention. More interesting than the four riders was the person watching them, hidden even deeper in the trees. This new person did not belong to the steel lord. He was dressed in dull greens and browns and appeared more like mud and bushes than a person. The mud person crept slowly through the forest, and never revealed himself to the steel people.

The raven's black eyes gleamed as he cocked his head to one side, scuttling back and forth on his branch to get the best view, but the mud person did nothing except watch, and the steel people did nothing except point and talk, and Bran croaked in disgust.

A slight swirl in the wind brought Bran a new smell and he twisted on his branch to find its source. A presence lurked in the forest behind the mud person, and Bran swooped through the branches, searching for it. The ancient trunk of a fallen tree, moss-covered and decayed, formed an archway dark with shadow, and Bran landed on its top, his talons sinking into the soft wood of the tree stump.

A moment passed, and the forest waited alongside Bran as he peered at the opening beneath the fallen tree. Then a shape slipped from the shadows and padded across the needle-covered dirt. The wolf was large and moved with an easy stride. Thick, black fur rendered the wolf practically invisible amongst the shadows on the forest floor, save for a streak of grey around the wolf's muzzle.

The wolf glided to the base of a tall pine and settled on its haunches amongst the tree's roots. The wolf scented the air carefully, slowly raising its long snout first one direction then the next, and its ears swiveled to follow each creak of a branch or hiss of wind across leaves.

The mud person had not noticed the wolf's arrival, and for a time Bran watched the wolf watch the mud person watch the steel people, and bobbed his head in silent laughter. Then he swooped to a low branch in the tree above the wolf, sending a small shower of needles fluttering about the wolf's head. The wolf craned its neck upwards and fixed Bran with its grey eyes.

Bran stayed on his branch, above the reach of the wolf's jaws, and soon the wolf turned his attention to the people.

The steel people took their time pointing at everything they could see, and midday had passed when they finally mounted their horses and rode off. The mud person waited until the sound of the hoofbeats had dwindled to nothing before he, too, moved away, a silent sigh of air through the trees.

Then, at last, the wolf departed. It did not follow the steel people or the mud person. Instead, the wolf descended the slope to the riverbank and began to lope through the woods next to the water, pausing frequently to dash to the shore and scent the ground. Bran watched it go. The raven did not understand why the wolf was searching, for it must have known its quarry was long gone, and its search hopeless. But the wolf's detours to the river grew more frantic, until the wolf raised its muzzle to the dark sky and howled mournfully, and Bran understood.

Bran spread his wings and let the south wind loft him into the air. He circled slowly, climbing ever higher, until the river was a silver snake and the hills no more than a wrinkled blanket, and then he let the wind carry him north, back to the steel people, happy that he had a new story to tell. He could feel his Whisper growing closer, quickly now, and the raven wanted to reach his treasure place before his Whisper arrived so that he could boast about his finds.

***

THE MARTYR'S TEARS

Karsha Hali blinked as the forest slowly swam into focus around him, the heavy swaying of the trees and the rush of wind in their branches shockingly wrong as they replaced the thick warmth and narrow confines of his small study. Karsha sank onto the soft bed of pine needles that covered the forest floor, and his fingers curled instinctively around the smooth roots that spread underneath him, clinging to the rigid wood as the forest teetered.

Why am I here? Karsha wondered. He pressed his boney fingers into his scalp and tried to rub a coherent thought into his head, but before he could do more than take a single, steadying breath, Bran landed on the ground in front of Karsha with a rush of wind and swirling leaves. The raven peered at Karsha as he folded his great wings neatly against his body, his eyes gleaming brightly.

Karsha sighed and leaned against the tree at his back. *I made it,* he realized. *I am with Bran. The journey is over.*

Bran croaked softly as he watched Karsha slowly gather himself. Karsha wished desperately to close his eyes and sleep away the heavy ache of weariness that covered him, but he forced his eyes open and rose unsteadily to his feet.

"What have you found?" Karsha asked the raven. Bran presented him with a small wooden tube clutched in the raven's talons, and dropped it into Karsha's outstretched hand with a satisfied croak.

Karsha broke the seal and deftly pulled the parchment free from the tube. He studied the message carefully for a time, watching patterns of words and letters flow backward and forward through the message, forming new meanings, until, with a sniff of disgust, he carefully replaced the parchment in the tube and tucked the container deep in his robes.

"I truly despise that man," Karsha told Bran, and the raven spread his wings and cawed his agreement. "Now, which way is Duke Campbell's camp? I must speak with him, and I would like you to watch. If I end up swinging from a gibbet by the end of today, I would ask you, as a last favor to me, to tell the Queen everything you have found. And tell her I died content that I did so in her service."

THE MARTYR'S TEARS

Bran chuckled and croaked, but Karsha shrugged away the raven's objections. "It is true," he insisted, "even if I scream and shame myself. Do not tell her that part, though."

Karsha followed the raven through the forest, his boney feet enjoying the soft prickle of the needles and the thick squish of the damp earth. Late afternoon had arrived by the time they reached the edge of the forest and saw the duke's pavilion sitting atop a gentle hill, surrounded by the tents of his nobles and their soldiers.

Karsha gathered his robes around him, checked the charms dangling from his chains, and meandered toward the encampment through a field of tall grass whose delightful soft tufts brushed against his hands as he strolled.

His walk was abruptly ruined by one of the sentries posted around the camp, and he was ushered quickly to Duke Campbell's pavilion through a cacophony of pounding hammers and shouted orders.

Karsha entered the pavilion and found the duke was not alone. Campbell sat at a polished table with a lord dressed in a long riding-coat and steel breastplate. His coat was pinned at his throat by a silver amulet shaped into a leaping dog. Silver goblets filled with dark red wine sat at hand, and there was the echo of earnest words in the studied quiet that lingered around the table.

"Karsha." The duke welcomed the southerner with a shake of his head. "I was astonished to hear your name announced, yet, here you are. I did not expect to see you here."

"It is good to be mistaken in such things," Karsha replied.

"Do you know Lord Arledge?" the duke waved Karsha towards the lord with an idle twist of his hand.

"I remember that Lord Arledge had a spotted hound who loved to have his chest scratched," Karsha said thoughtfully as he shuffled to the table.

"I do indeed," Lord Arledge agreed with a smile. "I have brought him with me, in fact. Doesn't do much more than lay about and eat, anymore, but I couldn't bear to leave him behind."

Karsha levered himself into one of the remaining seats and gazed wistfully at the bottle of wine, but the duke appeared unaware of the southerner's interest.

"Why have you come to southern Albyn?" the duke asked.

"The Queen wished to know how you progressed with her orders."

"You have wasted your journey, in that case," the duke replied. "I have sent her detailed accounts. I am surprised you have not seen them, but perhaps they arrived after you were sent."

"Yes, that is likely true," Karsha agreed easily. "Even so, I am anxious to hear for myself."

"I do not have time to satisfy your curiosity," the duke said shortly. "You may travel with us if you must, but unless you have something useful to offer…" The duke rose from his seat and indicated the entrance to the pavilion with a curt gesture.

"Oh, I do," Karsha assured the duke. He burrowed in his robes for a moment, careful to find the correct message, and placed a silver scroll case on the table.

The duke frowned as he retrieved the parchment from the case and read it.

"The Queen says to please satisfy my curiosity," Karsha said helpfully. "She feels this will be useful to her."

The duke scowled and dropped the scroll on the table. Arledge took his turn reading it and nodded his agreement.

"Very well," the duke said magnanimously. "What would you like to know?"

"Why are you marching so many soldiers east?"

"Bandirma is to the east."

"This is true," Karsha agreed. "But why do you march to Bandirma?"

"Do you not recall the Queen's order to seize the temples?"

"Of course, I remember it well. It did not say to march an army to Bandirma. Unless you are thinking to seize that temple as well? I am no general, or duke, but I do not think you have enough soldiers for that."

"It did not," the duke agreed, his voice cold. "But when the Temple decides to re-take their temples, their army will come from Bandirma. Most of my soldiers are spread across all of Albyn, holding the temples, but what few we could gather here will block the Temple army when it emerges. It is the only way to defend ourselves from their response."

"Ah, so you are preparing for the best place to war?"

"Yes. With proper fortifications, we may be able to hold against the Temple here."

"I see," Karsha frowned. "The Queen does not want a war. Send your soldiers back before one begins."

"What?" the duke asked sharply, and he leaned on the table with closed fists. "When the Temple army comes, do you think they will shrink from battle?"

"No," Karsha agreed. "So, move your soldiers far enough away so that they cannot be attacked. Then there will be no battle."

"This is not a game!" The duke slapped the table with an open palm, and the goblets jumped. "You play with lives."

"No, we play with words."

"Is this how you give counsel to the Queen?"

"We hear the story we wish to hear, no matter the words of the bard. The Queen is wise to know that seeking the truth will provide many stories for listening."

"I am not the Queen, nor am I a squire in need of tutoring."

"Not even the gods think they have no more to learn."

"The Temple is in no mood to negotiate with us," the duke pointed out. "If the Queen wishes to hold their temples, it will come to steel."

"Ah, yes, this is an excellent point." Karsha bobbed his head in agreement. "It is my next question! The Queen is most upset that priests and soldiers were murdered in her name in Littleford. She wonders how you allowed it to happen."

The pavilion grew quiet, the thick flap of its heavy canvas in the wind the only sound as the duke glared at Karsha, his eyes dark slits. Karsha busied himself with his charms, carefully selecting a silver spiral that fed endlessly into itself to polish with his thumb as he waited.

"I did not 'allow' it to happen," the duke said stiffly. "Sir Cathan overstepped his orders."

"You have told the Queen about your great family and your prestige with the nobles of Albyn. If your command is not as you claimed…"

"It was a tragedy, but I have punished Cathan for it, and it will not happen again," the duke bristled.

"How have you ensured this?"

"I have sent more soldiers, my soldiers, to every temple to make sure there are no more incidents."

"You do not trust the knights who hold the temples?"

"I trust my soldiers more."

"And this has worked?"

"There have been no more attacks like Cathan's."

"Ahhh… but that is not all. I have read a message from Newbridge."

"Yes," the duke agreed impatiently. "There have been attacks on our soldiers holding the temples by Temple soldiers hiding in the forests around Newbridge."

"And your soldiers have stopped these attacks?"

"No, not yet. But they will."

"Hmmm," Karsha grumbled to himself, and he selected another scroll from his robes and set it on the table. "More fighting in the Queen's name, and an army readying for a war she does not want. I think she will not be happy."

"Did she think there would be no strife as we seized the temples?"

"No, she knew there would be. But it continues to grow, and is far worse than it should have been." Karsha pushed the scroll onto the table and sat back, watching the duke and the baron carefully. His hand closed around the spiral charm as he waited.

"What is this?" the duke asked.

"The Queen commands that you return to Kuray to explain yourself. Immediately."

"You dare to mock me?" the duke asked through clenched teeth. "You have played your game, all the while with that in your pocket." The duke ignored the scroll, but Baron Arledge leaned across the table and retrieved it, and quietly unrolled the parchment to read.

THE MARTYR'S TEARS

"I hoped I would not have to show you it," Karsha said consolingly. "It would go into the fire tonight, never to be mentioned. Alas, that story was not to be."

"You will regret that choice." The duke rose from the table and strode to the pavilion's entrance. He pulled the flap open and gazed across the encampment, his hands clasped behind his back. "Whose orders do you think are followed in this army?" the duke asked. He faced Karsha and shook his head. "Not yours."

Karsha's thumb found the small catch on the silver charm that would break the endless spiral. But before he could draw breath to respond to the duke, Baron Arledge interrupted with a discrete cough.

"I am sorry, your Grace, but it is not his order. It is the Queen's," he said, offering the scroll for examination. "It is quite clear, and her seal was unbroken."

Campbell snatched the scroll from Arledge and read it quickly, his eyes darting from line to line. "You cannot think this gives him the right to issue commands to me?" he demanded of Arledge.

"Her Majesty's seal is on it. It is treason to deny her commands," the baron pointed out, his words precise and clear.

"They are not her commands," the duke snarled. "She mouths whatever thought this charlatan puts into her mind."

"I believe Her Majesty may take counsel as she pleases, your Grace, and it is her command—"

"Don't be absurd, Arledge," Campbell cut the baron off. "Our families are the true rulers of Albyn. For millennia, we have guarded the realm. A piece of parchment signed by some bitch Arian bedded while he was in Venaissin doesn't change that.

"Since His Majesty married Lady Gabrielle, I believe it does," the baron said sternly. "I feel sure the other lords and ladies would agree, if I were to ask them. Shall I summon them, and read them Her Majesty's command? I should caution you to choose your words more carefully when you refer to Her Majesty in their presence. We in the south do not tolerate such disrespect."

The duke regarded the baron silently. Karsha perched on the edge of his seat, wondering what story would play out before him.

"You are a disgrace to Albyn," the duke said slowly. "How dare you side with these two foreigners over your own people?"

"I serve the Silver Queen," Arledge said simply, "as I have always served the rightful monarchs of the realm. I urge you to do the same, for the sake of your family name. You knelt and offered her your sword as I did." The baron's face softened and his voice was gentle as he continued. "Your Grace, I know it leaves a bitter taste to depart the army, but no one can question your loyalty and the strength of your leadership. Explain yourself to the Queen and be done with it, and you will be welcomed back upon your return."

The duke glared at Karsha and the baron for a moment longer, then strode from the pavilion. Karsha hopped down from his chair and stood in the entrance to watch the duke call for his horse.

"Perhaps an escort for his Grace?" Karsha mused. "A shame if he were diverted from his journey to Kuray."

Baron Arledge called to a knight wearing the baron's sigil. "Ten soldiers to escort Duke Campbell to Kuray," the baron instructed. "And, Sir Connor, make sure he gets there."

The knight nodded and raced to join the duke with his men as they thundered through the camp to the road. They disappeared westward, and Karsha finally allowed himself a sigh of relief.

He helped himself to a silver goblet from the sideboard and returned to the table to join Baron Arledge. Wine sloshed onto the tabletop as he poured, and he popped his fingers into his mouth to rescue the drops clinging to them. He left the small puddle gleaming in a shaft of low evening sun, and he watched it slowly creep along the table's grain toward the edge.

"I feared a sad ending," Karsha told the baron. "Thank you for your loyalty to the Queen."

"It might have been very sad indeed, if he had his soldiers in camp instead of scattered to all the temples," the baron tapped the scroll on the table. "This parchment would not have saved you, I fear."

"No, not the parchment," Karsha agreed.

THE MARTYR'S TEARS

"What now, my lord counsellor? Do you have a scroll in your pocket for me, as well?"

Karsha grinned at the baron. "Perhaps we have had enough scrolls for today? Tell me, my lord… when two of your dogs, that you love and cherish, when they snarl and fight with one another, what would you do?"

"Perhaps they quarrel over a choice piece of meat?"

"No," Karsha said sadly. "It is more serious than that. They have bitten at each other, and drawn blood."

"I see." The baron sipped from his goblet as he considered. "That is very bad. They must be separated, before more harm can be done."

"Would you strike at them, and curse them, to drive them apart?"

"Not at all," the baron replied with a frown. "You would ruin the dogs that way. They would fear you, and cower, and perhaps bite out of terror. No, they need a voice they can trust, and firm guidance from a master they love. That will bring them together into a pack, again."

"A familiar, caring voice." Karsha bobbed his head happily. He slurped noisily from his mug, enjoying the rich taste of the wine as he gazed through the pavilion's entrance at the bustling camp. "If only we might spend our day with your noble hounds. But we must consider the problems that have so displeased the Queen, instead."

The baron chuckled softly. "I thought we were."

"I was speaking of dogs," Karsha disagreed. "Why, have you found a course of action in our musings?"

"Yes, my lord counsellor," the baron smiled. "First, I would suggest separating the dogs, so that they must stop fighting. As you mentioned to his Grace, we could return the army to Littleford, or further."

"It seems a fine suggestion, to me." Karsha took another deep gulp of his wine.

"Where we cannot separate the dogs, we must use a familiar voice. Replace Duke Campbell's men in the temples with soldiers who were raised in those towns and villages, soldiers who know the people, who know the priests, and who are known by them. Nothing breeds contempt faster than a stranger with a sword."

"Will that stop all the quarreling?"

"Perhaps not, but it will restrain it where it has already begun, and delay it where it has not. Friendship will do that."

"But, Sir Cathan was from Littleford, was he not?"

"There are ruined dogs, that is certain. They must be put down when they are found. But what happened in Littleford is the exception, thank the Maker."

"Ah, Littleford," Karsha sighed. He shook his head sadly. "And what do you suggest for a dog that has been badly wounded. Surely it will not forgive so easily."

"A gentle hand that treats its wounds is soon trusted again," the baron pointed out. "In all the temples, the soldiers should work to help the people. Building, repairing, plowing… anything but guarding. Especially in Littleford."

Karsha finished his wine and smacked his lips noisily. He rummaged in his robes until he found another scroll, and placed it on the table. "You show great wisdom in your suggestions, my lord, but it is not for me to decide." Karsha pointed at the scroll on the table. "It is for you. The Queen asks you to take command, and wishes you good fortune."

Baron Arledge took the scroll but did not open it. "I shall do as the Queen wishes, of course, but Duke Campbell was right. If the Temple army comes forth to retake their temples, there is little I can do to stop them."

"Then, do not stop them," Karsha shrugged. "The Queen does not want a war. Now, before it comes to that, we must try to convince the Temple to give us what we want, but the gods only know if we have enough time."

"I understand," Baron Arledge replied.

"I have only one suggestion for you, my lord, and then I must go," Karsha said. "In each temple, choose at least one of our soldiers to discipline for acting against the Queen's commands. Whomever has gone beyond their orders."

"What will their punishment be?"

"Whatever is appropriate. Do not be harsh where it is not warranted. Perhaps they can serve the people of the area in some way. But it should be public, as should the reason," Karsha grinned. "Even the gods like to watch someone humbled."

"Yes, my lord counsellor." The baron rose and walked with Karsha to the pavilion's entrance. "Where will you journey, now?"

"I must visit the other dogs," Karsha said with a sigh, "and find some way to help them, as well."

"I hope you have some scrolls in your pocket for them."

"I might," Karsha laughed.

Wyn

"Well, it *feels* like a storm," Danielle insisted. Icy spray tore from the tops of the wind-whipped waves and sliced across the boat, stinging Wyn's cheeks. The boat lurched heavily as the wind caught her sails, and Wyn whooped in glee as water foamed over the bow and swirled across the deck.

"It does, a bit," Wyn conceded as she clung to her hood and the rail of the boat with equal strength, "but there's worse to come. There's a proper blizzard in those clouds, I'd say."

"If the wind grows stronger, we will need to find shelter or turn south to sail with the wind." Danielle was barely visible within her deep hood, with a thick scarf wound around her mouth and nose. "We could find ourselves back in Greymouth if the gale lasts more than a few days."

The boat staggered again as a fierce squall drove her far over on her side. Wyn rode the surge with legs braced wide, delight and terror twisting through her like the whirlpool she felt certain was about to open directly under them.

"How much time do we have before the blizzard arrives?" Danielle gazed worriedly upriver, into the wind. Wyn scrambled to the windward rail and peered ahead. The surface of the wide Abhainn Albyn was grey and white as the wind drove spray across it, and the distant embankments faded quickly into a murky haze as mist and rain swept across them. But Wyn could clearly see the dark mass of powerful clouds looming to the north, as if evening descended without regard for compass or time.

She watched, fascinated, as a frenzied whorl of spray flew across the river surface toward the boat. It hit with a shriek of wind through the lines, a sharp crack as the sail snapped at its tethers, and an enormous crash from somewhere inside the small cabin. The boat foundered for a moment, its bow once again plunging into the waves, before it heeled far onto its side, so far that Wyn grabbed the rail without thinking and clung to it despite the twist of pain that snaked through her left hand.

The boat did not tip, although Wyn was not sure how, and Danielle held the boat steady until the sails could capture the wind and send it knifing across the choppy water.

"Could you pull in those lines, there." Danielle's voice was calm even as she shouted above the wind. "That one, and that one there, to shorten the sail before we go over?"

Wyn scrambled to obey, and she scowled as the pain sharpened and stabbed up her arm as she gripped the line. *Too bad, you stupid arm. Get better and then it won't hurt.* Wyn squeezed out the pain and cursed bitterly as she fought to pull in the rigid line.

"Good, that should do for a while," Danielle appeared satisfied with the reef, "but we should find shelter while we have the time. Search for any inlet, or cove. Any place we can dock with any shelter from the wind."

"Oh, and look." Wyn held out her hand to catch a whirling flake. "Here's the snow. Lovely."

A freezing mixture of snow and rain hissed across the surface of the river and lashed at the two companions. The grey banks drifted in and out of visibility through the downpour, and the wind whipped the stinging ice nearly horizontal as it screamed through the boat's lines.

THE MARTYR'S TEARS

Wyn began to laugh uncontrollably as shivers wracked her body. "It really does feel a bit like a storm!" she shouted between chattering teeth.

"There!" Danielle cried out, and she pointed into the swirling snow to the west. "An inlet, I swear!"

"Wishful thinking," Wyn predicted, but as the bank became clear, Wyn had to admit to herself that it did indeed appear as if there was a small fold in the hills along the shore, where an inlet could certainly hide.

"I think there is a dock," Danielle squinted against the snow pelting her face, "at least, there is some kind of structure, there along the shoreline."

"We don't want a dock, do we?" Wyn glanced at Danielle. "Aren't we hiding?"

"I do not care," Danielle shook her head miserably. The noblewoman's hand was shaking on the tiller, and she had curled into as tight of a ball as she could on the wooden seat at the rear of the cockpit.

"Come on then, let's get off the river and find a nice fire and get you warm," Wyn said sympathetically. She ooched across the cockpit and settled onto the seat next to Danielle and they huddled together for warmth. "You're shivering as much as I am!"

"Well, I am cold," complained Danielle from within her hood.

"Me too," Wyn agreed, shivering as the wind knifed across her ears.

As they neared the shoreline the structure Danielle had spied became clear. The remains of a jetty jutted into the river where a wrinkle in the hills created a natural breakwater. Crumbling stone pillars poked above the water along the quay, showing where a dock once extended, but there was no sign of any wood left attached to the stone. A tall arch rose amongst the trees on the embankment behind the jetty, straddling a few moss-covered steps of fitted stone that climbed the hillside.

Wyn traced the path of the steps through the swaying trees until it disappeared entirely, no more than a dozen steps into the forest. After that, the trees had grown over it so completely that there was no sign a path had ever existed.

"I don't think we need to worry about hiding—" Wyn began, but as she spoke, a ferocious blast of wind tore a hole in the thick curtains of rain and snow over the hill, and a dark shape was briefly revealed. A tall tower, jagged in silhouette against the cold clouds, loomed over the hilltop, no more than a long bowshot from the ruined pier.

"Maker's breath, did you see that?" Wyn scowled. "Another bloody black tower. Bandits and trolls, and probably a bunch of horrible wights and magi. Martyr's tears, I've had enough of that lot. Can we go someplace else?"

"I believe we are stopping here, no matter what we should like," Danielle answered as she swung the boat behind the breakwater. "Our poor boat is starting to list. I fear that crash may have hurt her."

Danielle avoided the jagged piles of submerged stone around the ruined pier and guided the boat toward a muddy embankment a stone's-throw away. Wyn hauled on the lines to drop the sails and scurried to the bow with a coil of rope. The shore crept closer as the wind shrieked and snapped Wyn's cloak, and to her disgust she hesitated, staring anxiously at the gap of water and the muddy slope beyond. *Martyr's tears, it's no more than a tiny hop. Useless girl.* But although her legs felt stronger, a nagging doubt lurked uncomfortably in the bottom of her stomach.

Wyn leapt before she could think about it again, furious with herself. She flew across the gap and landed far up the embankment, but stumbled and fell to her knees as tangled roots caught her boots. Wyn felt her left arm give way as she tried to catch herself, and she ended up face-down in the wet leaves and slick mud. Wyn spat mud and curses as she sprang to her feet, angrily whipped the rope around a thick tree truck, and knotted it tightly.

She returned to the boat with even more determination, and scrambled her way into the cockpit, hoping against hope that Danielle had not seen her fall. But Danielle was not able to conceal the concern in her eyes.

THE MARTYR'S TEARS

"Have you not seen someone fall before?" Wyn glared at Danielle with fists on her hips. "I'm fine, by the way, so you can stop staring at me as if I were a Korrigan popped fresh from its hole. What is so funny?" Wyn stamped her foot as a smile began to spread across Danielle's lips.

"It is just, you have a few, leaves…" Danielle ventured, and she reached a tentative hand to Wyn's hair and gently removed a handful of wide, brown leaves.

Wyn's hands flew to her head and found wet leaves clinging to her hair in fistfuls. She pulled one free in astonishment, then could not help laughing. "I must look spectacular. Plus, I've ruined your nice cloak. What a mess."

"That is what cloaks are for," Danielle pointed out. "Now, we need to see what has happened to our boat."

As soon as the small hatch to the cabin was opened it was obvious why the boat was listing. The iron stove had come loose from its mountings and rolled across the cabin, demolishing the bunk and wedging itself against the hull. Pieces of shattered wood and tangled blankets were strewn across the floor, and there was a slowly growing puddle where water oozed between two of the stove-crushed planks.

"Are we going to sink, then?" Wyn eyed the small puddle with suspicion.

"No." Danielle traced her fingers over the divot the stove had carved from the hull. "It will be a bit damp over here but the leak will be small. It might have been much worse. Our bunk saved us with its sacrifice."

"The stove is dead, I think." Wyn held up a twisted piece of metal. "We'll need a smithy to fix some of this."

"We cannot stay here, then." Danielle began shoving blankets and food into a pack. "We will freeze without a fire."

"We're going to go to the tower, aren't we?" Wyn rolled her eyes to the ceiling. "When we're all killed and eaten don't blame me."

"I am sure it will be fine, and it is the only shelter," Danielle smiled. "Think of the fire we can build."

By the time they returned to the deck the storm was fully upon them. The trees creaked and groaned as they bent in the wind, and snow streamed in horizontal sheets. The wind howled and shrieked through the boat's rigging, and the boat heeled to the side despite being safe behind the breakwater.

They struggled up the path from the old archway, searching for the few remaining stones that poked from the forest floor to guide them along the long-abandoned trail. Wyn saw grey shapes lurking amongst the trees, statues of knights in heroic poses now weathered and moss-covered. One had toppled off its plinth when its great stone base had split from roots and cold, and Wyn laughed gleefully as she pointed out the thorny shrub that now grew from between the statue's spread legs.

But the laughter passed quickly as they reached the top of the trail and approached the tower. Sheets of snow obscured its highest ramparts, but what could be seen was foreboding enough to force a curse from Wyn. A jumble of stone buildings perched on top of the hill and their steeply peaked roofs peered at Wyn over the top of a thick wall. In the center rose the tower, its sides encrusted with small turrets like knots on a tree. Jagged battlements bristled from the top of every tower and along every wall, and slit windows peered blackly at her from every direction. Wide gates of heavy wood and iron were sealed beneath a grim barbican tower, with a rusted portcullis for fangs and a horned forehead of a battlement.

Wyn pulled open a small postern door in the gate. It creaked on rusted hinges, allowing them entrance into the gloom of the tunnel and inner courtyard. As glad as Wyn was to be sheltered from the wind and snow, she could not bear to stand under the dark murder holes in the curved ceiling, and slid forward to the end of the tunnel while Danielle tried to light the lantern she had carried from the boat.

The courtyard was narrow, barely wide enough to fit a cart, and followed the outer wall as it wrapped around the tower. The dismal sky was a mere slit above the courtyard, filled with whirling snow that eddied and swirled as if pulled by puppet strings. The walls' feet stood in deep shadow, so shrouded in gloom that Wyn wondered if evening had not suddenly descended while they were passing through the tunnel.

Wyn slipped into the darkest shadows of the walls, guarding against any ambush or concealed watcher, but the black slits and jagged ramparts remained empty, bare vestiges of a time when the tower could guard.

Danielle led them farther into a tight maze of courtyards trapped between towering walls. Behind a tight turn, they found a heavy door set between two thick towers gashed with arrow slits. The door's iron hinges were warped and rusted, but together they forced open the door wide enough to slip through.

They found themselves in a hall filled with bare stone and squat pillars, with cold echoes whispering to them from its gloomy depths.

"Lovely." Wyn wrinkled her nose in disgust as she glanced around the barren hall.

"What is this place?" Danielle walked slowly to the center of the hall and turned in place to examine each direction. Breath wisped between Danielle's lips, a curl of white against her soft, dark skin, that drifted past her cheek and dissipated against the fur lining of her hood. "It is old, but not old enough to have collapsed. Who would build such a fearsome castle on the banks of the Abhainn Albyn?"

"No telling," Wyn dismissed the unfathomable ways of high-muckities with a shrug, "but it doesn't smell of troll, or smoke, or anything, really. Just empty stone."

"I suppose that is good news," Danielle smiled in relief. "In my heart, I was convinced we had found yet another Crunorix tower. Had there been stairs leading into the earth I believe I would have sat down and cried."

"I'd have joined you." Wyn shook the memory of the dark catacombs beneath the High Fells from herself with a furious shiver and was once again aware of her numb feet and frozen nose. "It's not any warmer than that bloody place was, is it?" Wyn blew on her clenched fingers. "Where do we go, then?"

"This way." Danielle pointed to a passageway that led from the entrance hall.

They followed the hall as it led them into the depths of the abandoned keep. The passage was narrow and twisted back and forth, the rooms they passed cramped and fashioned from rough-hewn stone.

They reached a room that once must have been a kitchen. An arched ceiling gave relief from the oppressive weight of the stone. Several cavernous fireplaces and an oven filled the walls. Scarred wooden tables stood under rusted iron hooks, grim without their pots and pans hanging from them.

"Fireplaces, thick walls to keep the heat in, and even fuel for the fire." Danielle's golden eyes flashed happily. "Yes, this is a fine place to stop."

They busied themselves with a hatchet and soon had a stack of table legs and struts piled haphazardly in the fireplace, and with the help of a liberal application of lantern oil, roaring, orange flames poured heat into the room.

Wyn found herself staring at Danielle as the noblewoman pulled back her hood and let the heat of the fire wash over her. Wyn's gaze followed the light of the fire as it gleamed from Danielle's wide eyes, and glowed bronze along the elegant curve of her high cheekbones and the beautiful, dark swell of her lips. Velvet shadow traced the long, graceful curve of her throat to the dark shadow at its base.

She's so lovely, Wyn sighed happily, *even cold and miserable and wrapped up in a coat.* She let her gaze wander lower, over the full curve of Danielle's tunic, past the sway of her hips, and along the leather leggings which clung to the length of Danielle's legs.

Danielle yawned deeply, her fingers pressed to her lips. "I am exhausted," Danielle sighed. She glanced at Wyn and smiled as she caught Wyn's gaze. "You look happy."

"I am," Wyn returned Danielle's smile.

"I am, as well." Danielle knelt by the fire and began to unlace a bundle of blankets from the boat. "Storm and ice and a stone floor for a bed, and yet I am quite content. If only we had some wine. Steaming hot. With spices." Danielle's fingers rested on the leather ties and she inhaled deeply. "I can almost smell the aroma."

"I can't help you there," Wyn apologized. She knelt next to Danielle and opened her own bundle, freeing a confusion of brown blankets. "Only blankets, I'm afraid. Must have forgotten the tasty spices."

Danielle laughed. "I do not mind. As long as you are here, I am happy. No matter where we are."

Wyn smiled, then she frowned, frustrated at her inability to put voice to the delicious glow that filled her heart. "I mean, it's really nice to be with you, no matter where. It makes me feel good… or… happy! Really happy. No, more than that. All the time. Oooo, I'm so terrible at words."

"You are my light, my heat, my every thought. You are my every breath, my every touch. You are the sun that warms me, the gentle breeze that carries me across the sea, and the bright star that guides me. You are my beginning and my end, my every in-between."

"Oh," Wyn gaped at Danielle in amazement. "See, that's what I wanted to say, really, but… words."

"They are not my words," Danielle laughed. "I wish they were, but I am not a poet. Nevertheless, they are what I feel, and I have longed to say them to someone for most of my life. Now I can, and I realize that even they are not sufficient."

"Well, they're pretty bloody good," Wyn sniffed. "That's a proper poem, is it?"

"Yes," Danielle said quickly, and she fastened her attention to her bundle.

"It's not from one of your reads, at all?" Wyn asked slyly, a grin spreading across her lips.

"Yes," Danielle answered reluctantly.

"That's all right," Wyn decided. "They're still better words than I could ever say."

"I recall a poet, a real poet, who wrote that love could never be expressed in mere words. I do not remember her name, nor exactly how she put it. Gabrielle was always the one who could remember every phrase from every poem and song."

"I like your words," Wyn told her. "They're better than any poet's, I'll wager."

"There, you have proven her correct, I am certain," Danielle laughed. "There has never been a poem that speaks of finding love in your lover's acceptance of a quote from a terrible read, yet I feel it there more strongly than in the most elegant verse."

"Well, that's not surprising, really," Wyn said. "Most poets are full of shite, I reckon. Still, none of that helps us with the wine, I'm afraid."

"No, it does not," Danielle sighed. "I wonder where my spice box has journeyed to. I left it at Nóinín Cnoc. Do you remember, I made wine for us, that night when I tried so desperately to catch your eye."

"I think I would remember a gorgeous lady batting her eyes at me. In fact, I do remember it, and it happened much later."

"I absolutely did, when we all gathered in my tent, the day Killock returned."

"When Bradon was so grumpy?" Wyn smiled at the memory. "And you yanked his beard and made him be still. That was a laugh."

"I did not yank his beard," Danielle corrected her. "I fixed it."

"If you say so, your Braidiship, but I remember when you 'fixed' *my* hair, and there was a lot less shouting."

"Of course," Danielle said. "When I was braiding Bradon's beard I wanted him to calm down and listen. When I braided your hair, I was thinking about… other things."

"I know what you were thinking about, you naughty girl." Wyn sighed in contentment. "You seduced me, that's the simple truth."

"I did not!" Danielle laughed. "I merely braided your hair and told you how I felt about you. You were the one telling stories about… milkmaids. And *you* kissed *me*."

"I was just a poor, innocent girl," cooed Wyn. "Overcome by your fancy ways."

"That seems extremely unlikely, but that is not the point. You do not remember what I was wearing that evening in the tent?"

THE MARTYR'S TEARS

"Um, I think so," Wyn said, puzzled. "No, not really. It was fancy, I remember thinking that."

"It was a blue dress, one of my favorites," Danielle smiled wistfully. "I brought it so that I would have something impressive to wear if we happened to go to Kuray. I remember I picked it because it very much flattered me, and I wanted to look stunning if we travelled to court where so many eyes would be upon me. I took the dress to impress the court, but I wore it that evening in that tiny little tent just to impress one person." Danielle held Wyn's gaze. "You. I clearly failed since you hardly remember it."

"Well, you look amazing in everything." Wyn raised an appraising eyebrow. "Also in nothing."

Danielle smiled in pleasure and Wyn saw a delightful blush begin to creep across her cheeks. They finished unpacking blankets and bedrolls in comfortable silence, and then they curled together in front of the fire.

"Will you tell me about the princess?" Wyn asked.

"Which princess?"

"The one in your read, that said that stuff about love being windy and so on."

"Oh, she was not a princess," Danielle corrected. "She was the elder daughter of a dowager countess."

"Very different, I'm sure," Wyn giggled. "Tell me about her. Did she have heaving ditties and was in love with a knight with an enormous sword?"

"Well, she was betrothed to his brother, and he to her sister, but that was when she was very young, and it was not until years later… are you sure you wish to hear this story?"

"Oh, yes," Wyn said contentedly. She snuggled closer, so that Danielle's breath stirred her hair and she could feel Danielle's heat pressed against her from fingers to toes. "Does she ever find out how big his sword is?"

***

Time passed slowly as the blizzard scoured the countryside, marked only by the gradually increasing distance Wyn and Danielle had to travel to find more furniture to feed into the ever-hungry fire.

They spent their days talking, laughing, and exploring the lives that had brought them together, or listening in comfortable silence to the gale moan across the far-distant chimney opening. They occasionally left the kitchen to explore the tower, watch the snow blow horizontally through the courtyard, or listen to the mournful howl of wolves beyond the walls, but they soon tired of these excursions. The tower was empty, the bare stone silent, and the sheets of snow immutable.

Wyn trained dutifully, driven by anger and frustration over her body's weakness, and she listened to Danielle speaking Venaissine. In return, she showed Danielle how to pick a lock and feel for the uneven weight of a die.

At last, the storm released its grip, the winds died away and became spiteful gusts, and the snow fell only in fits. Danielle and Wyn wrapped themselves up and tromped through the fresh pack to the ruined docks to inspect the damage the storm had done to their boat.

It had weathered the blizzard surprisingly well. It listed slightly to the side from the water that had leaked through the damaged hull, and trees had dropped branches onto its deck. But otherwise, it appeared unharmed. The tightly furled sails remained tied, and the hundreds of lines had remained in their channels.

They spent the afternoon bailing icy water from the cabin, and together, they rolled the stove across the boat and lashed it to the other bulkhead. Its shifted weight raised the damaged hull slightly, and although water still dripped through the dented timbers, the flow was less. Once underway, Danielle believed she could keep that side mostly out of the water.

As the short day drew to a dreary close, they trudged through the snow to the tower, weary and cold with thoughts of fire and blankets pulling them up the trail. But as they approached the outer gate Wyn stopped dead in the middle of the path and gaped at the tower in shock.

"Bloody hell…" she whispered.

"Wyn, are you all right? You are as pale as ash." Danielle peered at her with a questioning frown.

"It's just, it's just, fuck me." Wyn shook her head to clear it. "Look at that."

Wyn pointed to a stone shield carved into the tower above the gate. It wore a fresh hood of snow, but its face was clear, and the grey light revealed it bore a sigil of a crenelated wall behind a smith's hammer.

"I didn't see it last time." Wyn could not take her eyes off the shield. "The storm, I suppose."

"Does it mean something to you? I do not recognize the sigil."

"Yeah," Wyn answered softly. "It was on Mum's letter…"

"Your mother?" Danielle said uncertainly. "Wyn, I do not understand."

"Mum had this letter," Wyn started to explain. "She kept it in her little box with her preciouses. The letter was old and crinkly, torn and such, but I remember it had a red seal on it. Mum told me that meant the letter was real, because it had a proper seal on it, so every time I snuck into the box I would look at that seal and think about kings and princes and the like. And that's the seal, right there over that gate."

"Where did your mother get the letter, do you know?"

Wyn laughed bitterly. "From my Da. Don't know where he found it. Stole it most like. He told Mum it explained where there was an old castle, full of armor and swords and treasure, all just waiting to be found. Mum always told me that's where Da had gone, to find that castle."

"What happened to the letter?"

"That's the best part," Wyn wrinkled her nose in disgust. "After Mum died I kept that box and I read that letter. It wasn't any map to any treasure. It was just some letter from some high-muckity Baron to some other high-muckity Baron, talking about where he was going to go and fight next summer and asking for help. Supplies and men and such. It was shite, all of it, everything he had told Mum. I burned it." Wyn could still see the parchment blackening and curling as the yellow flame crept across it and the red wax bubbled and ran like blood.

"Perhaps your father learned of this castle's location in some other way," Danielle said thoughtfully. "Perhaps he really did find it."

"Not him," Wyn snorted. "He's stabbed to death in a tavern in some shitty village, too drunk to know he's dead, I'd bet your sister's shiny silver crown on it. Still, I wish he could have known I found his castle for real. I'd love to see him try to swallow that. Be like watching a rat choke on a turd."

"But it is right on the river," Danielle ventured. "It must be marked on maps. It would not have been difficult for your father to find."

"If he'd had to lift a finger it would have been too much effort. In any case, there's nothing here to take," Wyn laughed again. "Right on the river… anything left behind would have been taken long ago. Trust Da to pick an ancient ruin full of treasure that isn't full of treasure. What a bucket of shit he was."

Wyn strode into the barbican tunnel before Danielle had a chance to ask her any more. The sudden intrusion of her father into her life had sent a churn of fear and surprise swirling through Wyn's stomach. *Da didn't come here*, she reassured herself. *I'll not find his corpse around the corner, with a bag of loot for Mum over his shoulder. He's dead in a damn ditch, stabbed for being a bastard, I know he is.* She shivered again, grateful that the freezing air was sharp and helped clear her head.

They walked in silence through the dark passageways of the keep until they reached their kitchen home. Wyn roamed the halls until long after dusk hunting for wood and brought back enough to last for several days. With the extra fuel, they banked the fire especially high and created a roaring conflagration that bathed the kitchen with warm, orange light.

Wyn had not said ten words since the gate, and Danielle gave her the quiet to weather the churn of her thoughts, but as they lay together under their blankets by the fire, Wyn felt some of the anger slip away, and with a sigh she let the strain in her shoulders and jaw pass with it.

"It's all right, Dani, you can talk to me," Wyn said ruefully. "I'll not bite your head off, I promise."

"I am not concerned," Danielle replied. "You had things to think about."

"I'm not mad at you," Wyn told her, suddenly anxious that Danielle might have misunderstood her silence. "You've not done anything wrong."

"I know." Danielle rolled onto her side and rested her head in her hand so that she could gaze into Wyn's eyes. "I have never heard you mention your father before."

"That's because Da was a lying piece of shit who left us when I was too little to remember him. Just took the few coins Mum had and left."

"I am so sorry, Wyn."

"Like I said, I don't remember him, but Mum always said that he was coming back, and for a while, I believed her."

"But he never did?"

"Not likely," Wyn snorted. "I tried searching for him a few years ago. And guess what? It turns out he was a lying piece of shit. Everyone who knew him said he was a mean drunk who would smile to your face and then hit you in the back of the head with a bottle. I met a cobbler who actually spat on me when I mentioned Da's name to him."

"You believe he is dead now?"

"I hope so. You know, the only person who said he was a good man was the person who should've hated him most. Mum always said she loved him. She even kept a pair of boots he had left behind, cleaned and brushed and ready by the door. He even managed to ruin Mum's life *after* he was gone. Always waiting for him."

Danielle took Wyn's hand in hers and Wyn grasped it gratefully. The warm, gentle pressure of Danielle's fingers made Wyn's eyes burn with hated tears, but she clung to their comforting touch. Wyn sniffed surreptitiously and wiped at her eyes with her bandaged hand before any shining drops could betray her.

"I guess your da is gone too since you're the Marquessa and such?" Wyn asked.

"Yes, he died when I was only eight, but I remember him. He was a kind man, and always very loving. He taught me to sail, and whenever he was home we would always go onto the ocean, just us."

"What happened?"

"He was killed by a young knight named Amaury Miquelon while he was in Vordoux. Amaury stabbed my father in the back while Amaury was dueling, drunk, in the street."

"Did they catch him?"

"Yes, eventually. Amaury fled the city once he realized what he had done, but my mother tracked him down. She never spoke of it, but I have heard that they dueled and that he begged her for his life on his knees."

"Did she kill him?"

"He received no mercy from her."

"And so that's when you got your title?"

"Oh, no. My father was not the Marquis. My title comes from my mother's family. She was the Marquessa before me."

"Oh. Your mum must've died too, then, I suppose."

"Just a year after my father. She never recovered from his death. Every day there was a little bit less of her left until she was gone."

"Your mum died when you were nine?"

"Yes, and Gabrielle was seven."

"That's how old I was when Mum died. She was sick too, for years really, but at the end it was terrible."

"I did not know."

"How about that, though? Both of us orphans, the same age and everything."

"I can tell you that servants and an enormous house do not make you miss your parents any less, but they do take away the worry of eating and surviving. And I had my sister. I do not know how you managed it, by yourself and on the streets."

"Oh, those streets aren't so bad, once you get used to them."

Danielle was quiet, and Wyn knew that her bravado had not fooled the noblewoman, any more than Wyn believed it herself. Terrible thoughts stirred deep within her, behind a closed door where she had locked away the memories of the pain and suffering of those first years on her own. Wyn had thought it safe to talk about her father, for all she felt for him was hatred and anger, and with Danielle beside her, holding her hand, Wyn had felt safe enough to mention, just *mention,* mind you, her mother's sickness and death.

But the memories were pressing against her door, and tonight they had a strength that she had never felt before, or perhaps the door was weaker. They grew upward in her chest and throat, and she wanted them to burst out and be gone from her, as if they were a sickness that festered in her stomach. But as they swelled she felt the panic and the pain that grew with them, and she tried to swallow them before it was too late and they overwhelmed her.

At their forefront was her memory of her mother's death. It had been the height of summer, with a golden sun in a clear blue sky that made people mop their brows with their handkerchiefs. Her mother had been in her bed for weeks, and the priests had come and one of the servants from the Temple had stayed in their house and helped her mother, as she had been too weak to walk to the privy and back.

And each day her mother had asked for Wyn. She had gone at first, a few times at most, but soon she had ignored the servant when she brought the requests, and then, when she could no longer stand the old woman's disapproval, Wyn simply snuck from the house and stayed away as long as she could.

Finally, there was a day when she came home to find the priests had returned, and one kindly greyhair had taken her hand and explained that her mother was with the Maker.

They took Wyn to the temple and gave her a small room to stay in, and she sat on the rickety cot as she slowly realized how many things she would no longer have a chance to say to her mother. As the small candle in the room guttered and dimmed, and the black night grew closer and closer, regret and shame descended on her until she could not bear it and fled the temple, running wildly through the streets until she collapsed in the road.

She felt that darkness closing in again, now, despite the bright fire, and the same feeling of terrible regret and shame churned and fought to break her, just as they had done ten years ago.

Wyn curled into a tight ball and gasped as a sob shuddered through her. She wanted to puke, to throw up the vile feelings that lived behind her door, but she feared what they would do if she let them free and could not get rid of them. Panic flooded over her as sweat broke out in fiery pinpricks all over her back.

"Oh, Wyn," Danielle's voice washed over her, so full of concern that Wyn could no longer stand to have such darkness within her, living next to the hope and love that had blossomed so recently. She let the door shatter, and the memories rushed out and broke her heart.

"She didn't deserve any of the things that happened to her," Wyn sobbed and clung to Danielle's hand. "All she did was take care of me, no matter what, and what did she get for it? Da shit on her. Then life shit on her and she got sick. And then I shit on her.

"Everything she did for me and then I didn't do anything for her when she was sick and she needed me. I couldn't wait for her to die, she was so sick all the time and I didn't help her.

"That's the sort of person I am. I'm just like my da. I should have helped but I didn't. I left her! And I deserve everything that's happened to me since, I know it. Everything except you. I don't deserve you, I don't deserve someone wonderful, and kind, and gorgeous. I deserve to be shit on, and I know that's what is going to happen. You'll find out who I really am and then good riddance to Wyn, and who could blame you?"

"Wyn, that is not true!" Danielle rose to her knees and drew Wyn to her. Wyn wrapped her arms around Danielle and held on, burying her face against Danielle's shoulder as silent sobs wracked her body. "Maker's breath, you were nine. Of course you wanted your mother back. And of course you had no idea what to do. Neither did I! I stood and watched and held her hand and wished it were over, every single day. But Wyn, we were little girls then. What matters is who we became because of what happened to us.

"And consider what you have done since then. You have helped every person who needed help, especially those who could not help themselves. You have dedicated your life to helping and defending those in need, that is *you*, now.

"I am so proud of the woman I love, and I know your mother would be proud of you, too. She would see who you have become and she would see herself, not your father. Someone who gives selflessly, who helps those who need it most, who defends those who cannot defend themselves, and does it without thought for herself."

Wyn held on tightly, but now she sobbed with relief, her grief finally given voice. And when she eventually caught her breath, she pulled back and gazed into Danielle's eyes.

"Are you real?" Wyn asked. "Or are you a dream?"

Tears streamed down Danielle's cheeks as well, and she gently swept hair from Wyn's face with her fingertips.

"I will always be here when you wake up, I promise."

Then Wyn kissed her, tenderly, feeling the warm, soft touch of Danielle's lips against her own as she tried to force every scrap of her love through the kiss so that Danielle might know how boundless it was.

"I love you, too," Danielle whispered when at last the kiss ended, and she pulled Wyn into her arms and held her until their soft breathing was the only sound.

***

Wyn dreamed of her mother's house. It stood dark and shuttered behind the weed-choked garden, its yellow door stained and cracked by rain. Wyn hesitated with her thumb on the latch.

What am I doing? I had something to tell Mum. Wyn frowned in concentration, then her face lit up with a smile. *Oh! I remember.*

Wyn lifted and pushed on the thumb latch at the same time in a practiced motion to free the latch from its twisted hook.

Wyn was surprised to see that the main room was filled with people. She rushed past a tall priest with a grey beard and the kind cooper's wife who lived three houses along on the left.

"Where have you been?" Danielle asked. She stood at the bedroom door garbed in long robes of diaphanous white that swirled in a gentle, warm breeze.

"I don't know," Wyn stared at Danielle. At first, Wyn thought that Danielle's robes were glowing, but as she watched she realized that the soft light came from Danielle herself, a nimbus that flickered and shifted like sunlight from the surface of an ocean.

"It is not too late," Danielle answered. "She's waiting for you."

Wyn slipped through the door.

The bedroom was dark, with only small candles on the old dresser to light it. Her mother lay in the bed, golden hair spread on the pillow, the thick quilt pulled up to cover her shoulders. Wyn crept across the floor, not wanting to disturb her.

"Mum?" Wyn's voice was that of a child, small and scared. She reached a hand for the blanket and her fingers remembered the feel of the old, patched quilt. "Mum? It's me."

Wyn's mother opened her eyes and noticed Wyn, and she smiled. The smile washed the pain from her eyes, it wiped the weariness from her cheeks, it pushed the terrible sadness from her mouth.

"Wyn, you're here."

"I have something to tell you, Mum." Wyn took her mother's frail hand in hers, the small fingers nothing but bone beneath the skin. But they still had a little strength left, and her mother gripped back and gently laid her other hand on top of Wyn's. Tears burned Wyn's eyes but she could not wipe them away.

"Mum, I'm sorry I left you. I should have helped you, but I didn't."

"It doesn't matter," her mother smiled again. "I love you, and I'm proud of you."

"It does matter," Wyn told her. "It matters to me, but I want you to know that I've not run away again, not from anyone who needed me."

"That's why I'm proud of you," she patted Wyn's hand gently. "You took care of everyone but yourself, Wyn. You've been so sad."

"Yeah, but I'm happy now, Mum, Dani makes me happy. She's kind, and strong, and brilliant, and fierce, but she's not crazy like me."

"She sounds lovely."

"She is, Mum. She loves me, you see, and I love her, and I wish that you could meet her."

"Not right now," her mother closed her eyes and relaxed onto her pillow. "Someday, when I am not so tired."

Wyn nodded her head and stroked her mother's hand as the candles dimmed, one by one, until the room was dark and all Wyn could feel was her mother's fingers curled in her own.

The Martyr's Tears

Karsha Hali

Karsha chewed thoughtfully on a nut as he watched the long grass that covered his perch flatten and spring back with the wind. A pile of shells filled his lap, testament to his long vigil, but he did not mind the wait. From his small hillock, he could see far across the sprawl of Bandirma to the white-flecked expanse of Loughliath and watch the smoke from the town's chimneys dance in the wind. Between Karsha and the town were rolling fields separated by long, graceful curves of stone walls and hedgerows, and Karsha grinned as he watched the farmers collect their sheep, the white herds flowing like mercury across the fields as the dogs brought them home.

Karsha cracked another nut open and fished out the tender flesh with a boney finger. Leaves swirled into the air over the muddy trail beneath his perch in a fresh gust of wind, and Karsha smelled ice on its breath.

A red squirrel eyed Karsha from the low branch of a tree across the trail, and he carefully dropped a nut from his shrinking supply into the grass at his feet. The squirrel was suspicious, but in the end greed overwhelmed caution, and it darted across the path and clutched the nut, staring with black eyes at the small wizard.

"Remember where you hide this one," Karsha instructed the creature, "or I shall regret my gift."

The squirrel blinked at Karsha and hopped into the trail. There it froze, staring toward the distant town.

"Hurry," Karsha warned. "She is almost here."

The faint rhythm of hoofbeats drifted to them between bursts of wind. The squirrel fled into the bushes with its treasure, and Karsha climbed to his feet amidst a shower of empty shells.

He pulled his hood over his head and peered along the trail. A flash of movement between the trees announced the arrival of the horse and its rider an instant before they rounded the bend and sped toward Karsha.

The rider was a slender woman garbed in a long dress with a deep hood that she had thrown back to let her black hair stream free in the wind. Silver gleamed from within her hair, and from an amulet hung around her graceful neck. A smile parted her dark lips with the joy of her ride, and her cheeks were flushed.

She slowed as she spotted Karsha standing beside the trail, and Karsha called out to her.

"Lady Rowenna."

The rider reined in her horse and graced Karsha with a puzzled smile. "Do I know you, sir?"

"You do, my lady," Karsha admitted. "But I hope you will treat me kindly, despite that."

"Why would I not?" Rowenna asked. Her smile faltered and a small frown appeared on her brow.

Karsha slipped off his hood and revealed himself, and saw Rowenna's eyes go wide with shock and recognition. Her hand flew to the hilt of her sword and it slid free from its sheath in a silver blur.

"Karsha Hali," Rowenna gasped.

Karsha bowed low, his hands spread wide to either side, his gaze fixed on the hooves of Lady Rowenna's horse, waiting for them to suddenly lunge. The horse stamped and shifted in the mud, anxious to run, but it did not step toward him, and Karsha dared to raise his head and meet the Templar's eyes.

Lady Rowenna scoured the trees behind Karsha with her gaze, searching for any sign of his allies, but the thin tip of her blade never wavered from his chest. Karsha waited until her gaze at last settled on him. Astonishment had given way to puzzled suspicion in her eyes, but Karsha did not see anger or fear.

"Every ranger and scout in Bandirma has searched for you for weeks," she said.

"Yes," agreed Karsha. "I am thankful they have looked in the wrong places."

"It is no coincidence to find you next to my path, is it?"

"No, my lady. I heard a story of a beautiful woman who enjoyed her ride through the forest every day, and I hoped today would be no different."

"Why did you come here? To surrender, or to do more harm?"

"Just to talk," Karsha shrugged. "To tell you the story you are searching for."

"Just to talk?"

"Yes. You and I, at first, and then others if you think it fitting."

"What if I said to come along and you can tell your story to the whole Council, right now?"

"No, not yet. One day they may be ready to hear my story, but that is not today. Today is for us to talk, or for us to say goodbye and return to our homes." Karsha fixed the Templar with an unwavering stare. "And nothing else."

Lady Rowenna nodded slowly, but she did not lower her sword, and she did not dismount. "Tell me, then."

"Wonderful," Karsha grinned. He settled back onto his patch of flattened grass and curled his feet beneath his robes.

"Long ago," he began, "far in the south of my land, there were two great kingdoms. The people of the sky lived in tall towers built from the brightest of clouds, and the people of the stone built mighty fortresses deep within the earth. The people of the sky and the people of the stone showed great kindness to each other, and gave gifts and aid that brought happiness to both kingdoms.

"In the tallest spire of the city of the sky people lived a wizard. He was old, very old, but his eyes still saw clearly, and he spent his days watching from the windows of his tower, for he could see the entire world from there, and could learn things that even the gods did not know.

"One day he saw a shadow far away. Of course, he saw many shadows every day as the sky people's city passed over the land, but this shadow was not cast by any cloud. It came from beneath the earth, was twisted and dark, and consumed whatever it touched. The wizard watched this shadow for many days, and wondered what could have created it, for he had never seen any shadow like it.

"Now, deep under the earth, the ruler of the people of stone lived in a vast cavern. It was so deep that the roots of the world came together there, and the ruler of stone built his throne so that he could sit and place his hands on the roots, and therefore know everything that the stone touched. He sensed the weight of distant mountains, the burrowing roots of wide jungles, the slow rub of winding rivers.

"One day he felt a dark touch against the stones, a shadow colder than the oldest rivers of ice, blacker than the deepest caves. It spread through the stone and consumed it, as if it were a maggot feasting on decaying meat. The ruler of the stone people watched this shadow for many days, and wondered what could have created it, for he had never seen any shadow like it.

"When the shadow did not pass, the wizard journeyed to the city of the people of stone and spoke with their ruler. 'I have seen a shadow on the world,' the wizard said, 'a terrible darkness that I have never seen before.'

"The ruler of the people of stone said, 'I have felt a shadow deep in the earth, a foul presence that consumes everything it touches.'

"And so the two spoke and decided that they would join as allies against the darkness, for it brought fear into both their hearts.

The Martyr's Tears

"Now, in the city of the people of stone lived a prince. He, too, spent his days searching the stone for knowledge, but he was a proud man, and he searched for power that he might wield for himself. The prince found the darkness, but he did not watch it. He spoke to it, and the darkness replied. No one knows what they said to each other, but the shadow's words twisted the prince's heart, and filled his veins with poison.

"When the prince heard that the people of the sky and the people of the stone had allied against the shadow, he was gripped by fear. He coated a dagger with black poison and went to speak with the ruler of the people of stone. The prince treated him with fair words, and swore he would help destroy the shadow. But when the ruler turned his back, the prince stabbed the ruler, and the black poison spread through his body and killed him before he could utter a sound.

"The black poison seeped into the stone and was carried throughout the stone city. Everywhere it went it took the prince's treachery with it, so that his lies were soon lurking in the hearts of many of the people of stone. Then the prince took his dagger and went to kill the wizard, so that no enemy of the shadow would remain.

"The wizard felt his approach and fled the stone city. But the sky people did not abandon their friends, the people of the stone. They have watched the spread of the black poison, and they see that it has not touched everyone who lives beneath the earth. The prince can be defeated, but the sky people know that soon his ally, the shadow, will grow too powerful to defy. Time grows short."

Karsha rubbed his hands together, trying to find some feeling in his fingers' icy tips. "This story has many endings. Some are sad, some are joyous, some I cannot bear to utter. Which ending would you like to hear?"

"What is the prince's name?" Lady Rowenna asked. Her sword had not wavered as she listened to the story.

"Ah! You would like the ending where the people of the sky and the people of the stone are reunited when the treachery of the prince is revealed."

THE MARTYR'S TEARS

"I would like the ending where the daughter of the river people forces the wizard to explain why the people of the sky have been butchering the people of the stone."

"That is a sad ending," Karsha said softly. "So full of regret and shame that it is difficult to tell."

"Try," insisted Rowenna.

"The people of the sky hoped that they could convince the people of the stone that the prince had murdered their ruler, but they knew that his poison was strong, and they feared what he might trick the people of the stone into doing.

"The people of the sky sought to capture the temples of the people of the stone, to trap the prince in the city. And, yes, to force the people of the stone to listen to their words. The wizard urged the people of the sky to do this."

Karsha sighed and plucked at the frayed hem of his robe. "I urged them to do this. I fear the prince, and I fear his master, the shadow. I thought it best… But there are evil men amongst both peoples, and one of the sky people committed a terrible crime. There is no excuse, only sorrow."

"Accidents happen?" Rowenna scoffed.

"No!" Karsha insisted. "A mistake was made. My mistake, for it was my counsel. I regret it for the harm it has done to those innocent people, but I regret it more for the harm it has done to the trust between us. The shadow is still out there. The Crunorix are still within your walls. This is what matters. All else must be pushed aside."

"I have heard that you are the Crunorix priest who murdered Bishop Benno. Your story does not change that."

"No, it does not," Karsha bobbed his head in agreement. "I wish only to tell you this story so that you know both, and can decide between them. There is proof, for all true stories leave their mark on the world. But you must know what you look for."

"Very well," Lady Rowenna said thoughtfully. "Then we are at the moment when you reveal your villain."

"It is Reverend Whitebrooke," Karsha said simply. He carefully watched Lady Rowenna's face as she absorbed the news, and saw careful consideration and resolve, but no defiance. *This is not a new thought for the lady, at least, not entirely. She has had suspicions that have laid a fertile ground for it to take root.*

"I see," Lady Rowenna replied. "Your proof?"

"My proof is my own eyes," Karsha assured her. "During the battle in the Queen's apartments, Whitebrooke challenged me with fuil crunor. He consumed the life of the soldiers in the room and used it to open an abyss to shadow. I was forced to flee…" Karsha sniffed and adjusted his robes. "…that time."

"Whitebrooke tells us that you were the one to use fuil crunor in that room."

"A good lie," Karsha admitted. "You must find your proof elsewhere."

"And what of Lady Danielle?" Rowenna asked. "Whitebrooke tells us that she is your disciple."

"A terrible lie," Karsha tutted. "Lady Danielle fought the magus in the catacombs and destroyed it. Only a fool would believe this lie. In any case, she stood beside me in the Queen's apartments when I felt the shadow summoned into Bandirma. She was sipping wine next to her sister, not practicing fuil crunor."

Lady Rowenna nodded thoughtfully, and at last her sword tip dropped. "Very well, I shall carry your story to my brother and others in Bandirma who seek the truth about our real enemy. But I can promise no more."

"This is a good ending," Karsha assured her. "May the gods grant you good fortune in your hunt. But, since the gods are fickle and cruel, I shall help you, as well." Karsha burrowed in his robes and drew forth a small wooden message tube.

"What is that?" Rowenna asked.

"A secret," Karsha smiled. "It belonged to Whitebrooke, but he sent it into the world and I took it."

Rowenna cautiously held out her hand and Karsha dropped the tiny container into her gloved palm. Rowenna opened the clasp and read the fluttering parchment, then glanced at Karsha in confusion. "You say this is Whitebrooke's secret?"

"Oh, yes," Karsha assured her. "You might ask Reverend Sebastian."

Rowenna rolled the parchment and placed it back in the tube, silent despite the puzzled questions crowding her face.

"If you wish to speak again, come to Littleford," Karsha told her. "You will be welcome."

Lady Rowenna sheathed her sword and wheeled her horse. "I hope I am not misjudging you, Karsha Hali."

Karsha grinned. "Tell me, before you leave… why are you the daughter of the river people?"

"I was born within bowshot of the Abhainn Albyn, not in a tunnel," Rowenna informed him archly. "We are not all Korrigans, you know."

"Ah," Karsha sighed happily. "Perhaps you will tell me the stories of the river people when we next meet."

"Perhaps," agreed Rowenna, and she put her heels to her horse and it leapt down the trail, vanishing quickly behind the trees.

Karsha left the remains of his sack of nuts on the ground for the squirrel and began his long walk through the forest. Clouds piled into dark cliffs in the west and wind gusted fitfully around Karsha's huddled form. The trees stirred uneasily, swaying and creaking with worry as the storm neared.

The first drops of rain stung his head with an icy touch before he had gone a dozen paces, and he glared at the black clouds.

Bran croaked at him from a nearby branch. The raven's glossy feathers blew in all directions in the wind, and his perch swayed precariously, but the raven cared only to laugh at the water trickling across Karsha's scalp.

"Will it snow?" Karsha asked the raven. "It feels cold enough." He shivered and hurried his steps. "Stop laughing and show me where I left the horse."

Bran swooped through the trees westward, and Karsha trundled after him, his robes flapping around his legs as the storm descended on Bandirma.

The Martyr's Tears

Killock

Water streamed from the wolf's shaggy fur as it clambered up the muddy embankment and slipped between the trees along the river's edge. The wolf's paws padded without a sound in the thick, new snow that coated the ground, and it glided through the shadows like a breath of air, its gleaming eyes and steaming breath the only signs that it was more tangible than a spirit of the forest.

Sharp scents curled around the wolf as it loped along the forest floor. A family of deer seeking water, an owl watching the wolf from its perch, a black rat cowering in the reeds. The wolf enjoyed the taste of the scents rolling across its tongue, but it did not turn to pursue them. They did not mark the trail it was searching for.

The wolf's path meandered with the river, never leaving the proximity of the river's edge, even when the forest thickened and an easier way presented itself. The wolf pushed through tangled branches with a low snarl, scrambled up moss-covered rocks, and leapt over fallen trunks without pause.

An inlet curled away from the river across the wolf's path. Thick trees crowded the edge of the inlet, and the water was so choked with rushes that only in the center was there a narrow gap of clear water, still and black as a gaping cave.

The wolf reached the water's edge, its paws sinking into the thick, frozen mud that oozed amongst the reeds. But the wolf did not back away, nor did it leap into the water to churn across, as it had every other time a stream had blocked its path. The wolf stood with nose raised above the rank smell of the mud, ears straining forward, as it probed the quiet backwater.

The wolf whined as a faint scent stirred against its nose. It sprang out of the mud and pushed its way further along the inlet, returning to the edge of the water again and again as it went.

The scent grew stronger as the wolf approached a bend in the inlet. The reeds had been flattened and broken in a long stretch, and the cove was filled with scents that did not belong in the forest. Oil and metal and old smoke. But there were also familiar scents, a blend of happiness and comfort that drew the wolf closer.

The wolf circled one of the trees, dug into the powdery snow, and snuffled the frozen mud beneath. A whine of excitement escaped its mouth. The scents clung to the tree, and the wolf knew the rough bark had been brushed against, had been touched, and recently.

The wolf trampled the snow until it had made a nest amongst the tree's roots and lay its head wearily on its paws, content for the moment to simply rest amidst the scent of its pack. The wolf had journeyed far since it had last found the trail, and worry had churned in its stomach with every stride that it would not find it again.

But as the wolf rested, another scent crept across the forest toward it. The wolf raised its head, and a low growl throbbed in its throat. The scent was leather and steel mixed, and it lurked in the shadows, and the wolf's hackles bristled.

The wolf rose and slipped into the darkness between the trees. The second trail encircled the inlet, probing carefully forward along the wrinkles in the forest floor until it reached the edge of the water where the reeds were flattened. There, the wolf found the sharp taste of steel and sweat pressed into the mud and smeared on the bark of the trees. The wolf growled again, then followed the trail as it departed the inlet, chasing the path of the river.

The wolf rushed after the trail, its weariness vanished as it pursued those who hunted its pack.

***

Killock watched the faint spark of a lantern wobble between the farmhouse and the barn. A fresh gust of wind stung his face with small crystals of ice and dappled the river's surface behind the line of trees where he crouched. The knight pulled his hood lower and wiped an icy drip from the tip of his nose, gave the farmstead one last, thoughtful stare, and rose from his concealment amongst the tree trunks.

Killock turned his back on the farm and retraced his steps to the riverbank. He picked his way between snow-capped rocks and over gnarled roots to the small cove he had discovered, and paused at the edge of the muddy embankment that bordered it.

In the dim morning light, the faint tracks he had found the night before stood out clearly. Beneath a pine at the water's edge, where the snow had not penetrated the thick branches, a pattering of light boot prints circled the tree and a fresh line had rubbed through the moss on the tree's trunk above a conveniently low branch. A broken branch trailed where a tree spread over the cove.

Killock pulled his hand free from its glove and ran his fingertips over the groove on the tree trunk. He could almost feel the rough thread of the rope that had rubbed the path in the moss. He crouched to examine the boot prints around the base of the tree more closely. They were small and barely left a trace in the soft mud, and their toes pressed in to reach the rope around the tree.

A young woman, tying up a boat. The knight traced one of the prints with his finger, gently feeling the mud run across his skin. *But was it my young woman?*

Killock listened to the branches rub against each other as he considered the marks left for him. They were similar to the tracks he had found at intervals along the Abhainn Albyn. A small boat whose occupants always chose concealment over an easy berth, always far from villages and farms. But concealment on a river bank could simply mean shelter for a boat caught by weather or the end of a day, and Killock had seen many small boats passing him by in his days of pursuing the river north from Greymouth.

There were other signs, however, that gave the knight hope that he was still on the right trail. He followed the boot prints up the embankment to the edge of the trees again, where they disappeared under the snow in the direction of the farm. This time, Killock did not hang back amongst the trees to observe. He followed one of the low, stacked stone walls toward the farm, bent almost double as he crept along its base.

Where the wall dipped into a small gulley formed by a stream, Killock abandoned it and crept toward the farm on a hunch, and found a single boot print where he expected it, behind the thickest of brambles that offered the best concealment to observe the farmstead. A single, long strand of golden hair waved from a hooked thorn, almost too faint to see. The knight watched it flutter for a moment, his grey eyes dark.

Killock pressed onward, following the stream until it curved away from the small rise the buildings sat on. The knight searched the buildings for the best approach, then hurried across a stretch of frosted ground to the shadows under the eaves of the farmhouse. The knight carefully brushed away the snow beneath a small, shuttered window, and the corner of his mouth curled slightly in satisfaction as he discovered a pair of small prints in the frozen mud. He pressed against the wall and cautiously eased the shutters open enough to peer inside.

Packed shelves surrounded the small room, filled with baskets and barrels and jugs. The heavy smell of cold meat curled through the gap along with the sweet scent of dried fruit and the thick aroma of fresh bread. A cloth covering a lump beneath the window caught his attention and he peeled it back. Killock's mouth watered and his stomach growled in sudden misery as he revealed a pie whose crust oozed trails of brown gravy across its flakey surface.

Killock let himself imagine a steaming slice on a thick slab of bread for a moment, then shook the vision away. The cloth over the pie was wide enough to also cover a suspiciously empty spot on the shelf next to the pie, and a circle of clean stone on the dusty floor next to a cluster of clay jugs also caught his eye.

The same as before. The boat is concealed, then a raid on whatever farm or village is nearby to obtain food. And the raider knows what she is doing. Always the best concealment, always the best route, never taking more than she can snatch and carry away quickly without notice.

Killock quickly retreated from the farmstead, following his own footsteps back to the small cove. He crouched once again next to the tree with its rope mark, and rested his fingers in one of the small boot prints next to the tree. *It is Wyn and Danielle… it must be.*

Killock crept carefully along the edge of the cove to a spot where a mossy boulder rose amongst the gnarled roots of a crooked tree. He knelt and examined another track he had found earlier. This one was heavy, a wide boot that had scraped the moss from the boulder and sunk deep into the mud at its base. One of the roots showed a mark where metal had scored its surface.

But for all the heaviness of the print, Killock found it difficult to follow the trail. It moved from stone to stone and root to root, rarely touching earth to leave an easy mark. If it had not been for the slight slip down the front of the boulder, Killock was not sure if he would have seen the tracks at all.

But now that he knew it was there, he persevered. The tracks led the knight around the cove, touching on the small boot prints where they circled the tree, and then up the embankment into the shadows beneath the thick canopy of trees. Here, the tracks were joined by other prints, and Killock carefully traced the overlapping marks until he was convinced he had identified the tracks of three different men, each as careful as the one the knight had followed.

After gathering together, the footprints headed north along the riverbank, sticking firmly to the concealment of the fringe of trees.

Killock stood and stretched his back as he stared at the ground at his feet. The fits of wind had died away, leaving the forest softly silent under its white blanket.

Three men now, whereas before there was only one. And they are closer to the women, only a day behind, now, perhaps two. Killock scowled at the boot print in the mud at his feet. *And perhaps two days ahead of me. Whoever they are, they move quickly.* Killock began to stride after the tracks, soon falling into a steady lope that devoured the long curves of the river. *But not as fast as I.*

Gwydion

Gwydion perched on the window sill and scrupulously arranged his robes so that a minimum of cloth touched any surface. He was willing to hazard the bird shit that adorned its stones, as well as the not insignificant chance of a plunge to a watery death. Both risks were preferable to being trapped inside Reverend Sebastian's study with the window shutters closed. He had forced the disappointed Bird Master to pen up the pigeons that otherwise would have flown, and perched, on whatever, and whomever, they pleased.

Relentless rain obscured Loughliath and the distant hills, and turned the roofs of the township a dull, sullen grey. Water ran along the lip of the window and dripped onto the sill, creating small, white puddles amongst the droppings, and Gwydion wondered if there was, in fact, any stone left beneath the shit, or if the entire ledge had slowly been replaced over the centuries.

Gwydion adjusted the small, gold brooch that held the collar of his robes in place, and turned his attention to the murky interior of Tithius' Tower, and the lord of its lofty spire.

Sebastian scurried around his desk, badgering two hapless acolytes as they struggled to serve tea and light lanterns at the same time. Only when both he and Gwydion had a tiny cup in hand and the center of his desk was as brightly lit as three lanterns could make it, did the Bird Master finally cease his fluttering and crouch with his nose virtually touching the surface of the desk, peering intently at the object that Gwydion had brought to him.

Gwydion watched Sebastian in silence, occasionally raising his cup to blow thin strands of steam from the surface of his tea, but never bringing it to his lips.

Sebastian muttered excitedly and tilted the object back and forth, cooing in delight. He suddenly rounded on the acolyte who stood nervously by the door to the study.

"Bring me the second volume of the Grand Duke's first exploration, quickly now!"

The acolyte fled as fast as her legs could carry her, and Sebastian beckoned Gwydion to join him at the desk.

"This is one of the finest representations of a phoenix I have ever seen," Sebastian crowed in delight. "Whoever carved this must have seen the real creature, without a doubt. Where did you say you found it?"

"I won it off a sailor in Greymouth, of all places. He claimed it was valuable."

"Very. Consider the detail captured in the feathers of the neck."

"I believe he meant the plating."

"Ah yes, the sculptor has used gold to indicate the brilliant plumage along its crest. A rather dull approximation of its real color, we are told, by all credible accounts."

"He named it a dragon bird, although I am not at all certain why I gave that any credence."

"They are sometimes called that, and I have read accounts of them breathing fire as if they were their mythical namesakes. But they are now properly recognized as the phoenix. My goodness, you can make out the patterns on its tail when the light reflects from the side, look."

"I had noted that very thing," Gwydion assured Sebastian.

"Astounding. The beak, and the talons. This is a raptor of the highest order, there is no doubt."

"I am thrilled you like it. I thought of you the moment he showed his cards."

Sebastian glanced up and met Gwydion's gaze for a moment, then returned to examining the small statue. "Did you? Most kind."

Gwydion contented himself with standing quietly at the end of the desk while Sebastian continued to mutter and turn the small statue back and forth, until the acolyte returned, staggering under a heavy, iron-bound volume that Sebastian hastily cleared room for on the desk. The Bird Master quickly found the passage he was searching for and poured over the page, his long, boney finger scratching across the vellum as he compared the description with the sculpture.

Then, finally satisfied, Sebastian perched on his chair, gently running his fingers over the line of the statue's wings. Gwydion moved to the only other chair in the room, eyed its dilapidated pillow with distrust, and merely rested one hand elegantly on its back.

"Tell me more about these cards that he showed," Sebastian croaked, never taking his gaze from the bird. "Did he show them too soon? One hears of it happening, but it seems unlikely, given the rigidity of the rules of such things."

"He thought he had a winning hand," Gwydion explained thoughtfully, "and so he grew careless. When he was caught, he tried to bluff his way out."

"Lies and threats?"

"Mmmm, and intimidation."

"He sounds like a foolish player."

"Careless, perhaps. Certainly overconfident that his lies, or rather, his bluff, would not be challenged. But as it turned out he played clumsily, and it soon became obvious what he was actually holding in his hand."

"I do despise an arrogant player. Too often they are shielded by the rules of the game, and one has no choice, does one?" The Bird Master glanced at Gwydion from under long, white eyebrows.

THE MARTYR'S TEARS

"Of course, one must play within the rules," Gwydion assured Sebastian. "One has no choice, obviously. Which makes it ever so much more satisfying when one does catch a poor player."

Sebastian bobbed his wrinkled head in agreement. "It is."

"Oh!" Gwydion placed his cup on the desk and began searching his pockets. "I have just remembered. Speaking of showing one's cards too early must have reminded me."

"Did it?" asked Sebastian. "How fortunate."

"Yes, here we are." Gwydion produced a small, wooden message container. "I rather think that this card was meant to stay concealed."

"May I?" asked the Bird Master. Gwydion deposited the message into Sebastian's talons and watched the priest unroll it carefully on the desk next to one of the lanterns. Sebastian looked it over briefly and glanced at Gwydion. "How did this come to be in your pocket?"

"Oh, more poor card playing, in a way," Gwydion explained airily.

"I see," Sebastian said. "Shameful."

"I knew you would think so," Gwydion replied with a smile.

"Of course, if this message was meant to stay concealed, if it did, for example, contain some hidden meaning, then I could hardly say, could I? Rules, you see."

"Ah, but—"

"No, there are no exceptions for such things. Much as I enjoy watching a poor player misplay his hand, I cannot break the rules, myself."

"Of course, you are correct," Gwydion frowned in annoyance. *What was the point in giving Rowenna this useless piece of paper if no one can tell us what it means?* he wondered. *Is Karsha Hali playing us for fools? Or am I the bad card player at this table?*

Sebastian shuffled around his desk to a stack of painstakingly ordered message scrolls.

"If we could speak of other things for a moment," he croaked, "I would like to ask a favor. I have these messages, you see. Usually, I would just send them down with an acolyte, but what with the rain and cold they have been kept so busy with keeping the cotes dry and warm that they simply have not had time."

"I would be delighted to take them for you."

"Marvelous, dear boy, marvelous. The messages are for Reverend Whitebrooke. Just came in this morning, one from Greymouth, another from Northwick. Poor creatures were half-drowned, but they made it."

"Then I am proud to bear their messages the final distance," Gwydion said grandly.

"Good. I knew I could rely on you, Lord Gwydion."

Sebastian picked up two message slips and passed them to Gwydion with trembling fingers, the dry parchment curling into a tight roll as he took them. Gwydion straightened one and read the brief, scrawled note.

"Apparently, a cheap supply of coal has been found in Greymouth, and in Northwick, no coal has been…" Gwydion raised an eyebrow and glanced at Sebastian. "Yes, well, I see."

"I knew you would, my lord," Sebastian croaked horribly, his shoulders shaking as if he suffered from a fit as he laughed. When his dry wheezing finally subsided, he replaced the message Karsha Hali had given Rowenna in its wooden container, and handed it to Gwydion. "I am sorry I cannot tell you any more about this message. If I were you, I would take it to Reverend Nesta. She might know more."

"I will make sure it is given to Nesta immediately."

"I knew I could rely on a man of your judgment."

Gwydion took his leave and descended the long, circling stairs immersed in thought, so that his arrival at the door to the bailey came as a surprise. He watched a long train of wagons slowly maneuver through the Tùr Abhainn and across the bailey to the massive doors of the warehouses. Drivers cursed each other, the soldiers and stewards who tried to organize them, and the chill rain that poured over Bandirma, turning the cobbles of the courtyard into a maze of small lakes and islands that quivered under the wheels of the wagons.

THE MARTYR'S TEARS

Spying a small gap in the procession, Gwydion dashed across the bailey and made the shelter of the wide doors to the temple with only a minor disaster to the hem of his robes and one boot, which he shook morosely in a vain attempt to rid it of the water that had seeped through every seam.

"Well, what did he say?" Rowenna asked, uncaring of his sartorial plight.

"Whitebrooke has indeed been playing shenanigans with secret messages."

"And did Sebastian tell you what they were?"

"Oh no, that would be against the rules. He explained it all to me at length. I feared I might never escape." Gwydion gave his boot one last shake, then gave up, promising himself a new pair instead. "But, look. Sebastian gave me these two messages that just arrived for Reverend Whitebrooke."

"They speak of coal supplies…" Rowenna held the message next to the one Karsha Hali had given them. "As does the one sent by Whitebrooke to Newbridge. Why is every town in southern Albyn sending Whitebrooke messages about coal?"

"He must have sent them all the same message as the one Karsha Hali found on its way to Newbridge."

"But, why would Reverend Whitebrooke be so interested in coal?"

"He wouldn't be, would he. Unless there really is a message concealed in it and they are all talking about the same thing back and forth."

"I suppose so."

"Ro, it must be. Karsha Hali didn't just give us that message for no reason. It was important, and he did it to help get proof against Whitebrooke, he said. And now we have these messages arriving for Whitebrooke talking about coal supplies. It must be some sort of cypher, and I bet Karsha knows what it's all about, somehow."

"Sebastian gave you the messages?"

"He did. Apparently, I am a man of great judgment."

Rowenna laughed.

"Great judgment," Gwydion repeated. "His words."

"Oh, yes. That is actually the very trait I think of first when I am asked to describe you."

"Of course it is. Shall we gather the others and take our treasure to Reverend Nesta, bless her tiny fingers?"

"Yes. And pray that they shed some light on Whitebrooke's guilt. They could be entirely unrelated. He won't have written down 'I am a Crunorix priest' and sent it to Newbridge, will he?"

"Perhaps not. However, Sebastian was certain that we would want Nesta to read these."

"And you trust him to know what will help us?"

"Well, he and I have a certain understanding, you know. In any case, I had just told this brilliant story about a card player bluffing and revealing his cards too soon, and Sebastian picked up on it right away."

"A card player?"

"Yes. You had to be there, Ro."

"I am very pleased I was not. There is shit on your robes, by the way."

"We all have to take risks," Gwydion declared grandly, and refused to say any more, secure in his place in the pantheon of heroes.

***

The rain relented as dusk gently descended over the farmlands south of Bandirma. A heavy, orange glow seared the clouds along the western horizon and painted the sheer cliffs of Bandirma with a thousand gleaming sparks of light. White mist clung to the fields and curled lazily amongst the trees that covered the distant hills, each rank growing hazier until they appeared to glow.

High on the side of the hill perched a small ledge carved into the solid stone of the cliff. Long ago, builders had deepened the ledge, raised a low stone wall around the outer edge, and smoothed the ground. An old statue of the Martyr stood in the center, contemplating the wide, southern view.

THE MARTYR'S TEARS

The shrine had been abandoned generations ago. The statue was terribly weathered, her features smoothed by centuries of wind and rain. Dirt and stones had trickled down the cliff above and clustered around her feet in silent worship. The outer wall had crumbled in one spot and left a crack wide enough to see through. A gentle breeze curled through the gap and rippled the puddles that lapped around the base of the statue.

"To the unknowing, that is peace," Faron's rich voice washed over the shrine. He stood at the low wall, arms folded across his chest as he took in the vista. Faron had donned his thick, grey cloak over his robes, and stood with feet braced wide, as if ready to claim the land for his own. He turned his back on the valley, and a broad smile split his face. "But it is a façade. A vortex lurks beneath our feet, my friends."

"This makes you happy?" Roland asked. He sat on a cracked stone near the cliff and laid his long sword across his thighs. The polished steel caught the evening light and shone as if it had been pulled from the forge moments before, and Roland's pale hair caught the blaze and turned white.

"The challenge stirs my blood," Faron replied, and he adjusted his cloak to drape in a dignified fall of cloth across his shoulders.

"The sooner this is over, the better," Rowenna's voice was strained.

"This is much better than meeting in our rooms," Gwydion announced, smearing mud across the edge of a paving stone with his boot. "Nice and dry and warm, and with wine to drink. Yes, thank goodness we came up here."

"What we must discuss should not be overheard," Roland reminded him sternly.

"Well, that is certainly not going to happen up here, I'll give you that."

Rowenna knelt at the statue's feet and gently wiped away a layer of wet leaves and grime, freeing her sandaled toes for another season. She then rose and did the same for the Martyr's face and hands, smoothing away the errant grime of winter as if wiping tears from her cheeks.

THE MARTYR'S TEARS

"Shall we, before we catch cold?" Gwydion prompted the others. "Why are we not simply taking these messages of Whitebrooke's to Reverend Nesta?"

"You trust Karsha Hali that much?" Faron asked. "We have only his word that Reverend Whitebrooke is a Crunorix priest."

"Hmmm, not quite, my lord," Gwydion corrected Faron. "We know quite a bit more than that, don't we? Only Whitebrooke can decipher the fuil crunor rituals. Only he claims to have seen the proof that Karsha Hali was responsible for the rituals. Only he claims to have seen the proof that Lady Danielle participated. Only he lives to report what happened in the Mountain. And yet we know from Lady Danielle that the rituals do not reveal who cast them, as Whitebrooke claims, and we hear from Reverend Meara that no one can decipher the rituals and that Whitebrooke knows nothing of her latest efforts. That he has banned her from the stone chamber in the archives, a chamber to which he has the only key, making him the only one who could have opened it on the day Benno was murdered.

"And none of that even touches on the ridiculous assertion that Lady Danielle is also a Crunorix priest. It's laughable. What did Karsha Hali call it, Ro?"

"A terrible lie."

"Exactly," Gwydion said.

"It damns him." Roland ceased polishing his sword and leaned against the stone at his back.

"It is damning," Faron corrected. "It is not proof."

"It is enough," Roland disagreed.

"That is what they said of Lady Danielle," Faron reminded them mildly.

Roland scowled and stood, returning his sword to its scabbard with a snap, while Faron waited silently, the breeze playing idly with his long, dark hair and the hem of his cloak, and his gaze weighed on Gwydion.

"Sir Killock searched Whitebrooke's rooms, and found no proof," Faron pointed out.

"Yes, and Killock is usually such a good finder," Gwydion agreed. "But, and I say this with all respect, how would he have any idea what to search for? What are the signs of a Crunorix?" he wondered. "Rituals and sacrifices, but those must be hidden, and even if Killock found a tome on fuil crunor, it could merely be the signs of the research Whitebrooke pursued. Killock only saw their works in the Black Grave, he doesn't know what they look like when they are the insidious poison concealed within the shell of a normal life.

"Faron, you are right, none of what I have said is proof, of course," Gwydion smiled thinly. "But I am not sure we really have much time for niceties. Let's go and find Whitebrooke and chuck him in the dungeon. Before the Queen shows up and decides to do the same to all of us. What do you say, Ro? Sounds like a lark."

"Being right about Whitebrooke and leaving him free is far worse than being wrong and letting him sit in a cell for a few days," Rowenna decided.

"Hmmm, that's a much better reason than mine," Gwydion admitted. "Let's say that, if someone asks."

"It is an expedient answer, but that does not make it a just one," Faron said solemnly. "Your conjecture does not explain why the Crunorix priest would have done the things he did, let alone tie those motives to Reverend Whitebrooke."

"Actually, we thought about that on our trip from the Mountain," Gwydion revealed grandly. "You tell him, Ro, it was you who first thought of this."

Rowenna finished her ministrations and faced the others. "I was thinking of what we said, all those days ago when we stood on Tuireadh Cnoc. We wondered if the Crunorix priest was desperate, or perhaps insane. 'Both' was what you said, Gwydion, and of course, that could still be true."

"Where did your thoughts lead you?" asked Faron.

"Well, they didn't, because I didn't know who to apply them to at the time. But let us say it is Reverend Whitebrooke, so what then can we determine? What did Reverend Whitebrooke gain from each of these actions? And where do they all lead?"

"Killing Benno threw the Council into disarray, and Whitebrooke was in position to take advantage. He guided them into blaming Karsha Hali and Danielle. He also gained the Bishop's Ring," Gwydion interjected.

"So that only he could speak with God," Faron murmured.

"Yes. But perhaps just as crucially, the Bishop's Ring would allow him to open the doors to the Mountain," Rowenna pointed out. "Blaming Danielle also did more than just conceal him. If that was all he wanted, then Karsha Hali would have sufficed. No, blaming Danielle gave him the Martyr's Blade. Whitebrooke isn't desperate. He's driven. Everything he's done furthers his goal."

"It is very tidy, isn't it?" Gwydion said excitedly. "He needed the ring to open the Mountain, and he needed the Blade. And as soon as he had both he travelled to the Mountain, and God was killed while he was there. But why did he need God dead? Perhaps it was this tree He guarded?"

"Perhaps," agreed Roland. "But whatever the reason, I believe we are closing in on his true goal."

"So, Faron," Gwydion smiled at the Templar. "My answer is yes, I do trust Karsha Hali, not because of his charming ways, but because all my reason and all that we have found points to the same conclusion Karsha Hali arrived at. And that is why I trust that whatever is in these messages will help bring Whitebrooke to justice. Now, can we take the messages to Nesta and try to convince her that Whitebrooke is not the person he claims to be?"

"Reverend Nesta already doubts," Faron assured them. "It is Maeglin we must convince, and he has a will of steel."

"Then let us hope these messages contain something to persuade him," Roland laughed sharply, a dry sound of rasping metal.

"Very well," Faron agreed. "We shall take the messages, and our suspicions, to Nesta."

"Now, correct?" Gwydion smiled as he felt his fingers tingle with excitement. "And I get to talk."

***

"We thought it crucial that you see these right away." Gwydion passed the small message parchments to Nesta.

Nesta took the parchments, gazing with bemusement at the Templars encircling her desk. Gwydion merely nodded his head in stern surety. Nesta gave them another moment of examination, then perched her spectacles on her round nose and peered at the messages.

Gwydion watched the high priestess closely as she read. An instant of confusion, then sudden understanding, and she began a much more attentive reading, holding her place with a precisely placed finger as her brow wrinkled in concentration. Concentration transformed into astonishment, then a scowl of anger, and Gwydion knew the contents had set the stage perfectly. *Bless you Sebastian, you boney old bird.*

Nesta set the parchments on her desk's blotter and pulled her hands away, hiding them in her lap, and she peered over her spectacles at the Templars in suspicion.

"Do you know what these say?"

"No, your Reverence," Gwydion shook his head seriously. "How could we? No, we are here to discuss something of grave importance with you." Gwydion paused dramatically, unable to help himself. "We have uncovered the Crunorix priest."

"Have you, indeed?" Nesta folded her spectacles and held them in her lap. "I have heard this before."

"You have, and yet the stories we have been told make less sense the more they are considered. As I am sure you have noted, yourself." Gwydion decided that Nesta's stern silence was all the agreement he was likely to get, and pressed on quickly. "And so we have probed these assertions, sought out the truth behind the tales, treachery, and deception."

"And?"

"It's Reverend Whitebrooke." Rowenna spoke softly, but her words filled the study, hard as steel.

"Reverend Whitebrooke?" Nesta's thin eyebrows arched sharply. But Gwydion saw a tightening in her lips that told him she was not as surprised as she acted, and she could not stop a quick glance to the message scrolls on the desk in front of her.

Ahhh, she did suspect, or at least, she doubted what Whitebrooke has told her. And the messages may not confirm our accusation, but whatever they do convey, they reinforce it.

"Yes, Whitebrooke," Rowenna repeated flatly. "To begin with, any story that claims Danielle had anything to do with aiding the Crunorix, betraying the Temple, or harming Benno is a lie. It has been said before, but it is no less true for its repetition. And knowing that, I have questioned every word the man who spread that lie has spoken."

"It may be difficult to believe, but we have no way to know," Nesta shook her head, unimpressed.

"Were you allowed to speak with Danielle?" Faron's resonant voice sounded merely curious.

"No," Nesta hesitated, "no, I was not."

"Driven away, before her voice could be heard. What could she have told you?"

"Are we being rhetorical, dear?" Nesta snapped, but again her gaze sought out the parchment, and Gwydion saw her lips tighten in disapproval. *Interesting.*

"No, your Reverence," Gwydion assured her. "Listen to what we have uncovered."

Gwydion spoke quietly, laying out all that they had discovered, and all that they had surmised, quickly and precisely, the low throb of contained anger lending a keen edge to his words. And when he was done Rowenna began to speak, explaining precisely how every action Whitebrooke had taken revealed his true purpose.

Nesta sat silently through it all, her hands resting in her lap, her green eyes searching the faces that surrounded her. And when Rowenna had finished speaking, the high priestess carefully placed her spectacles on the blotter and frowned at them as she gathered her thoughts, and Gwydion knew they had not convinced her.

"It is all conjecture, as much as the claims against Karsha Hali and Danielle," Nesta smiled apologetically.

"Not all," Gwydion pointed out reasonably. "His claim to be able to tell who created each ritual. It was Revered Meara who told us that she had found no such thing, and that Whitebrooke had not even talked to her about her research. Are we to assume he found this knowledge on his own, then did not share it with the person he instructed to examine the rituals? And it is not conjecture that he controls the only key to the room in which the first ritual took place. You heard that from Meara yourself, your Reverence." Gwydion took a breath and decided to gamble. "Then there's that..." and he pointed to the message scrolls on the desk.

"Yes, there is that," Nesta agreed, and she skewered Gwydion with a penetrating stare. "Are you sure you don't know what they say?"

"No, your Reverence."

"Well, you are a bloody good guesser. They do not speak to the points you just made, not directly, but they certainly raise questions that must be answered."

"Shall we ask them, and demand answers?"

"Yes, dear, but this is something for the whole Council to hear."

Nesta tidied her desk, walked briskly to the door, and issued orders to her aides waiting outside. "Find the other Councilors, and tell them to please come immediately to the Chamber." Nesta faced the Templars and indicated the door. "Are you coming?"

The Councilors arrived quickly and took their seats, all save Sebastian, who sent word he would not be attending. Whitebrooke was the last of them, and he strode to his chair with a dark scowl across his face.

"I trust there is good reason for this summons," Whitebrooke growled. "I have had to interrupt a delicate divining that will not be easily replicated."

"There is," Nesta assured him, then turned to the acolyte who had been sent to find Sir Maeglin, and who had returned alone. "Where is Sir Maeglin? This concerns him, as well."

"His officers say he left early this morning, ma'am, and they don't expect him back until tonight."

"Very well," Nesta dismissed the messenger. "Sir Roland," she called to the knight. "If you wouldn't mind..." and she indicated the center of the dais.

The Templar walked slowly to the spot and faced the ring of chairs.

"Sir Roland," Nesta began, "do you know a man by the name of Calder?"

If the knight was surprised by the question he did not show it, hesitating for only a heartbeat before answering. "I do. The Calder I knew was sent to me for training as a knight."

"Did he have the skills to become a knight?"

"He did. He was a skilled swordsman, and a better woodsman. I sent him to train with Sir Killock as a ranger."

"What happened to Calder?"

"Sir Killock threw him out of the Temple."

"Why?"

"He was vicious, remorseless. A dangerous man. He attacked a man over a spilled drink."

"And that is when Sir Killock expelled him?"

"Yes, and we sent him to the sheriff in irons."

Nesta sighed and tapped the tight roll of the message parchments the Templars had given her on the arm of her chair. "I am very sorry to tell you that he was not, in the end, expelled from the Temple."

"He wasn't?"

"No. He was recruited back in, for a group that is as closely a guarded secret as anything in the archives. A group whose duty is to take care of problems that cannot be solved in any other way, and yet the solution is something that the Temple cannot sanction."

"You mean assassins," Roland said the word flatly, but Gwydion felt it twist in his stomach and heard a sharp intake of breath from his sister beside him. Most of the Council appeared equally shocked, with open mouths and ashen skin. All but Whitebrooke, Gwydion noticed. The Archivist's scowl had deepened, and his beard bristled as he stared at Nesta, but he was clearly not surprised by the news that the Temple was secretly employing people to do exactly what they had always condemned as unforgivable. Roland bowed his head in thought, then raised his gaze to Nesta's. "You are saying that Sir Killock and I trained an assassin."

"Many," Nesta told the knight, and Gwydion saw Roland's shoulders slump. "Those you train as rangers, and as... other agents... leave the training with many of the skills they will require. It is only a question of finding those with the right nature. Some you find for us and expel. Some we find ourselves, and we convince them to withdraw from service."

"Who? Who finds them? Who instructs them? Who knows of this?" Reverend Dougal was furious, and he banged his fist on the arm of his chair with each demand.

"Bishop Benno. Every Bishop knew. And Reverend Whitebrooke, for the Archivist keeps the codes and records their actions. And there must always be a third Councilmember, which was me."

"The two of you should resign *immediately*," Dougal spluttered, pointing a finger shaking with rage at Nesta and Whitebrooke. "This is unforgivable!"

"We can't all live in a tower, Dougal," Whitebrooke rumbled. "The Temple deserves better guardians than that. The world demands it."

"Unforgivable," Dougal insisted, pronouncing each syllable. "And if either of you thinks that you have a chance at becoming our next bishop, you should know that the Convocation will never vote for—"

"They are not going to know," Nesta interrupted him, "because no one here is going to tell anyone. Now then, this is not the time to discuss succession, I think we can all agree."

"Did He know?" Rowenna asked quietly.

"My mind tells me He must have," Nesta said sadly. "But my heart tells me He could not have. Benno was always cautious never to discuss it with Him, in any case."

"Nesta, why are you telling us this?" asked Reverend Hayley.

"Because Calder has found Lady Danielle, and it is Calder whom Reverend Whitebrooke ordered to kill her."

"You son of a bitch," Sir Roland spat into the stunned silence that followed Nesta's announcement.

THE MARTYR'S TEARS

"That is absurd!" Whitebrooke bellowed, and a chorus of shouts and commands filled the room, cries for reason mixing with strident calls for order.

"Is it?" Nesta asked amidst the chaos, and she held up the messages. "Your order, Reverend Whitebrooke, and the reply from Calder that he had found her in Greymouth. Perhaps you can explain why you sent this order, when we had agreed that no harm was to come to Lady Danielle? When the search had already been called off? Why was it so crucial to you to silence her?"

"Absurd!" Whitebrooke bellowed again, and he rose from his chair.

"I do not believe it is," Nesta said simply. "Councilors, Templars, I call for Reverend Whitebrooke's arrest and immediate confinement for daring to issue these murderous orders in direct violation of this Council's wishes."

"Damn your eyes!" Whitebrooke cursed. "How dare you!"

"Second," Reverend Liadán said clearly, and Whitebrooke suddenly became deathly silent, staring at the priestess in fury.

"Guards!" Nesta called, and the wide doors to the chamber opened and two knights wearing polished steel and wielding long spears entered the chamber.

"I am the one who will lead this Temple into the future!" Whitebrooke found his voice again, and he jabbed his thick finger at the Councilors. "Not you, with your pathetic faith in the teachings of a fraud, and you will regret siding with that bitch against me."

"We will see," Roland promised, and he stepped toward Whitebrooke. The Archivist desperately tugged at his robes, groping for the hilt of his own sword trapped beneath them, and Gwydion hoped that the priest would find it in time. *Then it will be over.*

But Roland's blade whispered from its sheath long before Whitebrooke found his own. The bright steel of Roland's sword blazed in the lantern light as he held it still as a shaft of light above his head, ready to strike, his pale stare locked on Whitebrooke's hand.

THE MARTYR'S TEARS

Whitebrooke froze, glaring furiously at the Templar. For a heartbeat there was no sound, not even a breath, and then Whitebrooke abandoned the search for his sword and yanked his robes roughly into place.

"You are all fools," he growled.

"Take him to the cells," Roland ordered, and the guards swiftly disarmed the Archivist and ushered him from the room. Whitebrooke strode ahead, as if they merely escorted him, his robes twisting in his wake as he swept his dark gaze across the chamber. As Whitebrooke's scowl settled on Gwydion, the Templar could not resist answering with a satisfied grin and a twist of his hand in farewell, but he could not deny the relief he felt as Whitebrooke finally looked away.

"Bloody marvelous," Gwydion whispered. He turned to Rowenna, and a wide smile burst across his face. "That was amazing. I think I shall go and kiss old Sebastian right on his beak."

But Rowenna paid no attention to her brother, and faced Nesta, her eyes shining with anguish. "Is Danielle dead?"

Nesta shook her head sadly. "No, but they have found her, and it will not be long, now."

Wyn

Wyn awoke with the fine hairs on the back of her neck raised and her fingers tingling. The night was long past its mid-point, and the fire they had banked in the kitchen's wide hearth had subsided to a hot glow of embers that did little to light the room.

She lay as still as ice, listening for the sound that had awakened her. Danielle breathed quietly beside her, slowly and evenly, an occasional pop from the fire cracked as the wood smoldered, and the faintest of echoes called from the far-away wind as it moaned around the towers of the abandoned keep, but otherwise the kitchen was as silent as it was dark.

Wyn waited a few more heartbeats, then slowly rolled onto her hands and knees. She bent low over Danielle, and gently woke her with a whisper and a finger over her lips.

"Someone's here," she breathed in Danielle's ear, and the noblewoman nodded silently, her wide eyes reflecting the glow of the fire.

Wyn slipped from the blankets and quickly pulled on her boots, never taking her gaze from the deep shadows by the room's door.

"Boots and cloak, in case we have to make a run for it," Wyn whispered, and Danielle quickly followed Wyn's example, staying as quiet as she could.

A faint echo of a sound caught the edge of Wyn's hearing, the chime of metal on stone. *Gotcha.*

Wyn led the way to the door and slipped into the dark hallway beyond. But she stopped after only two steps as she caught a slight scent of oil.

A shape stirred within the shadows in the narrow hallway, a hooded form that moved with only the faintest whisper of cloth. Wyn had only a heartbeat to react.

She lunged with her dirk and the point tore through cloth and scraped across hard leather as the hooded form twisted away from her. Wyn spun after her foe, diving to the floor as a blade sighed through the air in an arc over her head.

She whirled into the hooded figure's legs and unleashed a sweeping kick that caught him in the side of the knee. His legs buckled and Wyn heard a grunt of pain as he stumbled to the ground.

Wyn rolled to her feet and leapt after the fallen figure, but her legs were too slow and a heavy kick to her midriff drove the air from her lungs and threw her into the stone wall behind. Wyn hissed in pain and rolled to her feet, dirk ready, as the hooded figure scrambled upright. The faint light from the kitchen caught the edge of a long sword in his hand, but Wyn could not make out any details of his face or clothes, only that he was tall and moved as fast as a snake.

Danielle threw herself onto his back, arms wrapped around his shoulder and neck. The impact knocked him to one knee, and Danielle clung to him as he thrashed and twisted to free himself. He threw a vicious elbow over his shoulder and caught Danielle on the side of her head, and she fell to her knees as he wrenched free of her grasp.

Wyn darted forward and stabbed twice with the dirk, sliding the point deep into his side over his hip. He shouted in pain and twisted away, and Wyn's third strike was blocked to the side by a parry that nearly wrenched the knife from her fingers. Wyn spun with the impact and her leg flashed out and there was a crunch of breaking bone as her boot caught him in the face. The hooded man staggered backward, clutching at his shattered nose. His legs gave way and he crashed into the wall and sprawled to the floor. Wyn landed on his back an instant later, driving her knees cruelly into his ribs, and she grabbed for the back of his head. But her bandaged fingers made her fumble, and she could not get a grip on his hood or the hair underneath.

She realized she did not need to. He was not moving, his body lay still. Wyn jabbed him with her dirk to make sure, but he did not respond, and she rose, disappointed.

Wyn hurried to Danielle. The noblewoman clambered to her feet, rubbing the side of her head gently.

"Oh, my poor head," Danielle groaned. "I shall have a lump, I am certain of it."

"Can you walk?" Wyn asked anxiously. "We need to get out of here, in case he had friends. They'll have heard this ruckus unless they're deaf as a post."

"I can, but should we not search him before we go? He may have weapons or supplies we can use, or even an indication of who he is," Danielle said.

"Grab his sword, then, but—" Wyn heard the creak of wood an instant before the twang of string, and had already leapt before the arrow ripped through the air. She collided with Danielle and knocked her from her feet, shielding her as they fell to the floor. Danielle cried out as the arrow tore cloth and flesh as it passed before cracking off the stone wall behind them.

Wyn rolled toward the archer, but before she could reach him there was the scuff of boots on stone from a different direction, and the sound of steel sliding from a scabbard.

Wyn hauled desperately on Danielle's arm. "Back to the kitchen!" Wyn hissed. Danielle stumbled to her feet, clutching her left arm high near her shoulder, and Wyn dragged her back through the door into the kitchen.

Another arrow snapped off the stone doorway as they ducked through, and footsteps followed quickly after them.

Wyn snatched an iron hook from its hanger and hurled it through the doorway, and took satisfaction as she heard a yell of surprise. *That should slow them down, I hope.*

Danielle regained her feet and the two women scampered across the kitchen, crouching low between the heavy tables as they raced to the door on the far side. An arrow struck the wooden door as they passed through with the dull sound of an axe hewing a tree.

They raced down the darkened passageway, neither knowing nor caring where it led, other than away from their assailants, until at last the sounds of pursuit had quieted. Wyn paused in a long chamber and became perfectly still, poised as she let the voices of the ancient tower come to her. Wyn focused past her thundering heartbeat, past her burning, panting breaths, past the small noises of Danielle waiting quietly next to her. But she heard no sign of their attackers.

"They're coming, slow and careful," Wyn whispered to Danielle.

"Is that bad or good?"

"Mostly bad." Wyn glanced about the chamber, seeking the darkest shadows and the best places for ambush. "It means they're not just bandits here for loot and a bit of tail. They know what they're doing, and so far, they've not made many mistakes."

"What shall we do? Do we fight them? I did not have a chance to pick up that man's sword."

"No. That first one fought well, and we got a bit lucky to surprise him. I don't want to fight two of them." Wyn turned to Danielle and took her hand. "Listen, Dani, here's the good part. Careful means slow, and as long as they think we're hiding and fighting back, they'll stay careful. But that gives us a chance to get away."

"So, we run?"

"Mostly. They'll figure out we're running and then careful goes out the window, so we need to trick them, make them think we're hiding to get a head start." Wyn gave Danielle's hand a reassuring squeeze. "So you head to the boat, fast as you can, and get her ready to sail. I'll lurk here and make sure they want to stay careful, then I'll join you at the boat, and we get clean away."

"You are going to fight them both, alone?" Danielle's whisper was a hiss of concern and denial.

"Nothing like that, never fear," Wyn lied. "I'll just make sure they spend the rest of the night jumping at shadows instead of chasing us."

"Wyn, I am not going to leave you to fight while I run away." Danielle's mouth set in a stern line and her eyebrows furrowed. "No more than you would leave me."

"Of course you wouldn't," Wyn agreed. "But this isn't a fight, it's an escape, and that means running. Don't worry, they'll not catch a glimpse of me. The Queen of Thieves, remember?"

There was nothing Danielle could say to that, as Wyn knew very well, and the noblewoman was forced to reluctantly nod her head and acquiesce to the plan.

"I'll see you at the boat, then," Wyn whispered.

Danielle gently stroked Wyn's cheek, then kissed her, Danielle's lips soft and urgent. "At the boat," she repeated quietly, and she released Wyn and ran from the chamber.

Wyn drew in a long breath, savoring the tingle that still throbbed in her lips from Danielle's touch.

Maker's breath, she sighed, astonished. *Well, now I know why all those silly knights are laying down their lives in those ridiculous reads Dani likes so much.*

Wyn took another deep breath, then let out everything she would not need for the fight ahead in a long exhalation. Fear, pain, exhaustion, worry—all were blown into the chill air. Rage and steel remained, and forged a fiery determination. *All right, you bastards, come and get me.*

Wyn slipped into the passageway that had led them to the long chamber, and found one of the small, dark rooms that they had passed, just a few steps from the end of the passage. She sank into the darkest shadows where the wall had crumbled into a jagged, black stain, and waited.

When the sound came, it was a whisper of an echo, felt more than heard. A stir in the air that brushed against Wyn's ear, and she became one with the stone that she lay against. Her heart slowed, her breath stilled, her body became motionless. Even her thoughts became hard and cold.

The doorway grew darker, and the air stirred as someone entered. There was a slight scuff of leather on stone as a fleck of rock was ground beneath a boot.

Then the presence was gone.

Wyn waited only a few heartbeats. She silently unfolded from her shadow and flowed to the doorway. She could see her pursuers, black shapes silhouetted against the dim light of the long chamber as they reached the end of the passageway. They paused there, peering into the yawning shadows of the chamber, wary of the perfect ambush spots that lay in front of them.

Wyn glided through the darkness toward them. Anger pulsed through her body, each throb accompanied by a flare of rage. Danielle's cry of pain as the arrow tore through her arm. The singing whisper as the blade had sought Wyn in the dark. *They hurt her. They tried to kill me. They tried to kill Danielle.* At the last moment, one of the men stiffened slightly, some inner sense warning him of the hunter's approach, but it was far too late.

Wyn's dirk rasped gently as it passed across the man's throat, and his gurgling cough shattered the stillness. She planted her boot in the small of his back and kicked hard. He staggered forward, clutching at his neck as blood shot through his fingers and splattered against the stones.

The second man twisted toward his companion and Wyn stabbed at him. But he reacted more quickly than she could have imagined, somehow sensing the attack from the shadows even as his companion collapsed noisily at his feet. Wyn's dirk tore through his clothes, the sharp point slicing through and into his ribs under his arm. But his reaction had saved his life. The knife jammed into the hard leather of his breastplate instead of his unprotected neck, and the armor blunted the attack.

The man struck back before Wyn could try again. His sword hissed over her shoulder as she threw herself sideways, then rang as it impacted with the stone floor as she rolled away. He was fast, and his blows were controlled and precise, and Wyn knew she faced a skilled swordsman.

She lunged to her left, then spun to her right, hoping for an opening, but his sword flickered through the shadows in front of her face, and she danced out of range, her dirk held ready to strike.

He advanced cautiously, using his sword's length to his advantage, thrusting and jabbing to keep Wyn on her toes as she ducked and weaved, hunting for an opening. She could feel her legs starting to weaken, far too soon, and her breath began to labor. He must have sensed it as well, for he began to press, his strikes coming more frequently, forcing her to react without pause.

Wyn snarled in frustration and willed her tired legs to obey. She let his sword jab past her shoulder instead of dodging away, and lunged as quick as thought, but he twisted to the side and shielded his head with his left arm, and her blade tore a long wound across his forearm instead of his face.

Wyn leapt after him. She spun into a high kick, but it was too slow, too low, and he caught it against his ribs and clamped down across her calf with his right arm, pinning her leg. He instantly stepped into Wyn and swung a heavy left fist that brushed against the side of her head as she ducked, her leg still trapped under his other arm. Wyn jabbed and felt the knife strike home into his abdomen, but she was off-balance, the blow weak with only the strength of her arm behind it, and the blade did not penetrate his armor.

He twisted to his left, and his backhand glanced off the back of her head and sent shards of glass pain stabbing through her skull. Then he charged, driving her backward with her leg still trapped high under his arm.

Wyn let him push, curled upward, grabbed a handful of hair and hood with her free hand, and slashed the dirk across his face. The tip dug into his cheek and tore a long gash before he could flinch away. He pulled back, straining against her grasp, and she let him hoist her high into the air before smashing her knee into his face. He cried out and desperately pushed her away, and Wyn felt pain lance through her weak left hand as he tore free. Wyn arched backward and rolled to her feet.

Blood dripped from his gashed arm and ruined face, but now he advanced purposefully with vicious cuts of his sword that left no opening. Wyn was once again forced to spin away, each dodge slower and harder than the one before as her legs burned with exhaustion.

So she ran.

A quick feint forward to make him guard, then she bolted into the dark passageways. Surprise gave her a head start, but it was a slim lead, and she could hear his boots pounding on the stone floor behind her.

Wyn reached the entrance hall, its wide pillars ghostly in the faint light that filtered through the high windows. The main doors stood waiting for her, but she ignored them and raced for the stone stairs that curved toward the ceiling from the center of the room. There was no use simply running to the boat—it would draw her pursuer to their one chance of escape, and now that her ambush had failed to eliminate their attackers, escape was what was needed. She had wounded her opponent, but she knew she could not overcome him, with her failing strength and his longer weapon and thick armor, not unless she got very lucky.

An arrow ricocheted from the stone banister of the stairs, spraying her with splinters as it snapped past her face. Wyn cursed and dove to the ground, sprawling across the stair landing. A second arrow flashed between two of the stone pillars of the banister and struck the stair above her head. Wyn scrambled desperately up the stairs on hands and feet, listening for the creak of his bow, throwing herself sideways just before the harsh twang of the string's release. She reached the top of the stairs, flung herself over the last step, and was instantly up and running again.

Another staircase loomed out of the darkness and she took it, vaulting upward in great bounds. She could hear her pursuer on the stairs below, his boots echoing on the cold stone, but her lead had grown while he stopped to shoot at her, and she was far enough ahead to stay concealed behind the switchback of the stairs.

Then she ran out of stairs. Gratefully, she hurdled the last few steps and raced down the short passage beyond as she gasped for every breath and her legs burned with fatigue.

A dozen quick steps and she reached a small wooden door. Wyn burst through it onto a narrow parapet high on the side of the tower. A thin layer of snow crusted the rotten ice that covered the narrow path, and the wind swirled and eddied as it gusted past the tower. Wyn scurried around the tower, peering over the edge into the night as she went. A quarter of the way around she found what she was hoping for. The tall, peaked roof of one of the wings of the tower rose to within an easy jump of the parapet. Its crest was pointed, and jagged shapes lined it, but it offered a quick way down.

Wyn vaulted the parapet and dropped to the roof. She landed lightly, her boots scrambling for purchase on the ice-covered slate for an instant before she regained her footing.

She sprinted along the narrow crest of the roof as snow stung her cheeks and the wind sighed as it passed through the twisted iron spikes that adorned the crenellations. Bottomless gulfs loomed on either side, disappearing into darkness beyond whirling flakes of dancing snow. Wyn pushed herself faster, her shoulders itching with anticipation of an arrow strike.

She leapt from the ridge and landed on the steep slope of the roof, sliding on hip and thigh as she accelerated toward the edge. Wyn twisted back and forth, keeping her boots free from the thick snow. Then the narrow ledge of stone at the end of the sloped roof was there, and she planted a boot and vaulted through the swirling snow toward a dimly seen mass that loomed on the other side of the chasm.

A steeply pitched metal roof emerged from the snow, the peak of a small turret on the side of the grim wall she flew toward. Wyn hit the peak of the tower and let her speed tumble her down the incline, then burst from the roll at the last moment and sprang over the jagged iron spikes that lined the edge of the roof. Her body knifed through the air and she spun as she passed the edge, extending perfectly to grab two of the spikes as they flashed by.

Pain shot up her left arm from her wrist as she swung her momentum into her hold. Her fingers could not hold on and slipped from the spike. She clung desperately with her right hand as her swing twisted her into the unyielding stone wall of the turret. The impact drove the breath from her lungs but she did not relinquish her grasp.

She thrashed against the stone wall of the turret with her boots, forcing traction from the sheer surface. Wyn pulled herself up using her good hand, then screamed a curse as the old iron groaned and twisted under her weight and ripped free from its rivets. She dropped a half of her body length before the nest of spikes caught, creaking, on the next brace.

Wyn held still, slowly twisting as she dangled from the end of the iron spike, her fingers clinging to the smooth shape. She could feel the vibration as the remaining brace pulled against its rusted rivets, and her fingers slipped down the spike a hand's-breadth before her grip regained its purchase.

"Knew I could make it," Wyn hissed through her teeth. She peered beyond her dangling feet. The turret wall fell into utter darkness without any ledge or interruption of any kind, but the massive stone blocks were rough-hewn, and might give her purchase. She delicately probed with her boots until they found the tiny cracks left between the stones. Wyn freed her left hand from its bandages with her teeth, jammed her fingers into a crack, then at last released her grip on the iron spike and began creeping across the face of the wall like a spider, hanging from her fingertips while her feet probed for their next purchase.

The weathered stones made for excellent hand-holds and Wyn quickly moved around the turret to the angle where it joined the main wall. Once there the climb down was simple, as she could wedge herself into the corner as she descended.

But it was tiring, and she was already exhausted from her escape. Sweat trickled between her shoulder blades while ice froze on her eyelashes, and her left arm throbbed with a dull ache that started in her wrist and extended into her elbow. Wyn gritted her teeth and cursed in a steady stream that never faltered.

Wyn dropped the final distance to the ground and brushed off her hands in satisfaction. Her fingers and face were numb with cold while her arms and legs and lungs burned with fire, and her hip and shoulder throbbed where she had collided with the wall, but she was satisfied. This pain was familiar, this pain would heal. She could barely see the roof from where she had leapt, and she had no idea where she was in relation to the main doors, so she reasoned that her pursuer would likewise have no idea where to go to find her again.

She jogged along the wall until she found a low tunnel and scrambled through it away from the central tower. The tunnel led to a small postern gate set on the side of the wall overlooking the river. A narrow trail led down the steep slope and Wyn followed it, huddled inside her cloak as she tripped and stumbled in the darkness and snow that concealed the path. She reached the woods after an eternity on the track and she hurried between the dark trunks as the trees creaked under their load of snow.

Stone statues loomed in the dark and welcomed her to the river trail. Wyn chuckled as she passed the statue with the thorns growing between its legs, and she knew she was nearly to the boat.

Danielle was waiting for her, pacing on the flat deck in front of the mast. When Wyn emerged from the dark forest Danielle leapt from the prow of the boat and wrapped Wyn in her arms, relief washing across her face.

"I was about to come searching for you," she whispered in Wyn's ear.

"No need," Wyn tried to smile through her chattering teeth. "I led them a merry chase, just like we planned. But I think it's time we were off."

"You are unharmed?"

"Bumps and bruises. Some will definitely need kissing, later."

"As soon as we are gone, I promise," Danielle's smile beamed relief.

They boarded their boat and Wyn shoved them free of the bank with a boat pole while Danielle raised a small scrap of sail, enough to push them slowly from the inlet. Wyn watched the ruined pier and stone arch recede until there was nothing left to see, then scurried to help raise more sail as they entered the river proper.

The canvas bellied and caught the wind, the boat creaked as it heeled onto its side, and Wyn curled into her cloak next to Danielle on the rough bench as the boat surged across the current and left the tower behind.

Grey light slowly lit the low clouds and revealed the dark silhouettes of the trees along the embankment. Wyn examined her left hand as the light grew, flexing her fingers and turning her hand this way and that, surprised by how small her fingers appeared now that they were free from their cocoon of bandages. Shiny pink skin ran along her little finger and curled in an arc to her elbow, but the skin was smooth and felt normal to touch. *Why does it hurt so bloody much, then? There must be something broken inside, and that won't mend soon, I bet. Still, it's nice to be rid of those bandages so that I can work properly. Except now my fingers are cold.*

Wyn tucked her hands into her cloak and wedged them under her arms. Danielle shifted slightly behind her, and Wyn twisted around in her seat. "Sorry if I was squishing you."

"Not at all," Danielle replied absently, her attention divided between holding the tiller and trying to peel back her cloak from her arm. "It is only that my arm is uncomfortable."

"Let's have a peek, then." Wyn gently folded back Danielle's cloak and frowned in concern as she saw the stain that glimmered wetly down the sleeve of Danielle's tunic. "Martyr's tears, that looks painful. Why did you not say?"

"I had not noticed." Danielle peered at Wyn's fingers as she gently rolled up the sleeve. "The running and the worrying took my mind away, I suppose. It hurts now, though." She bit her lip. "Quite a lot. Would it be frail of me if I started to cry? I do not think I have much choice…"

"Oh, Dani, I think this needs help," Wyn fretted. The arrow had sliced deeply across Danielle's arm, and blood still trickled from the gash. "What should I do? All I know is to wrap it tight."

"It must be stitched, as if you were mending a tear."

Wyn snatched her hands back. "You've seen my clothes, right?"

THE MARTYR'S TEARS

"I have, but it needs to be done, and I will tell you how. It must be easier than opening a lock or lifting a purse. But we should hurry before the pain grows too much."

Wyn took the tiller and guided the boat to the shore, where she found a small, sheltered bank and quickly tied the boat to a tree. Danielle retrieved the small box that had contained the bandages and salves she had used on Wyn's hands from its place in the boat's lockers. The box was sadly empty of anything that could clean or protect Danielle's wound, as they had used all their supplies on Wyn's burns, but it did still have a supply of thread and thin needles. Wyn blanched as she saw the long, silver shapes laying on the cloth that Danielle had unrolled on the boat's table.

They used wine to clean the wound as best as they could, as they had no means of boiling water, and trusted that the needles and thread had been properly prepared before they had been stored in the box. Then Wyn picked up the needle that Danielle had selected.

"As small as you can, please, and deep so they do not tear free," Danielle instructed, her voice trembling despite her best efforts. "Keep the edges tucked in, or else they may fester, and it will leave a smaller scar."

Wyn pushed her hair from her face and leaned close to Danielle's arm. The needle shook as she pressed it to Danielle's skin, and Wyn paused to push her hair away again. "Oooo, Maker, here we go," she breathed, and she began to stitch. Danielle guided her for the first few, but then she turned pale and grew quiet, and Wyn worked diligently in silence. Her tongue became numb where she was biting it and her jaw ached, but she kept going. Her fingers responded with quick, delicate movements, until, sooner than she could believe, Danielle was whispering to tie off the thread, and she was done.

They rested together on the floor of the cabin, Wyn with her back propped against the bulkhead, Danielle resting comfortably in her embrace, and they fell soundly asleep.

***

THE MARTYR'S TEARS

Wyn awoke to the sound of water lapping against the hull and the gentle rustle of trees stirring in the wind. Danielle still slept, warm and soft next to Wyn, and Wyn contented herself with gently stroking Danielle's dark hair, feeling the long, silken locks flow smoothly under her fingers.

When at last Danielle stirred, she simply gave Wyn a sleepy smile and then snuggled alongside her, her free hand seeking Wyn's to entwine their fingers together.

"How is your arm?"

"I think I will survive," Danielle murmured.

They lay in comfortable silence as Wyn traced Danielle's touch up and down her fingers. Wyn wanted to stay curled together forever, with Danielle's head pillowed on her chest, the warmth of Danielle's breath on her neck, and the gentle movement of Danielle's breathing pressing softly against her side. But a thought that had lain dormant deep within her mind began to resurface, and it would not leave her alone. She wrinkled her nose in frustration, but could not drive the thought away.

"Dani…" she began, unable to help herself.

"Yes?"

"Those men who attacked us last night," Wyn continued, and she felt Danielle grow still against her. "Do you remember I said I didn't think they were bandits?"

"I do. You said they were not just after some loot."

"I think I was right."

"This surprises you?"

"Ha ha. I've been thinking. First, why would some baddies be lurking in the middle of nowhere, in a ruin with no loot in it?"

"Perhaps they sought shelter, as we did?"

"After the storm? Anyway, why were they anywhere near the place? There's nothing out here but, well, nothing. Second, they didn't care about any of our stuff. When we ran away, they came right after us. I have a pretty good idea why a bunch of bastards would chase after you even if there was a pile of gold in the way, but it was dark and they couldn't have known they were chasing after the most gorgeous girl in the world, right? All some roaming baddies would have known was that someone had conked one of their gang on the head. Anyway, they weren't chasing after some tail, they were methodical, hunting us.

"Third, they were serious fighters. Mean, yeah, but also well-trained, and they knew how to move. And they didn't give up because they got bloodied, they kept coming."

"If they were not bandits, then who?"

"I think they were after us. I mean, I think they knew exactly who we were, and they followed us there to kill us."

"Followed us? From where?"

"From Greymouth. I think it was the Temple assholes you spotted stalking us in the market. They followed us."

"To kill us?"

"Who knows, but they certainly didn't wait too long to try."

Danielle stayed silent after that, and Wyn bit her tongue to leave Danielle to her thoughts. Finally, when Wyn thought she might possibly burst with the need to blurt something out, Danielle pushed herself against the cabin wall and wrapped her arms around her knees.

"They will never stop, will they?" she asked softly, but now there was fierce anger lurking amongst the quiet words.

"Not until Shitebrooke is done in. He'd have a tough time whispering bullshit into everyone's ears with his throat slit."

"I really thought we were safe." Danielle rested her head against the bulkhead, her eyes closed in weariness. "I thought we had escaped, that no one would be searching for us anymore. But no matter where we go, they would find us, would they not?"

"Probably," Wyn admitted. "Now that they have a trail."

Danielle remained with her eyes closed for a dozen breaths, then she lowered her head and met Wyn's gaze, her eyes sad, but her mouth set in a fierce, determined line.

"No more fleeing, no more hiding," she said. "We must turn and fight, and finish Whitebrooke."

Part Two

Cormac

The bodies swung gently under the twisted branch of an old oak tree, suspended from ropes that creaked painfully as the branch swayed in the wind.

Thick trees loomed over the road and sighed mournfully as they rustled together, but the ravens perched on the corpses had no such sympathies. They croaked angrily amongst themselves as they tore at the exposed faces and hands of the bodies.

Cormac watched the birds gorge themselves. His horse stamped her hoof impatiently in the soft earth of the road, anxious to escape the smell of blood, but Cormac soothed her and she snorted her acceptance.

He dismounted and walked slowly across the road until he stood beneath the bodies. They could not be more than a day old, so fresh was the blood that pooled in the mud beneath them. Both bodies still wore armor, and good winter boots and cloaks. An oddity if they were the victims of bandits, but Cormac doubted that they were.

They had died of arrow wounds, although the arrows themselves had been taken, and the men had been dead by the time they were trussed and hung from the branch, a small mercy. Cormac had seen defeated enemies treated far worse. A sign was hung around the neck of one of the bodies. 'MURDERERS'.

"Whose soldiers are they?" Eilidh asked quietly. She twisted in her saddle, eyes scanning the dense forest around them as her fingers played over the hilt of her sword. "Do you know their sigil?"

"Newbridge." The grey bridge on its blue field was still visible under the brown stains that now defaced it.

"Queen's men."

"Aye, their lord would be vassal to the Queen."

Sir Eilidh nodded, her brow furrowed as she took in the bodies once more. There was no hesitation in her gaze, nor disgust, just appraisal as she considered the corpses. Cormac could practically see the shining armor that she should be garbed in, rather than the simple wool clothes that she currently wore. She sat her horse easily, with straight back and head held high, and her hand never strayed far from the hilt of the sword at her side.

"A strange choice of victims for bandits, surely?"

"Not bandits," Cormac agreed. "Whoever they are, they are not timid."

"No, they are not," Eilidh pointed at the sign. "This is retribution."

Cormac returned to his horse and mounted. Eilidh pondered the bodies in silence as the ravens hoked and ate, and Cormac waited patiently, content to watch her. Eilidh had discarded the bandage that had wrapped her head since Littleford, leaving the long, stitched wound that slashed down her forehead over her right eye proudly exposed. She had gathered her blonde hair into a ragged knot to keep it from falling into her face, and loose ends wafted in the breeze that stirred the trees around them. Her lips were set in a thin line, her strong jaw clenched so that Cormac could see the muscles under her ear twitch as she ground her thoughts, and her high cheekbones caught the dim light that filtered through the trees.

A strong face, Cormac decided. *A warrior's face.*

Eilidh caught his gaze and held it.

"Do you not agree?" Eilidh's voice was sharp.

Cormac felt a smile tug at the corner of his mouth. "Yes, sir."

Eilidh dropped her gaze at that. "Of course you do. I am sorry, it is just..." Eilidh raised her head and took a long breath that released some of the strain that corded the muscles of her neck into long ridges. "It is just that I cannot help but think that this could be more of what we witnessed in Littleford, and in every village since."

Cormac agreed with that as well. They had yet to pass a village on the Rathad an Thuaidh without seeing its temple occupied by soldiers of the local lord, the Temple priests and soldiers held hostage as if they were prisoners of war. Nowhere had they seen the bloodshed that had happened in Littleford, but they regularly saw other signs of fighting. Soldiers and prisoners alike with bandaged wounds, and the remains of pyres that still smelled of ash and smoke. *Why should Newbridge be any different? I remember it as a large town, I would wager its temple was a large one, and likely well-garrisoned.*

"Well, we will find out when we get there," Cormac said, and guided his horse in a wide circle around the bodies and then urged her into an easy canter. Eilidh followed, and they departed to a chorus of croaking ridicule from the ravens.

***

Newbridge stood on the site of an ancient hill fort, built millennia ago by the same forgotten people who had constructed the great henges and placed the standing stones on Tuireadh Cnoc. There was no sign of the fort save for the circular hill upon which the town sprawled. A great earthen ring surrounded the town, pierced by deep culverts to allow access to the hill. The ring was softened by meadows and herds of grazing sheep, but its sides were still steep enough to provide a breathless ride for the town's children when it snowed.

Within the outer ring stood another earthen ring, this one higher than the first, and then another, higher again. The town nestled on the flat spaces behind the rings, three tiers of buildings that rose above the fields.

Cormac and Eilidh rode through the town gates as the light rain that had pattered on their hoods for most of the day finally relented and became a chill mist that congealed around the hill. The streets were mostly deserted in the frozen gloom, as a few locals hurried through the lanes without pause.

Plenty of soldiers, though.

Town guards stood at the gates of each ring and ignored the wet and cold long enough to question visitors passing through the gates. Soldiers in livery that bore the grey and blue of Newbridge patrolled the lanes in pairs and stood watch over the marketplace. The first tavern Cormac approached had no room for them.

"I'm sorry, lad," the tavern keeper wiped her hands on her apron and shook her head consolingly. "Sir Alroy took all my rooms, and his men have the common room. You'll have to try elsewhere."

Cormac guided them through more twisted lanes until they reached the marketplace. The square was quiet, with only a few merchants and farmers peddling their wares to the thin trickle of townsfolk who braved the mist. Cormac ignored the stalls, drawn by a shape at the far end of the marketplace.

Two torches smoked in the damp air on either side of a cage made of black iron suspended from a scaffold. The cage was small, barely the width of a man's shoulders, and much shorter than a man was tall. At least, shorter than the man who was wedged into it. The cage was not wide enough for him to bend his knees, nor tall enough for him to stand upright, so he hunched awkwardly and pressed against the iron bars for support. His skin was torn and raw where his shoulders and back rubbed against the cage, and blood had oozed to form a stain beneath it.

A placard was hung around the man's neck. 'TRAITOR', it read.

Cormac hoped the man was dead, but feared he may yet live. Two soldiers stood sentry on either side of the cage, ignoring the water that ran from their steel helms.

"Who is he?" Cormac grabbed the arm of a boy as he passed.

"One of the rangers," the boy replied as he pulled against Cormac's grip. "They finally caught one."

"What rangers?"

"The ones from the Temple who wouldn't surrender when Sir Alroy took it."

"Did they fight Sir Alroy?"

"Not really, I suppose." The boy gave another tug and then gave up. "They hid in the forest, at first… but now they've been raiding storehouses and burning what couldn't be taken."

Cormac released the boy and he scurried off as Cormac lingered by a stall that was selling a few scrawny rabbits and pigeons. Now at least the bodies in the forest made sense. *Kill one of ours and we kill two of yours. The logic of war.* Once violence began only escalation remained, never compromise, and if the rangers thought to drive off Sir Alroy and his soldiers by depriving them of their food, Cormac knew the people of Newbridge would bear the brunt of the hardship. *Soldiers are always the last to starve.*

Cormac's mouth set in a grim line as he turned his back on the ranger and caught Eilidh's gaze. The knight's face was colorless, her body rigid as she stared silently at the caged prisoner, her eyes dangerous with fury.

Cormac moved to her and stood close, between her and the cage. He rested his hand on her shoulder. Through the thick wool of her cloak and tunic, he could feel the smooth muscles of her shoulder twist and pulse as she gripped her sword.

"There's nothing we can do for him," Cormac murmured, his voice pitched to carry to her ear and no farther. But she did not seem to hear him, and her piercing gaze was unrelenting.

"A cage, damn them," she muttered through lips compressed into a thin line.

"There's nothing we can do," Cormac repeated, still with no effect. He leaned closer and spoke more forcibly. "Eilidh!"

She jerked as if slapped and finally her gaze pulled from the cage and met his. "They tortured him, Cormac. They put him in a cage. Displayed like a criminal, worse, a traitor." Her eyes shone with tears of anger and pain.

"I know." Cormac kept his gaze locked on hers, and she could not glance away. "Eilidh, I know, but there is nothing we can do except die alongside him."

Eilidh shook her head, still rigid with fury, but she turned and strode away, her horse trotting behind her so quick was her step.

Cormac risked one last glance behind him. The soldiers still stood unmoving, seemingly unaware of how close their death had been, and Cormac let his own hand loosen on the hilt of his brother's sword. He patted the neck of his horse and followed Eilidh from the market.

They finally found lodging close to the marketplace. A sign that bore a painting of a befuddled sheep and the carved words 'Damn Ewe' hung over a thick oaken door that opened to the glow of a warm fire and the sound of a raucous fiddle. They pushed through the smoke-filled common room to a bench near the fire.

The Damn Ewe was filled with the roar of conversation shouted over the fiddle. Townsfolk mixed with farmers in town for the market, with a smattering of travelers in the throng. Cheers and the pounding of mugs on the wooden trestles followed each of the fiddler's tunes, and groans met each new tune as it began. The tavern keeper bustled from table to table, scolding the locals and keeping a wary eye on the travelers.

Cormac had finished his meal and started a fresh mug when a man sat down across the table from him.

Their neighbors quietly left without comment and were replaced with the man's companions. Cormac watched them go, finished his mouthful of ale, and waited on his new tablemates.

The two who sat on either side of Cormac and Eilidh were soldiers. Grey steel rings rustled under their thick cloaks, and swords hung from their belts. The knight across from Cormac was younger than his men. He wore a cloak with a fur-lined hood and a padded jacket with the grey-and-blue sigil of Newbridge on its chest. His cloak was held by a silver badge with the Queen's arms engraved on it.

The man deliberately ignored Cormac and Eilidh and made a show of listening to the fiddle until the tune ended. Then he turned casually to Cormac.

"New to town?" he asked disinterestedly. He smoothed his trim mustache as he watched Cormac.

"Yes, m'lord. Arrived not an hour ago."

"And are you passing through? Or staying?"

"Just the night, m'lord."

"Travelers." The man pulled off his black leather gloves and carefully laid them on the table. "You do not have the appearance of merchants."

"No, m'lord," Cormac agreed.

"I'd say you have the bearing of soldiers." The man held Cormac's glance.

"Aye, m'lord," Cormac agreed again, but offered no more.

"Not Queen's men, though, are you. Where did you do your soldiering?"

"I was a soldier, m'lord, but not anymore." Cormac traced a finger across the spiral of five black dots around his left eye. "Served with Duke Thornton in the Ironbacks. Three years, and that was enough snow and ice for me." Cormac kept his voice diligently dull and subservient.

"Three years? Yes, I imagine it would be." The man tapped his fingers on the tabletop as he considered Cormac's story. "And what do you do now that you aren't soldiering?"

"Take messages places. Find people," Cormac lied. It was an easy story to believe. Many soldiers did exactly that when they left the army, working as errand boys or bounty hunters for the highest bidder for their skills.

"I see." The man's fingers stopped tapping. "And which is it that brings you to Newbridge? Hunting or carrying?"

"Carrying, m'lord," Cormac answered easily.

"I see," the man repeated himself. "And what of your lovely companion? Your wife?"

"No, m'lord," Eilidh laughed scornfully. "I'd not take this one."

"Obviously a woman of taste." The noble turned to face Eilidh more directly. "Did you also serve with Duke Thornton?"

"No, m'lord," Eilidh said with a grimace. "It's cold enough down here."

"Indeed it is. Do you also carry messages? Find people?"

"Aye, m'lord, or rather, we do, together. To make sure, as it were."

"Might I see this message, just to confirm you are who you say you are?"

"I'm sorry, m'lord," Cormac shrugged apologetically and tapped the side of his head. "It's in here. If you're going to write it down you might as well send it on a bird, after all."

Cormac waited patiently and offered nothing more. He had been questioned before in various villages across Albyn. Usually by a watchman, or perhaps the constable himself if it were a slow day. Cormac knew he appeared as a man accustomed to fighting, and with no badge or sigil, that made him dangerous. But he had never rated being questioned by a nobleman.

The man rapped the table firmly with his knuckles and stood. "Very well. But I would be disappointed to hear that you were still here at sundown tomorrow. I would take it as a sign that your story was not wholly truthful. That you might be here to create trouble. Am I understood?"

"Yes, m'lord. Leave tomorrow, m'lord."

The man hesitated for a moment, and Cormac wondered if he had not kissed his ass sufficiently. He could usually manage to sound at least neutral when ass kissing. Captain Alistair had always declared that it was Cormac's greatest skill as a soldier. But in the end, the knight appeared satisfied with Cormac's performance and left before he could notice the steel core concealed within Cormac's gaze.

Cormac was glad. He had not been in the mood to embarrass the idiot in front of his men. There were always consequences for doing something like that.

"You did well," Cormac congratulated Eilidh. "I was convinced you were a hardened mercenary."

Eilidh snorted in contempt at her performance, but she could not stop a smile from twitching at the corners of her lips. "I joined the Order of Knights so that I wouldn't have to bend my knee to haughty pricks like him." She shook her head in disbelief. "Yet here I am, still simpering like a little girl."

"A good soldier always knows how to butter up an officer," Cormac said thoughtfully. "Otherwise how else could they get them to stay out of the way? Sir."

Eilidh smiled properly at that and nodded her head in defeat.

The seats around them remained empty while they finished their drinks, as the locals stayed clear of whatever trouble had attracted the attention of the lord and his men. They left the Damn Ewe as soon as they were done, Cormac to return to the marketplace, while Eilidh retrieved their horses from the stables. They needed just a few supplies, some wine, and some oil for the lantern. Food, Cormac could hunt, and the sooner they were gone from Newbridge the better. *Tonight, if possible.* Cormac did not need a bed in a tavern, and he certainly did not need the trouble that being strangers in a town looking for enemies would bring them.

Cormac found wine quickly and purchased a small cask of a bitter swill that reminded him of happy times in the barracks of Irongate. But oil proved more problematic, and he peered about the remaining stalls while considering how necessary the lantern was.

Then he saw her.

At first, he did not recognize her. She was wearing a long cloak with a deep hood, lined with fur, that appeared warm and soft, and a fetching tunic embroidered with silver thread that glinted in the light of the lanterns hung from the stalls. But then she laughed at something the stall owner said to her, and the light caught her smile and her golden hair peeking from her hood, and her laughter echoed brightly through the market.

Cormac walked toward her, unbelieving. She laughed merrily again, leaned close to the merchant, and laid a gentle hand on his arm for support, completely befuddling him. Then she turned and sauntered toward Cormac.

"Wyn?" he called to her.

Wyn glanced at him in surprise, and the color drained from her face and her eyes widened in shock. Her bag dropped to the cobblestones with a thunk.

"Corlath?" her voice trembled, and her hand covered her mouth.

"No, it's Cormac," Cormac reassured her. "Wyn, it's me."

Wyn closed her eyes in relief and color rushed into her face. She grinned joyfully and punched him in the shoulder.

"Damn it, I thought you were your brother! Did you cut your hair?" Wyn punched him again. "It's not funny! You scared me to death."

"If you'd seen your face, you'd know it was funny," Cormac insisted. "I didn't know eyes could get that big."

"Martyr's tears," Wyn rolled her eyes, "I think I had another heart attack."

Cormac gathered Wyn's bag from the ground and carried it for her as they walked through the market. Wyn relented after just a few steps and linked her arm through his and held it tightly.

"What are you doing here?" she asked. "It's so good to see you! Where's Killock? Did you manage to get Mairi and Aileen home? How did you find us?"

"The girls are safe with their families. I am not sure where Killock is. We parted ways after Twin Pines." Cormac decided to keep Killock's destination to himself until they were somewhere that a furious Wyn would not attract quite so much attention. "As to the last, I didn't really find you," Cormac explained. "I was searching for you, but I was going to Kuray to find you there. I didn't expect to see you here in Newbridge. Is Lady Danielle with you?"

"Of course she is," Wyn pfft'd at him. "I'm going to tell Dani that you tried to kill me by being mean and pretending to be your brother. But where's Killock?"

"Lady Danielle is here in the town?" Cormac suddenly felt a clutch of worry in his stomach. As happy as he was to have found

Wyn and Lady Danielle, the last place he wanted them to be was in a town with a strong force of Temple rangers lurking nearby. He had not heard any news that made him think the Temple was not still searching for Lady Danielle as a murderer and a traitor.

"Of course not," Wyn took playful offense at the suggestion. "She's safe in the boat down the beck while I came to get some food. Wouldn't want anyone to see her, after all. We're not completely helpless without you, you know. We did make it all the way to Bandirma and then all the way here without you."

"I heard," Cormac said softly. "I was in Bandirma shortly after you left, and I know what they were saying. Wyn, I am so sorry I wasn't there to help you and Lady Danielle."

"That's all right," Wyn patted his arm. "Yes, we just about died three or four times, and had to escape twice, and we fought a shadow demon all on our own, oh, and some wights. They were bitey." Wyn frowned. "And we even found out who the Crunorix is. But other than that, it was really quiet."

"You discovered another Crunorix priest?" Cormac stopped dead in his tracks and gripped Wyn's arm.

"Of course!" Wyn grinned gleefully. "Leave it to the girls, and we'll take care of it."

"But who is it?" Cormac glanced around nervously, although none of the passersby appeared interested in anything but pushing past on their way to someplace dry and warm.

"His name's Shitebrooke, or something like that, I forget, actually." Wyn shrugged. "Dani will remember. He's a priest. Oh! He's the Archivist, I remember that."

"A priest, in Bandirma…" Cormac shook his head. "Did you tell anyone?"

"Well, no, actually," Wyn frowned fiercely at him. "Seeing as how he mostly killed us and we barely escaped and all, we thought maybe going back was a bad idea."

Cormac nodded. Bandirma had not felt like a place where people were ready to listen to reason and logic when he had last been there. He had been stopped three times on his way into Bandirma by soldiers who were searching for fugitives, and Cormac had felt a knot of dread twist in his stomach long before he crossed the bridge over the Abhainn Fuar to discover Bandirma in an uproar.

The Bishop dead, magi loose in the temple, a battle inside the Royal apartments, disappearing royal guests. But none of it had stunned Cormac more than the news that Lady Danielle was one of those responsible for the death and destruction. Not because he believed it… but that anyone would.

Cormac had left Bandirma before anyone could question his story too closely or draft him into the search effort.

"I am glad you are here now, and that we somehow found each other. I almost didn't recognize you, you look so different in those clothes."

"I know, right?" Wyn laughed. "Dani says they suit me, but really I think she just likes to look at my bum. Although she won't admit it, the shy thing."

Cormac nodded silently, although Wyn had completely befuddled him. He was fairly certain Wyn was speaking of Lady Danielle, although trying to think of her as shy was not possible, and he struggled to reconcile what Wyn's posterior might have to do with it.

Wyn did not seem to notice his confusion. She hummed to herself and stopped to "Oooo" over a tray of small tarts to the delight of the proud baker.

Cormac laughed softly to himself as they continued their walk, and Wyn raised a questioning glance. "It's just I never imagined finding you happily shopping for food. Everything seemed so dire, I pictured you and Lady Danielle hiding in the forest, or desperately running for your lives, cold and wounded. I am just glad to see you safe, and to hear Lady Danielle is safe, as well."

"Of course she's safe, she had me," Wyn declared, and a sly smile crossed her lips. "Quite a few times, actually." She waited expectantly, then her eyes widened in sudden glee. "Maker! You don't know, do you! That was after you left!"

"What was?" Cormac wondered if he appeared as confused as the Damn Ewe.

"Her Ladyness and me." Wyn clutched her hands and swooned dramatically, then lost herself in helpless giggles.

"You're having me on," Cormac laughed. "I don't believe it."

"You don't believe that we're luv-ers?" Wyn sang. "What, a girl can't be tricksy? Honestly, the longer I think about it the more I wonder what I ever saw in you lot."

"No, I just can't believe her Ladyship has such bad taste," Cormac said thoughtfully.

"I know!" Wyn agreed. "Terrible, but I did try to warn her off."

"Now I really don't believe it," Cormac shook his head.

"Awww, did you fancy her, too?" Wyn consoled him. "Well, of course you did, she's gorgeous. But she's mine, and anyway, you're not her type. Because, parts."

"Well, there it is," Cormac shook his head. "The story of my life."

"Oh yes?" Wyn said incredulously. "I don't think. I'll wager that the pretty girls in those mountain villages couldn't keep their knees together when you and your brother came calling, with all your mysterious tattoos and your smile and all."

"Perhaps," Cormac smiled. "But I'll not kiss and tell. Not like some."

"Oh? You'd like it if I did, though?" Wyn blinked wide eyes at him. "Wish for it all you want, because wishing is all you'll have to take to your bedroll tonight." Wyn grinned at him.

"I suppose so," Cormac gave in. "Although, do you think if I pointed out to that baker's daughter that I have mysterious tattoos, her knees might pop open?"

"The red-head with the ribbon?" Wyn scoffed. "I'm surprised she didn't have a go at you right there over the tarts, the... tart. Wait... she looked sweet as... no." Wyn shook her head in disgust. "That should have been an easy one. Oh! Speaking of tarts..."

Wyn fished two of the small pastries from her bag and they munched contentedly as they walked, savoring the sweet burst of the hot currants in the flaky shell.

THE MARTYR'S TEARS

"Come on then." Wyn popped her fingers into her mouth one at a time to get the last of the sticky syrup. "I'm off to the boat with this lot. It's not far."

Cormac hesitated, finally forced to make the decision that had churned in the back of his mind since he had recovered enough from his shock to think through the consequences of finding Wyn and Lady Danielle.

"There's a slight… problem," he started hesitantly, then trailed off as Wyn regarded him with a raised eyebrow.

"Oh, yes?" she asked, intrigued.

Cormac sighed, frustrated with himself. He had passed every opportunity to tell Eilidh about his search during the journey from Littleford, certain each time that he needed just one more day to make sure he could convince Eilidh that Lady Danielle was not a traitor. *I thought I had more time*, was his only defense, and it sounded weak and pathetic even as he thought it. *I hoped I had more time… not just to tell Eilidh about Lady Danielle and Wyn. Just… more.*

The time had come, and he was still uncertain what Eilidh's feelings might be toward these two fugitives. *She hasn't mentioned them, which makes sense, seeing as how they were no more than the subject of strange messages from Bandirma about faraway events as far as she was concerned. But she is so unyielding when it comes to her duty, I fear what she will do.*

Cormac knew the simple solution was to abandon Eilidh, right now, and simply disappear. She would never suspect it had anything to do with Lady Danielle. But even as he thought it, Cormac knew he could not leave her. *I've brought her so far from safety.* There were other feelings that stirred beneath his protestations of responsibility, but Cormac did his best to ignore them.

"Martyr's tears, Cormac, out with it," Wyn fussed impatiently. "It can't be that awful."

"It isn't," he began again. "I met a woman in Littleford, and she's been traveling with me…" Cormac trailed off as Wyn began to laugh, a huge smile spread across her lips.

THE MARTYR'S TEARS

"Is she a milkmaid?" Wyn managed to ask amidst her laughter.

"No," Cormac answered, completely baffled by the turn the conversation had taken.

"Well, that's something," Wyn giggled again. "The lasses are quite friendly in Littleford, aren't they? But why is that a problem? Bring her along. If she's come this far with you and hasn't run away in the night, it must be true love."

"It's not like that, Wyn," Cormac said quickly. "She's a knight. A Temple knight."

"You don't mess about, do you?" Wyn blinked wide eyes at him. "Does she like to ride? I bet she does, strong lass like her."

Cormac laughed despite himself. "I swear, it's not what you think. We had to fight our way out of Littleford together, and we've been helping each other ever since." Cormac hoped he sounded sincere. The last thing he needed was Wyn crowing about true love the first time she met Eilidh.

"If you say so," Wyn frowned. "But you still haven't said why she's a problem. We could use another shiny sword, I'd say."

"She's a Temple knight, Wyn," Cormac explained. "The last she heard, Lady Danielle was a traitor to be arrested and taken back to Bandirma."

"Oh, well, explain it to her," Wyn shrugged, unconcerned.

"And if she doesn't agree?" Cormac asked. "She'll know Lady Danielle is here."

"Then explain it to her, *better*." Wyn poked a finger into his chest to emphasize her words. "Martyr's tears, Cormac, you're as useless as a lad asking for a dance. 'Ohhh, what if she says no?' I've seen you take on a wight without a thought, but this is what scares you?"

Cormac pinched the bridge of his nose, hoping to push his frustration into his gut where it belonged. "I don't want to put Lady Danielle in any danger," he explained. "I promised Sir Killock I would protect you both."

"She's really got you by the prick, hasn't she?" Wyn shook her head. "All right, I'll do the talking, so don't you worry about a thing. She'll see it straight."

THE MARTYR'S TEARS

"No, I think I'd better do it." Cormac collected himself. He realized he had little choice in the matter, and the understanding brought some small relief with it.

"If you're sure," Wyn shook her head. "Well, go on then, before we freeze to death."

The walk back through the marketplace took far less time than Cormac thought possible, and before he had a chance to think of how he might explain everything to Eilidh she was standing before him, a cloaked figure stamping her boots to keep warm as she waited with the horses in the street.

She turned as he approached, and Cormac saw a brief sign of a smile of welcome before her face closed and resumed the grim intensity she had worn since Littleford.

"Maker, you took your time," she greeted him. "I thought I might have to rescue you, for a change."

Cormac tried to smile, but it was as weak as her attempt at humor, and she turned to her horse, embarrassed.

"Eilidh, wait," Cormac stopped her before she could swing into her saddle. "I found someone, in the town. That's what took me so long."

She faced him, a puzzled frown deepening the furrow between her brows.

"Found someone?"

Cormac squared his shoulders and said a quick prayer.

"You know I am searching for someone."

"I'm not going to forget something like that," Eilidh scoffed. "I only agreed to help you because you told me how vital it was."

"Of course." Cormac busied himself with the clasp on his cloak, suddenly unable to meet her gaze. "Well, I found them. At least, I found one of them, and she knows where the other person is."

"You did?" Eilidh could not keep the surprise from her voice. "Here, in Newbridge? I thought you said we were going to Kuray?"

"I thought we would need to, but as it turns out…" Cormac trailed off, lost for a path around the irrelevant details.

"Is that not good news?" Eilidh asked.

THE MARTYR'S TEARS

"It is, very much so." Cormac sighed. *Best to get this over with.* "Eilidh, the person I was searching for, I didn't tell you their name, because I feared you wouldn't help me if you knew who it was."

"Why wouldn't I want to help you?"

"Because the person I've been trying to find is Lady Danielle." Cormac forced himself to meet Eilidh's gaze. "I'm going to help her, even if it means keeping her safe from the Temple."

Eilidh's face remained stone, but Cormac could see the strain in her posture, and she crossed her arms and shook her head slightly as she considered his words. "Lady Danielle. The traitor who killed Reverend Benno."

"That isn't true, I know it. I can't prove it to you, any more than I can prove that tomorrow will be cold. But I have no doubts." Cormac tried to fill his words with absolute certainty, but he feared he merely sounded zealous.

"That's it? I trust you, or… what?"

"I can't take you to her, not unless you tell me that you will not act on the accusations."

"Because you believe they cannot be true?"

"That is all I can say," Cormac spread his hands helplessly. "I hope that you know you can trust my word, and my judgment. At least to come and determine your own thoughts."

"And if my thoughts are that she should return to Bandirma to face her accusers?"

"Then we will part ways, and after that, you may do as you wish. But it won't come to that. We have fought together, and I know you to be a woman of honor and righteousness, and hope that you will see what I see."

"Very well then," Eilidh nodded her head curtly.

"Are you certain?" Cormac could not keep the surprise from his voice, so sudden was her acceptance.

"Am I certain that you are right? No, how could I be?" Eilidh reached a hand and gripped his shoulder firmly as she held his gaze. "But I know the man who returned for me when he could have run, who aided me when I asked him to, and who fought beside me. And that man I trust. So I will come with you, and if you are right, then I will gladly help. And if you are wrong, then I will gladly save you from the folly you have stupidly led us into."

They led their horses down the street in silence, each caught in their own thoughts. Wyn waited where Cormac had left her, a small circle stamped into the slush mute testimony to her growing impatience.

When she saw them approaching, she ceased her pacing and met them with an astonished expression that quickly changed to a friendly smile.

"Wow, you're… tall," Wyn blinked as she stared at the knight.

"Wyn, this is Sir Eilidh," Cormac introduced them.

"Do I know you?" Eilidh asked Wyn, a small frown creeping across her face.

"I think I'd remember meeting you," Wyn laughed.

Eilidh nodded slightly, her brow still creased in concentration. "Pleased to meet you."

"Well, that's because you don't know me yet, but it's sweet of you to say," Wyn grinned at the knight. "Are we ready, then, or shall we freeze a bit more?"

They mounted their horses, Cormac pulled Wyn onto the saddle behind him, and they rode west across the three low, stone arches of the bridge that gave the township its name.

Wyn guided them south along the bank of the Gleann Beck. They followed the river trail carved from the earth by the oxen that pulled barges upstream from the Abhainn Albyn, past fields of stubble and into the thick forest.

As they passed under the trees Wyn twisted to watch Eilidh, then leaned close to Cormac's ear. "Are you sure it's not what I think?"

"I'm certain, Wyn."

"Yes, but she looks like, oh, I don't know, like a statue someone carved to show what a warrior should look like, you know? Tall and strong and fierce and icy cold. Or are you telling me you didn't notice?"

"I noticed," Cormac admitted.

"Well then."

Cormac didn't respond and spent the remainder of the ride enjoying Wyn's tortured silence as she squirmed with the need to tease.

The boat was tucked into a small inlet amongst thick reeds and willows that trailed their branches in the still water. Light shone from a small window, and the smell of a wood fire hung in the trees. *The Martyr must watch over these two. Docked next to a path with lights and smoke, and no one standing guard on the trail.*

"It's me!" Wyn called merrily, and hopped onto the boat. She slid the small hatch open and warm light spilled into the cockpit.

"What wonderful things did you find for us this time?" Lady Danielle answered, and Cormac paused a moment to thank the Maker for bringing him to them.

Cormac helped Eilidh tether the horses and followed Wyn onto the boat as he listened to her bubbling voice bounce from the cabin.

"You'll not believe it, but I found us some tarts! There may be a few less than when I started, but still, tarts! And some carrots, boring, and bread, also boring. A cheese, very smelly. I did have some eggs, but I dropped the bag, so there's no telling. And I got us a duck, but I had to pay for that because it still had feathers and such and it was staring at me, so I asked the butcher to make it nice."

"You paid for the duck, but not the others?"

"Maker, no," laughed Wyn. "What a thought. Oh, but I saved the best for last. You'll never guess what I found, not in a year of guessing."

"Shall I start the year right away? I will guess you found a cask of Venaissine wine, a delightful red that tastes of summer sun."

"I was supposed to get wine, wasn't I?" Wyn hardly paused. "Bother the wine. No, I found a Cormac!"

Cormac thought briefly about hanging back for a moment to spoil Wyn's fun but decided the consequences were far too dire. He stepped down the ladder into the cabin and was greeted by an astonished smile, a joyful embrace, and more questions than he could possibly answer.

"And this is Eilidh, I think, yes that's right, who's Cormac's friend, a lass from Littleford, there's a little laugh for me. Plus, she's a knight, although of course she is, easy to see that."

Lady Danielle greeted Eilidh warmly as the knight hesitantly entered the cabin.

"Sir Eilidh," Lady Danielle took her hands and smiled in greeting. "I am very pleased to meet you."

"Lady Danielle," Eilidh returned the greeting awkwardly, then plunged ahead. "I must tell you that I am here only because Cormac has vouched for you. He swears that the charges against you are false, but if I feel that he is deceived I will carry out my duty and arrest you."

"You'll try," scoffed Wyn.

"I understand, Sir Eilidh," Lady Danielle replied. "Cormac is right, the story you have heard is nothing but lies, spread by Reverend Whitebrooke to conceal his own treachery. I have nothing but my word to offer you as proof, but my word must suffice, for I have no intention of leaving myself at the mercy of that pig."

"Reverend Whitebrooke? The Archivist?"

"The same. A murderer and a traitor." Lady Danielle refused to release Eilidh's gaze as she appraised the knight, and her accent grew pronounced as her words flowed. "Sir Eilidh, do you truly trust Cormac, or do you simply give us the benefit of the doubt? We do not have time for someone who says they are with us, yet doubts and questions our cause. We are fugitives, yes, but we fight to rid our Temple of this bastard, even if it means fighting against our friends who are deceived."

"I trust him," Eilidh answered without hesitation, and she met Cormac's eye before quickly glancing away.

"As do I," Lady Danielle said.

"I will help you, until the instant you show me that his trust in you is misplaced," Eilidh stated flatly.

"Of course," Lady Danielle agreed, and smiled as she finally released the knight's gaze.

THE MARTYR'S TEARS

The boat was quiet for a moment, the only sound the gentle lapping of the stream as it flowed past.

"Phew!" Wyn exclaimed into the silence, and she grinned around the room.

Lady Danielle laughed, and Cormac felt himself relax as tension drained from the cabin at the sound.

Cormac was relieved to see that Wyn had spoken truly. Both she and Lady Danielle appeared happy and safe, far from the grim visions that had driven him along the Rathad an Thuaidh. Wyn glowed with cheerful energy, and Lady Danielle was radiant. He smiled as he saw the tenderness between them, the small touches, the way their eyes lingered on each other, their soft smiles of contentment. He had been convinced he was the victim of an elaborate trick, but it was clearly not so.

Cormac managed to get them away from the duck before they could ruin it, and listened quietly as Wyn and Lady Danielle helped each other tell him of their travails since they had parted ways in Dolieb.

"I am so glad you have found us," Lady Danielle told him at the end of the tale. "I have hated sending Wyn alone into the villages when we have needed food, but I have dared not accompany her since we left Greymouth, and now we are faced with abandoning our boat and trying to find some horses to bear us instead."

"Thank you, m'lady," Cormac found himself grinning in return. "I am very happy as well."

"Ha! You'll not be so cheerful after a night on the deck I'll wager," Wyn teased.

"There is plenty of room in here if we move some things around," Lady Danielle objected.

"What, and have him gawking at us?" Wyn wrinkled her nose at the idea. "I already swore he'd get no closer than a wish of that."

"I am not sure what you mean," Lady Danielle muttered quietly, and she blushed a lovely dark red from her throat up the sides of her neck. *Ah. Shy. There it is.* Cormac kept his face carefully neutral, as if he had unexpectedly stumbled across two officers discussing strategy.

"Oh," said Wyn, and she examined the toe of her boot for a moment. "Are we not telling anyone, then? Because I thought after we told your sis we were bedding each other…"

"Wyn!" Lady Danielle's blush rushed to cover her cheeks.

"Sorry! I meant, after we told her we were *sleeping* together…"

"Oh, my Lord." Lady Danielle covered her face with her hands and started to laugh.

"… that it was all right to say," Wyn concluded lamely. "Oooo, I'm so confused. I can't help it, Dani, it bubbles out of me, I'm sorry if I messed it up."

"It is fine," Danielle said from behind her hands. "We are no longer keeping anything a secret, but I had not thought to engage a crier to make sure everyone knew immediately."

"I never told everyone!" Wyn exclaimed indignantly. "Just this one, and that was just by mistake seeing as how I mostly forgot he didn't already know. And now her as well, I suppose."

"I do love you, Wyn," Lady Danielle peeked out between her fingers. "And as it appears that it is not possible to die of embarrassment, I think all shall be well."

Cormac could barely restrain his mirth as, to his disbelief, it was now Wyn's turn to blush.

"Well, all right then, your Ladyness. I, err, I fancy you too, you know."

"Oh, *now* you run out of words," Danielle laughed again.

"Martyr's tears. Iloveyoutoo," Wyn blurted out, and she glared at Cormac. "Not a word from you."

"Of course not," Cormac reassured her, although he felt his grin might have spoiled the effect.

"Well, you have heard our news," Lady Danielle's fingers searched absently for something around her neck but returned to her lap unsuccessful in their quest. "All of our news. But now it is your turn. Were you able to find Mairi's father and Aileen's parents? Where is Sir Killock? You must tell us your tale."

"The girls are with their families," Cormac assured her. "And I managed to find this." He unbuckled his pack, drew out the water-stained bag, and presented it to Lady Danielle.

"My bag!" she cried joyfully. "You wonderful man, you found it! Everything is still here. My Devices, my medical chest, oh thank you, Cormac!"

"My pleasure, m'lady." Cormac fastened his pack as he resumed his tale. "After Twin Pines, my travels are easily told. I came to Bandirma as quickly as I could, hoping to join you, only to find the Temple in disarray. After hearing your story, I would guess that I arrived mere hours after your escape from Reverend Whitebrooke. Since then I have ridden for Kuray, hoping that was your destination. You were wise to stay to the rivers. The roads are no longer safe."

Cormac told them of Littleford and his escape with Eilidh, and of the capture of the temples across Albyn. "We saw bodies of soldiers strung from a tree alongside the Rathad an Thuaidh, m'lady, revenge for the attacks on the temples, I would say. I fear things will grow far worse if Whitebrooke is not revealed as the one responsible for the attack on the Queen."

"That's what we're going to do," Wyn announced. "We're going to kill him, and also tell everyone he did it, he murdered the Bishop, he is the one using fuil crunor, we fucking saw him do it. As soon as we're not running for our lives from every idiot in the Temple who believed him when he said we did it." Wyn crossed her arms and glared at Eilidh as if daring the knight to challenge her.

"Wyn, that is not fair to Sir Eilidh," Lady Danielle chastised softly. "She is here now, once given the choice and the truth to make that choice. I am sure others will do the same, just as I am sure there are others who are unconvinced by Whitebrooke's lies."

"I suppose," Wyn relented grudgingly. "Shouldn't be that hard to figure out."

"Perhaps some have already done so," Lady Danielle consoled. "Even the drover we met in Greymouth was unwilling to believe that the Temple could have had anything to do with an attack on the Queen."

THE MARTYR'S TEARS

"M'lady, if you don't mind, you mentioned that something happened in Greymouth?" Cormac asked.

"We were hopeful," Lady Danielle smiled sadly at Wyn, "and we nearly paid for that hope with our lives. We thought we could hide and be safe in Greymouth, so far from Bandirma," she explained. "So we visited the market and a tavern for food without any concern for concealing ourselves, and a man recognized me.

"We left immediately, but I saw him again on the docks. I hoped that we had left him there, but when we were forced to take shelter from a storm we were attacked by several men. They must have been following us."

"Could they have been bandits?"

"Not this lot," Wyn shook her head. "They knew how to fight, and sneak, and they chased us rather than nick our gear. Plus, we were in the middle of nowhere, in the middle of a blizzard. I've never met bandits that hard up for a bit of thievery. No, they were there to kill us, that's for sure."

"The orders from Sir Maeglin said to capture you, Lady Danielle, not kill you," Sir Eilidh informed them.

"There is no telling what Whitebrooke has been ordering," Lady Danielle ventured, "and why else would they follow us for days up the river, if they had not been ordered to do so?"

"Look, it doesn't matter, does it?" Wyn demanded. "Whoever they are they're still out there, likely a bit angrier than before, so we know they're still after us. There's nothing to be done except head back to Bandirma and fix old Shitebrooke."

Cormac nodded thoughtfully. "Then, m'lady, perhaps I can suggest we douse the fire and the lanterns, and I'll stand watch until we can leave."

"It is too cold," Lady Danielle was dismayed. "You will freeze to death. We should all takes turns watching."

"I've been sleeping outside for days," Cormac said reassuringly, "and believe me, I'm accustomed to standing a watch. This is best."

"I think I know how to stay hidden." Wyn scowled. "Only done it for years and years without your help."

THE MARTYR'S TEARS

"I know," Cormac reassured her. "But guarding against attackers is different from staying concealed, and there's no hiding this boat."

"You've convinced me," Wyn laughed. "You go on and freeze outside, I'll stay warm and snug in here."

"I will stand watch with you," Eilidh said, and Cormac nodded, hoping that the knight would not see the enormous grin and exaggerated winks that Wyn cast in their direction.

They took blankets for themselves and their horses and left the boat, and Cormac slid the hatch closed behind them. The dappled grey nuzzled his hand appreciatively and he rewarded her with a carrot, then settled the blanket across her back.

"Regrets?" Cormac asked Eilidh quietly as they settled their gear.

"Not yet," Eilidh replied thoughtfully. "They are either consummate liars, or they believe they speak the truth. What did Wyn mean when she said that she had seen Reverend Whitebrooke use fuil crunor?"

"You noticed." Cormac watched Eilidh closely. Aside from the crease between her eyebrows caused by the small frown that she sometimes wore, the knight appeared only to be concerned with settling the blanket around her shoulders in such a way that it did not impede her sword. But Cormac caught a quick glance from her that slid away as fast as it had arrived.

"I did," Eilidh finally replied. "Isn't that what they called the dark magic in the stories about Ruric's war?"

"Yes," Cormac agreed. "I swear I will tell you the entire tale when we have the time for it."

"Then tell me as much as we do have time for." Eilidh finished with her blanket and stood easy, one boot placed firmly on the gnarled root of a nearby oak.

"Is that an order? Sir?"

Eilidh finally met his eye, and a trace of a smile graced the corner of her lips. "If you'd like."

"Yes, sir, I like orders." Cormac matched her with a grin of his own, but continued before the silence could stretch. "We were sent by Bishop Benno to investigate some rituals, up near a town called Dolieb. Lord Bradon, Lady Danielle, Sir Killock… and hundreds of soldiers. They were worried that it was the Crunorix, just like in those stories."

"And was it?"

Cormac nodded silently, his thoughts lost in endless black stone catacombs and the stare of burning red eyes. He took a deep breath and let the chill air burn the images away. "It was. We found them. It was just like those stories. Dark magic and undead creatures. And at the end, there was this Crunorix high priest, a magus they called it. I saw it with my own eyes, and it was worse than anything I'd ever heard of in any story. Over a dozen of us journeyed into the mountains, and only four came out. My brother died in there. So did Lord Bradon and Captain Alistair, and nine of the best warriors I have ever seen."

"I watched Lady Danielle and Wyn fight for their lives against the Crunorix. I watched Lady Danielle kill the magus when no one else could. She saved us down there.

"The only question we couldn't figure out was who had revived the fuil crunor rituals, who was responsible. But it seems Lady Danielle and Wyn found him when they returned to Bandirma. It was one of us, this Whitebrooke, and they know because he tried to kill them. So, when I hear that they are accused of killing Bishop Benno, I know who is really responsible."

"You know how that sounds?" Eilidh asked.

"It's hard to believe," Cormac granted, his hands spread helplessly wide, "but there's no chance the woman on that boat, the woman I saw risk her life to fight and destroy the magus, who grieved for those who were slain, could possibly be a traitor."

"You are correct, it is hard to believe," Eilidh agreed, but her voice did not sound as if she condemned.

They began their watch then, as Cormac could say no more, and Eilidh had retreated to her own thoughts. They moved slowly through the trees along the embankment, pausing at unpredictable intervals to watch and listen, but they remained in the dark shadows under the trees, and always in sight of the boat.

THE MARTYR'S TEARS

A light wind began to blow in the hours before dawn, and Cormac heard the screech of an owl hunting farther into the forest, but no other signs of life disturbed them.

When the grey dawn revealed the difference between land and water, Cormac and Eilidh made a wider patrol and visited the spots they had been scrupulous to avoid during the night. These perfect hides showed no signs of use.

They departed soon after. They gathered the few items they needed for their journey and left the boat concealed in its inlet, but only after Lady Danielle had meticulously scrutinized every line and knot and hatch to make sure they were as diligently secured as possible.

Wyn mounted behind Lady Danielle on Eilidh's horse, while the knight joined Cormac on his dappled grey mare. Eilidh settled behind him without a word and wrapped an arm around his chest, and he could not help but feel her body press against his back, strong and hard, yet soft and warm at the same time.

They followed the ox track to the bridge and spurred the horses into a gallop as they turned south on the Rathad an Thuaidh, returning over the long distances he and Eilidh had just crossed. But Cormac felt a fierce energy coursing through him, urging him onward, far different from the grim worry that had driven him northward. He had found Lady Danielle and Wyn, Eilidh had joined them, and now they rode to bring justice to the one that had caused so much grief and misery.

The horses appeared to share his passion, for they stepped high and surged forward, ears back and tails streaming as they raced toward Bandirma.

Killock

The trail wound between the trees, the different scents of the men weaving together and then separating again as they spread across the forest. When the trails diverged, the wolf ignored the others and followed the path that smelled of blood. The other paths always rejoined it, and the wolf knew that it had found the leader of the men.

The wolf moved cautiously now, slipping from shadow to shadow through the forest. The scent was very fresh, and the wolf would often pause and listen intently, disturbed by what it sensed ahead. All night the wolf had drawn steadily closer to its quarry, but now that bright daylight danced between the branches of the thick pines, the wolf hung further back.

A great tree had long ago fallen across the path the men had taken. Its trunk rested against a small rise of earth, creating a tunnel beneath it that the men had used to avoid the detour around the tree's long trunk.

The wolf hesitated at the edge of the deep shadow beneath the tree. It sniffed and whined and paced across the entrance to the short tunnel, but would not enter. The trail was unhesitating as it plunged beneath the tree, but there was a fleeting smell that was much fresher.

The wolf lowered its head and crept forward. The smell of metal danced across its nose, so faint that it could barely taste it, but it was there, and the wolf whined and growled as it fought against the urge to flee.

The leaves beneath the tree were deep and sodden, the detritus of years of accumulation. The wolf pushed forward gingerly, as if the leaves were sharp thorns.

Its paw found something hard under the loose surface, and the wolf leapt back as the ground exploded with the harsh snap of metal against metal. Razor teeth glinted amidst the shower of dirt and leaves as the wolf cringed away.

Wood creaked from the top of the small hill, and the wolf lunged forward. The air hissed behind its head and the rotten wood of the tree trunk disintegrated as it was struck. The wolf streaked between the trees and behind bushes, its ears laid flat and its tail streaming behind. The wet earth ripped under the wolf's claws as it swerved and another hiss sliced through the air.

The wolf found a dark space beneath a moss-covered boulder and slid into it. Its instincts screamed to run, to fly through the forest faster than any pursuer, but instead it held still, listening.

Leaves rustled and a twig snapped as two men hurried down the hill to the fallen tree. They peered into the forest in the direction the wolf had fled, but they could not see its unblinking eyes gazing back at them from the concealing shadows.

"Almost," one of the men grunted.

"You think Calder will be pleased with 'almost'?" the other sneered. "What the fuck were you shooting at, anyway? I've never seen a worse shot."

"I didn't see you hit it, neither," the first man said reasonably. "And I wouldn't have had to shoot it if it hadn't found your trap, now would I?"

"We'd better go and tell him."

"Don't shit your panties," the first man replied. "So the wolf got away? It ran off, and it'll not come back, I reckon. Calder won't care."

THE MARTYR'S TEARS

"You think? That wolf has followed us for two days now. You think it'll give up because we shot a few trees sort of near it?"

"It's a fucking wolf. We'll get it next time, if it comes back."

The second man seemed unconvinced, but he followed his companion as the two men hurried away.

The wolf eased from its hide and slipped after the men, gliding silently through the shadows.

***

Only the faintest of sounds betrayed the river in the dark, a tiny trickle as the water stirred heavily against the muddy bank and a gurgle as it eddied amongst the roots of a stand of ancient willows. The water appeared black, and its smooth surface gleamed slick as ice in the sharp light of a frozen moon.

The branches of the willows trailed thickly in the river, dragging on the water as if to stymie what little current remained. Beneath the branches the shadows were as dark as a cave, wet and slick against the skin. Killock breathed the damp air deep into his lungs and let its touch seep into his skin as he became indistinguishable from the knotted shapes around him.

The far bank of the river was no more than a bow shot away, a confused tangle of black shapes glimpsed between the branches of the willows. But there was a tinge of oiled wood and damp canvass drifting on the air, and a taste of old smoke in the back of Killock's throat, that told him there was more in the jumble of shadows than trees. He watched patiently, and slowly the shadows gave up their secrets to him. A long, low shape nestled amongst the rushes, and a tall shaft swayed gently amongst the branches of the trees.

Still Killock waited, unmoving. The boat concealed across the river appeared abandoned. No light gleamed from a crack, no sound creaked from a plank. But Killock knew the boat was not empty. A weight moved slowly within the boat, tilting the mast against the branches behind it, and Killock felt the hair on the back of his neck rise as he peered into the blackness beyond the boat. Something lurked in those shadows. Killock could feel its gaze.

Killock carefully removed his Diviner from its pouch and aligned two of its hoops. He formed his Word slowly, like the creep of ice across the surface of a pond, so that its whisper was lost amongst the lap of the river against the bank and the stir of the trees in the breeze.

Figures crouched in the darkness beneath the trees, six of them, spread across the embankment around the boat. They were shrouded in cloaks and clothing the color of earth, and were as still as stone, merging into the divots and hollows of the forest as easily as Killock.

A seventh figure slipped from the boat and joined the watchers. He turned and gestured to bring the others from their hiding places, and Killock caught his breath as the man's face was revealed for an instant. An ugly wound carved across his jaw and cheek, but Killock recognized the eyes set deep under a heavy brow, and the gaunt cheeks and crooked nose.

The seven figures briefly came together, then slid between the trees upriver, until not even Killock's Diviner could find them. Killock let his Word fade away, disassembled the hoops, and packed them back into their wallet.

Calder... Killock felt his jaw clench. *He should be rotting in a cell.*

Killock rubbed at the weariness in his jaw as he stared at the vague shape of the boat. *Why is Calder pursuing Wyn and Danielle? What could he possibly have to do with them?* Killock shook his head angrily. *Does it matter? They are in terrible danger, and they may not know it. I must reach them before Calder does.*

If it is Wyn and Danielle's trail. If it is their boat.

Killock slipped into the water with barely a ripple and crossed the narrow stretch with gentle strokes that made no sound, emerging amongst the deep shadows beneath a patch of twisted shrubs. He crept along the embankment to where the boat bobbed gently in the reeds against the shore. Although it listed slightly to one side, the decks were clear of branches and leaves, the lines still coiled neatly, the sail wrapped in a tight bundle along the boom, and it gave every sign of being only recently abandoned.

Killock stared grimly at the cover of the small hatch. Given time, the knight would have preferred to wait until he was certain that no one lay concealed within the boat, but the Templar knew he had little choice. There was no time to lurk safe and hidden in the shadows, not while Calder and his men were drawing ever closer to Wyn and Danielle. *At least I will find out if Calder left someone to watch for a tail. And, if they are here, they are not hunting.*

Killock hopped onto the boat with only a moment's hesitation and crouched in the cockpit as the boat rocked and pulled gently against its tether.

The dark interior of the boat beckoned and Killock padded down the short steps that led inside. He paused at the bottom, his gaze penetrating the thick shadows that filled the small cabin. Freezing water pooled on one side, and a thin mattress rested on the deck away from the water. A battered stove with a broken door and a twisted pipe was braced against the bulkhead by thick wedges of wood, and a small pile of firewood was secured in a basket nearby.

Killock eased into the cabin, alert to every movement of the boat, every creak of wood. The cabin was neat and tidy, save for the dark puddle of water, but there were signs of a final hurried farewell. There were no blankets for the bed, nor food in any of the cabinets, and Killock found a long bandage discarded on the cabin floor behind the mattress. Blood had stained the thick fabric of the bandage, and Killock slowly wound the length of cloth around his hand until the red patches lay on top of one another. *An arm,* Killock decided, noting the narrow width of the wrap. *A very slim arm.* Killock removed his gauntlet and tested the stain. The blood was not wet, and the cloth smelled clean and without any scent of infection.

Killock gently flattened the bandage and sat on the mattress, suddenly overwhelmed as relief and anxiety swelled within him. *They were here,* he thought. *Right here.* For weeks, he had hoped. For days, he had been certain. Now he knew. The cabin was filled with their presence, and he had only to close his eyes to hear

THE MARTYR'S TEARS

Wyn's chatter as she sat on the mattress beside him, or imagine Danielle laughter as she warmed her hands by the fire.

Were they here last night? No more than the night before, he decided. *All of these days, all of these weeks, and it comes down to the slimmest of margins. The smallest decision, one way or the other, will decide who wins this race.*

Killock ran his fingers through the ragged tangle of his hair and took a last, lingering breath, seeking to draw the happy scent of the cabin deep into his chest. He suddenly paused, his head twisted to the side as he listened without breathing, holding as still as stone. The boat creaked and shifted, a subtle movement that had nothing to do with the lap of water against its hull.

Killock waited silently. The boat creaked again, and the puddle on the cabin floor crept slightly closer to the stove's feet.

He left watchers to guard his trail, Killock shook his head wearily. *Does Calder know that he is being followed, or is it just unfortunate caution? Either way, they have sprung their trap.*

Killock stood, careful not to touch the low ceiling, and slid slowly toward the hatch, pacing himself with the brush of movement on the deck above his head. He collected the broken stove door, then eased into the shadows against the bulkhead.

The hatch opened with a sigh of air. Killock waited quietly, until he heard the soft creak of a bow string stretching. Then he raised the stove door and stepped dramatically into the open hatch.

The iron in his hands shrieked and bucked twice in the space of a heartbeat. Pain tore across the knight's cheek and buried itself into his hip, but Killock brushed the sting aside and leapt up the steps and into the cockpit without hesitation. Movement tugged at the corner of his eye and he twisted and hurled the stove door toward it. A cry of pain rang out as the door struck heavily.

Killock did not wait to see the results of his attack. Another great stride brought him to the stern of the boat, and he leapt from the rail, arcing through the air in a flat dive. He curled by instinct, hit the embankment in a roll, and was up and running before the spray of mud had reached its apex.

Trees rushed at him out of the darkness and branches tore at his hands and face. He weaved suddenly to the side and dropped into the black shadows beneath the twisted shell of an ancient trunk.

Running footsteps hurled themselves toward him through the forest, his pursuers still unaware that their quarry had halted his flight. He guessed at two men and slid his sword free. The first leapt over Killock's hide, landed an arm's-length away, and was gone without pause. The second followed a heartbeat later and a step further away. Killock uncoiled in a long lunge, his blade a hiss in the air as it sank cleanly into the man's side under his arm. Killock felt the point grate against bone and then plunge deep, and the man's weight dragged the tip down as he went limp.

Killock tore the sword free and raced after the first man. A dozen churning steps brought him close, and he called softly to his prey.

The man lurched to a stop and turned. Some instinct screamed a warning and his sword tip rose as Killock fell on him. Killock brushed the sword aside with his own, and steel rasped against steel in a long hiss. Killock twisted and buried his shoulder into the man's chest, driving him backward off his feet to smash into a tree with such force that his breath burst from him in a choking cry and his head cracked into the wood.

The man stumbled forward, his sword lunging awkwardly at Killock as its wielder fought to regain his balance. Killock swatted the blade aside and whirled away, his sword a silver blur that sliced through the man's neck and left an arc of dark blood hanging in the air. The man took another step as his hands clutched at his throat, then he sank to his knees, choked, and collapsed.

Killock slipped behind a tree and watched the last twitches of the man's leg in the mud as he listened for any other sounds of pursuit. At last, satisfied that the two men had been on their own, Killock carefully peeled back his tunic and examined the wet slick of blood spreading across his hip. He slowly pulled a long piece of wood from his side, the splintered shaft of one of the arrows that had struck his improvised shield. He tossed the wood away and wiped experimentally at his cheek, finding his gauntlet wet with blood when he pulled it back. He pushed the pain of both wounds far away.

The others are not far ahead, but there is no telling how long they will wait for these two, if they wait at all, he realized. *I must move quickly.*

***

The men's trail led the wolf upstream through the forest to a stone bridge that crossed the river toward a smoke-crowned city perched on a high, muddy hill. Three of the men waited there, hidden in the shadows of the trees near the bridge, but the wolf was cautious, and the men did not see it as it slunk through the underbrush and settled on its belly a stone-throw away, waiting to see which way the men would leave.

At last the wolf's patience was rewarded. A man appeared, running across the bridge, and as he approached the three men rose from their concealment and joined the newcomer on the road at the end of the bridge.

"We're going," the new arrival informed the other three.

"They haven't come back, yet."

"He says 'now' and he didn't seem like he wanted a discussion. They can catch us up if they can, but we need to go."

The other men nodded acceptance and the four of them hurried across the bridge. But their voices lingered clearly as they departed.

"Does that mean we've found them?"

"Close. The guardsman said he remembers them coming through this morning. Says they took the Rathad an Thuaidh south towards Littleford. Says they had horses."

"South?" The men's voices were fading, but the wolf could easily hear the confusion in the question. "Why the fuck are they going south, now?"

"Who cares?" The wolf strained to hear the last traces of the men's words. "We'll catch up easy…"

The wolf ran to the edge of the bridge and back to the trees, whining in dismay as the men reached the far end of the bridge and entered the city between the tall gates on the other side. Then it suddenly sprinted to the river and leapt into the water, churning across its slow-moving surface until it reached the far shore. The wolf shook a shower of water from its heavy fur and raced along the curve of the earthen city wall, darting amongst the fields and farmyards that clustered against it.

The wolf did not slow until it spied the flickering glow of lanterns ahead, marking where another gate pierced the city walls. It swerved away from the gate and streaked across an open field. At the far end of the field was a low wall made of piled stones covered in brambles, and on the other side the beaten earth of a road that emerged from the gate and disappeared into thick forest in the other direction.

The wolf scrambled through the thorny brambles and began to search the road, racing from side to side. The puddles and mud frustrated it, and the road stank of men and horses and cows and sheep in an overwhelming brew. The distant sound of metal clashing against metal caught the wolf's attention, and it stared at the distant gates as they were slowly opened and five horsemen emerged onto the road.

The wolf growled, then swallowed its anger and began to trot along the road, keeping close to the border. The sound of hoofbeats stirred the hair on the back of the wolf's neck, still faint, but slowly and steadily devouring the distance between the wolf and the horsemen.

The wolf pressed on, then suddenly stopped. The feeblest of scents caught its attention, and it sped forward in a rush, racing ahead of the horsemen into the forest as it followed the trail of its pack.

THE MARTYR'S TEARS

Maeglin

S ir Maeglin rapped impatiently on the polished wooden door and brushed past the steward who answered without pausing to reply to his greeting.

The Knight Commander strode along the small corridor and into the drawing room at its end, Sir Hollis close behind bearing a roll of maps. The Knight Commander would have preferred meeting the Council almost anywhere else. The deep armchairs and warm fire of Reverend Nesta's room seemed to encourage endless discussion and ponderful silences, but the Council was meeting, and Sir Maeglin would not wait until their next formal session.

The Council had taken up residence in the chairs around the fire, and Reverend Ail and Reverend Dougal were already sipping wine from crystal glasses when Maeglin entered the room. Maeglin ignored the remaining chair and stood beside the fireplace, so that the Council could not help but face him from their arc of chairs.

"Knight Commander," Reverend Liadán greeted him softly. Maeglin nodded curtly in reply. He had never known what to expect from Liadán, which made him wary of her. She managed to remain quiet and aloof, but Maeglin knew the priestess had spent many years leading congregations in the largest temples while the rest of the Council were already entrenched in the bureaucracy of Bandirma, so there had to be more to her than her formal veneer. But Maeglin had never seen it, and it disturbed him to know that he might not understand her inner thoughts. *Preferable to the bleating from Reverend Ail, or Reverend Dougal's muttering,* Maeglin considered. *Or Reverend Hayley's endless arguments.* Maeglin glared at each of the Council in turn.

"Your message mentioned that you have urgent business," Reverend Ail prompted.

"Yes," Maeglin replied. "As you all know, there were a thousand soldiers on the road to Bandirma a brief time ago. I had hoped that Duke Campbell would be foolish enough to challenge us here, but he did not, and the army turned back to Littleford." Maeglin paused to make certain that he had their attention. "Where, for the most part, it has disappeared. Along with the Duke."

"How do you mean?" Ail asked.

"There are less than five hundred soldiers in Littleford now, and I have multiple reports that Baron Arledge is their commander."

"Where have the rest gone?"

"To our temples, all over the south. A dozen here, twenty there. They have scattered."

"Why?" Ail asked. "What could a few more soldiers in each temple accomplish?"

"Quite a lot, it appears. They are plowing fields and building outhouses and repairing roofs. All over the place. My scouts tell me that the farms around Littleford are ready for sowing, and the soldiers have moved to paving the roads and shearing the sheep."

"What?" Reverend Dougal peered at Maeglin as if he were seeing an apparition. "Shearing sheep?"

"Yes."

"Good for them," Reverend Hayley said firmly.

"Good for us, as well," Maeglin added. "I have also received some interesting news from the north." Maeglin gestured to Sir

Hollis, and the knight quickly bent and unrolled the map across the small table in front of the chairs, pushing cups and glasses aside. Hollis weighted the map with a teapot and a saucer and stepped back.

"We have received messages from our temples in the north," Maeglin continued. "Just a few, but all are temples between Newbridge and Dalby Combe, and all say the same thing… the soldiers have departed. The temples are back in our hands."

"Departed?" Hayley could not keep the excitement from her voice. "Just… gone?"

"Yes," Maeglin agreed.

"But, where did they go?"

"Here," Maeglin pointed to the map. "Dolieb."

"Dolieb?" Dougal asked. "Why Dolieb?"

"Because that is where General Boone is," Maeglin announced. "A large force was seen passing through Dolieb, almost a month ago, heading north. The report swears the general was with them."

"North?" Ail asked. "North of Dolieb?"

"Boone is going after Sir Lochlan," Hayley muttered, and Maeglin gave the priestess a grudging nod.

"It seems likely. Boone cannot like having a Temple army lurking in the north while the nobles poke us in the eye here in the south."

"Or, the general is going to help Sir Lochlan guard the exit to the catacombs," Reverend Nesta said reasonably. "Bishop Benno and the Queen reached an agreement to ally against the Crunorix before his death, don't forget."

"He reached an agreement with Karsha Hali," Maeglin corrected her. "Maker only knows if the Queen knew anything about it, or if she feels bound by it now if she did. In any case, I have sent a message to Lochlan warning him to watch his flank. Hopefully the birds will arrive in time."

"General Boone was in Dolieb a month ago, but our temples were only recently released?" Liadán asked softly. "Why do you think those soldiers are joining Boone?"

"They haven't come south, and Boone will want as many reserves as he can get. The High Fells are not an easy place to make war."

"Sir Maeglin, I see that this is all very interesting," Reverend Dougal grumbled. "Dolieb, Boone, outhouses… but you've sent a bird to Sir Lochlan already. What was so urgent it could not wait until tomorrow?"

"Arledge is here, in Littleford," Maeglin slammed his finger onto the map, rattling the saucer. "He has no reserves. They are scattered to the winds. There are no forces to relieve him. The closest are in Irongate, and Boone has taken all the rest into the High Fells."

"You wish to attack," Hayley realized.

"Yes," Maeglin agreed. "A quick strike on Littleford will capture the only force of any size arrayed against us, and then we can retake our temples and destroy the rest of the Queen's army in detail as we wish."

"And what happens when Duke Thornton arrives from Irongate, and General Boone arrives from the north?" Reverend Hayley asked contemptuously.

"Boone is months away from being able to field a force against us, and Thornton's soldiers are spread across the west in the Stone Shield waiting for the Ironbacks to thaw. We can free our temples and still have months for you to reach an agreement with the Queen."

"And at the end of that time we will have accomplished what, exactly?" Nesta asked.

"We will have freed our temples," Maeglin replied shortly.

"Freed them from what?" Nesta asked. "From having their roofs repaired?"

"Do you think this is a joke?"

"No, of course not," Nesta replied. "But nor do I see it as a call for escalation. I cannot imagine a more benign occupation."

"They have violated our sovereignty," Maeglin insisted. "Our temples. There is bitter fighting around Newbridge, worse every day. And Littleford—"

"None of that matters," Hayley interrupted. "We will solve the first through diplomacy, not warfare. The second is insignificant compared to the misery you would propose. And the third was a tragedy that has not been repeated, and the criminal responsible is in our cells. No, what matters is what Bishop Benno died fighting, what Lord Bradon died fighting, what the Queen is begging us to join her against… what matters is ending this ridiculous standoff and standing against the Crunorix."

"Well said," Ail congratulated the priestess. "Yes, don't you think we should be talking about finding the Crunorix, instead of spending all of this time on plans for attacking Baron Arledge?"

"The Queen tells us it is one of us. We tell her it is one of hers," Maeglin told Ail coldly. "Shall we draw lots for who we turn over to the Queen, and simply hope we have time to find the real culprit before it is too late?"

"Well, no," Ail glanced around the room for support. "But perhaps we could focus on finding the proof a bit more, and on the Queen's army a bit less. There hasn't been a real threat from the army in weeks, after all, and the Templars have made some very compelling arguments—"

"They have no proof," Maeglin interrupted the priest. "Do you now wish to set aside Temple law at your convenience?"

"Reverend Ail did not suggest anything of the sort," Hayley insisted. "He said we should be focused on the pressing threat, which is not a campaign against Baron Arledge."

"Do you wish for a formal vote?" Nesta asked.

"Yes," Maeglin insisted, his jaw clenched. "I want your voices on record."

"Very well," Nesta said quietly. "In favor of authorizing the Knight Commander to pursue his plan of attack."

Maeglin listened to the fire crackle for a moment. "I want to hear the nays."

"Those against," Nesta obliged him.

"Nay," Hayley said immediately.

"Nay," Ail agreed.

"Nay," Liadán said softly.

"And 'nay' for me," Nesta said briskly. "Dougal, dear, do you wish to vote as well? We have the four we need if you don't want to."

"Abstain," Dougal said gruffly. "He's not wrong, you know. If we want to get the temples back, now's the chance."

"We will get them back, and we will do it without more bloodshed, without turning on those who are our allies against our true enemy," Hayley scoffed.

"I didn't vote 'aye'," Dougal complained.

"Was there anything else, Knight Commander?" Nesta asked.

"No." Maeglin gathered his map. "If that will be all?"

"Yes, Knight Commander. Thank you for your advice and time."

Maeglin strode from the apartment and stood quietly in the hallway beyond, his fists on his hips as he stared at the stones beneath his boots. Hollis waited patiently, knowing better than to interrupt the Knight Commander.

They wish me to focus on finding proof... as if every effort had not already failed. My soldiers found nothing, their priests found nothing, the Templars found nothing. What good will sending the troops through the temple one more time achieve? How can we force an archivist to read more books in a day? They still do not even know how to open Whitebrooke's chamber in the archives.

Maeglin walked slowly toward the doors to the Inner Temple, his teeth grinding together under the strain of his clenched jaw. *The Templars are not wrong. Whitebrooke's actions are suspicious, to say the least. His claims are unsupported. His motives, especially regarding Lady Danielle, have been suspect from the start. And he still has not explained his orders to assassinate Lady Danielle, nor his unwillingness to open the chamber in the archives. I am wrong,* Maeglin realized, *there is something more we can do.*

Maeglin raised his head and strode forward, his boots harsh against the stone floor.

"Sir, where are you going?" Sir Hollis asked.

"It's time to get the truth out of Whitebrooke," Maeglin's lips twisted in fury. "That bastard has been lying to my face for months."

"Sir?" Sir Hollis hurried in front of Maeglin and halted the Knight Commander with a raised hand. "Sir, Reverend Whitebrooke has yet to stand trial. He stands accused, only."

"Don't worry, Hollis, there will be enough of him left to try," Maeglin pushed past the knight and continued to stride down the hallway. "Come with me if you'd like. We'll find out how much justice means to each of us."

But Sir Hollis did not follow, and Maeglin nodded in satisfaction. *He knows it needs to be done, yet he will not cross that line. That is good to know.*

Whitebrooke had been imprisoned in a section of the dungeon reserved for prisoners who warranted particular care and consideration. The cells were located against the northern wall of the Temple, where the prisoners could have a window to soothe them, and the cells were dry and well-heated, boasted a proper bed, and their own privy. But for all that, they were as secure as any other cell.

Three soldiers were on duty in the small guardroom and they leapt to their feet as the Knight Commander entered. Maeglin glanced at them for a moment, then gestured to the one he wanted.

"Vaughn, come with me."

The soldier joined him as Maeglin retrieved a ring of iron keys from its hook, and followed the Knight Commander into the cells. Half-way along the passage, Maeglin stopped in front of one of the doors, jammed the key into its lock, and twisted it open.

The room beyond was brightly lit by lanterns, and a cheery blaze snapped in the fireplace. The room smelled of meat and sage from a platter of food set on the heavy table in the center of the room.

Whitebrooke glared at the Knight Commander from his place at the table. A book was spread open beside the Archivist's plate with a candle next to it, and his fork and knife poised over a bloody steak.

"It's time to answer some questions, Whitebrooke," Maeglin said coldly.

The priest finished his cut and raised a piece of steak on his fork. He considered it for a moment, placed it in his mouth, and chewed thoughtfully as he watched the two soldiers enter his cell. Then he placed his utensils on the plate and carefully wiped his lips with a napkin

"I have nothing to say to you, Maeglin," Whitebrooke rumbled. "Get out."

"We will see," Maeglin replied, and he sat facing Whitebrooke across the table. "Have they told you that they have set your trial date?"

"It will be a farce, whenever it is," Whitebrooke waved away the trial with a sweep of his massive hand. "I did what needed to be done, when no one else would do it." Whitebrooke's eyes gleamed beneath his heavy brows as he watched Maeglin. "Perhaps you have felt the same urge?"

"Lady Danielle had to be killed?" Maeglin asked. He filled a cup from the bottle on the table, sampled the wine, and sipped again. "This is better than we get in the barracks."

"You should speak with your steward," Whitebrooke replied.

"I shall." Maeglin turned to the soldier standing rigidly next to the door. "Vaughn, do you care for wine?"

"No, thank you, sir."

Maeglin watched Whitebrooke's gaze linger on the tall soldier while the knight enjoyed another sip.

"Farce or not, I do not like your chances," Maeglin told the priest. "Do you know the punishment?"

"If it were a slap on my wrist, it would still be an injustice."

"Oh, it's worse than a slap on your wrist," Maeglin chuckled. "It is unfortunate that you do not have one of Killock's agents as a bedmate. Then you might be able to escape, as Lady Danielle did." Maeglin enjoyed Whitebrooke's silent glare while he sipped from his cup again. "Why do you think the girl helped Lady Danielle escape? Was she in thrall to Karsha Hali, as well?"

"Perhaps she was in thrall with having Danielle spread her legs for her? Who knows?"

"Well, you couldn't blame her for that, now could you? What do you think, Vaughn?" Maeglin watched Whitebrooke's gaze involuntarily return to the soldier at the mention of his name. "Would you blame someone for setting Lady Danielle free if she spread her legs for them? You'd let her go if she let you fuck her, wouldn't you?"

"No, sir, I'd not free a prisoner, not for a fuck."

"Not even a prisoner as beautiful as Lady Danielle?" Maeglin asked.

"Well, sir, if she asked sweet enough I'd fuck her, but she wouldn't be getting out afterwards. There's plenty of tail in the world, and none of it's worth hanging for."

"Very wise, Vaughn," Maeglin laughed. "I'd heard that you didn't mind if the prisoners weren't treated as our honored guests."

"No, sir... they're all fucking scum, sir, no need to tuck them in at night, is there, sir?"

"No," Maeglin agreed. "None at all." Maeglin paused to take another swallow of wine. "Tend to the fire, please, Vaughn. It is smoking."

The soldier obediently moved to the fireplace and began prodding the wood, and Whitebrooke twisted to watch.

"Lady Danielle was fortunate that Killock's people are not as loyal to the Temple as my soldiers are, I suppose," Maeglin mused. "Tell me more about why she had to be killed?"

"What?" Whitebrooke's glare snapped to meet Maeglin's. "She is a threat to the Temple. She is a Crunorix priestess who is adored by the Council and the Templars. No one would have the balls to deny her. No one but you, and I."

"You gave the order to kill her... to protect the Temple?"

"Yes, of course." Whitebrooke's chair creaked perilously as he leaned back. "You know as well as any the crisis we face. God is dead, our Bishop is dead, the Queen is manipulated by a Crunorix priest, her army on our doorstep. There is no Ruric to defend us this time, no Martyr to save us. We must craft a new Temple, a stronger one, and I could not allow the Council to welcome her back, no matter how it saddened me to give the order."

THE MARTYR'S TEARS

"And that is also the reason you will not tell us the Word for this?" Maeglin pulled a key made of polished stone from his pocket and laid it on the table. "To protect the Temple?"

"There is no telling what lies beyond that door by now," Whitebrooke slammed his fist on the table, sloshing wine from both their cups. "It was folly to interrupt my work."

"Was it?"

"Of course!" Whitebrooke thundered. "Do you think the Temple will survive, clinging uselessly to the teachings of a failed God? There are other powers, Maeglin, greater powers, and we can use them to build anew. I have seen it, Maeglin, I have seen the faint embers, hidden beneath the ashes of failed lies. All we need do is fan them, and the blaze will be ours to master."

"A new Temple, built from ancient powers?"

"Why not?" Whitebrooke demanded, his chin lifted arrogantly, his bristling brow furrowed. "They are there, they are real, not like the half-truths we have been taught all our lives. If we master them, never to be used as the Crunorix do, but to defeat our enemies, to raise up the Temple, to welcome a Golden Age… can you imagine it, Maeglin? That future is there, in our grasp, if only we have the vision, if only we are courageous enough to grasp it."

"I don't want to imagine it. I want to see it for myself. Give me the Word to the key."

"Have you not been listening?" Whitebrooke scoffed. "It is far too dangerous for anyone to open except for me."

"I have heard enough," Maeglin replied. "Give me the Word."

"No, I shall not," Whitebrooke sneered.

"Very well," Maeglin shrugged, and he nodded to Vaughn. The soldier did not hesitate. His fist smashed into the back of Whitebrooke's head, driving the priest against the table. Plates and bowls and cups crashed to the floor, and the bottle smashed in a shower of glass shards and dark red wine. Whitebrooke roared and twisted to find the soldier, but Vaughn moved faster, and wrapped his arm around the priest's neck and pulled it tight with his other arm. Whitebrooke's face turned red and veins

THE MARTYR'S TEARS

stood purple against his skin as he strained against the soldier's arm.

"Hold him," Maeglin said as he rose to his feet, his hand gripping the hilt of his dagger.

Whitebrooke kicked savagely at the table with such force that it twisted upward and slammed into Maeglin. The knight stepped quickly back, but the edge of the table caught him across the leg, and he stumbled against the wall.

The priest lurched from his chair, carrying the soldier on his back, and hurled himself backward, smashing Vaughn into the wall behind him. Vaughn grunted with pain, but hung on, and grimly bore down on the priest's neck.

Maeglin scrambled to his feet as Whitebrooke snapped his head backward. Vaughn's nose smashed and his grip slipped, and Whitebrooke tore himself free.

Vaughn cursed and struck the priest in the face, heavy blows that landed with the sound of a cleaver in a butcher's shop, but Whitebrooke snarled and spat blood in the soldier's face. Vaughn clawed desperately at his eyes as Whitebrooke fell on him. The priest's huge fist smashed into the soldier's jaw, spinning him around, and Whitebrooke grabbed the soldier by the hair and smashed his head into the wall.

Maeglin hurdled the table and leapt toward Whitebrooke. The priest released the soldier, and with a snarl he lunged at Maeglin, faster than the Knight Commander had expected from a man of Whitebrooke's size. The priest's hands reached for Maeglin's throat, fingers curled into grasping talons.

Maeglin stepped past the clutching fingers, twisting to the side as Whitebrooke's hands scrabbled at his shoulder, then he straightened and slammed his fist into Whitebrooke's jaw, putting the strength of his legs and arms and hate into the blow.

Whitebrooke's teeth cracked together with the sound of a tree splitting in a deadly frost, and his head snapped back as blood sprayed from his mouth. He staggered to the side and collided with the table. Maeglin followed him, grabbed a fistful of the Archivist's shaggy hair, and yanked the priest's head back. Whitebrooke grabbed for Maeglin's hand, twisting backward, and

Maeglin struck downward with a blow that snapped the Archivist's nose, forcing him to one knee.

Maeglin struck again, his mailed fist driving into the unprotected flank of the priest, but Whitebrooke did not collapse. The priest roared in fury and lurched to his feet, one huge fist exploding upward into Maeglin's abdomen. The blow lifted the Knight Commander from his feet and drove the air from his lungs despite his mail shirt, and he crashed to the floor amidst the scattered debris of Whitebrooke's dinner.

The Archivist was on him in a heartbeat. Maeglin had only time to scramble to his hands and knees before the priest's hands clamped like steel on the collar of his shirt and Maeglin was whirled into the air to slam cruelly into the stone wall beside the fireplace.

Maeglin fought to draw breath as he pushed himself off the stone floor. He regained his feet and searched for the priest, finding Whitebrooke over the prone body of the soldier, Vaughn's short sword naked in his hand.

"Let's see if you're as arrogant once I've pricked you in the belly," the priest spat.

Maeglin did not reply. He sucked in a readying breath, clenched his jaw, and waited for Whitebrooke's attack.

The blade sliced through the air, the shining steel precisely extended toward Maeglin's chest.

The Knight Commander took the sword's edge on his vambrace and stepped into the priest. The steel blade shrieked against thick armor as Maeglin's fist smashed into Whitebrooke's cheekbone, splitting the skin and rocking the priest backward.

Whitebrooke hacked blindly with the sword as Maeglin circled to the side. He struck the priest in the throat, then again in his jaw. Whitebrooke choked a curse and swung wildly, tearing steel scales from the Knight Commander's chest with the tip of his sword.

Maeglin stepped away, then lunged forward as Whitebrooke raised the sword. His fist smashed into Whitebrooke's mouth, spraying blood across his chest and the floor.

THE MARTYR'S TEARS

Whitebrooke staggered to the side and his sword scraped sparks from the stone with its tip. Maeglin followed him, stomped on Whitebrooke's blade, and wrenched the hilt from the priest's hand. Whitebrooke grabbed for it, bending low, and Maeglin struck with a blow that caught the Archivist behind the ear, driving him to one knee.

Maeglin fell on him before Whitebrooke could gather the strength to rise. Another blow to the side of Whitebrooke's face finally dropped him to the floor, and Maeglin rammed his knees into the Archivist's chest, pinning him on his back. The priest refused to give in, and he grabbed at Maeglin's arms and face. Maeglin bared his teeth and unleashed his rage into Whitebrooke's face, smashing blow after blow as blood drenched the Archivist's beard and streamed from twisted nose and torn skin, until at last Whitebrooke lay still.

Maeglin rose, his chest rising and falling as he gulped air. Blood stung his eyes and pattered onto the floor from his fists as he surveyed the battered form of the priest. Whitebrooke groaned and rolled heavily onto his stomach, but did not rise.

Maeglin spat onto the priest's back and stepped away. Vaughn was back on his feet, blood dripping from his nose and mouth, his face ashen under a web of bright red droplets as he stared at the priest. Maeglin snatched a cloth from the wreckage of the dinner table and began to wipe his face and neck.

"Make sure he doesn't choke to death," Maeglin snarled. "He never answered my question."

The soldier nodded as Maeglin tossed the sodden cloth onto Whitebrooke's back and strode from the room.

THE MARTYR'S TEARS

Danielle

A malicious wind blew through Littleford, causing chaos in the bustling marketplace and along the narrow, rush-choked river that meandered around the town. The wind gusted suddenly, setting the tall fir trees swaying and creaking. It swept flattened patches of churned water across the river, bending the grasses and reeds that grew in the shallows, and caused the small fishing boats on the river to spin and foul each other's lines. In the marketplace, it ripped awnings and pulled hats and bonnets free, and sent up a chorus of banging shutters along the streets.

When the sun shone upon the town the buildings and streets sparkled. Drops of frost clung to every surface, glittering in the sun and trembling in the wind. Bright flowers of purple and orange swayed in tubs placed around the market, freshly burst from their bulbs. But when the sun fled behind a cloud, the dull grey of winter returned, and with it sharp drops of rain that whipped through the town on the wind and stung the unwary face.

Despite the wind, the marketplace was filled. With the end of winter a rumor on everyone's lips, the farmers had swarmed the town to prepare for the spring. The smithies were buried beneath harnesses to be mended, ploughs to be straightened, and hoes to be sharpened. The first loads of freshly shorn wool had arrived with some of the more entrepreneurial farmers, who were more than willing to give their flock a few cold nights in exchange for a good profit.

Littleford was accustomed to the famers' pilgrimage, but no preparation could have readied the town for the overwhelming deluge of soldiers that now crowded the streets, filled every tavern, and clogged the market. The long hill across the river was covered by their encampment. Circles of tents clustered around cooking fires, long horse lines ran in front of the trees, and a sturdy wooden palisade encapsulated the whole.

Danielle stared in wonder at the crowds from the entrance of an inn that stood along the river bank. She had taken shelter in a small eddy in the jostling stream of people created by a stack of barrels, content to watch the bustle as she waited for Wyn to return.

Remarkably little trouble marred the busy streets. Danielle heard some good-natured shouting and saw exasperation in the faces of those caught in the throng, but the soldiers appeared to be behaving themselves, and more smiles than scowls graced the faces of the townsfolk.

Wyn appeared through a small gap in the crowd as if by magic, hopping between a plodding mule and a soldier on horseback. The sun caught her hair in a blaze of gold, and her cheeks were crowned with pink spots from the breeze. She grinned and waved as she caught sight of Danielle, and hurried to her.

"Phew, what a scrum," Wyn giggled. The bright sunlight had brought out Wyn's freckles in a faint band across her cheeks and nose, and Danielle suppressed an urge to stroke them with her fingers. "I haven't seen so many people in one place since Kuray."

"I remember Littleford as a very quiet town," Danielle said, astonished, as a jostling crowd of eager customers surrounding a vendor of sizzling sausages forced her to press herself against the brick wall of the inn. "What are all the soldiers doing here?"

"Well, it's a bit strange, really," Wyn shook her head, baffled. "One lot is working on re-paving the ford, as we saw on the way in, and another lot is out in the fields every day plowing, and everyone's laughing about how they've had their roof patched, or barn fixed, or a new sty built. It's bizarre."

"An army came to fix the town?"

"Apparently, and from all over. There were some lads from a village near Northwick, and another lot from Ráthmór. I even saw one old bastard from Glen Walden who would run us out of the market whether or not we'd done anything, the old troll."

"It is not what I was expecting," Danielle admitted. "From what we heard from Cormac and Sir Eilidh, I had imagined a very grim scene."

"Well now, there is still a bit of a rumble about that, if you listen hard enough," Wyn said quietly, so that Danielle leaned close to hear her. "The townsfolk are none too pleased, although they keep it amongst themselves, as it were. But it wasn't these soldiers that did that... those were all hauled off, and some were murdered in their home, long before this lot began to show up."

"Maker's breath... it is hard to believe."

"It is, but I heard similar from others." Wyn brushed fluttering strands of hair from her face as she peered at the crowded street. "Do you think it's safe for Eilidh to come into town, since it's different soldiers, and all?"

"The townsfolk will still recognize her," Danielle pointed out. "And the soldiers are still loyal to Gabrielle, even if they are not the same ones that attacked the temple."

"I suppose," Wyn said, unconvinced. "The townies will never give her up, will they?"

"I do not know," Danielle sighed. "Everyone is so friendly, it is hard to imagine she would be in danger. I think we were right to be cautious, and it is only for one night," Danielle said thoughtfully. Her gaze wandered across the busy street as she watched the passing soldiers. *Dozens and dozens... no, hundreds... all serving knights and lords pledged to Gabrielle. And the temple abandoned. We may have found the safest town in all of Albyn.*

"... Dani?" Wyn's voice interrupted Danielle's reverie.

"I am sorry, I was lost," she apologized.

"You were, a bit," Wyn laughed. "Were you able to get a room, or do we need to find a stable to sleep in?"

"I did manage to persuade an innkeeper to give us a room," Danielle said proudly, then her face clouded. "But we do not have much money, now. I had to promise the innkeeper almost all we had left."

"Do we have enough for food?"

"I think so."

"Never mind, then," Wyn shrugged. "Some tasty tuck and a warm bed and tomorrow will sort itself. There's plenty more silver out in that mob, that's certain, and few enough rooms left in town. Speaking of, how did you persuade him to give us a room? Did you do like I said?" Wyn asked Danielle, her grin spreading.

"A bit," Danielle said sheepishly.

"I wish I'd seen," Wyn sighed wistfully. "Maybe you can persuade me later."

"I would like that," Danielle said softly, and she felt the strain of their ordeal begin to slip away, soothed by the safety of soldiers filling the streets and the comfort of Wyn's happy smile. *It has been so long... so many weeks of being frightened, and cold, and hurt.* "I have missed you."

"Martyr's tears, me too," Wyn's eyes widened as her smile spread. "Come on, is this the place? I'm starved and aching for a bonk, and standing in the street's not helping either."

"Yes, this is the inn," Danielle replied. A vibrantly-painted sign hung from iron hooks over the front door, featuring a shaggy black bear on its hind legs, balancing a mug in one paw and a fiddle in the other, and the words "The Dancing Bare" over its head.

The tavern beneath the inn was already filling with hungry patrons ready for their evening meal and a mug drawn from a freshly-broached cask. The tavern was spacious, with long tables surrounding a wide, empty floor in the center. Heavy, smoke-stained beams sat upon rough-hewn wooden pillars rubbed smooth by countless leaning shoulders and steadying hands, and an old staircase led to the rooms above.

The tavern keeper hurried over and made a show of ushering them to a small table near the tavern's windows.

They were brought fresh bread that steamed as it was cracked open, and a tender cut of pork nestled amongst potatoes roasted golden brown.

"And there's bacon for the morning," the tavern keeper assured them with a wink as he departed.

"This place will do," Wyn decided. "Oooo, they have butter!"

The roar of the tavern grew as more people squeezed through the door, townsfolk and soldiers alike pushing good-naturedly into the tavern. Three fiddlers stamped and wailed a merry tune, and the room filled with cheers and whistles at the end of each song.

By the time they had finished their meal, the tavern had filled to bursting. The room exuded energy, a happy expectation that made the people laugh, and smile, and greet each other exuberantly as if seeing old friends for the first time in months.

A serving lad who could not meet Danielle's eyes brought her a cup of wine, and she leaned against the wall and let the noise and warmth and joy wash over her.

Wyn called the lad over and spoke with him, her words lost amidst the hubbub. Danielle saw him frown in puzzlement, then gesture toward the center of the tavern with a mug.

"No!" Wyn clapped her hands together and her eyes widened with joy. The boy nodded, and Wyn turned to Danielle with a smile.

"Dani, you'll never guess what today is," Wyn said gleefully.

"I do not know. Market day?"

"Not that! It's First Day!"

"It is?" Danielle asked, bewildered. "When was Midwinter?"

"I suppose it was months ago," Wyn laughed. "We missed it in a cave or someplace horrible, I expect."

"It is impossible to tell when winter ends, here in the north," complained Danielle. "If it ever does."

"Well, it rains instead of snows," Wyn said helpfully. "Although, not always."

"I cannot believe a year has passed, already," Danielle admitted. "I have lost all track of time. Will they do something to celebrate?" Danielle gazed hopefully around the crowded tavern. "At home, we would fill the rooms with flowers."

"Not flowers," Wyn said, her smile widening even further. "Dani, they are having a céilí!"

"Are they?" Danielle said brightly, her smile fixed. "When?"

"Right now! Tonight! Isn't that amazing?"

"Amazing," Danielle agreed.

"Oh, no! You promised. Twice!" Wyn insisted. She pulled off her boots and added them to the pile of her cloak and thick jacket, leaving her clad in only the slim tunic and leather leggings that Danielle had bought for her in Cillian's shop. "You will love it, I swear. Oh, please, Dani, please dance with me."

Danielle sought for some excuse, but there was none to be had, and with a last, despairing glance she allowed Wyn to pull her from her seat and guide her through the crowd to the center of the tavern, where a wide square surrounded by watchers had formed.

The lines of dancers formed quickly as the fiddlers played the call. Wyn squeezed Danielle's hand and flashed her a happy smile, then led her into the line.

"What do I do?" Danielle whispered.

"Don't worry, I'll show you," Wyn told her happily.

Danielle held Wyn's hands tightly. The touch of her skin against Wyn's buoyed Danielle and sent nervous tingles of excitement through her.

Then the first notes tumbled out, fast and powerful, and the dance began. Heels stomped, toes pointed, and twirling stars formed and re-formed as the lines came together and pulled apart.

The tavern throbbed with the wail of the fiddles and the pounding rhythm of the dancers, urged on by the crowd of watchers who clapped and cheered. The heat was stifling, the roaring fire now aided by the thundering hearts of dozens of dancers and the cheering, happy throng.

Danielle had never experienced dancing like this. She had been to countless balls as she grew up in Venaissin, always invited as the young Marquessa and budding beauty who was the topic of so many conversations, expectations, and marital machinations. But the dances of her homeland were slow, precise, and cold, with dozens of dancers in intricate patterns that could be followed even when encumbered by ornate dresses and robes.

The pace in the Dancing Bare that night was fast, loud, and hot. Spinning and leaping and laughing, with clapping and cheering all around. She felt awkward placing her hand on Wyn's hip at first, exposing herself in front of so many people. But she soon lost herself in the simple intimacy of moving together, holding each other, guiding each other through the dance. She began to leap higher, skip faster, and laugh and cheer with each new tune. The smiles and laughter of the other dancers, and the chilled mead swallowed hastily between tunes to cool off, soon soothed away any last fears. *No one cares,* she realized. *No one is agape over the fact that the Marquessa d'Lavandou has brought her common lover into public. No one is staring with disapproval.* The realization freed her more than she could have predicted. She had thought herself long past any such concerns, since she had exposed her love for Wyn to Gabrielle, but now she understood that unwinding the knot of secrecy and fear she had diligently woven over so many years would not be so simple. *I will have many firsts in my new life, and this is one of them. The first time we have shown others how we feel. There, that loop is freed and blows away on the wind. What will be next?*

Of course, I am not the Marquessa d'Lavandou anymore, am I? I am just Danielle, who is in love with Wyn. She knew that was too simple a thought, and far from the truth. Nevertheless, for the moment, for the time of a dance, she could cling to it and to Wyn, and banish the paragon, the adept, the wielder of the Blade, the hunted traitor, and simply be a young woman dancing in a tavern with her love.

As Danielle's worries fled before the laughter and the music, she found herself watching Wyn, her eye drawn to the way Wyn moved, to the way the light fell on her face and hair, the way she smiled and laughed and teased as she slipped through the dancers. The silver threads in her tunic flashed as Wyn danced, whirling and leaping, lovely and graceful as if she were a faerie being who did not need to touch the ground as a mortal did.

Wyn caught her gaze and grinned at her with wide eyes. Danielle felt her heart beat heavily, and longing stirred deep within her breast as heat rose into her throat. She nearly glanced away, so sudden was the urge. But she did not. *I can look at her any time that I want!*

Wyn's grin spread into a wide smile of pleasure, and she blew a kiss, winked and spun away.

Danielle watched Wyn go, mesmerized by the golden curl of Wyn's hair around her long neck.

Danielle smiled as the heat of embarrassment became an ache of another sort, that made her breath grow short and her heart pound. She spun her way clear of the line and stood in the ring of watchers, clinging to a cup of cold, honeyed mead, as she let the feeling wash over her.

As the music ended Wyn skipped across the floor to Danielle, happy and grinning, and stood, shifting from one pointed foot to the other, as if unable to stop dancing.

"Are you all right?" Wyn asked breathlessly.

Danielle nodded happily. "Yes, I am very well, but I could not continue for a moment."

Wyn executed a quick blur of pointed toes and twisting feet that magically moved her closer, and she leaned forward and kissed Danielle, her touch a tingling sparkle on Danielle's lips.

"Yum," Wyn licked her lips. "That's tasty, that is."

Danielle offered her cup and watched Wyn drink deeply, the shining perspiration on her neck shimmering in the lantern light as she swallowed.

Wyn passed the cup back and ran an appraising gaze over Danielle's face. "You look like a cat with a little feather caught on her whiskers, really happy and sly, all at once."

Danielle nodded again, then leaned forward and brought her lips to Wyn's ear. Small strands of blonde hair tickled against her cheek, and she breathed in Wyn's warm scent.

"I have been watching you," she whispered.

"Oh yes?" Wyn giggled softly next to her. "You managed to have a bit of a peek, did you?"

"I have been practicing," Danielle assured her gravely. "Diligently."

"It's nice to practice, isn't it?" Wyn laughed. "What did you look at? Was it nice?"

"It was very nice," Danielle closed her eyes and breathed out a heavy, satisfied sigh.

"Oh, now I'm jealous, you naughty girl," Wyn pulled back and pouted dramatically.

"You said for me to share," Danielle reminded her, and she lifted the cup to her own lips and let the cool, sweet liquid slide across her tongue, her gaze never leaving Wyn's over the rim of the cup.

"Mmmm, that I did," Wyn smiled and squirmed luxuriously. "Now my nips are all crinkly. Do they show?" Wyn peered down and began to rearrange her tunic, much to Danielle's delight, trying to pull the clinging cloth free from her damp skin, but Wyn only succeeded in pulling it taut against her lithe form in fascinating ways. "How is it that yours aren't?" Wyn demanded crossly. "There's no way you could get away with it, not with the way you fill out a shirt. Stupid things, why don't they wait until we can do something about it? Unless…" Wyn glanced up and Danielle hastily raised her gaze to meet Wyn's. "Unless you're thinking about a trip upstairs? For a visit downstairs?"

Danielle shook her head. "There was a promise of dancing. I should like more."

"C'mon then, your Danciness, they're getting ready again." Wyn led Danielle by the hand back onto the floor and they stood ready for the music, Danielle's fingers entwined in Wyn's. "You do know they'll play forever yet. Midnight, easy. That's a long time to wait."

"I do not mind," Danielle declared, sweeping her hair from her face with a shake of her head. "I am enjoying myself very much."

"That's what you said," Wyn winked.

"Not just that." Danielle smiled and gazed around the room. "All of this. The sound, the movement, the excitement. The happiness. I did not realize."

"I'm glad to hear it." Wyn squeezed her hands as the fiddlers gave a long note to settle the dancers in their places. "But what you also don't realize is that I've got a present waiting for you."

"A present? What is it?"

"I'll give you a clue." Wyn gazed innocently at the ceiling and nibbled on her lip in a show of profound thought. "It's all wrapped up very snug, and it's a bit fuzzy."

The fiddles launched into the dance before Danielle had a chance to reply, which she gave thanks for, as she felt sure she would have stammered and made a silly fool of herself, and instead she was simply able to enjoy another warm flush of excitement kindle itself deep within her.

They danced until long after the middle night bells rang in the town square and Danielle's dark skin gleamed with perspiration. The last patrons departed, the last guests retired, and still she and Wyn danced. With their last silver pennies, they persuaded one of the fiddlers to stay, and with a generous helping of convincing from Wyn, they persuaded the innkeeper to sweep the floors and wipe down the tables around them.

But at last they wore the poor fiddler into surrender, and he stumbled from the tavern with aching fingers. Danielle did not want to let go of Wyn, and they stood quietly in the middle of the empty floor, hand in hand, until Wyn gave her a grin and a tug on her hand, and pulled her toward the stairs.

They crept up the steps, but the wood was so old and worn that Danielle could not help but make them creak and groan, no matter how delicately she placed her feet where Wyn was pointing, and they were giddy with stifled laughter by the time they made it to the upstairs hall. They had been given a room with a high window that overlooked the front of the inn and a door that led to a small balcony that faced the river and the ford. The bed was wide enough to sleep four, with a thick, down cover, far more luxury than they had seen in many weeks.

As Danielle fumbled with the latch she suddenly froze. The snores of some unknown guest carried clearly into the hallway from a distant room, and Danielle could no longer suppress her giggles. "Perhaps we are sharing our inn with a boar," she whispered.

Danielle managed to get the door open, and then firmly shut it behind them. A single candle guttered on the small dressing table, its tiny nub barely higher than the pool of wax that had spread around its base. Danielle lit a second candle before the first one died completely away, then took a soft cloth and dipped it in the water bowl that sat on its stand next to the table. She ran the cloth down her neck, enjoying its cool touch as it wiped away the tickles of sweat. Rivulets trickled down her throat and into the deep curve between her breasts and left behind a tingling fire.

When she turned to face the room, she saw that Wyn was sitting on the edge of the bed, watching her with dark eyes.

"Do you know how gorgeous you are?" Wyn asked. She rose from the bed and padded on bare feet across the floor to stand in front of Danielle. "How are you real? I can't believe I can just reach out, and touch you..."

Wyn did just that, and stroked gentle fingers along Danielle's neck and deeply into her hair across the back of her head, and Wyn gazed into Danielle's eyes, a small frown betraying the intensity of her thoughts.

"I love you, Danielle," Wyn whispered.

Danielle felt a smile spread across her lips, and her heart beat heavy in her throat. "Thank you for taking me dancing."

Wyn smiled and her serious demeanor fled. "It was fun, I told you. And you did well. It's not easy the first time."

"I went wherever you pointed me." Danielle let her fingers glide across Wyn's cheek and guide her hair behind her ear. "I hope I did not appear too foolish."

"No, not foolish." Wyn's eyes grew wide. "You looked a long way from foolish, never fear."

"I am happy to hear it, but you were by far the most amazing person in that room tonight. The way you moved, so gracefully. Ethereal, except that is not right because you were strong and alive. I kept thinking of the stories of the forest spirits," Danielle smiled. "I have already told you what watching you did to me."

"Yeah," Wyn laughed. "I haven't really been able to think of much else, since."

"I could not help it. You are so lovely, and I could imagine… I pictured…" Danielle felt heat rise to her cheeks. "Oh, Martyr's tears, why is it so difficult for me to say these things? You must think me ridiculous to have such problems."

"I don't mind," Wyn shrugged. "I'm embarrassing enough for the both of us, so it's probably for the best."

"It is silly, but I cannot help it." Danielle took a deep breath to gather her will. "You…" *A fine start,* she chastised herself, and rolled her eyes in exasperation.

"You don't have to say anything." Wyn took Danielle's hands and placed them on her waist. Danielle could feel the ridge of Wyn's hips and the gentle curve of her waist through the soft fabric of her tunic, and Wyn's fingers rested lightly on the back of Danielle's hands, a gentle pressure to go further. "It's all right, I promise."

"I want to." Danielle took another deep breath. The words were so clear in her mind, and the ache in her chest so strong, that she felt the words should simply pour out when she opened her mouth. *But they do not… it is so unfair.* "I wish to tell you what I see when I watch you, what I feel. I want you to know how I desire you, that there is love, yes, and also passion, and that you stir such thoughts within me. It is not right that you should not know what you do to me, and what… what I wish to do… to you."

"Go on then." Wyn's smile grew with anticipation.

"You promised me a gift," Danielle managed to get the words out without dropping her gaze. "I have been thinking of it all night. I have thought of nothing else, and I would… and I would like it very much."

Wyn nodded silently, then pushed against Danielle, her lips seeking Danielle's, and Danielle pulled Wyn toward her as their kisses became urgent. Then their fingers were scrabbling with laces and buttons until Danielle's clothes sighed to the floor alongside the crumpled pile of Wyn's clothing, and they came together again, pressing skin against skin, their hands buried in each other's hair as their mouths locked together. Wyn's lips tasted of honey, and her neck tasted of salt, and her pale skin was hot as she pressed against Danielle.

Wyn laughed and stepped away in a graceful, slow turn, with pointed toe and arched back, and Danielle allowed herself to stare, to consume Wyn with her gaze, etching every line, every curve, every shadow, into her memory. The fall of golden light over the curve of her skin, the high arc of shadow over her hips, the long rise of lithe muscles along her back and shoulders. Wyn held out her hand, and Danielle joined her and lost herself in Wyn's touch.

***

Danielle was deep in satisfied sleep when the soft knock on her door came, and for a moment she hoped she had dreamed the sound. The bedroom was utterly dark, the candle long since extinguished, and the only sound besides the omnipresent rush of the nearby river was the gentle breath of the young woman beside her.

The knock came again, soft but insistent in its duration, and Danielle slowly disentangled herself from Wyn's outflung legs and padded softly to the door, remembering half-way there to detour to the foot of the bed to search for her clothes. The knock came a third time before she could distinguish whether she was holding her leggings or Wyn's tunic, and she abandoned them all for one of the blankets pulled from the bed that she wrapped around her shoulders and which trailed behind her across the floor like the train on a formal dress.

Danielle paused at the door and pressed cautious fingers against its smooth wood.

"Yes?" she called softly.

"Danielle, it's Killock," came the whispered reply.

Danielle stood frozen in shock, staring at the faint yellow glow coming through the keyhole. Then her fingers were fumbling to open the latch and keep her blanket secure at the same time. Light from a candle sliced through the open crack and Danielle blinked and squinted against its unwelcome glow.

A hand shielded the small flame and Danielle saw that her ears had not deceived her. Killock was seemingly unchanged from the last time she had seen him, months ago. A scraggly beard streaked with grey covered his jaw, and deep wrinkles surrounded his eyes as he smiled.

"Oh, Killock, it is you," Danielle sighed, and she pulled him close in an awkward tangle of blanket and arms. The buckles of his arm guards pressed coldly against her back, but she did not care. The knight smelled of leather and earth, and Danielle could feel his wiry strength holding her safe, and relief from a strain she had not realized existed suddenly washed over her, leaving a burning sting in her eyes.

They stood quietly for a moment, with only the sound of Danielle's breathing and the creak of leather disturbing the silence. Then Danielle carefully disentangled herself and her blanket with an apologetic smile.

"It is so wonderful to see you," she whispered. "How did you know we were here?"

"I have been following you," Killock murmured. "I am sorry, Danielle, but we must leave, immediately."

"But it is the middle of the night…" Danielle shuddered as a yawn overwhelmed her. "Can we not leave in the morning?"

"No, we do not have much time. Can you gather your things and meet me in the tavern? I will explain everything, I promise."

"Yes, of course," Danielle assured the knight. "I will only be a moment."

Danielle eased the door onto its latch and felt her way to her pack. She crouched and searched through it, her fingers confident as she found everything in its expected place. She stood, once again yanking the recalcitrant blanket into proper position. The heavy amulet was cold in her hand as she took a deep breath to clear the last vestiges of sleep from her mind and prepared her Word. It was a delicate pattern, as the amulet was not well-suited for subtle work. It was designed to unleash its power in a great rush, but Danielle wanted a far different result. The Word formed slowly, hanging in her mind like distant stars on a summer night, and Danielle whispered the Word and let it flow into the amulet.

The Device stirred as its bindings released, and heat bloomed deep in its interior, rushing to escape. But Danielle's Word channeled it and tempered it, and released only a small, emerald flame that danced across the surface of the amulet and climbed her hand until it perched, trembling in the slight breeze, on the tips of her first two fingers.

Satisfied with the low, steady glow, Danielle crossed the room to the bed and sat on the edge next to Wyn. Wyn lay face down, her hair a blonde sprawl across her pillow, the cover twisted and wrapped around her arms and legs. Danielle stroked Wyn's back gently, tracing delicate shapes across her pale skin until she groaned and burrowed deeper into the pillow.

"Wyn, wake up, Sir Killock is here, and he says we must leave."

"Bother Killock," Wyn mumbled.

Danielle began tracing the basic stanza of runes on Wyn's back, beginning at the base of her spine and working her way up between her shoulder blades.

"You may sleep later, I promise, but Sir Killock says it is urgent."

A single eye blinked balefully through the flop of Wyn's hair. "What do you mean, 'Sir Killock says'?"

"He is here, waiting for us. I promise."

Wyn slowly pushed herself upright, then sat, slumped and yawning, as she rubbed furiously on the sides of her head with her hands.

"Where on earth did he come from?" Wyn complained. "Does he show up when we're stuck in an old ruin filled with men trying to kill us? No. He waits until it's the middle of the night, and we're completely knackered…" She stopped rubbing long enough to peer through her hair at Danielle. "Is your finger on fire?"

"Yes," Danielle replied, embarrassed. "I could not find the candle in the dark, and in any case, we have no taper—"

"It's wicked," Wyn assured her, and she staggered to her feet and trudged to the pile of clothes at the foot of the bed. "Where's my knickers? Bother the knickers, where's my pants?"

THE MARTYR'S TEARS

Danielle left Wyn to teeter her way into her leggings and readied herself. She gently placed the flame onto the candle and let it settle there, turning a gentle yellow, then quickly donned the warm traveling clothes that she had worn since Bandirma, once beautiful, now sadly worn; leather leggings, soft boots, a long, red tunic that reached almost to her knees, covered by embroidery in silver thread, and a thick, quilted jacket and lined cloak. A wide belt, fastened snugly around her waist, and she was ready.

Wyn had managed to don her leggings, and wiggle her arms and head into her tunic, but had then given up and simply gathered her boots, knife, belt, and cloak into an ungainly bundle.

Danielle collected the rest of their belongings and the candle, and led the way down the stairs to the common room.

The tavern was empty, with only the feeble glow of the smoldering logs in the wide fireplace to light it. Sir Killock stood next to the fire, warming his hands, a darker patch in the shadowy room.

But before Danielle could do more than draw a breath to greet the Templar, Wyn had dropped her bundle with a clatter, bounded across the floor, and hurled herself onto Killock. She wrapped her arms around his neck and let her momentum swing her feet in a wide circle as the knight hugged her and swung her around three times before setting her on her feet.

"…and I talked to God, and He didn't say anything about how naughty I've been, even though I thought He might, but no, and I escaped from Bandirma, twice for goodness' sake, plus we know who the Crunorix is, plus I tried to kill him but I got killed instead but it was all right in the end, plus we went all the way to Greymouth and back, and look at these fancy clothes that Dani bought me to meet the Queen, and she didn't even know I was wearing her knickers, there's a laugh—"

"I am overjoyed to see you, too, Wyn," Sir Killock spoke quickly when the young woman paused to draw breath.

"Where have you been?" Wyn asked.

"I have been… a very long way. And I will tell you all about it," he continued hurriedly as Wyn indignantly drew breath to object, "but first, you said that you discovered who the Crunorix is?"

"Oh, yeah, no problem," Wyn said airily. "His name is Shitebrooke. Or something like that. I've forgotten again."

Killock laughed harshly. "Whitebrooke."

"Yes, that's the bastard."

"You do not sound surprised," Danielle told the Templar.

"No," Killock ground the word through a clenched jaw. "I suppose I am not. His accusations against you, Danielle, were full of inconsistencies and falsehoods, but I could not prove that they were lies, nor did I find any evidence that he might be the Crunorix priest."

"Bad luck," Wyn consoled. "Well, I saw him do it, and he told Dani all about it, all gloating and such, the shit stain. You ask her, she'll tell you, so there's your proof."

"It is true," Danielle said stiffly, her jaw clenched against the memory of Whitebrooke's sneering laugh. "He performed fuil crunor in front of us, and boasted that he would lead the Temple into a new age, founded on the power of the Crunorix."

"I believe you," the Templar said thoughtfully. He glanced at Wyn. "You don't seem disappointed to hear there is still doubt as to his crimes?"

"You're joking, right? I'm the one who's going to stick a knife in him and let his juices run out. I was worried you were going to have all the fun without me."

"She has come up with quite a few ideas along those lines," Danielle nodded appreciatively. "Some of them very interesting."

"You say the sweetest things," Wyn beamed at her.

"I am sure she has." Killock stared, unseeing, at the floor in front of his feet. "Who else knows?"

"Just us," Wyn answered. "Oh, and Cormac, and Sir Eilidh. That's it, on account of having to run for our lives and never being safe and all. But we're on our way to Bandirma to finish Shitebrooke off properly, and spit in his face while we're at it, so we'll soon not have to worry about him."

"Who is Sir Eilidh?" Killock asked.

"Oh, she's a knight that Cormac is sweet on, though he won't admit it, so he brought her with him all the way from Littleford," Wyn said mischievously, then suddenly creased her faint eyebrows with a frown. "Although that sounds a bit strange, now."

"Good," Killock said absently, his attention still far away.

"Killock," Danielle said gently. "You said we had to leave."

"Yes." Killock's gaze regained its focus. "We are in danger. I have followed you for days, and in Newbridge I discovered a group of men who were also tracking you. They had found your boat, and your trail leading south."

"They must have been the men who attacked us when we took shelter from the storm." Danielle frowned at the memory. "I hoped we had seen the last of them when we escaped."

"They have not given up, nor will they," Killock said grimly. "I recognized one of them at the boat, a man I trained years ago who I expelled from the Temple because of his cruel nature. Unfortunately, his skills have not faded. He will find you again."

"What can we do?"

"We run, and with luck I can hide our trail."

"From a few bastards?" Wyn asked incredulously. "Why don't we wait right here by the fire and give them a thrashing when they show up."

"You say that you have fought them before… you know that they are not simple thugs."

"There were three of them attacked us last time, and I killed one of them and almost got another, even though I was not my best."

"You did?" Danielle asked, and she felt her throat close with sudden fear. "When? You said you would stay far away from them."

"Oh, shit…" Wyn looked stricken. "I didn't mean to say… I'm sorry, I didn't want you to worry, but we were never going to get away, not with them right behind us and with a bow and all. It was our best chance, and it almost worked. I killed one of the bastards and left the other with a mark he'll never be rid of, I was that close."

"Then tell me that," Danielle pleaded. "Do not lie to me just to shelter my feelings."

"I'm sorry, I promise, I really am," Wyn assured her, but Danielle could barely hear the words over the sound of her heart, and she swallowed against a surge of panic.

She stayed behind, alone in those pitch-black tunnels, and fought two men just so that I might escape. And her only thought was not to worry me. How many times has she risked her life for mine, and never once hesitated to do so?

Danielle slowly became aware that Killock and Wyn were arguing, and forced herself to listen.

"How is it any different?" Wyn asked.

"In the tower, they had already caught you. You had little choice, and your ambush took them off-guard," Killock said patiently. "Now, we have a chance to get away, and we should take it. Remember, they do not seek to defeat us, they only seek to kill Danielle. One shot from the shadows will be all the chance they need."

Danielle felt the skin between her shoulders creep in anticipation of a sudden strike, and she swallowed heavily. "Please, can we not let them do that?"

"Fine," Wyn said angrily. She pulled on her boots, ramming her feet into them and yanking the ties so fiercely Danielle feared they would snap. "We'll just run forever, then."

"Wyn, there are many of them, and only three of us," Danielle said reasonably. "And I know I shall be useless, worse than useless, as you will have to take care of me as well as fight."

"I did find something in Bandirma that might help if it comes to fighting," Killock told Danielle. "I thought you might be missing these." Killock rummaged in his bag and placed two Devices on the table, a thin shaft with a grip of swirling waves, and a small, grey egg.

"Oh…" Danielle gasped, speechless, and her eyes gleamed with happy tears. "I thought I had lost… I never hoped…" Danielle gripped Killock's hands and squeezed them, then gently picked up the Devices, suddenly fearful they would crumble into dust at her touch.

"Now old Shitebrooke is for it," Wyn giggled gleefully. "He'll fry up like bacon."

"I thought you were going to stab him?" Killock asked.

"I don't mind watching Dani cook him up with… does it have a name yet?" Wyn asked.

"It does not. I have hardly had time to think," Danielle complained.

"Oooo, how about Shadowbane?" Wyn's eyes went wide. "Or, no, Maker's Touch? No no no… Last Laugh, or Sun Spear, or Shining Death?"

"Now who has been reading ridiculous stories?" Danielle asked. "I would feel absurd telling someone those names. 'Maker's Touch' does not even make sense."

"Be picky, then. The Lady's Touch, oh, Dragon's Breath!"

"Perhaps later?" Danielle suggested gently. "I thought we were fleeing?"

"Still? Even though you have Thingy?"

"It will not stop an arrow," Danielle pointed out.

"Bloody arrows," Wyn grumped, and pulled her hood firmly over her head. "I'm ready."

"Check the back," Killock told her, and Wyn hurried to the kitchen and slipped through the door.

Danielle raised her Diviner. "Where do we want to go?" she asked.

"To wherever Cormac and this Sir Eilidh are waiting. If we can throw our pursuers off our tracks, I can get us to Bandirma without being found again. If not, then there will be five of us to face them."

Danielle nodded, and closed her eyes to concentrate on the small Device's Word. Shining patterns assembled quickly in her mind, familiar patterns of an intricate, delicate structure forming instinctively at her command. *Show me the way*, she whispered to the Word, and the lights pulsed as they flowed into the Device, and its bindings unfolded.

Golden light filled the rings of engraved symbols around the Device, and Danielle began to alter her Word, crafting it to match her needs. *Lead me away from them, lead me to safety, lead me to a place to hide.* The golden symbols floated above the Device's grey surface and spiraled into new patterns. Danielle watched them combine and re-combine, altering her Word to match them, until they settled into place again.

"North," she told Killock. "Across the river."

"North?" the Templar asked, puzzled. "That's the way they are coming."

"It says north," Danielle insisted.

Wyn returned as Killock struggled with the unexpected guidance, and she frowned at the glowing Device in Danielle's hand.

"I missed it," she pouted.

"Is the back of the tavern clear?" Killock asked.

"All quiet," Wyn said. "Horses are happy in the stable." Wyn wrinkled her nose and shoved strands of her hair back under her hood. "I dunno. It felt a bit weird."

"Could they be here, in Littleford, already?" Danielle asked.

"I would be surprised." Killock frowned. "But it is possible."

"It says north," Danielle held up the glowing Device. "If our pursuers are already here, perhaps they are expecting us to flee southward, and are awaiting us in that direction."

"North?" Killock asked again.

"Yes."

"All right. Let's go."

Killock led them through the darkened kitchen and out the back door of the inn. Danielle smothered the Diviner with her cloak and followed the knight along the side of the building, sticking to the darkest shadows. At the corner of the inn, Danielle chanced a peek at the Diviner. It pointed away from the stables, directly north across the river.

"Leave the horses," Danielle whispered.

Her guide led them to the riverbank and across the ford, using the wooden bridge the soldiers had built while they paved the crossing. Killock led the way, bent low in the shadow of a gnarled hedgerow that bordered the road, avoiding the silver light of the wide moon as it shone through a gap in the scurrying clouds.

They had not gone more than one hundred paces when Danielle felt the Diviner twist away from her Word. She peeled back a corner of her cloak and peered at the Device. Its golden runes swirled aimlessly around its grey shell, and her Word could not bring sense from the patterns.

"Wait," she whispered to Killock. "Something has changed. There is no clear path."

Wyn appeared abruptly from the shadows behind Danielle. "They're coming," she hissed.

Killock pondered the news for a heartbeat before deciding. "The temple." The knight pushed through a small gap in the hedgerow and hurried toward the dark shapes of the abandoned buildings on the slope above them. Danielle squeezed after him, the twisted limbs of the bushes scratching and grabbing at her hair and cloak. They followed a muddy path between two fences that led to the low barn, now empty and cold. Killock ignored the stalls and raced across the cobbles of the temple's yard to the main building. A small door gaped open forlornly, and Killock ushered them inside, then closed the door and slid the bolt behind them.

The interior of the temple was bitterly cold and musty. The floorboards creaked under their boots as if anxious to give up all the pent-up strain of lonely weeks, and the air stirred only reluctantly as they passed.

The light of Danielle's guide showed them a path through narrow hallways and past abandoned bedrooms and a scriptorium, until they reached the heavy, iron-bound door to the main temple, itself. The hinges scraped as Killock swung the door open, and they stepped into the echoing emptiness of the temple.

Shafts of cold moonlight speared through tall windows set high in the walls, turning the pews and pillars of the temple silver and black.

Killock reached the main doors and stopped, his hand on the heavy iron rings, his head cocked to the side. Then he turned back to the room and urged Wyn and Danielle away from the doors. "They are outside… hurry, the armory…"

Steel hissed as blades came to hand, and Killock led the way, hurrying toward the end of the room. Danielle took a dozen steps and then Wyn suddenly leapt into the air and collided violently with her, knocking Danielle to the ground between two of the pews. There was a soft thrum of sound, and the snap of an arrow shattering on the stone floor where she had stood a heartbeat before.

More bows fired from somewhere behind them, and Danielle instinctively ducked and covered her head with her arms as the volley ripped into the wood protecting her. Wyn scrambled desperately for the cover of a pew as more ricocheted from the stones around them.

"On the left!" Killock shouted, and Danielle saw figures materializing from the shadows behind the long line of pillars. They wore black cloaks and black leather armor, and their blades wore soot to dim their steel. The attackers rushed toward them without any shouts or cries, eerily quiet, as if they were shadows or smoke. They leapt over the pews and darted forward, covering the distance so quickly that Danielle barely had time to draw a breath to ready herself.

One of the assailants swerved toward her, his gaze locked on hers from within the shadows of his hood.

Danielle stumbled back as the man vaulted the pew and landed an arm's-length away, and Danielle gasped as she recognized him. A red, puckered wound now slashed across his cheek and into the hair above his ear, but Danielle could still see his dark eyes watching her in the market in Greymouth, and his silhouette standing on the quay as they sailed away.

The scarred man lunged forward, his blackened blade ripping the air as Danielle threw herself backward. He drew back for another strike, and Danielle raised her hands in desperate defense.

"Calder!" A shout drew his gaze, and his blade hesitated for a heartbeat. Then another figure crashed into him from the side. Danielle caught a glimpse of a faded cloak and grey hair, and then Killock and the scarred man tumbled over the pew with a crash of splintering wood.

THE MARTYR'S TEARS

Danielle grabbed the back of the pew and began to struggle to her feet. An arrow slammed into the wood next to her hand with a crack and a shower of splinters, and Danielle flung herself to the floor again and scrambled away on her hands and knees. More arrows struck the wood around her, quivering with the force of their impact. One of the small cushions on the pew was torn apart by the razor tip of an arrow, and a cloud of down feathers swirled incongruously into the air.

Danielle reached the end of the pew and lunged for the safety of a stone pillar and the shadows behind it. One last arrow ricocheted from the stone a hand's-breadth from her head as she dove, sprawled across the floor, and slid behind the pillar.

She quickly scrambled to her feet, and, pressing against the pillar as closely as she could, Danielle peered into the temple.

Several archers perched in the balcony and the air was filled with the vicious snap and sizzle of their shafts as they fired into the room.

Directly in front of her, Killock was locked in combat with Calder, the man who had pursued her across half of Albyn. Even as she watched, Killock scrambled to his feet, slipping on the splintered wood that littered the floor, and managed to face his opponent as Calder lunged with his sword. Killock jerked backward and knocked the blade to the side at the last moment. But Calder followed relentlessly, and his return blow sent Killock dodging low as the blade whistled through the air above his head.

Calder lunged again, and again, but each time Killock knocked his blade aside, skipping backward to keep his distance as Calder pressed to close.

Danielle searched for Wyn, but could not find her in the shadows. Her lance was in her hand, although she had no memory of pulling it from her pack, its familiar weight a comfort. The first patterns of its Word began to take shape in her mind, the Word delicate in its complex power. Danielle was dimly aware of the flash of steel to her right as Killock spun past his opponent and left an arc of crimson blood hanging in the air from the tip of his blade, and of the wood of the pew in front of her trembling under the impact of quivering arrows.

More of the Word's shining pattern slotted into place, but there was a strange blur of movement, and Danielle turned, trying to keep the pattern balanced delicately in her mind as she searched the shadows behind her.

A figure with a long, blackened blade loomed, Danielle twisted to escape the blow at the last instant, and the blade struck a shower of sparks from the pillar. The figure slashed at her as she dodged away, and Danielle heard tearing fabric across her back. She struck the ground hard and her knee banged against the stone and twisted underneath her. Pain shot through her leg but she rolled away as the blade struck the floor where she had been an instant before.

Her opponent slid forward, his sword ready to strike, then he parried desperately as Killock fell on him from the side, the Templar's sword a dancing, silver flame as it scythed through the air. The blades shrieked as they ground against each other, then Killock drove his fist into his opponent's face, shattering his nose, and sent him stumbling into the wall. Before Killock could press his advantage, Calder followed him from the pews, and Killock was forced to dodge backward. Their swords rang like a smith's hammer against the anvil as they clashed. The second attacker spat blood on the floor and joined his companion, lunging to force Killock to parry while Calder circled to flank. Killock feinted high and slipped between them as the man with the broken nose flinched away, but before Killock could take more than a single step, Calder's blade sliced across Killock's shoulder, ripping through the sturdy leather guard the Templar wore.

Danielle clambered to her feet, her knee screaming in agony. An arrow sliced past her shoulder and tugged her hood, and she ducked and scrambled toward the next pillar in line. Each step sent stabs of agony through her knee, but Danielle forced herself to run.

Arrows snapped off the floor at her feet and ripped the air around her. Splinters showered her face and hands as she reached the pillar and flung herself behind it.

A cloaked shape suddenly loomed out of the shadows, directly in her path, and Danielle flung out her hands as she plowed into her assailant. They stumbled and crashed to the floor. Danielle tore at his gloved fingers and twisted his hand, and his sword slipped free and clanged to the stone floor. Danielle reached for it, scrambling desperately over the attacker's thrashing body, but his hand knotted deep in her hair and yanked her head brutally back as she clutched at his fingers and pain scored her scalp.

The attacker pulled Danielle onto her back on top of him, and she heard the whisper of steel on leather as he drew a knife. She twisted with wild strength and smashed her elbow into his face, and his hand convulsed open and released her hair as he flailed at her arm. Danielle rolled and drove her knee between his legs, then reared back with her fist clenched, ready to slam it into his bloody face.

But he struck first, and his knife scored across her ribs, slicing through her heavy coat and into the flesh beneath. Danielle cried out as searing pain flared, and she rolled desperately away.

She pressed one hand to the wound and managed to push her legs under her, but the room pitched and swayed, and her legs did not seem to have the strength to hold her steady. Blood oozed between her fingers and ran to their tips, and drops began to patter to the floor beneath her. Danielle watched, mesmerized by the vibrant color as it traced a meandering pattern on the polished stone. She fought to rise to her feet and lurched to the side as the room swayed again, and drops of blood spattered across something lying on the floor. Danielle stared as darkness pushed at the edges of her vision and she clung to consciousness. *Why is a sword here?* she wondered, before recognizing the simple guard with the blackened blade that she had wrenched from her attacker's hand. She reached for the blade and then slowly straightened, sending fresh agony across her ribs. The sword felt heavy and awkward in her hand, but the weight sent strength through her and she clenched her hand around its hilt as she turned to her assailant.

He was on his feet again as well, and he watched her warily as he wiped blood from his shattered nose with the back of his gauntlet. Danielle saw that he was not a large man, only a hand's-breadth taller than she, but his face was as rugged as stone, and he moved with a quick, wiry strength that reminded her of the way Killock fought. He was older than she had expected. His clean-shaven face showed the wear of wind and cold in the long, thin lines that grew from his fierce scowl, and Danielle realized with a sinking heart that she faced a true veteran. The long, straight blade of his knife never quivered as he pointed it at her, ready to slice or thrust.

Danielle raised her sword and let her weight sink into her thighs. She focused on the center of her attacker's chest, half-remembering the low rumble of Bradon's voice across a snapping campfire many years ago, wishing she could recall any further details of the Templar's long-forgotten advice on swordplay.

Her attacker moved toward her with a smooth step, his knife gliding from right to left, drawing her blade with it. Danielle thrust, attempting to use her sword's greater weight and reach to advantage, then swung across and back as her opponent dodged away and to the side, waiting for an opening.

Where is Wyn? Where is Killock? The thoughts echoed in her mind, but Danielle kept her gaze riveted to her opponent.

He lunged forward suddenly, and Danielle leapt away, but her boot caught on a chunk of wood from a shattered pew, her knee buckled, and she stumbled. Her attacker followed her relentlessly, his blade scything towards her. Danielle screamed and drove upward, pushing with her legs and back, thrusting desperately toward him. The point of her sword slammed into the hard leather of his breastplate with a shock that ran up her arm and into her jaw, then tore through the armor and sank between his ribs. The sword twisted in her hand and ripped free of her grasp as his weight collapsed onto it.

He crashed into her and she sprawled across the floor, and her cheek struck cruelly against the smooth stone. Fresh pain spread from her ribs and knee, and Danielle groaned as she rolled onto her stomach and slowly drew her knees under her.

An arrow cracked off the floor in front of her, and she paused to glare at the balcony before lurching to her feet. Danielle left the sword stuck in her attacker's body and stumbled toward the wall and the line of sheltering pillars. She reached their shadow and pressed her cheek against their cold stone, gasping for breath as she peered into the temple.

Killock's duel with Calder continued, but two more assailants had joined his opponent, and all three harried the knight, driving him back despite the never-ending silver blur of his sword.

At least the archers had stopped shooting, and Danielle saw that Wyn had somehow vaulted into the balcony. Danielle caught a glimpse of her spinning between the archers, her knife leaving a thin spray of blood across the white stone as she passed. But even as Danielle watched, the archers abandoned their bows, drew swords, and began to close on Wyn despite whatever wounds the knife had sliced into them.

Danielle reached once more for her lance but hesitated as her fingers brushed against the heavy amulet in her pack. *There are so many of them, moving so quickly, I will never be able to hit them all with the lance. Not before the Word is drained. Not before they realize where the threat is coming from.* She left the lance and drew the amulet from the pack, and Danielle let her pain pass from her as she filled her mind with its Word. She knew she would have little chance to repeat her Word, not once their assailants were alerted to her presence, and so she built the Word into a structure as powerful as any she had attempted before with this Device. She felt the amulet respond, its fire seething against its bindings.

Somewhere on the edge of Danielle's senses, light and shadow swirled and steel rang out. *Now,* Danielle whispered to the amulet, and the Shape of Fire responded. Bindings released deep within it and an emerald inferno blasted into the room. It roared across the floor, dancing to Danielle's Word, and engulfed the black-garbed figures, who screamed and raised their hands in useless desperation.

The river of flame branched and leapt. A seething torrent washed across the balcony and turned the archers into blazing torches. A cyclone of brilliant fire twisted around Killock, encircling him with a shield that sent his attackers reeling back, clutching at their seared flesh and blackened skin.

A scream tore from Danielle's throat, a cry of rage, pain, and sorrow, and with it, she unleashed a final eruption of flame, a towering pillar of fire that reared into the air, its roar thundering against the arched ceiling. Danielle's gaze met Calder's in the instant before she struck with the breath of a dragon, pouring fire onto him until he flared white hot.

Then she released the Word, and the flames faded, and they became a score of flickering yellow fires spread across the room. A great gust of scorching air blew through the room and Danielle let it wash over her, streaming her hair behind her, the heat a balm to her pain and fatigue.

Then the wind passed and Danielle slowly limped to the center of the room, pausing only to yank her sword from its former master, unwilling to abandon the blade that had saved her.

Killock shouted commands at the two surviving attackers, but they sat unresisting as he bound them, too shocked and wounded to flee.

The rest would never rise from the floor of the temple. Danielle forced herself to look at them.

Then Wyn was at her side, her smile white within the blood smeared across her face and matted in her hair. But as she approached, Danielle saw her smile falter, and she quickly guided Danielle to a pew as she called for help.

"My side hurts," Danielle told her, and Wyn sucked in her breath as Danielle peeled back her hand to let Wyn see. Wyn rummaged in Danielle's pack for a moment, then pressed Danielle's circlet onto her head, making Danielle wince as fresh stabs of pain lanced across her tender scalp.

"Do the thing," Wyn urged. "Dani, quick, you have to look and tell me what to do."

Danielle nodded wearily and forced her exhausted mind to form the circlet's Word, thankful that it was as familiar as only an old friend could be. Memories flooded her, lifetimes of skill and training at her command, and with the eyes of generations of healers, Danielle finally examined the long wound that gaped across her side.

THE MARTYR'S TEARS

"Oh," she said from far away. "It bleeds far too much. Wyn, it needs pressure, and heat to cauterize the worst of it that will not stop. Then stitches deep in the tissue, before stitching the skin, or else it will tear again."

"I can't do all that!" Wyn's eyes were wide with fear. She clamped her cloak to the wound and twisted to search the room. "Killock! Hurry, she needs you!"

The Templar arrived with the smell of blood and leather, and Danielle ran an appraising glance over the score of wounds that crossed his body and arms as he, in turn, listened to Wyn repeating Danielle's words.

"She will be fine," Killock reassured Wyn. "I have done this before, many times."

"She likes the stitches small," Wyn told him urgently. "She said 'small' last time."

"I will make them small, I promise," Killock said, his voice sturdy and serene as a mountain.

"Is anyone else hurt?" Danielle asked faintly as Killock began heating his knife over a hastily assembled fire.

"I think everyone," Killock told her. "But you first. Then you can help the rest of us."

Danielle lay still as Killock worked on her, and she did not cry out as Killock pressed the tip of the glowing knife to the places in the wound that would not stop bleeding, and she did not groan as he carefully pulled the wound together with thread, although she could not stop the tears that ran across her cheeks and into her hair.

By the time Killock had finished, Wyn had spotted lanterns approaching from the direction of the army camp at the top of the hill, summoned by the thunder of Danielle's Word and the flare of the amulet's light from the temple windows.

"They will have healers," Killock suggested gently, "and will surely treat the Queen's sister with the utmost care and concern."

"What about a Templar?" Danielle asked.

"That, I am not so certain of," Killock admitted. "It will depend on who their lord is. I have seen blood spilled too often between Temple and Crown to risk being taken prisoner, not now, not when we know who the Crunorix in our midst is, and we are so close to vanquishing him."

"Then I am coming with you."

"Let's get you back to the Bare," Killock agreed.

Danielle tried to rise, but her leg refused to support her, and she gagged with the pain from her knee. Danielle clung to Killock's shoulder and tried to limp along beside him, but their pace was agonizingly slow, and the knight soon swept her off her feet and held her cradled in his arms as he began to lope toward the river through the temple fields. His pace never faltered, and his arms never lost their steel strength. Danielle clung to Killock as pain spurted from her side with every jarring step.

She was dimly aware of the rush of the river and the sudden heat of the inn's kitchen, somehow unchanged since she had last seen it, a lifetime ago.

The stairs creaked loudly under Killock's boots and then he laid Danielle onto the soft mattress of her bed. Lanterns were lit, and the tavern keeper woken to summon a healer, an older man with a thick beard and a scar across the bridge of his nose.

The healer examined Killock's work and wrapped bandages around Danielle's torso, and ripped open the seam of her leggings to expose her leg despite her protests to spare the material. Her knee was already purple and swollen, but the healer declared that the kneecap was whole, and the tissues that held it in place felt intact. He wrapped it tightly, and then Danielle insisted he help Wyn, who had driven away all other attention while she hovered anxiously over Danielle.

Danielle eased upright and glanced wearily around the room as Wyn taught the healer some new curses. It was bright and clean, a dream from a time before blood and pain and charred bodies. Danielle shuddered and struggled from the bed despite the healer's frown of disapproval, and staggered to the balcony door, clutching at bed post and chair to keep herself from putting weight on her throbbing knee.

Killock stood silently in the shadows outside, watching the glowing dots of lanterns spread slowly across the hillside beyond the river. Dozens more lanterns shone from the walls of the temple, and its windows glowed with light.

"Do you think the two prisoners will tell them who we were?" Danielle asked.

"I doubt they will say a single word."

Wyn joined them a few moments later, and they listened to the rush of the river and watched the lanterns together, until Wyn grew bored.

"What now?" she asked. "Because if we're just standing here, I'm going back to bed."

"Now?" Killock chuckled quietly and leaned on the balcony railing. "There is only one thing left to do, isn't there?"

Danielle nodded to herself. "Yes, only one," she agreed softly. "Finish Whitebrooke."

The river's rush filled the night air as Danielle's words lingered. Then Wyn shuddered with a yawn.

"Excellent," she said wearily. "I'm off to bed."

THE MARTYR'S TEARS

Gwydion

Loughliath slumbered beneath leaden clouds, nearly motionless. Its wide, grey surface lapped placidly at the shoreline, stirring an endless, soft tumble of rocks in a gentle surge that was easy to discern even on the heights of the balcony above.

Gwydion strolled slowly along the long, curved rail of the balcony. The towering archive windows behind him had their drapes drawn back, and yellow light from the bright lanterns on the other side of their thick panes glimmered faintly in the thin, morning light, as if frozen by the icy air that clung to the grey stone.

Steam curled from the delicate cup Gwydion carried carefully in one hand, and he sipped gratefully as he walked, enjoying the slow warmth of the liquid as it spread through his chest.

Gwydion reached the center of the balcony's long arc and paused. He burrowed his free hand even deeper into his pocket and shivered, but he did not hurry back to the relative warmth of the archives. Instead, he drew in a deep breath of icy air and listened to the distant wash of water on stone, and grinned wryly at the comfort they brought him.

A harsh clack broke Gwydion's reverie as a door opened. Hard footfalls approached, and he greeted the newcomer with a smile.

"Look, Roland, I swear you can see the Mountain, just peeking through the clouds, right there."

The knight joined Gwydion at the railing and considered the claim with a slight frown and a nearly imperceptible nod. "It is possible, although it is more likely to be one of the lesser peaks, closer to us."

"Ah, well, some mountain, in any case," Gwydion shrugged, unconcerned. He glanced toward his companion before returning his gaze to the vista, and sipped thoughtfully at his tea. Roland appeared weary, although the knight stood tall and his eyes were clear as he gazed at the distant glimpses of snow-capped rock. Deep lines ran from the corner of Roland's eyes and, for the first time in Gwydion's memory, the knight had not shaved, the soft gleam of golden stubble making Roland look far older.

"Have you slept, at all?" Gwydion ventured.

Roland glanced sharply at him, then shook his head. "No, not much. We have searched Whitebrooke's rooms, but we did not find anything."

"I suppose there isn't really a rush, is there? Whitebrooke is in the dungeons, perhaps not for the charge we would wish, but for one with grave consequences, nonetheless."

Roland nodded absently.

"Excellent," Gwydion declared. He sipped his tea, then pointed across the great lake. "Look, there is some sort of little boat. Can you imagine? They must be absolutely frozen."

"Why are you out here?" Roland asked.

"They say fresh air helps to clear the mind," Gwydion replied easily. "It has certainly brought me clarity that I was sadly lacking this morning, although I now find myself entirely concerned with my frozen ears."

"You have not found success in the archives?"

"None," Gwydion admitted with a scowl. "No golden trees. Only that Reverend Ambroise ordered the window in the Cathedral built with a golden tree on it, but no explanation of why he chose that design. Ah, the secret is somewhere here, but we will need an army of researchers to find it."

"We could form such an army."

"We could if we trust them. How many of the surviving archivists do we think Whitebrooke has corrupted?"

"I don't know. Do we have a choice?"

"Not really. Not if we want to find anything out quickly."

"Then we should."

"I agree." Gwydion spent a moment re-arranging the collar of his robe so that it was slightly more snug. "Which brings me to the one useful thought that all this standing about and shivering did produce. There are other places we could search."

"Such as?"

"The Guild archives are the most obvious. They must have built the tree. But there are certain challenges involved with them, of course."

Roland laughed softly. "I would agree. Criénne is months away, even on a fast ship, and the Guild would not let us into their archives if we made the trip."

"Ro and I had a little plan for that, actually, but it was rather based on the Grandmaster having a strong heart, so it might not work out. We could also send a message asking the Guild about a tree, but I do not think it very wise. I am not sure we should be alerting the Guild as to what we have found. Not until we know something about it."

"I agree."

"There are also the royal archives, in Kuray. Those were built during the reconstruction, so it is reasonable to assume that they should contain many references to Ruric's war and the Blade. Perhaps that extends to the forge that created it? Lastly, I wonder if Lady Danielle's family might have hidden more than the Blade, all these years."

"Vordoux is practically as far away as Criénne."

"I believe that is the case. Which, it pains me to say as I shiver and think of far-away vineyards, leads me to suggest we try the royal archives first."

"You are aware that the Queen is not thrilled with the Temple right now?"

"That is no reason for her to be unhelpful. I am certain that I can convince her that we all want the same outcome."

"You are volunteering to go?"

"Of course, who else?"

"And Lady Rowenna?"

"Oh, she's coming too. I'm not about to do all of that research on my own."

Roland nodded thoughtfully as Gwydion regretfully finished his tea. "There are many of the Queen's soldiers between us and Kuray," the knight said at last.

"I believe Karsha Hali said we would be welcome in Littleford. At least, Ro was. I am certain he meant to invite me."

"I meant, are we not tasked with defending the Temple?"

"Oh, that," Gwydion dismissed the thought with a shrug. "If you think it more valuable for us to stand about and glare at people than to prove to the Queen that we are her friends and uncover the secrets of the Martyr's Blade's origin, then, of course, I am happy to do so."

"There may be call for more than an angry gaze. Sir Maeglin urges the Council to take back our temples, and I wonder how long he will accept their refusal."

"You think Maeglin will listen to my counsel? No, of course you don't. You are the only one of us he might heed, and that depends on whether Maeglin has forgiven you for being the Council's first choice for Knight Commander."

"And if it comes to swords?"

"It won't."

"If it does?" Roland insisted.

"Then I will likely regret not being here for the rest of my life," Gwydion sighed. He swirled the dregs around the bottom of his cup, watching the tea leaves clump and slide. Then he tipped them over the edge of the balcony. "So much for fate," he declared.

Roland smiled to himself. "I don't believe in fate."

"Nor do I," Gwydion laughed. "Takes all the credit."

***

Gwydion considered the packed streets in wonder as he rode slowly through the town. Littleford had always been a quiet town, the temple an excellent place for reading, with the sounds of the river flowing over the ford and bees busy in the meadows as a humble accompaniment to the book. Even an evening trip to a tavern in search of a decent bottle of wine and a blushing maiden to court had a tranquil and cozy ease.

There was no hint of that serenity in Littleford now.

"No one cares a bit about us, though, do they?" Rowenna laughed as she fended off a soldier trying to press a clump of heartsease into her hand.

"No, they don't," said Gwydion thoughtfully. "It is extremely disturbing, actually."

The Templars reached the town square and were forced to dismount and lead their horses through the throng, until, at last, they found the curved street that led to the ford. Prosperous shops lined this street, along with the best inns that Littleford could provide.

"Do you suppose we will be able to convince one of these establishments to part with a room?" Gwydion wondered.

"We could ask Sir Killock."

"What?" Gwydion stared at his sister in puzzlement.

"He's standing right there, waving at us."

Gwydion followed Rowenna's extended finger and found Sir Killock in the cobblestoned yard of one of the inns, next to two horses, saddled and ready for the road. The knight beckoned to him, and Gwydion began the slow process of leading his horse across the street.

"Where on earth has he popped up from?" Rowenna asked.

"Some place very muddy, from the look of him," Gwydion decided. Killock had not shaved in days, the ragged stubble on his cheeks forming a wiry beard, and his grey-streaked hair hung in confused tangles about his shoulders. A fresh bandage peeked through a tear in his cloak over his shoulder, and dried mud streaked his boots and leggings.

As they approached, Killock's companions drew Gwydion's gaze. A young woman with a wide smile and hair the color of the sun, whose leather leggings did little to conceal her slim shape, and a young soldier with cropped hair and a spiral of marks tattooed around his left eye.

"Sir Killock," Gwydion greeted the knight. "Do you simply loiter in streets waiting for us to arrive?"

Killock nodded, a small smile the only indication that he had heard Gwydion's words, and the knight turned to introduce his companions.

"Wyn, Cormac, I would like you to meet two friends of mine, Lord Gwydion and his sister, Lady Rowenna."

Gwydion took the blonde girl's hand in his and swept it to his lips. "I am shattered to think that I have not had the pleasure."

"Nice to meet you too, your... wait, what?" Wyn stared intently into his eyes, and a grin began to twitch at the corner of her lips.

The young soldier, Cormac, nodded formally when introduced, and would have been easy to dismiss as just another suit of armor if it had not been for a glimmer of a smile twinkling behind his eyes.

"You must be the Wyn we have heard so much about," Rowenna guessed. "I am so pleased to see you safe."

"Aren't the two of you flash," Wyn announced. "Or, you know, not flash. Brilliant! Or something. No... oooo, I don't know words."

"Erudite?" Gwydion suggested helpfully. "Urbane? Intriguing, perhaps?"

"Pompous?" Rowenna supplied.

"I like 'flash'. I think I shall stay with that," Gwydion decided.

"What are you then?" Wyn asked. "I mean, you're not likely to be a pair of boring high-muckities, are you? Not when Sir Killock says you're his friends."

THE MARTYR'S TEARS

"We are *also* boring high-muckities, but I believe the real answer to your question is that we are Templars, like your Sir Killock, and like your friend, Lord Bradon. In fact, I very much liked Lord Bradon. We both did. Knowing that you were his friend, and stood beside him at the end, says more for you than you could know."

"You know about all that?"

"Of course," Rowenna assured her. "Killock has told us about the terrible time you had in the catacombs. I am amazed by what you have accomplished."

"These two can stay," Wyn smiled at Killock.

"I am glad they meet with your approval."

"Were you, ah… entirely successful… in your search?" Gwydion asked Sir Killock.

"Yes, I found them both," Killock nodded. "Lady Danielle is resting while we ready the horses."

"I wondered if you might be leaving. Where are you off to?" Gwydion asked.

"Bandirma."

"I see. All of you?"

"Yes," Killock frowned at him. "Gwydion, do you have something to say?"

"Always," Gwydion assured him. "Perhaps we could have a quick drink before you go, and we could talk a bit more easily. Is this a good inn? We could stay here, what do you think, Ro? Where's the stable boy?"

With the horses stabled they left the yard and wound their way through the throng toward the entrance to the inn. Wyn began skipping lightly between the puddles, making a game of it, and murmuring a strange mixture of Venaissine and Common under her breath. Gwydion strained to make sense from the words, which seemed dedicated to a boat with brown sails.

"You speak Venaissine now?" Killock asked.

"Dani's been teaching me," Wyn replied, her eyes sparkling with mischief. "She says I have a wonderful tongue…" Wyn's voice faltered and the grin fled her face. She was having trouble meeting Killock's eye. "Anyway…"

THE MARTYR'S TEARS

Now, that is interesting, Gwydion thought. *I fear I am sadly out of the running already. Shame. I wonder if Lady Danielle returns her worship?*

"Your accent is good," Sir Killock appeared unaware of Wyn's hesitation and the blush that was shining on her cheeks. "I would say it is better than your Common."

"Thanks, I think," Wyn laughed loudly.

"And you seem extremely happy. You have grown so much since we said farewell in Dolieb."

"It's just, a few things have changed a bit, that's all. Good things, though, yeah? Dani told me…" Wyn hesitated, glanced uncomfortably at Killock, and clearly changed her mind about what she had been about to say, "… some things. And I, you know, thought about them. A lot." Wyn pushed hair from her eyes and chewed delightfully on her lip, reminding Gwydion, strangely, of a young priestess who had worked in the library of the small temple in the village of Chluaidh.

They reached the front door to the inn before Wyn could say any more, much to Gwydion's disappointment, and she led them inside.

"I think they may have…" Gwydion stopped and laughed when he saw the sign with the painted bear hanging beside the door, but the others entered without pause, and he found himself speaking to a young boy with a wicker basket clutched in his arms and an expression of terror in his wide eyes. "I suppose one might hope that the sign makers did, in fact, know what they were writing. It would certainly make for a livelier evening, would you agree?"

The boy nodded mutely, and Gwydion patted his head. "Of course you do." Gwydion waved the boy past, gave the sign a rap with his knuckle, and followed the others inside.

The shutters along the street had been thrown open, and dust danced in the beams of brilliant light that shone through, illuminating the splintered wood floor and the oily black of the cooking pots hung over the fire pit.

The room rumbled with the happy murmur of conversation, as the tavern was packed with both soldiers and townsfolk enjoying bowls of the creamy soup that bubbled over the fire.

Nonetheless, his companions had secured places at a table in the far corner, and Lady Danielle was soon summoned from her room to join them. She walked gingerly down the stairs, aided by a cane made from polished driftwood and a statuesque blonde warrior with high cheekbones sculpted of marble, whom he was to learn was Sir Eilidh, and sat carefully at their table with a smile of relief.

Gwydion left them to their delighted squawking and found the bar, where he placed silver coins on the polished wood until the tavern keeper whisked away the first bottle of wine he had offered and presented a second with great solemnity, dusting off the label with the brown cloth he kept draped over his belt.

Gwydion tucked the bottle under his arm and gathered a collection of cups before winding his way to the table, where he enjoyed a gentle embrace from Lady Danielle.

The chattering amongst the ladies continued unabated, only occasionally wandering to accept a word from Killock or himself, but Gwydion did not mind and lost himself behind a contented grin as he considered how much Lady Danielle had changed since he had last seen her.

She had lost none of her beauty, but the months of hardship had carved away some of the softness and left behind a strength that had previously been concealed. She was noticeably leaner, with a play of muscle under her dark skin that would not have dared to appear on the smooth arms of the noble Marquessa he had known before. And she appeared weary, with frayed bandages wrapped around several of her fingers, her nails ragged and torn, and her flowing hair escaping from the most basic of braids, a far cry from the intricate sculptures that he knew she favored.

The strength suited her in a way that surprised Gwydion. *She is no longer unearthly and remote,* he realized, as he watched her golden eyes flash with laughter. *No longer a goddess. She is real. Such divine cruelty.*

Gwydion laughed to himself and then suddenly stood, holding his glass aloft until he had the gaze of everyone around the table.

THE MARTYR'S TEARS

"To old friends and new," he proposed, and then continued with a wide smile. "To beauty, strength, wit, courage, love, and laughter. May you all one day be as blessed in these as I."

Glasses clinked amongst groans and laughter, and the toast was repeated. Wyn drained her glass and smacked her lips in satisfaction, and Gwydion happily filled her glass again.

"What good fortune has brought you to Littleford?" Danielle asked. "We have not seen a friendly face in weeks, and now we are surrounded by friends."

"We are off to Kuray, to beg your sister to let us pilfer her archives," Gwydion caught Wyn's eye and winked, and the blonde girl snorted in mirth.

"I did that once," Wyn giggled.

"Did you, indeed?" Gwydion congratulated her.

"Wasn't so hard," Wyn boasted. "Although I was a bit worried she might recognize me when Dani and I talked with her, but, no, it was just 'it's forbidden' and no dungeon for me, so all's well."

"How very nice for you." Gwydion appraised the vehement stare that Danielle was directing at Wyn, tamed the smile that was threatening the corner of his mouth, and asked, "What was forbidden, exactly?"

"Things," Wyn said airily. "But after we explained, not forbidden, so no worries."

"That is good to hear," Killock said mildly. "I am happy you both realized how you felt about each other."

"What?" Danielle stared at Killock in surprise.

"Although it took you an extremely long time," Killock considered thoughtfully.

"Realized... wait... you bloody knew!" Wyn glared at the knight, her hands on her hips. "How? You left before it happened!"

"I hoped you would find each other," Killock replied.

"Did you really?" Danielle asked, her surprise giving way to a soft smile. "I thought I had concealed my feelings so well."

"You cannot conceal such a thing," Killock said gravely. "I only worried that you would never speak your heart."

"I stopped myself from doing so, many times. I cannot remember why, now," Danielle sighed.

"Well, I didn't suss it out, and nor did anyone else, I'll wager," Wyn laughed. "It's like an awful adventure read. Forbidden love and all that."

Oh my goodness, 'love' is it? But I fear so, she's like a puppy bounding in a field. I shall be amazed to see Lady Danielle in such a state.

"It's marvelous," Rowenna offered joyfully. "I am so happy for you both."

Maker, give me strength, Gwydion forced himself to smile banally and offer his congratulations, but he found it difficult to stop himself from searching the room for anyone willing to bring him a new bottle of wine. *Even a mug of ale. Anything.*

Gwydion sighed. *Come to think of it, I believe I have had this very nightmare before. Trapped with lovely women forbidden to me. And with my sister watching me. And nothing but vinegar to drink, I remember that part very well.*

Much to his relief the talk soon moved on to other topics, all much less cloying, as stories were told of storms and deserted castles, of ancient towers and lost lands rediscovered, of dark days and light.

Gwydion amused himself by watching Killock watch Wyn and Danielle as they chatted and laughed, their heads close together, their fingers entwined. A proud smile insisted on spreading across the weathered knight's face, no matter how frequently he banished it.

"... and in the end Reverend Sebastian simply gave the messages to Gwydion," Rowenna finished a fairly awful retelling of their part of the tale.

"Whitebrooke found them extremely difficult to explain," Gwydion chuckled. "Especially with Sir Roland's sword hanging over his head."

"Oh, no!" Wyn groaned. "Why does no one *ever* wait for me? Did he whack Shitebrooke with it?"

"Tragically, he did not," Gwydion finished his glass and tried to let the tart liquid touch as little of his tongue as possible on its way past. "Whitebrooke surrendered before any whacking could commence, and now resides in a cell."

"He got off easy," Wyn scowled. "Those were some hard bastards he sent after us."

"Ah, so they managed to catch up with you? Reverend Nesta sent out orders to call them off immediately, but I did wonder if it would be in time."

"Far from it," Killock said grimly. "Was that what you wanted to tell me, out in the yard?"

"Partly." Gwydion examined the dregs in his glass and wondered what they were and where they could have come from. "I assume your intent is to stand beside Lady Danielle as she accuses Reverend Whitebrooke of being a Crunorix priest."

"Yes, that is right," Killock agreed, and Danielle nodded as well, a frown of concentration knitting her brows. "He may be in a cell, but that has done nothing to satisfy justice, or the Queen."

"No, I quite agree," Gwydion assured him. "But I thought I would point out that we have already accused him of that same thing, to no avail."

"There is a difference between the word of Karsha Hali and Danielle's testimony," Killock countered.

"I wonder if Maeglin will agree with you," Gwydion mused.

"Killock, Danielle," Rowenna added gently, "Gwydion is right. Maeglin will put Danielle into the dungeons the moment she reaches Bandirma, and keep her there until some proof of Whitebrooke's treachery is found. Until the Convocation, there is no Bishop, and Sir Maeglin has taken that as license to do whatever he wills."

"What's a Maeglin, anyway?" Wyn asked.

"The Knight Commander," Gwydion explained. "Tall man, always angry. Has a little sea serpent on his armor."

"A sea serpent?" Wyn pushed hair out of her eyes. "That's the bastard who put us in the dungeon the first time."

"Another victim for your stabbing list?" Gwydion asked.

"I…" Wyn hesitated, visibly uncertain for the first time. "I think we stay away from that one. There's something wrong with him, something scary."

"He is extremely fierce," Danielle agreed, trying to soothe Wyn.

"It's more than that." Wyn chewed on her lip as she considered. "He's a killer. You see it in their eyes, the ones to watch out for, and you don't mess about with them. Stay out of their way, or kill them quick, before they can do you."

"He is a soldier," Danielle tried.

"Yeah, maybe," Wyn shrugged, unconvinced.

"Gwydion, what are you suggesting," Killock asked grimly. "That we leave this to the Queen and Karsha Hali to take care of for us, and hope it works out for the best?"

"No, not at all," Gwydion chuckled. "What fun would that be?"

"We could sneak in and stab Shitebrooke in the stomach," Wyn mused.

"A tempting thought, but one that does not necessarily convince the Temple to admit they were wrong to accuse Karsha Hali, which is an annoyingly crucial step in getting everyone to put their swords away," Gwydion pointed out. "No, I suggest allowing Lady Danielle to accuse Whitebrooke, hope that her testimony is enough to convince Maeglin, and stay out of the dungeons while you do it so that you can stab Whitebrooke in the stomach later, if it doesn't work."

"Mmmm, that's wise, that is," Wyn agreed thoughtfully.

"How do we do that?" Danielle asked.

"Oh, I would ask for help. I will take care of that this afternoon, never fear," Gwydion assured them. "Although I think I will need your assistance, Lady Danielle, if you don't mind. People tend to listen to the Queen's sister."

"No one could possibly think I am the Queen's sister," Danielle laughed, staring at her travel-worn clothes. Her leggings were torn to the thigh, her long, red tunic bore a gaping rent that revealed the flash of white bandages beneath, and she wore a long sword hanging from her hip, far from the exotic dresses of shimmering silk Gwydion was accustomed to seeing her wear.

"Well, we will need to make a grand entrance," Gwydion sat back with a contented smile. "So you rather need to go shopping."

THE MARTYR'S TEARS

"Shopping, Maeglin…" Wyn complained, and slumped onto her elbows. "Bloody hell, I'm never going to get to stab that bastard, am I? Is there any chance of any of this happening before summer?"

***

Gwydion guided his horse warily across the ford, making sure that no water splashed to soak his boots or the hem of his cloak. He had donned his most splendid robes, long and black and elegantly fitted, with silver thread woven into the high collar and around the hems, and had polished his boots until they gleamed as brightly as the dancing water in the crossing.

Lady Danielle rode beside him, now garbed in the best that Littleford could offer.

She had chosen a dress of pale lilac and grey with a bodice that Wyn had declared 'unfair', a long, fitted coat of the same material, and a wide belt that encircled her waist snugly, adorned with silver disks engraved with intricate knot-work. Rowenna had helped her comb out her hair and had pinned it into thick waves and a few artfully sculpted ringlets that curled across her shoulders. "I feel as if I am being presented to yet another suitor," Danielle had rolled her eyes as she was subjected to review in her room. "Maker, I thought I was past that particular horror."

A young soldier crossing the ford in the opposite direction stepped from the paved surface in his distraction and floundered into deeper water, much to his companions' glee. "One imagines that you witness such frolics all the time," Gwydion chuckled.

Danielle smiled as the soldier called out to her with a proposal of marriage, but her smile turned quickly to a grimace of pain and she pressed her hand to her ribs. "It is not fair to make me laugh," she complained.

"I shall be banal beyond belief once we reach the encampment," Gwydion promised, "but if your injuries are unveiled, I very much doubt we shall be allowed to—"

THE MARTYR'S TEARS

"I understand," Danielle snapped. She drew in a careful breath. "I understand," she repeated, more gently. "No one will know I am hurt, and the dress will bind me, no matter how many stitches come free."

The dress had a stiff corset that held the deep wound in her ribs together, and long gloves concealed the scratches on her hands and arms. The skirt disguised the thick bandages that wrapped her knee, and Danielle swore that she could walk a short distance without her cane, if Gwydion supplied his arm.

The road climbed the gentle rise beyond the ford and wound through green pastures, but Gwydion and Danielle were not riding that far today.

"You are certain of this?" Danielle asked as they approached the gates to the army encampment.

"Of course," Gwydion reassured her with his best smile. "In fact, more than ever. Do you see the three puppies playing on that banner above the pavilion? That is the rather ridiculous sigil of Baron Arledge, one of my father's great friends. We may die from listening to endless hunting stories, but that is the worst we have to fear."

"That is not what I meant," Danielle whispered. "Are you certain it is the best idea to rely on me?"

"Never worry, you will be marvelous."

"I will not be marvelous, I will be hopeless. It is all very well to say 'persuade him to help us' but what am I meant to tell this baron to convince him?"

"He will convince himself, we will merely guide him to that conclusion," Gwydion replied. "Simply imagine you are persuading your innkeeper to give you a room."

"It is not the same thing at all," Danielle muttered. "He is a baron, entrusted to carry out Gabrielle's orders, not an innkeeper. He will not be befuddled by a smile."

"You have rather too high an opinion of barons," Gwydion chuckled. "I find most innkeepers to be far more astute. No, Arledge is no fool, that's true, but neither is he to be feared at cards."

THE MARTYR'S TEARS

"In any case, all I did with the innkeeper is what Wyn told me to do," Danielle objected.

"Then, may I suggest the same course of action? Do what Wyn told you to do."

"Martyr's tears," Danielle sighed. "I cannot imagine how this could be more terrifying."

The gates were crowded with mounted soldiers coming and going, and a train of empty wagons departing the camp, but a knight in a spotless surcoat of snowy white quickly guided them through the crowd and apologized for the inconvenience before politely asking for their names and business.

"Viscount Dúnchluaidh and the Marquessa d'Lavandou. Please tell Lord Arledge we need to speak with him."

"Yes, my lord, please come with me and I will announce you."

The knight quickly guided them to a wide pavilion that sat on a small rise above the ordered chaos of the camp. A rippling banner with three snarling dogs embroidered on it snapped above the pavilion, and men-at-arms with long spears and tall shields stood guard outside.

Danielle dismounted gracefully, but Gwydion saw her face grow pale with the motion, and she grasped his arm as he escorted her into the pavilion's interior. She walked with slow dignity, her head up and a smile on her lips, but Gwydion could feel her fingers trembling against his arm.

Thick rugs covered the floor, and heavy wooden chairs and tables filled the space as if an ancient hall's study had been somehow magically transported into a field and covered with a tent. Braziers filled with glowing coals produced a hazy heat around the interior, undisturbed by the heavy stirring of the pavilion's thick canvas.

Two enormous wolfhounds lay near the braziers, their muzzles streaked with grey. They barely lifted their heads to gaze sleepily at the newcomers, content to thump heavy tails on the thick rugs and sigh happily as they returned to dozing in the heat.

Gwydion and Danielle were greeted by a thin man dressed in a long coat and sweeping cape, both bearing embroidery of a leaping dog. Baron Arledge appeared no different than the last time Gwydion had seen him, although that had been years ago. The same dignified mane of grey hair, the same bristling brows, the same lined face and sculpted nose. Baron Arledge smiled in greeting, but his eyes were watchful as he approached, quickly appraising the two figures standing before him.

"Gwydion!" Arledge placed a friendly hand on Gwydion's shoulder. "I am pleased to see you, my boy. How is the Earl?"

"Father is well, I believe."

"Still not speaking?" Baron Arledge tutted. "Never mind, I am sure you will sort it out."

"Yes, my lord," Gwydion agreed. "My lord, may I introduce Lady Danielle, the Marquessa d'Lavandou?"

"I am very pleased to have the privilege of your acquaintance, your Ladyship," Baron Arledge bowed low, and Danielle somehow curtsied gracefully, "although, of course, I have heard Her Majesty speak of you many times. I am honored to receive you, and I beg your forgiveness for these humble surroundings."

"Not at all," Danielle replied graciously, and Arledge ushered them into chairs near the braziers, and ordered wine for them to sip while they talked.

"Your Ladyship, if you will forgive me, I was amazed to hear your name announced by young Daren."

"Were you, my lord?"

"Yes." Arledge leaned forward and ruffled the ears of the dogs at his feet as he considered his guests. "Her Majesty has commanded her lords to scour her kingdom for any news of you, and all have failed. But here you are, arrived in my camp unlooked for."

"It has been a hard journey, my lord."

"I have no doubt. And yet, here you are with Lord Gwydion."

"And yet," Danielle agreed pleasantly.

"And yet," Arledge repeated, "Her Majesty was concerned that you should be found before you might be discovered by the Temple."

THE MARTYR'S TEARS

"Yes, my lord, that is why we sought you out." Gwydion paused to place his glass solemnly on the oak table. "There are those in the Temple who are deceived and unknowingly serve Her Majesty's enemies. But there are also those, like myself, who seek to unearth those traitors and bring justice upon them."

"Well said," Arledge nodded solemnly. "It does you great credit to be here, my boy. Your father would be proud."

"Thank you, my lord." Gwydion managed not to roll his eyes. "We have come to you to tell you this, and to inform the Queen that her patience will be rewarded. We will soon bring the traitor to justice."

"Will you, now?" Arledge's thick eyebrows arched in surprise, and he glanced from Gwydion to Danielle and back.

"Yes, my lord," Danielle sat forward, her hands clenched in her lap, "and to tell my sister I am safe, of course."

"I will send birds at once." Arledge nodded quickly.

"Thank you, my lord. I shall mention your help to my sister." Danielle sighed and sat tall and straight in her chair, and Gwydion noticed a small stain glimmering wetly on the tight fabric over her ribs.

"Do not trouble yourself, my lady," Arledge replied. "It is my honor to help, and my happy duty to send your news to the Queen. Think nothing of it. Now then," the baron continued, "what shall I tell Her Majesty you are going to do?"

"Lady Danielle knows the truth of who is behind the attack on the Queen," Gwydion told Arledge proudly.

"Does she?"

"Yes, my lord," Danielle agreed. She glanced nervously at the entrance to the pavilion and lowered her voice so that Arledge leaned forward to hear her. "It is the same man who falsely accused me, and had me imprisoned."

"Good Lord, did he really?" the baron asked, shocked.

"Yes, my lord," Danielle nodded sadly. "I was fortunate to escape."

"I should say so," the baron said thoughtfully.

"We travel to Bandirma to confront him," Gwydion said grandly.

THE MARTYR'S TEARS

"My lady, Gwydion, your courage does you both credit, but I am afraid I cannot allow you to proceed."

"No, sir?" Gwydion frowned thunderously.

"I do not think the Queen would look favorably on me if I allowed her sister to return to the clutches of the man who was responsible for mistreating her so poorly in the first place." Arledge shook his head to forestall their protests. "Which is undoubtedly what would happen."

"But, my lord, this time I will have Lord Gwydion and Lady Rowenna at my side, and I shall accuse him in front of the entire Council," Danielle disagreed. "I must try, my lord."

"My lady, I am sorry, but I do not think you understand what a craven, devious, wretched creature this man you would accuse must be. He has convinced the Temple to draw swords against Her Majesty, he can certainly convince them to arrest you a second time, or worse," Arledge said ominously. "It is out of the question."

"But, my lord, what can we do?" Danielle asked, stricken. She leaned toward Arledge and rested her fingers on his arm for support. "My lord, will you help me?"

Gwydion carefully watched the baron's face. Arledge's stern visage melted into a proud smile and a kind gaze, and he patted Danielle's hand to comfort her. "Of course, my lady, of course. I will help you, never fear. I just could not bear to think of you two risking yourselves needlessly."

Danielle nodded, apparently too overwhelmed with gratitude to speak.

"Thank you, my lord," Gwydion said solemnly. "I knew we were right to seek you out."

"Of course," Arledge brushed away such details with a wave of his hand. "Now then, will you and your sister be visiting us this summer? That magnificent boar is still roaming the glen above the tor, but I believe I now have just the dog to lead the hunt…"

***

The Martyr's Tears

It was long after dusk when Gwydion and Danielle at last returned to Littleford. Gwydion had feared that Danielle would not be able to bear her wounds, the baron had kept them so long, and Gwydion knew that they would never be allowed to leave if Arledge had realized how hurt she really was.

But Danielle had chatted and smiled and endured tale after tale of stags and dogs and boars without complaint, and had made it back onto her horse without incident when the baron had finally sent them on their way with promises of plans and help on the morrow.

"You were bloody marvelous," Gwydion told Danielle as their horses splashed across the ford.

"I had a good teacher," Danielle said wearily. "Honestly, I did not know if I could do it."

"You were superb," Gwydion assured her. "When you asked him for help, well… there isn't a man alive that would not have been swayed."

"I thought I was going to fall out of my dress," Danielle laughed softly. "That would have been amusing."

"My dear, I hope you take this in the spirit of friendship in which it is offered. It was a beautiful sight, and I can only express my profound envy of your charming consort."

"Oh, Gwydion, are you terribly disappointed? I did not know."

"Shattered," Gwydion assured her. "But I am buoyed by the knowledge that no man could have succeeded in my place, and, of course, by the joy I feel at your happiness."

"You can be very charming when you try, you know."

"That is precisely what I have said for years."

Sir Killock and the others awaited them in the stables of the Dancing Bare, and the knight helped Danielle dismount while Gwydion summoned the stable boy to collect their horses.

"Did your visit to the encampment pay off?" Killock asked.

"Oh, yes," Gwydion smiled as he offered Danielle his arm for support. "Lady Danielle was perfect. Baron Arledge was convinced it was his idea to help us by the time we finished."

"What will he do?"

THE MARTYR'S TEARS

"We will find out tomorrow."

Gwydion had hardly opened the door to the inn when he was startled by a wailing shriek followed by a roar of approval from the crowded room within.

"Oh, they're going to play again!" Wyn said happily.

"The music has such energy," Danielle sighed. "I should not be sad, I know, but I wish we could spend the night dancing, again."

"You danced? To that… noise?" Gwydion asked her in astonishment.

"Of course," Danielle laughed, "until the musicians begged for mercy, and the tavern keeper sent us away."

"Well, I never," Gwydion replied. "You are absolutely full of surprises tonight, my lady."

"I am finished being surprising," Danielle declared. "I hurt all over, and I am too tired to stay awake, so I will go upstairs and lie down."

"I'll go with you," Wyn said quickly, although Gwydion noted a strained lightness in her tone.

"No," Danielle told her kindly. "Please go and have fun, and do not worry, and wake me to tell me all about it when you come to bed."

"Are you sure? I don't mind."

"I am." Danielle gave Wyn a tender kiss, retrieved her driftwood cane from Killock, and walked with slow dignity across the tavern and up the stairs.

The tavern was packed and noisy. The narrow paths between the filled benches oozed a constant stream of patrons pushing past those who had given up on a seat and stood to enjoy their ale. Barmaids weaved their way expertly through the crush and kept the guests well-supplied with ale, wine, and mead. A whole deer rotated on a spit over the blazing fire, constantly attended by the innkeeper himself, a red-faced man with a booming laugh and a shirt that failed to cover his massive gut, who alternated between bathing the deer in butter and wiping the sweat from his bald head.

The Martyr's Tears

Gwydion escorted the women through the throng, paused to flash a smile at a barmaid, and was rewarded by a cup of wine and a chorus of moans from the patrons who had been bypassed by the girl on her way to him. A few silver coins and a quick whisper in her ear secured Gwydion a table and excellent service for the rest of the evening.

Gwydion took a long draught from the cup, decided it was only fairly awful, and joined the others at the table.

More screeching noises filled the room, and dancers flocked to the floor to the cheers of the watching crowd.

"Good Lord." Gwydion blinked as a particularly high note assaulted his ears.

A very earnest young soldier begged for Wyn to join him, and Gwydion watched them spin gracefully around the floor together, enchanted by their fluid movement, the speed and rhythm of their steps.

"If a Venaissine marquessa can do it, do you think we might be able?" Gwydion asked his sister, but Rowenna only laughed, and graciously accepted a hand from a tall lad with dark curls and freshly polished boots who triumphantly led her past his awestruck friends into the line.

"Don't tell me you are going to join in?" Gwydion asked Sir Killock. "My world will absolutely shatter from the strain."

"No, the musicians tend to object to the noise my knees make."

"And I am quite content to watch, as well," Gwydion tapped his cup against Killock's and leaned against the wall next to the knight. "Although the fiddles remind me of pigs being fed."

"They play a lively tune, at least. You have fed many pigs?"

"One can imagine it. It's certainly very fast, but it doesn't seem to be ending any sooner for all that."

"Oh no, they are just getting started. Watch."

Rowenna glided gracefully past, her smile a radiant flash of white as she moved elegantly through the line, and then Eilidh and Cormac promenaded into view, Eilidh stamping out the steps with precise measure and a glowing smile on her lips, Cormac flowing easily through the moves with supple grace and a gleam in his eye.

"The ladies are making a good accounting of themselves, are they not?" Gwydion chuckled.

At a break in the music Wyn hurried to the table and gulped her ale, her chest rising and falling like bellows as she caught her breath.

"I'm quite puffed now." Wyn sank onto the bench between Killock and Gwydion. "Still not all the way back, but not so bad, really."

"You dance marvelously," Gwydion assured her.

"I was hoping for a proper céilí to take Dani to for ages," Wyn sighed happily. "She promised, you see, because I had a bath."

"Did you, indeed?" Gwydion asked her. "How splendid. I understand you and your paramour made quite the showing last night."

"My what is showing?"

"I merely meant that I heard that you and Lady Danielle had exerted yourself until deep into the night. I salute you both on your amazing stamina."

"You're not joking," Wyn nodded appreciatively. "I could barely move by the time we were finished."

"I can imagine," Gwydion said thoughtfully. "You seem very happy together."

"Yeah, bizarre, right? I'd pinch myself, but that'd be bloody stupid if I was dreaming, wouldn't it?"

"Very wise. I am always astonished when confronted by two people in love. It seems so mythical when I consider it."

"You don't think a high-muckity nob could love someone like me, is that it?"

"Not at all. Well, actually, yes, but not for the reasons you think. Most of my, I shudder to say, peers, lost the ability to feel any emotion for anyone aside from themselves long ago. But in this case, knowing the nob in question, I refer only to the general astonishment of witnessing love between any two people."

"How often do you go around witnessing love between people, then?"

"Very rarely, come to think of it."

THE MARTYR'S TEARS

"So, all that pervy stuff about what high-muckities get up to in their castles isn't true?"

"No, it's all true. Quite unlike the wholesome celebration of life that you find amongst the good people of the farms and villages, of course."

"Yeah, celebrations. It might be different in your palace or whatever, but out here it seems like most folks have a shit life."

"Yes, my whatever is certainly different. There's never any threat of a shit anything at home, mostly because there's never any threat of any change at all. Ancient crumbly things all over the place. And that's just my family. The furniture is worse. And just wait until I tell you about the tea parties."

"That does sound really awful," Wyn rolled her eyes.

"A room full of insipid peacocks, ass-licking and squawking and waiting for the moment to spur you in the back. No, they were delightful soirees."

"Awww, does it sting to have to pucker up? Well, you have some lucky servant to wipe the spittle from your arse, and gold knickers to put on afterward, don't you? It's a bit worse when it's a real knife in the back, I promise you."

"I suppose that's true," Gwydion laughed. "I had forgotten about the gold knickers."

"Exactly. High-muckities always complain about how tough it is to have gold shit all over them."

"You've chosen an interesting companion if that is how you feel."

"She's different."

"Hmmm, true, but in what way exactly has she avoided your wrath?"

"Well, she cares about normal people, not just always looking down on us like we're all scum and not real people like the rest of your lot."

"You are delightfully un-self-aware. But I do agree, painting others with such a sweeping brush is extremely judgmental."

"Yeah," Wyn said uncertainly, then pressed on. "Plus, she doesn't care about titles and money and such."

THE MARTYR'S TEARS

"That certainly makes her unique amongst the nobility, I will grant you."

"That's what I'm saying," agreed Wyn. She caught a beckoning wave from the floor and stood to leave, but hesitated for a moment and turned to Gwydion. "You're a bit strange, aren't you? I mean, you're not much like a real nob either, even though you sound like one until you listen to the words you're saying."

"Don't let me fool you, my dear. I am quite the privileged ass, I'm afraid, though not for lack of trying. Just ask my father."

A sly grin flashed across Wyn's face. "We'll see, your Nobiness."

Wyn scampered across the room, and Gwydion turned to Killock. "What a charming girl," he mused. "I adore her already. How on earth did you survive her training?"

"She's a handful, that's for certain," Killock replied thoughtfully, then his frown deepened. "Two handfuls, actually."

Maeglin

Sir Maeglin planted both hands on the slick stone of the parapet and leaned forward as if being an arm's-length closer would bring clarity. The crest of the Tower of Tithius was hushed as it waited for the Knight Commander. Even the pigeons stifled their incessant cooing as if sensing the gravity of the moment. The long banner atop the beacon slapped soddenly against its pole and the distant roar of the Abhainn Fuar swirled in the misty rain around them, but the wide vista before him was as silent as a painted tableau.

Beyond the gleaming rooftops of the town, a patch of colorful tents and pavilions sprouted in the green fields. A strong company of riders formed a long row between the tents and the town and waited patiently beneath a thicket of tall spears adorned with drooping pennants.

"What is your count?" Maeglin asked.

"No more than one hundred, all mounted," Sir Hollis replied without hesitation.

"And how many are in the hills that we cannot see?"

"None," Logan snorted and spat over the parapet. "We haven't spotted a single scout on the roads west or south, and the forests are undisturbed. There's no one between us and Littleford."

"Who are we looking at?"

"I see the banners of most of the southern lords," Sir Hollis answered.

"Are these the same riders that were reported leaving Littleford?"

"Likely," Logan grunted. "It would be a hard ride, but they could have covered the distance this quickly."

"What are they doing?" Reverend Ail asked.

Maeglin turned from the parapet and confronted the group clustered in the small space left clear by the tower's innumerable coops. The Council stood cold and wet in their fine robes, huddled together under their hoods, but the two Templars appeared unaware of the chill mist and stood near Maeglin at the parapet as they examined the distant riders.

"They are waiting," Maeglin told the high priest coldly. The mist stirred around the tower and droplets brushed the Knight Commander's face, but their chill touch felt refreshing, and he pushed back his hood so that they could coat his head and neck.

"What are they waiting for?" Ail asked.

"To see what we will do," Maeglin replied.

"If they've come all this way to watch us freeze to death on top of this tower, I'd say we are doing them a favor," Reverend Dougal huffed.

"No, we have had quite enough watching, I believe," Reverend Nesta replied. "Knight Commander, what is your suggestion? One hundred knights waiting in a field is hardly a threat to us, is it?"

"No," Maeglin replied. "We have twice that number ready to ride out at this moment, as well as infantry." Maeglin peered at the distant pennants. "Most of the southern lords… are they the lords themselves, can you tell?" he asked Hollis.

"I'm not sure, sir," the knight answered.

Maeglin nodded, his thoughts racing through the mist toward the distant riders like a cavalry charge, calculating distances and movement. *Some might escape, but…*

"Knight Commander," Reverend Nesta interrupted him, "I do not intend to sit here for days, waiting to find out what they are going to do. Will someone please go and tell whoever is in charge to speak his mind, or kindly remove his army from our fields. We have planting to do."

"Very well," Maeglin replied.

"Perhaps we should send someone to speak, ah, diplomatically, as well?" Reverend Ail spoke up.

"The Queen is holding our temples. There is nothing to negotiate until they are released," Maeglin insisted, and Nesta nodded cautious agreement.

"Sir Roland and I will accompany you," Lord Faron intoned, and Maeglin shrugged his acceptance.

"Come if you wish, Lord Faron."

The three horsemen rode quickly through town, their horses' hooves ringing loudly from the cobbles as their riders urged them on. Maeglin led them along the Rathad an Thuaidh until they were well within bowshot of the awaiting knights before halting on the crown of a slight rise, glaring impatiently at the line of horsemen.

"You do not fear them," Faron observed, "and you bring no escort. You dare them."

Maeglin snorted in amusement but did not deign to answer the Templar. Lord Faron settled on his horse, his dark eyes sweeping the riders before them, his face expressionless as he waited.

Sir Maeglin's horse was not as sanguine about being kept standing in the soaking mist, and it stomped its hoof and snorted to let its displeasure be known. Maeglin held the horse steady and patted its neck. "Wait when I wait," Maeglin told the stallion. "Fight when I fight." The horse snorted once more but settled under the firm voice and reins.

Sir Roland's saddle creaked as the knight sat high, peering ahead. "They are coming."

A group of horsemen broke from the line and turned toward Bandirma when they reached the road. Three riders led the way, followed by a small escort of knights bearing snapping pennants on the ends of their lances, cantering easily towards Maeglin and the Templars.

Even at a distance, Maeglin recognized Baron Arledge's sweeping mane of grey hair, but it was the two other riders that made Maeglin suck in his breath in fury.

"You treacherous bastard!" Maeglin rose in his stirrups and thundered. Maeglin's horse whinnied and reared at the sudden sound, but Maeglin barely noticed, merely shifting his weight so that he could keep his gaze focused on the object of his wrath.

Sir Killock reined in a stone's-throw from Maeglin alongside Arledge and Lady Danielle. The knight appeared not to have heard Maeglin's outburst at first, as his face was impassive as a stone, but Maeglin could see the glint of the Templar's eyes following him.

"Sir Maeglin," Baron Arledge called out. "I had hoped that we could have civil discourse. Will you be able to hold your blade, or shall we postpone our talks until another day?"

"I will hold it until that faithless dog slinks from your side. Then I will run him down."

Arledge glanced to Sir Killock, then back to Maeglin. "Very well, though you do Sir Killock an injustice."

"He stands by you, instead of with the Temple," Maeglin insisted. "I give him what he is due."

Arledge considered Maeglin's words for a moment, then walked his horse forward to meet the Temple riders. Lady Danielle and Sir Killock followed him.

"Sir Roland, Lord Faron," Arledge greeted each in turn. "I wish that we met under better circumstances."

"Perhaps the circumstances will prove to be better, in the end," Faron told the baron, and Arledge accepted the point with a small nod.

"Why are you here, Baron?" Maeglin asked curtly. "Have you come to return my prisoner?" Maeglin glared at Lady Danielle. The noblewoman's face was pale and drawn, but she returned his gaze fiercely. He turned his ire onto Arledge. "Are you here to return the temples you have illegally seized?"

"You know why we are here," the baron replied sternly. "The Temple is harboring a Crunorix priest, whose machinations have threatened us all. The Temple has attacked the Queen, although Her Majesty is willing to accept that you were deceived by this Crunorix priest. But you will not have her pardon any longer if you continue to defy Her Majesty. Present the priest to us, or allow us solve the problem for you."

"As you did in Littleford?" Maeglin snarled.

"Littleford was a terrible mistake, Lord Commander. Do not make an even worse mistake now."

"Such as opening my gates to you? As far as I know, your Karsha Hali is the Crunorix priest. There is as much evidence to support that claim as any other."

"That is not the case." Arledge paused, but Maeglin refused to respond and waited silently for the baron to play his hand. "We know who the priest is, and we have proof."

"Proof, Baron? Or accusations?"

"No, my Lord Commander. I have witnesses. Two people who have seen the priest use fuil crunor magic, and they name the same man."

"Who are these witnesses?"

"The first is the Queen's counselor, Karsha Hali, who witnessed the Crunorix priest use fuil crunor during the attack on the Queen's apartments in Bandirma.

"Who is the second?"

"I am," Lady Danielle replied for the baron. "Sir Maeglin, the Crunorix priest is Reverend Whitebrooke. I saw him perform fuil crunor. He boasted of murdering Bishop Benno. There is no doubt."

"Hearsay is not proof," Maeglin barked. He frowned at the Templars sitting beside him. "Even if it does conveniently match other accusations. Have you shared your theory with Sir Killock?"

"He left long before we concluded our investigation," Lord Faron replied. "As you well know."

"An investigation that also found no proof," Maeglin snorted in disdain.

"Sir Maeglin, I saw him. That is no hearsay. I witnessed him, I heard him admit to it, I heard him gloat of the power it would give him," Lady Danielle said coldly. "We all name the same man… what more proof could you wish for? Where is your reason?"

"Whitebrooke accuses you of the same," Maeglin snapped.

"And you were willing to act on that, or have you forgotten?"

"I remember." Maeglin felt his skin burn across his cheek, as if a fly had stung him, and he angrily scratched away the irritant. "I have questioned Reverend Whitebrooke, and I will continue to question him until I am satisfied. Until then, he will rot in a cell." Maeglin glared at Lady Danielle. "Which is where you should be, so that I may question you, as well." A sudden vision of her lying helpless in chains on a stone floor beneath him disconcerted the Knight Commander, and Maeglin swallowed heavily and pushed the image away.

"You have already heard the only answers I would give you," Danielle replied.

"Lady Danielle is under my protection, Sir Maeglin," Baron Arledge declared. "There is no more need for questioning. You have your proof."

"Her testimony may be enough for you, but it is not proof, and thanks to Fionn's Law, the Temple does not have to bow to your judgment on the matter."

"Fionn's Law?" Killock frowned in astonishment. "Maker's breath, Maeglin, he's asking you to deal with a murdering bastard, not break an ancient law."

"You would do well to hold your tongue, traitor."

"You named me that before," Killock replied coldly. "I grow tired of it."

"You stand next to those who have killed our people and taken our temples. Does the truth taste bitter in your mouth?"

"I stand by those who can see the truth, who wish to defend those we love and who seek justice for those who threaten them. You are a fool to think otherwise."

Breath hissed into Maeglin's lungs through bared teeth, and his hand snapped to the pommel of his sword without thought.

THE MARTYR'S TEARS

Before he could draw, Lord Faron spoke, his voice a soothing rumble of rolling thunder, and Maeglin found himself listening without moving.

"This is not for us to decide, Baron. What message would you have us take to the Council?"

"You have it plain before you. You were made fools, and you chose the wrong horse. Now you must pay for your wager. Try Whitebrooke for the crimes of the murder of Bishop Benno, of attacking the Queen, of falsely accusing Karsha Hali and Lady Danielle, and of practicing fuil crunor. Do it now, and do not mutter about Fionn's Law. Gaze up the road, and see that the lords and ladies of Albyn are watching. It will not protect you from their justice."

"You know Whitebrooke did it," Killock met Maeglin's glare. "All reason tells you he did. Arledge is asking you to do justice, that is all. End this now, with Fionn's Law intact, and we can unite against the Crunorix."

"You disgust me, Killock." Maeglin spat on the road between them. "Run back to your new master."

Killock hesitated one final heartbeat, and his gaze sought out the other Templars. Then he wheeled his horse and the three riders clattered back to the watching nobles.

Maeglin did not wait for the three to reach them. He pulled hard on the reins and spurred his horse, and the stallion leapt into a gallop toward Bandirma. Maeglin did not slow the horse until he had thundered across the bridge and through the long tunnel of the River Gate, scattering mud and soldiers with equal disregard.

Maeglin swung from the saddle before the horse had come to a halt, and strode toward the entrance of the Tùr Abhainn, but the Templars had matched his speed, and now Sir Roland confronted the Knight Commander.

"Where are you going, Sir Maeglin?"

"To ready my men," Maeglin replied shortly. "The lords and ladies of Albyn, Sir Roland… sitting there, in our grasp. Perfect hostages for the return of our temples."

"Only if you gain the Council's approval, Sir Maeglin."

"This is a matter regarding the defense of the Temple. It is not their concern."

"Tell them, Sir Maeglin, or I shall, and I will not be as convincing as you might hope. If you wish to keep your title, let us deliver Arledge's message to the Council, and then you can gain their approval for your plan, if you are able."

Maeglin glared at Sir Roland. *Has he kept his skill with a blade, I wonder?* Maeglin angrily brushed the thought away. *That is not helpful.* "Very well... Arledge isn't going anywhere, in any case."

Maeglin led the way to the Council chamber, the black scowl of rage on his face clearing a path through the hallways with ease.

They found the chamber empty, save for an acolyte dusting the Council's highbacked chairs who held her duster tightly in both hands as Maeglin descended on her, as if it were a shield against his grim expression.

"Where is the Council?" Maeglin demanded.

"I'm not sure, sir, I'm just—"

"Find them," Maeglin growled, and the girl fled.

"A fearsome foe, indeed," Lord Faron mused. "Worthy of your wrath."

Maeglin disregarded the Templar's mocking tone. "It is too hot in here, and she stared at me like a fish." Maeglin unbuckled his cloak and dropped it unceremoniously on one of the benches encircling the chamber.

They waited in silence after that, until the doors to the chamber opened and admitted the five members of the Council.

"Who was it?" Reverend Dougal barked. "Who is leading them? Who did you speak to?"

"Baron Arledge," Maeglin replied. "And he claimed the knights were the lords and ladies of Albyn, although we were not close enough to know if this was true."

"What did he want?" Reverend Hayley asked.

"He brought fresh demands... that we hand Reverend Whitebrooke to them to be tried for being a Crunorix priest, or we do it ourselves."

"And he brought fresh proof," Lord Faron rumbled. "Lady Danielle and Sir Killock stood with him."

"Lady Danielle is alive?" gasped Reverend Liadán. "Thank the Maker."

"Yes, and it was she who brought the proof against Reverend Whitebrooke," Lord Faron continued. "She witnessed him use fuil crunor, and heard him admit to the murder of Bishop Benno."

"Then… that's it, isn't it?" Reverend Ail beamed at the other priests. "We have our proof. We can end this terrible standoff with the Queen."

"It isn't proof," Maeglin corrected the priest angrily. "It is just more accusations."

"Well, yes, but it is Lady Danielle who is our witness, and we already know Whitebrooke tried to kill her. Now we know why."

"You think you know why. We don't know."

"Sir Maeglin, this is absurd," Reverend Hayley said sharply. "Reverend Whitebrooke lost all credibility when he ordered assassins to kill Lady Danielle against the wishes of this Council, and we have all heard the compelling theories of Lady Rowenna."

"Circumstantial," Maeglin disagreed. "I will continue my questioning of Reverend Whitebrooke, and we should demand that Lady Danielle be returned to my custody, so that I may question her as well. Then we will find proof. Then we will have justice."

"I have heard how you questioned Reverend Whitebrooke," Hayley challenged him. "That is not Temple justice."

"That is disgusting," Reverend Liadán said softly.

"Did you see what happened to Bishop Benno? To the archivists? To my soldiers? That is disgusting."

"Your heart is torn with grief, my brother," Faron folded his arms across his broad chest, unperturbed. "You are not yourself."

"Do I mishear you, Faron?"

"You seek payment for the crimes done against Bishop Benno and your soldiers? For the harm brought to all who have suffered?"

"Of course."

"As do I. But I will not accept my payment in their coin, nor will I accept partial recompense." Faron's eyes blazed with the intensity of his fervor, and he swept his hands wide as if to embrace the warmth of some hidden sun. "Nor do I believe you would."

"I would not give in to Baron Arledge's demands. I would not throw Fionn's Law into the mud."

"Well said," Reverend Dougal huffed, but Reverend Hayley's voice carried further.

"We are not giving in to his demands, Sir Maeglin. We are finally exercising our own law, as we should have done, instead of sitting and taking no action while you tortured prisoners to no effect, and assassins are sent to commit murder. Fionn's Law… for Martyr's sake."

"In any case," Reverend Ail said soothingly, "we cannot exactly demand they leave our temples or send Lady Danielle to us. Why would they listen?"

"We make them listen," Maeglin said harshly. "The lords and ladies of Albyn are sitting by themselves in the fields outside of town. They would make excellent hostages to force the release of our temples."

"You think you can capture one hundred armed knights without bloodshed?" Reverend Haley asked.

"There may be some… what did Arledge call Littleford? 'A terrible mistake.' I am certain we can make our apology sound just as sweet."

"And when word reaches the Queen and the lords who are not here, you believe they will be sanguine about our escalation?"

"They should have thought of that before they took our temples."

"They broke the Fionn's Law for what they believe is a true cause. You want us to break it for retribution," Nesta admonished softly. "Well, we will take a formal vote if you wish, but if you insist we do then I will also call for a formal vote on your rank and title."

"The defense of the Temple is my responsibility," Maeglin spat between his bared teeth.

"You think attacking and capturing the nobility of Albyn will make us safer? I have never heard such nonsense. No, it is over, Sir Maeglin. We have the proof we need to vote on Reverend

Whitebrooke's guilt… and any other formal matters put before the Council. Are there any?"

Maeglin's hand shook with the need to grasp the hilt of his sword, and sweat poured from his skin in waves that left burning trails behind. He clutched the brooch that adorned his breastplate and gripped the coiled serpent until its sharp pin sank into the flesh of his palm, and the bright pain overwhelmed his need to draw steel. He swallowed his bile and shook his head in response to Nesta's prompt. "No."

"Good," Nesta said. "I declare that there is sufficient evidence to accuse Reverend Whitebrooke of the murder of Bishop Benno, the murder of Temple soldiers, the crime of treason against Her Majesty, the Queen, and most vile of all, of practicing fuil crunor. I call for him to stand trial for these crimes immediately."

"Second!" chorused the rest of the Council, and they nodded in satisfaction to each other. Maeglin pressed the pin into his hand a second time, and a third, as he stood silently and listened to the Council congratulate each other. Then he strode from the chamber, no longer able to bear the prickling heat.

Sir Hollis was waiting anxiously in the hallway outside the chamber and he fell into place beside Maeglin as the Knight Commander stalked along the passageway.

"Send word to the knights to be ready to ride on my signal," Sir Maeglin told Hollis. "They are to divide their forces as they clear the town. One group will ride directly to the Rathad an Thuaidh and hold it, the other will charge the Queen's knights, and either take them prisoner or drive them into the first group."

"How large should the force be?"

"I want hostages. Send as many as you can ready, so that the nobles will surrender. Overwhelming force, Hollis."

"Yes, sir."

"And, Hollis… no messengers are to be sent to Baron Arledge's camp without my approval, understood?"

"Yes, sir. And where will you be, sir?"

"I am going to speak with Reverend Whitebrooke. I feel like asking him some more questions."

Hollis nodded silently and hurried away.

Maeglin clattered down the stone stairs to the dungeons, threw open the heavy door that led to the cells, and halted. The guard room was deserted, bright lanterns glowing cheerfully on a bare table and an unused cot against the wall. Steel whispered into Maeglin's hand without thought.

He crossed the room and pushed open the door to the privy with the tip of his blade, but it was empty, and the Knight Commander strode to the thick gate that barred access to the cells. It swung open at his touch, and as he peered into the quiet hallway he noticed the empty iron hook next to the door, from which usually hung the keys.

Maeglin walked cautiously down the passageway. Light shone into the hall through the cells' open doors, creating bright patches across the dull stone floor. Maeglin paused to peer into each cell as they passed, but all were empty, and he pressed on without searching them.

The two cell doors at the end of the hall were closed, casting the passageway into gloom, but Maeglin could see huddled forms sprawled on the floor, and he approached slowly, his sword poised.

The first body lay on its back, with its legs twisted underneath it. A jagged wound gaped in the soldier's neck beneath his uselessly clutching hands, and a thick pool of blood had formed around his head. The soldier's sword was still in its sheath.

The second soldier had managed to draw her weapon halfway from its sheath before dying. She, too, bore a gaping wound across her neck, this one a cruel slash drawn through her throat, and she had staggered backward, seeking to flee, judging from the spray of blood across the floor.

A twisted laugh muttered into the hallway through one of the closed cell doors. Maeglin stepped to the door and swung it open, and it crashed into the stone wall with a bang that echoed down the passageway.

The cell stank of wet death. The bodies of three soldiers lay in a pile in the center of the floor, and long trails showed where they had been dragged together. All three had been eviscerated, and the glistening coils of their entrails sprawled freely around them.

A figure jumped to his feet as the door slammed open, although for a moment Maeglin could not tell if it was a man or some beast, so covered was it with swathes of blood and gore. But man it was, standing naked, his body covered in weeping cuts and jagged tears, and blood plastered across his face and chest. He snarled at Maeglin, a feral noise that had no trace of speech, and leapt toward the knight, his arms outstretched, his fingers bent into hooked claws.

Maeglin swept the man aside with a precise cut of his sword, the heavy blade tearing through flesh and muscle in a long wound across the man's chest. He crashed to the ground with a gurgling scream, and Maeglin's thrust took him in the center of his back, piercing the heart, the steel blade not pausing until it struck stone.

Maeglin pulled his sword free and rolled the corpse of his assailant over with his boot. The face was disfigured with torn skin, livid burns, and blood, but Maeglin recognized him. *Vaughn.*

He was despoiling the bodies, Maeglin realized. The Knight Commander examined the corpses on the floor. *These are soldiers sent to relieve the guard.*

Where are the prisoners? Where is Whitebrooke? Maeglin stared across the hallway at the last door, still closed.

Maeglin found the ring of keys in the back of the room, discarded on the floor. He retrieved them and approached the last door. The key ground against the iron lock as the heavy pins pushed into place. Maeglin adjusted his grip on his sword, then hurled the door open, sending it smashing into the wall with a crash that shook dust from its hinges.

The room beyond was dark, with only the light from the hallway falling in a thin shaft across its floor. A pale leg lay stretched across the patch of light, and a band of black markings, their strokes sharp and jagged. Maeglin fetched a lantern, and its light revealed what he had feared. Seven corpses laid out like spokes in a giant wheel, their flesh carved into bloody gashes that formed the symbols of fuil crunor, their blood painted into the wide ring of markings that surrounded them. An eighth corpse lay torn apart in the center of the pattern, its chest gaping open, its abdomen ruptured.

Eight... two prisoners are missing. Maeglin passed the lantern's light around the room, and paused, staring intently at the dark corners where the shadows appeared to flicker and move against the light.

Maeglin left the lantern on the floor and raced back to the stairs. He summoned the first soldiers he saw.

"Call out the guard. Everyone. Two prisoners have escaped, Reverend Whitebrooke and Sir Cathan. They must be found."

"Yes, sir!" The soldiers turned to go, but Maeglin held one behind. "No one is allowed in there, not until I send someone to begin the investigation, is that clear?"

The soldier nodded her head grimly, and took station at the entrance to the stairs as Maeglin strode toward the gates of the Temple, his mind churning. *Maker knows how long he has been gone, but it took time to do all of that. He cannot be far. Whitebrooke cannot have escaped the Temple already.*

Maeglin forced himself to calmly review every memory of the Archivist he could dredge up. Images raced past Maeglin as his memories churned. Whitebrooke boasting of his victory over Karsha Hali as he stood amongst the defiled remains of Maeglin's soldiers; standing in a hidden cave, sneering at Maeglin's efforts to find Lady Danielle; gleefully showing Maeglin the Blade taken from Danielle's room; blustering as he threatened Maeglin and Nesta in the high priestess' study.

Maeglin opened his eyes. *I know what he wants*, he realized. *It was the first thing he took after Benno's death, and the first thing he asked for when he awoke. He wants the Martyr's Blade.*

Cormac

Eilidh held still as Cormac pushed his hands slowly down her back, his fingers searching carefully along her spine.

"You have done this before?" Eilidh asked.

"Yes," Cormac assured her. "It's just a bit… tight."

"It is supposed to be." Eilidh twisted impatiently and grabbed his wrist. "Here, let me show you."

"No, I have it." Cormac pushed her hands firmly away. His fingers grasped the buckle and pulled it two notches tighter, and the bright steel backplate settled into place.

"Much better," Eilidh agreed. "Now, there will be buckles under the pauldrons. Make sure that they lay secure against the breastplate, and above the vambrace. If they are loose they are useless."

"I have done this before," Cormac muttered quietly as he shoved his hand under the steel shell of the pauldron and gave several hard tugs on its buckles. Eilidh faced him so that he could reach the front straps, a satisfied smile on her lips as she watched his eyes.

Cormac settled the pauldrons against her breastplate and fastened them tightly, then strapped the gorget into place around

Eilidh's neck as she held her hair out of the way. A final adjustment to the straps along her ribs and waist and Cormac stepped back.

"There, my lady, your squire has finished."

Eilidh gave a satisfied nod and strode in a tight circle, settling the weight on her shoulders and hips. She came to a stop facing Cormac, a wide smile lighting up her eyes.

There had never been any concealing the fact that Eilidh was a knight. There was no hiding Eilidh's strength, nor her proud confidence, no matter how much drab wool and scuffed leather she wore.

But now Eilidh had removed even that thin ruse and replaced it with shining steel, and Cormac realized that the knight appeared more comfortable in a suit of armor than she ever had in her simpler clothes.

"It is very well-crafted." Eilidh raised her arms and inspected the join under the pauldrons.

"It looks as if it were made for you," Cormac assured her.

"Now, a new sword." Eilidh turned her attention onto a rack of blades with a savage grin, and Cormac joined her in carefully examining the edge and heft of every weapon.

Baron Arledge had brought an extensive collection of weapons and armor with him, as well as his personal armorer, and the baron had given them free-run of his armory.

Cormac had chosen a vambrace of overlapping steel plates for his shield arm and a jerkin of steel scales over hardened leather to replace his worn leather breastplate, thick enough to turn aside all but the heaviest of blades, light enough to be worn on a long march, and flexible enough to allow him to move as he wished.

Eilidh had not compromised in any way. Her gaze had been drawn immediately to the polished steel of the heaviest of plate, layers of metal that would, to Cormac's eye, take hours to polish every night.

"Hello! You're both looking very ferocious," Wyn greeted them as she sauntered into the tent.

"It's good to have some steel around me again," Eilidh agreed.

THE MARTYR'S TEARS

"I see you've changed as well," Cormac noted, grinning broadly.

"Well, I've mostly ruined my nice clothes, poor Dani had to stitch them up so many times, and anyway, I wanted something a bit dark and lurky if we're going off to be wicked, right?" Wyn said reasonably. She had selected black leather leggings, and low boots, easy to kick off if required, and had opted for a simple, black, woolen tunic and a long, hooded cloak that reached to her ankles. "Anyway, what's so funny about my clothes?"

"Nothing at all," Cormac reassured her, "except when Baron Arledge said we could have our pick of the quartermaster's stores, he didn't mean 'find some old farmer's togs'."

"Pfft, shows what you know, then, doesn't it?" Wyn laughed. "This kit's perfect for skulking about, never fear."

"I am glad to see you have put on at least a bit of armor," Eilidh said approvingly.

"Her Ladyness made me. She said it was 'perfect'," Wyn complained, peering at the hardened leather vest that she was wearing. Wyn was clearly not as convinced as Lady Danielle. "It rubs all along here, and it jabs me in my pits when I try to bend or twist."

"It is not tight enough," Eilidh told her. "You have pulled out all the ties. Here, let me fasten them."

"Not tight enough? I can't breathe and it's smooshing my ditties as it is," Wyn pouted. "It gets in the way of everything. I hate it."

"It could save your life," Eilidh said sternly. "Even leather can turn a blade."

"The only reason it might need to is because it slowed me down enough for someone to poke me. It's coming off the moment we're someplace her nibs can't see."

"You will get accustomed to its weight," Eilidh tried again.

"Not with it shoved into a sack, I won't," Wyn informed her.

"She can hide behind us," Cormac interceded, handed another sword to Eilidh to inspect, and glanced at Wyn slyly, "just like always."

Eilidh nodded absently as she drew the sword from its leather sheath and held it to the light, turning it as she peered along its length. Its unadorned blade was as broad as her hand and tapered to a fine point. Eilidh tried its weight, then slid it into its sheath with a snap. "Excellent," she announced with a smile as she buckled the wide, leather belt around her waist.

"Is there anything over there that I might be able to lift?" Wyn asked hopefully, slipping her long dirk from its place across her back. "I've been carrying this thing around for ages, and it's fair for a soldier's prick, but I don't think it would do much in a real tussle."

Cormac laughed and threw open a chest resting against a wagon wheel, revealing a trove of knives, daggers, dirks, and short blades beyond Wyn's wildest dreams.

"Babies!" Wyn cooed, and began rummaging through the pile, oooo-ing and ahhh-ing at each new find. At last, she claimed a pair of long knives with curved blades and hilts small enough to fit comfortably in her hands, and she spent a moment twirling them through her fingers before nestling them in a cross against her back.

"All is well," she declared with a satisfied sigh.

They left the armory then and stood for a moment outside its entrance, gazing across the green fields that separated the tents of the Albainn nobles and the town of Bandirma.

Wyn brushed at the long strands of hair wavering in her face. "What's going to happen?" she asked softly, staring toward the high walls of the Temple on the far side of the river. "We'll not really go to war, not over fucking Shitebrooke, will we?"

"I wish I knew," Cormac replied, shaking his head in frustration, "but Arledge can't just camp here forever. Perhaps Sir Maeglin will listen—"

"Bloody Sir Maeglin," Wyn spat. "He can kiss my pucker. He's done nothing but help Shitebrooke, and that's a fact. He'd be for the block too if it were up to me."

"Someone will see reason," Eilidh said firmly, "now that the truth is known. It will take time for the sting of pride to fade, but once it does, they will see reason."

"Pride can kiss my pucker, too," Wyn muttered. "We're likely fucked, then. Pride's all these high-muckities care about, and that's a fact, too."

"I am sure they will send a message soon, they must," Cormac tried again, but his reassurance did little to raise Wyn's glum spirits. They began to walk toward the quarters they had been assigned, watching the life of the encampment around them. Wyn glared at her boots at first, but by the time they stopped to watch a group of squires challenge themselves to leap over each other's shoulders, Wyn was laughing and applauding along with the rest of the crowd.

Eventually, their steps returned them to the farm that Arledge had taken for himself, a prosperous spread of buildings on a slight rise in which they had been given rooms. They obtained bowls of steaming broth thick with carrots and potatoes, and a hunk of heavy, black bread, and Wyn carried a supply up the creaking stairs to the bedroom in which Lady Danielle had been invalided.

With Wyn gone, Cormac and Eilidh were left to themselves in the farm's dining hall, a narrow room with whitewashed walls covered to the rafters in racks of antlers that grabbed spitefully at cloaks and sleeves as the diners passed.

"How does the man find time to farm?" Eilidh wondered.

The musty silence weighed heavily as they ate, and Cormac wished for the ease of the road, where the quiet passage of fields and forest had only brought him closer to the woman riding next to him. *What did we talk of, all those days? Nothing, and everything, and now I cannot think of anything of interest to say when I need to.*

His thoughts returned to the first night he had met Eilidh, when she had bent his ear across a trestle table in the refectory at Littleford long after their empty bowls had been cleared away, excitedly outlining the minutia of her plan for training her new troop. *I thought her young and enthusiastic,* he remembered. *Now I see her passion and drive, although I wish more of the girl's excitement and joy had survived.*

"It will rain tomorrow—" Cormac started.

"I think I shall—" Eilidh began, then smiled as they both stopped. "You said…?"

"Only that I am certain it will rain tomorrow," Cormac repeated, embarrassed. *Is that really what I wanted to say to her?* "More polishing," he concluded lamely.

"Yes, more polishing," Eilidh agreed. "Speaking of… I must go and see to this armor, or else I shall be up all night."

"You need a squire to help you with it," Cormac volunteered.

"I will have to make do," Eilidh replied, then rose abruptly and left with a hurried, "Good night."

Cormac finished his meal and then sat back and contemplated the spread of antlers over his head. *Well done, you.*

He left the dining hall and wandered aimlessly until he spotted Wyn, perched on the rough, wooden rail that encircled the pig pen. Cormac leaned on the rail beside her and watched her slowly push small chunks of bread into her bowl of stew until it more resembled a thick porridge than soup. Wyn sighed and donated the bowl to the pigs.

"Not hungry?" Cormac asked.

"No," Wyn agreed.

"How is Lady Danielle?"

"The same, I suppose. She's been asleep all evening. She had them make her some medicine that knocks her right out."

"Has she given up pretending not to be hurt?"

"Yes, it was too much on the ride here… although I don't think she's really let on how bad her side is."

Wyn was quiet for a moment, and Cormac waited patiently. "I was thinking about your brother," she started, her voice hesitant and uncertain. "When we first met, do you remember?"

Cormac nodded silently and began to scrape mud from his boot onto the lowest rail of the fence. He remembered the long column of soldiers winding through the snow, and the satisfaction of being called to ride ahead with Lord Bradon, certain that the dull march had ended and the campaign had finally begun. And he remembered the thin girl waiting to guide them, shivering in her threadbare clothes, tiny as she perched atop a massive horse that someone had certainly given her as a joke, scowling fiercely at the soldiers as they rode by.

"What made you think of that?"

"Just, I suppose, seeing you all kitted out in your fancy armor again, it reminded me, is all." Wyn pressed her lips together as a slight tremble passed through them. "You looked the same that day."

"I'm surprised you noticed us."

"He smiled at me," Wyn explained.

"You looked like you wanted to hit us," Cormac smiled to himself. "I suppose Corlath thought a smile might let you know we were nice."

"You did it, too."

"There you are."

"Well, you were all so big and fierce and scary, with all your tattoos and such. Do you remember Captain Alistair's lovely dragons?"

"I do."

"He never did tell me his stupid dragon story," Wyn grumbled. She watched the pigs snuffle the empty bowl for a moment as her shoulders drooped.

"Why did Corlath do it?" she whispered. "He hardly knew me, but he…"

Cormac was silent for a moment, then glanced at Wyn from the corner of his eye. "He smiled at all the girls, so don't feel special or anything."

Wyn's laugh became a sob, and she sniffed uselessly. "Yes, that's what I was talking about."

Cormac examined his hands before continuing. "He always fought for those who needed someone to fight for them. That's why he liked you, because he saw the same in you. A villager he had never met. His brother. And I don't just mean me, I mean all of us in Captain Alistair's troop, we were all his brothers."

"Brok was his brother then, too."

"Corlath knew that wasn't true anymore. He knew who his family was in that room, and it wasn't Brok. It was a sister, and there was no way Corlath wasn't going to fight to save her."

Wyn wiped at her nose again. "I want to remember him, Cormac, I want to let people know what Corlath did, but it's hard because I have to remember everything else."

"He would understand," Cormac nodded to himself. "I understand." He turned so that the faint light from the farm buildings caught the side of his face, and ran a finger across the spiral of dots and swirling flames that were tattooed above his left eye. "You know what these are?"

Wyn shook her head.

"Each one is a story." Cormac touched each of the dots, his finger unerring even without a mirror to guide it. "Each one a foe that must be remembered. But the stories are never easy ones to tell. Pain and fear and sorrow as well as celebration. They are worthy of remembering nonetheless, and that is why we honor them, so that the telling of the story will always be there, no matter how we may shrink from it."

Wyn nodded again, her eyes unfocused as she gazed into dark memories, and tears ran across her cheeks and hung, quivering, from her lip.

"Can you help me?" Wyn suddenly asked, and wiped fiercely at her eyes with the back of her hand. She tapped a finger above her left eyebrow. "I have some stories I want to remember."

"Are they worthy of you?" Cormac asked. "The markings are to honor you… you should only mark those that bring you honor, for the ceremony makes their death a part of you."

"You know the first," Wyn told him, "and that's to honor Corlath, not me. I just wish that shit-hole Brok knew that he ended up a little dot on my forehead," Wyn grinned fiercely. "The second one… that's from a long time ago."

"I can help you," Cormac nodded. "I can make the ink, and I know the words to say."

"Good," Wyn said with satisfaction, and she hopped off the fence. "Let's go."

They took needles and a pestle from the healer's tent, ink and powder from a scribe's desk, and found a sheltered nook within the first sweep of trees on the side of the forested hills, far from the pickets Arledge had placed around the encampment.

Cormac fashioned a small fire within a ring of rocks, and soon the grove was dancing with the yellow light of its flames as the warrior carefully ground the colored powders into a few drops of water until he had a palette of reds, oranges, and yellows to go with the jar of pure black ink they had stolen. He cleaned the needles with vinegar and flame, then motioned for Wyn to sit cross-legged by the fire so that the light fell fully on the side of her face.

"Just on my face, right?" Wyn skewered him with a steely gaze. " 'Cause I've heard about what those clan women do, and you're not touching my boobs with those things."

"Just your forehead," Cormac assured her.

Cormac knelt close, and gently tucked her hair behind her ear. Her cheek felt warm and soft against his hand, and he watched her eyes narrow as the first small darts of pain began to rain across her skin.

"The flames are the breath of Ddraighnall, the white dragon, through whose fire all must pass to be judged," Cormac explained as he worked. "It is he who will judge these lives you offer to him, and it is his breath that will consume them for all eternity if they are found to be wanting."

"Dani told me about him," Wyn said softly. "That's where they are now, both of them. Burning forever."

"That is for Ddraighnall to decide," Cormac reminded her, and paused in his work as Wyn snorted with contempt. "But you are probably right," he conceded. "Now, hold still, stupid, or you'll end up with a huge cock tattooed on your face."

"You wouldn't dare," Wyn decided, but she stayed still and silent, just in case.

Cormac began to hum as he worked, resonant and slow, a tune full of strange rhythm. The hum became a chant in the language of the Ironback clans, a sound like boulders grinding against one another, but the words suited the song, and Cormac found it soothing and soon lost himself in his work.

Midnight passed, and then dawn, and the work paused only to allow Cormac to mix fresh ink and to massage his aching hand. Finally, the flames were finished, a long braid of red and orange and yellow that encircled her eyebrow and descended to the top of her cheekbone in a wide arc.

THE MARTYR'S TEARS

"Now we place them in Ddraighnall's flames to be judged." Cormac took up the needle one last time. "Name them."

"Brok," Wyn said firmly.

"Who is Brok, that he must be judged by the dragon?" Cormac asked formally.

"Brok was…" Wyn bit her lip, then started again. "Brok was a soldier. He was a father. He had daughters, I dunno how many, little ones that he talked about all the time, and he was always laughing and was so strong you knew nothing bad would ever happen to him. Brok was a soldier, and a father, and a friend. Brok was a murderer and a rapist. He killed his friend, he tried to rape me, and he would have killed me too, except Corlath stopped him."

Cormac sang and the needle branded the story into her skin with a precise circle of black ink.

"Name them," Cormac said again when the first small circle was complete.

"Quinn," she said.

"Who is Quinn, that he must be judged by the dragon?" Cormac repeated.

"Quinn killed women and children so that people would be scared of him. He made slaves of those who were weak, and he murdered those who were strong. He beat children just for begging for food in the wrong place. He cried when he died. He was so scared he cried and begged on his knees, and he was just a little boy in the end."

Cormac sang again, and the needle danced across her skin one last time.

"There," he said, and he stood and stretched his back. "It will be sore for a day or two, I remember."

Wyn climbed to her feet and joined him in stretching. The mist had turned into a steady drizzle that was soaking the forest, and only the thick leaves of the tree above them kept them from the dripping wet. She stepped from beneath their shelter and let the rain slowly trickle across her face and neck, its cool touch soothing.

THE MARTYR'S TEARS

Cormac packed their supplies and smothered the charred remains of the fire, then joined Wyn.

"So, how does it look?" Wyn asked.

"It suits you, actually," Cormac smiled. "Very fierce."

"I am the Queen of Thieves," Wyn murmured, profoundly pleased.

They began the walk down the hill toward the encampment, but they had only taken a dozen steps when Wyn suddenly stopped in her tracks.

"Oh no," she sighed in resignation, and closed her eyes. "Killock is going to kill me. Bit hard to blend in with tattoos all over my face."

"Just one," Cormac replied helpfully. "In any case, it's not Killock you should be worried about. Wait until you show Lady Danielle."

"Oh… shit."

***

They gathered in the parlor of the farmhouse as the rain became an insistent roar against the slate tiles of the roof, and squires hurried to bank the fire with a healthy supply of wood. The room was a large one, with tall windows overlooking the darkened valley and massive beams, stained with ancient smoke, crossing overhead, and the heat from the snapping flames could not quite reach the damp corners of the room. They clustered near the fire and waited in the hushed murmur of quiet conversation for the squires to depart.

Danielle had made the trip downstairs, aided by two knights, and now sat stiffly in one of the low-backed chairs, shifting back and forth uncomfortably as she tried to find a position that did not strain her wound.

Cormac and Sir Eilidh stood to Danielle's side, while Wyn took up station to her right, ready with small pillows scavenged from other chairs should they be needed. Across from them stood Baron Arledge, with stooped shoulders and his hands clasped behind his back.

Only Sir Killock did not join the circle. He leaned against the outer wall between two of the windows, his face lost in shadow beneath his hood.

Cormac took advantage of the Baron inquiring of Lady Danielle's health to take Wyn a step aside.

"How did her Ladyship…?" Cormac whispered in her ear. "Is she still talking to you?"

"She thought it was lovely," Wyn replied quietly.

"Really?" Cormac frowned. "She's not furious with me?"

"She said it was beautiful and wonderful, and oooo'd and ahhh'd," Wyn assured him. "Then I told her why I wanted it and she got all weepy, and then I got all weepy. It was sweet, so no laughing."

"That's better than I expected. I was fairly certain I was going to spend a significant part of today being told off."

"Not a bit," Wyn smiled slyly. "If I'd thought for a moment, not likely, right, but *if*, I'd have remembered, which, by the way, I'll not ever speak to you again if you tell her I told you, that Dani quite likes all that mysterious warrior silliness."

"She does? I don't believe it."

"It's romantic, you berk."

"Well, you are the expert on that."

"I am," Wyn told him. "Anyway, it all turned out well, no worries. In fact, I'll just point out that I was right, again, so there."

"You were? I doubt it. About what?"

"I was, too," Wyn said fiercely. "I *told* you that a mysterious tattoo would make a girl's knees…" Wyn suddenly stopped, her cheeks blushing a pale crimson, and glanced quickly at Lady Danielle, fortunately oblivious to the whispered conversation. "I mean… never bloody mind what I mean, I was just right."

The doors to the room closed with a heavy thud behind the departing squires, sparing Wyn from further interrogation, much to Cormac's disappointment.

THE MARTYR'S TEARS

"I have been speaking with Sir Killock about what to do," Arledge began without preamble. "Some of the nobles counsel summoning the army from Littleford, saying that we appear too weak without them. Others counsel returning to Littleford as a show of good faith. Most wish to return to their lands to oversee the spring planting."

"You should grant their request," Sir Eilidh said firmly. "Holding the temples has not achieved anything."

"Perhaps," Arledge dismissed the concern and carried on, "but I am convinced that Sir Maeglin will not listen to reason. I had hoped, we all did, that the Council would be more open, but there has been no message from them for almost a day, now, and while there still may be one any moment, Sir Killock and I have been discussing what we might do to resolve this conundrum for the benefit of both Crown and Temple."

"I am pleased to hear it," Lady Danielle said. "What have you decided?"

"We're going to go in and get Whitebrooke," Killock's voice rasped softly from the other side of the room.

"And kill him?" Wyn asked hopefully.

"That will be up to him."

"The Queen wants him to stand for treason," Arledge instructed, "so everything possible must be done to bring him here alive."

"He'll fight, though, don't you think he'll fight? I think he'll fight."

"How do we do it?" Cormac asked, his mind already absorbed in the details of dark, narrow passageways, a struggling prisoner, and gates and walls and locks.

"We know where he is being held," Killock replied. "We enter through the cisterns, the same route that Wyn and Danielle escaped through. Just us, none of Arledge's men. The Temple will take care of this, so Maeglin has no one to blame but us. If we are successful, Maeglin can rage about proof until he passes out, but the baron won't have attacked anything, and maybe this can end tonight."

"Tonight?" Lady Danielle repeated, shocked.

"Yes," Arledge said gravely. "The fighting around Newbridge has escalated. Every day we delay could bring with it more death, and that could easily start a war."

"Do you believe abducting Whitebrooke from the Temple's dungeon and trying him for treason will end this confrontation?" the noblewoman wondered.

"Whitebrooke is the cause of all of this, my lady," Arledge said. "Setting us at each other's throats, killing and murdering. Once he is gone, we can once again unite."

"Yes, my lord, I am aware that Whitebrooke is the cause," Lady Danielle said sharply. "I doubt that executing him will convince those who do not think my word or Karsha Hali's word is enough. They may be relieved in their hearts, but they will still wonder."

"They'll get over it," Wyn assured her, and Lady Danielle gave a slight smile. Then she shook her head.

"Not until they see something they cannot ignore."

"What can we show them?" Killock asked, his voice a sigh in the shadows. "He has hidden any proof away, and I will wager it's behind that stone door in the archives that cannot be opened."

"It will open eventually, and then all doubt will pass," Arledge declared. "We simply cannot wait that long to act. It is too dangerous. We can deal with any ruffled feathers until then."

"You misunderstand me," Lady Danielle said wearily. "I agree, we cannot wait. Which is why we should also try to breach that chamber while we are in the Temple. If we can manage that, we have the proof *and* that bastard in our hands."

"My lady," Baron Arledge spoke gently, as if to a child to be consoled, "of course we agree that finding irrefutable proof would be for the best. Nonetheless, we are told that the finest minds in the Temple have failed to find a way into the stone chamber, so I am not sure…" Arledge spread his hands helplessly.

"They are trying to open the door," Lady Danielle gave Arledge a thin smile. "I say we should destroy it."

"Can it be done?" the baron asked, and he glanced around the room seeking a sign of corroboration for this glimmer of hope.

"Of course," Lady Danielle replied simply. "It is stone, and Veils, and Wards, but all may be overcome by a Weapon if it has the power. My lance, for example—"

"You can't go," Wyn scolded her. "You can't even walk without hurting yourself, and you want to sneak into the Temple? Your insides will plop right out before we reach the tunnel, no chance. Oh! And it's reckless! That's what it is."

"There are medicines to numb the pain—"

"Your insides will fall out!"

"My lady, I hardly think the Queen would look favorably on us if we were to allow you to go straight from the sick bed to the Temple," Arledge frowned.

"Exactly, what would your sis say?" Wyn agreed quickly. "Oh! Plus, we have to be sneaky to get all the way to wherever this door is, and you're horrible at sneaky…" Wyn faltered as Lady Danielle shot her a withering glare. "I mean, not horrible, just, you know, a bit loud, in parts…"

"You are taking those two," Lady Danielle complained, pointing at Cormac and Eilidh, looming on the other side of her. "No one could hear my tiny footsteps with the… the… oh, what is the… the great clanking and bashing they will make."

"Commotion, my lady?" Arledge supplied helpfully, and Wyn glared at him until the lord glanced away in embarrassment.

"Yes, the commotion," Lady Danielle agreed, and sat back in a triumph only somewhat spoiled by a flinch of pain.

"They will not be coming into the Temple with us, for precisely that reason," Killock said into the silence that followed. "They will take the entrance to the tunnel, and then hold it open until our return."

"See?" Wyn nodded her head emphatically. "Please, Dani, you can't go. Think about how far you will have to walk between the tunnel and wherever this door thing is. I know you would do it if we had to, but we don't need whatever is in there, we can just do what the baron said. Please, Dani, you're too hurt, it's crazy."

"This, from the woman who traipsed into Littleford to spy with hands all wrapped in bandages and not able to breathe," complained Lady Danielle, but Cormac heard a note of defeat in the noblewoman's voice.

"Let's not, um, talk about that *right* this moment," Wyn said quickly, and she glanced at Sir Eilidh, who was frowning in concentration.

"In any event, I was not actually suggesting I would accompany you," Lady Danielle continued sulkily, "just my lance."

"My lady, what good would that do?" Arledge frowned, perplexed.

"They carry it to the door," Lady Danielle took a deep, resolute breath, "and then I empower it. From here."

"Is that possible?" Arledge glanced around the room, searching for confirmation, and finding only bafflement to equal his own.

"It is possible," Lady Danielle replied. "The Device does not need to be held in your hand to empower it. The Word is not conveyed by touch."

"It just gets harder the further away you are," Sir Killock explained. "Much harder."

"Have you ever attempted such an endeavor?" Arledge asked Lady Danielle. "Has anyone?"

"It does not matter," Sir Killock cut across any reply that might have come. "If Lady Danielle thinks there's a chance, it is worth the risk. *After* Whitebrooke is secured."

"There remain some practical details," Arledge apologized. "How will you know when they have reached the chamber door, my lady?"

"I will not," Lady Danielle replied. "We must have a signal. Will midnight be enough time to get there?" she asked Sir Killock, and the Templar nodded silently. "Then at the midnight bells, I will empower the lance."

"Twice," Sir Killock added. "To be certain."

"Twice," Lady Danielle agreed, but Cormac saw her blanch.

The baron gave them the rest of the short afternoon to 'ready yourselves', but Cormac was not sure what he needed the time for. *We're not planning an assault on a fortified position,* Cormac groused to himself. *Follow the guides, hold the position. Ready. Now, what am I supposed to do until nightfall?*

Cormac decided the correct answer was sleep, but he spent a moment conferring with Sir Killock, making sure he understood what the knight wanted of him. However, Sir Killock cut Cormac off after only a moment.

"You know what to do, Cormac," Killock said kindly. "Hold the entrance to the tunnel until we return with the prisoner, then keep him subdued while Wyn and I open his room in the archives."

"And if we are discovered?"

"Hold it as long as possible, but make sure Whitebrooke gets to Arledge. Wyn and I can find another way out if it comes to that, so don't get caught."

"Yes, sir," Cormac nodded, and left the Templar to himself. Cormac strode from the room and through the house, his steps a heavy thunder on the wooden boards. When he reached the cobbled yard, he stopped and examined the heavy, somber sky.

"All set?" Eilidh stepped next to him.

Cormac glanced at her from the corner of his eye. She stood tall, her head tilted back and one eyebrow cocked. He could imagine dragon fire curling across her brow, and his fingers twitched toward her, ready to trace the flame's path over her skin. Cormac forced his hands together and instead massaged the lingering ache from his fingers. *Perhaps one day.* Cormac realized he had turned mute as he gazed at Eilidh, and quickly turned his thoughts to the coming night.

"Yes, it's simple enough. Guard the tunnel, guard the prisoner." Cormac frowned, and forced himself to listen to the rain patter off her cloak, trying to will a calm he did not feel over his jumbled thoughts. "I do not like them going into the Temple without us. After we have Whitebrooke as our prisoner, when Killock and Wyn need to go much farther, I understand. But they will need us at the beginning, when they go to the dungeons to collect Whitebrooke, and the risk of being overheard in that short distance is small."

Eilidh nodded her head sympathetically. "You should say as much to Sir Killock. He will listen to you."

"I will," Cormac decided, and they stood quietly for a moment, content to watch the rain.

"Cormac..." Eilidh hesitated, then appeared to come to a decision and continued, "I wanted to tell you—"

"Hello!" Wyn announced as she stepped lightly around the worst of the puddles in the cobbled yard. "Are you not afraid you will drown? Another beautiful day in the mud." Wyn squinted into the rain, then pulled her hood firmly over her head. "I'm off to get some nosh before we go. Do you want some?" Wyn suddenly held up her hands and her eyes widened. "Whatever it was, it wasn't me. Or, if it was me, I didn't mean it, I promise."

Cormac glanced around, bewildered at the sudden turn of the conversation, and realized that Eilidh was glaring sternly at Wyn, with her arms crossed and her brow furrowed.

"I remembered you," Eilidh told her. "It took me a little while, but I remembered in the end. Mairi."

"Got there, did you?" Wyn laughed, completely unfazed at being discovered. "I wondered if you would. What gave me away?"

"Your scar." Eilidh traced a finger across her eyebrow and cheek. "It's so faint I didn't notice it when we met in Newbridge, but you can still see it, and when Lady Danielle mentioned the injuries to your hands I remembered the poor girl with the bandaged hands and the same scar."

"You've got a good eye," Wyn nodded in approval. "I about had to pick my jaw out of the mud when Cormac led you down the street."

"You recognized me right away?"

"I remember all the ladies who slip me silver," Wyn winked, "and I didn't even need to dance for it that time. You seemed nice, and the coins were sweet. Plus, I remember faces, somehow, I don't know how. Everything else just falls right out, but faces stick."

"I didn't think you had noticed the coins."

"I thought I was going to have to help you get my purse open," Wyn laughed, "before someone saw you rummaging in there and called the sheriff on you. Bit hard to explain you were trying to put coins *in* someone's purse. I may try that next time. Or, you know, if that ever happens, I mean."

"I see," said Eilidh. "You don't mind, then?"

"I don't mind what?"

"That I know what you did."

"Nooo... good on ya."

"Some might feel some shame for taking advantage of my compassion for an injured girl who needed help."

"Well, 'some' are pretty daft, then."

"Or they have a sense of honor."

"Are you serious?"

"Of course I am."

"It's easy to talk about honor when you're the one with the shiny armor and sword." Wyn rolled her eyes in disgust. "Some of us can't just shout and get what we want on a plate made of gold."

"You see no difference between deceit and open confrontation? And do not say swords. I mean in speech and action."

"Time and a place for everything," Wyn replied. "Right now, being pretty open. Earlier, not so much. Anyway, you come off well in the telling. Kind heart for the unfortunate and all that. You should be chuffed. Most folks, I have to get them pissed before they'll help."

"Wyn, it has nothing to do with how I come off in the story. Do you not see that it demeans you when you take advantage of others, deceiving them to get your way?"

"I think it just might have something to do with how you got taken advantage of, actually. A bit sensitive?"

"It does not. When I became a knight, I swore to honorably defend the weak, the commoners who cannot defend themselves. Not to lie and connive and take the expedient path. You say that you fight to help the unfortunate as well, but if you do not fight honorably, your cause has no honor."

"Well, let's see. First," Wyn ticked off her points on raised fingers, "I'm not a knight, you may have noticed, so I haven't sworn to be a good little soldier marching about shouting 'honor!' and never thinking for myself. Second, you sound a bit of a poncy twat when you say 'commoners'. Third, I said when we met that you wouldn't like me once you got to know me, and I guess I was right." Wyn faced Cormac and shrugged. "I don't know what you see in her," she said, and walked away.

Eilidh watched Wyn disappear into the bustle of the camp and then sighed. "That went well."

"I thought so."

"Am I wrong? Does how not matter as much as why?"

Say nothing, Cormac instructed himself unnecessarily.

But Eilidh was having none of it and fixed Cormac with a piercing stare. "Well?"

"How does matter as much as why. I agree."

"You do not sound convinced."

Idiot, Cormac chastised himself. *Eilidh is angry and embarrassed, and all she wants to hear right now is 'yes, sir.' Try harder, or shut up.*

"I am convinced. Saying you fight for a cause means nothing. How you fight means everything."

Eilidh continued to glare at him, and Cormac wondered what more he could say to escape.

"That's how she fights," he explained. "That's how everyone she knows fights, and it's how she has survived and how she has saved others. And she's been taught that it is the right thing to do, not just by what happened to her as a child, but by Sir Killock, who deserves our respect. You judge how she fights differently, and differently from Sir Killock, and even Lady Danielle, so it is difficult for her to condemn all of that just because you might find it dishonorable."

"Do you find it dishonorable, too? Or do you find that it is worthy of respect?"

Say nothing! It was too late for that, however, and Cormac knew it. *Perhaps it is for the best. There has always been something between Eilidh and Wyn. They have never warmed to each other, and perhaps this is how that gap can be crossed. Or at least, the start of a crossing. They need to trust each other, and perhaps they can become friends, or at least return to tolerating each other, or else my life is going to be an unending trial.*

"I think that a knight's righteous adherence to duty and virtue is one way to fight, but there are others. It is whether your heart is wicked or kind that matters when you deliver a blow or deceive an opponent. Far worse would be to compromise, to fail to use every means to fight for your cause."

"You think I fail to use every means to fight?"

"I have never seen you compromise," Cormac assured her, "never seen you back away from what you think is righteous. But nor have I ever seen Wyn do that. I hope that you can come to see that, too. As Sir Killock did, as I have, and as Lady Danielle has."

"Are you in love with her?" Eilidh asked, then suddenly frowned, embarrassed, and shook her head. "I'm sorry, I should not have asked you that. It's none of my business."

"In love? With whom?" Cormac wondered, completely baffled. "Lady Danielle? I think that would be a bit optimistic of me," he smiled.

"No, not Lady Danielle," Eilidh said shortly. "It doesn't matter, forget I said anything."

"Wyn?" Cormac laughed. "Why would you think that?"

"It was foolish, I see that now," Eilidh said gruffly.

"You have to tell me why you thought that. It's only fair," Cormac insisted.

"Martyr's tears, Cormac, very well. It's the way that you two talk with each other, always smiling and laughing and happy together. The way you are vouching for her now. And what you did for her last night. Whoever did that cared for her."

"I do care for her. And I suppose I do love her, in a way, but not as you mean. In fact, I would say that she is an exasperating, teasing, hilarious, wonderful pest."

Eilidh laughed, and at last the anger began to leave her. "You just described three of my sisters."

"We didn't have a sister. I think our parents decided that we were enough."

"Count yourself lucky. Sisters are terrible. And I love all five of mine."

"Five? Are they all like you?"

"Oh, no, not at all. Cadhla is beautiful and ladylike and good at everything she tries. Daireann and Darcy are so alike that Mum gets their names wrong, as sharp as tacks and wicked as the day is long. They're the ones the boys chase. Endewyn is number four. She has the sweetest heart, but she's not the brightest, poor thing. She married a farmer who is exactly like her, and they are very happy. Saoirse is the youngest of us, but she's the fiercest, and never backs down from anything."

"Why do you say they are not like you?"

"Oh, well, I am tall and strong, and loud, but that's about it. I'll never be as gorgeous or graceful as Cadhla, nor as smart as the Ds, nor as kind as Endewyn. And I wish someday to be as brave as Saoirse. No, I knew that my only chance was to become a knight. And here I am, throwing that away for a… for a cause."

"Well, I don't know about all of that," Cormac said thoughtfully. "I'm not sure you are as loud as you think you are."

"Thanks," Eilidh replied, but Cormac could see she was smiling, just a little, and a weight appeared to have lifted from her shoulders, for she now walked with head up, watching the life of the encampment with interest as they passed it by.

"It feels good to be back in camp," Cormac realized. "The rain and mud… feels like the start of the spring campaign. Makes you feel like a soldier, again."

"I am not sure what I am, anymore. How can I be a woman of the Order of Knights when I am about to draw steel against the Temple? Could a knight truly feel in her heart that this is the right thing to do?"

"I don't know. But if your heart says this is right, then does it matter? I don't think I've ever fought for the Temple. I fought for my brother, for the soldiers around me, and for Captain Alistair and Lord Bradon, and I did that because they fought for what's right, what my heart said was right, and that's all that mattered. Now I fight for Lady Danielle, for the same reasons."

THE MARTYR'S TEARS

"And you know that this attack is the right thing to do? Your hand will not waver if it must draw the blood of a Temple soldier?"

Cormac walked in silence as he gathered his thoughts, and Eilidh gave him the time he needed. "I know what is evil. I have seen it, and I know it is worth sacrificing everything to overcome. If someone stands against me in that, then I will not hesitate, even if my heart breaks with every blow. That, you may count on."

She raised her hand and rested it on his shoulder, her hand strong against him as she gripped him firmly, and a small smile lifted the corner of her lips and made the skin next to her eyes crinkle happily. "Well said," she murmured. "You make me proud to stand beside you, and you push all of my doubts away. Thank you, Cormac."

Cormac caught his breath as a surge of tingling flowed across his skin, as if his limbs had suddenly awoken from an unbroken sleep, and he felt his heart thudding beneath his ear.

The rain had plastered Eilidh's blonde hair to the side of her face, and her braid had come loose and hung, sodden, down her back, but her green eyes shone and she stood uncaring of the chill drops that slid down her neck, and Cormac's hand ached to take her hand in his, and wipe the rain from her skin. He was taken aback by the urgency of the feeling, and he feared that it would show in his gaze.

Eilidh smiled again, squeezed his shoulder a final time, and then released him, his skin still warm where her hand had rested, ever-so-briefly. Eilidh glanced about, as if taking in the commotion of the camp for the first time, but Cormac found it difficult to take his eyes off her. *Why do I not tell her? For weeks we have traveled together, never apart, and never once...*

Cormac drew breath to speak and realized that he did not know what he would say. *I don't know my own thoughts*, he berated himself. *I know I long for another day on the road, feeling her pressed against me as we ride. I know how often I have imagined her sliding her tunic from her shoulder so that I may trace my fingers along her neck. And if that were all, if it was just desire... ahhh, Corlath, I need your advice. I will fuck this up on my own, I know it.*

THE MARTYR'S TEARS

Eilidh suddenly began to walk, gesturing for Cormac to follow. "Come on," she said, excitement bubbling in her voice. "You can help me get accustomed to this sword before I have to actually use it."

They hurried through the steady drizzle to the barn and Eilidh laughed as Cormac and a helpful goat chased frantic chickens into pens against the back wall, leaving the wide, hay-covered floor to the two of them. Cormac draped his cloak and padded coat over the railing of one of the stalls and walked slowly to the center of the floor, stretching his shoulders with a series of energetic twists. Eilidh joined him there, also clad only in leggings and tunic, and she raised an eyebrow at his flailing.

He smiled in return, slipped Corlath's sword free, and tossed the sheath to the side. Eilidh mirrored him, and the wide blade she had acquired from the smithy sang like a tine as its tip cleared the leather. Her sword was similar in length to his, but wider, and would deliver a heavier blow, and he knew better than to think that its weight would slow her.

They circled the center of the room, their gaze locked on one another, their boots muffled against the hay and packed dirt of the floor.

Cormac struck first, wagering that Eilidh would think that he would grant her the first blow. Her sword caught the thrust easily and turned it aside, and she skipped away, her green eyes flashing in the dim light. He chased her with a long lunge that was a feint, ready to trap her parry, but she danced easily away again and refused his offer with a disgusted roll of her eyes.

"I thought we were testing your sword, not your boots," he teased, backing away and spreading his hands to his sides.

"I wasn't sure if you were ready for me. Were those meant to be real attacks?"

"No, just making sure you had figured out which end was the sharp one."

Eilidh launched herself at Cormac, a fierce grin on her face, her sword a gleaming blur. Cormac was ready for the attack, and stepped into it, his parry high and strong as he took her tip against the base of his blade. Steel shrieked as the swords ground against each other for an instant, then Cormac countered with a short jab that required no pause in his motion.

But Eilidh moved as quickly, turning inside his sword as she whipped her blade backhanded in a long arc. The steel sang in the air, and Cormac was forced to hurl himself sideways, ducking under the blow, before catching his balance again.

"Now who is running?" Eilidh asked sweetly, waiting for Cormac to come to a stop.

Cormac saluted her with his sword, then lowered into guard as the knight began a purposeful advance. Cormac slid to his right, then forward to meet her. Her sword swept out first, and Cormac conceded the attack to the heavier blade, trapping it against the base of his own blade with short, precise parries. Steel crashed and his sword rang with the strength of her blows, but such was his sword's balance that his stance never faltered, his grip never wavered. Two, three, four times she struck, with such speed and strength that it drove Cormac backward.

Then he countered, a quick thrust between the rhythm of her blows. She knocked his sword aside with hardly a pause, and again he backpedaled as he probed for another opening. A quick step forward forced the opening, and he cut high at her shoulder. Again she caught the thrust and turned it, and again her riposte put him on the defensive.

Cormac gained some distance between them with another feint and spun away. She pursued him, but Cormac had gauged her tactics now. *She is strong and fast, and her form is excellent, and that is enough for most opponents,* Cormac realized, *but she fights to set up the perfect finish, instead of taking what is offered her. A winning tactic for the practice field, perhaps, but it is a weakness to be exposed.*

Cormac initiated the next exchange as Eilidh neared, a low thrust offered as perfect bait for an inside parry, and Eilidh did not disappoint, instantly taking his sword's point away and returning the attack with a slashing uppercut. Cormac let the pattern continue, building the textbook replies to each move until a rhythm pulsed faintly in their motion. Then he broke the pattern, a short jab at her face, awkward and rushed and unexpected, then the true strike, and he stepped into the downward slash as she twisted to catch the jab, off-balance and off-guard.

Eilidh bent like a blade of grass and cried out in fierce denial. Somehow, she wrenched her blade to catch his over her shoulder, her strength enough to turn his sword slightly, and she took advantage, exploding into his chest with her shoulder, driven by the strength of her legs. Cormac felt his weight leave his feet, and then there was a mad tangle of limbs as he grabbed her shirt and she clutched at his legs, and then the ground hit him in the back and her shoulder drove the breath from his lungs.

They thrashed madly on the ground, their hands clenching and pulling at their tunics, their backs arching, their legs shoving for purchase. Eilidh grinned fiercely at him as they struggled, and he matched her, locking one hand around her wrist while he thrust with his other arm, bending her backward. But she surprised him, ducking inside his arm so that her shoulder pressed against his elbow while twisting and dragging her other arm across his body, and he could no longer keep her away as his arm bent over her shoulder. Her arm slid under his chin and pressed against his neck, and she hissed in triumph as he tapped against her arm in surrender.

Eilidh pushed herself up with her hands on his chest and held herself there, staring at Cormac through a ragged cascade of blonde hair, a wide smile lighting up her face. Cormac let his arms flop onto the ground on either side and sucked in deep draughts of air. Eilidh nodded in weary agreement and blew out her cheeks, and her head drooped as well. Her hair fell about his face, and with it came the scent of rain, and sweat, and hot leather, and he suddenly became aware of her weight across his hips, and the strong length of her thighs pressed against his waist as she straddled him.

Cormac watched a drop of sweat run around her neck and over the long ridge of her clavicle. Her tunic had been wrenched far to the side in their struggle, and Cormac gazed at the play of muscle across her neck and shoulder through the skewed collar as she breathed, and then followed the long run of the bead of sweat

THE MARTYR'S TEARS

as it left its perch and traced the smooth swell of her breast until at last it disappeared beneath the cloth.

Eilidh slowly pushed herself back, letting her weight settle on his hips, and pushed her hair out of her face with her hands, her eyes fixed on Cormac's, never blinking. Eilidh's chest rose and fell as she caught her breath, and her tunic clung to her, pulled taut against her shape. Cormac felt an urgent ache that pushed against her warm weight, and he dared to raise his hands and place them gently on Eilidh's waist, feeling the play of smooth muscle curve to meet the sharp ridge of her hips.

Eilidh closed her eyes and tilted her head back, then let her hands drop to rest on his for a moment, and the two warriors held still, absorbed in the feeling of their breathing moving themselves gently against each other. Then she stooped quickly and pressed her lips against his. They were warm and soft, and there was the sharp taste of salt as her lips opened in the instant before she pushed herself back, smiled, and quickly rose to her feet.

She held out a hand and he took it as he scrambled to his feet, and held it for a moment longer, feeling her long fingers curl around his palm. She squeezed his hand, then let it go and began to straighten her clothes, and he followed suit, refastening belts and bemoaning the loss of buttons torn from their thread. No word was spoken until they had donned their coats and cloaks and buckled their swords around their waists. Then they stood in the open doors of the barn and watched the rain slowly fill the yard with murky puddles.

"Thank you," Cormac said at last. "I didn't know what to do."

"I still don't know what to do." Eilidh frowned and adjusted her cloak against the mist that drifted into the barn. "But now we know, and we can figure it out, together, when we return from tonight."

"Good," Cormac said softly. "I would like that."

They stood quietly for a while, then Eilidh sighed and faced Cormac.

"Almost time," she said. "We need to get our armor on."

Cormac nodded, gazing into her eyes. She was nearly as tall as he, and when she took a step forward and pressed against him, she had only to raise her mouth slightly to meet his. Her hand slipped behind his neck, and his hands slid behind her and pulled her close. He felt the firm press of her breasts against his chest, and her stomach against his, and her fingertips traced lightly along his jaw as her lips opened against his.

At last, she pulled back and gave his cheek a gentle pat. "I am sorry. I could not help it."

"Understandable," Cormac grinned at her.

She smiled in return, then stepped away and donned her hood against the rain. "Come on then, armor," she said, "or else we'll be fighting as naked as one of your clansmen."

"That's no good," Cormac said sadly as he followed Eilidh into the downpour. "I don't have time for more tattoos today."

Maeglin

"Oh, the Martyr's Blade is well-hidden, never worry," Reverend Dougal chuckled contentedly. "This old hill has nooks and crannies that no one has seen, nor heard of, for centuries and centuries. No one, that is, who is not as well-versed in the histories as I am."

Dougal waved impatiently to his acolyte. The tall boy stepped next to the priest's lectern and held his candle as close to Dougal's book as he dared. "That's better, that's better," the priest mumbled to himself as he peered at the elegant scrawl of ink on the brittle pages before him.

"Not even the Archivist?" Maeglin asked.

"What?" Dougal glanced at the Knight Commander and blinked in surprise. "Maeglin, I am very busy right now. Would you mind if we continued at another time?" The priest returned his attention to his book, and Maeglin caught the flicker of a smile at the corner of the acolyte's mouth as the boy glanced quickly away from him. *Not a boy,* Maeglin corrected himself as he glared at the acolyte's lowered face. He could see the shadow of a vague patch of damp hair on the acolyte's lip. *He only looks like a child.*

"It is important, Dougal." Maeglin forced steel calm into his voice.

"I would never reveal where the Blade is hidden to Whitebrooke," Dougal replied, his mouth pursed in disapproval.

"I did not accuse you," Maeglin ignored the priest's bluster. "Interesting that you thought I had."

"You make your thoughts clear, Maeglin," Dougal grumbled. He pushed himself away from the book and met Maeglin's scrutiny. "You always have. No, I did not tell Whitebrooke where the Blade was hidden."

"But he could know of the place you chose? Someone as well-versed in the histories as he is?"

"Perhaps," Dougal snapped. The priest's gaze slid away from Maeglin's. "Even if he did, he could never guess that we hid the Blade there."

"You know that Whitebrooke knows this place," Maeglin stated. "You are certain of it."

"I never told him the Blade was there," Dougal insisted, his voice strident. For a moment, he glanced at Maeglin with his eyes wide, but he turned away in an instant. "Never!"

Weak, Maeglin thought, the need to grasp the priest by his ornate robes writhing through his hands. *His pride chokes him, and I have no time to loosen his throat.*

"If Whitebrooke finds that Blade, we are all fucked," Maeglin forced the words through his clenched teeth. "Tell me where it is, damn you, so that I can stop him."

"I did not tell him!" Dougal said desperately, his eyebrows arching in fear. The priest rose from his chair in a rush, scraping its feet across the stone floor of the study. "Now, leave me, or I shall call for a formal reprimand from the Council."

Maeglin spun the priest around by the shoulder. Dougal staggered, teetering on one withered leg as his hands flailed uselessly against Maeglin's arms.

"No!" Dougal gasped in terror, but Maeglin sneered at the priest's pathetic cry and slammed his hand into Dougal's chest, sending the old man sprawling onto the floor.

THE MARTYR'S TEARS

"Knight Commander!" Dougal's acolyte shouted in horror and stepped forward, his hands raised to forestall the knight. Maeglin smashed an armored fist into the acolyte's stomach and watched in satisfaction as his arrogant face crumpled into pain and shock. The acolyte sank to the floor in misery, and Maeglin turned to Dougal.

"What…?" Dougal gasped as he slowly clambered to his knees. He raised shaking hands above his head as Maeglin's shadow fell on him.

Maeglin seized Dougal's hand and twisted savagely. The priest shrieked in agony and crumpled to the ground.

"Maeglin, please!" he begged, and the Knight Commander grinned in satisfaction. *His pride is gone, now we will find the truth.*

"What does Whitebrooke know?" Maeglin demanded.

"He knows of the place!" Dougal sobbed. "He does, but I swear I never told him that's where we concealed the Blade!"

"You know this how?" Maeglin applied more pressure against Dougal's hand.

"He told me about it!" Dougal cried out, his voice cracking. "He was the one, he told me."

"You hid the Blade in a place that Whitebrooke told you about?" Maeglin spat.

"Yes!" Dougal wailed. "But I never told him!"

Maeglin released the priest's hand and watched Dougal cradle it against his chest. "You chose a place that Whitebrooke suggested." Maeglin's mouth twisted as he forced the words out. His hands burned and he clenched his fists against the pain.

"How could I know what he was?" Dougal whimpered.

"You know now," Maeglin snarled, "and yet you said nothing."

"Why would I?" Dougal asked, his voice shaking. "He doesn't know I showed it to Ail, I swear, how could he know the Blade is there?"

"When did you last speak to Whitebrooke about this place?"

"I don't remember—" Dougal stopped himself and glanced at Maeglin for a terrified instant.

THE MARTYR'S TEARS

"Damn you," Maeglin cursed. He seized the priest and flung him onto his back. Dougal screamed in fear and flailed at Maeglin's arms, but the Knight Commander ignored the thrashing and pinned the priest under his armored knee. Dougal gasped in pain, and Maeglin thrust his thumb into the priest's mouth. Dougal's teeth ground against the steel bands of Maeglin's gauntlet as the priest tried to twist free, but Maeglin hooked Dougal's jaw and yanked his head still.

"Don't bite, you bastard," Maeglin whispered to the priest, "or you'll lose your teeth."

Dougal froze, his eyes wide as he stared in terror at Maeglin.

"Now then, where's that lying tongue?" Maeglin asked, and he pushed his thumb deeper into Dougal's mouth. The priest gagged and grabbed Maeglin's wrist with his feeble fingers, but his mouth gaped open, revealing wrinkled gums and worn teeth.

"When did you last speak with Whitebrooke about this place?" Maeglin asked again quietly.

"After—" Dougal choked.

"After you hid the Blade there?"

Dougal nodded miserably. The soft bags of skin under his eyes pulled with Maeglin's grasp to reveal swollen red flesh, and tears ran freely into the maze of wrinkles that crossed his sagging cheeks.

"What did you say to him?"

"Thank... thank you," Dougal choked out.

"You thanked him?" Maeglin asked. Dougal nodded, unable to speak, his gaze never leaving Maeglin's. "For telling you of this place?" Dougal nodded again.

Maeglin shook his head, disappointed. "You should have come to me immediately," he told the priest. "There was no need for all of this." Maeglin pressed his thumb into the priest's palate, as if to remind him of which he spoke. Dougal gasped in pain and clutched at Maeglin's wrists, and the Knight Commander struggled to suppress a smile. *Pompous fool. When I have finished with Whitebrooke, there will be another traitor to hang.*

"Now," Maeglin told the priest. "I need to know where the Blade is."

THE MARTYR'S TEARS

***

Water roared through the brick channel, frothing and churning as it passed, and its thunder echoed from the low, arched ceiling of the tunnel. A narrow path ran above the water alongside the channel, and as Maeglin strode along it, his lantern sent swaying shadows dancing across the rough brick walls.

Iron bars crossed the passage, thick and gnarled with rust like the swollen fingers of an ancient man drowning beneath the turbulent waves. The freezing water sprayed around the bars as it passed, coating the walls and ceiling with drops that glistened in the lantern's light. Maeglin turned into a side tunnel as he approached the bars, a small shaft which forced Maeglin to bend low to avoid the ceiling. His boots splashed in the trickle of water that ran down the center of the curved floor, and the tunnel filled with the sound of steel scraping against stone as his armored shoulders brushed against the walls.

The tunnel ended in a square room with unfinished walls that still showed the deep scores of the miner's cuts. The floor was ankle-deep in black water, still and cold as ice. Maeglin stepped into the room and waited for the arrival of the faint footsteps that had followed him from the temple.

"Where are we?" Roland's dry rasp slid above the echoes of the water.

"The sewers," Maeglin smiled grimly. "This one was never finished. The miners found something when they were digging, and they hid it away and dug in a new direction instead."

"Why are you in the sewers, Knight Commander?"

"Because this is where those fools hid the Martyr's Blade. They thought someplace concealed was better than someplace secured, but they did not think to ask how Reverend Dougal came to know about it in the first place." Maeglin knelt in the chill water and cupped handfuls over his head, seeking to soothe the heat that stung his skin. He let the trickles run down his neck into his armor, then opened his eyes and glanced at Sir Roland. "Why are you in the sewers, Templar?"

"The Council asked me to follow you." Roland held his lantern close to the wall and examined the glistening stone.

"Why?"

"They spoke with Reverend Dougal. What is your intention?"

"To find Reverend Whitebrooke." Maeglin rose to his feet. "He wants the Blade and he knows it is here, thanks to Dougal. What else?"

"Perhaps you seek the Blade for yourself?"

"That is ridiculous. Who thinks such a thing?"

"The Council is not inspired by your actions." Roland finished his inspection of the wall and faced Maeglin. His hand rested on the pommel of his sword. A casual gesture, but one that caught Maeglin's eye.

"May they choke on their righteous bullshit," Maeglin snarled. "If Whitebrooke is here, I will capture him. If he is not, I will move the Blade to somewhere safer, where we can guard it. That is all."

"I don't think they want you moving the Blade anywhere," Roland said flatly. "That is why I am here."

"I see," Maeglin said quietly. "You are their lapdog, now? I mistook you for a Templar."

Roland did not reply, his pale eyes never blinking as he returned Maeglin's gaze.

Maeglin snorted with amusement and stepped to the far wall. The surface gleamed with a thousand small cuts like faces on a gemstone, each one flat and smooth. Maeglin traced his fingers along the wall until he found the small crack, invisible amongst the shifting shadows, that revealed the concealed door.

He slipped the blade of his knife into the crack and felt the small latch click open, then placed his shoulder against the stone and pushed. The door rumbled as stone ground against stone, and it slowly slid back, no more than the width of a finger. Then hidden counterweights were released, and the door rose gracefully into a dark recess, revealing a tunnel that dove deeper into the ground.

"Dougal told me that they found it when they first began to tunnel into the rock beneath Bandirma." Maeglin raised the lantern again and stepped into the tunnel. The shaft was circular, its walls as smooth as ice, and the stone glimmered in the light as if a thousand crystals were embedded in its surface. "Dougal says that it was formed eons ago by molten stone that burst through the earth and created the hill, but I don't know how anyone could know that. In any case, the tunnels seem to be endless, always down, so they sealed it up."

The tunnel twisted slowly through the ground until the entrance was lost from view and they neared the chamber that Dougal had claimed would hold the Blade. Maeglin quickened his pace and strode around the final bend in the tunnel and into the chamber beyond.

Curved walls arched to a smooth, domed ceiling, as if a blister had long ago swelled within the stone. The floor formed a natural mound in the center, and dark mouths of tunnels gaped from the walls.

"I take it this was where the Blade was kept?" Roland's voice rumbled from the side of the room, and Maeglin saw that the knight stood over the remains of a shattered chest, long splinters of wood and twisted hinges all that was left of the ancient Device.

"It must be." Maeglin's jaw clenched as he glared at the remains. *Too late...*

A soft brush of sound brought Maeglin's gaze to the far side of the chamber. Dark openings in the wall led into the rock, but nothing stirred in their shadows as Maeglin probed each in turn with his lantern's light.

Maeglin set the lantern down and slipped his shield from its place across his back. The bright metal settled comfortably on Maeglin's arm, a welcome weight.

"You have the left," Maeglin told Sir Roland. He met the Templar's gaze briefly. "There may be—"

The attack came with no more warning than a gentle stir of air. Maeglin saw Roland's eyes go wide as the Templar stared past his shoulder, and he twisted with shield raised. Maeglin caught a glimpse of a mass of squirming shapes gleaming blackly in the lantern's light before his shield was struck with a blow that bent the steel rim and numbed his arm with jagged sparks of pain.

Maeglin staggered away as the dark shape reared above him. Serrated limbs ripped across his shoulder, screeching against his steel armor. Maeglin lashed out with his sword, but the shining blade sighed cleanly through empty air as the dark mass moved with impossible speed. A flicker of motion caught Maeglin's gaze and he swung his shield to meet it. A long, heavy, segmented shape lashed from the half-glimpsed mass of limbs and struck the shield a colossal blow. The metal tore as a long spine thrust through the shield's face, and black liquid sprayed from its tip across Maeglin's breastplate.

Maeglin twisted away as acrid smoke stung his nostrils and burned his throat. Then Sir Roland leapt to the attack, his sword a faint gleam in the lantern's light as it streaked through the air. Its edge ground across the black carapace in a long line, and Roland's reverse thrust slid deeply between two of the overlapping shells. The creature shrieked and was gone in a whirl of shadow before Roland could follow, leaving behind only the slow drip of black ichor from the edge of Roland's blade.

Maeglin regained his balance as he swept the shadows with his gaze. A small trickle of pebbles and the scuttle of limbs across stone sounded in the shadows near one of the tunnels, then again in the rippling stone of the chamber's domed ceiling.

Maeglin stared upward, willing his gaze to pierce the mottled shadows of the chamber roof. *There...* a shape stirred, and Maeglin felt a surge of fire pass through his limbs with a great pulse of his heart.

Gleaming armor and serrated limbs raced across the ceiling faster than the eye could follow. Maeglin caught a glimpse of long, segmented legs covered by cruelly curved barbs that moved with the implacable rush of a spider, as dark as the shadows that clung to the deepest pits beneath the mountains, and a lashing tail longer than the creature's body, thick and plated with chitinous armor, ending in the long spike that had pierced Maeglin's shield.

Maker! Maeglin felt a thrill stir within his chest. *At last, I may test myself against the works of the Crunorix.*

THE MARTYR'S TEARS

As if it had heard Maeglin's challenge, it leapt from the ceiling, and Maeglin twisted to meet it. Long barbs curled around the edge of his shield, and the steel boss rang with a hammer blow that sent shards of pain lancing into Maeglin's shoulder. He staggered back with the impact, and a serrated claw scraped across his chest, ripping at the steel plates.

Maeglin grunted and his sword flashed in a tight spiral, its edge biting deep into the black shell of the creature's limb. Maeglin ducked forward, his shield held high against the blur of death that crashed upon it, and thrust between the limbs, the silver steel of his blade plunging deep and then slicing free in a spray of dark, foul liquid as the creature tore itself away and vanished in a blur of movement.

Maeglin turned warily, his point searching for his opponent. A patter of black rain raced across the floor toward Roland, and suddenly the creature plunged onto the Templar.

Roland hurled himself away from the creature's attack, and its scythes shredded cloth instead of flesh. Roland's sword bit deeply into the demon's unprotected flank, ripping free a chunk of armor with the sound of rotten wood breaking.

Maeglin took a step toward Roland, then swung his shield high as a blur of movement flashed from the shadows. The creature's tail crashed onto Maeglin's raised shield and the steel rim bent around his vambrace. Maeglin was swept from his feet and hurled into the stone wall, his shield arm numb. The creature fell on him before the knight could find his footing, and Maeglin dove desperately to the side as sparks flashed like lightning from the stone above his head.

The creature's breath hissed as it followed, its limbs a blur through the shadows. Maeglin arched his back as a point gouged a scar across his pauldron, and let his momentum take him into a leaping roll away from the demon. He came to his feet smoothly, and his blade slashed across the creature's flank, then twisted and struck upward, jamming home beneath one of the creature's legs. The creature wrenched away, and Maeglin bellowed and followed the thrust, stabbing desperately after the fleeing shape.

THE MARTYR'S TEARS

Maeglin pulled back to thrust again, but the creature moved faster. A massive claw clamped around Maeglin's neck with steel strength, lifting the knight into the air, and smashed his head against the wall. Maeglin felt the room spin around him, and red pain streaked across his vision as his fingers scrabbled against the crushing grip. He caught a glimpse of the long, dripping spike thrusting upward toward his stomach, and Maeglin parried desperately, his sword screeching as his hilt locked against the base of the spine.

The shadow demon suddenly released Maeglin, and the knight staggered back, drawing air through clenched teeth. Roland's sword sliced across one of the creature's legs, knocking it away from Maeglin. Roland lunged forward, his sword seeking the creature's body, but its arms swept in a blur, knocking aside the Templar's sword with unnatural strength.

Black liquid stained the Templar's pale skin in a spray across his neck and cheek, and blood seeped from beneath the thick armor over his arm where a jagged wound gaped through the steel.

The demon began to circle the knights, its limbs tapping on the stone floor. A whisper of air leaked from it as it slipped through the shadows.

"It seems unslowed by its wounds," Roland's voice ground quietly beside Sir Maeglin.

"I will claim the same," Maeglin snarled. "What do we face? Did Sir Killock mention battling such a creature in the catacombs?"

"No," Roland admitted. "Perhaps it is as vulnerable to fire as the other creations of the Crunorix."

Maeglin glanced toward the lantern, glowing warmly on the stones near the entrance to the chamber, but he doubted he could reach it before the creature would reach him.

"If you can hold it off me, I will show it something better than flames," Sir Roland said.

"All right, Templar, impress me." Maeglin banged his sword against the remains of his shield and strode toward the shadow demon.

THE MARTYR'S TEARS

The creature reared, its bladed limbs quivering in readiness. With a rush, it sprang at the knight.

Maeglin leapt to meet it, his blade slicing through the air. The creature's tail curled menacingly above the seething mass of its razor limbs, but Maeglin was prepared for its speed and its strength now. He stepped to the side and his sword flickered twice as the tail struck at him, his blade's razor edge slicing shallow cuts across the creature's steel-hard shell. The impact made his sword quiver in his hand and numbed his wrist, and Maeglin bought himself more room by leaping away.

The demon pursued him, then twisted away with a scream of fury as a Word pulsed through the cavern's stone.

Sir Roland brought his sword to guard. The sword trembled as a shock ran through its steel, and smoke the color of ash lapped along its surface, clinging to the blade's edge before curling into the air around it. A smile flickered at the edge of Roland's lips as the shadow creature hurled itself toward him.

The demon reached him in a blur, its limbs a writhing mass of barbs and blades as it swarmed across the floor and raised to strike at the Templar.

Roland struck first, an arcing blow that landed heavily amongst the demon's limbs. The demon's armor shattered as if it were glass hit by a boulder. Cracks fissured across its surface in a wave, then it exploded in a shower of twisted flesh. Another pulse and the blade ripped free. Drops of foul liquid sprayed in an arc across the floor at Roland's feet and the demon tumbled away, its limbs thrashing wildly against the stone floor until it collided with the far wall, but its claws scraped uselessly on the stone, and it could no longer climb the smooth surface.

Maeglin retrieved his lantern and removed its oil reservoir, then stalked the scrabbling mass of the wounded demon to the corner of the chamber. The demon hissed as the oil splashed over its ruptured skin, then shrieked as Maeglin struck sparks from the floor with his sword and the oil caught with a greedy roar. Maeglin watched in satisfaction until the demon's limbs stopped beating on the floor, then he turned to the Templar.

"Did you learn that in Priest school?" Maeglin grunted to Roland.

The Templar smiled thinly and shook his head. "It was my father's. My inheritance."

Maeglin nodded his head, then abruptly turned on his heel and strode into the tunnel.

They walked in silence as they climbed back through the sewers to the brightly-lit hallways of the temple. Quick commands sent soldiers hurrying into the sewers to search the endless tunnels beyond the hidden chamber, but Maeglin had little hope that they would find anything. *If Whitebrooke knew of those tunnels, then he knows that no other entrance was ever found. Unless he wishes to bury himself, he came back to the surface. He is still here inside the walls, and as long as he is, I have a chance to kill him.*

"What now?" Sir Roland asked. The Templar's black armor was scored from the shadow demon's serrated limbs, and sweat plastered his pale hair against his scalp, but Roland's eyes showed no weariness.

"We search." Maeglin became aware that he still gripped his sword in his hand, and thrust it angrily into its sheath. "We search every room, every tunnel. We question every steward, soldier, acolyte, knight, and priest. Whitebrooke is here, somewhere."

"Do you think you will find him?"

"We might," Maeglin shook his head grimly. "He's a priest, not a trained spy."

"That has not betrayed him, so far," Roland observed, and Maeglin scowled at the Templar.

"What do you suggest, Sir Roland?" Maeglin asked quietly.

"Nothing, save that you were right to anticipate his desire for the Blade. Perhaps speaking with the remaining archivists might reveal some similar goal."

"You do that," Maeglin dismissed the Templar. Sir Roland's gaze lingered on the Knight Commander, his brow furrowed.

"You cast others aside so easily, Maeglin," the Templar rasped softly. "Yet you need our aid. Tonight has shown that clearly."

THE MARTYR'S TEARS

"I need aid, not useless hindsight and ponderous musing," Maeglin snapped.

"If you wish for my aid, I will be in the archives," Roland replied, and he strode away.

Maeglin issued his orders and watched the hallways fill with running soldiers and shouted commands, and it was not long before a messenger arrived, summoning him urgently to the warren of small cells that made up the quarters of the junior clergy.

Two soldiers stood guard outside one of the cells, and three more watched within. Maeglin pushed past them into the room.

A body lay at his feet, dozens of gashes crossing his arms and chest and abdomen, his tunic slick with blood. Maeglin frowned and tilted his head to examine the corpse's face, then stared slowly around the rest of the tiny room.

Books and parchment covered the small cot, the cramped desk, and most of the floor, save for a patch of space around the body which had been splashed with blood. Two young women were on the floor. One lay sprawled, her arms and legs awkward and splayed, and her head rested in the lap of the second girl amidst a halo of bright red hair. A blanket was wrapped incongruously around the supine girl's shoulders.

The seated girl met Maeglin's gaze, and her brow wrinkled in a puzzled frown.

"Can you help her?" Her voice was weak, and Maeglin crouched to hear her. "Aine won't wake up, and I don't know what's wrong with her."

Maeglin examined the other young woman more closely. Blood matted her red hair behind her ear, but he could see no other signs of harm, and her chest was rising and falling under her robe.

The seated girl's robe was splattered with blood, and there was a spray of dried specks across her neck and cheek. A scalpel lay on the floor next to her, its blade stained red.

"Can you tell me what happened?"

"He hit her," the young woman replied.

"Is that how her head was hurt?"

"Yes. Can you help her?"

"I can. These men will take her to a healer, and then you and I can talk."

The young woman nodded, and Maeglin signaled two of the soldiers to take the unconscious girl away. Maeglin waited impatiently, his fingers exploring the mat of dried blood and swollen flesh on the side of his head without thought.

"Why was Sir Cathan here?" Maeglin asked once the soldiers had gone. He examined the dozens of gashes that crossed the knight's corpse.

"He came for me, but then he hit Aine, and he said he would kill her, so I killed him."

"He told you how to do this?" Maeglin asked, and he held up a stained piece of parchment with fuil crunor markings drawn on it in exquisite detail.

"No," she replied, and she reached out for the parchment. "It's my research, I deciphered it."

"Research?" Maeglin asked, and his eyes narrowed. "What is your name?"

"Meara. Reverend Meara."

Maeglin let her have the page. "I know you, Meara. You're an archivist. You're the one Whitebrooke sent to research the ritual in the archives."

"Yes."

"Who sent Sir Cathan here, Meara?"

"Reverend Whitebrooke."

"Do you know where he is now?"

"No. He's too strong, but I tried and I stopped him. Reverend Whitebrooke told Cathan I was one of his priestesses."

Maeglin rose slowly to his feet and stared at the young woman kneeling beneath him in her blood-spattered robes.

"What shall we do with her?" one of the soldiers asked quietly.

"Do?" Maeglin asked, puzzled. "She's a Crunorix priest. Throw her in the dungeons, and make sure she is chained. I will interrogate her, and then she will hang."

THE MARTYR'S TEARS

"Sir?" the soldier asked. "She doesn't seem to be a threat, sir."

"Tell that to him." Maeglin pointed at the corpse of Sir Cathan. "Get on with it."

"Yes, sir," the soldier saluted, and they helped Meara to her feet and guided her out of the room. Maeglin glanced around the room once more, then pulled the gauntlet roughly from his left hand. The skin across his fingers and the back of his hand throbbed in bright red lines, stinging unbearably with a burning heat. Maeglin glared at the swollen flesh in distaste, drew his dagger, and pressed the tip into one of the long marks. The point cut deliciously into the skin, the bright pain a clean, welcome relief from the throbbing torment, and blood ran freely down his wrist. Maeglin guided the blade slowly back and forth, until the pain washed the burning away. Then he jammed his hand back into his gauntlet and returned to the hallway.

He left the last soldier to guard the room and walked slowly toward the main halls, deep in thought. *Always chasing you, Whitebrooke, no matter what I do. I found your disciple, but do you care? You have your Blade, but do you dare use it? It nearly killed you last time, so why do you want it again?*

His steps took him through the Atrium and into the bailey. Night had fallen, and a steady rain was pouring from the black sky. Puddles crept toward the entrance of the Atrium across the broad stones, and stewards rushed to stem the flow with mops. Maeglin leaned against one of the colossal pillars that framed the entrance and watched the lanterns of the Tùr Abhainn transform into wavering streaks of gold behind the sheets of rain. With each gust of wind, drops struck him, pattering against his cropped hair and pinging from his armor. The chill water stung as it washed the blood from his hair, and he blew drops from his lips with relish, savoring the energy the cold brought him.

He strode across the bailey, ignoring the hurrying forms around him with their hoods held hopelessly over their heads, and entered the Tùr Abhainn, passing quickly through hallways packed with troops to the suite of rooms given to the Captain of the Gates. Sir Hollis stood as Maeglin entered.

"Knight Commander," Hollis greeted Maeglin.

"Sir Hollis, send messengers to every captain at every post. I want a report on their status, right now. Every detail, no matter how small. Tell them to send it here."

"Yes, sir. Is there something you are hoping for, sir?"

"He's been one step ahead of us at every turn," Maeglin scowled. "He's left a trail if we can find it, and someone, somewhere, is staring at it right now without knowing it."

Sir Hollis nodded and left to bellow orders into the hallway, while Maeglin moved to Hollis' desk and leaned on it with clenched fists.

I will find you, he promised. *I will find you.*

Rowenna

Shafts of golden morning light blazed through the tall windows of the dining hall as heavy drapes were thrown back. Dust swirled in the beams, a vortex of glowing stars chasing each other in circles and eddies. The light reflected off a polished table that ran the length of the hall, its surface as brilliant as a mirror's, and cast wavering patches of brightness across the somber paintings and dark wood of the wall.

"I am sorry about the dust, my lady," the butler sniffed. "If we had known you were arriving last night, Eithne could have prepared the rooms."

"That is quite all right, Edmund," Rowenna assured him, but there was no way to tell if her words had any effect on the tall, dour man. Despite the early hour, the butler was dressed impeccably in a heavy, dark jacket and polished shoes, and he watched with a disapproving frown the bustle of the parlour maids and the footmen as they set silver platters of food on the long sideboard at the head of the room.

Rowenna moved to one of the windows while she waited for the quiet rush to subside. Below her was one of the narrow parks that wound through the New City of Kuray, its winding paths and groomed trees starting just a few steps from the white pillars and wrought iron posts of the manor's gates. Beyond the trees, Rowenna could see snow-covered hills on the far side of the valley, and the shining white marble of the Baths at the foot of the Silver Keep. The castle itself could not be seen from the dining room, but Rowenna knew that if she should require such a view, the drawing room and its wide terrace would provide it.

"Breakfast, my lady," Edmund announced. Rowenna filled a silver plate with warm bread, an egg, and a pot of precious marmalade and carried it to the table. One of the parlour maids filled a cup with tea, and Rowenna gratefully sipped the scalding liquid.

"Has Father been up to visit?" she asked as she spread thick swathes of the sweet preserves across the bread.

"Not since two summers ago, my lady," Edmund replied. "I fear the winter is a hardship for his lordship, although I expect we will see him this summer."

Rowenna nodded and chewed in silence, her thoughts far away in the arbor of Castle Chluaidh on the Abhainn Albyn where she had last seen her father, still tall, but now stooped as he leaned heavily on his cane, a thick cloak wrapped around his shoulders to shield him from a slight autumn breeze.

"Maker's breath, Edmund, it's a bit cold in here, don't you think?" Gwydion rubbed his hands together and crossed to the food, not waiting for a reply. "Don't tell me there's no marmalade?"

"I believe the pot is on the table already, my lord," Edmund replied.

"So it is," Gwydion agreed, and brought his plate to sit opposite Rowenna. "Is there any left?"

"No," Rowenna replied.

"Shall I send for some more from the pantry, my lord?"

"No, Edmund, she is just being cruel." Gwydion stretched across the broad surface of the table and retrieved the pot. "There is plenty here."

They ate in silence, the house utterly still as the servants disappeared, all except Edmund, who stood quietly next to the sideboard, ready with the pot of tea, should it be needed. The sun slowly slid across the table, sparkling on the plates' silver crests as it passed.

Only one morning, and already I am anxious to leave again. I wonder if I shall ever come to think fondly of this sterile silence.

Gwydion sat back in his chair, patted his mustache with a napkin embroidered with the family crest in gold thread, and watched Rowenna, a knowing smile peeking from behind the cloth. "The house is exactly as I remember it, Edmund. Well done."

Rowenna raised her own napkin to hide her smile, and nodded her approval to Gwydion as Edmund offered a gratified "Thank you, my lord."

"Now, would you please send a note to the castle to let Her Majesty know we have arrived? Thank you, Edmund."

Rowenna rose and strolled onto the terrace that ran the length of the drawing room, and snuggled deep into her shawl as the chill morning air drifted across her shoulders. Gwydion joined her, and leaned nonchalantly on the rail, staring at the tall towers of the Silver Keep, shining brilliantly against the pale blue sky.

"I suppose we will find out if Baron Arledge's bird made it to Kuray," Rowenna mused.

"We're not enemies, Ro," Gwydion replied. "The Queen knows that, even if the message never arrived."

"When did you become an optimist?"

"I am just seeing what it feels like, never fear. I am sure I will have thought of something extremely cynical to say by the time we meet with the Queen."

"The thought of spending the next month buried under a mountain of old books doesn't dampen your spirits?"

"I quite like old books, Ro, and I admit I have wanted a snoop in the Royal Archives for some time. In any case, there are other perquisites for being in Kuray."

"You won't be much good if you are sleeping off a hangover every day."

"You wound me," Gwydion laughed. "Are you saying you do not intend to grace society with your presence? I have never seen you miss a gala or ball."

"Oh no, I asked Eithne to prepare several dresses for me. But I can hold my drink. Not like some."

"Very true," Gwydion laughed again, "and it would be a shame if you weren't able to show Kuray your new dancing skills. Do you think you could convince Countess Odhra to dance a reel?"

"Is that the wager?"

"If you'd like."

"I shall have to think of an appropriate stake."

Gwydion nodded and returned his gaze to the castle, absorbed in his thoughts.

An image flashed into her mind, the two of them, no more than ten and six, standing upon the same terrace listening to their father recite the names of the towers for them, his resonant voice imbuing each name with a rich history that she still felt today. *I wonder why I thought of that?* she wondered, but the answer followed quickly on the heels of the question. *Because I was thinking of Father at breakfast.*

"We could visit Chluaidh on our way home."

Gwydion was silent for a moment, and Rowenna wondered if he had heard her. Then he glanced at her from the corner of his eye, and she saw that his mouth had set into a thin line.

" 'On our way home', you say," he laughed coldly. "How very ironic of you."

"You know what I mean," Rowenna said sharply, then stood quietly while she breathed away her ire. She understood all too well the chill in her brother's voice, but his retort had raised her hackles. "In any case, you heard Edmund. If Father is too frail to travel anymore…"

"Good," Gwydion said softly. "Less chance of meeting him accidentally."

Rowenna nodded quietly and joined Gwydion at the terrace railing. The trees in the garden below shielded white streaks of snow in their shadows, and the breeze was chill as it hushed through the thick needles and drifted onto the terrace. Rowenna readjusted her shawl and laid a gentle hand on Gwydion's shoulder.

"I do understand. I lived in that house, too. But there might not be many more chances, and I thought…"

"You thought what?"

"Just that he is alone there, now."

"I hope he has enough of his wits left to realize that he did that to himself."

"However much he hurt you, he is still our father."

"He's a bastard. And it wasn't just me he hurt."

"I know," Rowenna whispered. "It just makes me sad."

"Ro, you care, and you forgive. Maker knows I count on it. But you should not be sad that son of a bitch is dying alone and unloved. Be sad that he deserves it, because he does deserve it." Gwydion wrapped a comforting arm around her shoulders. "It doesn't matter. He doesn't want me there."

"He's not unloved," Rowenna told Gwydion, and she held his gaze until he glanced away. "How else could he cause so much pain?"

Gwydion sighed and shook his head. "You go if you want. Hold his hand and tell him all is forgiven. It will ease your heart. But I am never returning to Chluaidh. I hope they use it as his pyre."

***

The summons came as noon bells echoed back and forth across the valley, each tower seeking to out-do its neighbors, leaving Rowenna with just enough time to prepare.

She chose a sweeping, dark red gown patterned with golden thread that shimmered as it caught the light, with a wide collar that left her shoulders bare. She pinned her hair with a green enameled leaf and nestled a chain of polished onyx stones in its thick waves. A necklace of gold, with a single onyx pendant, and a wide armband that matched, completed the preparations.

"You do realize we are just having a chat with the Queen?" Gwydion asked, astonished, as Rowenna joined him in the hall.

"It is a trip to court, you ninny. And I see you have brushed yourself up as well, so you are one to talk."

Gwydion beamed, a flashing smile that lit up his face as he bowed low. He had donned a heavy robe of dark green over an embroidered doublet of rich black, and a wide leather belt with a silver buckle. The high collar of the doublet rested snugly around his neck and accented the grey streaks in his dark hair and trim beard.

"One does one's best," he allowed. "And you look mostly all right, yourself."

"Nonsense." Rowenna fixed Gwydion with a stare and a raised eyebrow. "I have it on good authority, quite recently in fact, that I am a 'good 'un', so there."

"Another of your dancing partners from Littleford that I need to interrogate? I hope I can understand this one's accent."

"Just remember, when he says 'feckin' eejit' he's talking about you," Rowenna said archly, and swept past Gwydion and down the steps to their awaiting carriage.

Two matched chestnut mares quickly pulled the carriage through the wide avenues of Morningside, home to the pinnacle of Kuray's elite, and up the switchback of King's Road to the arched gates of the Silver Keep. There they were met by a tall knight in silver armor so polished that Rowenna had to glance away as he turned and his epaulets caught the sun. The knight escorted them through the public rooms of the keep, filled with the hushed murmur of conversation and the soft swish of rich fabrics, and up sweeping stairs to a series of elegant rooms dominated by tall ceilings and dark portraits.

Here they waited briefly until the paneled doors were swept open and the Queen entered, flanked by two knights.

The Queen was stunning in a flowing white dress that complimented her dark skin, a belt of chorded gold thread, and a simple silver chain around her neck that held a silver ring as a pendant. Her hair cascaded across her bare shoulders and down her back like a waterfall of black fire, and a thin silver circlet rested on her brow.

Rowenna curtsied low and saw Gwydion sweep into a bow beside her, but the Queen took Rowenna's hands in hers to draw her up, smiled in welcome, and Rowenna bent slightly to touch her cheek to the Queen's.

"Your Majesty," Gwydion smiled brilliantly when the Queen turned to him. "You are radiant, a sun that warms us all. I give thanks that I have had the good fortune to know you and your sister, both. Speaking of Lady Danielle, she sends her love and begs me to tell you that she is well, and thinking of you."

Rowenna rolled her eyes dramatically at Gwydion over the Queen's shoulder, for that message had been given to her to deliver, not her brother, but he appeared unabashed.

"You have seen her recently?" Queen Gabrielle asked, leading the siblings to elegant settees arranged before a wide fireplace. A tidy fire crackled behind the screen and cast a pleasant heat. Gabrielle gathered her dress and sat gracefully on the end of a settee.

"In Littleford, Your Majesty," Gwydion replied, and he perched elegantly on the edge of a high-backed chair facing her, allowing Rowenna the comfort of the other settee and its white cushions. "She had just completed an arduous journey, unjustly persecuted, I am ashamed to say, by my Temple." Gwydion paused for a heartbeat, letting the silence provide weight to his words, then continued, "Yet she was untouched by her hardships, unrivaled in spirit and form, saving, of course, for yourself, Your Majesty."

The fire popped merrily in the silence as the Queen absent-mindedly pressed the silver ring to her lips as she considered the Templar.

"That did not take long," Gabrielle said. "I had not thought to hear a forthright admission of the Temple's guilt. I am quite unprepared. We do not even have tea, yet."

"There is no point in denying the suffering inflicted upon Lady Danielle, and yourself, Your Majesty, by the Temple," Rowenna said softly. "We can only beg your understanding, and pray that you know that we are your friends. We are all deceived by the same enemy."

Gabrielle played with her ring for another moment, twisting its smooth shape through her fingers, before letting it rest against her chest again. "Danielle sent several birds, but there are only so many words one can fit onto a scrap of parchment, no matter how tiny the script. How is she? I know she tries to shield me from worry."

"She was hurt," Rowenna replied, "but she says the wound will pass, and her spirit is still strong."

Gabrielle nodded slightly, her golden eyes unblinking as she watched Rowenna.

"This is what Baron Arledge tells me as well." The Queen finally glanced away, turning her gaze on the fire. "He does not seek to shield me."

"I'm sorry, Your Majesty," Rowenna said softly.

"No, I am grateful. And her friend, Bronwyn, is she also…"

"Very much so," Gwydion smiled. "Inseparable, the whole time. An arduous example to try to live up to, if you ask me. Insufferable."

Gabrielle smiled gently at the fire, then drew a breath and faced the Templars once more.

"The baron also says that you wish to see the archives and that I should grant you leave, although he could not trust to say why in a letter."

"No, Your Majesty, for we may have discovered an invaluable secret in our fight against the Crunorix, if only we can unearth its origins."

Rowenna told the Queen of what they had found in the cave deep within the Mountain, of the pool filled with the soft glow of shining water, of the golden tree, and of the long shape nestled deep in its roots.

"There is a painted window above the altar in the Bandirma cathedral," Rowenna told the Queen, "that shows a tree in a cave deep underground, but no one knows the story of it, and there is no explanation in the Temple archives. We believe that the Tree is a Device of great power that forged the Martyr's Blade, somehow using this pool of water that washed away the touch of fuil crunor.

"If we can find some hint of the Tree in your archives, some clue as to how it works, or how to use it, perhaps we can forge another Blade."

"Perhaps we can make a dozen!" Gwydion laughed. "As many as possible, until there is a forest of flaming Blades ready to drive the Crunorix back into the Black Grave."

"Why do you think the knowledge is in the archives here?"

"We don't, not really," Rowenna admitted. "However, the Silver Keep was built immediately following the war, and if there were a record of the forging of the Blade, a copy might well have been placed in the archives here for safekeeping."

"Who would wield this forest of Blades?" the Queen asked. "Or do you believe it is as easy as this?" She snapped her long fingers in the air.

"We have no idea," Gwydion said wryly. "Maybe Ro and I could do it. We're not the same class of adept as your sister, but neither is that bastard Whitebrooke, and he was able to empower the Blade, so we know it's possible for others to do so."

"Of course, it put him into a coma for days and days," Rowenna pointed out, "so perhaps not the best example."

"Well, he lacks my charm," Gwydion countered. "Unfortunately, Your Majesty, finding a wielder is hardly the first hurdle. Assuming we find information in your archives we will still need to craft the swords, and that is something far beyond any of our abilities. That is when we will need a Guild master, and who knows what they will ask of us for that service."

"A kingdom," the Queen mused to herself.

"Perhaps," Rowenna agreed cautiously. "We know they created two for Ruric when the need was paramount. If they can be made to see that we are facing a similar crisis, perhaps they will help again."

"Two?" the Queen asked, puzzled.

"Ruric's sword, and of course the Martyr's Blade," Gwydion explained. "We know those two Weapons are the only two that

THE MARTYR'S TEARS

ever hurt the Nameless King, so it seems likely they were forged from the same mold."

The Queen nodded in silence, then sighed and smoothed her dress across her lap. "I hope you are right. I asked Danielle to wield the Blade for me, but I would gladly pay much more than a kingdom to give that burden to someone else."

"Well, I wouldn't tell the Guild that," Gwydion said helpfully.

"No, perhaps not," the Queen agreed with an amused smile, and Rowenna groaned inwardly. *He will be insufferable. More insufferable.*

The Queen stood, and the Templars joined her. "Very well, you may have access to the archives, and Maker guide your search. I only ask that you convey all that you learn to my archivists."

"Of course, Your Majesty," Gwydion agreed. "Thank you, Your Majesty."

Queen Gabrielle rang a small, silver bell that stood on the mantel, which was immediately answered by a servant dressed in the black robes of the Queen's household. "Write out an order allowing Lord Gwydion and Lady Rowenna full access to the archives, and then take it to Lady Sionna," the Queen ordered her, and the servant curtsied and sped from the room. "You wish to start immediately?" the Queen asked the Templars.

"Well, I rather thought that tonight—"

"Yes, Your Majesty, immediately is perfect," Rowenna interrupted her brother. "We must retrieve our tools from our father's house in Morningside, but if it pleases you, we should like to start as soon as we can return."

***

Rowenna scratched her quill across the blank parchment, her elegant, precise script filling line after line as she painstakingly transcribed an extensive account of the First Conclave by a priest with the somewhat unlikely name of Reverend Athair Mór. At last, she reached the end of the passage and returned the quill to its stand, blew carefully on the parchment, and stretched her arms above her head, trying to loosen the ache that lurked deep within her shoulders. One of her candles guttered and smoked as it reached its stub, and Rowenna pinched out the flame before the smoke could sting her eyes. *They are tired enough without that.*

The walls of the study loomed darkly around her. Tall shelves of books rose past the limits of the candles' glow toward a dimly lit ceiling of vaulted stone. The wide table at which Rowenna sat dominated the center of the floor, ponderous tomes and the scattered shapes of scroll cases covering its surface, the product of Lady Sionna's energetic compliance with the Queen's command.

Rowenna realized she had not seen the Royal Archivist in some time, and wondered how deep into the night they were. She did not recall hearing the midnight bells, but she admitted it was likely she had missed them. Rowenna stood, sliding her heavy chair out of the way, and peered into the coal bin next to the fire, hoping for fresh fuel, but she was disappointed. The study had not started warm, and with the fire gone, her fingers felt like ice as she held them against her cheek. Before returning to the Silver Keep she had changed into the long, thick robe and leggings that she used for travelling, but still she shivered as a low moan circled the room and stirred the candles, reminding Rowenna that the Royal Archives perched atop a spire surrounded entirely by ice-cold air and endless winds fresh from the high glaciers that slid slowly down the surrounding mountains.

Rowenna returned to the table but did not sit, gazing at her notes as she kneaded feeling into her hands. She reluctantly faced the pile of books still waiting for her on the table, and sighed.

Reverend Athair's book was a heavy one, with metal end plates and pages an arm's-length tall, and enough pages of cracked parchment that it was a hand's-breadth thick. But Rowenna managed to heft it as high as her shoulders before letting it drop onto the table next to Gwydion's head.

The crash was thunderous, and so exceeded her expectations that she screamed in surprise, then burst out laughing as Gwydion leapt to his feet, stumbled over his chair, and fell, flailing, to the floor.

"Martyr's tears!" Gwydion stared at Rowenna in shock. "I've pissed myself, thank you very much."

"Your face was absolutely marvelous," Rowenna clutched the chair and snorted with laughter. "Oh, dear, I can't help myself, but honestly you deserved it for snoring all through bloody Reverend Athair."

"Reverend who?" Gwydion picked himself off the floor and straightened his robes, trying to restore some dignity. "I could be at Countess Odhra's ball, but instead I'm playing silly wankers with you."

"Well, I hope that will teach you to do your fair share," Rowenna laughed again.

"I read all of those," Gwydion complained, waving his hand at an ungainly pile of scrolls scattered across the floor by his awakening. "Useless, all of them."

"I haven't found anything, either," Rowenna admitted. "But we never thought we would figure it out on the first day."

"I thought we might find something," Gwydion finished tidying his robes and peered across the table at Rowenna's notes. "You've been busy, though. What is all this?"

"Probably nothing," Rowenna sighed. "I don't know. But Reverend Athair is the second person from the Conclave who referred to giving something to the Guardian. He calls it a Word, but Lord Yorath called it the Source. And Yorath said that Lord Adlar was distraught that it was already in the Guardian's possession before he arrived."

"It's not exactly 'and there was a Tree which didst make a Great Blade', is it?"

"No, not at all. And both Yorath and Athair are useless. They don't explain what they are talking about, and it's all mixed in with things that took place years apart. I don't know. It just stood out a bit. Mostly because Lord Adlar was a Guild master. But I did think that perhaps 'Guardian' referred to Lady Danielle's ancestor who took the Blade and hid it. Although Athair says 'Guardian' as if it were a name, not a title, so perhaps not."

"Well, that clears it up."

THE MARTYR'S TEARS

"Sorry. I'm a bit tired. I haven't had a nice nap, like some people."

"Yes, it was extremely restful, what with all that banging and falling on the floor. In any case, let's see if this doesn't make more sense after a good night's sleep, shall we?"

"Ohhh, that does sound good…" Rowenna yawned and gathered her parchments into a leather folio.

They took the candelabra with them to light their way, as the passageways and long, spiral staircase of the archives were deserted and unlit. At last, they reached the base of the tower, and the heavy wooden door that was the entrance to the archives, its panels home to the twelve scenes of the Elvhen Song of Sorrow, dominated by the lamentation of the Elvhen lords as they discovered the passing of the Maker. The sculptor had rather fancifully decided to represent the Elvhes as creatures of the world, wolves with swords in their hands, deer with crowns on their heads, fish in silver armor, even a dragon with what appeared to be a shining sun clutched in its claws. Rowenna had never seen such a personification of the Elvhes before, and she found that she liked it much better than the typical carvings that showed them as a human might appear, dressed in robes and armor that could be found in any court in the land.

The doors closed with a gentle thud, reuniting the two halves of the Song, and Gwydion led the way along a curving passage with tall windows set between pillars on its outer wall, swearing that he remembered the way to the main tower. Silver moonlight bathed the passageway through the panels of thick glass, creating patches of grey and blue amongst the dark shadows.

"Just a bit farther, I believe," Gwydion muttered, and Rowenna sighed to herself. "Or, perhaps we should have turned?"

"It's a tower," Rowenna pointed out. "Just peek out the window. I am sure you will see…" She frowned, peering beyond the window she had pointed to. The small panels of glass were thick with frost, but an orange glow pulsed behind several of them, lending a ruddy tint to the stone that framed the window. "What on earth is that?"

Gwydion stepped to the window and rubbed his fist across the glass. "I'm not sure."

They stared through the patch wiped clear by Gwydion's glove. The glow looked like a coal, waxing and waning in the heat of a fire, but that made no sense, perched as they were so high in the air. Dark shapes appeared silhouetted against the light and Rowenna realized what she was seeing.

"The city is on fire," she gasped as scale and distance snapped into focus. "The northern ridge, it's on fire."

"That must be near the market," Gwydion muttered.

The glow suddenly pulsed, flaring redly against the dark shapes of the buildings that surrounded it, and Rowenna could now clearly see the vast sea of roofs that covered the market, and the long streets of buildings adjacent, lit in orange as flames engulfed them.

"How is it spreading so quickly?" Rowenna asked, her voice strained with concern. "Is no one fighting it? Where are the bells to call for help?"

"I am not sure..." Gwydion's voice trailed off and he leaned against the glass, straining to see across the distance. "My God, Ro, look! The streets are full of people... but they are just running past the fire! What..."

Rowenna could see that Gwydion was right. Figures silhouetted against the flames dashed along the street, dozens of them, too far away to make out more than the surge of motion as they crossed before the flames. But clearly none were stopping to challenge the fire's spread, and merely ran past and onward toward the dark bulk of the sleeping city.

"It's an attack," Rowenna whispered. "The city is under attack."

Wyn

The rain thundered on the wooden tiles of the steeply-pitched roof a hand's-breadth above her head, tireless in its quest to drown the city. The gutters flowed calf-deep already, swirling and frothing as the stone-lined channels attempted to carry the water to the river. Streets and courtyards rapidly became lakes, and the small islands of the cobbles disappeared under the seething surface as sheets of rain cascaded into the rising flood.

Wyn glared balefully from the small, dirt-encrusted window tucked under the peak of the warehouse's roof. Below her, the river docks were deserted, their stone quay already lost beneath the unending torrents. Beyond the piers, Wyn could hear the roar of the Abhainn Fuar, but the river was concealed by darkness and passed unobserved. *Probably for the best,* Wyn decided. *It's likely to burst its banks and drown us all.*

Across the river, Wyn could see the massive river walls of the Temple. At least, she could see the blurry glow of the torches that hid in deep alcoves within the river gates, wavering behind curtains of rain. The bridge itself was invisible, its lanterns unlit.

Wyn blew on the tips of her fingers and then adjusted her new gloves, a prize found in the bottom of a chest of forgotten gear in the back of a tent. They were soft and long and slim, and the black leather was only a bit cracked and worn. Best of all they left her fingers free to work, just like her treasured wool gloves, lost long ago. But, like those older gloves, these left her fingers perpetually frozen, and she tucked her hands beneath her arms in a long-practiced gesture as she watched.

This is daft, she grumbled. *There's no one mad enough to be about on a night like this. Except us, of course.*

She had promised to watch, however, so she did, for what seemed like ages, until eventually a faint voice called out to her from the shadows of the warehouse floor beneath her. Wyn gratefully scurried along a beam, dropped quietly to the top of a pile of stacked crates, and vaulted to the ground.

"Anyone?" Cormac's voice came softly to her from the shadows.

"Not likely. The gates are all closed, tight as a countess's, uh, purse, and there's none but fishes about."

"Sir Killock," Cormac called out quietly. "It's clear."

There was a general stirring in the darkness as soldiers became alert. Arledge had sent twenty of his best with them to the warehouse, as it was far too close to the bridge for his liking. "A quick strike by cavalry and you are all taken," the baron had decided, although how, exactly, the sentries above the gates were supposed to have seen them quietly moving through the deserted streets and into the warehouse, Wyn was not sure. *Still, I'm glad he did, since Dani insisted on coming. Now she has all these lads to look after her.*

Danielle had scoffed at the idea of staying in the encampment and had archly pointed out that traveling with the party to the river docks put her as close to her lance as she could possibly be when she needed to empower it, making it impossible to argue with her.

Wyn slid through the crowd of soldiers in their blackened armor to where Danielle sat wearily on a small crate, gingerly holding her ribs.

THE MARTYR'S TEARS

"What did I say?" Wyn whispered.

"My insides have not plopped out in the slightest," Danielle pointed out. "I may have a small faint in a moment, that is all."

"I suppose it is my turn to carry you across the river docks," Wyn chuckled. "We could've just stayed here all this time, instead of doing all that running about. There's a man who sells fried bread, very tasty. We could've lived off that."

"I enjoyed the journey," Danielle objected. "In any case, I should be quite plump if we had eaten nothing but fried bread, and none of my clothes would fit."

"No, that's a point," Wyn agreed.

Danielle held out the object she had been cradling in her lap. "My lance," she said.

"I'll get Killock, then—"

"No, Wyn, I want you to carry it."

"Me? Martyr's tears, I don't think that's a clever idea." Wyn put her hands firmly behind her back.

"Of course, you."

"I can't use that," Wyn insisted.

"You will not have to, that is the point." Danielle pushed the Device toward her. "Please, Wyn. I must know that, whatever happens, wherever you are, at midnight you will have this to help you."

Wyn extended a hesitant hand, her fingers recoiling from the slim shape on their own accord.

"Wyn, it will not hurt you."

"I know that," Wyn insisted, and she took the Weapon gingerly. "What do I do?"

"Hold it, as if it was a sword or your knife," Danielle explained, "extended toward your enemy. With your hand, Wyn."

"What, now?" Wyn asked.

"Yes, now," Danielle smiled. "It will not do anything until we tell it to." Danielle stood carefully and stepped behind Wyn. "Hold it in your right hand."

"Maker's breath," Wyn muttered, and peered at the thin blade of the lance, nearly invisible in the dim light.

"Do not worry, Wyn."

"I'm not scared," Wyn shook her head. She was not sure how to explain what she was feeling. Nervous, yes. So nervous that her fingers trembled on the cool metal of the Device. But far more powerful than that was the rush of heat to her neck and the delighted quiver across the muscles of her stomach.

Wyn curled her fingers around the sculpted hilt of the Weapon, searching amongst the curved ridges for the proper grip.

"Yes, like that," Danielle nodded. "Except… here, let me show you."

Danielle pressed against Wyn and ran her hand along Wyn's arm until her fingers lay along Wyn's. Wyn let Danielle guide her fingers into place, and they held the Weapon as one.

"There," Danielle whispered into Wyn's ear, and Danielle gripped Wyn's hand fiercely. "Extend toward your target as if you are thrusting with your knife."

"Mmmm, I like thrusting with you," Wyn sighed contentedly and wiggled against Danielle, enjoying the feeling of Danielle's firm softness pressed against her back. "Do we have time for you to show me where to put my fingers a bit more?"

Danielle laughed softly. "Not nearly enough, my wonderful Queen of Innuendo."

"In-my-end what?" Wyn bit her lip to keep giggles from bursting forth. "Sounds interesting. I can't wait."

"Oh, I have already said it is not fair to make me laugh," Danielle groaned. "My poor ribs. Have mercy, I surrender." Danielle collected herself with a deep breath and a shake of her head to sweep her hair behind her shoulders.

"So," Wyn ventured, and held up the lance, eager to hear more about the Weapon that was to be hers to wield. "After I point it…"

"Aim it at whatever you wish to destroy," Danielle smiled, a gleam of white in the dark.

"That's all?"

"Yes. Oh, and do not be surprised by the feeling. It is quite powerful. That is how you will know it is time, and you have just a moment before it fires."

'Aim it at whatever you wish to destroy...' I can't wait, oh, Maker, I can't wait. Just, please don't let me fuck it up.

"Think of my hand with yours," Danielle sat carefully and leaned tenderly against the crates behind her. "That is not far from the truth."

Wyn tucked the Weapon carefully into her pack, glancing behind her as she heard her name called. Cormac was hovering nearby, gesturing for Wyn to join him and the others near the warehouse door.

"I think we're about to go."

Danielle nodded mutely, her eyes bright in the shadows across her face.

"I'll be back in two shakes," Wyn assured her, "and this will all be over."

"Promise me."

"Two shakes, I promise."

"I will be here."

Wyn hurried across the warehouse to join Cormac, refusing to glance behind her as she went. *Poor thing, she sounds ever so sad.*

"I have her lance," Wyn boasted proudly. "She says I should carry it. Better that way, she said."

"Don't lose it," Killock told her.

Wyn frowned. "You must be thinking of someone else. I find things, I don't lose them."

"Then let's go and find Whitebrooke," Killock replied.

Wyn pulled her hood firmly over her head and wrapped her cloak around her shoulders before following Killock out of a small side door and into the downpour. Chill water instantly soaked the thick fabric and began to run down her skin, and she cursed as her boots filled in the first dozen steps. They rounded the end of the warehouse and stopped behind a row of tables near the edge of the building. Water poured from the lip of her hood and roared on the soaked fabric, making it impossible for Wyn to see or hear anything in the deluge. She wiped uselessly at her eyes, but more rain instantly sprayed into her face, and she cursed again in frustration.

THE MARTYR'S TEARS

"Get the door to the tunnel, Wyn," Killock shouted in her ear, and Wyn nodded. She scurried beneath the tables on hands and knees until she could dart behind the low rails that bordered the pier. From there she was hidden from the wavering lights of the river tower, and she squatted down and began to feel under the pooling water for the metal grate she knew was somewhere nearby. Her fingers were numb, but she could easily tell flat stone from iron bar, and she soon found the grate, and then the small latches concealed under its lip. A slight pressure from her fingers in just the right order and the latches released. Wyn pulled with all her might against the weight of the iron and the water on top of it, until with a great rush the pool suddenly emptied through a yawning gap, and the concealed door beneath the grate came free.

Wyn glanced toward the tables and saw the others scampering toward her. She giggled as she watched the forms of the two warriors, massive in their steel armor, as they tried to be sneaky.

Wyn waited until the others drew near, then dropped into the dark hole. There were a few steps, then a short, low tunnel that ended in another iron door. Wyn's boots splashed noisily as she stepped to the door, and she began to blow and rub her fingers to return some feeling to them. But a shadow caught her eye, and she reached cautiously out to the door and gave it a gentle tug. The door swung open with only the resistance of the water pooled around her feet to stop it.

"That was quick," Cormac told her as he crammed into the tunnel behind her.

"Yeah," Wyn agreed with a frown. "It was open."

The street door closed above them with a heavy clang and they were plunged into pitch black. The noise of the rain faded, replaced by a deeper roar, a low vibration that echoed from the darkness ahead. Wyn heard the squeak of metal and the scrape of a lighter, and sparks lit the stone walls as Cormac tried to light the tiny lantern he had carried inside a leather bag to keep it dry. The lighter rasped again, and this time the spark took hold in the wick, and a dim yellow glow filled the tunnel.

"Are we ready?" Eilidh asked.

THE MARTYR'S TEARS

"Wyn says the door was already open," Cormac informed the other two.

"What does that mean?"

"Someone has passed this way recently," Cormac decided.

"Let's get moving," Killock's voice carried from the back of the tunnel.

"You're up," Wyn told Cormac, and the warrior grinned and pushed past her, leading the way with the lantern, his sword already in his hand.

Eilidh came next, and Wyn molded herself against the wall of the tunnel to give the armored knight room to pass. It was still a tight fit, and Wyn let out a squeak as the knight squeezed past.

"You've left your armor behind," the knight observed once she was through the gap.

"I, uh, forgot it," Wyn shrugged. "Good thing too, or else we'd be stuck in here like a cork."

The knight followed Cormac, and then Killock moved beside Wyn.

"Off you go," the Templar told her, and Wyn scuttled after the other two.

The tunnel sloped downward into the earth, and eventually broadened enough that Wyn could walk upright, although the others had to stoop to avoid the ceiling. The heavy roar grew louder, until they had to shout to be heard. The soldiers glanced warily at the walls, but Wyn laughed.

"The river!" she yelled at them. "We're under the river! Don't be so scared!"

"That doesn't make me feel better!" Cormac shouted back, and he began moving more quickly.

They had not gone much farther when the soldier suddenly halted, and Wyn peered past Eilidh and saw the sloping tunnel ahead was filled with water. The lantern reflected across the tunnel's ceiling in shining waves, but Wyn did not notice as she stared, aghast, at the dark, still pool.

"He's flooded it," Killock growled behind her, and all three turned to the Templar. "Maeglin's flooded it."

"It could be the rain," Eilidh offered hopefully. "Perhaps it does not extend much further."

"No," Killock shook his head. "It runs flat all the way to the cisterns. It is designed to be flooded from there." The Templar tore his cloak free from its clasp and began to remove his boots.

"What are you doing?" asked Wyn.

"I will swim to the other end, and release the door. The tunnel should drain into the cisterns."

"Are you joking?" Wyn asked, astonished. "It's all the way across the river! Plus, do you remember the door? It's not exactly got a doorknob, you know."

"I know how to release it." Killock dropped his sword belt to the floor with a clang that echoed sharply from the stone walls.

"And there's the lock. He'll have locked it, sure as anything, so it's not just popping the latches."

"I can open it."

"You'll drown, that's what you'll do. This is mad."

"If you think I am going to let you go instead of me, you're the one that's mad," Killock shook his head. "You're not the only one who can pick a lock."

"Oh?" Wyn crossed her arms and stared icily at the knight with one eyebrow arched. "You'd like a race to see who's fastest, is that it? I'll go. I'll do it, because you know I've got the best chance to get that door open, in the dark, underwater, quick enough not to drown while I'm doing it."

"Wyn…" Killock ran a hand across his face, pushing aside weary frustration. "It's too dangerous."

"Sir Killock," Cormac's voice was hard and formal, and Wyn saw that his mouth was set in a grim line. "If I may, I think Wyn is right. She has a much better chance of opening that door, and waiting to find another way, at some future time, carries its own set of risks. This is the right choice for the mission, sir."

Killock stood quietly for a moment, his gaze locked on the stone floor at his feet. "No, it is too dangerous," he said finally.

"Too dangerous for me, but not for you?" Wyn asked. "Why, because I'm a girl?"

THE MARTYR'S TEARS

"No, Wyn," Killock sighed. "I cannot lose you, it's that simple."

"One, if I start to drown I'll just come back, two, even *if* it goes tits up you could replace me with any of a dozen just like me from any gutter in Kuray. Bit harder to find another Templar, I'd say."

"You are not listening," Killock said softly, and then he nodded his head, resigned. "You are right, you should go."

Wyn waited in shocked silence for more, but Killock only stooped to recover his discarded gear from the floor at his feet and began to put it back on.

"Wyn," Cormac said softly, and she yanked her gaze from the Templar and saw the soldier offering a small coil of rope. "We can tie this around your waist, and if you are in trouble, yank it and we can pull you back right away."

Wyn stared at the end of the rope dubiously. "Really? That sounds like something from a silly read. It can't possibly work."

"It will work," Cormac promised.

"Huh," Wyn said uncertainly. "A first time for everything, I suppose."

Wyn removed Danielle's lance from her pack and handed it to Killock, then removed her cloak and the wide leather belt that held her pack and knives and placed them carefully on the floor away from the lip of the pool. She stood on the heels of her boots until they slipped free, and added her prized gloves to the pile. The stone floor was freezing, and she clutched her hands to her chest as shivers wracked her body.

Cormac passed the rope around her waist and cinched it tight, and Wyn stepped to the edge of the pool. The dark water was perfectly still, and despite the lantern, Wyn could not see the bottom more than an arm's-length ahead.

"Don't forget my stuff," she told Cormac. "I'll need that."

"I won't," he assured her. "Two hard tugs to let us know you are there, all right?"

Wyn stepped gingerly into the water with her toes and gasped as the cold burned her already frozen skin.

"Cold?" Cormac tried uselessly.

"It's lovely," Wyn shivered through chattering teeth.

She glanced behind her and met the gaze of the other three. Cormac's eyes were filled with concern, his brows furrowed, despite his weak smile of reassurance. Eilidh met her gaze and held it, and then bowed her head to Wyn in approval and understanding. Killock's face was expressionless, but his eyes shone in misery, and he would not turn away.

Wyn faced the filled tunnel and took a step, and then another, the water lapping greedily up her calves and gurgling around her thighs.

"What am I doing?" Wyn muttered breathlessly.

The water climbed her stomach and then her chest, and now her toes were slipping on the slick stones of the tunnel floor, and her skin was on fire. "Fuck!" she cursed as her fingers dipped into the water, and she clenched her hands miserably in front of her mouth. She stood on the tips of her toes, the water lapping against her neck and beneath her arms, and nothing ahead of her but a hand's-breadth of ceiling.

She breathed deeply, once, twice, three times, gulping the chill air into her lungs until she felt like she might burst, then she plunged beneath the surface.

The water stung her eyes and there was nothing to see but grey walls and a yawning darkness ahead. She kicked strongly and clawed the water with her hands, shooting forward until the weak light was gone and she could no longer see even the dim shadows of her own arms. The water tugged and dragged on her tunic as it flowed past, and the rope felt determined to pull her backward on every stroke.

Wyn's fingers grazed stone and she realized that she had swum into the floor. Her toes scrabbled for purchase and she lunged forward again, knowing that she had reached the point where the tunnel leveled out far beneath the river.

Half-way? she pleaded, trying to remember. *Half-way.*

Her lungs began to ache with the need to gasp, and Wyn clenched her teeth against the urge. She was not a good swimmer, she knew, and she pulled furiously with her arms and kicked savagely with her legs, trying to make up with strength what she lacked in skill. *Dani would be at the door already,* she thought feverishly, *I bet she swims like her porpoise.*

Hard stone grazed against her shoulders and rapped her knuckles as she pushed blindly into the ceiling, and Wyn thrashed downward.

Her lungs gagged against her sealed throat, and Wyn knew she could not make it. Unless her fingers touched the door on the next stroke, she would not be able to open it in time. But she pulled further into the blackness, bitter fury driving her deeper. *Fuck you, Shitebrooke, I'm coming for you. Fuck you Maeglin, and your fucking tunnel,* she screamed as she swam.

She collided with the ceiling again, striking her head cruelly against the stones, and to her surprise heard a splash. She blinked her eyes desperately but could see nothing. Her ears and skin told a different story. Water lapped against her cheeks as she struggled, and there was the slap of water against stone in an empty space. She pressed her lips against the ceiling and opened them a crack, and only a few drops of water ran into her mouth. She gasped, pulling air into her lungs in deep draughts, as she stood on her toes and clutched at the narrow cracks in the stones to anchor herself in place.

Wyn began to giggle in relief, and kissed the stone loudly between breaths, laughing again at the echoes of the wet smack. "Knew I could make it," she told the tunnel. She wrapped one arm around the rope and pulled hard, twice, then released it after a faint tug returned down the rope in reply.

But already the air was growing stale, the small pocket good for only a few more breaths. *So, decide, you stupid girl. I'm half-way, or a bit more if I'm lucky, but I'm too slow. I'll not have time to open the door, not if it's as far as I've just come, and I'll not likely find another breather on the way.*

The rope is too heavy, she decided, remembering the lethal drag on every stroke. *And it's getting heavier, the more I pull with me.*

Wyn's fingers were slipping the knot before she could think it through, and the rope uncoiled from its loop around her waist and sank before she could change her mind.

THE MARTYR'S TEARS

All right then. Wyn patted the ceiling next to her face, breathed in as much as she could, then pushed savagely away from the small pocket of life, streaking through the pitch black. The water seemed to froth around her arms and legs as she struck out, so dramatic was the difference of the weight of the discarded rope on her tired limbs. As the rush of her launch slowed, however, and the muscles of her shoulders and thighs began to burn once more, she wondered if it would make enough of a difference to see her to the end of the tunnel.

There's no way back, so keep going, she reminded herself, and she thrashed forward with desperate strength. Her lungs began to gag for air, and a shining sound began to shriek in her ears, and still the tunnel would not end. Wyn's shoulders burned with a fire that the chill water could not soothe, and she wondered if somehow the tunnel had branched, and she was swimming farther and farther from the gate.

Then her hands collided with iron.

Wyn ran desperate fingers across the surface, finding strange shapes, unlike anything she was expecting. Panic flared redly in her chest, and she half-turned to flee down the tunnel before she gathered her will and continued her search. A narrow indentation with a small toggle within it, at last, gave her a landmark.

First, the lock, hurry! Wyn slid her fingertips across the door until she found the thick plate that housed the door's handle and the series of small indentations that guarded the release. She triggered them in precise order, then popped the plate free. Behind it was the small gap that would allow a pick into the door's tumblers. Wyn retrieved her pick from her waistband, then guided the hooked tip of the steel needle through the gap with her other hand. Water bubbled against the pick as it leaked into the door's inner workings, but Wyn did not have time to curse. Already her chest was spasming against her sealed throat, and the singing noise had become blinding pain drawing a red mist slowly across the pitch-black water.

The bolts on the door were heavy steel, but Wyn ignored them. The handle would twist them out of the way. Instead, she felt for the delicate pins that locked the bolts in place, and the trembling point of the pick found them, small pressures on the thin shaft that passed one by one as she eased the pick against them, clicking them into place.

Now the latches... the thought was a lazy one, slow and far away, and Wyn wondered at its nonchalance. The sequence for the latches swam murkily through her mind, and she found her fingers tracing the door without knowing if she had actually pressed the metal toggles or not. She kept on, knowing that to start again was death. At last the final pair snapped into place, and she grabbed the handle with both hands and twisted.

The handle was wrenched from her hands as the door flew open and she was hurled through the doorway in a frothing torrent of water that exploded into space beyond. Wyn felt herself crash into the ground and tumble before being swept up in a great wave that launched her high in the air. She caught a ragged breath as the wave turned to foam, then she plunged downward and hit deep water. She was driven down and tugged and rolled, and she thrashed upward until her head burst free. She was still being swept along, but more slowly now, and she gazed around in numb astonishment.

Above her head rose the tall arches of the cisterns. A roaring waterfall arced over the cistern from a doorway on the walkway above, a thundering rush that sprayed in a great torrent over the surface of the cistern's pool. Wyn swam wearily to the edge, dragged herself onto the walkway, and lay there, watching the cascade slowly lose its force as the tunnel drained.

Water overflowed the pool and began to lap around her where she lay, and Wyn dragged her knees under her, crawled to the nearest pillar and rested against it as the water slowly climbed to cover her sprawled legs.

She waited there as the waterfall trickled to a gentle stream. There was no other sound in the vaulted chambers save for the echo of water stirring in the darkness, and no light save for a few scattered lanterns, tiny stars that reflected off the black water and made lonely, wavering sparkles and shifting glows on the stone ceiling.

THE MARTYR'S TEARS

Soon, however, she was rewarded by the sound of splashing footsteps growing rapidly nearer, and light shone from the doorway as a lantern approached, swinging madly from side to side.

Wyn clambered to her feet to meet them, clutching her hands in front of her mouth and shivering miserably, as her clothes clung to her like sheets of ice no matter how many times she pulled the sodden cloth away from her skin. Killock was first out of the doorway, and he found her an instant later. His boots pounded through the ankle-deep water as he raced to her, and he enveloped her in his arms and held her quietly. Wyn rested her head against his chest and felt the thin wool of his tunic warm against her cheek. She could hear his heart racing, pounding fast and strong, and she closed her eyes and breathed in old leather and warm earth and oiled metal.

"You can go, next time," Wyn whispered, and Killock laughed with relief.

"I am so proud of you," Killock told her, and he gently wiped long, dripping tails of her hair from her face.

She shivered again, her toes now aching in the chill water. Killock picked her up as easily as a child and carried her to the end of the walkway, where steps led up to a higher level, above the swollen surface of the pool.

There they halted again, and Cormac presented her with her abandoned clothes and gear, and she pulled them on gratefully, although her cloak and boots were soaked from the rain, and did little to warm her.

"Are you all right to continue?" Killock asked her.

Wyn nodded mutely, not daring to open her mouth for fear of her teeth chattering.

Killock held out Danielle's lance for Wyn, and she took it gratefully, relishing the return of its elegant weight to her care. Then the ranger led the way through the cisterns, passing from walkway to walkway without hesitation, until they found the iron grate that concealed the tunnel to the dungeons. Killock released it and they were soon in the low passage.

"How did you do it?" Cormac whispered to Wyn as they walked. "You were gone forever, and then when we pulled the rope and it was loose…"

"I held my breath," Wyn managed between bouts of shivering. "I didn't like the other choice."

Cormac chuckled and let her be after that, which suited Wyn. She was quite happy not to think about endless black water for a while. *Maybe not ever,* she decided.

They ascended a tight, spiral staircase, its iron rungs coated in dust, so narrow that Wyn feared that Eilidh's armor would stick fast, wedged forever between the central pillar and the stone walls.

When Killock at last released the hidden door at the top of the stairs, Wyn was amazed to see that the door opened into a luxurious cell appointed with a feather bed and walls lined with bookshelves.

Killock crept to the door and pressed his ear against the small iron portal set into the thick wood. He paused for a moment, then signaled silence to the others as he listened. Wyn decided to be quiet near the fireplace but was disappointed to find it full of cold ash instead of glowing coals.

Killock slid soundlessly from the door and rejoined the others.

"Something has happened," he said, his voice a low growl. "There are voices from the far end of the hall, and people coming and going in a great hurry."

"What kind of people?" Cormac asked.

"Many soldiers," Killock replied. "A few stewards, a few priests."

"I'll go and find out, shall I?" Wyn asked.

Killock nodded, but Cormac and Eilidh shared a bewildered glance that made Wyn snort in amusement.

A quick rummage in the tall wardrobe at the side of the room revealed an assortment of priestly raiment, and Wyn selected a simple brown robe, common for both priests and acolytes to wear. She quickly discarded her cloak and wiggled into the robe. It was too long for her, but she folded the sleeves and decided no one was likely to notice the hem dragging a bit. Wyn pulled the collar open and dangled a pendant on a chain around her neck, a golden labyrinth that would sparkle and draw the memory away from her face. She adopted a bright-eyed and innocent expression, and at the last second remembered to pull her bangs over her new tattoo. *Won't pass a careful peek, but it should do nicely for a quick chat in a dark hallway,* she decided.

A leather folio filled with sheets of vellum and a long quill taken from the writing desk completed her disguise.

"How do I look?" she asked, standing tall and serene for inspection.

"Very good," Killock approved. "A junior priestess, or perhaps an acolyte sent to scribe. The quill is a nice touch. Very proper."

"Very proper, *your Reverence*," Wyn intoned formally. "Right, be back in two shakes."

Killock quietly unlocked the door while the hall was empty, fixing Wyn with a stare and a raised eyebrow as the lock clicked open with a gentle rake of his pick.

"Pfft, try it under water," Wyn scoffed, and she slipped into the hall.

Wyn adopted a hurried walk with tiny steps, bustling and confident, and made sure to clutch the folio prominently in front of her.

A quick glance as she passed showed her that the cells were all unoccupied, and she ignored them and pressed on. At the end of the hall, two soldiers stood guard outside the final pair of doors, and she could hear the rumble of subdued voices emanating from beyond them.

As she approached, one of the soldiers stepped forward and raised a hand. "I'm sorry, your Reverence, no one is allowed any farther."

"But, Reverend Nesta said I was to come," Wyn told him and glanced from one to the other of the soldiers in confusion. "She asked for a full report," she explained, offering the soldier the folio and flashing her best apologetic smile. "Right away."

The soldier glanced at his partner, but before the second soldier could weigh in, Wyn tilted the folio and let the sheaf of parchment cascade onto the floor. She made a wild grab for them and succeeded in batting a handful into a wide spray.

"Oh, Martyr!" Wyn exclaimed, and fell to her knees, making a hopeless mess of holding the folio and trying to grab the parchments at the same time.

"Here," the soldier immediately stooped and began to help, and his partner joined in, gathering the pages Wyn had knocked toward him.

"Thank you," Wyn said breathlessly, then made a grab for the same page as the soldier and banged her head on his helmet. She sat down abruptly and stared in shock at the soldier, who instantly knelt, his eyes concerned.

"Are you all right, your Reverence?"

"It was my fault," Wyn assured him, rubbing her head gently and allowing tears to gleam in her eyes. She squinted as much as she dared, trying to force a drop onto her cheek, but it would not come, and she returned to wide-eyed helplessness.

The two soldiers finished gathering the sheets as Wyn silently stacked them back in the folio. "Thank you," she said warmly and made a show of straightening her robes.

"You're welcome, your Reverence, and I'm very sorry about knocking your head."

"No, you have been ever so kind," Wyn assured him and laid delicate fingers on his forearm.

"Thank you, your Reverence, but, um, I'm afraid I have to insist that no one is allowed in, right now. I can ask Sir Breandán if you'd like, but I know what he'll say."

"What should I do?"

"Bring a note from Reverend Nesta, I can show that to Sir Breandán if you'd like."

"Oh, yes, thank you," Wyn smiled happily and hurried down the passage, pausing to wave cheerily at the guards as she rounded the corner.

She passed four soldiers escorting an ashen-faced steward in the opposite direction, waited for the hallway to clear, then ducked back inside the cell concealing the others.

"We're fucked," she said furiously.

"What did you learn?" Killock asked as they crowded near.

"He's escaped," Wyn scowled. "Shitebrooke's bloody escaped."

"How is that possible?" Cormac gasped, but Killock remained silent, his brows furrowed, and the Templar paced quietly away from the other three as he listened.

"They're not sure. Some ponce named Breandán was in there, running his mouth the whole time I stood outside. I think he was supposed to be questioning these guards that were in there, but all he was doing was asking about the same stuff he already knew, over and over."

"What did he ask?"

"Oh, useless shit, like, 'why didn't you come and check when Vaughn didn't return to the barracks after his shift' and so on. Some guard went mad, killed his friend, set Shitebrooke free, then they killed all the other prisoners in some ritual that was behind a door I couldn't see past. Sounds like he did the next few guards who showed up too. They finally caught him, but Shitebrooke was gone by the time that happened, and no one knows where."

"Did you see anything?"

"Of course," Wyn replied. "Threw some papers right in front of the door and trotted over to pick them up. Bit of a bloodbath in there. Looked like four down, three guards and the mad one. He was laid out in the middle, and they'd done him no favors. Completely naked, and cut to pieces. Very gory."

"And all they are saying is that he was crazed? That's it?"

"Well, that's all Breandán was saying, but that's bollocks. Because as much as they had chopped him up, you could still see he was all covered in bright red marks, all over his skin. You remember, Cormac. Just like Brok."

Cormac's eyes widened in shock, and he nodded slowly. Killock whirled to face Wyn, an astonished expression on his face. "What was like Brok?"

"His skin. After Brok killed Reverend Assus he got all these terrible blotches all over his skin like he'd been whipped. Meghan too, poor thing. He said they itched something fierce, but Dani didn't know what to do about them."

"This was right before he attacked you?"

"I suppose so."

"And this guard, just now. You are sure he bore the same marks?"

"Well, in different places, but yes, the same. This one had them on his neck and all down one arm and side. Brok had them all over his face and arms and neck."

"Blood of a priest," Killock whispered. "Damn."

"What is it?"

"Damn it,Ránnach even told me…" Killock shook his head angrily. "The blood of a Crunorix priest can infect people, drive them to do… what you have seen.Ránnach said that they sacrifice priests to make armies of fanatics."

"So, what, Shitebrooke threw some blood at the guards?" Wyn said skeptically.

"No, but if he was injured when they arrested him, or if he struggled with the guards, they would have gotten it all over themselves."

"Now what?" Sir Eilidh asked, her arms crossed firmly and her face grim. "If Whitebrooke is gone, and the whole Temple is already searching for him, there is little chance we will catch him."

"No," Killock agreed. "No, we don't search for him. We go to the one place we know he doesn't want us. The stone chamber, just as we planned. With any luck, he's hiding there now, but even if he isn't, we know it's concealing something he doesn't want us to see, and I am more convinced now than ever that we need to expose it."

"We stick to the plan?" Eilidh asked.

"We stick to the plan," Killock agreed. "You two return to the cistern tunnel and make sure our escape route is still open for us. Wyn and I will go to the chamber and open it."

"The Temple will be in an uproar, searching for Whitebrooke," Cormac pointed out.

"It will. Be careful."

Cormac nodded, the two soldiers squeezed into the concealed stairway, and Killock fastened the door in place behind them.

THE MARTYR'S TEARS

"You have been quiet," Killock said to Wyn as he returned to the center of the room.

"I've been praying," Wyn told him.

"Praying?" Astonishment warred with bewilderment across Killock's face.

"Yes." Wyn's brow furrowed in concentration. "I'm praying Shitebrooke is hiding in that chamber so that I can kill him."

Killock laughed. "Do not get your hopes up. That chamber has been guarded at all hours since the attack on Benno. I'm not sure how Whitebrooke could have gotten in there."

"That's why I'm praying." Wyn shot an exasperated look at Killock. "For a miracle."

"Fair enough," Killock conceded. "I think I shall join you in taking up ecclesiastic garb."

"I did what now?" Wyn asked, puzzled.

Killock opened the wardrobe and pulled out a formal robe, heavy with embroidery. "Here we are."

The Templar stripped away the leather guard he wore on his arm and then donned the robe, settling it comfortably on his shoulders. "What do you think?"

"You look like someone who's just stolen a priest's robes."

"With my young acolyte beside me, no one will think twice," Killock insisted. "In any case, I actually deserve to wear these, unlike you. Although it has been an extremely long time."

"What? Oh, Maker, of course, you're a Templar. Did they make you wear robes? When you were anointed? You must have felt daft."

"A bit," Killock admitted. "There was chanting."

"Awww, I wish I could have seen it. It must have been precious."

"It was hot," Killock frowned. "Shall we go? I believe we have an appointment."

Wyn's hand flew to the pack concealed under her robes. "Let's."

They were forced to wait until the passageway was clear, then slipped out and into the wide halls of the Temple unobserved. Killock strode ahead, his robes billowing around him dramatically, and Wyn clutched the folio to her chest and scurried after him, her feet pattering in rapid accompaniment to the heavy tread of Killock's boots.

The Temple was alive, as Cormac had predicted, but Wyn and Killock were either waved past or ignored by the countless patrols and sentries, and the pair soon reached the archives.

A few priests and acolytes still worked in the reading room, their lanterns making small pools of warm light in the vast darkness of the vaulted space. Only the small scratches of pens on parchment and the dry rustle of turning pages disturbed the silence.

Wyn followed Killock down the wide steps that led to the lower room and they padded between the long tables. A single acolyte blinked owlishly at Wyn as she passed, but her light-dazed eyes saw only a vague shadow and quickly returned to her work.

The Templar paused at the heavy wooden door that led to the archivists' study, but he heard no sound from beyond. The door was not locked, and Killock slipped through and closed it behind Wyn with only the rustle of his robes to betray him.

They moved with more care now, passing silently down the hallway and into the stacks, the labyrinth of small rooms and twisted passageways filled with the treasures of the archives. The musty scent of old leather and polished wood seeped from every corner, and Wyn's gaze was caught by an endless procession of intriguing boxes and chests, just begging to be explored.

There was no time, however, for any such delights.

Killock knew his path through the maze and did not hesitate at any turn, door or side passage. Soon they stood before the massive iron door that guarded the way into the vaults that housed the most precious knowledge, the most valued artifacts. Here the Templar paused, as the iron door was always locked, and was sealed with a Word that only the senior archivists knew.

But Killock had wanted to know what lay beyond the door from the moment he first saw it, decades ago, and what Killock desired to discover was soon revealed. Too many priests and priestesses knew the Word for it to be kept secret, and less than a month from the time he had first seen the iron door, Killock had breached it.

Killock quickly formed the Word, its cunning patterns sliding easily into place. Killock whispered and let the Word pass into the door's lock. Deep within the ancient iron, wards clicked open and the seal released.

The physical lock, a heavy iron bar with delicate pins, yielded to Wyn's pick within a few heartbeats.

Killock led them through the iron door, then down a dark stairway past imposing doors on every landing.

"What's behind them?" Wyn whispered, pointing to one of the ornate wooden doors, its panels covered in engravings of a priestess confronting a snake-headed man wielding a forked whip.

"Secrets," Killock replied, and continued down.

At last, Sir Killock halted on one landing, removed his robes, and concealed them in the corner of the small room.

"I'll not get any further pretending to be a priest," he explained. "But I may as a Templar."

One last flight of stairs and Wyn understood. The next landing was brightly lit, with a squad of soldiers guarding the approach to a single doorway set into the curved wall of the landing. The knight commanding the soldiers stepped to meet Killock and Wyn, then suddenly stiffened to attention as he saw the Templar's face.

"Sir Killock," the knight greeted them.

"Sir Niall," Killock replied without breaking stride, and Wyn hurried in his wake through the open door.

Beyond was a featureless room, the walls seemingly carved from a single block of stone, with only a massive door in the far wall to interrupt them. Killock closed the door behind them, a slab of stone identical to the one blocking their path, and it thudded home with a boom that shook the floor. Wyn stepped to the far door, ran her fingers across the faint line that was the only sign the door was not simply a part of the wall, and investigated the small hole in the center of the door.

"Is it just needing a key?"

The Martyr's Tears

"Yes, but the lock requires its Word as well as the proper key. And we have neither."

"Can I have a go, anyway?"

"I thought you knew better than to play with Wards?"

Wyn snatched her hands away from the door. "Shit. Speak up a bit quicker next time, if you don't mind."

Killock simply smiled and sat with his back against the wall to wait. Wyn ignored him and peered intently at the keyhole from a safe distance, chewing on her lip as she did. Her fingers tucked her hair behind her ear without her noticing, then she faced the Templar with her arms crossed firmly over her chest.

"Won't it just kill me as soon as we use Dani's lance on it?"

"Wards typically protect their contents. I've never heard of a Ward that behaved like the one you described Whitebrooke as having, that attacks those who try to break it."

"So, this one won't do that?"

"No. Probably not."

"Oh, wonderful. And what if Whitebrooke is in there? Do I hit him with the second shot?"

"It depends."

"On what?"

"How much you believe in Danielle."

"Why is that?"

"It will be her Word that releases the power of the lance, and Whitebrooke's Word that releases the power of his Ward. A master can easily overwhelm a novice, even if the novice has a far superior Device. They are dependent on each other, the adept and the Device, so you must ask yourself, do you think Danielle, wielding her lance, can overcome Whitebrooke, wielding his Ward?"

"Yeah, no problem."

"In that case, you should hit him with the second shot."

"Perfect. Of course, you know that you're asking a fish about which knife is best. I've no idea, but, I know Dani is better than old Shitebrooke. She used the Martyr's Blade, and you said when he did it he was knocked out for days."

"True. So..."

"So, I shoot him."

"Good. I would as well."

"When?"

"When what?"

"When do I get to shoot him? How much longer do we have to wait until midnight?"

"Not long."

Wyn took the lance from her pack, and held it awkwardly, unsure of whether to keep it poised and ready or to try and relax. In the end, she tried to do both, sitting next to Killock against the wall while keeping the lance pointed at the door. But she soon grew bored with her pose and began experimenting with small thrusting motions of the lance.

"Oh!" Wyn's eyes suddenly widened in surprise as the lance stirred in her hand. It pulsed as if alive and the patterns along its shaft began to glow with a rich, golden light. Wyn leapt to her feet as if stung by a wasp. "She's doing it!"

"Point it at the door, Wyn," Killock said urgently as he scrambled to his feet.

"I am!" Wyn extended her arm fully and turned her face as far from the lance as she could. But she could not help peeking back, excitement warring with fear. The Weapon thrummed again, fainter this time, and the bright markings dimmed.

Come on Ladykiss, or whatever your name is. Wyn adjusted her hold on the Weapon's hilt, her grip suddenly slick with sweat. "It's not working!" she called out.

"Danielle is too far from us. She needs help."

"Here!" Wyn thrust the Weapon toward Killock.

"No, Wyn, you have to help her."

"Me?" Wyn gasped. "I don't know how to do this!" As if in response, the lance stirred in her hand, but with little strength.

"Yes, Wyn, you," Killock assured her. "Do not think about the Weapon. Danielle is reaching out for you. Help her. Find her."

What does that mean? Wyn thought desperately. *Find Danielle?* Wyn swallowed panic. *What did Dani say? 'Think of my hand with yours'...*

Wyn closed her eyes and pushed away the stone walls of the chamber around her, seeking a darkened corner of a warehouse and the warm grip of Danielle's hand. When the touch came, Wyn nearly jumped in surprise, so real was the sensation of Danielle's fingers resting on her own. *Dani, I'm here!* Wyn called, but she did not need to. Danielle stood next to her, Wyn knew it with a certainty that astonished her. Wyn could feel Danielle's arm alongside her own, Danielle's breath on her neck.

The lance quivered in their hands.

Dani, Wyn breathed. Wyn could feel Danielle's hands holding hers as she gently wrapped bandages around Wyn's fingers, Danielle's hands on Wyn's waist as she guided Danielle across the dance floor, Danielle's arms tight around her shoulders as she held Wyn safe as she wept.

The lance shook again, and golden markings flared anew along its blade.

Wyn could no longer tell where she ended and Danielle began. They spiraled around each other, entwined so closely that Wyn could feel Danielle inside of her, in her heart, in her mind, in her thoughts. A shining image filled the darkness behind Wyn's eyelids, a constellation of stars and silver light more beautiful than she could have imagined.

Danielle breathed out the Word with Wyn's lips, and the bindings within the lance released. Wyn's eyes opened wide and a wild grin spread unchecked across her lips.

"Oooo, here we go!" The fine hairs on Wyn's arm stood on their ends as a vibration throbbed deep within the lance.

Wyn shrieked with glee as the lance erupted and a beam of brilliant radiance poured from it, bathing the chamber with its golden blaze. The stone door boiled under its touch, and molten rock splattered across the floor. Wyn moved the lance slowly, carving a trail of destruction across the door until the light began to wane. A massive section of rock sheared free and crashed to the floor with an impact that shook the room and opened a wide gap into the chamber beyond the door.

"Maker's breath, Dani." Wyn took a deep breath and blew out between pursed lips.

Freezing air and the scent of death from an ancient tomb rushed through the rent in the door. Wyn felt the shadows stir beyond the smoking hole, as if recoiling from the glare, and she heard a long rasp of something sliding across stone.

"Ummm," Wyn started, and she stepped away from the hole. "She said she would do it twice, yeah?"

"Yes," answered Killock, but he had drawn his sword.

"All right…" Wyn raised the lance and pointed it at the gaping hole. "Come on, Dani, give it a tickle," she whispered, but it stayed inert in her hand.

Now figures were clearly moving in the chamber on the other side of the hole she had carved. White skin slid past the opening, and black eyes stared at her from the shadows. Black talons wrapped around the smoking edge of the hole and scraped slowly against the stone. *Of course Shitebrooke has a horrible wight to guard his hole… why would I think otherwise?*

"Anything?" Killock asked over his shoulder.

Wyn shook the lance helplessly, but it made no difference. "I think I broke it!" she cursed.

The wight slid into the chamber and Killock met it instantly with rune-carved steel, slicing the creature across its face and chest. The wight screamed in rage as the blade bit deep, cutting through skin and bone as hard as stone as if it were no more than normal flesh.

The wight hurled itself upon the knight, but Killock spun past its claws and landed a whirling backhand that scoured across the wight's skull and trailed foul ichor in a long arc through the air.

More figures followed the wight into the room, withered husks whose gaping mouths and white eyes searched the room for their prey.

The Templar leapt to attack the wight, hurrying to finish it, but the wight had gauged this new threat of steel that could pierce its skin. The wight met Killock with its inhuman strength, and its blade knocked Killock's savagely aside. He staggered, regained his stance, and countered as the wight reached for him, stabbing his sword into its ribs at full extension. But he was forced to dance backward to avoid the deadly arc of the wight's counter.

"Damn it," Wyn muttered to herself, and she slid her knife free and started toward the fray. As she took her first step she felt a tremor from the lance, and she stopped dead in her tracks, staring hopefully at the long, thin blade.

"I think it's working," Wyn called out.

"Hurry," Killock urged. He lunged between two husks, tore a long gash across the chest of one and impaled the second as he dodged away from the pursuing wight. But the wight leapt after him, and Killock desperately blocked its pale blade as it flashed toward him. He took the parry two-handed, but the strength of the blow lifted him into the air and hurled him into the wall with a shock that drove the breath from him in a grunt.

The lance quivered slightly in Wyn's hand, then pulsed strongly, and once again a golden glow climbed along its shaft, growing brighter with every heartbeat.

"Here it comes!" she shouted to Killock. The wight turned to her at the sound and hissed through bared fangs. Wyn carefully aimed the lance at its chest as it bounded toward her, its blade sweeping through the air as it closed with terrifying speed.

"Bye-bye," Wyn crooned as she felt the pulses in the lance build to a climax. Blazing sunlight speared from the tip and sliced through the wight. The creature's skin split open as the beam passed. Its flesh boiled and black smoke poured from the wound. The wight shrieked as it was consumed in fire, and Wyn laughed in delight. It howled and tried to escape but Wyn adjusted her aim quickly as the creature moved, and it was immolated in the beam's golden light.

"Quick, into the chamber!" Killock shouted, and Wyn raced to the gaping hole, holding the lance pointed directly into the lurking shadows beyond. She hopped through the gap and stared around the chamber in revulsion. The remains of a Crunorix ritual lay spread across the floor, the bloody writing brown and crusted. Husks lurched toward her, but a sweep of the lance destroyed them utterly, their parchment skin erupting into flame at the slightest brush of its brilliant touch.

Against the back wall of the chamber stood a stone altar, and upon it was a hideous iron-bound book. Wyn's stomach twisted as she glanced at it, its wrongness an ache that made her stumble and lose her balance. The lance's beam wavered across the ceiling, leaving a glowing trail of melted stone in its wake.

Wyn clenched her teeth in a snarl and lowered the beam onto the book. Fire spattered from it and the air around it hissed and boiled. Great clouds of smoke erupted from the point of impact, and a scream of rending metal filled the room. Wyn ignored the noise and heat and kept the lance steady as its golden light burned away the smoke and shadow that enveloped the book until it touched the ancient parchment. Flames raced across its surface, searing and greedy, and an inferno twisted and rose high above the book.

Finally, the lance drained and its blaze flickered and expired, but the book continued to burn. Its pages curled into ash, and its bindings melted.

Killock stood beside her, although she had not noticed his arrival. He watched the book burn for a moment, a satisfied smile lurking under his grey whiskers.

"Was that his book?" Killock asked.

"His Soggywhatsitsname? I think so," Wyn laughed quietly.

"I imagine that will not make him happy."

"I imagine not," Wyn agreed. "But you know what? Fuck him." Wyn sighed happily and peered around the room. Thick smoke filled it, but the book was blazing brightly enough that she could see the far end of the chamber. A small crease appeared between her eyebrows. "No Shitebrooke though."

"No," agreed Killock.

"So, what do we do?"

"We go."

"That's it? We just give up?"

"Unless we want to be here when Maeglin comes to investigate, we must." Killock lost his smile and his face settled once more into its stern lines. "It's time to leave."

"I suppose." Wyn sadly tucked the lance away in her pack. "It's a shame we can't go and lurk a bit in his bedchamber, in case he comes back. Or maybe in his privy, that would be a laugh to see his face when he comes for a piss."

"Don't worry, you will have your chance," Killock assured her.

"Promise?" Wyn asked.

"Of course," Killock replied, and strode for the door.

"That was not a promise," Wyn complained, and chased after him.

THE MARTYR'S TEARS

Gabrielle

Frozen air moaned and curled around the highest towers of the Silver Keep, the white stone of their peaked roofs gleaming in the silver light of the moon as if the tall castle was made of ice. Within the Royal Apartments, the candles had long been snuffed, the lanterns quenched. The tall paintings of brooding lords gazed into thick shadows filled with dark shapes that had been elegant furniture and gleaming silver when light had filled the hallways.

A faint noise disturbed the ancient wood and stone. The well-oiled click of metal turning within the latch of the wide doors of the Queen's bedchamber whispered cautiously into the hall, then the gentle brush of heavy wood eased across carpet as one of the doors swung inward.

Candlelight gleamed against the polished wood of the door. Long, graceful fingers quickly shielded the flame, and a tall, slender figure slipped into the hallway.

"Your Majesty," a deep voice greeted her.

"Shush," Gabrielle admonished Sir Liam. The knight stood in the shadows beside her bedchamber door, his steel armor reflecting hundreds of small yellow sparks from its polished surface. "If you wake Bryn or Aithne, I shall never hear the end of it."

"No, Your Majesty," Sir Liam agreed, his voice now a soft growl. The young knight smiled at the gentle rebuke, his teeth flashing white in the shadows.

Gabrielle led the way down the passage, her slippers padding softly on the thick carpets that covered the ancient wood of the hall. Her private study was only a few steps away, and she eased the door open with as much care as she had used on her bedchamber door.

The study smelled of cold ash and polished wood. Its arched ceiling disappeared beyond the reach of the candle's small flame, and a distant moan of wind escaped the wide fireplace as Gabrielle entered.

"Oh, my Lord, it is so cold." Gabrielle shivered and gathered her soft woolen robe more tightly around her shoulders, suddenly wishing she had taken the risk of dressing instead of sneaking out in her nightclothes. "I am… frigid?" she tried.

"No, Your Majesty. The air may be frigid, but you are not," Sir Liam corrected. "Your Majesty may be frozen, or chilled, or bitterly cold, or we sometimes say we are bitten by the frost, if we wish to exaggerate."

"I am all of those at once," Gabrielle decided. "What is frigid, then? Is it not like ice?"

"For the air, it means cold, as Your Majesty said." A smile crept onto the corner of Sir Liam's mouth. "But for a lady, it is taken to mean passionless, as if her heart were made of ice."

"Ah! She is unloving?"

"Yes, Your Majesty."

"This is not me," Gabrielle agreed. "So many words for cold," she shook her head in astonishment. "But my heart will soon be ice, I think, if we do not have a new fire."

"Yes, Your Majesty." Sir Liam fetched a steward while Gabrielle lit more candles, and the fireplace was soon snapping with fresh flames, filling the small room with dancing light and heat.

Gabrielle settled at her desk, a small table with gently curving legs made of golden wood that Gabrielle had commissioned from a carpenter in the Old City. It was far more comfortable than the imposing slab of ancient wood that lurked in the Queen's official study, where she sat to sign decrees, even though it had not been crafted from a piece of the old Kuray Castle's gates as her official monstrosity had.

Gabrielle shifted through the messages of the day. All had been read, and responded to, but they clung to her thoughts like tar and would not let her rest. She set aside all that dealt with the minutia of the kingdom, banishing them to the polished wooden box that her secretary would collect in the morning, and was left with two small stacks. One contained a dozen sheets from General Boone, each with a few precise lines of words. The other stack contained as many sheets, but each was covered on both sides in a spidery hand that wandered to fill the available space.

Gabrielle sighed and pulled a fresh sheet of smooth vellum from a stack, dipped a quill, and began her second attempt at copying the latest piece of Karsha's message, straining to translate his hurried scratching into actual letters and words. There was no indication of which piece might come first or last in sequence, and they had been arriving one pigeon at a time over the last three days. So far, Gabrielle had pages filled with a story about a troll and a very dim-witted sheep, more pages on a spirit, or a spider, or a spider spirit, she was not sure, who was searching Bandirma for the Martyr's Blade, and several more, improbably, concerning a dancer in the Old City whom Karsha was adamant the Queen should find and speak to.

And only a brief mention that Danielle and Arledge have left Littleford for Bandirma. That is all... Gabrielle had Baron Arledge's official report, but she wished that Karsha had added his thoughts. *Perhaps in the next sheet.*

"Your Majesty, do you require anything else?"

Gabrielle glanced up at Sir Liam and smiled. "No, Sir Liam, thank you."

"Yes, Your Majesty."

Sir Liam escorted the steward out of the study, and Gabrielle's gaze lingered on the tall knight until the door closed behind him. Then she drew a deep, satisfied breath and returned to her transcription.

Her fingers were aching by the time she finished the page, and she frowned at her work, as illegible as the original with crossed out words and scribbles between lines as she tried out new guesses as to what Karsha had written. *At least I now know what happened to the troll.* She sighed and set the letter aside.

A map drew her attention next. It was bound in soft leather ties, and bore a note from Lady Sionna that gave a brief history of each location described in Boone's reports. Gabrielle spread the map open and arranged the General's letters near the places they described, forming a trail that marched from inked fields and villages into areas filled with images of twisted trees and craggy peaks. *There is even a troll,* Gabrielle thought, wondering at the link between the two letters.

She placed the last of the General's letters and stood to better peer over the map. The spread of fearsome mountains and lonely forests suddenly made her feel very alone. *They are so far away from me.*

Gabrielle covered a yawn with her fingers and glanced forlornly at the stack of books awaiting her attention. Another gift from Lady Sionna, they told the story of the Conclave held after the defeat of the Nameless King. Speaking with Lady Rowenna and Lord Gwydion that afternoon had stirred the Queen's thoughts toward ancient history, and Gabrielle had asked the Archivist to bring her what books she felt would be the most informative. But the sight of the tomes, which had filled her with an eager excitement when they had arrived earlier that evening, now produced a knot of worry in her throat.

Gabrielle carefully opened the top book in the stack and gazed with dismay at the tiny, cramped writing that filled every page.

The midnight bells sounded in the distance, echoed by the silver chime of a timepiece on the mantle, and Gabrielle's gaze wandered to a small book almost concealed under a carefully placed stack of parchment. The book was a leather portfolio wrapped around a loosely-bound sheaf of parchment, tied with long, red ribbons whose ends tucked between the pages. The timepiece finished its song as Gabrielle decided it was a sign that allowed her to abandon the Conclave for the comforts of the small book.

She carried it to the settee, kicked off her slippers, and curled up on the end closest to the fire. The fire popped cheerfully, the pages crinkled as she turned them, and she discarded her robe as the room warmed. Her long fingers played absently with the ring on its silver chain around her neck as she was transported to a faraway forest, where a brave young woman felt the first confusion of her heart's desire for the mysterious woodsman who had saved her.

Gabrielle was deep into a very descriptive passage that had her frequently checking to make sure the door was closed when her reverie was disturbed by a distant bell. It rang discordantly, without the laborious tolling of the time bells, nor the joyful clangor of the announcement bells. But it was persistent, and Gabrielle paused with her finger on the page as she tilted her head to listen.

The door to the study crashed open, startling Gabrielle so that she gasped in shock. Sir Liam strode into the room, his handsome face grim, followed by five soldiers wearing tabbards of snowy white.

"Your Majesty, there is an alarm," Sir Liam told her.

Gabrielle blinked at the knight in surprise. More soldiers hurried past the open door, filling the room with the clash of metal and the thud of their boots on the thick carpets.

"An alarm?" she asked. "What has happened?"

"I do not know, Your Majesty," the knight replied. He closed the door and twisted the key in the lock. "We will stay here until we know."

"Stay here?" Gabrielle asked. "Should we not go to help?"

"No, Your Majesty, not until we know what is happening."

"But—" Gabrielle started, before a pounding knock on the door interrupted her. Liam spoke briefly through the door and Gabrielle heard Sir Ceridwen's answering rumble. Then Liam unlocked the door and turned to Gabrielle.

"Your Majesty, the Silver Keep is under attack. There is fighting around the main gate. We must go to the citadel."

"Sir Liam, I do not understand—"

"At once, Your Majesty," the knight insisted. He held out his hand, beckoning to her.

Gabrielle closed her mouth with a snap, her mind suddenly clear. She strode across the room and snatched up the long sword that rested on its stand behind her desk. Its silver pommel bore the royal arms of Albyn, its cross-piecce a leaping dolphin, and its grip was fitted perfectly to her hand.

The knight held her gaze for a moment, and smiled encouragement to her. Then he turned to the door. "Sir Ceridwen, we are ready."

"Very good, Sir Liam," Ceridwen answered. "Time to go."

Sir Liam led Gabrielle into the hallway, the five soldiers crowding close behind. More soldiers awaited them outside the door, and they closed in ahead of her, so that she was closely surrounded as they hurried down the hallway.

"Sir Liam, Bryn and Aithne…" Gabrielle asked the knight.

"We have them, Your Majesty," the knight replied quickly. "They will follow with the next group."

Gabrielle twisted to see and caught a momentary glimpse of more soldiers filling the hallway behind. There was a flash of red hair that must have been Aithne, but Gabrielle was rushed onward before she knew for certain. She saw more soldiers ahead, calling out at each door, and Sir Ceridwen's grave countenance as he commanded each turn, each rush forward, each sudden wait.

They reached the wide stairs that led to the formal chambers of the Royal Tower where they were joined by another squad of soldiers. Sir Cerdiwen conversed with the newcomers' leader for a moment before striding to join Sir Liam and the Queen.

"There is fighting in the ballroom and around the throne room," the knight reported in a flat voice so full of menace that Gabrielle almost stepped away before she could reassure herself that the knight's rage was directed at those that dared to threaten her.

"How did they get in the gates?" Sir Liam asked.

"I don't know. It doesn't matter," Cerdiwen growled. "They're inside, and they're pushing forward. We need to move quickly if we are to make the citadel before we are cut off."

"And if we already are?" Sir Liam asked.

"Then we will make for the Small Gate," Sir Ceridwen decided. "If we can rally troops there we can hold an entrance into the Silver Keep. If not, it will allow us to flee."

"Let us not speak of fleeing," Gabrielle frowned.

"No, Your Majesty."

"Who are they?" Gabrielle asked. She felt dread gather in her throat, and Danielle's voice whispered in her memory. *'I have seen one, a magus...'* Maker, not the Crunorix...

"We don't know, Your Majesty, it is very confusing. They may be disguised as soldiers from your vassal lords. We need to hurry."

"Should there not be—" Gabrielle began, then held her breath as a vibration pulsed through the stone under their feet.

The knights exchanged worried glances.

"What was that?" she asked them.

"A Weapon," Sir Ceridwen replied. "Do you recognize its voice?" he asked Sir Liam.

"No, but it is very faint... perhaps—" Another throb of distant thunder trembled in the stone, and the knight frowned. "No, Sir Ceridwen, I do not recognize it."

"Nor I," the older knight agreed. "Ready your shield."

Sir Liam nodded, and drew his shield onto his arm. His gaze rested on the shield as he gathered his thoughts and grew still. The he spoke the shield's Word. The shield rang like a bell as its bindings opened, and Gabrielle felt her nightdress billow as the air thrummed in response.

Sir Ceridwen nodded satisfaction and ordered the squad forward, and Sir Liam pulled Gabrielle along with them. They plunged down the stairs and along one of the wide halls lined with pillars that marked the formal rooms of the Keep, so quickly that Gabrielle did not have a chance to do more than sprint along with them. Her bare feet stung as they slapped the cold stone, and her nightdress fluttered around her legs, and she gripped her sheathed sword in one hand and Sir Liam's strong hand in the other.

Servants fled through the halls around them, some chasing after the soldiers, others quickly darting through doorways to disappear from sight. Gabrielle heard cries of panic, and then the distant clash of metal echoing up a stairwell. Ceridwen did not hesitate, and turned the squad away from the sounds of fighting toward a more circuitous route to the citadel.

Gabrielle had never liked the citadel. Its heavy, grey stone formed a castle within a castle, unreachable save through a gate guarded by a steel portcullis and walls built as thick as the outer walls of the Keep itself. The rooms and halls within the citadel were cramped and rough, with few furnishings and fewer luxuries, but Gabrielle raced toward them without hesitation.

They turned a corner and Ceridwen ordered a sudden halt. Bodies lay scattered across the floor of the hallway ahead of them, dozens of soldiers slaughtered in close, bitter fighting. Blood stained the portraits on the walls and pooled on the white marble floor.

Sir Ceridwen led them forward cautiously, and Gabrielle stared at the fallen soldiers as she passed. Many had died with their weapons still sheathed, but a dozen had fought savagely, pressed together shoulder to shoulder against the wall of the hallway. Terrible wounds tore their bodies, weapons still lodged in their flesh. And here were also the corpses of their foes. Soldiers in white tabards so like the defenders' that Gabrielle had to peer closely to tell them apart.

Sir Ceridwen bent to one body and rolled it onto its back. The black sigil of crossed swords beneath a crown showed clearly on the blood-stained field behind it.

"Campbell..." Gabrielle gasped, and she felt a chasm of despair open within her.

Cries of alarm suddenly rippled through the soldiers. Boots pounded toward them from a side passage, and Gabrielle caught a glimpse of a formidable force of soldiers with drawn blades.

Her soldiers rushed to confront them. Steel rang on steel as they clashed, swords shrieking against armor and blade.

Gabrielle drew her sword and discarded the sheath. The blade's familiar weight sent strength surging up her arm, and she bared her teeth in a fierce grin.

But Sir Liam dragged her away from the fight. Ten soldiers surrounded them and charged down the hallway with Sir Ceridwen leading the way. A squad of soldiers poured into the hall as they passed, and Gabrielle staggered as her defenders were pushed into her by the savage impact of blades against them. A soldier fell next to her, but the others closed the gap and surged forward.

More attackers appeared ahead of them. Sir Ceridwen did not pause. The knight swept two aside with a shining slice of his blade, then drove another back into his comrades. Gabrielle's soldiers rushed into the gap with fierce cries, slicing and stabbing at the invaders. Gabrielle was shoved and jostled and struck by armored limbs as her soldiers struggled against their attackers.

The right side of her protection collapsed, and an enemy soldier rushed at her, his sword raised high above his shield. Gabrielle twisted and raised her sword to guard. She saw the enemy's eyes widen in confusion as he was suddenly confronted by the strange apparition of a beautiful woman clad only in her nightclothes. He stopped in his tracks, uncertain, and Gabrielle hesitated as well, unable to attack this young man who so clearly should not be her enemy.

Sir Liam did not hesitate. The knight's sword slid cleanly over the lip of the soldier's shield and into his throat. Blood burst from the young man's mouth and he collapsed, his eyes still locked on Gabrielle's as they filled with pain and helpless confusion.

More invaders swarmed forward, and Liam met them boldly. His shield rang from their blows, and his sword was a shining blur as it arced through their desperate parries. Its blade tore flesh and struck sparks as it passed.

Gabrielle wrenched her gaze from the dead soldier's face. More enemy soldiers were filling the hallway from both sides, but Sir Ceridwen and Sir Liam had forced open a wide gap in the attackers, and her soldiers were pressing through. Gabrielle staggered forward with them, her sword clutched in her hand.

Then they had broken free from the invaders and they raced toward an open chamber at the end of the hall. Sir Ceridwen and Sir Liam flanked her as they burst into the open. Gabrielle recognized the wide, curved walls and sweeping stairways of the Silver Tower, balcony after balcony ascending upward toward the magnificent chandelier and arced ceiling. The wide floor was made of white marble, unmarked save for the black stag and crown of the royal sigil in the center.

Knights in bright armor awaited them there. A dozen garbed in steel that blazed in the light of lanterns hung around the chamber. Behind them stood a rank of soldiers wearing Campbell's sigil, and Gabrielle's heart sank at the sight.

"Back," hissed Ceridwen, but the hallway behind was blocked by soldiers, and Gabrielle knew they could never win through before the knights fell upon their backs.

One of the knights stepped forward and removed his helm. His armor was as black as a well, his cloak as white as snow, and his breastplate bore his sigil in white enamel.

"Surrender," Duke Campbell commanded, his voice rising clearly above the clash of metal. "Lay down your sword, my lady, or your soldiers will all die, and I will take it from your hand."

"Do not," Sir Ceridwen muttered. "We will force a passage for you."

Gabrielle glanced at the craggy face of her knight. His eyes were flickering over their foe, gauging a thousand blows in his mind to find the right course. She turned further, and saw Campbell's soldiers closing on all sides, his knights in the forefront, their shining steel dazzling.

"For me, or for us all?" she asked.

"Your Majesty, please," Sir Ceridwen said roughly. "You are all that matters, you know that."

Gabrielle tried to smile at the grizzled knight. "No. I will need you when we find the right time to fight, a time when we can win."

"No, Your Majesty," Ceridwen pleaded, but Gabrielle had already turned her back on him and begun to walk toward the center of the room.

Her steps took her to the black stone of her sigil, and she stopped with her feet planted on the proud back of her stag. She bent and placed her sword on the ground at her feet, and heard Ceridwen curse as Campbell's knights moved to encircle them.

Gabrielle's skin crept as the chill air brushed across her, unimpeded by her nightdress. The polished floor burned like ice against her bare feet, and the cold stares of the surrounding soldiers seemed to pierce the thin silk as easily as the air did. She fought a nearly overwhelming urge to clutch her arms across her chest, and instead forced herself to stand as proudly as she could, her head high as she glared at the duke.

"Good," the duke announced. "Very good, Your Majesty."

The leather straps of Campbell's armor creaked as he slowly approached, his footfalls echoing heavily from the marble floor. He stopped an arm's-length in front of her, so close that she could smell him, oil and leather and stale sweat. The lanterns gleamed from the glossy steel across his shoulders, and his thin lips curled slightly as he matched her gaze.

"Sir Ranald, her sword," the duke commanded. A towering knight with a ginger beard stepped to the duke's side and retrieved the Queen's sword from where it rested. He offered it to the duke, but Campbell waved the knight away, uninterested in the blade, his gaze never leaving Gabrielle's.

"How dare you," Gabrielle said defiantly. "How dare you draw your sword against me. You are a traitor, and a shame on your family name."

Campbell frowned in displeasure, his eyes as cold as the blue ice at the heart of a glacier. "Bring her," he ordered, his voice stern. "Sir Ranald, secure the rest of the Keep." He strode from the chamber and a squad of soldiers closed around Gabrielle. She followed the duke with as much dignity as she could muster, the echoes of her feet lost amongst the heavy footsteps of her escort.

Campbell led them quickly through the Keep to the Royal Tower and mounted its long staircase. Gabrielle realized that they

THE MARTYR'S TEARS

were returning to her apartments, and her heart fell. *All those deaths, all that fear, just to end up back where I started.*

The duke entered the private study and strode to the fireplace, his hands clasped behind his back as the flames shone from his armor. The door closed behind Gabrielle with a soft thump, startling her. She glanced behind her and discovered the soldiers had waited in the hallway.

Gabrielle's gaze came to rest on the heavy, silver candelabra that stood beside the settee. She stepped toward it without thinking further than the need to have its weight in her hand, but before she could take a second step, the duke swung to face her, a dark silhouette framed against the flames behind him.

"It is over," the duke informed her.

"Over? When General Boone has destroyed your army, when the lords of Albyn have condemned your family, when you kneel in chains awaiting the axe, that is when it will be over. You have sealed your fate."

"You think so? You think the great families of Albyn will condemn me? They will flock to me. It is long past time the mockery of your rule is ended, and a true Albainn sits on the Silver Throne."

"A true Albainn?" Gabrielle scoffed. "Does a true Albainn pledge his loyalty and then break his word?"

Campbell's lips drew into a thin line, and Gabrielle knew that she had scored. *Although it will do me no good.*

"My loyalty is to Albyn," Campbell said, his resonant voice rising to fill the room. He stepped closer to Gabrielle, so that she had to raise her chin to keep his gaze, and he filled her vision with steel. "You are a beautiful woman, and I understand why the King brought you to Albyn. I am certain you would have made him a noble wife. I would have served your children as I served him. But misfortune took him from us, and I will not allow a girl who knows nothing of Albyn, and who is in thrall to a wizard from some savage jungle, to sit upon his throne." The duke shook his head in disgust. "No matter how shapely is the posterior she perches on."

THE MARTYR'S TEARS

Gabrielle felt the blood rush from her face and flood, tingling, into her fingers. Her breath shortened, and her hand itched to slap the duke.

Campbell watched her for a moment, studying her as if she were no more than a curiosity, then he drew a scroll from his belt and offered it to Gabrielle.

"Sign this."

"What is it?" Gabrielle kept her hands firmly by her side.

"It is your order commanding that I be made regent, to rule in your name."

"You are insane," Gabrielle said, shocked.

"If you truly love the kingdom as you claim, you will sign."

"Why would I?"

"If you do, I will spare the soldiers who are still fighting for their misplaced loyalty. If you do, I will allow you to remain here in the Silver Keep, unharmed, until a suitable time has passed. Then we shall marry, and you will abdicate in favor of your husband, your king. Sign it, and your children will still rule this kingdom."

Gabrielle clenched her jaw shut against the words she wished to hurl in Campbell's face. Instead, she took the scroll from his hand, unrolled it, and stared, unseeing, at the black ink scrawled across its surface. *Abdicate... give Albyn into the hands of this posturing, cruel, vindictive man... Martyr's tears, to give myself to him, to bear his children...*

Gabrielle took a calming breath, raised her gaze to meet the duke's, and ripped the parchment in half.

Campbell's eyes narrowed to slits beneath his deep brows. He twisted savagely and the back of his mailed fist caught Gabrielle across her mouth before she could flinch away.

The impact exploded into her head so that her vision dimmed and wavered. The floor struck her face and arms and blood burst sickeningly into her mouth. The world tumbled dizzyingly around her, something smashed with the tinkle of broken glass, and she sprawled helplessly on her stomach, the thick carpet rough against her cheek.

THE MARTYR'S TEARS

Somewhere in the distance she could hear Duke Campbell speaking, but she could not understand the words. Her hands stung as if they had been thrust into a bowl of icy water, but a much deeper throb of pain was blooming across her mouth and jaw. She struggled to drag her hands and legs under her, and blood dripped across the intricate weave beneath her face as she rose unsteadily to her knees.

Campbell's voice grew clearer as the world swam slowly into focus. "... remember your place and there will be no need for this pain. Do you understand?"

Yes, Gabrielle thought desperately. Her lip screamed with pain, and her jaw throbbed. She swallowed the blood that filled her mouth and slowly stood. She brought her fingers to her lip, and examined the glistening red that coated them.

The duke was watching her with disdain etched into his face, and Gabrielle felt anger burn away the last traces of confusion from her.

"I am unhurt," she declared, careful to tame her accent and the slurring her lips seemed intent on forcing on her words. "My corsets are much worse than your blow." She smoothed her nightdress back into place while she waited for Duke Campbell to respond.

The duke's expression did not waver, but nor did he strike her again. "Very well, I will leave you to consider your answer while I dispose of the last of your defenders, but you should ponder the cost of your defiance. There are others who will bear the brunt of your pride."

The duke stepped to the door and called for his soldiers. Gabrielle felt a flood of relief as Aithne and Bryn were prodded into the room, but it was fleeting as the duke directed the soldiers to collect the books and messages from Gabrielle's desk and search the room for any weapons before they left. *All of Boone's reports, Karsha's plans...* she thought in dismay. *And my seal...*

"She is to remain in the private study until I speak with her again," Campbell ordered, his voice stern and cold.

At last her handmaidens were released and they ran to Gabrielle's side as the door closed behind the soldiers. They had not been harmed beyond scratches and bruises, and anger and concern fought for dominance on their faces as they examined the damage Campbell had done to Gabrielle.

Aithne gently cleaned her lip with a cloth and cool water, but Gabrielle could not help wincing despite the red-haired girl's care.

"It needs to be stitched, Your Majesty," Aithne told her. "Will they allow a healer?"

"I do not know," Gabrielle replied. *If I ask, and they refuse, then I am truly a prisoner. Am I ready to know this? It can make no difference, can it?* Gabrielle ran her tongue along the inside of her lip and probed her teeth. *All there. I am lucky.* "I do not need a healer," Gabrielle decided stubbornly.

"Yes, Your Majesty," Aithne agreed, and she continued her ministrations until Gabrielle was ready to beg for mercy.

"I'm sorry, Your Majesty, they won't let me go to your chamber to get you new clothes," Bryn announced as she returned from a shouted conversation through the door, frowning in anger. "Just look at your poor dress."

Gabrielle peered at the white fabric. Blood had stained the elegant embroidery on the collar and the soft cloth over her chest, and left long streaks on her skirts, but there was little to be done.

"Will you take my clothes?" Bryn asked. "They aren't much, but—"

"No, Bryn, thank you but there is no need," Gabrielle assured her hurriedly. Gabrielle could not stand the thought of asking one of the young women to wear her blood-stained dress.

"At least take my housecoat," Bryn insisted. "You are frozen, Your Majesty."

"Then you will be frozen." Gabrielle shook her head. "In any case, I believe I had a robe when I was reading…" Gabrielle frowned, befuddled by the thought that so little time had passed since she had put down her book, although it seemed a lifetime ago.

Bryn brought her the long robe of soft wool and Gabrielle gratefully wrapped herself in it, and Aithne retrieved Gabrielle's slippers from beneath the settee, which did little to soothe the aching cold that had turned Gabrielle's toes numb.

She moved as close to the fire as she dared, and slowly turned in place as she glared at the rich carpet under her feet, her thoughts filled with words she should have hurled at Duke Campbell and actions she should have taken that would not have left her locked up in her nightclothes while her kingdom was betrayed.

Maeglin

Lightning flared so brightly outside the windows of the cluttered room that the lanterns were completely overwhelmed, and the books and furniture that filled the room were etched into the Knight Commander's gaze in stark black and white.

Maeglin scowled at the thick windows as thunder rattled them in their frames, and rain struck the panes hard enough to sound like hail thrown violently against them.

"He's not here, sir." A soldier stepped into the drawing room of the Archivist's apartment, frowning in disappointment.

"Get out," Maeglin dismissed him, and the soldier hurried from his glare. *No, Whitebrooke is not here, hardly surprising since we have searched his rooms a dozen times, and guards have watched the doors continuously since he was imprisoned.*

Maeglin idly picked a book from a side table and examined the binding, then carried it with him into Whitebrooke's study. *Whitebrooke is not here, but there must be something to tell me where he has gone. He must have left some trail for me to read.*

Maeglin swept the room with his gaze. It was all too easy to picture the Archivist at his desk, hunched over the neatly stacked books, scribbling hurriedly on the sheets of parchment that appeared to rest on every flat surface. Maeglin slid a parchment aside with his finger and examined the sheet which lay underneath it. It was written in no language Maeglin could read, but he had been assured by those who could that the research was innocuous and unhelpful. The Knight Commander could tell for himself that the parchment contained no diagrams of Crunorix rituals, nor, indeed, did any of the hundreds of books and scrolls they had found in the Archivist's rooms.

Maeglin slid the parchment back into place and tapped it with his finger as he brooded. *No hint of fuil crunor, but might there not be a hastily jotted note regarding a long-forgotten room, or a message to an accomplice, worded so as to throw off suspicion?*

Maeglin glanced again at the book in his hand. It was a thin volume of bound vellum, painstakingly lettered and illustrated, purporting to be an account of the construction of Saint Cionaodh's bridge.

It will take days for the priests to read through all of these, Maeglin realized, shaking his head as he gazed at the volumes filling every wall and table, *let alone find any note that might pertain to where Whitebrooke has gone.* Maeglin was not sure what he had hoped to find, only that he was convinced he could and would find it. *And we have found no other trace of him, no matter how we search.*

His hands suddenly flared with a burning itch. Maeglin's face twisted and he hurled the book across the room. It fluttered and tumbled, and pages ripped free as it smashed into a shelf bowed with the weight of the ancient lore it carried. Several volumes crashed to the floor, but that was suddenly not enough for Maeglin. He strode to the shelf and swept books from it with both hands, sending them careening through the air. A small side table stood next to the shelf, and Maeglin lashed out with a kick that smashed the carved wood into splinters and sent a tall stack of books sliding to the floor in a rush.

Maeglin returned to Whitebrooke's desk and cleared its surface with a violent sweep of his hands, and glass shattered as the Archivist's lantern smashed amongst the ruins of the former side table. The Knight Commander grabbed fistfuls of

Whitebrooke's notes and hurled them into the fireplace, and watched with satisfaction as the pages curled and blackened in the flames.

"Knight Commander, is everything all right?"

Maeglin glanced to the doorway, where the two guards stood with drawn blades, staring about the room in confusion.

"Go back to your post."

"Yes, sir, only Sir Hollis is here with a message for you."

"Very well."

Maeglin shoved a pile of books off a chair near the fire and sat to watch the flames dance. His knife no longer brought any relief from the torment of his swollen hands, and his cheeks and neck were almost as intolerable. Sweat beaded across his skin, no matter how often he splashed water onto his head. *Why now? I have no time for sickness...* Maeglin clenched his jaw and forced his hands to rest peacefully on the arms of the chair. *It will not master me. It is just pain.*

Maeglin detached his mind from the throbbing as he had so many times before with pain and wounds. He listened to his breathing, the snap of the fire, and found a small, dark thought that was cool and quiet.

Maeglin closed his eyes and let his mind enter the thought.

There was no disturbance, only a small, wet noise that came and went. Cool, damp air caressed his skin, and he drew it deep into his lings.

The wet noise came again, a drip against stone, and Maeglin let his mind search the dark space for its source. A figure drifted in the shadows, and he approached it, his heart beating in anticipation.

She hung naked from chains fastened around her wrists, so that her toes barely brushed against the floor. Manacles also encircled her ankles, fastened to iron rings sunk deep into the stones beneath her. Her skin glistened with moisture, rivulets of water trickling over her beautiful body. Blood dripped between her full lips, and her hair fell limply in a curtain around her bowed head.

THE MARTYR'S TEARS

Maeglin grabbed her hair and pulled her head back, and her golden eyes stared wide and desperate into his.

"Please," she whispered.

Maeglin laughed. His dagger was in his hand, already slick with blood, and he slid its point over her stomach. Her dark skin parted and bright blood flowed.

"Please," she gasped, her lips open. Maeglin brought his mouth savagely down onto hers, tasting the salt of her blood as it coated his tongue. He thrust with his dagger, feeling the point slide deep into her stomach. She gasped again, and her blood flooded his mouth.

"Please," she moaned, and Maeglin rammed his knife into her again—

"Sir?"

Maeglin started and stared at his hand in revulsion, the sensation of his dagger clenched in his fingers so real that the sight of his empty hand felt twisted and wrong.

He clenched his hands into fists and swallowed the sour bile that surged in his throat as the images of his vision clustered behind his eyelids. *What is wrong with me? What vile place do such disgusting visions come from?*

"Sir?" Sir Hollis repeated himself. The knight moved to the fireplace with a sheaf of small parchments held carefully in his gloved hand. He frowned in concern as he glanced at the Knight Commander. "I have the latest reports from most of the patrols, sir."

"Most?" Maeglin swallowed again as fresh revulsion stirred in his stomach. He forced himself to ignore the image of long legs streaked with blood and focus on the knight standing before him.

"Three patrols have not sent a report, Knight Commander."

"Send runners to find those three, and tell their leaders to report to me in the Tùr Abhainn."

"Messages have been sent to all three, already, sir. I will send for you immediately when the patrol leaders arrive."

"Good. What have the other patrols reported?"

"They have found no signs of Reverend Whitebrooke, nor of any further fuil crunor rituals. Not since Reverend Meara was discovered. In fact, all they do report are a multitude of small issues and unrelated items."

"Such as?"

"Well…" Sir Hollis sorted through the dozens of pieces of parchment in his hand. "Two casks of wine were found to be filled with water, and the quartermaster questioned. One patrol reports seeing lights moving across the farmlands to the south, but could not say with certainty how many, nor how far away. The cisterns appear to have flooded, so they are checking the sluice gates. And a soldier managed to slip and fall from the roof of the kennels while he was searching it, and cracked his skull. The healers send word that they do not expect him to survive the night. There are many more… do you wish to hear them all?"

"No. What is his name?"

"Sir?"

"The soldier who fell."

"Orin, sir."

"The one from Dalby Combe?"

"Yes, sir."

"Very well."

Maeglin watched the last traces of parchment curl and rock in the draft of the flames, his thoughts already testing the delivery of the news of Whitebrooke's escape to Baron Arledge. *He will insist on making his own search of the temple. He will not trust that Whitebrooke truly escaped, and will suspect we abetted his flight. How may I deny Arledge's request? He cannot be given authority over us. Will he accept merely observing our own efforts?*

"There is another messenger ready to leave," Sir Hollis informed him. "If you have time to review his message."

"Who's message?"

"From the Council… again."

"I will read it later."

"Yes, sir, only this is the third waiting for you. What shall we tell the Council when they ask why we have received no response from Baron Arledge?"

"I will deal with it when the time comes. We need to find Whitebrooke before then."

THE MARTYR'S TEARS

"Sir, what about the knights you ordered ready?" Sir Hollis asked. "With this weather…"

"Let them stand down, all but a score. We must wait until the storm ends."

"Maker's breath," Sir Hollis said admiringly, as incandescent fire etched the clouds over Loughliath, and the window panes shook as thunder smashed into them. "Arledge's nobles will likely be washed away by morning. It's no wonder the cistern flooded. We're lucky it wasn't worse."

"Worse?" Maeglin frowned. "How bad is the flooding?"

"The patrol reports that water has covered the walkways in the Reservoir, but that the other cisterns are still at normal levels."

"Only the Reservoir?" Maeglin asked.

"Yes, sir."

Maeglin leapt to his feet and strode quickly from the room, summoning the guards from the door as he passed. "Come with me. Sir Hollis, take a squad and search the warehouses along the river docks."

"Yes, sir," Sir Hollis replied. "What are we looking for?"

"Whitebrooke," Maeglin shouted in return, as he began to run down the passageway. "We've found him."

***

The narrow stairs echoed with the sound of heavy boots on stone and the creak and rub of metal armor. Sir Maeglin hurried down the steps, his sword drawn, and his men followed as quickly as they could.

Now we will see if good fortune has finally turned away from Reverend Whitebrooke, Maeglin grinned to himself. *However he learned of the tunnel under the Abhainn Fuar, he could not have anticipated the storm. He will be hiding nearby, or perhaps in the tunnel still, waiting for the tempest to pass.*

Chill, damp air greeted them at the bottom of the stairs as they entered the cisterns, a maze of deep recesses and branching paths divided by thick stone pillars and low archways that disappeared into the gloom in all directions.

Maeglin knew where to go. He followed a wide walkway into the darkest recesses of the cisterns, where the deep Reservoir lay beneath the massive river gates that linked the cisterns to the Abhainn Fuar. Beside those gates stood a small door that gave entrance to a chamber which housed part of the gate's great mechanism, as well as a concealed door that was known to only a few.

They dropped down a short flight of steps and Maeglin's boots splashed into water, the walkway flooded to his ankles.

I was right. This is no flood, Maeglin thought with grim satisfaction. *If the river gates had breached, the entirety of the cisterns would have flooded.* Maeglin was certain, now, where the water had come from. He had pulled the lever himself, opening a sluice gate to flood the concealed tunnel, and had listened to the roar of water filling the narrow passage on the far side of the steel door that secured its entrance. *Someone has opened the door to the tunnel, and released the water that filled it. Someone trying to escape.*

The Knight Commander ran forward, water exploding upward at every step. Then, faintly, Maeglin heard sounds of fighting, steel clashing with steel and shouts and cries so distorted as they echoed that they were unintelligible. He slowed his pace, listening intently. *Did the patrol examining the river gates find him?* Maeglin wondered. *The fighting sounds fiercer than I would have imagined. Does Whitebrooke have still more of his creatures protecting him?*

Maeglin rounded a pillar and ahead the chamber was filled with figures locked in combat. Two warriors held the entrance to a high platform along the chamber wall against a squad of soldiers clad in the dark green and gold of the Temple, and swords rose and fell in the dim light.

Maeglin's gaze darted across the mass of battling forms and the Knight Commander quickly made sense of the chaos. The two enemy warriors had positioned themselves well. They had caught his men at a pinch-point, where the squad's superior numbers could not be brought to bear, and they held the high ground, defending a short flight of steps up to the raised platform while the Temple soldiers struggled on the flooded walkway below. The two warriors had secured their retreat as well, as the door to the gate-controls room, and the entrance to its concealed tunnel, stood open along the far wall, a short sprint beyond the platform on which they fought.

Maeglin gave orders to change all of that.

He split off two of his soldiers to round the cistern so that they would approach from the far side, either denying the enemy their escape or forcing them to fall back. He set two more soldiers as archers with orders to pepper the distant platform with arrows if the enemy gave them a clean shot. Their meager volley would not be truly effective, Maeglin knew, but in the dark, they would be hard to ignore. Then he pressed along the lower path with his remaining two soldiers to join the fight on the platform from the flank.

The archers were as effective as Maeglin had hoped. The two warriors on the platform ducked and hesitated as arrows cracked off stone and metal around them, and neither glanced into the flooded cistern to see Maeglin's approach.

A short, narrow stair led to the wide platform and Maeglin paused at its base, dropped his visor, and vaulted up the steps. He burst onto the platform bellowing war cries and smashed into the invader's flank.

One of the enemy warriors slid sideways to meet Maeglin, his shield raised and his sword poised to strike. Maeglin did not give him time to set. The Knight Commander knocked the warrior's shield aside and drove its bearer backward with a long thrust, then blocked a heavy blow from the second enemy, a tall knight in full armor, and sliced the knight across her breastplate.

Two of his men had engaged the first invader, driving him back across the platform, so Maeglin challenged the knight. She met him eagerly, her sword lashing out with a speed that belied its weight, and Maeglin stepped to his right to take the blow on his shield, then quickly parried low as her second blow swept under his shield, tearing through the jerkin of chain metal links he wore under his plate.

The knight put her shoulder into his shield and drove him back a step, raining overhand blows over the top of it. Maeglin parried two before suddenly raising his shield and jabbing his sword into the thin armor over her hip. His blade bit deep and metal crunched, and the knight lurched away, her sword in high guard. Maeglin pursued her, lunged low to draw her blade, then swung his shield into the side of her head. Her return stroke was clumsy and wild, and Maeglin knocked it to the side with ease. Before she could recover, the Knight Commander leapt forward and smashed his sword into her shoulder, his blade grinding across the join of pauldron and gorget with a shriek of twisting metal. The knight staggered and raised her sword, but Maeglin did not pause and hewed with his sword into the same spot a second time, then a third. Her blade beat against the vambrace on his sword arm but he paid it no heed and struck again as if he were chopping wood. Her armor bent and tore free, her sword spun out of her hand, and blood sprayed against the side of her helm.

Maeglin twisted at a cry of warning, and caught the other warrior's sword with the top of his shield and the ridge of his pauldron as his enemy's silver blade ripped through the air, screeching as its edge flashed across Maeglin's steel plate. A second blow followed instantly upon the heels of the first, then a third, the warrior's sword a gleaming blur, and sparks arced from Maeglin's armor as steel rang on steel.

Maeglin did not wait for another attack. He struck first, a crushing blow that the warrior barely caught on his shield, then another that knocked the warrior's blade to the side, and another that tore steel scales from the warrior's chest. His enemy flung himself back, but Maeglin followed, raining savage blows upon his foe. An awkward parry left the invader's sword hanging for an instant, and Maeglin locked it with a deft twist and struck across the warrior's wrist, sending the blade clanging to the stone floor. Two heavy blows on the warrior's shield drove him to his knees, and Maeglin stepped back as two of his soldiers rushed forward to subdue the man.

THE MARTYR'S TEARS

Maeglin returned to where the warrior's sword lay on the stones and pushed it around with the tip of his blade until the pommel faced him and the Queen's arms flashed silver in the lantern's light. *Queen's Guard?* Maeglin wondered. *I do not recognize him. Who is this man, and why would the Queen's Guard be aiding Whitebrooke to escape?*

"Just these two?" Maeglin asked.

"Yes, sir. Just the two of them, sir." One of the soldiers from the patrol who had been fighting when Maeglin's reinforcements arrived nodded his head. The soldier was cut above his eye, and a sheen of blood ran down his right arm beneath his breastplate. Only three soldiers from the original patrol were now standing, the others unconscious or wounded, although Maeglin saw no injuries that would not be survived.

Two warriors, waiting in the cisterns by themselves, one bearing the Queen's sigil. I expected, at best, to find only Whitebrooke, at worst, to find the way barred by more of his foul creatures, or another priest turned traitor, such as Meara. Something is amiss here.

Maeglin cast his gaze across the platform and the wide pool below them. *Only three of the patrol still able to fight, and of my soldiers...* Maeglin frowned. The two soldiers who had raced to the platform with him were there, although one was laid out on the stones, apparently senseless, to judge from his vaguely moving hands. *Where are the two I sent to take the rear of the platform?* Maeglin's eyes narrowed fiercely. *Where are my archers?*

The chamber was quiet and empty away from the soldiers grouped on the platform, the pool of water a shimmering mirror.

There was a sound of scraping metal and a heavy crunch, and Maeglin turned in time to see the soldier he had been speaking with sink to the floor without a sound, his eyes showing whitely through fluttering eyelids.

Behind him stood the enemy knight. Bright blood ran freely from the seams and joins of her armor, all along her right side and arm, spreading like spilled wine over the shining steel surface. She had removed her helm to use it as a club, and it dangled from her left hand as she surveyed its effectiveness on the unconscious soldier. Her blonde hair was matted with blood and sweat, and more blood flowed from a long, jagged cut across the side of her head and ear.

But her injuries did not seem to concern her. She stood tall, and a satisfied snarl curled the corner of her lips as she locked her gaze with Maeglin's.

"We're not done yet, Knight Commander," she told him.

Maeglin snorted once, a mixture of respect and amusement.

"You wish to end it?" Maeglin asked.

"My blade is the fire of justice. I shall never lay it down," the knight intoned. Maeglin frowned in confusion. Her words were the beginning of the vow of the Order of Knights, the pledge taken by all Temple knights when they were knighted. "My shield is the ramparts of honor. I shall never lay it down," she continued, her gaze never leaving Maeglin's. "My strength is a shelter for those who suffer and cry out for succor. I shall never waver."

"Eilidh, no!" the other invader cried out, and he surged to his feet against the two soldiers who restrained him.

"Eilidh?" asked Sir Maeglin. Now he knew the enemy knight, her name completing the familiarity her face had stirred, and the realization baffled him. *I thought her lost along with the Littleford garrison. How did she come to be here, guarding Whitebrooke's escape?*

Maeglin drew in his breath sharply as he realized the only truth that made sense. *They are not here to aid an escape. They fight for Arledge. The tunnel is open, our walls are breached... and there must be others within the temple.*

The helm dropped from her hand and she stepped to her sword, lying where it had fallen to the stones. Maeglin nodded acceptance, and the knight collected it awkwardly in her left hand.

"Good for you," Maeglin told her, and he hefted his sword and stepped toward her.

"Maeglin."

The voice was low, a feral growl from the shadows at the far end of the platform that sent fire coursing through Maeglin's arms and chest.

The Knight Commander took a long, satisfied breath, then faced the source of the voice.

"Killock," Maeglin snarled.

Maeglin crossed the distance between them in a rush and his sword flashed out, fast and low. Killock knocked it aside and slid to Maeglin's right, away from his shield, and countered. The Templar's blade was a silver blur as it struck twice. Maeglin heard a crunch as the sword bit through the steel scales over his shoulder, but the wound was shallow. He knocked the second attack aside with a high parry which flowed into an attack that ripped downward through the air onto Killock's shoulder.

But the Templar twisted underneath the blow, his sword arcing wide to strike across Maeglin's back. Maeglin turned into the attack and barely had time to raise his shield to deflect the strike, and his own sword swept low with the speed of his turn and forced Killock to abandon his attack and leap away to avoid the blow.

Maeglin lunged after the Templar, but Killock moved faster. The air filled with the blur of their blades as Killock launched a flurry of attacks. The Templar's sword sliced high, slid past Maeglin's guard, and reversed to impale the Knight Commander. Maeglin met each attack, his own sword flashing silver as he deflected Killock's blade and countered.

Maeglin felt his sword tip catch and tear through Killock's jerkin, but was rewarded only by hot fire traced across his shoulder as Killock slid his sword neatly over Maeglin's shield and between the join of his breastplate.

Sir Maeglin grunted in pain and lunged forward with his shield, catching the Templar heavily across the chest and shoulder. Killock staggered from the impact and dropped to the ground, rolling away from Maeglin.

Maeglin pursued instantly with an overhead strike. But Killock rose smoothly to his feet from his roll and parried the attack high, then continued his rise, up and into Maeglin, the Templar's shoulder and hip guiding the Knight Commander's weight and momentum. Maeglin felt his feet leave the ground, the world spun around him, and he crashed heavily to the stone floor.

His helm twisted with the impact and for an instant he was blind. He tore it off just in time to roll away as Killock's blade struck sparks from the stone floor where he had lain. Maeglin lunged awkwardly from his knees to drive the Templar back but Killock did not hesitate. He guided the clumsy thrust to the side and then locked Maeglin's sword in his guard. Killock grabbed the Knight Commander's hand and twisted. Pain lanced from the trapped wrist and Maeglin's fingers convulsed open.

Sir Maeglin surged to his feet and slammed his shield into Killock's face. The Templar stumbled back, spitting blood, and Maeglin followed. He tore his hand from Killock's grasp and slammed it home into the Templar's chest. Maeglin heard the breath rush from Killock as his armored fist smashed into him. Maeglin struck again with his shield, hoping for a final crushing blow, but Killock ducked under it and thrust upward. Maeglin felt the Templar's steel blade tear through the scales over his ribs and bite deep.

He made Killock pay. He leveled the Templar with a haymaker to his jaw. Killock sprawled across the stone floor, tried to rise, and fell again as his legs splayed uselessly under him.

Pain lanced across Maeglin's ribs and made him suck air through his teeth. His steel shield hung heavily from his arm and he could not raise it, so he ripped it free and discarded it to bang on the ground. Blood flowed through the seams of his breastplate and made a wet sheen across his ribs and hip. Maeglin tucked his arm close to his side, then bent to retrieve his sword.

He turned to Killock. The Templar had risen to his hands and knees but no further. His head was bowed and his cloak hung over it in disarray. Maeglin could see Killock shift as he strained to gather himself, but his movements were slow and uncertain.

Mine as well, the Knight Commander thought as he moved cautiously forward. Every step sent spears of red pain through his ribs no matter how hard he pressed with his arm against the wound. Maeglin placed one boot on the blade of Killock's sword and pinned it to the ground. He pressed the tip of his blade under the Templar's hood and pressed upward. Killock slowly rose onto his knees. His beard was soaked with blood and his eyes were dazed and unfocused as he tried to steady himself.

THE MARTYR'S TEARS

"You treacherous bastard," Maeglin snarled.

Maeglin caught a glimpse of movement from the corner of his eye. Something black and fast. He flinched away, and the motion saved his life.

Blackened steel sliced across his jaw instead of through his neck. He struck with his sword at his half-glimpsed opponent. A swirl of blonde hair ducked under the thrust and pain stabbed into his outstretched arm. Maeglin retreated a step and brought his sword around in a flashing arc.

Rage flared behind his eyes as he recognized the lithe figure of Danielle's thief. Her teeth were bared in a fierce grin and her eyes were slits of fury. Her black cloak swirled as she slid impossibly low under his blade. Maeglin twisted to chase her with his sword, but pain ripped from his side and he staggered.

That was all the opportunity the girl needed. Maeglin caught a glimpse of long, leather-clad legs as she leapt at him, then felt her curl around his shoulders and neck. She twisted and her momentum wrenched Maeglin backward. The world pitched and they landed heavily, the young woman on top. Strong legs clenched tightly around his neck and Maeglin felt his vision go dim as blood swelled impossibly to his head. His right arm was trapped against her thigh, but his left was free and he strained to pull her leg from his throat.

She spat a curse at him and stabbed at his face with a long knife. Maeglin desperately blocked it with his arm and the blade gouged the thick armor along his forearm. He grabbed her wrist and twisted, and she screamed and her knife clattered to the ground. Maeglin pulled hard and felt her leg lock loosen slightly. He let go of his sword and grabbed a fist-full of her tunic with his right hand and pulled with that as well. Slowly she twisted away. She rained blows on his arm with her other knife and he felt pain flash as the tip found its way through the metal scales, but he gritted his teeth and strained his powerful shoulders and arms against her and ignored the pain.

Then suddenly she let go and rolled away and Maeglin sucked air into his starved lungs. He clambered to his feet and spun to find her. She came at him from behind. The tip of her knife sought his neck above his gorget. He caught her wrist as the tip of her blade sank in behind his clavicle. He wrenched her arm back, then twisted it to the side. She spiraled with the motion, her body twirling through the air like an acrobat's. When she landed, she whirled faster than he could follow. Her leg whipped around with the spin and extended into a thunderous kick that exploded under his chin.

Maeglin did not feel himself crash to the ground, flat on his back. He lay stunned, his hands held weakly above his face. Blood filled his mouth and he choked and tried to sit up, but his body would not respond.

She landed on him. Knees ground into his arms, pinning them, as she sat on his chest. Light flickered across her face and hair as she leaned over him. Her green eyes flashed pure hatred.

He felt her blade slide under his chin.

"I remember you, snake knight," she whispered to him, and she tensed to slip the knife home.

"Wyn," Killock's voice was a thick snarl through smashed lips. "Let him go."

Maeglin felt the young woman freeze, the tip of her knife trembling against the thin skin under his jaw.

"This is the one that took me and Danielle to Shitebrooke," she replied. Her gaze never left Maeglin's eyes. "Why should he live?"

"Trust me, Wyn," Killock stepped to her shoulder.

Wyn hesitated a moment longer.

Maeglin spat blood. "Do it, or get back on your leash, but make up your mind before I choke to death."

Wyn drew in breath sharply, then stood in a quick, smooth movement. She stepped away as Killock squatted next to Maeglin.

The Knight Commander stifled a groan and rolled heavily to his side, then drew his knees under him. The world swayed and fire dripped across his ribs and arms. He searched for his soldiers, only to find them on their knees or sprawled on the ground, the warrior with the Queen's sword and the wounded knight standing over them.

THE MARTYR'S TEARS

"You're going to do something for me," the Templar's low growl returned Maeglin's attention to the man hunched next to him.

Maeglin coughed heavily. "I don't think so."

"You will because you will want to do this," Killock leaned close. "Maybe you should see what Whitebrooke has been hiding behind the stone door in the archives. Where Benno died. The door is open now."

How does he know that?

Then Killock was gone. Maeglin crawled to the wall and painfully hauled himself upright. His soldiers were retrieving their weapons, asking for orders, but he ignored them, his thoughts turned toward whatever secret lay behind the stone door.

Gabrielle

The lock to the study door clicked and the door swung open to admit Aithne into the room. The tall handmaiden strode stiffly through the doorway, her fists clenched at her sides. Her cheeks were pale save for an angry blush that matched her hair, and her lips had compressed into a thin line.

The two soldiers that had escorted Aithne into the study quickly closed the door behind her, but not before Gabrielle glimpsed the swollen red skin that crowned one of the soldier's cheeks.

"Aithne, are you hurt?" Gabrielle stepped to the handmaiden's side, but the young woman quickly shook her head.

"No, Your Majesty, I am well," Aithne replied. She glared over her shoulder at the closed door. "I had to instruct one of them in proper etiquette, that is all."

"Did you, indeed?" Gabrielle asked. She took Aithne's hand and gently spread her fingers. The handmaiden's knuckles were as red as her cheeks. "I do not remember this lesson. It sounds much more interesting than the ones you insist on teaching me."

"Yes, Your Majesty. He will not be so smug when addressing a lady, the next time."

"But, whatever happened?" Gabrielle asked. "Were you able to find any hope for our escape?"

"No, Your Majesty, I'm sorry," Aithne scowled. "There are six of them guarding us, and two insisted on escorting me the entire time. I never had a chance to slip away, even for an instant."

"Damn," Gabrielle sighed. She had hoped for better news, some sign that the soldiers might be inattentive in their duty, or might not consider the three noblewomen worthy of careful guard.

"Yes, Your Majesty," Aithne agreed.

Gabrielle paced to the fireplace and glared at the cheerful blaze. Her fingers brought her silver ring on its chain to her lips as she pondered her plight. *What now? Dawn is not far away. How long do I have before Campbell returns? If we cannot avoid our captors' watch, do we risk a more desperate plan? A weapon snatched in passing, and hope that surprise will overcome armor? Or that a threat of violence would force them to submit meekly?* Gabrielle shook her head. *It is beyond unlikely, and yet, biding my time in the hope that a better chance will arise seems as hopeless. Campbell is not likely to relax his guard once I have his full attention.*

A Word suddenly pulsed from beyond the study doors, rattling them against their frames. Lightning flared through the narrow gap beneath the doors and the keyhole, flashing and vanishing so that dark lines lingered in Gabrielle's vision no matter how she blinked.

A second Word was spoken, this one sharp and ringing, like a hammer on metal, and it echoed in a pulsed rhythm that struck as fast as a drum and then was gone.

Gabrielle held her breath, listening to the pounding of her heart in her ears, until she felt she must burst. At last, a sharp click from the door's lock, and the bolt was withdrawn.

The tall doors to the hallway opened and a figure in long, elegant robes stepped through with a sword in his hand, a second figure behind him. Gabrielle barely had time to recognize the dazzling smile of Lord Gwydion before Aithne closed on the Templar from the side, a candlestick poised to strike.

Lord Gwydion's smile fled as the handmaiden lunged at him. He raised his hands and shouted, "Friends! Friends!"

"Aithne, wait!" Gabrielle called out. "Lord Gwydion? Lady Rowenna?"

"Martyr's tears, I thought she was going to brain me," Gwydion drew a deep breath.

"Yes, my lord, that's right," Aithne told him with a satisfied smile. "But I'll hold off for now."

Gabrielle urged the Templars into the room. She caught a glimpse of the bodies of soldiers strewn across the hallway behind them, but the two Templars appeared to have survived unharmed. Lord Gwydion's robes hung perfectly about him and not a hair was disturbed from its beautiful sweep, and Lady Rowenna glided into the room and curtsied as gracefully as if she were at a society ball. As Lord Gwydion took Gabrielle's hand and brushed his lips against the back, Gabrielle suddenly felt very aware of the throbbing pain of her swollen and split lips, and the thin, bloodstained cloth of her nightclothes.

"My lady, my lord, why are you here?"

"Well, Your Majesty, the castle is under attack," Gwydion said lightly. "We rather thought we should find you and see if we couldn't be of some help."

"I am very pleased that you did," Gabrielle admitted. "Although I cannot tell you how sorry I am that you were forced to risk your lives to do so."

"Think nothing of it. Soldiers are of little concern, to us," Gwydion assured her.

"They didn't really seem to care about two nobles wandering around," Rowenna explained, frowning at her brother's boast. "For the most part they just yelled at us to join the others."

"Exactly," Gwydion agreed. "Except much more exciting than she made it sound."

"The ones in the hall were the first that actually tried to stop us." Rowenna winced sympathetically as her gaze drifted to Gabrielle's lips. "Were they the ones who attacked you, Your Majesty?"

"No, it was their master, Duke Campbell. He is responsible for tonight, the traitor."

"He hit you?" Gwydion asked, aghast.

"Duke Campbell did not take kindly when I told him, 'No'."

"What does he want?" Rowenna asked.

Gabrielle laughed bitterly. "He wants to marry me."

"He…?" Gwydion paused and shook his head. "Although I cannot fault the man for his infatuation, this is the most damnably strange proposal I have ever heard of."

"Oh, he does not want me," Gabrielle scoffed. "He despises me. He wants my throne."

"I see," Gwydion frowned in displeasure. "Then, my lady, he is a fool."

"Thank you, my lord," Gabrielle replied, pleased.

"What shall we do, Your Majesty?" Aithne asked.

"Is there still fighting, Lady Rowenna? Do loyal soldiers still resist?"

"I didn't see any, Your Majesty, I'm sorry."

"Campbell's soldiers were still running about quite urgently, though, weren't they," Gwydion said thoughtfully. "There must be some fighting still, somewhere. But we didn't see it, I'm afraid, Your Majesty. I don't think there can be many still fighting back."

"They will be in the citadel, if anywhere," Gabrielle said. "That is where we were going when Campbell caught us."

"Is that where you wish to go, now?"

"We would be as trapped in the citadel as we were in this room," Gabrielle decided. "No, we must escape, so that I may announce the truth of his attack to the realm, instead of awaiting his pleasure as his hostage."

"Yes, Your Majesty," Rowenna agreed.

"Sir Ceridwen mentioned something called the Small Gate," Gabrielle said thoughtfully. "He said it was a way out of the castle."

"Did he happen to mention where it was?" Gwydion asked.

"No."

"I know where it is, Your Majesty," Bryn spoke up. "It's in the west gardens, beyond the stables."

"Excellent," Gabrielle congratulated her. "You will lead us there."

"Yes, Your Majesty. If we're going outside, we will need proper clothes."

Gabrielle and her handmaidens hurried to their rooms, stepping over the bodies of the soldiers in the hallway as they went.

Once in her dressing room she tore through her clothes, choosing soft leather riding leggings, a thick woolen tunic, and a warm jacket that reached to her thighs. She added sturdy boots that she had received for a trip to Irongate, a cloak lined with ermine, and drew a wide leather belt tight around her waist to complete her gear.

Bryn and Aithne had chosen similarly, preferring sturdiness and warmth over rich colors and elegant designs.

"Bryn, armor, Aithne, swords, as quick as possible," Gabrielle told the handmaidens.

"Yes, Your Majesty, except Duke Campbell has your sword. I'm so sorry, Your Majesty."

"Never mind, Aithne," Gabrielle sighed. "Fetch King Arian's sword from above the mantle in the audience chamber, instead."

"There are quite a few to choose from lying around in the hall," Gwydion suggested.

"Good. See what you can find, Aithne, for you and Bryn, but I am not leaving King Arian's sword for Campbell."

They hurried to obey, and for a moment the study was quiet. Gabrielle retrieved her book from the settee and regretfully placed it on her desk. *I wonder if I shall ever find out if Aveline reveals herself to Conrad...* Gabrielle banished the read from her thoughts as Bryn returned to the room laden with steel and leather and insisted on helping Gabrielle don her armor first, a long tunic of steel and silver chain so finely crafted that it appeared to be made of shimmering cloth.

Gabrielle staggered as the handmaiden pulled the armor's straps, and she frowned in irritation. "It is fine," she instructed Bryn, but the young woman paid her no heed.

THE MARTYR'S TEARS

Aithne returned with King Arian's sword, a heavy blade crafted for splitting shields and unhorsing knights, and Gabrielle hefted it with both hands wrapped around its thick hilt. It was far heavier than the elegant sword Campbell had taken from her, and its blade was weighted to fall forward in a disconcerting rush, like a boulder tipped from a cliff. The grip was also far too long, even with both hands clutching it, and the pommel tried to gouge her forearm as she let the tip fall. "We must hurry, or I shall be too exhausted to do more than drag this behind me when we reach the fighting," she said bravely, but only Gwydion could muster a smile at the thin joke.

Aithne and Bryn helped each other into their armor, steel rings over polished leather breastplates and skirts, and the young women buckled on short swords with wickedly sharp points. Gabrielle lingered in the doorway for a moment, thrusting from her thoughts a dozen suddenly remembered preciouses which cried out to be collected.

"Your Majesty, should you not empower your armor?" Lady Rowenna's voice was quiet but insistent. "There may not be time if we are attacked without warning."

"Oh…" Gabrielle's fingers drifted to the delicate engravings that covered her breastplate beneath her throat. "Should we not wait? The Word might not last, and they might hear it if I did it now," she said in a rush.

"Well, they didn't hear us shouting just then, did they?" Gwydion pointed out. "Go on, Your Majesty, there's little sense in wearing that and not using it."

"No, of course not, yet…" Gabrielle's voice trailed off, and she sighed in resignation. "Oh, very well, but I forbid you to laugh."

Gabrielle tried to clear her mind of pain and anger and dread, and dredged her memory for the delicate structure of stars that would unlock the bindings of her armor. But the pattern was elusive, and concealed itself behind the throbbing of her lip, the smell of polished wood, the contented murmur of the fire, and the silent anticipation of the two Templars.

Pay attention, she chastised herself. *You have managed this before.* Slowly she dragged the Word into place. A spiral of shining threads surrounding a star that blazed like liquid silver, each thread carefully linked until they appeared to be a rush of water over the edge of a fall. Clouds of distant sparks hovered around the spiral, but Gabrielle could not spare a thought for them, and they remained hazy and diffuse.

Quickly, before it falls apart. Gabrielle whispered the Word and with her breath the bright constellation of silver light flowed into the delicate structures of her armor. Deep within the layers of metal, bindings opened in a precise sequence. The Word washed through the steel, following the elegant threads of metal, and spiraled into a gossamer web that encircled her.

Gabrielle opened her eyes and drew in deep breaths of air. A faint warmth radiated from the mesh of steel that covered her, but there was no other sign of her work, and she wondered if her Word had truly empowered her armor. *It must have. I felt it release…*

Gabrielle hesitantly sought out the eyes of Lady Rowenna, dreading what disappointment she might find there.

"An intricate Word, Your Majesty," Rowenna said kindly. "You spoke it beautifully."

"I did not," Gabrielle sighed in exasperation. "I barely got it out, and, I assure you, that is quite an accomplishment." She glanced involuntarily toward Lord Gwydion, then quickly back to his sister, unable to meet his eye. *If he mocks me, I shall not be meek in my response, I swear it.* But, to her surprise, Gwydion remained silent. "I do not understand," Gabrielle admitted to Rowenna. "Learning the Words was always so easy for Danielle, but no matter how I try, I cannot say them like her. I cannot tell you how many people I have disappointed. I am afraid you are merely the latest in an extensive list."

"Not at all, Your Majesty," Rowenna replied. "It is a gift, like any other, and there is no knowing why the Maker gave this gift to some, and different gifts to others."

"You may tell that to my instructors. They were ever disappointed in my efforts, compared to Danielle."

"I know exactly how you feel," Lord Gwydion said conspiratorially. "Ro showed off whenever she could. It was galling, to say the least."

Gabrielle glanced hesitantly at Lord Gwydion, uncertain if he teased. "I do not believe it, my lord. You are a Templar."

"Oh, absolutely true. She was unbearable. But I make up for it in other ways. As do you, Your Majesty," Gwydion assured her.

Gabrielle risked a small smile to Gwydion, and he answered in kind, a dashing grin that made her smile real.

"You have kind hearts," Gabrielle thanked the Templars, "but royal feelings aside, my effort was very poor."

"With your permission, Your Majesty," Rowenna said softly. "Lord Gwydion or I could attempt it."

"Please," Gabrielle urged them.

"You do it, Ro. I could not possibly improve on the Queen's Word," Gwydion insisted gallantly.

Lady Rowenna closed her eyes for a moment and breathed in, slowly and deeply, her chin raised. Gabrielle was struck by her delicate, elegant beauty, and was suddenly reminded of a graceful statue of Eloriel, the Elvhen seer, which stood in the gardens of Gabrielle's home in Lavandou.

Rowenna opened her eyes, and Gabrielle saw that they were wide and dark as the Templar gazed on the Word she formed in her mind. Then Rowenna whispered the Word, and Gabrielle's armor thrummed with its force, a resonate surge that pulsed deep into her chest and tingled in her fingers. Crystal chimed all around the room, the windows rattled in their frames, and the fire subsided with a crackling roar.

"There," Rowenna sighed. "What a lovely Device, Your Majesty."

Gabrielle gathered her wits from the daze the Word had cast on her. "It was made for Queen Aoife, centuries ago. I was told that she wore it when she fought King Otho on the river of ice."

"May it protect you as well as it did her," Rowenna replied.

"And may we not meet anyone like Otho, tonight," Gwydion added solemnly.

They raced down the stairs, but had barely reached the base of the Royal Tower when they were spotted by soldiers guarding the rotunda, and they had to flee.

Bryn led them along a curved hall, then quickly down a side passage, but although there were no longer footsteps directly behind them, they could hear the calls of soldiers echoing from every direction, and glimpsed hurrying figures matching their progress at every intersection.

Bryn turned again, and they burst through wide double doors into the ballroom. Elegant chandeliers hung above the polished wood, and chairs with rich cushions and delicately curved legs lined the low balcony.

Gabrielle had not yet taken a step into the ballroom when soldiers burst in, their swords drawn.

"Halt!" the leader of the soldiers cried out, and Gabrielle hefted her massive sword into guard above her head. But Lady Rowenna did not hesitate. Gabrielle felt the concussion of the Templar's Word in her chest as she stepped toward the soldiers, her long robes swirling behind her.

The soldiers leapt to attack, but Rowenna's Weapon matched their speed. The blade sang through the air, a precise silver line drawn across limbs and body, and steel and flesh parted in long fissures. The remaining soldiers flung themselves away from the web of pain the sword drew across their path, but the blade trembled with a faster rhythm, and slid deep into them, piercing them a dozen times before the the first soldier could fall.

More boots thundered on the stairs below them, as soldiers rushed to the cries of their comrades. Lord Gwydion strode to the top of the stairs to meet them. Brilliant light leapt from his fingers like sparks from a forge, and the skin of the soldiers spat and boiled as the light touched it. They shouted in pain and clutched their eyes, staggering and tumbling as they tripped over the steps and the struggling limbs of the fallen soldiers.

"Come on," Gabrielle shouted to the handmaidens, and they sped across the ballroom floor after Lady Rowenna.

But before they could reach the far side, the great doors opened, and more soldiers rushed in. In their center strode a lord dressed in bright armor lined with flashing gold and a long cape made from golden cloth. He bore a long spear, more suitable for jousting than for fighting in the halls of a castle, and Gabrielle wondered at it until she saw the lord kneel and lower the tip of the lance toward them.

The lord spoke a Word, and crimson flame rushed up the lance and exploded from its tip. The bolt sizzled across the ballroom as fast as an arrow, directly at Lady Rowenna, standing alone at the vanguard of their small group.

Gabrielle leapt without thinking. She collided with the Templar, knocking her aside as red brilliance burst around her. Gabrielle felt a hammer blow against her back, and scorching air blasted against her face. She raised her hands against the blaze as it surged around her, but in a moment it was gone, and only the smell of hot metal remained.

Gabrielle hurriedly searched for Rowenna, but the Templar was already on her feet, unhurt, and Gabrielle realized with a shock that she was, as well. The great Wardpact crafted into her armor had shrugged the Weapon's fire aside, leaving the Queen untouched.

"Thank you, Your Majesty," Rowenna said.

"We are not quite done, Ro," Lord Gwydion interrupted. "Perhaps we should finish with Lord Goldenrod here, first."

"Perhaps you should deal with him," Rowenna snapped back, annoyed. "He did bring some soldiers with him, so I will be a bit too busy to do everything. Again."

"Are you still miffed about Reverend Athair?" Gwydion asked, bewildering Gabrielle. "Honestly, he can't possibly have been as boring as you are being now."

"You wouldn't know, would you?" Rowenna replied sweetly before she turned to face the approaching soldiers, her sword ready.

"My lord, the Weapon…" Gabrielle reminded Gwydion.

"Never worry, my lady," the Templar assured her with a grin. He stepped slowly toward the golden lord and smoothed his long robes into place, one arm casually held across his back, the other poised as if to strike a backhanded blow against his distant foe.

THE MARTYR'S TEARS

Gabrielle heard the golden lord's Word pulse across the room, but at the same moment Gwydion spoke the same Word, sharper, harder, like lightning to the golden lord's thunder. Crimson flame burst from the lance and was hurled toward Gwydion, but the fire curled and twisted like a pennant in a gale instead of arcing smoothly across the floor.

Gabrielle felt Gwydion alter and twist his Word, and the lance's fire reared into the air high above the polished wood. The golden lord matched him, and the flame danced like a kite on a string, roaring like a great beast, then lurched toward the Templar.

"He's strong, but I don't think he has ever dueled before," Gwydion said calmly. "Shall we find out?"

Gwydion unleashed another Word, and then another, each one sending shock waves through the air that blasted the twisting flame backward. Gwydion did not relent, and his voice rang out with a final Word that tore the flame into a dozen torrents which arced high into the air and then screamed toward the golden lord.

The lord bellowed desperately, and his Word was enough to send one of the trails of fire into the elegant chairs that lined the balcony. But the other streams were unaffected, and they burst over him in an impact that drove him to the floor. He screamed as the fire consumed him, and strove to rise to his feet, but the heat was too intense, and he collapsed before another heartbeat had passed.

As the thunder of the fire flowed away into the distant recesses of the hall, Gabrielle became aware that she was holding her breath, and let it out with a rush. She glanced quickly around, but the fight was done. Six soldiers lay sprawled at Lady Rowenna's feet, and the rest had fled from her steel and the dismaying fate of their lord, and were even now bolting from the room.

Maker's breath... a duel, a real duel! Gabrielle thought, overwhelmed by what she had witnessed. "Lord Gwydion, you showed no fear, my lord, no hesitation..."

"How could I, my lady, with you at my side," Gwydion smiled dazzlingly.

THE MARTYR'S TEARS

Gabrielle could not control the smile that burst across her lips, and she winced as pain stabbed in response, but she found that she did not mind.

"Shall we go, before they decide to send more soldiers to see what the ruckus was all about?" Gwydion asked.

"Yes," Gabrielle agreed. "Bryn, can we reach the garden without passing through so many of the main halls?"

"Yes, Your Majesty," the young woman nodded. "Follow me."

They left the ballroom and the grand, public galleries, and descended into a maze of smaller halls, filled with the stale smells of old varnish and ancient cloth. Tall paintings in thick oil loomed on the walls, and silent statues of cold marble stared disinterestedly from their alcoves as Gabrielle hurried past.

At every juncture, Bryn chose the path that appeared the least used until Gabrielle wondered if they were the first people to tread on the long carpets since they were first laid.

But Bryn could not keep them hidden in the far reaches of the Silver Keep forever, and at last, they were forced to cross a wide plaza, frosted white under sharp stars, to reach the west gardens. In the plaza, they found the remains of bitter fighting. Bodies of soldiers lay amongst the ornamental shrubs, their armor rent, their bodies torn by uncountable wounds, and the tale of surprised guards drowning in an overwhelming rush of death was clear to see.

Beyond the plaza, Bryn led them through a narrow garden tucked beneath the looming mass of the outer walls until they reached the base of a squat tower that guarded the flank of the Keep. Here, a steel portcullis guarded a heavy door of reinforced wood hidden in the shadows of the thick stone that flanked it.

As they hurried toward the shadowy entrance, figures suddenly emerged from the darkness around them. Gabrielle saw the faint glint of moonlight on naked blades as the figures closed in and a harsh voice demanded, "Lay down your swords, you bastards!"

"I think not," Lord Gwydion responded, his voice dripping with disdain. "We can kill all of you without trouble, so I think I must insist that you lay your weapons down, instead."

"Lay them down, I said," the leader of the shadowy figures insisted, but Gabrielle heard a distinct hesitation in her voice. The deep shadows made it difficult to be sure, but Gabrielle could see no more than six figures surrounding them.

Whose soldiers are they? Gabrielle wondered. The silhouettes sported helmets and spears that looked as if they were the same as she had seen every day since she had moved into the Silver Keep, standing constant guard in every hallway, but Duke Campbell's soldiers appeared little different, even in the light. *Let us find out,* she decided.

"I believe you mean, 'lay them down, Your Majesty'," she declared in her most regal voice, rich with encouraged accent.

Steel rustled around the circle of figures as the soldiers glanced at each other, and Gabrielle swore she saw their weapons sag.

"Your Majesty?" the leader of the soldiers asked, her voice hesitant and baffled.

"Sir…?" Gabrielle asked.

"Sir Geraldine Carollan, Your Majesty." The knight dropped to a knee.

"Geraldine?" Lady Rowenna asked the knight hesitantly.

"Lady Rowenna?"

"Yes, it's me. I hardly recognized you, you've grown up so much…" Lady Rowenna paused, awkward for the first time in Gabrielle's memory. "… how is Gérard?"

"He is well, your Ladyship. I'm so sorry I didn't recognize you, your Ladyship, Your Majesty. Please forgive me."

"There is nothing to forgive," Gabrielle said kindly. "Stand, and tell us, is the Small Gate still safe?"

"Yes, Your Majesty." The knight climbed to her feet with a creak of metal against metal. "We've been here since the alarm bells rang, and no one has passed save for a healer and some stewards carrying away two wounded soldiers. They were the ones that told us we were betrayed by Duke Campbell. Is it true, Your Majesty?"

"Yes, it is," Gabrielle replied. *Five soldiers and a knight who sounds as young as I am… not the most inspiring of armies.* "Send two soldiers through the tunnel, as fast as they can, to make sure the far end is safe, Sir Geraldine. We will follow as soon as they have departed."

"All of us, Your Majesty?"

"Yes. We must remain free to rally the loyal lords to us. That begins tonight by fleeing, though it stabs cruelly to say it."

"Yes, Your Majesty," the knight agreed, and she quickly gave orders to scout the tunnel.

Gabrielle refused to glance backward as she passed the steel portcullis and entered the tunnel. Steep stairs descended into freezing darkness and Gabrielle stepped cautiously, her hand pressed firmly against the rough stone wall as her toes sought out the next step. The soldiers lit lanterns as soon as they felt the light would be shielded from the entrance, and they moved more quickly after that.

The stairs finally disgorged into a small tunnel, roughly hewn from the raw stone of the mountain. The lantern's light glistened on shards of bright stone buried in the grey rock, sparkling as if the bare surface was covered in frost. The tunnel was barely wide enough for two to walk abreast, and Gabrielle feared for Lord Gwydion's head against the low ceiling.

The tunnel exited through a small, fortified tower that overlooked the plateau on which the Silver Keep stood. It was ungarrisoned now, its iron gates unbarred, and they swung open easily, allowing the group access to the concealed switch-back path that led the short distance to the plateau.

The Silver Keep rose serenely above them, its white walls shining in the moonlight. No sign of the chaos and death within leaked from behind its stone façade and Gabrielle wondered if some strange Device had transported them through time, to a more peaceful night when her soldiers were not dying upon the swords of their trusted allies.

THE MARTYR'S TEARS

Her miniscule retinue crossed to the wide road that led to the New City, and the idyllic deceit was shattered. Black smoke, thick with whirling ash, roiled upward from a blaze that licked greedily at the base of the cliff beneath the Keep, and cries and screams carried faintly to Gabrielle. Torches swarmed in the roads, dancing rivers of flickering light that clustered around the fires, and bells rang in confusion and alarm from hundreds of towers, an unending cacophony that echoed from the valley walls.

Whitebrooke

Lightning flared across the sky, for an instant revealing the heaving, white-flecked surface of Loughliath below and the heavy coils of boiling, black clouds above. Thick curtains of rain connected the wind-swept water and the churning sky, shining like silk in the lightning's glare. Then the lightning faded and the night fell back into a deeper darkness than before the recent illumination. Rain lashed against Whitebrooke's face as if the stinging drops were angered by being momentarily revealed. The savage wind hurled the drops like flung stones that struck painfully against his exposed skin.

The tower perched on the northern side of Bandirma, halfway up the sheer cliff. An ancient watchtower, it was completely abandoned, its iron doors locked and sealed for centuries. The top of the small tower was only a few steps across and littered with the detritus of long abandonment. Crumbled rock from the cliff face above piled against the back wall and clogged drains had turned the floor into a lake of thick mud, save for a few islands near a crack in the parapet through which the water could escape.

Whitebrooke ignored the rain and his soaked robes and gripped the parapet in front of him with his powerful hands as if he wished to tear the stones free from their crumbling mortar.

A new era of the Temple. Whitebrooke thought bitterly. *A vision of eternal life, freedom from the curse of death. I had but to reach out and claim it and cast aside those who cling to the lies of the past.*

How has it come to this? I am a fugitive within my own Temple, hounded by lesser men of no vision, and all I have striven for has slipped through my fingers.

He cursed and shoved himself away from the parapet. He had hoped the lash of the freezing rain and the sizzling dance of the lightning would scour away the despair that dragged at his every step, but the storm's violence only heightened his sense of helpless fury.

Whitebrooke left the roof of the tower by way of a narrow staircase that wound into its depths, dark and crumbling so that each step invited disaster. The current residents of the tower, flocks of starlings that filled the old embrasures with their nests and covered the stairs with their droppings, fluttered madly about Whitebrooke's head as he descended, driven mad by the storm. He cursed at the birds, but he was not free of them until he reached the small chamber at the tower's base.

The cracked surface of the floor had been brushed clear of dirt and debris in a wide circle. The rain had blown through a wide gap in the outer wall where the chamber ended in a plunge to the gale-lashed surface of Loughliath. A dark puddle had formed there, extending wavering fingers into the room along the seams between stones, but the rest of the floor was dry, and showed the chalk outlines of a dozen fuil crunor rituals, the scribbled explorations of a talented mind gradually understanding the complex, jagged patterns.

In the center of the floor a small ring of symbols was drawn in the crusted brown of dried blood, a crowning achievement of insight and brilliant reasoning that still astounded Whitebrooke.

Yet the patterns gave him no comfort, and only served to remind him of what had been lost. The *Sanguinarium*, safe in its stone chamber, protected, yet it might as well have been the bait at the center of a snare, watched by hunters eager to catch a glimpse of their prey.

They were foolish enough to trust Reverend Ail to keep the Martyr's Blade safe, but dare I risk that they are as careless a second time, when it comes to guarding the archives?

He scowled at the simple ritual in the center of the floor. He had mastered much more complex rituals, yet he knew he had barely begun the ascent to the heights of power the *Sanguinarium* could teach him.

There is no choice, he realized. *I must have it. It is worth any risk. The only question is, when? When do I dare the archives?*

The lives he had taken from his fellow prisoners were long spent, used to overwhelm the Wards placed around the Martyr's Blade. The last dregs he had crafted into a demon of shadow, left to conceal his theft of the Blade for as long as the demon could kill those who came seeking it. It had seemed an ingenious plan, at the moment, but he now regretted it. A demon would have been a useful ally in negotiating whatever trap awaited him in the archives.

But there were equal risks in waiting while he prepared another ritual. There was no ready supply of sacrifices waiting in their cells, or dutifully arriving at his summons. No squads of soldiers rushing to their death, and no wight to feed on them, if there were.

And Whitebrooke would have to prepare the ritual and gather the victims alone. Neither Sir Cathan nor Vaughn had arrived at the tower. He was not surprised that Vaughn did not appear. The soldier had been driven insane long before Whitebrooke had left him, and there was no chance he would be anything but a feral, vicious animal by now. *Little different from when I first saw him,* Whitebrooke decided, his lip twisting in a sneer.

But Cathan's absence irked him. *How could he have failed such a simple task? I could use his brutality, but I need an acolyte of Meara's ability now, more than ever.*

Still, none of them were here, and lingering while he waited for some unlucky chance to reveal the sealed-away path to the abandoned tower accomplished nothing.

THE MARTYR'S TEARS

Again, there is no choice. I must trust, as ever, in my own hands. Whatever Nesta and those simpletons thrust in my path I shall deal with, and if I can reach the stone chamber, I will have my wight to aid me.

Whitebrooke strode to the door and unlatched it. The ancient steel groaned and scraped as he dragged it open, revealing a narrow stairwell that dove into the heart of the hill.

The stairs led into a little-used passageway far from the noise and lights of the main temple, but Whitebrooke proceeded cautiously nonetheless. He slipped from shadow to shadow, waiting patiently for distant voices to pass from his hearing before proceeding, until he reached a passage that gave him sight of the archive's wide doors. To his surprise, no soldiers guarded them, and they stood invitingly open.

Is Maeglin such a fool as to leave the archives unwatched? Perhaps he has searched them and found that I was not there, or perhaps he thought I would not dare return. Or, perhaps, it is a trap.

Whitebrooke strode to the doors and through them, his hand on the pommel of the great Blade at his side. But there were no cries of alarm at his appearance. The cavernous reading room was deserted, swathed in shadow with heavy drapes pulled across the windows against the storm.

He hurried along the upper floor. A smaller staircase at the end of the room gave him access to the lower floor and from there the door that led to the stacks.

Once he was safely inside the cluttered labyrinth, he found and lit one of the small lanterns that were kept there. Its tiny beam fluttered across stacks of books and gleamed from polished wood and metal as he strode down the tight passageways, following a twisting path that would have appeared goalless to one who did not know the stacks as well as the Archivist did. His steps quickly led him to a heavy steel door set into the far wall of the stacks, and here, again, Whitebrooke paused and listened patiently for any sign of guards. There were none, and he deftly opened the door with a quick Word that slipped from his mind as easily as breathing.

Beyond the door lay the wide, curved stairs that led to the hidden heart of the archives. Landing after landing he passed, each one silent and still in the shadows, each one sealed by an armored door locked by steel and Device.

He halted for a moment above the last landing, straining his ears for any sound that he was not alone. But there was no light, no faint clink of metal on stone, no cough or sigh, and when he, at last, crept down the last curve of the stairs, he found himself on an empty landing, facing a stone door that gaped open before him.

Whitebrooke stepped through the doorway and stopped. On the far side of the antechamber, a ragged hole gaped open where the second door once stood. A dim light came from beyond it, enough to show him that the stone around the hole was blistered and scorched, and there were bodies heaped on the floor in front of it.

He stepped cautiously forward. A foul smell filled the air. Here was the wight that he had left to guard his sanctuary, horribly burned so that it was barely recognizable as more than blackened flesh. A dozen steps brought him to the opening, and at this range, he could see that the door had been sundered by some powerful Weapon.

What could have…

Whitebrooke stepped through the gap into the stone chamber beyond, and his shoulders slumped.

The light in the chamber came from a lantern placed on the floor in front of the pedestal. Its light was bright enough that he could see, even from the doorway, that only a charred mass now rested where he had reverently placed one of the most glorious books ever written. Whitebrooke approached the pedestal slowly, his mind reeling in disbelief. *How could they have destroyed such a relic? Who would…*

Whitebrooke brushed the remains of the *Sanguinarium* with a gentle finger.

A creak of leather sounded from the thick darkness in the back of the chamber, and Whitebrooke whirled to face it. Footsteps sounded, slow and purposeful, the hard soles of heavy boots against stone, and a figure emerged from the shadows, his armor gleaming in the faint light of the lantern.

THE MARTYR'S TEARS

"You had your Blade, you could have tried to leave, but you didn't," Sir Maeglin said. "Why do you need this book?"

Whitebrooke gingerly turned the charred pages, and they cracked and turned to ash between his fingers.

"It is not just a book, Maeglin. These were Lazarre's words, every pattern, every structure, a life-time's work. A Grandmaster like no other, an adept like no other. Can you conceive of the secrets this book contained?"

"That's it? Research?"

"No," Whitebrooke sighed, and let the ashes slip through his fingers. "I needed the rituals it contained. A few I have mastered, but many more are still beyond me."

Maeglin laughed harshly.

Whitebrooke considered the knight cautiously. Blood soaked his face and neck from a long cut across his jaw, and a deep wound in his throat glistened darkly. Blood shone in a wide swathe on the steel plates over his ribs and hip. Maeglin's stance was slightly twisted, favoring that side, and his left arm was pressed against his ribs, his hand wedged into his belt. But most intriguing were the livid welts along his neck, a web of inflamed skin that crept onto the Knight Commander's cheeks. *His body has already been beaten, tonight. I wonder if his will has survived?*

"I am not the only one to have suffered a defeat this night," Whitebrooke offered magnanimously. "There is no need for us to be at each other's throats. We want the same future, a strong Temple, a Temple led by people of power and vision, who need not bow to the mewling of petty queens and weak-minded priests."

"Ahhh, I wondered if it would be offered." Maeglin's mouth twisted into a smile. "Did you give Benno the same speech?"

"I did. Benno was a man of quality, and I took no pleasure in his refusal. He chose to follow the lies of his false god, but I wished it otherwise."

"Who else? Lady Danielle, I suppose. I can guess what she said, as you ordered her death."

'*I see you have forgotten your wife.*' Danielle's voice mocked him mercilessly, but Whitebrooke stared defiantly at the scars on the back of his hand. *Never. Not even for a moment.* "What does it matter?"

"I know Sir Cathan said yes, but he's dead." Maeglin shook his head sadly, but his eyes were cold. "Didn't die well, either. I know your little disciple said yes, but she's in the dungeon. Has anyone else joined you? It sounds nice, 'people of power'… but, are there any?"

"You mock me," Whitebrooke snarled.

"I was hoping to make my life easier as I hunted down all of your pathetic followers. But it appears that I already have, doesn't it? It's a list of one, and he's standing in front of me, all alone, no great leader of a new age, after all."

"I do not stand alone. My lord is the Nameless King, his servants are the magi, and there are none who can stand against them."

"Except, you've lost your book," Maeglin pointed out. "I thought you needed that?"

Whitebrooke scowled, enraged at the knight's defiance. "You gloat over others' work, and claim to be their equal, but you are not."

"I will gladly clean the privies if it means I can flush you down the drain," Maeglin spat back.

Whitebrooke's hand grabbed the pommel of the Blade at his side, and he stepped toward the knight. But he stopped suddenly at what he saw.

Maeglin held his sword motionless, as straight as a shaft of sun pointed at Whitebrooke's chest, his stance balanced and strong. "Please," the Knight Commander urged.

"I think not." Whitebrooke released the Blade and gathered his robes around him. *His will endures… remarkable.*

"That's a shame," Maeglin smiled. "I thought I was going to cross that last name from my list."

"You will not have that pleasure." Whitebrooke settled his arms across his chest and sneered at the knight. "I told you, I do not stand alone."

Maeglin's eyes narrowed an instant before they widened with pain and shock. A blade of shadow erupted from his chest, and the Knight Commander cried out and dropped to his knees, struggling to pull free. Shadow curled around the knight like smoke and whispered in his ear, and his sword clanged on the stones as his fingers lost their strength. Maeglin collapsed to the floor, his eyes staring dully at the stone in front of them.

"My lord." Whitebrooke bowed low.

The King's shade emerged from the darkness and lingered over Maeglin's form. The shade wavered amongst the shifting shadows that cloaked it, a transient presence hardly more substantive than the gaps in mist, but when the lantern's steady light fell on it, the shade's black shape was unaffected and stood in sharp contrast to the thinner shadows behind it.

It slowly drew away from the body, crumpled in its blood-stained armor, and approached Whitebrooke, its steps silent, shadow streaming from it like smoke in the wind. Whitebrooke waited for its touch, but the shade passed him and approached the charred remains of the *Sanguinarium*.

"They destroyed Lazarre's book, my King." Whitebrooke rose and faced the shade. "The rituals are lost."

"Not lost," the shade whispered, and Whitebrooke shivered as ice dripped down his spine. "Merely hidden from you."

"Yes, my King." Whitebrooke bowed. "I am sorry. What shall I do?"

"Do? You will swallow the bitter taste of your failure."

"Centuries of belief in a lie are not so easily overcome," Whitebrooke muttered as a small flame of anger stirred against the frozen touch of the King's words. *So close… a slip of damn parchment, and the misfortune of having it flutter directly into Nesta's withered grasp. That is all… where was aid, when I needed it?*

"You are not my only servant. While you have let all we achieved here slip through your fingers, I have freed the most powerful of my magi from imprisonment. It is disappointing that you were not as successful."

"Yes, my lord, yet they have won but a small skirmish, when I was alone and they were many. Still I tore their false god away from them and freed you. When they realize that truth, they will no longer praise themselves, but will curse their failure."

Whitebrooke scowled as a note of sullen defiance spoiled the resonate note of his delivery.

"Perhaps. At least you have managed to regain the Martyr's Blade. Her loss would be unforgivable. You must bring the Blade to me, immediately."

"Flee?" Whitebrooke could not help but frown thunderously at the news.

"You are displeased with my command?"

"It galls me to leave, to run from these dogs as if they had defeated us. If they will not join us, they should be destroyed! Smother them with shadow, consume them all, my lord, and let their precious Temple become a throne worthy of you, worthy of your priests." Whitebrooke grinned savagely. He gripped the long hilt of the Martyr's Blade fiercely and twisted it in his hand. "Or let me burn them away. Scour the halls with fire and leave nothing but ash. No one will deny us, then. They will fall to their knees in the soot and beg to worship us."

"She is not for you, priest. She is mine," the shade hissed, and Whitebrooke shivered as tendrils of shadow brushed against him and he felt the touch of the endless abyss. But within the shadow, there was a flash of memory, a dream of flame curling between lips as a voice spat fierce denial. *'I am not for you, priest'... she said the same...*

"What is this?" The shade's voice scraped across the chamber's stone, and its shadow curled around Whitebrooke, so suddenly he had only the chance to flinch uselessly away as its touch enveloped him. "She has spoken to you, and you dare to conceal this from me."

"No..." Whitebrooke groaned. His bones ached as ice slithered deep into his limbs, and he sank to a knee, teeth grinding as he strained to remain upright. "I did not know... it was a dream..."

"You fool." The voice crept through Whitebrooke, a whisper that seemed to lurk deep within his mind as much as it brushed against his ears.

"Who is she?" he gasped, refusing to bend any lower, though the stone floor wavered and swam in his darkening vision.

"She is mine," the shade repeated. For an endless instant more Whitebrooke shuddered under the frozen touch of the shade, then the shadowy figure swirled away and returned to the remains of the *Sanguinarium*, leaving the priest to push himself slowly to his feet as the burning cold slowly leeched from his body.

"You have seen your fate if you try to possess her," the shade whispered, and Whitebrooke clenched his curled fingers into fists as he remembered the vision of them burning to charred stumps as her flame spread over them. Yet, the golden light of the fire was beautiful, its heat an ecstasy as it flared white hot.

He shook his head, forcing thought through numbing ice and smothering heat. "She is the Blade? But, I have commanded it, before, and it did not burn me."

The shade sighed like wind rasping over the icy crust of ancient snow. "You are a fool. You mistake the shadow for the shape that formed it, the light for the fire that cast it."

Deep lines furrowed Whitebrooke's bristling brow as he ran his thumb gently over the tapered pommel of the Blade. *Not the Blade, but the fire…* His gaze fell to the back of his hand and the three scars that gleamed there amidst the black hair, and he clenched it until his knuckles turned white.

"I will not lick my wounds!" he snarled. "If all else is lost, then I will take what risks remain. The *Sanguinarium* is gone. I am to bring you the Blade. Where, then, is my vision, your promise, life immortal? I will not abandon it so easily." He stared at the white scars, mocking him with their clarity. "Where is Aislin? She was shown to me in my dream… can the Blade tear the shroud and release her?"

The shade faced Whitebrooke and for a moment the priest felt that he stared into a pit that disappeared into endless darkness, and he feared he would fall. But the vertigo passed and he felt the shade's frozen touch withdraw.

"Perhaps I have misjudged you," the shade said soothingly. "Perhaps you are ready to be taught the Word of Life."

"What? I…" Whitebrooke stilled his mouth and frowned, taken aback by the sudden turn of the conversation. But he could not deny the stir of excitement that smothered the anger that had flared so brightly a moment before. "Yes, I am ready. Show me, my lord."

"It is not an easy thing to master. Only twelve have ever done so, although hundreds have tried."

"And when I master it, I will be able to destroy the curse of mortality?"

"You will, although it is not so simple as to merely train your mind to speak the Word, as if it were no more than a Device. It is that and also fuil crunor, ritual and Device, together, the epitome of both in power and intricacy."

"I do not understand."

"Few have. Those that do not are destroyed by the teaching of it. Do you still wish to be shown the Word?"

"Yes."

"Good."

"And the shroud?"

"Bring me the Blade," the shade replied. "You will need time to master that which you will be shown, tonight. When you have joined me, you will perform the Word, and I will tear the shroud with the Blade."

'... *with the Blade.*' Whitebrooke stilled his thoughts. "I am ready, then."

The Nameless King's shade billowed outward as if a strong wind blew through its midst, and deep within its shadow a form began to slowly emerge, and red eyes were revealed. Whitebrooke felt frozen air rush around him, so cold that it must have come from a place so deep that the sun's warmth had never penetrated to it.

The shadow slowly pulled apart and disgorged a towering figure. Its terrible shape loomed over Whitebrooke as he stepped away in fear. Its red eyes pulsed from within a tall helm of blackened steel, crowned with jagged spikes, and it wore ancient armor covered in twisted runes. The figure was wrapped in a cloak of swirling shadows, but within it, Whitebrooke could see its flesh was blackened and burnt.

THE MARTYR'S TEARS

Whitebrooke stumbled against the pedestal. His stomach churned as the gaze of the red eyes found him, and the stone under his boots seemed to bow and stretch. He sought frantically for the door, but the figure stood between the priest and escape.

A sound came from within the steel helm as if a razor were dragged across rough stone, and Whitebrooke realized the figure laughed.

"Whitebrooke," the magus rasped, "do you fear me? You have called to me, you have begged to join me, yet now you tremble like a child."

"Who are you?"

"I am Lazarre, first of the magi."

Whitebrooke gaped at the corrupted figure before him. He had felt the chilling touch of a magus before, through the rituals he had created to summon it, but he had never dreamed of the hideous strength of the presence that towered over him now. *It says it is Lazarre... can it have once been a man?*

"I am here to teach you, priest," Lazarre's voice seeped like smoke from his helm. "To show you the Word of Life, so that you may join us."

Whitebrooke groped for a reply, but his throat would not utter a sound, and his heart labored in his chest. He could not take his gaze from Lazarre's blackened, corrupted flesh and the oily shadows that leached from it. Whitebrooke's throat filled with sour bile, and he choked.

"Do you fear to join with us? Shall I tear your gift from you instead?" The magus stepped toward him.

"No!" Whitebrooke recoiled, and forced himself to meet Lazarre's gaze. "The King judged me ready to be taught the Word of Life, and I shall earn eternity with it."

"Perhaps. Or perhaps you will fail, and I shall consume your flicker."

"You shall not!" Whitebrooke clutched at the hilt of the Blade.

The magus laughed again, but it drew no closer. "Did not our Lord instruct you that the Blade was his? He will feast on her.

He will eat her fire and at last satiate his hunger… and you wish to deny him this?"

"No, he shall have it."

"Good, for there would be no mercy from him," the magus rasped, "nor from me." In one swift step the magus closed with the priest, and a hand covered in ancient steel enclosed Whitebrooke's throat.

Whitebrooke shouted in terror as the magus' shadow enveloped him and the cold of the crypt washed over him. He staggered away from Lazarre and sprawled to the stone floor, flailing as he crawled from the nightmare that loomed over him. He had reached the doorway before he realized that the magus did not follow. The priest clutched at his throat, which burned as if a collar of molten metal had been fastened around his neck, but his fingers found no wound, and as he gazed, unbelieving, at his fingertips, he slowly realized that there had been no touch from Lazarre's grip, no dreadful strangulation. Only cold.

Whitebrooke climbed to his feet and controlled the trembling that had overcome his hands. He forced himself to examine the magus more closely, though his every fiber urged him to flee. Shadow streamed from Lazarre like smoke to form a boiling cloak around him, but Whitebrooke realized that it was not just the cloak that was shadow. The magus itself wavered and grew translucent as if its edges were ink blotted with water.

"You are not here," Whitebrooke gasped.

"No," Lazarre agreed. "Our King merely shows you my shape. Count yourself fortunate, priest, for if I were to stand before you, you would fall to the ground and beg me to end your suffering, and I would do so without hesitation."

Whitebrooke found defiance in the feel of the Blade's pommel against his fingers. "We will see."

"Then prove your worth, and join us. But do not come before me clothed as a worm and expect mercy. Now, listen to the Word of Life."

The magus exhaled, and with its breath came darkness and light, intertwined in a Word beyond anything Whitebrooke could have imagined. His mind screamed as the Word flooded it, a wave of fire that threatened to shatter his skull. He clutched at his head and sank to his knees, but the Word continued to grow, until he wondered if it had no end, and despaired.

But, at last, he became aware of freezing air upon his neck, and the odor of decay, and slowly his senses brought him back. He sprawled in the center of the fuil crunor ritual that he had carved into the chamber floor.

Whitebrooke groaned and rolled slowly to his hands and knees, to be greeted by Lazarre's rasping voice.

"Your mind survived."

Whitebrooke was not sure if there was respect or disappointment in the magus' words, or merely disdain. He struggled to his feet, his thoughts whirling with the Word he had been shown. *A Word crafted from ritual… a Device empowered by fuil crunor… a ritual encapsulated by a Device…* His mind ached with the overwhelming intricacy of the Word of Life, its arcane depths seeming to grow ever more complex the more he sought to focus on them.

And yet, the shining patterns of light resonated with an echo of the familiar. *They are similar to the Word of the Martyr's Blade,* he realized. *What could link these two Devices, that their Words are cousins?*

Whitebrooke snarled with the effort of dragging his thoughts back to the stone chamber, as if he fought off a blow to the head.

"Yes," he forced through lips that felt too clumsy for normal speech, let alone shaping part of a Word. "I told you I would."

"Many have boasted the same. Few have survived the teaching. Fewer still have survived the speaking of the Word of Life. Save your boasts for when you join the magi. Until then, you are a worm, and you must burrow deep until you are safe from the sharp beaks of those who pursue you. Burrow until you come to our Grave, and lay the Blade at our King's feet. But do not take too long. Our Lord desires the Blade, and I will not be so merciful when he sends me to you the next time."

"It will come to no harm, I swear it."

"Harm? You are truly a fool if you think the Blade can be unmade as if it had been cast in a blacksmith's forge. Now go, worm." Shadow swirled and then stilled, and Whitebrooke felt the magus' terrible presence recede and dissipate.

Whitebrooke's stomach churned and he retched until his fingers clutched at the stone floor in desperate need for breath. The sour stink of nausea oozed around him, and his body heaved again, but there was nothing left in him, nothing to join the foul puddle beneath his face but the drip of thick mucus. At last, Whitebrooke could breathe, a bubbling, choking gasp that shook his heavy frame and squeezed tears of rage and shame from his eyes.

He slowly climbed to his feet and straightened his robes, settling the cloth on his wide shoulders and carefully smoothing the heavy embroidery. He spat the sour taste from his mouth, and ran thick fingers through his hair and beard.

Then he drew the Martyr's Blade. The long Weapon rang sweetly as its tip cleared the sheath, and Whitebrooke gazed at the hilt, brushing its spread wings of elegant metal with his thumb, tracing the line of engravings along its blade with his finger as his thoughts stilled and his mind found focus.

"Who is she?" he murmured. *Not the Blade, but the fire... not the light, but the fire that cast it. And so precious to them.* That thought was as clear as ink on fresh parchment. *Bring me the Blade, or I shall destroy you... bring me the Blade, or it will burn you... put the Blade aside, and I will show you the Word of Life... bring me the Blade, and I will tear the shroud.*

He gripped the hilt with both hands and watched the lantern's light gleam from deep swirls of metal on the surface of the Blade. Then he sheathed it and drew his robes tight around it, satisfied with the pressure of its hilt tucked beneath his arm.

His glance caught the remains of the *Sanguinarium*, and he paused to frown at the charred pages. He could only see Lazarre's blackened, cracked skin as he looked at it, and he could find no trace of the loss he had so recently felt at the book's destruction. He cleared more bile from his throat and spat on the page, then shoved the book violently from the pedestal. It crashed to the floor and shattered, bursting apart into ash and blackened flakes as the twisted bindings rang and bounced.

"She is mine," he whispered.

He strode from the chamber and mounted the stairs, but halted on a landing only a few flights above. The thick door released on a whispered Word and the Archivist stepped into a long corridor lined with small alcoves, each containing a treasure of the Temple displayed on a pedestal.

Whitebrooke hurried to the end of the corridor, ignoring ancient tomes, ivory handled scrolls, engraved weapons, and peerless sculptures. At the end of the corridor was a small, open space, with three chests made of wood, steel, and silver, seated upon low platforms of stone, each more ornate than the previous. All were engraved with an ornate crest depicting a broken chain, the sigil of Saint Rowenna. He selected the wooden chest and passed his hand over its carved top as he whispered its Word. Thick latches withdrew with a muffled clunk and the lid swung open under the lightest of touches.

Whitebrooke reached into the chest and withdrew the single Device within from its silken nest. He turned it back and forth and watched the light of his lantern glimmer on its black gem. He tucked it into a pocket deep within his robes, but examination of the Device had stirred his thoughts, and his gaze dropped to the hilt of the long Blade at his side.

They offer me immortality for it, a reward I have craved, to be sure, but I realize now, that prize falls short. I see the truth of it in the Word they revealed to me. An eternity of consuming the gifts of others to survive. That is not conquering death, it is feasting upon it. And yet they boast that only twelve have achieved it… that is twelve too many to share my destiny with. I count my fate to be higher than that, to lead humanity into an age of true immortality, not to stand in the shadows with a dozen who have settled for so much less. And to do that… to do that I must tear the shroud.

Whitebrooke retrieved a second Device from its pedestal as he hurried from the chamber. The Weapon's leather grip fit snugly in his hand, and its small, snake-shaped guard coiled around his fingers. There was no blade of any kind, just the gaping mouth of the viper and its fangs, but that was all it required.

He sealed the door behind him and mounted the steps, his strength returning with each stride. *There is still a path that leads to my vision for a new Temple. I shall stand at its head in glory. But it is not the one the Nameless King envisioned, with me a corrupted servant in his shadow.* Whitebrooke laughed grimly under his breath as he climbed. *Whatever power resides in this Blade, it will be mine. Power to tear the shroud, and release humanity from its imprisonment. Lazarre and the King think that I am helpless, that I have no choice but to hand over the Blade. That she will burn me if I dare to unleash her fire.*

They are wrong... I know where her fire was first tamed.

Once beyond the archives, he moved more cautiously, choosing little-used paths in the farthest reaches of the temple to climb higher and higher, away from the bright lanterns and scurrying soldiers and toward the gardens that crowned the hill. A final staircase took him to a small, locked door, its thick wood braced by iron bands. Whitebrooke twisted the latch free and shouldered his way through the door, forcing its warped shape open with a shriek of metal on stone.

Rain lashed against Whitebrooke's face through the doorway, soaking his beard and streaming from his hair, and he squinted against its stinging touch. He was drenched again after a few steps, and his robes clung wetly to his skin. Whitebrooke pressed on, uncaring, letting his robes slap against his legs in the wind. His path skirted the gardens, dark and deserted where tidy trees and shrubs twisted and thrashed in the storm, but he soon left them behind and followed a trail around the flooded lake and through the farmlands beyond.

A farmhouse loomed from the rain without warning. Its windows were shuttered and dark, and beyond it, nothing but an endless chasm, filled with curtains of slashing rain. For a moment, Whitebrooke feared he had found the wrong building. There was no sign of any inhabitants, no sign of any guards, but Whitebrooke realized that there would not be.

'Do you not know where we are?' Maeglin's gloating voice echoed in Whitebrooke's memory. *I do, thanks to you, Knight Commander. The Geata Thoir, the fabled East Gate. Thank you for revealing its location*

to me, although I did not guess, at the time, that I should have occasion to use it, myself.

Whitebrooke could vividly remember the heavy, steel door that Danielle had somehow opened during her own escape, as well as Maeglin's didactic recounting of the keys required to open it.

Whitebrooke unsheathed the Martyr's Blade and strode to the farmhouse door. He paused there and his hand closed around the grip of the snake-headed Device and drew it from his robes. Its two small sapphire eyes gleamed coldly in the rain as Whitebrooke prepared its Word. It was a simple Word, for the Device was a simple one in its effect, but it was powerful in its focus. Whitebrooke formed the Word quickly and spoke it to the Weapon, and its bindings clicked open.

Whitebrooke heard a shout from within the house and knew they had felt the Word. His boot took care of the simple latch that held the door, and he leapt through even as the door was crashing against its frame.

Four soldiers were in the room. Two were seated at a rough table in the center, polishing gear that had been neatly laid upon the table's surface. A third crouched next to the small stove, a lump of coal held in the tongs in her hand. The fourth had nearly reached the door, and his hand was on the hilt of his sword.

Whitebrooke swung the Blade at the nearest of the soldiers in a flat arc. The soldier tried to draw his sword, but he was far too late, and the Blade's heavy edge tore through the soldier's arm and raked across his abdomen, sending him staggering backward as blood sprayed across the floorboards.

The other soldiers came to their feet in a rush. The two at the table quickly snatched up the weapons they had been polishing, so Whitebrooke attacked them first. He raised the snake-headed Weapon and its power flared. There was a sharp crack of sound and blue sparks showered from the chest of one of the soldiers. He screamed and arced backward over the table, scattering the cups and daggers and buckles that covered it as he thrashed to the floor.

Whitebrooke brought the Weapon to bear on the third soldier, and again the viper spoke sharply, with the snap of a great whip, and the soldier dropped as if felled by a club.

The last soldier sprinted toward Whitebrooke, her sword raised high. He twisted to face her and swept the Blade to meet her attack, but she was too quick and her edge ripped through his robe and sliced into the flesh of his shoulder. Whitebrooke bellowed and slammed the viper-headed Weapon into her chest and twisted its Word. Lightning flashed and she was hurled away from him, crashed into a thick pillar that supported the roof, and slumped to the floor.

The soldier that Whitebrooke had cut with the Blade still thrashed on the ground, moaning in agony, and Whitebrooke silenced him with a quick thrust, then winced as pain stabbed from his wounded shoulder.

Whitebrooke pulled his robes away from his shoulder and cursed as he saw the long gash the soldier's sword had left behind. Blood flowed freely from the cut, and a throbbing ache was already beginning to pound from the wound, which Whitebrooke knew would soon turn to burning agony. Whitebrooke ground his teeth and tried to lift his arm, then cursed again as pain washed through him.

Damn me for being careless. Whitebrooke stalked to the soldier who had wounded him, gripping the hilt of the Blade in fury. But she was dead already. Wisps of smoke rose from twisted patterns of blackened skin, and with it came the smell of burnt flesh. Whitebrooke stared at her, breathing hard, then spat in her upturned face and watched the spittle gleam against her unseeing eye. *Damn you for your impudence. Just a guard who didn't know when she was supposed to die.*

Whitebrooke checked his shoulder again. It clearly needed a healer's attention, but there was no time for that. Whitebrooke pressed a wadded tunic from one of the soldier's packs against it and tried to ignore the pain.

He searched the soldiers until he found the steel key for the gate, and he helped himself to the largest of the thick winter cloaks that hung by the door. It would be a long walk, he knew, but the storm would cover his tracks, and there was no chance of being spotted by an alert sentry. *They are huddled by their fires, staring forlornly at the wavering lights of the Queen's army. They have only attention for bravado or fear, not a lone priest slipping along the shore. I must remember to thank the baron, for without him and his useless army I would be facing a much more perilous journey.*

***

The steady clop of hoofbeats echoed from jagged stone outcroppings as Whitebrooke's horse plodded up the road. The horse's nostrils gaped wide as it struggled for breath, and red-tinged foam dripped from its mouth around its bit, but Whitebrooke urged it relentlessly upward.

I am nearly there…

Whitebrooke had not halted for rest since leaving Bandirma, pushing his steed through day and night along the Rathad an Sliabh as it climbed ever higher through the hills of the Cnoic Ban. The storm had expired on the first day, leaving behind a blanket of thick mist that crawled from the surface of Loughliath and crept through the hills. As the road climbed higher, the constant patter of wet plops as the mist dripped from the trees gave way to a thick silence as the fog draped the lichen-covered stones in a concealing blanket.

Whitebrooke shivered as a switchback in the road took them into another thick band of mist, sparking a fresh wave of nauseating pain from his shoulder. The throbbing sting of the wound had become a burning ache that pulsed the length of his arm and across his chest, and every stumbling step of his weary horse sent fresh agony through him.

The horse gained the final rise of the road and plodded into the narrow ravine that led to the doors of the Mountain. The horse's head drooped and its hooves scuffed the ground, but Whitebrooke cursed and kicked it into a trot.

The ravine widened until the rock walls became ashen grey in the mist. The twisted limbs of the few hardy pines that clawed the thin soil loomed like skeletal fingers as Whitebrooke passed. The harsh cry of a raven disturbed the silence and a flurry of wings sounded sharply within the fog.

Whitebrooke's horse snorted in fear and shied from the trail. Whitebrooke yanked on the reins as he fought for control, but the horse would not obey and staggered further away.

A shape appeared in the mist behind Whitebrooke, slipping through the thick curtains like a shadow. For a moment, the priest thought the shape no more than an eddy in the fog, but as it flowed toward him, he saw it more clearly.

The wolf was virtually silent as it padded along the trail. Its fur was dark with moisture and streaked with grey around its muzzle, and it moved with an easy lope that appeared effortless.

The wolf slowed as it came through the mist, and its grey eyes watched Whitebrooke as the horse twisted against its reins.

Whitebrooke cursed and abandoned his terrified horse. He landed heavily and staggered, and the wolf darted forward. Whitebrooke ripped the Martyr's Blade from its sheath and raised it to strike, but the wolf swerved to the side and circled away. The horse fled into the mist, and for a moment Whitebrooke thought the wolf would follow it, but the beast turned back to him, and its jaws gaped wide in a long snarl that made Whitebrooke clench the hilt of his sword.

The wolf was larger than any that he had seen, but now that it was closer, Whitebrooke could see that it, too, bore signs of a hard road traveled. Blood trickled from long scratches along the beast's legs and streaked the fur on its muzzle. A slight limp betrayed another wound to its hind leg. But it brazenly challenged Whitebrooke despite the heavy blade he held ready, and another long growl throbbed between its fangs.

Whitebrooke's lip curled into a smile. "You think I am the prey?" he spat at the wolf. Whitebrooke reached into his robes and freed the snake-headed Weapon.

The wolf appeared to sense its danger, for it hunched, ready to leap, and its snarl doubled in ferocity. Whitebrooke kept his sword poised as he prepared the Word. *Come to my blade, or wait for my Word, but I shall have your pelt for a cloak, you dog.*

Whitebrooke thrust the snake-headed Weapon toward the wolf and spoke its Word, but even as he did, a dark shape streaked from the mist behind him. Black wings slapped at Whitebrooke, and talons raked his arm, and he saw a gleaming black eye and a gaping beak. The Weapon spat lightning as the wolf leapt away, and the spark threw a shower of dirt in the air where the wolf had stood a moment before.

Whitebrooke cursed and swung his sword at the madly beating wings of the raven, but the bird fled his reach with a raucous cry.

Whitebrooke twisted to find the wolf. Its shadow streaked through the mist between the trees, and he chased it with lightning, but the beast was gone. Whitebrooke sucked air between his teeth in fury and waited with Weapon ready, but the wolf did not return.

A harsh cry startled the priest and he spun on his heel, searching for the source of the sound. The raven perched on a jagged boulder split from the canyon wall. The bird's black eyes gleamed as it watched him, and its beak gaped open as it tasted the air. It cried out again, its call echoing between the stone walls of the canyon, and then a third time, furious and harsh.

Whitebrooke watched the bird cautiously, for the raven was unnatural in its size and in the unwavering focus of its gaze. It was at least as tall as Whitebrooke's knee, and its gleaming eye followed his every move.

The bird suddenly spread its wings and plunged across the narrow canyon toward Whitebrooke. The priest threw up his hands and the bird swerved, cawing harshly as its wings slapped at his head. Sickening pain tore through Whitebrooke from his injured shoulder, and he sank to a knee, helpless to do more than watch as the raven swooped around the canyon, screaming and calling.

Whitebrooke slowly rose to his feet as the raven settled once more on its perch, croaking in triumph.

It doesn't matter, the horse will be nearby when I am finished here. Whitebrooke readied the snake-headed Device. *And I can deal with this bird right now.*

The Martyr's Tears

The raven did not linger. With a final mocking cry, it launched once more into the air, its wings churning the mist as it skimmed over the lip of the canyon and was gone.

Damn you, then, he cursed the raven. Whitebrooke breathed in fiercely, settling his pain and anger as he wrapped his robes solemnly around himself. *It was just a bird, do not let it disturb you, at this most momentous of times.*

Whitebrooke strode forward, and his steps soon brought him to the wide stone bowls that guarded the door to the Mountain and the tall gates themselves.

The doors stood open, a narrow gap that stared blackly through the grey mist. Whitebrooke paused to light a lantern, then stepped through.

The entrance chamber waited silently, its distant walls and ceiling shrouded in shadows. The bleak light from the doorway painted a narrow strip across the chamber floor. Whitebrooke walked slowly to the center of the chamber, where the stone floor was shattered in a wide circle, crumbling testimony to his duel with the Templar Rúreth.

Echoes whispered to him from far away, and a distant thunder groaned through the stone beneath his feet. Whitebrooke paused, searching the gaping mouths of the tunnels for any sign of movement, but they remained empty. Another tremor pulsed in the stone, and the sound of crumbling rock cascading to the ground filled the air.

"Dust and pebbles!" Whitebrooke shouted into the echoing, shadows. "That will not stop me."

Whitebrooke waited for some response to his challenge, but there was none, save for the shifting sigh of dirt raining down from the ceiling. He laughed and spat to clear his mouth. Sweat poured from his brow, but at last the hall was still, and he paused to retrieve the Device he had removed from the wooden chest in the archives.

A black gem the size of a walnut, smoothed and polished into a perfect sphere, was contained within thin bands of silver metal, covered in small runes and elegant patterns. The bands were crafted so that they might turn about the gem freely, and the whole was surrounded by a silver setting.

The Wardpact did not lash out at those who sought to breach it, as Whitebrooke's old Wardpact had done. Whitebrooke suspected that exquisite Device was unique in that manner, and regretted its loss. But the black gem in his hand now had protected Saint Rowenna from the snake-god of Setisthor, and Whitebrooke judged it might well be the more powerful of the two Devices.

Whitebrooke strode heavily down the passageway that led deeper into the Mountain. *Nearly there. The sanctuary chamber, then the deepest door, and beyond that the heart of the Mountain.*

Whitebrooke's lantern sent shadows arcing across the walls of the sanctuary chamber as he swung it from side to side. Bodies littered the floor, the desiccated remains of Temple soldiers, their withered flesh blackened by jagged marks and gaping wounds. But the colossal body he expected was no longer there. The ground on which it had lain was empty, the stone unmarked.

Whitebrooke paused, uncertain what its absence could mean. He raised his lantern high and slowly swept the room with its light. The chamber was empty and still, yet a presence brushed against his mind like a breath of wind and was gone before he could react. He spun again, the Blade ready, but only stone pillars and shadows faced him.

Whitebrooke strode into the chamber until his lantern revealed the great door that led deeper into the Mountain. It gaped open as if welcoming him, but Whitebrooke hesitated at its lip, listening to the echoes of his footsteps fade to nothing. The tunnel beyond the door was silent and empty, and Whitebrooke could not help but feel a thrill of excitement as he gazed down its length. *I know what lies beyond, yet its presence is still undeniable. Is it simply the strange sight of the door standing open, or do I sense something of the ancient works awaiting me at the other end?* Whitebrooke smiled grimly. *Or perhaps I feel fate building to a crux. All I have striven for is in my grasp if only I can close my fist.*

Whitebrooke settled his robes on his shoulders, and he passed through the door and into the unknown.

The Martyr's Tears

The long tunnel beyond the door curved as it descended, the walls so smooth they glistened as if they were wet. Whitebrooke pressed onward, his strides lengthening as he neared his goal.

Gradually a light appeared ahead, a glow that reflected off the walls from some source yet unseen around the curve of the tunnel. Then, incongruously, an echo of a voice singing in a strange language. Whitebrooke stopped to listen, perplexed. The voice was guttural, yet not harsh. It crooned and chanted rather than seeking pure notes, and the song was somehow rich and soothing. But the words were as foreign as the melody to Whitebrooke's ears, and he could learn nothing from listening. He moved farther down the tunnel, more cautiously now, but the singer did not seem to be aware of his approach, and the song did not waver.

At last the tunnel opened ahead of Whitebrooke. He saw a wide natural chamber filled with warm light. In the center stood an ancient tree, its arching branches filling the cavern. Its leaves shone golden in the light of a lantern at its base, as did its bark, and as the leaves shifted in some unfelt breeze the light shimmered as if it were a summer sun reflected from the surface of a lake.

But as Whitebrooke entered the chamber his attention was drawn away from the tree to a small figure who sat amongst the tree's gnarled roots. The figure's black robes were a blot against the tree's light, and his hunched form mocked the tree's grandeur. In his hands was a small box made of black wood. The box was open and the figure was singing to whatever might be inside.

Whitebrooke laughed, a booming, harsh sound with no humor in it. "I have been looking for you."

Karsha Hali let his song trail off and met the Archivist's gaze, but he did not rise from his twisted-root throne.

"Not very hard," the little man replied with a gap-filled grin. "I waited for you to leave your temple, but you took so long that I grew bored and came here instead."

"I should have known that was your work above." Whitebrooke placed his lantern on the floor of the chamber and drew the black gem into his hand. The last time he had confronted the wizard he had dispatched him easily, but he knew this time would be more of a challenge. *Only my own strength to feed the fuil crunor, so I must rely on Devices.* He began to ready the Word for his Wardpact. Its complex shape slowly began to form in his mind, each tendril shining as it fell into place.

"The spirits of the Mountain are angry," Karsha shook his head sorrowfully. "They despise the corruption you brought into their midst. They feel the pain of the rift you created. They know the touch of the black shadow. No, it was not my work. I merely sang them the song of awakening, so that they might greet you when you arrived."

"Whatever you did, it failed. Noise and dust will not stop me, nor will your beasts and birds." Whitebrooke moved warily into the chamber, vigilant. Nothing stirred in the room, and Whitebrooke wondered if the wizard had finally run out of tricks.

"We shall see. The story is not over, yet," Karsha cackled.

"No?" Whitebrooke growled. "You have something in that box that you think will save you?"

"This?" Karsha glanced at the box in his hands as if he had forgotten it existed. He turned it over and then presented it to Whitebrooke. "No, this is empty. It is a nice box, though. It is made from the wood of the xexak tree. You have heard of this tree? No?" Karsha tutted in disappointment. "It is a great tree, found only in the deepest jungles. Each xexak tree has a spirit that guards it, so none can ever be felled. But if the tree dies, the spirit remains in the wood, so it is the strongest wood. Of course, because of this, it is difficult to craft, so extremely rare."

"You seek to stop me with an empty box?" Whitebrooke scoffed. He searched again for the trick that the wizard must be readying for him, but there was no sign of it. No Words, no swirling spirits, just a tiny man, and a small, empty box.

"Ha!" Karsha cackled again. "Would you be frightened of such a thing? I did not think so. No, a box of xexak wood can hold things that are far too powerful for normal wood, or even metal, or stone."

THE MARTYR'S TEARS

"And you have such a powerful thing in your box?" Whitebrooke strode toward the wizard, the Blade raised, the Word for his Wardpact at last ready to be spoken.

"No, it is empty, as I said." The wizard shook his head sadly as he once again showed the Archivist the box. "I set Nharghrod free while you were still upstairs."

Something stirred in the shadows behind Whitebrooke and he froze. A predatory hunger leaked into the room, primal and merciless. Whitebrooke twisted to face it. A vast shape slipped through the shadows of the room as if they were tall grass, and yellow eyes returned his gaze. Behind the eyes stretched a long body, sinuous and powerful with muscles rippling along its length, a deep orange covered in black stripes. Beneath the eyes white fangs, as long as Whitebrooke's hand, gleamed in front of a red tongue.

Whitebrooke shouted his Word as the shape flowed toward him and his Device exploded into motion. The shape struck at him, faster than thought, and pain flooded his mind as his Wardpact strained and tore. He lashed out desperately with the Martyr's Blade, but it was swept aside in a tremendous blow that ripped it from his hand and sent it tumbling across the floor. Whitebrooke screamed as long claws tore his flesh. The terrible fangs fastened around his skull and agony flared for an endless heartbeat.

THE MARTYR'S TEARS

Ranald

Sir Ranald strode down the long curve of the street, his boots splashing in the puddles that had collected amongst the cobbles during the long, misty afternoon. Grey clouds hung thickly in the valley that held Kuray, as if the city was unwilling to give up the memory of the smoke that had filled it, only days ago.

Wide stones had been laid down the center of the road for drainage, and the trickle of water along that channel competed with the steady drips from the eaves of the houses clustered against the lane.

A few hooded figures hurried through the gloom, and the plaintive bark of a dog echoed against the wet stone.

Two women clutching heavy wicker baskets gave Sir Ranald quick curtsies as he stepped aside for them, but as he passed a woodcutter pushing his cart, the man made no effort to conceal the sullen glare he gave the knight, nor the heavy glob of phlegm he spat onto the stones in the knight's wake. Sir Ranald gritted his teeth and stayed his course, although his shoulders itched under the furtive gazes he imagined behind every shuttered window.

He entered a narrow lane that curved between the tall, stone walls of the buildings that loomed over it. Bridges crossed between the buildings at frequent intervals, creating low tunnels of brick that forced Ranald to duck as he walked. A lantern that hung from a curled iron post cast wavering light amongst the cobbles and made the ancient stone walls gleam as if they were covered in frost. Cloaked figures clustered in the pool of light, and Ranald heard laughter as he approached. Two of the men wore the black cloaks of the city watch, but the knight received no more welcome from them than from the rest of the group.

A sodden wad of parchment lay on the stones at their feet, and Ranald recognized the smeared ink on the torn scroll. The same crossed swords and crown sigil that Ranald wore proudly had been crudely defiled on the parchment so that only the crown remained, and the proud proclamation of Duke Campbell's regency slashed by a knife until the parchment was mere tatters and then wrapped around a dead rat.

Ranald scowled at the older of the two guardsmen. "What has happened here?"

"We were just asking that, sir," the man replied easily. "These notices have been coming down faster than we can nail them up, but these lads didn't see who did it, so there's nothing to be done about it, I'm afraid."

"Is that right?" Sir Ranald swept the three other figures with his gaze. Two of the young men smirked and glanced at each other, but the third stared defiantly at the knight.

"Yes," the guardsman answered. "Sir."

I have no friends here, Ranald realized. He nudged the limp bundle with his boot. Dead rats had appeared across Kuray, hung from the same posts as the duke's proclamation, even hurled at the duke's soldiers as they patrolled the city. *At least the rats are dead.*

"Very well," Ranald told the guardsman. "Then perhaps you should send these boys home, if they are no help."

"We'll do that," the guardsman replied.

"Perhaps you should go home, too." Ranald was not surprised the words came from the young man with the defiant glare, his voice as cold as his eyes. "Seeing as you're no help, either."

"You do not wish the Queen to be protected?" Ranald shot back.

" 'Protected', is it?" the young man snorted, and Ranald thought for a moment that he would spit.

"We'll send them home," the guardsman intervened. "You can be on your way. Sir."

Ranald held the young man's stare a moment longer, then stomped away. Stifled laughter followed him, and he clearly heard someone mutter, "Fucking rat." The knight thought it was the guardsman.

Ranald entered a side alley before they could think to throw the rat at his back. *It will take time,* he tried to soothe his anger. *They will see that Duke Campbell is here to help the Queen, to help the realm. They just need to give us a chance.*

A heavy door sunk into the ancient wall of the alley appeared in the gloom, and Ranald pushed through it.

A haze of smoke and the smell of sizzling fat filled the room with a damp heat that clung to the thick beams that bowed across the low ceiling. Benches clustered around tables made from a wood so stained with age and spilled drinks that they appeared black. Candles seated in mountains of melted wax on each table lit the room with a dim glow, bright enough for Ranald to see the tavern was crowded, the barmaids busy scurrying from table to table with improbable numbers of slopping tankards clutched in their hands.

Ranald peered through the haze for a moment and found his soldiers, seated around a long table against the far wall. He pushed his way through the room and stood at the end of the table with a disappointed frown twisting his face.

"I've never seen such a deplorable bunch of wastrels," he informed the soldiers.

"Thank you, sir," one of the soldiers replied, and hoisted a mug to a murmur of agreement and a call of "Hear him!"

Ranald smiled in return. "How is the beer?"

"It'll put hair on your chest," the soldier said happily, and smacked his lips appreciatively. "But be sure you drink it through your teeth."

"Only the best for you," Ranald nodded in satisfaction. He caught the eye of the tavernkeeper, a young woman with a bright smile and endless energy who greeted Ranald cheerily despite the sour looks the knight received from many of the patrons.

"Good evening, m'lord, will you be drinking with us tonight?"

"No, unfortunately not. I must drag these misfits out on patrol. Perhaps tomorrow."

"A shame, m'lord. I've a nice bit of mutton on the spit."

"It made my mouth water the moment I stepped through the door," Ranald assured her. He fished in his purse and produced a handful of silver. "Now, what do I owe for the lads' room and board? You have been extraordinarily patient."

"Twelve and six bits, sir," the tavern keeper accepted the coins with a smile, "and will they be needing the rooms much longer?"

"Tired of them, already?" Ranald asked lightly.

"No, m'lord, I only thought they might be more comfortable in the keep."

"Oh, I don't think so… the food's no match for yours."

The tavernkeeper grinned and sauntered away with Ranald's silver jingling in her purse.

A barmaid arrived with freshly-pulled mugs, but Ranald had to disappoint her. "Sorry, lass, these ones need to finish up and head out in a moment."

"Oh… will you be coming back, later, m'lord?" she asked.

"I may," he said, flashing her a brilliant smile.

"Yes, m'lord," she curtsied prettily and left as Sir Ranald was treated to a round of chuckles and teasing from his soldiers.

"Warm bed, tonight, sir," a soldier congratulated him.

"Can you teach me a posh accent like yours, sir?"

"You'll need to learn how to have blue eyes, as well," laughed another.

THE MARTYR'S TEARS

"It's not the accent, Haerden," Ranald corrected him, "it's that I bathe occasionally. You might try the same."

"Nah, I reckon it's the accent," the soldier replied, and a chorus of laughter flowed around the table.

The soldiers finished their meal and donned their cloaks and weapons. Ranald stacked a few more silver coins on the table and followed the soldiers into the street.

The gloom of evening had turned to full night by the time Ranald led the squad to relieve the soldiers who guarded the streets during the day. He watched them pair off and disappear into the twisting streets with pride. They had endured day after day of hard travel as Duke Campbell had marched on Kuray, capped by the brief, bitter fighting against the Queen's deluded defenders. But there had been few complaints, and their morale was high.

Sir Ranald began his return through the city, musing on the advantages of returning to the tavern over the longer walk to his quarters in the Silver Keep. He was exhausted, but the bright smile of the barmaid lingered in his thoughts, as did the thought of a rich beer that had to be strained through his teeth.

"One mug, then, and off to bed," he told himself with a smile.

The knight retraced his steps into the maze of the Old City. His path wound through twisted alleys and dark lanes, but he knew his way, cutting through narrow gaps and taking each turn with confidence.

As he passed a dark opening between two ancient buildings, a muffled sound tugged at him. It was no more than a wet thud, but there was a slap of flesh on stone lurking amidst the noise that caught his ear, and he paused, peering into the shadows of the alleyway. Dark shapes of abandoned planks and a broken barrel jutted from the shadows, but he saw no sign of what might have made the sound.

Ranald stepped carefully into the alley, his head cocked as he listened amongst the wet sounds of water on stone. The scuff of leather against stone whispered from further in, and a choking gasp of pain.

THE MARTYR'S TEARS

Ranald crept forward, peering into the gloom. He turned a sharp corner, and ahead he saw a huddled figure in the middle of the alley.

The figure crouched on its hands and knees over the body of a fallen man, its head buried in the ruins of the man's abdomen. Wet, tearing noises slapped against the stones of the alley as the figure wrenched against the man's body, ripping free a dripping hunk of meat.

Sir Ranald's sword whispered from its sheath. At the sound, the figure raised its head and twisted toward the knight. Blood and flesh dripped from its mouth, a sucking hole lined with teeth like needles, but there was no face. Where eyes and nose should be, there was only smooth skin the color of bone, rising to a rippled crest that ran like a wound across the top of the figure's skull.

"Maker..." Ranald gasped, and he raised his sword.

The figure twisted with the speed of thought and leapt to the wall of the alley. Sir Ranald glimpsed long, white fingers as sharp as knives scrabbling against the pitted stone of the wall and then the figure was on the roof and gone.

Ranald raced to the wall in two great strides and hurled himself upward. His arm hooked over the top of the wall and his boots scrambled for purchase. But there was no sign of the figure on the warped slate roof, nor amongst the shadowy eaves of the surrounding buildings, and Ranald dropped back into the alley with a curse.

A wet, choking gasp from the body lying in the alley caught Ranald's ear, and he hurried to the fallen man.

The man's mouth worked soundlessly, gaping like a fish, but his eyes shone with desperate terror and a plea for help that spoke as clearly as any cry.

His body appeared as if it had been ravaged by a savage animal. Great wounds tore through his stomach and chest, revealing raw meat and shattered bone in twisted, gleaming shapes. Blood pulsed thickly amongst the carnage and spread across the cobblestones. Thin threads of a black substance formed a web of veins across the pallid skin surrounding the wounds, and buried into the ragged flesh within. The threads trailed from the body and lay curled and knotted amongst the blood and offal that had spilled from the man.

Sir Ranald stepped to his side and knelt, horror and revulsion churning in his stomach. "What was it?" he asked, but there was no understanding left in the savaged flesh on the ground before him, and Ranald took him from his misery with a quick thrust of his sword.

As the man died, the black threads shriveled like paper curling in a fire and disappeared into a wisp of smoke that vanished like a shadow, leaving behind only a stain of blackened flesh.

Sir Ranald rose and stepped quickly away, the back of his hand pressed firmly over mouth and nose as he fought against the sour churn of his stomach.

A whisper of sound from the dark recesses of the alley made Ranald whirl, his sword ready. For a moment, the alley was still. Then the hideous figure emerged from the blackness of the alley's depths. It stood like a man, no longer furtive, predatory as it moved slowly into the dim light. An arm uncurled from the shadows, knotted and ridged as if it were bone, and it now gripped a knife with a pale blade. White mist drifted from the blade as if it were ice exposed to fire.

Ranald gripped his sword tightly in his gauntleted hand, the weight of the steel a reassurance. The knight backed toward the alley's end, seeking both a wider space to swing his sword and the chance for allies.

The figure slid quickly toward him, and Ranald stepped to meet it with his blade. His swing sighed in a silver blur and sliced through the shadows surrounding the figure. Ranald felt the sword's edge catch and grind heavily across flesh as hard as bone.

He reversed his cut and lashed out again, his sword scything through the air in a deadly arc.

The figure moved faster. Its blade cut across Ranald's chest, parting the steel rings of his jerkin like shattered ice and slicing into the skin and muscle beneath. The cold blade burned Ranald, and he staggered, gasping in agony.

The figure leapt at the knight and slammed him backward. Long fingers as hard as bone clutched at him, tearing into the flesh of his shoulder. His boots caught on a cobble and he crashed to the ground amidst splintered wood.

Ranald lashed at the figure as its shadow swirled around him. The knight's bellow of rage twisted into a shriek of agony as the creature buried its mouth in his stomach. Fangs tore through his flesh. Ranald gouged at the creature with his sword, and his legs strove desperately against the cobbles, but the thing tore into him again and again, and the knight's strength streamed from him in waves of terror and pain. His fingers ground uselessly against the hard shell of its hideous head as it began to feast, gorging itself on dripping meat as the knight's screams became mewling, animal noises.

As the faceless creature consumed the knight, its shadow seeped over the knight's skin, coalescing into knotted veins that slowly burrowed into his flesh. The veins branched and spread and grew thicker. Where they touched against the thing's mouth and ashen fingers the veins clung to them, spreading faster as it ate, until the black threads covered both bodies like a diseased growth. Where they pierced the knight, the threads grew thick and the flesh withered, as if it were drained to feed the web's growth.

Soon, there was little of the knight's body left except shriveled meat that the creature continued to consume, until only a glistening pool of blood remained, soaking into the torn remnants of Sir Ranald's clothes.

The web of shadows began to pull on the skin of the creature, and its crest split with the sound of rotten wood. Flesh gleamed within as the shell tore further, and huge pieces ripped apart. The creature's long fingers curled and twisted and split, and a foul liquid splashed on the cobbles. More wounds ripped open as the black threads pulled the creature's skin apart, until, with the sound of splintering bone, the creature was torn in half.

As the jagged pieces fell away, the creature slowly stood. Pale skin now covered a man's form, powerful muscles lining its limbs and chest. A ginger beard clung wetly to its jaw, and its blue eyes glanced around the alley. It stooped to collect Ranald's sword from the blood-soaked cobbles before it slipped into the shadows of the alley, loping toward the distant bulk of the Silver Keep high on its hill above the city.

Danielle

The column of soldiers tramped steadily through the streets of Bandirma. Sunlight from a freshly-washed sky reflected off steel helms and bright spear-tips as they marched, and a sharp breeze from Loughliath spread the long pennants they carried into rippling, snapping waves of color.

Three riders preceded the column. The Queen's nobles had demanded their right to lead the way, but Arledge had denied them, and only Danielle and Wyn accompanied the baron as they approached the bridge to the temple.

Danielle wished that she were back at the encampment with the nobles.

She had forced her anxiety onto Wyn in the form of an elaborate braid. Her hair twined down her back in long, threaded streams that shone in the sun, the result of a sleepless night. Her green tunic had been cleaned and mended properly, and its silver thread sparkled as she moved in rhythm with her horse.

But Danielle had refused any attempt to treat herself similarly. Her hair streamed free in the wind in a dark mass of shining black, and she had refused all offers of beautiful dresses and had donned the torn, stained tunic and leggings she had worn during her long escape. White bandages shone through the long tear in her tunic like a badge of recrimination that she wore with fierce pride.

The baron turned his horse aside when he reached the foot of the bridge and allowed Danielle to proceed ahead of him.

The thick stones of the bridge throbbed with the thunder of the swollen river's passage, and a thin haze of water danced and shimmered in the wind over the roadway. Danielle's cloak tugged and flapped as it tried to free itself from its clasp, but she barely noticed.

The tall river gates were open. The tunnel beneath the Tùr Abhainn gaped darkly ahead, and Danielle could not turn away from it.

"My lady?" Arledge asked, and Danielle realized that she had allowed her horse to wander to a stop in the center of the bridge. "My lady, you must enter first."

Danielle nodded slightly. *I know… it was agreed that would be best.* But she could feel the judging gaze of the hundreds of slits in the tower wall above her, and she felt her breath grow short as dread churned in her stomach.

"Do you think they'll actually kiss our asses?" Wyn asked thoughtfully. "I'm not sure I'd like that, now that it comes to it. Do I have to bend over? I'm not dropping my pants, I don't care what the rules say is proper."

"Thank you," Danielle said softly, and she smiled at the young woman beside her.

"Well, I just want to make sure," Wyn beamed.

Danielle took a deep breath that stabbed pain across her ribs, and gently prodded her horse forward.

The Tùr Abhainn echoed with the clop of iron-shod hooves and the tramp of boots as they passed through the tunnel into the bailey.

Rows of Temple soldiers filled the courtyard, and a group of figures in green and gold stood at the top of the steps in front of the wide doors to the temple. Danielle rode determinedly forward, her gaze locked on the robed figures, not daring to glance to either side. As she reached the foot of the stairs, two squires rushed forward to take the reins of their horses, and

Danielle painfully swung from the saddle and lowered herself gingerly to the cobblestones.

Behind her, the steady march of the Queen's soldiers came to a sudden halt, and the surrounding Temple army drew to attention in a clash of steel that made Danielle flinch.

Arledge stepped to her side, and they climbed the low steps together.

The Council waited at the top, dressed in their most formal robes. Sir Roland and Lord Faron stood with them, tall and stern, and Danielle wished again that she were far away as she reached the top step.

Reverend Nesta stepped forward and extended her hands to Danielle. Danielle took them, although her arms ached to remain at her side.

"I am so sorry, my lady," the priestess said softly, and she gripped Danielle's hands firmly. "May you someday forgive us."

Danielle forced a smile to her lips, but she could not reply. *All the words I have imagined, all the anger, all the pain, all that has been lost, and none will come forth.* There was a deep sadness in the high priestess' smile, and tears shone in her eyes, and Danielle knew that Nesta could also feel the rift that had opened between them. Danielle wondered if it would ever heal.

Nesta released Danielle's hands and stepped back. "Welcome home, Lady Danielle," Nesta announced in a clear, ringing voice, and her gaze swept across the bailey.

Home. Danielle swallowed against a sharp pain that stabbed her throat and made her eyes burn, refusing to reveal it to those around her. Her gaze flickered to the massive doors that led into the Temple, flung wide in greeting, and to the cool passageway beyond the doors, lined with its silent saints. Those doors and the high walls had meant safety to Danielle for so long, their solid weight a shield that protected warmth, comfort, and friendship.

But now the doors yawned like a gaping mouth, seeking to swallow her, and the walls were a trap that she yearned to be free of. It took all her will not to turn to make sure the River Gate still stood open.

THE MARTYR'S TEARS

Instead, she met the gaze of the high priests and priestesses. She saw kindness, and sorrow, and pain in their expressions, but there was also guilt. And in the nervous glance of Reverend Dougal, she felt the same suspicion that seemed to burn her skin from every dark window and every carefully blank face in the gathered crowd watching her. *Do I hate them?* she wondered. *They did nothing to help me, when I most needed their help. They are good people, kind, whom I called my friends. How could they have let that happen? Martyr help me, I do not know if I can forgive them.*

Home. Danielle swallowed firmly again as she stared down the saint-lined gullet of the Temple. *This was my home. I thought I had saved it, but it has been taken from me.*

Sir Roland stepped forward. "Where is Sir Killock?" he asked quietly.

"Gone," Danielle answered. *Disappeared into the storm, the moment he returned from Bandirma.*

"He hunts," Lord Faron declared. "There is no rest for him until he has found his prey."

"Nor should there be, for any of us," Sir Roland said grimly. The Templar turned to Arledge and bowed formally. "Baron, you are welcome to Bandirma. Will you aid us in our search for the fugitive priest, Reverend Whitebrooke?"

"We will, my lord," the baron announced.

Orders rang across the bailey, and Sir Roland and Baron Arledge led the Queen's soldiers into the temple, side-by-side with precisely the same number of Temple soldiers. The Council followed them through the doors, and the remainder of the Temple soldiers were dismissed in a ripple of steel.

Danielle remained on the steps in the shadow of one of the tall pillars. She could not bear to think of the stained ruin of her rooms, nor of enduring the questioning gaze of the priests and soldiers who lined the halls of the temple.

"I think I'm ready to get an apology if we can get them all back out here for a bit," Wyn scowled at the retreating backs of the departing Council.

"Please, may we leave?" Danielle asked Wyn.

"Yeah," Wyn shrugged. "I was just hoping to see a bit more high-muckity groveling. I don't know where they took our horses, though. Shall I go and find them?"

"No. I shall scream if I stay another moment."

They walked slowly across the bridge and into the town, joining the stream of townsfolk eager to return to their homes, and found rooms for let in a tall, white house with a snug drawing room and a small, walled arbor.

"The market's open," Wyn announced, with her fingers pressed against the front window. "Slim pickings yet, though." Her fingertips tapped absently on the glass panes for a moment, then she turned and surveyed the room. "Will we be here for a while, then?"

"I have not thought," Danielle replied. She opened the doors to the arbor and stepped into the cool hush of the garden. The trees had already begun to bud and provided dappled shade across trim shrubs and a gravel path that wound between them. The moss-covered walls blocked the sounds of the town, and for a moment Danielle could close her eyes and imagine she stood in the flower-covered gardens of her home, or on the deck of a boat near a faraway sandy shore.

"Is it not lovely and quiet?"

"Yes." Wyn glanced quickly around the enclosure, and a small crease appeared between her brows. "Bit boring, though. Do you think they will find Shitebrooke in the temple?"

"I do not know," Danielle sighed, annoyed that the peace of the garden had been trampled. "I am certain they will find him if he is there."

"I suppose," Wyn said, unconvinced. "We should have gone with Sir Killock, if only he'd waited."

"He did not wait."

"Yeah. Bit of a habit with him. But we could follow along, couldn't we?"

"I can hardly walk, let alone pursue Sir Killock across the wilderness," Danielle said bitterly.

"Fair enough, fair enough," Wyn held up her hands defensively. "Stupid idea. But we're going to help catch

Whitebrooke, right? We'll not just…" Wyn's voice trailed off as she sought the right word, and she waved her hand aimlessly around the small garden.

"Why not?" Danielle asked. "Do we not deserve peace and solitude to heal?"

"Well, someone once told me that bodies heal faster when there's a bit less moping, so I thought—"

"I believe I know what is best for my own healing," Danielle said sharply.

"Yeah, it was a stupid idea," Wyn said quietly, and she watched her boot scuff lines into the pristine surface of the gravel path for a moment in silence. "I'll just go and see Cormac then, shall I? Make sure Eilidh's all right?"

Wyn was gone in a swirl of her cloak before Danielle could reply, and the front door of the house clicked shut before Danielle could take a breath to call to her.

Danielle let out her breath in a rush and glared around the arbor. The tranquility she had sought was gone, and she wondered if it had ever really been there. The walls felt as confining as a cell, the cozy rooms no more than a fragile shell on a storm-churned sea.

"Imbecile," she muttered to herself, and she left the garden to stare morosely from the front window.

She was not sure how much time had passed when a knock roused her from her thoughts, and she answered the door with trepidation.

"Lord Faron," Danielle said in surprise. Of all the people she had imagined who might wish to disturb her privacy, the somber Templar had not featured anywhere on the list. Danielle welcomed him into the drawing room, where she carefully sat on the edge of one of the ancient armchairs.

Lord Faron chose not to sit, and the floor boards creaked as he examined the small trinkets displayed on the mantel.

"You chose not to enter the temple," Faron began without preamble. He reached with heavy fingers and plucked a crystal charm from its stand to hold it to the light.

"My wounds…" Danielle said vaguely.

"Yes," Faron agreed solemnly. He faced Danielle and examined her thoughtfully. She found it hard to meet the gaze of his brown eyes and pretended interest in a small tear in the silver hem of her tunic. "You are wounded, my lady," Faron continued, his voice deep and calm. "Great harm has been done to you, and the wound may yet fester."

"I do not think so," Danielle replied quietly. "The cut was clean, and was bound immediately."

"Was it?" Faron wondered. "I believe the wound was ragged and remains unsewn. I saw it tear further as you spoke with Reverend Nesta, and I feared for you."

"I do not know what you mean."

"No?" Faron stood quietly by the fireplace, but he appeared to fill the room with grey steel and strength. His dark hair spread across his wide shoulders and his gaze never left hers. The noise of the town quieted to match the Templar's solemn presence. "I saw the knife's final twist this very day."

"How so?" Danielle snapped. "Perhaps you did not hear Reverend Nesta's words?"

"I did." Faron gazed slowly around the small room, "and yet I saw that Whitebrooke's poison still lurked within you, and Nesta, and all who failed you. I saw it drive you from the temple to hide behind these little walls."

"I am here because I am weary, no more."

"That is a lie."

"What do you want me to say?" Danielle stood in a rush, furious that the somber lord would not relent. "That I wish I had stopped Whitebrooke when I had the chance? I do. That I grieve over the friendships that have been shattered with distrust? I do. That I am saddened to find no comfort in a place that I thought was my home? I am. Does this satisfy you?"

"No. I take no satisfaction in such things. Find your righteous fire, my lady. Burn away Whitebrooke's poison." Faron gazed silently at Danielle for a moment, then walked slowly to the door. He paused with his hand on the latch. "Whitebrooke should fear your coming. The shadows he serves should fear your coming. The Temple should tremble in dread at the thought of your ostracism. Find your fire, my lady. Do not seal away your light behind these walls of sorrow."

The Templar departed, and the door closed softly behind him. Danielle became aware that her mouth was open to voice some word that had never been formed, and she closed it with a snap and shook her head in bewilderment.

Did he think to cheer me? Maker's breath. Bradon, you always said that Faron was a strange man, but you did not do him justice. Danielle walked to the window and stared unseeing at the quiet street beyond. She ached to have one last reply for Faron, to somehow make him understand how hard she had fought, the fury she felt when she thought of Whitebrooke still free. *Faron would know that I will not be content with simply driving Whitebrooke into hiding.*

But Danielle felt a twinge of disquiet worm its way through her stomach. She could not deny the sorrow she had felt when she had turned her back on the doors of the temple, nor the craving to draw the drapes and hide from the pain she felt when she thought of the life she had lost, that she had thought she had regained through so much struggle. Even now, her thoughts raced further away, to tall cliffs and the wide terraces of her home.

Perhaps I shall just go mad, instead. Danielle laughed, then stopped suddenly as she heard a tinge of hysteria leak free.

A loud crash and the tinkle of broken glass made Danielle whirl to face the room once more. A delicate lantern lay in ruins on the floor near the open garden doors, its shattered panes a sea of sparkling shards against the dark rugs. An enormous raven perched proudly on the table where the lantern had stood, its black eye gleaming as it watched Danielle.

"Oh, you terrible creature!" Danielle exclaimed, and she hurried to the small closet under the stairs and returned armed with a broom.

The bird had moved to the back of an armchair, and began hopping back and forth with wings spread, one leg held toward Danielle in offering.

She approached cautiously, the broom held ready. A flash of pale ivory clutched in the bird's talons caught her eye, and she hesitated. The raven croaked happily and ceased its fluttering, and

Danielle dared to reach out and let the raven drop the small tube onto her palm.

The bird contented itself with preening as Danielle twisted the end of the tube open and retrieved the small roll of parchment within. The writing was hurried, scrawled, and practically illegible. Danielle strode to the garden and held the parchment to the light to decipher it.

She let the paper curl back into a roll as she considered the words, and smiled as the first rush of excitement she had felt in many days pushed aside the worry that had weighed on her. She took a careful, deep breath to test her ribs, and winced. *Not too terrible,* she decided. *I will survive.*

***

The raven croaked impatiently at the riders from its perch on a small boulder above the trail.

"Oh, bother that bird," Nesta grumbled. "I am quite fed up with listening to it shriek at us."

"It would like us to hurry," Danielle decided. She shifted uncomfortably in her saddle as she tried to ease the ache across her side. "I wish it were a bit more sympathetic."

The raven cawed loudly and launched from its perch in a flurry of beating wings. It skimmed the rocks lining the edge of the switchback road and soared into space, wheeling over the rugged green hills below. Danielle watched it play in the swirling air currents until it was no more than a black speck that eventually vanished into the distant haze. *He will find us again when it pleases him.*

The riders rode in silence as their horses climbed toward the sky. The quiet was strained, and Danielle wished she could imitate Wyn, who was tucked into a ball beneath her cloak as she swayed easily in her saddle, the soft snores of contented sleep drifting from beneath her hood. But the pain from Danielle's wound made rest impossible, and Danielle grimaced as she adjusted her seat once again. *I should be grateful that I can ride,* she chastised herself, *and it is not much further. We should reach the Mountain before midday.*

Their goal had not been so clear-cut as they departed Bandirma. Arledge had wasted little time in gathering an escort and readying to ride, much to Danielle's surprise. The mere mention of the raven who had brought the message had been sufficient to convince the baron, and he had paused only long enough to wait for representatives of the Temple to join them.

When at last the three riders from the Temple arrived, the raven had led them north along the Rathad an Thuaidh, frequently disappearing for long stretches, only to reappear unexpectedly as thoughts of abandonment began to stir.

The clatter of hooves on the stones of the trail ahead broke into Danielle's thoughts, and in a moment a trio of riders galloped into view around a tight bend, the scouts that had been sent ahead that morning to investigate the road.

But it was the figure mounted behind one of the scouts that Danielle's gaze was drawn to, and she felt a smile burst across her lips.

Killock dropped neatly to the road beside the scouts as they reined to a halt. The knight had somehow become more travel-stained than usual. Dirt smudged every scrap of exposed flesh and had settled into black lines across his face that followed the deep creases in his skin. Fresh scratches marked his cheeks and the backs of his hands, a network of tiny lacerations, and Danielle noticed that he walked with a slight limp.

But a smile split his ragged whiskers as he approached, and he stood tall and unbowed in the center of the road, his hand resting easily on the pommel of his sword.

"He's quite pleased with himself, isn't he?" Wyn sniffed as she stifled a yawn and uncurled from her ball.

"I had not hoped to see you for another day, at least," Killock replied.

"You knew we were coming?" Danielle asked. "Have you found Karsha?"

"I did. I have. He awaits us in the Mountain, claiming his knees are too old to come and greet you."

"But, what has happened? Karsha's message was not very… clear."

"Is it Shitebrooke? Did you find him?" Wyn interrupted impatiently.

"He was here, but you need not concern yourself with him anymore."

"You're not saying that you killed him without me? Are you bloody joking?"

"I did not kill him. I was too late to stop Whitebrooke entering the Mountain."

"Reverend Whitebrooke is in the Mountain? Sir Killock, explain yourself. What has happened?" Nesta asked.

"It will be better if Karsha Hali explains, Reverend," Killock replied. "It is his tale to tell."

"This is worse than listening to a bard waiting for her cup to be filled," Nesta complained.

Killock swung easily onto the back of Wyn's horse, and they resumed their climb.

"I cannot tell you how happy I am to see you," Danielle told the knight softly. "None of Arledge's scouts, nor any of the Temple's rangers, could find a trace of Whitebrooke's trail. They claimed the storm had washed it away, and I feared you might face him alone."

"I was fortunate to find an ally already here," Killock replied. "Has the breach between Temple and Queen finally been sealed?"

"It has begun to heal," Danielle told Killock. "All is formally forgiven, and the Temple has welcomed the Queen's help in hunting Whitebrooke. I am not certain how long it will take to set things aright in our hearts."

"You didn't miss much," Wyn snorted. "Lots of fuss and bother. And not enough grovelly apologies!" Wyn finished loudly.

"You may have a formal apology from the Council as soon as we return to Bandirma," Nesta said expansively, "with the entire Temple packed into the Council chamber, if that is your wish. And, of course, my personal regret for the terrible slander and harm that was done to you in the Temple's name. In the meantime, don't scowl, dear, it makes your nose wrinkle."

"I'm not," Wyn muttered furiously, rubbing her nose with both hands.

They reached the doors to the Mountain soon after, and the silence of sheer rock and old ice spread to dampen their voices, and only the flutter of the raven's wings in the frozen air could be heard.

Sir Roland reached for his sword, but Sir Killock stayed him with a raised hand.

"There is no more danger here," Killock assured Roland. "The Mountain is quiet, once again."

Killock led the way through the great doors into the Mountain. Danielle breathed deeply to steady herself and followed, but her step faltered as she gazed around the entrance hall. She had thought herself prepared for seeing the Mountain abandoned and dark since hearing the news from Rowenna and Gwydion. The reality of the cracked stone and cold shadows was far worse than Danielle had expected, an abomination where warmth and welcome had always greeted her.

"Sliabh Mór may be quiet," Lord Faron pondered in a deep voice, "but it is not at peace."

"How can it be, when its heart has been torn from it? When it has been so foully desecrated?" Roland scowled.

Danielle reached for Wyn's hand and held it fiercely as she fought against despair. The touch of Wyn's fingers wrapped around her own gave Danielle the strength to step forward.

Killock lit a lantern and strode deeper into the Mountain. The lantern's flame created a pool of illumination in darkness so deep it appeared to be formed of black stone. Only when thick pillars loomed from the shadows did Danielle know that they had reached the sanctuary.

The lantern abruptly revealed the tall door that stood in the farthest wall of the sanctuary. The door swung easily at Killock's touch, and the Templar stepped through before Danielle's voice could halt him.

"Killock, where is He? Rowenna said He lay in the sanctuary. Can we not pause for a moment to pay our respects?"

Killock faced her, and his eyes shone redly in the lantern's light.

"I do not know where He is," Killock said quietly. "There is no sign of Him, either in the sanctuary or beyond."

"But, who would have taken Him?" Danielle wondered.

Killock only shook his head in silence and resumed his trek down the long, curved passageway beyond the door.

The passage seemed to wind interminably into the earth, until, at last, the tunnel opened into the wide chamber that Rowenna had described.

But no words could have prepared Danielle for what met them. The leaves of the golden tree stirred in a bright susurration of metal against metal as if a gentle breeze passed through its spreading branches, and the chamber was filled with dancing light as the tree's leaves reflected their lanterns in every direction.

Karsha Hali scrambled to his feet from his perch amongst the tree's knobbly roots and hurried to meet them, his black robes fluttering around his ankles like tattered wings.

"Lords and ladies and reverends, at last, you are here."

"Where is he? Where is Shitebrooke?" Wyn called out before anyone else could speak.

"Ah! Bronwyn… look at your marvelous flames," Karsha exclaimed in wonder.

"What? Oh, I mean, yeah, they're lovely, but—"

"May I hear the stories you carry?"

"Well, I suppose, but will someone please tell me where Shitebrooke is? And can I please stab him?" Wyn pleaded.

"He is gone. Consumed in pain and fear."

"This can't be happening," Wyn groaned.

"He suffered greatly. Perhaps this will soothe you?"

"A bit," Wyn grumbled. "It's so unfair…"

"Karsha, are you certain?" Danielle asked. She held her breath, suddenly desperate to hear that Whitebrooke was dead. She forced a breath past her lips. "Please, I must hear it plainly."

"Whitebrooke is dead," Karsha told Danielle with a gentleness that surprised her. "I am certain."

Relief burst from Danielle in bright laughter, and she covered her mouth in surprise. "I am sorry," she stammered. "I do not mean to take joy in his death. He caused so much sorrow…" she tried to explain. Whitebrooke's voice echoed in her thoughts, as if he stood in the chamber next to her, ranting, gloating, seeping with malice. But Danielle could not recall his words. All she could remember was Wyn's head resting in her lap, Wyn's body lying twisted and still on the stone floor, and the feel of Wyn's heart fading under her fingertips. *He nearly killed her, and now he is gone.* The laughter Danielle held back grew heavy in her chest and dragged a shuddering breath into her lungs. Her eyes burned and a sob choked her.

Concerned faces wavered in golden splotches, but she waved them away and forced herself to smile. "I am fine," she insisted, and fiercely wiped the tears from her cheeks. "I grieve for the pain he caused."

"We are most grateful to you, my lord Counselor," Nesta thanked the wizard.

"My heart soars to hear it," Karsha faced the priestess, a twisted grin once again firmly in place. "May I stand beside Bronwyn in the Council chamber to also receive the humble apologies of the Temple?"

"How…?" Nesta frowned. "If you would like, I would be pleased to offer you our most profound apology, and to beg your forgiveness for the accusation of fuil crunor."

"You have forgotten also murder," Karsha reminded the priestess helpfully. "You wish also to beg forgiveness for saying I murdered Bishop Benno, whom I liked very much."

"Yes, that as well."

"No. Sadly, I have no interest in such things."

"I still have interest in such things, even if he doesn't," Wyn pointed out.

"Of course, dear. I would not think otherwise."

"Karsha, why are we here?" Arledge interrupted. "Was it just to hear that Whitebrooke is dead?"

"No, of course not. I have a story to show you, although Sir Killock tells me that part of the tale is known to some of you already." Karsha led them across the chamber to the foot of the golden tree and stood next to the small pool of shimmering water. A long, steel shape lay amongst the undulations of the tree's roots.

"Is that…?" Sir Roland asked.

"Yes, the Martyr's Blade. Whitebrooke carried it here, although not even the gods know what he intended," Karsha replied.

"Why is it on the floor?" Wyn asked.

"It lays where it fell from his hand."

"He died right here? You said there was pain… I don't see even a tiny spot of blood," Wyn accused the wizard.

"No, there is nothing of him left. Even the gods have only his name to remember him by."

"Well, that does sound sort of nasty, I suppose."

"Horrendous," Karsha agreed with a grin. He gathered his ragged robes around himself with a tinkle of metal charms and turned his gap-toothed smile on the others. "Do you wish to hear the story of the stone gods?"

"Please," Nesta replied.

"Long ago, there was a great battle here," Karsha began. "How long, I cannot say. To the spirits of the mountain, the years have no meaning. They do not know of day, or night, nor of winter, or summer. They know only of the long journey from the great fire to the cold sky.

"But this battle the stone gods remember. They warred against the lords of water, who gnawed on the stone gods in the darkness, and carved great wounds. This chamber is one such scar.

"The lords of water were defeated, and the stone gods still revel in their triumph, even though the battle happened before the dragons curled around the roots of the mountains, even before the Children of Light first walked on the earth."

"Karsha," Arledge interrupted. "Is there more than ancient myth in this story? How do dragons and whatever a Child of Light is help us now?"

"Of course there is more," Karsha huffed. "But this is a story of stone. It would take a lifetime to tell it properly."

"Perhaps we could try a version that ends before supper?" Nesta suggested. "Most of us do not have an entire lifetime left."

"How true!" Karsha cackled. "Very well, I shall tell the tale with thoughts of meat and wine driving my words.

"While the stone gods celebrated their victory, the songs of the Children faded, and the age of the scrapers came. This is a long time, with many stories, but we will not speak of them now for fear of rumbling stomachs. I will say only that the stone gods remained undisturbed for all the ages of mankind."

"What's a scraper?" Wyn asked.

"We are. To the spirits of stone, we are fleas, scratching on the surface"

"Fleas don't scratch," Wyn pointed out. "They bite, and then you want to scratch them, that's certain. Or squeeze them until their heads pop. Or you can put them under a tin cup and heat it with a coal until—"

"May we hear the rest of Karsha's story?" Danielle interrupted gently.

"Yes, because we have come to the middle," Karsha nodded his head earnestly. "Perhaps later you will please tell me the story of the tin cup and the fleas. Now, I have told you that the stone gods dreamed of their victory over the lords of water. But after many years their solitude was disturbed. A goddess came to the mountain and followed the paths cut by the water spirits until she came to this chamber. She stood just where you are standing, now, Lord Faron. She was hidden inside a scraper, but the stone gods saw through her mask and knew her true face. They name her Danu, the Creator, the Maker's Breath, Sister of Darkness.

"The last of the Children of Light walked beside her as she entered the chamber, and many scrapers, as well. The scrapers built the tree, which the stone gods call the Twisted Vein. Then the last Child of Light spoke a Word of creation, and his voice still echoes in the stone. You can see it, here, where the sound of the Word first touched the stone." Karsha hopped from his perch and ambled to the center of the chamber. He stopped at the edge of the pool and squatted to trace the shape of the strange rune that disturbed the stone there.

THE MARTYR'S TEARS

"The Word tore Danu the Creator from her disguise, and she wept," Karsha continued. "The Twisted Vein caught her and shaped her into a shaft of light. Her tears quenched the shaft, and the Child of Light took her up as a Weapon and left the mountain."

Karsha stood slowly and sighed. "He never returned, but this story is not ended. Because Danu did return, now reunited with her brother. The scrapers had built a Guardian to contain them, and there they remained, entwined. They grappled one another, locked in an embrace of rage and lust that neither could end. The scrapers built the great halls above us and sealed the Guardian away, hiding it in the heart of the Mountain.

"Long years passed, but I am a stone god, and time is only a flicker for me to ignore. I close my eyes for only an instant, and I open them to witness the end of the story.

"Shadows enter the Mountain. Not the blackness of the deep dark in which stone is born, but the darkness of the abyss, where all is consumed. The shadows stain the rock and the stone gods rage against their touch. Shadow and flame shatter the Guardian and tear Danu from her brother. The shadows take her brother and flee into the abyss that is his home, while the flame takes Danu and returns her to the shape that the Twisted Vein had crafted for her. She calls out to her brother, eager to fill his darkness with her light until there is no more shadow, and all is flame."

Silence and confused glances greeted the last of Karsha's words, but the wizard was unconcerned with the reception and appeared taken with a sudden need to pluck at loose threads on the hem of his robes.

Danielle could not take her gaze from the Martyr's Blade. It lay awkwardly amongst the twisted knots of the tree's roots, and she ached to move it to a more dignified rest. *If I pick it up, I shall never put it down*, she realized. *Is that why I hesitate? One last moment in which to flee from this cave and run until I reach home and can pretend I am free? I thought such daydreams had passed, but I fear they have not.*

"I am more confused now than when we started," Nesta complained. "A goddess? A Child of Light? What does any of that mean?"

"I do not know," Karsha admitted happily.

"Can these spirits be trusted?" Arledge asked.

"I do not know," Karsha laughed.

"That is not very helpful," Nesta frowned at the wizard.

Danielle stepped to the edge of the pool of water and knelt. Tiny waves splashed musically against the lip of the basin, darkening the stone.

"Rowenna drank from this pool, and it washed the shadow from her wound." Danielle dipped her hands into the water and felt its chill touch flow gently around her fingers. She raised her hands and watched the water trickle down her arm, each drop shimmering and sparkling as if it were a precious stone, bright against her dark skin. "Are these her tears? Karsha, you said she wept, and the Blade was quenched in her tears."

Karsha squatted beside Danielle, his charms chiming to match the burbling song of the spring. He held his hand over the surface of the water, and smiled as a splash crowned his wrinkled paw with a spray of glimmering drops. "I do not know," he murmured.

"Can a goddess weep?" Danielle asked.

"Of course," Karsha replied sadly. "Sorrow, pain… these are burdens that not only mortals suffer. A goddess concealed within a mortal would weep such tears that I cannot bear to think of it."

Danielle slowly twisted her hand back and forth for a moment, and watched the shining drops quiver and chase after each other. Then she rose to her feet. "Of course," she sighed. "Why should any of us be exempt from pain and sorrow?"

"They are the Maker's gifts," Karsha replied. He straightened and settled his robes around his thin shoulders. "Without pain, there is no pleasure. Without sorrow, no joy. Without death, no life, and the Maker loved us too well to deny us those." Karsha graced Danielle with a gap-toothed grin. "The Maker's love is a terrible gift, but I am glad for it."

THE MARTYR'S TEARS

Danielle glanced at the Martyr's Blade, patiently awaiting her at the edge of her vision. *And without burden, no ease? What must I do to claim that tranquility as a reward?* Danielle closed her eyes and lost herself for a moment in the steady throb of her heartbeat in her throat. *Perhaps that is just a dream.*

Danielle opened her eyes and gazed at the Blade. *I am going to pick it up,* she realized. *Was there ever any choice?*

"Danielle, has the Blade changed?" Killock asked her quietly. "Does it seem different, in any way?"

"Why do you ask?"

"Karsha said the goddess has returned to the Blade," Killock said thoughtfully. He held Danielle's gaze for a moment longer. "I would expect that to make a difference."

"I do not see a change." Danielle breathed in deeply and exhaled, letting all thoughts of home and rest flow between her lips on her breath. She stepped toward the Blade and knelt at its side.

"I don't like this, Dani," Wyn's voice stopped Danielle's fingers as she reached for the Blade's hilt. "Who knows what Shitebrooke did to it."

"There is no shadow, here," Danielle assured her.

"Maybe not, but he was a devious shit."

"I will be cautious, I promise." Danielle retrieved her guide from her pack and held the small egg-shaped Diviner in one hand. The guide was not intended to unravel the nature of a Device, but it could find one, and Danielle trusted it to pierce any Veil Whitebrooke could have empowered. She whispered a Word to the guide and glowing runes pulsed into life across its surface in a web. Danielle adjusted her Word and the threads shifted and flowed around the guide until she was satisfied that there was no hidden Device protecting the Blade.

She let her Word expire and replaced the guide in her pack. She clenched one hand into a fist on her lap and extended her other to the Blade.

Her fingers brushed against the metal of the cross-piece and a surge passed through her and was suddenly gone, as if she woke from a dream. Danielle snatched her hand away, but as quickly as the sensation came it faded, and left Danielle wondering if she had truly felt something, or if she had imagined it. *No,* she decided, *the feeling was real. But what was it? It was not pain, nor heat, nor cold.* Danielle rested her fingertips on the Blade again, but she felt only the smooth coolness of steel under her fingers.

"You felt her presence?" Karsha asked.

"I felt… I am not sure. It is gone, now."

Danielle curled both hands around the long hilt of the Blade and raised it. The soft light from the pool rippled in the whorls of the sword's blade as if the light shone deep beneath the surface. *It was joy… rapture. And yet it was also longing… but for what?*

Mairi

The pristine snow was churned into mud in the narrow gap between the bushes. Blood speckled the few patches of white that remained, and Mairi could not help skipping as she rushed forward to see what had caused the mess.

"Another rabbit!" Mairi grinned in triumph. She knelt in the snow and released the leather noose around the unfortunate creature's throat. "Three already. I told you this was the spot."

Colin held the bag open and tucked the rabbit in with the others while Mairi gathered up the snare. "You were right," he answered softly.

"Yes, I was," Mairi muttered to herself as she coiled the snare around its stake, but she was not sure who she was talking to. Colin had not actually argued with her over where to place the snares, he had simply followed her around the small meadow and held out a snare when she had asked for one. In fact, Colin had said little, either the day before while setting the snares or today while checking them, and Mairi found it hard to fill the awkward silences.

"After we finish checking the snares would you like to have a go with your bow?" Mairi tried. Colin had brought his small hunting bow with him on both trips, although he had never taken it off his shoulder. "We can go by the beck to see if there are any ducks."

"Sure," Colin said disinterestedly.

Mairi finished tucking the snare into her pack in silence, disheartened. When her father had mentioned that Colin was still distraught over Meghan's death in the catacombs of the Sliabh Log, Mairi had volunteered to help him at once. *Didn't I bring Aileen all the way through the catacombs? And Aileen is only ten.* Mairi knew exactly what Lady Danielle would say to Colin, and was ready with the coin trick Cormac had shown her if talking failed. And if that did not work, then she had some new words she had learned from Wyn to try on Colin.

None of it produced more than a few small smiles that quickly gave way to brooding silence again.

"So, you miss her, I guess?" Mairi asked hesitantly, unsure if it was all right to talk about such things.

"Yeah," Colin offered. Mairi waited, but there did not seem to be more coming.

"She was nice," Mairi tried again. "I'm sorry."

"Why are you sorry?" Colin asked, frowning. "It weren't your fault."

"I mean I'm sorry it happened, is all." Mairi glanced at Colin and then quickly at the trail before he could notice. "Everyone tried their hardest to get us all out. It wasn't anyone's fault."

"Not everyone," Colin scowled. "No one in the camp did anything. I didn't do anything. We just waited for someone else to come along."

"What were you supposed to do?" Mairi wondered. "All those soldiers got killed, even Lord Bradon. There's nothing any of us could have done on our own."

"We could've tried." Colin kicked at a snow bank angrily and sprayed snow in the air. "We should have all attacked Reverend Crassus the first time, when he killed Thorley. Then at least we would've had a chance of killing him. But I guess we're just cowards."

"That's stupid," Mairi blurted before she could help it.

"Easy for you to say," Colin snapped back. "I heard you killed one of those things, and you saved Aileen. You fought. I didn't. I'm a coward, that's it."

"No, that's *not* it." Mairi felt like punching Colin, or screaming at him, or giving him a hug. She did not know which. "You'd just have died. That's why it's stupid. Just throwing your life away. You know what? Dying is terrible. I've seen it. I would have died too if not for Sir Killock. But I didn't. I fought, we all fought, and even when I thought we couldn't go another step, we went ten more, all so that we wouldn't die. You fight to live, not to die, and that's all you would have done if you'd have fought Reverend Asses. So maybe we should have done more, me too, because I didn't do anything until I had to, but what we shouldn't have done is just throw our lives away for nothing."

Mairi glared at Colin. The boy stared back, wide-eyed, shocked, and Mairi wondered if she had gone too far. *Well, I don't care.*

"Sorry," Colin said, and he lowered his gaze.

They walked in silence. Mairi alternated between pride and embarrassment at her outburst. *I don't think that's how Lady Danielle would have helped Colin. Maybe it was how Wyn would have, though.*

"Reverend Asses?" Colin asked, and Mairi though she heard a faint smile in his voice.

"What? Oh, that's what Wyn always called him. Did I say that?" Mairi asked.

"Yeah," Colin replied, and then was quiet for several steps. "What was it like?" Colin asked eventually. "When Meghan… died."

Mairi glanced at him and Colin looked quickly away. She brushed her hair from her face with her mittened hand as she considered how to answer.

"I don't think she was there anymore," Mairi eventually tried. "She didn't know what was happening. It was just terrible for the rest of us."

Colin nodded quietly to himself. Mairi thought he appeared more sad than angry, which felt better somehow.

THE MARTYR'S TEARS

They slowly trudged down the slope toward the Gylden Beck, wading through snow that came to their knees at times. Tall fir trees receded into the white mist around them like ephemeral towers, and the forest was quiet save for the snow crunching under their boots.

The stream wound through a gully choked with boulders at the bottom of the slope, a favorite panning spot in the summer as the giant stones forced the tumbling current into pools and eddies that snatched smaller pebbles from the torrent. Mairi did not see any ducks waddling across the stream's frozen surface, but Colin did not seem disappointed.

"Don't really want to shoot right now," he shrugged.

"That's all right." Mairi pressed on the ice at the shoreline with the toe of her boot and watched for any signs of movement. It was as solid as stone.

"I just wish I could've helped," he blurted out, and wiped his nose furiously with the back of his glove.

"Me too," Mairi said softly.

She walked cautiously onto the ice. Mairi loved sliding on the ice with the other children of the settlement, but even more, she enjoyed simply standing over the center of the stream and turning to gaze at the forest from a spot she could not reach at any other time of year. She listened intently as she stepped, ready to freeze at the slightest creak or groan or crack, but the ice was firm. She reached the center and knelt. A few swipes of her mitten and the loose snow was brushed aside. She could see the weeds swaying in the current along the stream bottom, and she waved to a startled fish that scurried away in terror.

"What do you see?"

Colin knelt beside her and peered into the stream.

"There's a little green fish, there in that clump of weeds."

Colin laughed. "I thought you'd found a nugget, you were staring so hard."

"No," Mairi smiled in return. "See, there he is."

They watched in silence for a moment until Mairi sat back with a sigh. "I guess we should go back."

Colin nodded. He clambered awkwardly to his feet and then helped Mairi up. They had begun the wary shuffle to the shore when she caught a rustle of branches that had nothing to do with a breeze. She peered into the forest. Branches cracked and rustled again. *Something big.*

"That's not a rabbit," Colin whispered. He took his bow from his shoulder and nocked an arrow. "Could be a deer."

"Could be a troll," Mairi cautioned. Her hand searched at her belt for the knife Wyn had given her.

"No, we would've heard them barking," Colin said with certainty. He raised the little bow and sighted into the bushes.

Mairi found that she was holding her breath, and forced herself to release it. *Please be a deer, please be a deer, please be a deer.*

"Oh," said Colin, and he lowered his bow. "It's somebody."

Mairi saw the bushes part and reveal the figure on the bank of the stream as if she were dreaming. Withered skin stretched like bleached parchment over bones, the foul remains of black teeth and gums filled a mouth under a gaping hole where a nose should be. The husk saw them at the same moment, and a wretched hiss oozed from its mouth.

"Run!" Mairi heard herself yell from far away, and she pulled frantically on Colin's arm. But the boy stood paralyzed with disbelief.

The husk plunged onto the frozen stream and scrambled toward them, its fingers scraping across the ice as it came.

"Run!" she screamed again, and Colin finally heard her. They turned together and slid and stumbled wildly across the stream. Mairi felt her boots slip and she crashed to her hands and knees. Colin grabbed her arm, but could find no traction in his haste, and spun uselessly to the ice. Mairi heard the scratch and scrape of the husk right behind her. Her boots pushed desperately on the ice and she half-crawled, half-slid forward.

Colin shouted in fear. Mairi risked a glance over her shoulder and saw that the husk was on him. Its fingers clutched at his feet. Colin kicked out and pushed backward. Mairi grabbed him by his cloak and hauled him toward the bank, kicking and sliding as her boots slipped on the ice.

A tree growing on the edge of the stream stretched roots over the ice, and Mairi clutched at the slender tendrils and pulled Colin to the shore. But the husk was too close. Skeletal fingers closed around Colin's ankle, and the husk dragged him back. Colin screamed and kicked with his other boot and struck the husk in the face, but it had negligible effect. The husk pulled him closer.

Mairi tore her knife from its sheath and threw herself at the husk. She landed smoothly on the ice and slid into the struggling bodies as the husk clawed at Colin's legs. She hacked at the hand clutching at Colin's ankle and felt the blade's razor edge slice through withered skin and shatter rotted bone. Colin lashed out with his freed leg and again caught the husk in the face, driving it back.

"Go!" Mairi screamed, and Colin wasted no time, rolling onto his hands and knees and scrambling away. Mairi followed as fast as she could, her boots and mittens thrashing on the slippery surface.

Steel-hard fingers wrapped themselves around her ankle and dragged her away from safety. She twisted onto her back as the husk pulled itself onto her, its ruined hand slapping against her arms as she warded off its clumsy blows. She kicked with her free boot and stabbed wildly at the husk's arm and chest, but the blows were useless against its endless strength.

Colin launched himself at the husk with a cry of desperation. He gripped a rock the size of his fist in his hand and smashed it into the side of the husk's skull as he crashed into the foul corpse. The impact drove the husk off Mairi, but it continued to thrash wildly and clutch at Colin. He drew back his hand and smashed the rock down again, and bone cracked with the sound of dry wood splitting.

"Die!" Mairi sobbed as Colin pounded the rock into the husk's skull a third time. Bone shattered, and the corpse finally collapsed.

They scrambled onto the bank, breathless, never taking their eyes off the remains of the husk sprawled on the ice. It trembled and twitched, but made no other move. But as their breathing began to return to normal, other sounds pushed their way forward. Branches groaned and snapped, and Mairi heard the heavy stamp of footsteps and the dry slither of skin against wood. Pale shapes drifted into view through the white mist, still distant but growing closer with each breath.

"We have to go," she whispered to Colin. "Quickly, before they find us."

Colin nodded, his eyes bright with fear, but he did not hesitate to follow Mairi as she hurried from the stream. They pushed through the thick snow and paused to cower against the trunk of a tree as more husks loomed into view on the slope above them. The hillside swarmed with the foul shapes, lurching with their strange stutter-quick steps. Several passed within a stone's-throw of their hiding place, and Mairi held her breath as they staggered by.

A brief gap in the swarm opened, and she silently pointed and received a grim nod from Colin in return. They waited for one last heartbeat, then leapt through the thick snow down the hill. Snow flew from Mairi's boots and hidden roots and stones twisted her ankles, but for five ragged breaths, nothing pursued them. Then a dry rasp passed through the silent trees, and the forest filled with the creaking and snapping of branches as the horde gave chase.

Mairi pushed harder, her lungs burning as she drew in gulps of frozen air. Colin kept pace next to her, leaping and scrambling through the underbrush.

They slid down a steep embankment and found a narrow game trail that wound along the ridge. They raced down it, ducking and weaving through the trees as branches clawed at their cloaks. Colin's boot twisted on the uneven ground and he sprawled heavily into the snow. Mairi grabbed his coat and dragged him to his feet.

"Come on!" she screamed to Colin. "Come on, run!"

Their legs were tiring now, and the stumbles came more frequently. Mairi could hear the husks closing in. But there was another sound drawing closer, a heavy noise of trampling and snorting. A horse burst through the low branches of the trees ahead of them with a rider in brown and grey urging it toward them. A second horse and rider appeared in its wake, and the two horsemen wheeled their mounts and stretched out hands to the fleeing children. Mairi staggered across the last distance and clutched the rider's arm, and he swung her onto the horse behind him.

She held tightly as the horse surged forward, racing between the trees as snow flew from its heavy tread. Pale shapes paced them on both sides for agonizing heartbeats, but the horses pulled ahead as the riders guided them expertly through the trees.

"Are you hurt?" the rider called to Mairi over his shoulder.

"No," Mairi shouted in reply, although it surprised her to discover that was true. Cuts from branches stung on her cheeks, bruises ached on her legs and arms, and one ankle throbbed from a twist, but there was nothing that qualified as a true hurt. She glanced behind and found the second horseman following closely, and saw Colin hanging tightly to the rider, arms locked around the rider in a death grip.

He looks unhurt as well. Mairi craned forward to yell in the rider's ear. "Where are we going?"

"To Twin Pines," the rider replied. "We must warn your people."

Mairi sat back, satisfied, and concentrated on hanging on as the horse plunged through the forest, hardly slowing as the rider maneuvered across the rugged terrain.

The rider did not relent until they reached the small clearing in the center of the settlement, where he finally reined in his mount amidst a flurry of spraying snow and snorting steam. He lowered Mairi to the ground as the settlers flocked to the clearing, drawn by the noise.

"Good people," the rider called to them. "You must gather your loved ones and flee. Do not waste any time. Death is on our heels."

A great commotion spread through the settlers, questions hurled from all around the circle at the two riders.

"It's the husks!" Mairi's voice carried over the noise and quieted it. "The husks have come. We saw them, Colin and me, hundreds of them, up by the pools."

A groan swept the crowd and the rider gave Mairi a puzzled glance. "Aye, the husks," the rider confirmed.

"Where should we go?" a woman's voice rose from the crowd, and Mairi saw that it was Morna who called out, her infant daughter perched on her hip.

"Our encampment lies to the east," the rider replied. "They will be headed this way as soon as we make our report, so travel in that direction and you should meet with the scouts. Do not stop to rest. Travel all night if you must."

"Are you Sir Lochlan's men?" Mairi asked. She remembered the soft-spoken knight in his shining armor, and still wore the sturdy, warm boots his soldiers had given to her when she had visited their camp near Dolieb.

"Sir Lochlan, aye," the rider replied, and he held Mairi's gaze. "Who are you, lass? How do you know of Sir Lochlan, or of the husks?"

"She knows more about them husks than you do, that's certain," Morna laughed bitterly. "She was in the Sliabh Log for days and days, and lived to tell of it."

Mairi saw the rider's face suddenly clear in understanding. "You're one of the girls who was with Sir Killock, back in Dolieb. I didn't recognize you, lass."

"That's where I saw Sir Lochlan," Mairi agreed, suddenly awkward under the attentive gaze of the whole settlement.

"Then you'll know not to stop running until you reach Sir Lochlan." The rider straightened in his saddle and addressed the circle of settlers again. "Leave now, take only what you need for the journey."

"What of our kin, those trapping and hunting?" Morna asked, and shouts of agreement echoed her.

"Pray for them," the rider replied.

Epilogue

The raven croaked serenely to himself as wind as cold as mountain stone gusted through the swaying branches of the small, twisted pine in which he perched, ruffling his feathers. From his vantage point, Bran could see rearing cliffs, massive ice rivers, rumpled lines of forested hills, and the wide, wind-stirred waters of the great, grey lake. His shining eye darted from one vast expanse to the next, greedily examining every facet of interest.

Tell the Queen what we have accomplished here, his Whisper told Bran, *tell her the priest is dead, the Temple allied, her sister safe. Tell her we are coming home.*

Bran spread his wings and let the wind loft him into the air. He soared from the ridge, the ground plummeting away, and his wings caught the river of wind that spiraled ever higher, bearing the raven upward until only the clouds and the barren mountain peaks could look down on him.

He heard the grumpy grumblings of the earth spirits slowly fading away as they returned to their long contemplation.

He saw the wolf, finally happy as its pup gamboled and teased around it, biting its tail and pretending to be fierce.

He saw the silver light of a goddess cradled in the arms of a raven-haired person, finally free from her dark sibling, finally free from her prison, finally free from her long years of unknowing, and he could feel her bright fire blazing as she stirred.

He thrust higher, his eyes scouring the world beneath him.

Far to the south, he saw a ship churning toward the wide mouth of a river, bearing new shackles for the goddess.

To the east, he saw a young woman approach a magnificent stone beneath an image of a golden tree, and watched the stone stir at her touch.

Far to the north, he saw a dark shadow oozing across the snow as it leaked from beneath the mountains.

And to the west, he saw a grim fortress of sharp stone open its gates, and fierce people clad in steel and fur pour forth.

Bran cawed a challenge to the wind and knifed northward through the air. The spirits of the sky answered his call, and chased him, and he chuckled to himself as they bore him for days across hills and forests with hardly a flap of his great wings.

At last the valley of the silver people's city appeared, gleaming white under a layer of recent snow, the smoke from hundreds of chimneys climbing like pillars into a silent sky. The silver people's castle stood cold and serene on its jutting prow of rock at the head of the valley, and Bran could see the high window in the tallest spire that had been his destination.

But the raven swerved aside with a harsh cry and dropped lower over the clustered chaos of roofs and towers huddled at the foot of the valley. Frozen air lingered in shadows that the sun never reached, a numbing blanket that swaddled the ancient buildings. Bran's wings beat furiously as he dove between the bowed stone walls, sending echoes swarming into the gloom of the narrow alleys and streets that wormed beneath the overhanging structures.

Bran spied a great pile of an ancient house, slowly collapsing toward the bottom of the valley. Several of its towers had fallen centuries ago, and two of its wings had long ago been pulled apart and reused across the city to patch walls and potholes. But the main hall still stood, and Bran squeezed through a crack in its vaulted roof and fluttered through its deserted hallways, heading ever downward until the rooms were lit only by the thinnest of sickly light from tiny, grime-covered windows high on the walls.

Dark figures moved furtively in the shadows, hurrying past on nefarious business, or lurked in doorways, watching like feral predators.

Bran ignored them all.

A narrow band of pale yellow light flickered into the hall beneath the warped planks of a wooden door. The door opened and Bran swerved through the crack. He cackled at the flailing arms of the tall man who had opened the door and swooped across the small room, landing on a table amidst a storm of fluttering paper and the crash of a candlestick falling to the floor.

Bran smoothed his feathers into place as the raven-haired Queen of the silver people stood from her chair next to the table and tentatively reached out with a curled finger to stroke Bran's breast. The raven croaked contentedly, then fixed her gaze with his gleaming, black eye, and saw her golden eyes go wide as he began to tell her his story.

THE END

THE MARTYR'S TEARS

Tales From the Martyr's World
The Thief's Tale

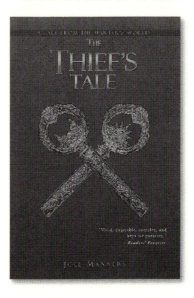

***

When an audacious burglary goes spectacularly right, Wyn expects her young life to change for the better. Glorious infamy and the respect and adulation of her underworld brethren will, at least, buy her a few drinks, and just might convince the other thieving vermin to keep their knives to themselves for a while.

But when her new-found reputation attracts the worst kind of attention, she is forced to take on an impossible heist, working for a vicious killer named Quinn, a man she has feared and hated since she was an orphan fighting for food on the streets.

Faced with the destruction of everything that holds meaning to her, Wyn vows to pull the greatest job of all, to beat Quinn at his own brutal game.

Available Soon

TALES FROM THE MARTYR'S WORLD
THE ARTIFICER'S TALE

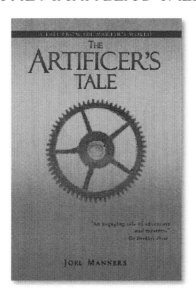

***

Rikard always dreamed of wielding one of the arcane Devices created by the enigmatic Guild of Artificers. Newly apprenticed into the Guild, he is now on the verge of mastering the closely-guarded secrets of creating the Devices.

But when one of the Guild's most venerable Wards is mysteriously activated, Rikard and his fellow apprentices are concerned. What ancient menace has returned a millennium after the Ward was created? Why are the Guild Grandmasters concealing the warning?

When Rikard and his friends find themselves in possession of a secret they never wanted, a dark truth hidden even from the Guild Masters, Rikard realizes their fate, and the fate of the Guild itself, rests in their hands.

AVAILABLE NOW

Books by Joel Manners

The Chronicles of the Martyr
The Martyr's Blade
The Martyr's Tears

Tales from the Martyr's World
The Artificer's Tale
The Thief's Tale (announced)

About the Author

Joel Manners has created rich worlds and memorable characters in video games for more than 30 years. He brings his talent for storytelling to the epic fantasy genre in his critically acclaimed series, *The Chronicles of the Martyr*. He lives in Austin, TX with his wife and two boys. And this dog his wife made them get, but honestly, she's pretty sweet. The dog. His wife too. Although he suspects that might change if she sees this.

Made in the USA
Columbia, SC
08 December 2018